GRACE LIVINGSTON HILL

Jumbo Reader #1

Aunt Crete's Emancipation
The Girl from Montana
The Story of a Whim
Because of Stephen
Lone Point

A BARBOUR BOOK

GRACE LIVINGSTON HILL JUMBO READER #1

ISBN 1-55748-416-3

AUNT CRETE'S
EMANCIPATION

Chapter 1
A Telegram and a Flight

"Who's at the front door?" asked Luella's mother, coming in from the kitchen with a dish towel in her hand. "I thought I heard the doorbell."

"Luella's gone to the door," said her sister from her vantage point at the crack of the sitting room door. "It looks to me like a telegraph boy."

"It couldn't be, Crete," said Luella's mother impatiently, coming to see for herself. "Who would telegraph now that Hannah's dead?"

Lucretia was short and dumpy, with the comfortable, patient look of the maiden aunt that knows she is indispensable because she will meekly take all the burdens that no one else wants to bear. Her sister could easily look over her head into the hall, and her gaze was penetrative and alert.

"I'm sure I don't know, Carrie," said Lucretia apprehensively, "but I'm all of a tremble. Telegrams are dreadful things."

"Nonsense, Crete, you always act like such a baby. Hurry up, Luella. Don't stop to read it. Your aunt Crete will have a fit. Wasn't there anything to pay? Who is it for?"

Luella, a rather stout young woman in stylish attire, with her mother's keen features unsoftened by sentiment, advanced, irreverently tearing open her mother's telegram and reading it as she came. It was one of the family grievances that Luella was stout like her aunt instead of tall and slender like her mother. The aunt always felt secretly that they somehow blamed her for being of that type. "It makes one so hard to fit," Luella's mother remarked frequently, and adding with a disparaging glance at her sister's dumpy form, "So impossible!"

At such times the aunt always wrinkled up her pleasant little forehead into a V upside down, and trotted off to her kitchen, or her buttonholes, or whatever was the present task, sighing helplessly. She tried to be the best that she could always; but one couldn't help one's figure, especially when one was partly dependent on one's family for support, and dressmakers and tailors took so much money. It was bad enough to have one stout figure to fit in the family without two; and the aunt always felt called upon to have as little dressmaking done as possible, in order that Luella's figure might be improved from the slender treasury. "Clothes do make a big difference," she reflected. And sometimes when she was all alone in the twilight, and there was really nothing that her alert conscience could possibly put her hand to doing for the moment, she amused herself by thinking what kind of dress she would buy, and who should make it, if she should suddenly attain a fortune. But this was a harmless amusement, inasmuch as she never let it make her discontented with her lot, or ruffle her placid brow for an instant.

But just now she was "all of a tremble," and the V in her forehead was rapidly becoming a double V. She watched Luella's dismayed face with growing alarm.

"For goodness' sake alive!" said Luella, flinging herself into the most comfortable rocker, and throwing her mother's telegram on the table. "That's not to be tolerated! Something 'll have to be done. We'll have to go to the shore at once, Mother. I should die of mortification to have a country cousin come around just now. What would the Grandons think if they saw him? I can't afford to ruin all my chances for a cousin I've never seen. Mother, you simply must do something. I won't stand it!"

"What in the world are you talking about, Luella?" said her mother impatiently. "Why didn't you read the telegram aloud, or why didn't you give it to me at once? Where are my glasses?"

The aunt waited meekly while her sister found her glasses, and read the telegram.

"Well, I declare! That is provoking to have him turn up just now of all times. Something must be done, of course. We can't have a gawky westerner around in the way. And, as you say, we've never seen him. It can't make much difference to him whether he sees us or not. We can hurry off, and be conveniently out of the way. It's probably only a duty visit he's paying, anyway. Hannah's been dead ten years, and I always heard the child was more like his father than his mother. Besides, Hannah married and went away to live when I was only a little girl. I really don't think Donald has much claim on us. What a long telegram! It must have cost a lot. Was it paid for? It shows he knows nothing of the world, or he would have put it in a few words. Well, we'll have to get away at once."

She crumpled the telegram into a ball, and flung it to the table again; but it fell wide of its mark, and dropped to the floor instead. The aunt patiently stooped and picked it up, smoothing out the crushed yellow paper.

"Hannah's boy!" she said gently, and she touched the yellow paper as if it had been something sacred.

Am taking a trip east, and shall make you a little visit if convenient. Will be with you sometime on Thursday.

DONALD GRANT

She sat down suddenly in the nearest chair. Somehow the relief from anxiety had made her knees weak. "Hannah's boy!" she murmured again, and laid her hand caressingly over the telegram, smoothing down a torn place in the edge of the paper.

Luella and her mother were discussing plans. They had decided that they must leave on the early train the next morning, before there was any chance of the western visitor's arriving.

"Goodness! Look at Aunt Crete," said Luella, laughing. "She looks as if she has seen a ghost. Her lips are all white."

"Crete, you oughtn't to be such a fool. As if a telegram would hurt you! There's nobody left to be worried about like that. Why don't you use your reason a little?"

"Hannah's boy is really coming!" beamed Aunt Crete, ignoring their scorn of herself.

"Upon my word! Aunt Crete, you look as if it were something to be glad about, instead of a downright calamity."

"Glad, of course I'm glad, Luella. Wouldn't you be glad to see your oldest sister's child? Hannah was always very dear to me. I can see her now the way she looked when she went away, so tall and slim and pretty —"

"Not if she'd been dead for a century or so, and I'd never seen the child, and he was a gawky, embarrassing creature who would spoil the prospects of the people I was supposed to love," retorted Luella. "Aunt Crete, don't you care the least bit for my happiness? Do you want it all spoiled?"

"Why, of course not, dearie," beamed Aunt Crete, "but I don't see how it will spoil your happiness. I should think you'd want to see him yourself."

"Aunt Crete! The idea! He's nothing to me. You know he's lived away out in the wild west all his life. He probably never had much schooling, and doesn't know how to dress or behave in polite society. I heard he went away off up in the Klondike somewhere, and worked in a mine. You can imagine just what a wild, ignorant creature he will be. If Clarence Grandon should see him, he might imagine my family were all like that, and then where would I be?"

"Yes, Crete, I'm surprised at you. You've been so anxious all along for Luella to shine in society, and now you talk just as if you didn't care in the least what happened," put in Luella's mother.

"But what can you do?" asked Aunt Crete. "You can't tell him not to come — your own sister's child!"

"Oh, how silly you are, Crete!" said her sister. "No, of course we can't very well tell him not to come, as he hasn't given us a chance; for this telegram is evidently sent on the way. It is dated Chicago, and he hasn't given us a trace of an address. He doesn't live in Chicago. He's very likely almost here, and may arrive any time tomorrow. Now you know we've simply got to go to the shore next week, for the rooms are all engaged at the hotel, and paid for, and we might as well hurry up and get off tonight or early in the morning, and escape him. Luella would die of mortification if she had to visit with that fellow and give up her trip to the shore. As you weren't going anyway, you can receive him. It will keep him quietly at home, for he won't expect an old woman to go out with him, and show him the sights, so nobody will notice him much, and there won't be a lot of talk. If he looks very ridiculous, and that prying Mrs. Brown next door speaks of it, you might explain he's the son of an old school friend who went out west to live years ago —"

"Oh Carrie!" exclaimed Aunt Crete, "that wouldn't be true; and, besides, he can't be so very bad as that. And even if he is, I shall love him — for he's Hannah's boy."

"Love him all you want to," sniffed her sister, "but for pity's sake don't let the neighbors know what relation he is."

"That's just like you, Aunt Crete," said Luella in a hurt tone. "You've known me and pretended to love me all your life. I'm almost like your own child, and yet you take up with this unknown nephew, and say you'll love him in spite of all the trouble he's making me."

Aunt Crete doubled the V in her forehead, and wiped away the beads of perspiration. Somehow it always seemed that she was in the wrong. Would she be understood in heaven? she wondered.

Luella and her mother went on planning. They advised what Aunt Crete was to do after they left.

"There's the raspberries and blackberries not done up yet, Crete, but I guess you can manage alone. You always do the biggest part of the canning, anyway. I'm awfully sorry about your sewing, Crete. I meant to fit your two thin dresses before we went away, but the dressmaker made Luella's things so much more elaborate than I expected that we really haven't had a minute's time, what with all the lace insertion she left for us to sew on. Perhaps you better run down to Miss Mason, and see if she has time to fit them, if you think you can't wait till we get back. You'll hardly be going out much while we're gone, you know."

"Oh, I'll be all right," said Aunt Crete happily. "I guess I can fix up my gray lawn for while Donald's here."

"Donald! Nonsense! It won't matter what you wear while he's here. He'll never know a calico from a silk. Now look here, Crete, you've got to be awfully careful, or you'll let out when we went off. There's no use in his finding out we didn't want to see him. You wouldn't want to hurt his feelings, you know. Your own sister's child!''

"No, of course not," agreed Aunt Crete, though there was a troubled look in her eyes. She never liked prevarication; and, when she was left with some polite fabrication to excuse her relatives out of something they wanted to shirk, she nearly always got it twisted so that it was either an out-and-out lie, which horrified her, or else let the whole thing "out of the bag," as Luella said.

But there was little time for discussion; for Luella and her mother had a great deal of packing to do, and Aunt Crete had the dinner to get and the house to set in order, surreptitiously, for the expected guest.

They hurried away the next morning in a whirl of bags and suitcases and parasols and umbrellas. They had baggage enough for a year in Europe, although they expected to stay only two or three weeks at the shore at most. Aunt Crete helped them into the station cab, ran back to the house for Luella's new raincoat, back again for the veil and her sister's gloves, and still a third time to bring the new book, which had been set aside for reading on the journey. Then at last they were gone, and with one brief sigh of satisfaction Aunt Crete permitted herself to reflect that she was actually left alone to receive a dear guest all her own.

Never in all her maiden existence had she had this pleasure before. She might use the best china, and have three kinds of pie at once, yes, and plum cake if she chose. Boys like pie and cake. Donald would be a big, nice boy.

What did it matter to her if he was awkward and from the west? He was in a large sense her own. Hannah was gone, and there was no one else to take a closer place. Who but his mother's sister should have the right to mother him for a while? He would be her own as Luella never had been, because there was always Luella's mother to take the first place. Besides, Luella had been a disappointing baby. Even in her infancy she had developed an independence that scorned kissing and cuddling. Luella always had too many selfish interests on hand to have time for breathing out love and baby graces to admiring subjects. Her frown was always quicker than her smile. But somehow Aunt Crete felt that it would be different with this boy, and her heart swelled within her as she hurried into the house to make ready for his coming.

The front hall was littered with rose leaves. Luella had shaken a bunch of roses to get rid of the loose leaves, and had found they were all loose leaves; therefore she flung them down upon the floor. She had meant to wear them with her new pongee traveling suit. It looked well to wear roses on a journey, for it suggested a possible admirer. But the roses had not held out, and now Aunt Crete must sweep them up.

A glance into the parlor showed peanut shells scattered over the floor and on the table. A few of Luella's friends had come in for a few minutes the evening before, and they had indulged in peanuts, finishing up by throwing the shells at one another amid shouts of hilarious laughter. Aunt Crete went for the broom and dustpan. If he came early, the hall and parlor must be in order first.

Luella and her mother had little time to waste, for the tickets were barely bought and the trunks checked before the train thundered up. It was a through vestibuled train; and, as Luella struggled up the steps of one car with her heavy suitcase, a tall young man with dark, handsome eyes and a distinguished manner swung himself down the steps of the next car.

"Hello, Luella!" called a voice from a pony cart by the platform. "You're not going away today, are you? Thought you said you weren't going till next week."

"Circumstances made it necessary," called Luella from the top step of the car while the porter held up the suitcase for her to take. "I'm running away from a backwoods cousin that's coming to visit. I'll write and tell you all about it. Good-bye. Sorry I can't be at your house tomorrow night, but it couldn't be helped."

Then Luella turned another gaze upon the handsome stranger, who was standing on the platform just below her, looking about interestedly. She thought he had looked at her more than casually; and, as she settled herself in the seat, she glanced down at her pongee traveling suit consciously, feeling that he could but have thought she looked well.

He was still standing on the platform as the train moved out, and Luella could see the girl in the pony cart turn her attention to him. She half wished she were sitting in the pony cart too. It would be interesting to find out who he was. Luella preened herself, and settled her large hat in front of the strip of mirrow between the windows, and then looked around the car that she might see who were her fellow passengers.

"Well, I'm glad we're off," said her mother nervously. "I was afraid as could be your cousin might come in on that early through train before we got started. It would have been trying if he'd come just as we were getting away. I don't know how we could have explained it."

"Yes," said Luella. "I'm glad we're safely off. He'll never suspect now."

It was just at that moment that the grocery boy arrived at the back door with a crate of red raspberries.

"Land alive!" said Miss Crete disappointedly. "I hoped those wouldn't come till tomorrow." She bustled about, taking the boxes out of the crate so that the boy might take it back; and before she was done the doorbell rang.

"Land alive!" said Miss Crete again as she wiped her hands on the kitchen towel and hurried to the front door, taking off her apron as she went. "I do hope he hasn't come yet. I haven't cleared off that breakfast table; and, if he should happen to come out, there's three plates standing."

But the thought had come too late. The dining room door was stretched wide open, and the table in full view. The front door was guarded only by the wire screen. The visitor had been able to take full notes, if he so desired.

Chapter 2

The Backwoods Cousin

Miss Lucretia opened the screen, and noticed the fine appearance of the young man standing there. He was not shabby enough for an agent. Someone had made a mistake, she supposed. She waited pleasantly for him to tell his errand.

"Is this where Mrs. Carrie Burton lives?" he asked, removing his hat courteously.

And, when she answered, "Yes," his whole face broke into dancing eagerness.

"Is this my Aunt Carrie? I wonder"; and he held out a tentative, appealing hand for welcome. "I'm Donald Grant."

"Oh!" said Miss Lucretia delightedly, "Oh!" and she took his hand in both her own. "No, I ain't your Aunt Carrie, I'm your Aunt Crete; but I'm just as glad to see you. I didn't think you'd be so big and handsome. Your Aunt Carrie isn't home. They've just — why — that is — they are — they had planned to be at the shore for three weeks, and they'll be real sorry when they know —" This last sentence was added with extra zeal, for Aunt Crete exulted in the fact that Carrie and Luella would indeed be sorry if they could look into their home for one instant and see the guest from whom they had run away. She felt sure that if they had known how fine-looking a young man he was, they would have stayed and been proud of him.

"I'm sorry they are away," said the young man, stooping to kiss Aunt Crete's plump, comfortable cheek, "but I'm mighty glad you're at home, Aunt Crete," he said with genuine pleasure. "I'm going to like you for all I'm worth to make up for the absence of my aunt and cousin. You say they have gone to the shore. When will they be at home? Is their stay there almost up?"

"Why, no," said Aunt Crete, flushing uncomfortably. "They haven't been gone long. And they've engaged their rooms there for three weeks at a big hotel. Luella, she's always been bound to go to one of those big places where rich people go, the Traymore. It's advertised in all the papers. I expect you've seen it sometimes. It's one of the most expensive places at the shore. I've almost a notion to write and tell them to come home, for I'm sure they'll be sorry when they hear about you, but you see it's this way. There's a young man been paying Luella some attention, and he's going down there soon; I don't know but he's there already, and his mother and sister are spending the whole season there, so Luella had her heart set on going down and boarding at the same hotel.''

"Ah, I see," said the nephew. "Well, it wouldn't do to spoil my cousin's good time. Perhaps we can run down to the shore for a few days ourselves after we get acquainted. Say, Aunt Crete, am I too late for a bite of breakfast? I was so tired of the stuff they had on the dining car I thought I'd save up my appetite till I got here, for I was sure you'd have a bite of bread and butter, anyway."

"Bless your dear heart, yes," said Aunt Crete, delighted to have the subject turned; for she had a terrible fear she would yet tell a lie about the departure of her sister and niece, and a lie was a calamity not always easily avoided in a position like hers. "You just sit down here, you dear boy, and wait about two minutes till I set the coffeepot over the fire and cut some more bread. It isn't a mite of trouble, for I hadn't cleared off the breakfast table yet. In fact, I hadn't rightly finished my own breakfast, I was so busy getting to rights. The grocery boy came, and — well I never can eat much when folks are going — I mean when I'm alone," she finished triumphantly.

She hurried out into the dining room to get the table cleared off, but Donald followed her. She tried to scuttle the plates together and remove all traces of the number of guests at the meal just past, but she could not be sure whether he noticed the table or not.

"May I help you?" asked the young man, grabbing Luella's plate and cup, and following her into the kitchen. "It's so good to get into a real home again with somebody who belongs to me. You know Father is in Mexico, and I've been in the university for the last four years."

"The university!" Aunt Crete's eyes shone. "Do you have universities out west? My! Won't Luella be astonished? I guess she thinks out west is all woods."

Donald's eyes danced.

"We have a few good schools out there," he said quietly.

While they were eating the breakfast that Aunt Crete prepared in an incredibly short space of time, Donald asked a great many questions. What did his aunt and cousin look like? Was Aunt Carrie like her, or like his mother? And Luella, had she been to college? And what did she look like?

Aunt Crete told him mournfully that Luella was more like herself than like her mother. "And it seems sometimes as if she blamed me for it," said the patient aunt. "It makes it hard, her being a sort of society girl, and wanting to look so fine. Dumpy figures like mine don't dress up pretty, you know. No, Luella never went to college. She didn't take much to books. She liked having a good time with young folks better. She's been wanting to go down to the shore and be at a real big hotel for three summers now, but Carrie never felt able to afford it before. We've been saving up all winter for Luella to have this treat, and I do hope she'll have a good time. It's real hard on her, having to stay right home all the time when all her girl friends go off to the shore. But you see she's got in with some real wealthy people who stay at expensive places, and she isn't satisfied to go to a common boarding-house. It must be nice to have money and go to a big hotel. I've never been in one myself, but Luella has, and she's told all about it. I should think it would be grand to live that way awhile with not a thing to do.''

"They ought to have taken you along, Aunt Crete," said the young man. "I do hope I didn't keep you at home to entertain me."

"Oh, no, bless your heart," said the aunt, "I wasn't going. I never go anywhere. Why, what kind of a figure would I cut there? It would spoil all Luella's good time to have me around, I'm so short-waisted. She always wants me to wear a coat when I go anywhere with her, so people won't see how short-waisted I am."

"Nonsense," said Donald. "I think you are lovely, Aunt Crete. You've got such pretty white hair, all wavy like Mother's; and you've got a fine face. Luella ought to be proud to have you."

Aunt Crete blushed over the compliment, and choking tears of joy throbbed for a minute in her throat.

"Now hear the boy!" she exclaimed. "Donald, do have another cup of coffee."

After breakfast Aunt Crete showed her guest to his room, and then hurried down to get the stack of dishes out of the way before he came down again. But he appeared in the kitchen door in a few minutes.

"Give me a dish and some berries," he demanded. "I'm going to help you."

And despite all her protests he helped her with such vigor that by twelve o'clock twenty-one jars of crimson berries stood in a shining row on the kitchen table, and Aunt Crete was dishing up a savory dinner for two, with her face shining as brightly as if she had done nothing but play the whole morning.

"We did well, didn't we?" said Donald as he ate his dinner. "I haven't had such a good time since I went camping in the Klondike. Now after we get these dishes washed you are going to take a nice long nap. You look tired and warm."

Aunt Crete protested that she was not tired, but Donald insisted. "I want you to get nice and rested up, because tomorrow we're going shopping. By the way, I've brought you a present." He sprang up from the table, and went to his suitcase to get it.

Aunt Crete's heart beat with anticipation as he handed her a little white box. What if it should be a breastpin? How she would like that! She had worn her mother's, a braid of hair under a glass, with a gold band under it, ever since she was grown up, and sometimes she felt as if it was a little old-fashioned. Luella openly scoffed at it, and laughed at her for wearing it, but no one ever suggested getting her a new one, and, if she had ventured to buy one for herself, she knew they would have thought her extravagant.

She opened the box with excited fingers, and there inside was a little leather case. Donald touched a spring, and it flew open and disclosed a lovely star made all of seed pearls, reposing on white velvet. It was a breastpin indeed, and one fit for a queen. Fortunately Aunt Crete did not know enough about jewelry to realize what it cost, or her breath might have been taken away. As it was, she was stunned for the moment. Such a beautiful pin, and for her! She could scarcely believe it. She gazed and gazed, and then, laying the box on the table, rose up and took Donald's face in her two toil-worn hands, and kissed him.

"I'm glad you like it," he said with a pleased smile. "I wasn't quite sure what to get, but the salesman told me these were always nice. Now let's get at these dishes."

In a daze of happiness Aunt Crete washed the dishes while Donald wiped them, and then despite her protest he made her go upstairs and lie down.

When had she ever taken a nap in the daytime before? Not since she was a little girl and fell from the second-story window. The family had rushed around her frightened, and put her to bed in the daytime, and for one whole day she had been waited upon and cared for tenderly. Then she had been able to get up, and the hard, careless, toilsome world had rushed on again for her. But the memory of that blessed day of rest, touched by gentleness, had lingered forever a bright spot in her memory. She had always been the one that did the hard things in her family, even when she was quite young.

Aunt Crete lay cautiously down upon her neatly made bed after she had attired herself in her best gown, a rusty black and white silk made over from one Luella had grown tired of, and clasped her hands blissfully on her breast, resting with her eyes wide open and a light of joy upon her face. She hardly felt it right to relax entirely, lest Donald might call her, but finally the unaccustomed position in the middle of the day sent her off into a real doze, and just about that time the telephone bell rang.

The telephone was in the sitting room downstairs. It had been put in at the time when the telephone company was putting them in free to introduce them in that suburb. It was ordinarily a source of great interest to the whole family, though it seldom rang except for Luella. Luella and her mother were exceedingly proud of its possession.

Donald was in the sitting room reading. He looked up from his paper, hesitated a moment, and then took down the receiver. Perhaps his aunt was asleep already, and he could attend to this without waking her.

"Hello; is this 53 M?"

Donald glanced at the number on the telephone, and answered, "Yes."

"Here you are, Atlantic. Here is Midvale," went on the voice of the operator at central.

"Hello! Is that you, Aunt Crete? This is Luella," came another girl's strident voice in hasty impatience. "What in the world were you so long about answering the phone for? I've been waiting here an age. Now, listen, Aunt Crete. For heaven's sake don't you tell that crazy cousin of ours where to find us, or like as not he'll take a notion to run down here to see us, and I should simply die of mortification if he did. This is a very swell hotel, and it would be fierce to have a backwoods relation appear on the scene. Now be sure you keep quiet. I'll never forgive you if you don't. And say, Aunt Crete, won't you please sew on the rest of that Val edging down the ruffles of the waist and on the skirt of my new lavender organdie, and do it up, and send it by mail? I forgot all about it. It's on the bed in the spare room, and the edging is started. You sew it on the way it is begun. You'll see. Now don't you go to sewing it on in the old way because it is quicker; for it doesn't look a bit pretty, and you've nothing much else to do, now we're gone, anyway. And say, Aunt Crete, would you mind going down to Peter's today, and telling Jennie I forgot all about getting those aprons to finish for the fair, and tell her you'll finish them for her? Do it today, because she has to send the box off by the end of the week. And Mother says you better clean the cellar right away, and she wondered if you'd feel equal to whitewashing it. I should think you'd like to do that, it's so cool this warm weather to be down cellar. And, Oh, yes, if you get lonesome and want something to do, I forgot to tell you I left those three flannel shirtwaists all cut out ready to be made in the upper bureau drawer of the spare room. Now don't read your eyes out the way you did the last time we went off and left you, and have to wear dark glasses for a week, because I have lots of things planned to do when I get home. I'm going to have Helena Bates for a week, and there'll be several lunches and picnics doing. Oh, say, Aunt Crete, Mother says, if there's any more pie cherries to be had, you better put up some, and be sure and stone them all. I just hate them with the seeds in. And I guess that's all, only don't forget you promised to have all those buttonholes worked for me in those underclothes I'm making, before I get back. Are you all right? Let me see. There was something else. Oh, yes, Mother says you don't need to get out the best china and make a great fuss as if you had grand company; he's only a country boy, you know. Say, Aunt Crete. Are you there? Why don't you answer? Aunt Crete! Hello! For pity's sake, what is the matter with this phone? Hello, central! Oh, dear! I suppose she's gone away. That's the way Aunt Crete always does!''

Donald, a strange, amused expression upon his face, stood listening and hesitating. He did not know exactly what to do. Without any intention at all he had listened to a conversation not intended for his ears. Should he answer and tell who he was? No, for that would but embarrass Luella. Neither would it do to call Aunt Crete now, for they would be sure to find out he had heard. Perhaps it was better to keep entirely still. There seemed to be nothing serious at stake. Ruffles and shirtwaists and gingham aprons for a guild and whitewashing the cellar! Nobody would die if none of them were done, and his blood boiled over the tone in which the invisible cousin at the other end of the wire had ordered Aunt Crete about. He could read the whole life story of the patient self-sacrifice on the one hand and imposition on the other. He felt strongly impelled to do something in the matter. A rebuke of some sort should be administered. How could it best be done?

Meantime Luella was fuming with the telephone girl, and the girl was declaring that she could get no answer from Midvale anymore. Donald stood wickedly enjoying their discomfiture, and was at last rewarded by hearing Luella say: "Well, I guess I've said all I want to say, anyway; so you needn't ring them up again. I've got to go out boating now." The receiver at the shore clicked into place, and the connection was cut off.

Then the young man hung up the receiver at the Midvale end of the line, and sat down to think. Bit by bit he pieced together the story until he had very nearly made out the true state of affairs. So they were ashamed of him, and were trying to get away. Could it be possible that they had been the people that got on the train as he got off? Was that girl with the loud voice and the pongee suit his cousin? The voice over the telephone seemed like the one that had called to the girl in the pony cart. And had his eyes deceived him, or were there three plates on the breakfast table that morning? Poor Aunt Crete! He would give her the best time he knew how, and perhaps it was also set for him to give his cousin a lesson.

Chapter 3

A Wonderful Day

Aunt Crete woke up at last from an uncomfortable dream. She thought Carrie and Luella had come back, and were about to snatch Donald away from her and bear him off to the shore.

She arose in haste and smoothed her hair, astonished at the freshness of her own face in the glass. She was afraid she had overslept and lost some of the precious time with Donald. There was so much to ask him, and he was so good to look at. She hurried down and was received warmly. Donald's meditations had culminated in a plan.

"Sit down, Aunt Crete; are you sure you are rested? Then I want to talk. Suppose we run down to the shore and surprise the folks. How soon could you be ready?"

"Oh, dear heart! I couldn't do that!" exclaimed Aunt Crete, her face nevertheless alight with pleasure at the very thought.

"Why not? What's to hinder?"

"Oh, I never go. I always stay at home and attend to things."

"But that's no reason. Why couldn't things attend to themselves."

"Why I couldn't leave the house alone."

"Now, what in the world could possibly happen to the house that you could prevent by staying in it? Be reasonable, dear Aunt. You know the house won't run away while you are gone, and, if it does, I'll get you another one. You don't mean to tell me you never go off on a vacation. Then it's high time you went, and you'll have to stay longer to make up for lost time. Besides, I want your company. I've never seen the eastern coast, and expect to enjoy it hugely, but I need somebody to enjoy it with me. I can't half take things in alone. I want somebody my very own to go with me. That's what I came here for. I had thought of inviting you all to go down for a little trip, but, as the others are down there, why, we can join them."

Aunt Crete's face clouded. What would Luella say at having them appear on her horizon? The young man was all right, apparently, but there was no telling how angry Luella might be if her aunt came. She knew that Luella preferred to keep her in the background.

"I really couldn't go, dear," she said wistfully. "I'd like it with all my heart. And it would be specially nice to go with you, for I never had anybody to go round with me, not since your mother was a girl and used to take me with her wherever she went. I missed her dreadfully after she was married and went west. She was always so good to me."

The young man's face softened, and he reached his hand impulsively across the table, and grasped the toil-worn hand of his aunt.

"Well, you shall have somebody to go round with you now, Auntie; that is, if you'll let me. I'm not going to take 'No' for an answer. You just must go. We'll have a vacation all by ourselves, and do just as we please, and we'll bring up at the hotel where Aunt Carrie and Luella are, and surprise them."

"But, child, I can't!" said Aunt Crete in dismay, seeing his determination. "Why, I haven't any clothes suitable to wear away from home. We were all so busy getting Luella fixed out that there wasn't any time left for mine, and it didn't really matter about me anyway. I never go anywhere."

"But you're going now, Aunt Lucretia," said he, "and it does matter, you see. Clothes are easily bought. We'll go shopping after breakfast tomorrow morning."

"But I really can't afford it, Donald," said his aunt with an air of finality. "You know I'm not rich. If Carrie weren't good enough to give me a home here, I shouldn't know how to make two ends meet."

"Never mind that, Aunt Crete; this is my layout, and I'm paying for it. We'll go shopping tomorrow morning. I've got some money in my pocket I'm just aching to spend. The fact is, Aunt Crete, I struck gold up there in the Klondike, and I've got more money than I know what to do with."

"Oh!" said Aunt Crete with awe in her voice at the thought of having more money than one knew what to do with. Then shyly, "But —"

"But what, Aunt Lucretia?" asked Donald as she hesitated and flushed till the double V came into her forehead in the old helpless, worried way.

"Why, there's lots of canning and housecleaning that has got to be done, and I don't really think Carrie would like it to have me leave it all, and run away on a pleasure excursion."

Righteous indignation filled the heart of the nephew. "Well, I should like to know why she wouldn't like it!" he exclaimed impulsively. "Has she any better right to have a vacation than you? I'm sure you've earned it. You blessed little woman, you're going to have a vacation now, in spite of yourself. Just put your conscience away in pink cotton till we get back — though I don't know whether I shall let you come back to stay. I may spirit you off with me somewhere if I don't like the looks of my cousin. I'll take all the responsibility of this trip. If Aunt Carrie doesn't like it, she may visit her wrath on me, and I'll tell her just what I think of her. Anyhow, to the shore you are going right speedily; that is, if you want to go. If there's some other place you'd rather go besides to the Traymore, speak the word, and there we'll go. I want you to have a good time."

Aunt Crete gasped with joy. The thought of the ocean, the real ocean, was wonderful. She had dreamed of it many times, but never had seen it, because she was always the one who could just as well stay at home as not. She never got run down or nervous or cross, and was ordered to go away for her health, and she never insisted upon going when the rest went. Her heart was bounding as it had not bounded since the morning of the last Sunday-school picnic she had attended when she was a girl.

"Indeed, dear boy, I do want to go with all my heart if I really ought. I have always wanted to see the ocean, and I can't imagine any place I'd rather go than the Traymore, Luella's talked so much about it."

"All right. Then it's settled that we go. How soon can we get ready? We'll go shopping tomorrow morning bright and early, and get a trunkful of new clothes. It's always nice to have new things when you go off; you feel like another person, and don't have to be sewing on buttons all the time," laughed Donald, as if he was enjoying the whole thing as much as his aunt. "I meant to have a good time getting presents for the whole family, but, as they aren't here, I'm going to get them all for you. You're not to say a word. Have you got a trunk?"

"Trunk? No, child. I haven't ever had any need for a trunk. The time I went to Uncle Hiram's funeral I took Carrie's old haircloth one, but I don't know 's that's fit to travel again. Carrie's got her flannels packed away in camphor in it now, and I shouldn't like to disturb it."

"Then we'll get a trunk."

"Oh, no," protested Aunt Crete, "that would be a foolish expense. There's some pasteboard boxes upstairs. I can make out with them in a shawl strap. I shan't need much for a few days."

"Enlarge your scale of things, Aunt Crete. You're going to stay more than a few days. You're going to stay till you're tired, and just want to come back. As we're going to a 'swell' hotel" — Donald reflected that Aunt Crete could not understand his reference to Luella's description of the Traymore — "we can't think of shawl straps and boxes. You shall have a big trunk. I saw an advertisement of one that has drawers and a hatbox in it, like a bureau. We'll see if we can find one to suit."

"It sounds just like the fairy tales I used to read to Luella when she was a little girl," beamed Aunt Crete. "It doesn't seem as if it was I. I can't make it true."

"Now let's write down a list of things you need," said the eager planner, "we'll have to hurry up things, and get off this week if possible. I've been reading the paper, and they say there's coming a hot wave. I need to get you to the shore before it arrives, if possible. Come, what shall I put down first? What have you always thought you'd like, Aunt Crete? Don't you need some silk dresses?"

"Oh, dear heart! Hear him! Silk dresses aren't for me. Of course I've always had a sort of hankering after one, but nothing looks very well on me. Carrie says my figure is dumpy. I guess, if you're a mind to, you can get me a lace collar. It'll please me as well as anything. Luella saw some for a quarter that were real pretty. She bought one for herself. I think it would do to wear with my new pin, and all my collars are pretty much worn out."

"Now look here, Aunt Crete! Can't I make you understand? I mean business, and no collars for a quarter are going to do. You can have a few cheap ones for morning if you want them, but we'll buy some real lace ones to wear with the pin. And you shall have the silk dress, two or three of them, and a lot of other things. What kind do you want?"

"Oh, my dear boy! You just take my breath away. I with two or three silk dresses! The idea! Carrie would think me extravagant, and Luella wouldn't like it a bit. She always tells me I'm too gay for my years."

Donald set his lips, and wished he could have speech for a few minutes with the absent Luella. He felt that he would like to express his contempt for her treatment of their aunt.

"I've always thought I'd like a gray silk," mused Aunt Crete with a dreamy look in her eyes, "but I just know Luella would think it was too dressy for me. I suppose black would be better. I can't deny I'd like black silk, too."

"We'll have both," said Donald decidedly. "I saw a woman in a silver-gray silk once. She had white hair like yours, and the effect was beautiful. Then you'll need some other things. White dresses, I guess. That's what my chum's grandmother used to wear when I went there visiting in the summer."

"White for me!" exclaimed the aunt. "Oh, Luella would be real angry at me getting white. She says it's too conspicuous for old women to dress in light colors."

"Never mind Luella. We're doing this, and whatever we want goes. If Luella doesn't like it, she needn't look at it."

Aunt Crete was all in a flutter that night. She could hardly sleep. She did not often go to town. Luella did all the shopping. Sometimes she suggested going, but Carrie always said it was a needless expense, and, besides, Luella knew how to buy at a better bargain. It was a great delight to go with Donald. Her face shone, and all the weariness of the day's work, and all the toilsome yesterdays, disappeared from her brow.

She looked over her meager wardrobe, most of it cast-offs from Carrie's or Luella's half-worn clothing, and wrote down in a cramped hand a few absolute necessities. The next morning they had an early breakfast, and started at once on their shopping expedition. Aunt Crete felt like a little child being taken to the circus. The idea of getting a lot of new clothes all for herself seemed too serious a business to be true. She was dazed when she thought of it, and so, when Donald asked what they should look at first, she showed plainly that she would be little help in getting herself fitted out. She was far too happy to bring her mind down to practical things, and, besides, she could not adjust herself to the vast scale of expenditure Donald had set.

"Here are some collars," said Donald. "We might as well begin on these."

Aunt Crete examined them with enthusiasm, and finally picked out two at twenty-five cents apiece.

"Are those the best you have?" questioned Donald.

"Oh, no," said the saleswoman, quick to identify the purchaser that did not stop at price, "did you want real or imitation?"

"Real, by all means," he answered promptly.

"Oh, Donald," breathed Aunt Crete in a warning whisper, "real lace comes dreadful high. I've heard Luella say so. Besides, I shouldn't have anything to wear it with, nor any place to go fixed up like that."

"Have you forgotten you're going to the Traymore in a few days?" he asked her with a twinkle in his eye. "And what about the gray silk? Won't it go with that? If not, we'll get something better."

Assisted by the saleswoman, they selected two beautiful collars of real lace, and half a dozen plain ones for everyday wear.

"Couldn't you go with us?" asked Donald of the saleswoman as the purchase was concluded. "My aunt wishes to get a good many things, and neither she nor I is much used to shopping. We'd like to have your advice."

"I'm sorry; I'd like to, but I'm not allowed to leave this counter," said the woman with a kindly smile. "I'm head of this department, and they can't get along without me this morning. But they have buyers in the office just for that purpose. You go up to the desk over on the east side just beyond the rotunda, and ask for a buyer to go around with you. Get Miss Brower if you can, and tell her the head of the lace department told you to call for her. She'll tell you just what to get," and she smiled again at Aunt Crete's kindly, beaming face.

They went to the desk, and found Miss Brower, who, when she heard the message, took them smilingly under her wing. She knew that meant a good sale had been made, and there would be something in it for her. Besides, she had a kindly disposition, and did not turn up a haughty nose at Aunt Crete's dumpy little figure.

"Now, just what do you want first?" she asked brightly.

"Everything," said Donald helplessly. "We've only bought a lace collar so far, and now we want all the rest of the things to go with it. The only things we've decided on so far are two silk dresses, a black one and a silver-gray. How do we go about it to get them? Do they have them ready-made?"

"Nothing that would be quite suitable, I'm afraid, in silks. But we'll go and see what there is in stock," said the assistant with skillful eye, taking in Aunt Crete's smiling, helpless face, lovely white hair, dumpy, ill-fitted figure, and all. "There might be a gray voile that would suit her. In fact, I saw one this morning, very simple and elegant, lined with gray silk, and trimmed with lace dyed to match. It is a beauty, and just reduced this morning to thirty dollars from sixty. I believe it will fit her."

Aunt Crete gasped at the price, and looked at Donald; but he seemed pleased, and said: "That sounds good. Let's go and see it. We'll have a gray — what was it you called it — voile? Remember that name, Aunt Crete. You're going to have a gray voile. But we want the silk too. Do they make things here? We want to go away in a few days, and would like to take them with us."

"Oh, yes, they'll make anything to order; and this time of year we're not so busy. I guess you could get a 'hurry-up' order on it, and have it done in a couple of days; or it could be forwarded to you if it was not quite finished when you left."

They stepped into the elevator, and in a moment were ushered into the presence of the rare and the imported. Aunt Crete stood in a maze of delight and wonder. All this was on exhibition just for her benefit, and she was Alice in Wonderland for the hour. Donald stood back with his arms folded, and watched her with satifaction. One thing alone was wanted to complete it. He would have liked to have Luella up in the gallery somewhere watching also. But that he held in anticipation. Luella should be made to understand that she had done wrong in underrating this sweet, patient soul.

The gray voile was entirely satisfactory to the two shoppers. Donald recognized it as the thing many women of his acquaintance wore at the receptions he had attended in university circles. Aunt Crete fingered it wistfully, and had her inward doubts whether anything so frail and lovely, like a delicate veil, would wear; but, looking at Donald's happy face, she decided not to mention it. The dress was more beautiful than anything she had ever dreamed of possessing. "But it won't fit me," she sighed as she and Miss Brower were on the way to the trying-on room where the garment was to be fitted to her. "I'm so dumpy, you know, and Luella always says it's no use to get me anything ready-made."

"Oh, the fitter will make it fit," said Miss Brower convincingly; and then, with a glance at the ample waist, whose old-fashioned lines lay meekly awry as if they were used to being put on that way and were beyond even discouragement: "Why don't you wear one of those stiffened waists? There's a new one on sale, has soft bones all around, and is real comfortable. It would make your dresses set a great deal better. If you like, I'll go get one, and you can be fitted over it. You don't like anything very tight, do you?"

"No," said Aunt Crete in a deprecatory tone, "I never could bear anything real tight. That's what puts Luella out so about me. But, if you say there's a waist that's comfortable, I should be so obliged if you'd get it. I'd be willing to pay any price not to look so dumpy."

She felt that if it took the last cent she possessed, and made all her relatives angry with her, she must have something to fit her once.

Miss Brower, thus commissioned, went away, and returned very soon with the magical waist that was to transform Miss Lucretia's "figger." If Donald could have seen his aunt's face when she was finally arrayed in the soft folds of the gray voile and was being pinned up and pinned down and pinned in and pinned out, he would have been fully repaid. Aunt Crete's ecstasy was marred only by the fact that Luella could not see her grandeur. Actually being fitted in a department store to a real imported dress! Could mortal attain higher in this mundane sphere?

When the fitting was pronounced done and Aunt Crete was about to don her discouraged shirtwaist once more, Miss Brower appeared in the doorway with a coat and skirt suit over her arm, made of fine soft black taffeta.

"Just put this on and let the gentleman see how he likes it," she said. She had been out to talk over matters with Donald and have an understanding as to what was wanted. She had advised the taffeta coat and skirt for traveling, with an extra cloth coat for cool days. Aunt Crete, with the new dignity that consciousness of her improved figure gave her, rustled out to her nephew looking like a new woman, her face beaming.

That was a wonderful day. Aunt Crete retired again for the black taffeta to be altered a little, and yet again for a black and white dotted swiss, and a white linen suit, and a handsome black crepe de chine, and then to have the measure taken for the silver-gray silk, which the head dressmaker promised could be hurried through. They bought a black chiffon waist and some filmy, dreamy white shirt-waists, simple and plain in design, and exquisite lace simply applied, fine handmade tucks, and finer material. Miss Brower advised white linen and white lawn for morning wear at the seashore, and gave Aunt Crete confidence, telling how she had a customer, "a woman about as old as you, with just such lovely white hair," who but yesterday purchased a set of white dresses for morning wear at the seashore. This silenced the thoughts of her sister's horror at "White for you, Crete! What are you thinking of?" Never mind, she was going to have one good time, even if she had to put all her lovely finery away in a trunk afterwards, and never bring it out again, or — dreary thought — were made to cut it over for Luella sometime. Well, it might come to that, but at least she would enjoy it while it was hers.

Two white linen skirts, a handsome black cloth coat, several pairs of silk gloves, black and white, some undergarments dainty enough for a bride, a whole dozen pairs of stockings! How Aunt Crete rejoiced in those! She had been wearing stockings whose feet were cut out of old stocking legs for fifteen years. She couldn't remember when she had had a whole new pair of stockings all her own. And then two new bonnets.

All these things were acquired little by little. It was while they were in the millinery department, and Miss Brower had just set a charming black lace bonnet made on a foundation of white roses on the white hair, that Donald decided she was one of the most beautiful old ladies he had ever seen. The drapery was a fine black lace scarf, which swept around the roses and tied loosely on the breast, and it gave the quiet little woman a queenly air. She was getting used to seeing her own face in strange adornments, but it startled her to see that she really looked handsome in this bonnet. She stood before the transformation in the mirror almost in awe, and never heard what Miss Brower was saying:

"That's just the thing for best, and there's a lovely lace wrap in the cloak department she ought to have to go with it. It would be charming."

"Get it," said Donald with respectful brevity. He was astonished himself at the difference mere clothes made. Aunt Crete was fairly impressive in her new bonnet. And the lace wrap proved indeed to be the very mate to the bonnet, hiding the comfortable figure, and making her look "just like other people," as she breathlessly expressed it after one glance at herself in the lace wrap.

They bought a plain black bonnet, a sweet little gray one, a fine silk umbrella, a lot of pretty belts and handkerchiefs, some shoes and rubbers, a handbag of cut steel, for which Luella would have bartered her conscience — what there was left of it; and then they smiled good-bye at Miss Brower, and left her for a little while, and went to lunch.

Such a lunch! Soup and fish and spring lamb and fresh peas and new potatoes and two kinds of ice cream in little hard sugar cases that looked like baked snowballs. Aunt Crete's hand trembled as she took the first spoonful. The wonders of the day had been so great that she was fairly worn out, and two little bright red spots of excitement had appeared in her cheeks, but she was happy! Happier than she remembered ever to have been in her life before. Her dear old conscience had a moment of sighing that Luella could not have been there to have enjoyed it too, and then her heart bounded in wicked gleefulness that Luella was not there to stop her nice time.

They went into a great hall in the same store, and sat among the palms and coolness made by electric fans, while a wonderful organ played exquisite music, and Aunt Crete felt she certainly was in heaven without the trouble of dying; and she never dreamed, dear soul, that she had been dying all her life that others might live, and that it is to such that the reward is promised.

They went back to Miss Brower later; and behold! the silver-gray silk had been cut out, and was ready to fit. Aunt Crete felt it was fairy work, the whole of it, and she touched the fabric as if it had been made by magic.

Then they went and bought a trunk and a handsome leather satchel, and Donald took a notion that his aunt must have a set of silver combs for her hair such as he saw in the hair of another old lady.

"Now," said Donald reflectively, "we'll go home and get rested, and tomorrow we'll come down and buy any things we've forgotten."

"And I'm sure I don't see what more a body could possibly need," said Aunt Crete, as, tired and absolutely contented, she climbed into the train and sat down in the hot plush seat.

The one bitter drop in the cup of bliss came the next morning — or rather two drops — in the shape of letters. One from Aunt Carrie for Donald was couched in stiffest terms, in which she professed to have just heard of his coming, and to be exceedingly sorry that she was not at home, and was kept from returning only by a sprained ankle, the doctor telling her that she must not put her foot to the ground for two or three weeks yet, or she would have to suffer for it.

The other letter was for Aunt Crete, and was a rehash of the telephone message, with a good sound scolding for having gone away from the telephone before she finished speaking. Luella had written it herself because she felt like venting her temper on someone. The young man that had been so attentive to her in town had promenaded the piazza with another young woman all the evening before. Luella hoped Aunt Crete would put up plenty of gooseberry jam. Aunt Crete put on her double V as she read, and sighed for a full minute before Donald looked up amused from his letter.

"Now, Aunt Crete, you look as if a mountain had rolled down upon you. What's the matter?"

"Oh, I'm just afraid, Donald, that I'm doing wrong going off this way, when Carrie expects me to do all this canning and sewing and cleaning. I'm afraid she'll never forgive me."

"Now, Aunt Crete, don't you love me? Didn't I tell you I'd stand between you and the whole world? Please put that letter up, and come and help me pack your new trunk. Do you want that gray silk put in first, or shall I put the shoes at the bottom? Don't you know you and I are going to have the times of our lives? We're going to run away from every care. Do you suppose your own sister would want you to stay here roasting in the city if she knew you had a nephew just aching to carry you off to the ocean? Come, forget it. Cut it out, Aunt Crete, and let's pack the trunk. I'm longing to be off to smell the briny deep." And laughingly he carried her away, and plunged her into thoughts of her journey, giving her no time the rest of the day to think of anything else.

Chapter 4
Aunt Crete Transformed

They locked the house early one morning when even the dusty bricks had a smell of freshness to them before the hot sun baked them for another day. The closed blinds seemed sullen like a conquered tyrant, and the front door looked reproachfully at Aunt Crete as she turned the key carefully and tried it twice to be sure it was locked. The lonesome look of the house gave the poor old lady a pang as she turned the corner in her softly rustling silk coat and skirt. She felt it had hardly been right to put on a new black silk in the morning, and go off from all the cares of the world, just leave them, boldly ignore them, like any giddy girl, and take a vacation. She regarded herself with awe and a rising self-respect in every window she passed. Somehow the look of dumpiness had passed away mysteriously. It was not her old self that was passing along the street to the station bearing a cut-steel handbag, while Donald carried her new satchel, and her new trunk bumped on a square ahead in the expressman's wagon.

It was a hot morning, and the great city station seemed close and stuffy, but Aunt Crete mingled with the steaming crowd blissfully. To be one with the world, attired irreproachably; to be on her way to a great hotel by the sea, with new clothes, and escorted devotedly by someone who was her very own, this indeed was happiness. Could anyone desire more upon the earth?

Donald put her into a cab at the station, and she beamed happily out at the frightful streets that always made her heart come into her mouth on the rare occasions when she had to cross them. The ride across the city seemed a brief and distinguished experience. It was as if everybody else was walking and they only had the grandeur of a carriage. Then the ferry boat was delightful to the new traveler, with its long, white-ceiled passages, and its smell of wet timbers and tarred ropes. They had a seat close to the front, where they could look out and watch their own progress and see the many puffing monsters laboriously plying back and forth, and the horizon line of many masts, like fine brown lines against the sky. Aunt Crete felt that at last she was out in the world. She could not have felt it more if she had been starting for Europe.

The seashore train, with its bamboo seats and its excited groups of children bearing tin pails and shovels and tennis-rackets, filled her with a fine exhilaration. At last, at last, her soul had escaped the bounds of red brick walls that she had expected would surround her as long as she lived. She drew deep breaths, and beamed upon the whole trainful of people, yelling baby and all. She gazed and gazed at the fast-flying Jersey scenery, grown so monotonous to some of the travelers, and admired every little white and green town at which they paused.

Donald put her into a carriage when they reached the shore. Half an hour off they had begun to smell the sea, and to catch glimpses of low-flying marshes and a misty blueness against the sky. Now every friendly hackman at the station seemed a part of the great day to Aunt Crete. So pretty a carriage, with low steps and gray cushions and a fringe all around the canopy, and a white speckled horse, with long, gentle, white eyelashes. Aunt Crete leaned back self-consciously on the gray cushions, and enjoyed the creak of her silk jacket as she settled into place. She felt as if this was a play that would soon be over; but she would enjoy it to the very end, and then go back to her dishwashing and cellar-cleaning, and being blamed, and bear them all in happy remembrance of what she had had for one blissful vacation.

She did not know that Donald had telephoned ahead for the best apartments in the hotel. She was engaged in watching for the first blue line of the great mysterious ocean; and, when it came into sight, billowing suddenly above the line of boardwalk as they turned a corner, her heart stood still for one moment, and then bounded onward set to the time of wonder.

Two obsequious porters jumped to assist Aunt Crete from the carriage. The hand baggage drifted up the steps as if by magic, and awaited them in the apartments to which they arose in a luxurious elevator. Aunt Crete noticed several old ladies with pink and blue wool knitting, sitting in a row of large rocking chairs, as she glided up to the second floor. It gave her rest on one point, for they all wore white dresses. She had been a little dubious about those white dresses that Donald had insisted upon. But now she might enjoy them unashamed. Oh, what would Luella say?

She glanced around the room, half-fearfully expecting to find Luella waiting there. Somehow, now she was there, she wanted to get used to it and enjoy it all before Luella came. For Luella was an uncertain quantity. Luella might not like it, after all! Dreadful thought! And after Donald had taken so much trouble and spent so much money all to surprise them!

The smiling porter absorbed the goodly tip that Donald handed him, and went his way. Aunt Crete and Donald were left alone. They looked at each other and smiled.

"Let's look around and see where they've put us," said Donald, pushing the swaying curtains aside, and there before them rolled the blue tide of the ocean. Aunt Crete sank into a chair, and was silent for a while; and then she said: "It's just as big as I thought it would be. I was so afraid it wouldn't be. Some folks next door went down to the shore last year, and they said it didn't look big enough to what they'd expected, and I've been afraid ever since."

Donald's eyes filled with a tender light that was beautiful to see. He was enjoying the spending of his money, and it was yielding him a rich reward already.

The apartments that had been assigned to them consisted of a parlor and two large bedrooms with private baths. Donald discovered a few moments later, when he went down to the office to investigate, that Luella and his aunt occupied a single room on the fourth floor back, overlooking the kitchen court. It was not where he would have placed them, had they chosen to await his coming and be taken down to the shore in style. But now that they had run away from him, and were too evidently ashamed of him, perhaps it was as well to let them remain where they were, he reflected.

"Aunt Carrie and Luella have gone out with a party in a carriage for an all-day drive to Pleasure Bay," announced Donald when he came up. "Aunt Carrie's ankle must be better."

"Well, that's real nice!" exclaimed Aunt Crete with a smile, turning from her view of the sea, where she had been ever since he left her. "I'm glad Luella is having a good time, and we shan't miss her a mite. You and I'll have the ocean all to ourselves today."

Donald smiled approvingly. He was not altogether sure he cared to meet that other aunt and cousin at all. He was not sure but he would like to run away from them, and carry Aunt Crete with him.

"Very well," he said, "I'm glad you're not disappointed. We'll do just whatever we want to. Would you like to go in bathing?"

"Oh, my! Could I! I've always thought I'd like to see how it would feel, but I guess I'm too old. Besides, there's my figger. It wouldn't look nice in a bathing suit. Luella wouldn't like it a bit, and I don't want to disgrace her, now I'm here. She always makes a lot of fun of old people going in and sitting right on the edge of the water. I guess it won't do."

"Yes, it will do, if you want to. Didn't I tell you this was my party, and Luella isn't in it? That's ridiculous. I'll take you in myself, Aunt Crete, and we'll have the best time out; and you shan't be scared, either. I can swim like a fish. You shall go in every day. Would you like to begin at once?"

"I should," said Aunt Crete, rising with a look of resolution in her face. She felt that Luella would condemn the amusement for her; so, if she was to dare it, it must be done before her niece appeared.

They went down to the beach, and for a few minutes surveyed the bathers as they came out to the water. Then with joy and daring in her face Aunt Crete went into the little bathhouse with wildly beating heart, arrayed herself in the gay blue flannel garb provided for her use, and came timidly out to meet Donald, tall and smiling in his blue jerseys.

They had a wonderful time. It was almost better than shopping. Donald led her down to the water, and very gently accustomed her to it until he had led her out beyond the roughness, where his strong arms lifted her well above the swells until she felt as if she was a bird. It was marvelous that she was not afraid, but she was not. It was as if she had that morning been transferred back over forty years to her youth again, and was having the good times that she had longed for, such as other girls had — the swings and the rides and the skatings and bicyclings. How many such things she had watched through the years, with her heart palpitating with daring to do it all herself! Her petulant sister and the logy Luella never dreamed that Aunt Crete desired such unauntly indulgences. If they had, they would have taken it out of her, scorched it out with scorn.

The white hair with its natural waves fluffed out beautifully, like a canary's feathers, after the bath, and Aunt Crete was smiling and charming at lunch in one of her fine new white dresses. She had hurried to put it on before Luella appeared, lest they might all be spirited away from her if Luella discovered them. She reflected with a sigh that they would likely fit Luella beautifully, and that that would probably be their final destination, just as Luella's discarded garments came to her.

But there was nothing to mar the lunchtime and the beautiful afternoon, wherein, after a delicious nap to the accompaniment of the music of the waves, she was taken to drive in the fringed carriage again, while a bunch of handsome ladies, old and young, sat on the hotel piazza in more of those abundant rockers, and watched her approvingly. She felt that she was of some importance in their eyes. She had suddenly blossomed out of her insignificance, and was worth looking at. It warmed her heart with humble pleasure. She felt that she had won approval, not through any merit of her own, but through Donald's loving-kindness. It was wonderful what a charm clothes could work.

"Put on your gray silk for dinner," said Donald with malice aforethought in his heart.

"Oh," gasped Aunt Crete, "I think I ought to keep that for parties, don't you?"

"If ever there was a party, it's going to be tonight," said Donald. "It's going to be a surprise-party. You want to see if Aunt Carrie and Luella will know you, you know."

So with trembling fingers Aunt Crete arrayed herself in her gray silk and fine linen, very materially assisted by a quiet maid, whom Donald had ordered sent to the room, and who persuaded Aunt Crete to let her arrange the pretty white hair.

It was surprising to see, when the coiffure was complete, that she looked quite like the other old ladies, who were not old at all, only playing old.

"I don't believe they will know me," whispered Aunt Crete to herself as she stood before the full-length mirror and surveyed the effect. "And I didn't think I could ever look like that!" she murmured after a more prolonged gaze, during which she made the acquaintance of her new self. Then she added half wistfully: "I wish I had known it before. I think perhaps they'd have — liked me — more if I'd looked that way all the time." She sighed half regretfully, as if she were bidding good-bye to this new vision, and went out to Donald, who awaited her. She felt that the picnic part of her vacation was almost over now, for Carrie and Luella would be sure to manage to spoil it someway.

Donald looked up from his paper with a welcome in his eyes. It was the first time she had seen him in evening dress, and she thought him handsome as a king.

"You're a very beautiful woman, Aunt Crete; do you know it?" said Donald with satisfaction. He had felt that the French maid would know how to put just the right touch to Aunt Crete's pretty hair to take away her odd "unused" appearance. Now she was completely in fashion, and she looked every inch a lady. She somehow seemed to have natural intuition for gentle manners. Perhaps her kindly heart dictated them, for surely there can be no better manners than come wrapped up with the Golden Rule, and Aunt Crete had lived by that all her life.

They entered the great dining hall, and made their way among the palms in a blaze of electric light, with the headwaiter bowing obsequiously before them. They had a table to themselves, and Aunt Crete rejoiced in the tiny shaded candles and the hothouse roses in the center, and lifted the handsome napkins and silver forks with awe. Sometimes it seemed as if she were still dreaming.

The party from Pleasure Bay had reached home rather late in the afternoon, after a tedious time in the hot sun at a place full of peanut stands and merry-go-rounds and moving picture shows. Luella had not had a good time. She had been disappointed that none of the young men in the party had paid her special attention. In fact, the special young man for whose sake she had prodded her mother into going had not accompanied them at all. Luella was thoroughly cross.

"Mercy, how you've burned your nose, Luella!" said her mother sharply. "It's so unbecoming. The skin is all peeling off. I do wish you'd wear a veil. You can't afford to lose your complexion, with such a figure as you have."

"Oh, fiddlesticks! I wish you'd let up on that, Ma," snapped Luella. "Didn't you get a letter from Aunt Crete? I wonder what she's thinking about not to send that lavender organdie. I wanted to wear it tonight. There's to be a hop in the ballroom, and that would be just the thing. She ought to have got it done; she's had time enough since I telephoned. I suppose she's gone to reading again. I do wish I'd remembered to lock up the bookcase. She's crazy for novels."

All this time Luella was being buttoned into a pink silk muslin heavily decorated with cheap lace. There were twenty-six tiny elusive buttons, and Luella's mother was tired.

"What on earth makes you so long, Ma?" snarled Luella, twisting her neck to try to see her back. "We'll be so late we won't get served, and I'm hungry as a bear."

They hurried down, arriving at the door just as Aunt Crete and Donald were being settled into their chairs by the smiling headwaiter.

"For goodness' sake! those must be swells," said Luella in a low tone. "Did you see how that waiter bowed and smiled? He never does that to us. I expect he got a big tip. See, they're sitting right next to our table. Goodness, Ma, your hair is all slipped to one side. Put it up quick. No, the other side. Say, he's an awfully handsome young man. I wonder if we can get introduced. I just know he dances gracefully. Say, Mother, I'd like to get him for a partner tonight. I guess those stuck-up Grandons would open their eyes then."

"Hush, Luella, he'll hear you."

They settled into their places unassisted by the dilatory waiter, who came languidly up a moment later to take their order.

Aunt Crete's back was happily toward her relatives, so she ate her dinner in comfort. The palms were all about, and the gentle clink of silver and glass, and refined voices. The soft strains of an orchestra hidden in a balcony of ferns and palms drowned Luella's strident voice when it was raised in discontented strain, and so Aunt Crete failed to recognize the sound. But

Donald had been on the alert. In the first place, he had asked a question or two, and knew about where his relatives usually sat, and had purposely asked to be placed near them. He studied Luella when she came in, and felt pretty sure she was the girl he had seen on the platform of the train the morning he arrived in Midvale; and finally in a break in the music he distinctly caught the name "Luella" from the lips of the sour woman in the purple satin with white question-marks all over it and plasters of white lace.

Aunt Carrie was tall and thin, with a discontented droop to her lips, and premature wrinkles. She wore an affected air of abnormal politeness and disapproval of everything. She was studying the silver-gray silk back in front of her and wondering what there was about that elegant-looking woman with the lovely white waved pompadour and puffs, and that exquisite real lace collar, to remind her of poor sister Lucretia. She always coupled the adjective "poor" with her sister's name when she thought of all her shortcomings.

Luella's discontent was somewhat enlivened by the sight of the young man that had not gone on the drive to Pleasure Bay. He stood in the doorway, searching the room with keen, interested eyes. Could it be that he was looking for her? Luella's heart leaped in a moment's triumph. Yes, he seemed to be looking that way as if he had found the object of his search, and he was surely coming down toward them with a real smile on his face. Luella's face broke into preparatory smiles. She would be very coy, and pretend not to see him, so she began a voluble and animated conversation with her mother about the charming time they had had that day, which might have surprised the worthy woman if she had not been accustomed to her daughter's wiles. She knew it to be a warning of the proximity of someone that Luella wished to charm.

The young man came on straight by the solicitous waiters, who waved him frantically to various tables. Luella cast a rapid side glance, and talked on gayly with drooping head and averted gaze. Her mother looked up, wondering, to see what was the cause of Luella's animation. He was quite near now, and in a moment more he would speak. The girl felt excited thrills creeping up her back, and the color rushed into her cheeks, which were already red enough from the wind and sun of the day.

"Well, well," said the young man's voice in a hearty eagerness Luella had never hoped to hear addressed to herself, "this is too good to be true. Don, old man, where did you drop from? I saw your name in the register, and rushed right into the dining room —"

"Clarence Grandon, as true as I live!" said a pleasant voice behind

Luella. "I thought you were in Europe, bless your heart. This is the best thing that could have happened. Let me introduce my aunt —"

Some seconds before this Luella's thrills had changed to chills. Mortification stole over her face and up to the roots of her hair. Even the back of her neck, where her bathing suit was cut low and square, turned angry looking. The pink muslin had a round neck, and showed a half-circle of whiter neck below the bathing suit square. But Luella had the presence of mind to smile on to her mother in mild pretense that she had but just noticed the advent of the young man behind. An obsequious waiter was bringing an extra chair for Mr. Grandon, and he was to be seated so that he could look toward their table. Perhaps he would recognize her yet, and there might be a chance of introduction to the handsome stranger. Luella dallied with her dinner in fond hope, and her mother aided and abetted her.

The lovely old lady with the silver-gray silk and the real lace collar and beautiful hair had her back squarely toward the table where Luella and her mother sat. They could not see her face. They could only notice how interested both the young men were in her, and how courteous they were to her, and they decided she must be some very great personage indeed. They watched her half enviously, and began to plan some way to scrape an acquaintance with her. One glimpse they had of her face as the headwaiter rushed to draw back her chair when she had finished her dinner. It was a fine, handsome face, younger than they had expected to see, with beautiful sparkling eyes full of mirth and contentment. What was there in the face that reminded them of something? Had they ever met that old lady before?

Luella and her mother brought their dallied dessert to a sudden ending, and followed hard upon the footsteps of the three down the length of the dining hall; but the lady in gray with her two attendants had disappeared already, and disconsolately they lingered about, looking up and down the length of piazzas in vain hope to see them sitting in one of the great rows of rockers, watching the many-tinted waves in the dying evening light, but there was no sign of them anywhere.

As they stood thus leaning over the balcony, a large automobile, gray, with white cushions, like a great gliding dove, slipped silently up to the entrance below them in the well-bred silence that an expensive machine knows how to assume under dignified owners.

Luella twitched her mother's sleeve. "That's Grandon's car," she whispered. "P'raps I'll get asked to go. Let's sit down here and wait."

The mother obediently sat down.

Chapter 5
Luella and Her Mother Are Mystified

They had not long to wait. They heard the elevator door slide softly open, and then the gentle swish of silken skirts. Luella looked around just in time to be recognized by young Mr. Grandon if he had not at that moment been placing a long white broadcloth coat about his mother's shoulders. There were four in the party, and Luella's heart sank. He would not be likely to ask another one. The young man and the gray-silk, thread-lace woman from the other dining table were going with them, it appeared. Young Mr. Grandon helped the gray-silk lady down the steps while the handsome stranger walked by Mrs. Grandon. They did not look around at the people on the piazza at all. Luella bit her lips in vexation.

"For pity's sake, Luella, don't scowl so," whispered her mother; "they might look up yet and see you."

This warning came just in time; for young Mr. Grandon just as he was about to start the car glanced up, and, catching Luella's fixed gaze, gave her a distant bow, which was followed by a courteous lifting of the stranger's hat.

Aunt Crete was seated beside Mrs. Grandon in the back seat and beaming her joy quietly. She was secretly exulting that Luella and Carrie had not been in evidence yet. She felt that her joy was being lengthened by a few minutes more, for she could not get away from the fear that her sister and niece would spoil it all as soon as they appeared upon the scene.

"I thought Aunt Carrie and Luella would be tired after their all-day trip, and we wouldn't disturb them tonight," said Donald in a low tone, looking back to Aunt Crete as the car glided smoothly out from the shelter of the wide piazza.

Aunt Crete smiled happily back to Donald, and raised her eyes with a relieved glance toward the rows of people on the piazza. She had been afraid to look her fill before lest she should see Luella frowning at her somewhere; but evidently they had not got back yet, or perhaps had not finished their dinner.

As Aunt Crete raised her eyes, Luella and her mother looked down into her upturned face enviously, but Aunt Crete's gaze had but just grazed them and fallen upon an old lady of stately mien with white, fluffy hair like her own, and a white crepe de chine gown trimmed with much white lace. In deep satisfaction Aunt Crete reflected that, if Luella had aught to say against her aunt's wearing modest white morning gowns, she would cite this model, who was evidently an old aristocrat if one might judge by her jewels and her general makeup.

"Somewhere I've seen that woman with the gray silk!" exclaimed Luella's mother suddenly as Aunt Crete swept by. "There's something real familiar about the set of her shoulders. Look at the way she raises her hand to her face. My land! I believe she reminds me of your Aunt Crete!"

"Now, Mother!" scorned Luella. "As if Aunt Crete could ever look like that! You must be crazy to see anything in such an elegant lady to remind you of poor old Aunt Crete. Why, Ma, this woman is the real thing! Just see how her hair's put up. Nobody but a French maid could get it like that. Imagine Aunt Crete with a French maid. Oh, I'd die laughing. She's probably washing our country cousin's supper dishes at this very minute. I wonder if her conscience doesn't hurt her about my lavender organdie. Say, Ma, did you notice how graceful that handsome stranger was when he handed the ladies into the car? My, but I'd like to know him. I think Clarence Grandon is just a stuck-up prig."

Her mother looked at her sharply.

"Luella, seems to me you change your mind a good deal. If I don't make any mistake, you came down here so's to be near him. What's made you change your mind? He doesn't seem to go with any other girls."

"No, he just sticks by his mother every living minute," sighed Luella unhappily. "I do wish I had that lavender organdie. I look better in that than anything else I've got. I declare I think Aunt Crete is real mean and selfish not to send it. I'm going in to see if the mail has come; and, if the organdie isn't here, nor any word from Aunt Crete, I'm going to call her up on the telephone again."

Luella vanished into the hotel office, and her mother sat and rocked with puckered brows. She very much desired a place in high society for Luella, but how to attain it was the problem. She had not been born for social climbing, and found it difficult to do.

Meantime the motorcar rolled smoothly over the perfect roads, keeping always that wonderful gleaming sea in sight; and Aunt Crete, serenely happy, beamed and nodded to the pleasant chat of Mrs. Grandon, and was so overpowered by her surroundings that she forgot to be overpowered by the grand Mrs. Grandon. As in a dream she heard the kindly tone, and responded mechanically to the questions about her journey and the weather in the city, and how lovely the sea was tonight; but, as she spoke the few words with her lips, her soul was singing, and the words of its song were these:

> Must I be carried to the skies
> On flowery beds of ease,
> While others fought to win the prize
> And sailed through bloody seas?

And it seemed to her as they glided along the palace-lined shore, with the rolling sea on one hand, and the beautiful people in their beautiful raiment at ease and happy on the other hand, that she was picked right up out of the hot little brick house in the narrow street, and put on a wonderfully flowery bed of ease, and was floating right into a heaven of which her precious Donald was a bright, particular angel. She forgot all about Luella and what she might say, and just enjoyed herself.

She even found herself telling the elegant Mrs. Grandon exactly how she made piccalilli, and her heart warmed to the other woman as she saw that she was really interested. She had never supposed, from the way in which Luella spoke of the Grandons, that they would even deign to eat such a common thing as a pickle, let alone knowing anything about it. Aunt Crete's decision was that Mrs. Grandon wasn't stuck-up in the least, but just a nice, common lady like anyone; and, as she went up in the elevator beside her, and said good-night, she felt as if she had known her all her life.

It was not until she had turned out her light and crept into the great hotel bed that it came to her to wonder whether Luella and Carrie could be meant by the ones in the hymn,

> While others fought to win the prize
> And sailed through bloody seas.

She couldn't help feeling that perhaps she had been selfish in enjoying her day so much when for aught she knew Luella might not be having a good time. For Luella not to have a good time meant blame for her aunt generally. Ever since Luella had been born it had been borne in upon Aunt Crete that there was a moral obligation upon her to make Luella have a good time. And now Aunt Crete was having a good time, the time of her life; and she hugged herself, she was so happy over it, and thought of the dear stars out there in the deep, dark blue of the arching sky, and the cool, dark roll of the white-tipped waves, and was thankful.

Luella and her mother had gloomily watched the dancing through the open windows of the ballroom; but, as they knew no one inside, they did not venture in. Luella kept one eye out for the return of the car, but somehow missed it, and finally retired to the solace of cold cream and the comforts of the fourth floor back, where lingered in the atmosphere a reminder of the dinner past and a hint of the breakfast that was to come.

As the elevator ascended past the second floor, the door of one of the special apartments stood wide, revealing a glimpse of the handsome young stranger standing under the chandelier reading a letter, his face alive with pleasure. Luella sighed enviously, and in her dreams strove vainly to enter into the charmed circle where these favored beings moved, and knew not that of her own free will she had closed the door to that very special apartment, which might have been hers but for her own action.

The next morning Luella was twisting her neck in a vain endeavor to set the string of artificial puffs straight upon the enormous cushion of her hair, till they looked for all the world like a pan of rolls just out of the oven. She had jerked them off four separate times, and pulled the rest of her hair down twice in a vain attempt to get just the desired effect; and her patience, never very great at any time, was well-nigh exhausted. Her mother was fretting because the best pieces of fish and all the hot rolls would be gone before they got down to breakfast, and Luella was snapping back in most undaughterly fashion, when a noticeable tap came on the door. It was not the tap of the chambermaid of the fourth floor back, nor of the elevator boy, who knew how to modulate his knock for every grade of room from the second story, ocean front, up and back. It was a knock of rare condescension, mingled with a call to attention; and it warned these favored occupants of room 410 to sit up and take notice, not that they were worthy of any such consideration as was about to fall upon them.

Luella drove the last hairpin into the puffs, and sprang to the door just as her mother opened it. She felt something was about to happen. Could it be that she was to be invited to ride in that automobile at last, or what?

There in the hall, looking very much out of place, and as if he hoped his condescension would be appreciated, but he doubted it, stood the uniformed functionary who usually confined his activities to the second floor front, where the tips were large and the guests of unquestioned wealth, to say nothing of culture. He held in his hand a shining silver tray on which lay two cards, and he delivered his message in a tone that not only showed the deference he felt for the one who had sent him, but compelled such deference also on the part of those to whom he spoke.

"The lady and gen'leman say, Will the ladies come down to the private pahlah as soon aftah breakfus' as is convenient, room number 2, second floor front?" He bowed to signify that his mission was completed, and that if it did not carry through, it was entirely beyond his sphere to do more.

Luella grasped the cards and smothered an exclamation of delight.

"Second floor front," gasped her mother. "The private parlor! Did you hear, Luella?"

But Luella was standing by the one window, frowning over the cards. One was written and one was engraved, a lady's and a gentleman's cards. "Miss Ward." "Mr. Donald Ward Grant."

"For the land's sake, Ma! Who in life are they? Do you know any Miss Ward? You don't s'pose it's that lovely gray-silk woman. Miss Ward. Donald Ward Grant. Who can they be, and what do you suppose they want? Grant. Donald Grant. Where have I, why —! Oh, horrors, Ma! It can't be that dreadful cousin has followed us up, can it? Donald Grant is his name, of course; yes, Donald Ward Grant. It was the Ward that threw me off. But who is the other? Miss Ward. Ma! You don't —"

"Luella Burton, that's just what it is! It's your Aunt Crete and that dreadful cousin. Crete never did have any sense, if she is my sister. But just let me get ahold of her! If I don't make her writhe. I think I'll find a way to make her understand —"

Luella's expansive bravery beneath the row of biscuit puffs seemed to shrink and cringe as she took in the thought.

"Oh, Ma!" she groaned. "How could she? And here of all places? To come here and mortify me! It is just too dreadful. Ma, it can't be true. Aunt Crete would never dare. And where would she get the money? She hasn't a cent of her own, has she? You didn't go and leave her money, did you?"

"No, only a little change in my old pocketbook; it wouldn't have been enough to come down here on, unless she bought a day excursion. Wait. I did leave five dollars to pay the grocery bill with. But Crete surely wouldn't take that. Still, there's no telling. She always was a kind of a child. Oh, dear! What shall we do?" The mother sat down on the tumbled bed beside the tray of Luella's cheap trunk.

"Well, we must do something, that's certain, if we have to run away again. It would never do to have those two appear here now. Mercy! think of Aunt Crete in her old black and white silk sitting next table to that lovely lady in gray. I should simply sink through the floor."

"We can't run away, Luella," snapped the practical mother. "We've paid for our room two weeks ahead. I didn't want to do that; but you thought if Aunt Crete should get any nonsense into her head about our coming home, we would tell we'd paid for the room, and that would settle it with her. So now it's done, and we can't afford not to abide by it. Besides, what good would that do? We couldn't afford to go anywhere but home, and that would be as bad as it was in the first place. We've got to think it out. If I just had hold of Crete a minute, I'd make her fix it up. She'd have to think of some way out of it herself without any of my help, to pay her for her stupidity in coming. I can't understand how she'd do it.''

"I didn't think she'd dare!" glared Luella with no pleasant expression on her face.

"I'll tell you what we'll have to do, Luella," said her mother. "We'll slip down those stairs in the back hall. I went down one day, and they go right out on the piazza that runs in front of the dining room. We'll just slip in the back door, and get our breakfast right away. It's getting pretty late. You better hurry. They've likely come up from town on that very early train, and they'll sit and wait for us. We'll ring for a messenger bellboy, and send down a note that my ankle is so much worse I can't come downstairs, and you can't leave me. We'll say: 'Mrs. Burton and Miss Burton regret that they cannot come down as requested: but Mrs. Burton is confined to her bed by a sprained ankle, and her daughter cannot leave her. Miss Ward will have to come up.' You write it on one of your visiting cards, Luella, and we'll send it down as quick as we get back from breakfast. Hurry up. The only thing about it will be that climb up three flights after breakfast, but it won't do for us to risk the elevator. Crete might recognize us, for the elevator goes right by that second floor front parlor. What I don't understand is how they got in there. It's only rich people can afford that. But, land! Crete's just like a baby; hasn't been out in the world ever; and very likely she never asked how much the rooms were, but just took the best she could lay eyes on. Or more likely it's a mistake, and she's sitting in that little reception room down on the office floor, and thinks it the second floor because she came up such a long flight of steps from the sidewalk. We'll have to tell the bellboy to hunt up the fellow that brought their cards, and take it to the same folks. Come on now, Luella, and go slow when you turn corners. There's no telling but they might be prowling round trying to hunt us; so keep a lookout.''

Thus by devious and back ways they descended to a late breakfast, and scuttled up again without being molested.

Luella wrote the note on her card as her mother dictated, and a small boy all brass buttons was despatched with careful directions; and then the two retired behind their ramparts, and waited.

Time went by, until half an hour had elapsed since they came back from breakfast. They had listened anxiously to every footfall in the hall, and part of the time Luella kept the door open a crack with her ear to it. Their nerves were all in a quiver. When the chambermaid arrived, they were fairly feverish to get her out of the way. If Aunt Crete should come while she was in the room, it might get all over the hotel what kind of relatives they had.

Mrs. Burton suggested to the chambermaid that she leave their room till last, as they wanted to write some letters before going out; but the maid declared she must do the room at once or not at all. The elevator slid up and down around the corner in the next hall. They heard a footfall now and then, but none that sounded like Aunt Crete's. They rang again for the office-boy, who declared he had delivered the message in the second floor front, and that the lady and gentleman were both in and said, "All right." He vanished impudently without waiting for Luella's probing questions, and they looked at each other in anxiety and indignation.

"It is too mean, Ma, to lose this whole morning. I wanted to go in bathing," complained Luella, "and now no telling how long I'll have to stick in this dull room. I wish Aunt Crete was in Halifax. Why couldn't I have had some nice relatives like that lovely old gray-silk lady and her son?"

Just then the elevator clanged open and shut, and steps came down the hall. It certainly was not Aunt Crete. Luella flew to the door at the first tap; and there, submerged in a sheaf of American Beauty roses, stood the functionary from the lower floor, with a less pompous manner than he had worn before. The roses had caused his respect for the occupants of the fourth floor back, to rise several degrees.

Luella stood speechless in wonder, looking first at the roses and then at the servant. Such roses had never come into her life before. Could it be — must it be — but a miserable mistake?

Then the servant spoke.

"Miss Ward sends the flowers, an' is sorry the ladies aren't well. She sends her regrets, an' says she can't come to see the ladies 'count of a drive she'd promised to take today, in which she'd hoped to have the ladies' comp'ny. She hopes the ladies are better this even'n."

He was gone, and the mother and daughter faced each other over the roses, bewilderment and awe in their faces.

"*What* did he say, Luella? *Who* sent those roses? Miss *Ward?* Luella, there's some mistake. Aunt Crete couldn't have sent them. She wouldn't *dare!* Besides, where would she get the money? It's perfectly impossible. It can't be Aunt Crete, after all. It must be someone else with the same name. Perhaps Donald has picked up someone here in the hotel; you can't tell; or perhaps it isn't our Donald at all. It's likely there's other Donald Grants in the world. What we ought to have done was to go down at once and find out, and not skulk in a corner. But you're always in such a hurry to do something, Luella. There's no telling at all who this is now. It might be

those folks you admired so much, though what on earth they should have
sent their cards to us for — and those lovely roses — I'm sure I don't
know.''

"Now, Ma, you needn't blame me. It was you proposed sending that
note down; you know it was, Mother; and of course I had to do what you
said. I was so upset, anyway; I didn't know what was what. But now, you
see, perhaps you've cut me out of a lovely day. We might have gone on a
ride with them.''

"Luella," her mother broke in sharply, "if you talk another word like
that, I'll take the next train back home. You don't know what you are talking about. It may be Aunt Crete, after all, and a country cousin for all you
know; and, if it is, would you have wanted to go driving in the face of the
whole hotel, with like as not some old shin-and-bones horse and broken-
down carriage?''

Luella was silenced for the time, and the room settled into gloomy
meditation.

Chapter 6
An Embarrassing Meeting

Meantime Aunt Crete in the whitest of her white was settling herself comfortably on the gray cushions of the fringed phaeton again, relief and joy mingled in her countenance. It was not that she was glad that Carrie's ankle was so bad, but that she was to have another short reprieve before her pleasure was cut off. Soon enough, she thought, would she be destined to sit in the darkened room and minister to her fussy sister, while Luella took her place in the carriages and automobiles with her handsome young cousin, as young folks should do, of course; but Oh, it was good, good, that a tired old lady, who had worked hard all her life, could yet have had this bit of a glimpse of the brighter side of life before she died.

It would be something to sit and think over as she scraped potatoes for dinner, or picked over blackberries for jam, or patiently sewed on Val lace for Luella. It would be an event to date from, and she could fancy herself mildly saying to Mrs. Judge Waters, when she sat beside her sometime at missionary meeting, if she ever did again, "When my nephew took me down to the shore," and so forth. She never knew just what to talk about when she sat beside Mrs. Judge Waters, but here was a topic worth laying before such a great lady.

Well, it was something to be thankful for, and she resolved she just would not think of poor Carrie and Luella until her beautiful morning was over. Then she would show such patience and gratitude as would fully make up to them for her one more day of pleasure.

It was Donald, of course, who had suggested the roses. When the message came from the fourth floor back, Aunt Crete had turned white about the mouth, and her eyes had taken on a frightened, hunted look, while the double V in her forehead flashed into sight for the first time since they had reached the Atlantic coast. He saw at once in what terror Aunt Crete held her sister and niece, and his indignation arose in true Christian fashion. He resolved to place some nice hot coals on the heads of his unpleasant relatives, and run away with dear Aunt Crete again; hence the roses and the message, and Aunt Crete was fairly childish with pleasure over them when he finally persuaded her that it would be all right to send these in place of going up herself as she had been bidden.

She listened eagerly as Donald gave careful directions for the message, and the stately functionary respectfully repeated the words with his own high-sounding inflection. It made the pink come and go again in Aunt Crete's cheeks, and she felt that Luella and Carrie could not be angry with her after these roses, and especially when everything was being done up in so nice, stylish a manner.

The drive was one long dream of bliss to Aunt Crete. They went miles up the coast, and took lunch at a hotel much grander than the one they had left, so that when they returned in the afternoon Aunt Crete felt much less in awe of the Traymore, her experience in hotels having broadened. They also met some friends of Donald's, a professor from his alma mater, who with his wife was just returning from a trip to Europe.

The bathers were making merry in the waves as they returned, and Aunt Crete's wistful look made Donald ask whether she felt too tired to take another dip, but she declared she was not one bit tired.

She came from her bath with shining eyes and triumphant mien. Whatever happened now, she had been in bathing twice. She felt like quite an experienced bather, and she could dream of that wonderful experience of being lifted high above the swells in Donald's strong young arms.

She obediently took her nap, and surrendered herself to the hands of the maid to have the finishing touches put to her toilet. It was the soft gray voile that she elected to wear tonight, and Donald admired her when she emerged from her room in the dress, looking every inch a lady.

A knock sounded at the door before he had had time to give Aunt Crete a word of his admiration; but his eyes had said enough, and she felt a flow of humble pride in her new self, the self that he had created out of what she had always considered an unusually plain old woman. With the consciousness of her becoming attire upon her she turned with mild curiosity to see who had knocked, and, behold, her sister and niece stood before her!

The day had been passed by them in melancholy speculations and the making and abandoning of many plans of procedure. After careful deliberation they at last concluded that there was nothing to be done but go down and find out who these people really were, and if possible allay the ghost of their fears and set themselves free from their dull little room.

"If it should be Aunt Crete and Donald, we'll just settle them up and send them off at once, won't we, Mother?"

"Certainly," said Mrs. Burton with an angry snap to her eyes. "Trust me to settle with your Aunt Crete if it's really her. But I can't think it is. It isn't like Crete one bit to leave her duty. She's got a lot of work to do, and she never leaves her work till it's done. It must be someone else. What if it should be those folks you admire so much? I've been thinking. We had some New York cousins by the name of Ward. It might be one of them, and Donald might have gone to them first, and they've brought him down here. I can't think he's very much, though. But we'll just hope for the best, anyway, till we find out. If it's Aunt Crete, I shall simply talk to her till she is brought to her senses, and make her understand that she's got to go right home. I'll tell her how she's mortifying you, and spoiling your chances of a good match, perhaps —"

"Oh, Ma!" giggled Luella in admiration.

"I'll tell her she must tell Donald she's got to go right home, that the sea air don't agree with her one bit — it goes to her head or something like that, and then we'll make him feel it wouldn't be gallant in him not to take her home. That's easy enough, if 'tis them."

"But Ma, have you thought about your sprained ankle? How 'll they think you got over it so quick? S'posing it shouldn't be Aunt Crete."

"Well, I'll tell her the swelling's gone down, and all of a sudden something seemed to slip back into place again, and I'm all right."

This was while they were buttoning and hooking each other into their best and most elaborate garments for the peradventure that the people they were to meet might prove to be of patrician class.

They had been somewhat puzzled how to find their possible relatives after they were attired for the advance on the enemy, but consultation with the functionary in the office showed them that, whoever Miss Ward and Donald Grant might be, they surely were at present occupying the apartments on the second floor front.

For one strenuous moment after the elevator had left them before the door of the private parlor they had carefully surveyed each other, fastening a stubborn hook here, putting up a stray rebellious lock there, patting a puff into subordination. Mrs. Burton was arrayed in an elaborate tucked and puffed and belaced lavender muslin whose laborious design had been attained through hours of the long winter evenings past. Luella wore what she considered her most fetching garment, a long, scant, high-waisted robe of fire-red crepe, with nothing to relieve its glare, reflected in staring hues in her already much-burned nose and cheeks. Her hair had been in preparation all the afternoon, and looked as if it was carved in waves and puffs out of black walnut, so closely was it beset with that most noticeable of all invisible devices, an invisible net.

They entered, and stood face to face with the wonderful lady in the gray gown, whose every line and graceful fold spoke of the skill of a foreign tailor. And then, strange to say, it was Aunt Crete who came to herself first.

Perfectly conscious of her comely array, and strong in the strength of her handsome nephew who stood near to protect, she suddenly lost all fear of her fretful sister and bullying niece, and stepped forward with an unconscious grace of welcome that must have been hers all the time, or it never would have come to the front in this crisis.

"Why, here you are at last, Luella! How nice you look in your red crepe! Why Carrie, I'm real glad you've got better so you could come down. How is your ankle? And here is Donald. Carrie, can't you see Hannah's looks in him?"

Amazement and embarrassment struggled in the faces of mother and daughter. They looked at Aunt Crete, and they looked at Donald, and then they looked at Aunt Crete again. It couldn't be, it wasn't, yet it was, the voice of Aunt Crete, kind and forgiving, and always thoughtful for everyone, yet with a new something in it. Or was it rather the lack of something? Yes, that was it, the lack of a certain servile something that neither Luella nor her mother could name, yet which made them feel strangely ill at ease with this new-old Aunt Crete.

They looked at each other bewildered, and then back at Aunt Crete again, tracing line by line the familiar features in their new radiance of happiness, and trying to conjure back the worried V in her forehead, and the slinky sag of her old gowns. Was the world turned upside down? What had happened to Aunt Crete?

"Upon my word, Lucretia Ward, is it really you?" exclaimed her sister, making a wild dash into the conversation, determined to right herself and everything else if possible. She felt like a person suddenly upset in a canoe, and she struggled wildly to get her footing once more if there was any solid footing anywhere, with her sister Crete standing there calmly in an imported gown, her hair done up like a fashion plate, and a millionaire's smile on her pleasant face.

But Luella was growing angry. What did Aunt Crete mean by masquerading round in that fashion and making them ashamed before this handsome young man? and was he really their western cousin? Luella felt that a joke was being played upon her, and she always resented jokes — at least, unless she played them herself.

Then Donald came to the front, for he feared for Aunt Crete's poise. She must not lose her calm dignity and get frightened. There was a sharp ring in the other aunt's voice, and the new cousin looked unpromising.

"And is this my aunt Carrie? And my cousin Luella?" He stepped forward, and shook hands pleasantly.

"I am glad to be able to speak with you at last," he said as he dropped

Luella's hand, "though it's not the first time I've seen you, nor heard your voice, either, you know."

Luella looked up puzzled, and tried to muster her scattered graces, and respond with her ravishing society air, but somehow the ease and grace of the man before her overpowered her. And was he really her cousin? She tried to think what he could mean by having seen and talked with her before. Surely he must be mistaken, or — perhaps he was referring to the glimpse he had of her when Mr. Grandon bowed the evening before. She tossed her head with a kittenish movement, and arched her poorly pencilled eyebrows.

"Oh, how is that?" she asked, wishing he had not been quite so quick to drop her hand. It would have been more impressive to have had him hold it just a second longer.

"Why, I saw you the morning you left your home, as I was getting out of the train. You were just entering, and you called out of the window to a young lady in a pony cart. You wore a light kind of a yellowish suit, didn't you? Yes, I was very sure it was you."

He was studying her face closely, a curious twinkle in his eyes, which might or might not have been complimentary. Luella could not be sure. The color rose in her cheeks and neck and up to her black-walnut hair till the red dress and the red face looked all of a flame. She suddenly remembered what she had called out to the young lady in the pony cart, and she wondered whether he had heard or noticed.

"And then," went on her handsome persecutor, "I had quite a long talk with you over the telephone, you know —"

"What!" gasped Luella. "Was that you? Why, you must be mistaken, I never telephoned to you; that is, I couldn't get anyone on the phone."

"What's all this about, Luella?" questioned her mother sharply, but Donald interposed.

"Sit down, Aunt Carrie. We are so excited over meeting you at last that we are forgetting to be courteous." He shoved forth a comfortable chair for his aunt, and another for the blushing, overwhelmed Luella, and then he took Aunt Crete's hands lovingly, and gently pushed her backward into the most comfortable rocker in the room. "It's just as easy to sit down, dear Aunt," he said, smiling. "And you know you've had a pretty full day, and must not get tired for tonight's concert at the Casino. Now, Aunt Carrie, tell us about your ankle. How did you come to sprain it so badly, and how did it get well so fast? We were quite alarmed about you. Is it really better? I am afraid you are taxing it too much to have come down this evening. Much as we wanted to see you, we could have waited until it was quite safe for you to use it, rather than have you run any risks."

Then it was the mother's turn to blush, and her thin, somewhat colorless face grew crimson with embarrassment.

"Why, I —" she began; "that is, Luella was working over it, rubbing it with liniment, and all of a sudden she gave it a sort of a little pull, and something seemed to give way with a sharp pain, and then it came all right as good as ever. It feels a little weak, but I think by morning it'll be all right. I think some little bone got out of place, and Luella pulled it back in again. My ankles have always been weak, anyway. I suffer a great deal with them in going about my work at home."

"Why, Carrie," said Aunt Crete, leaning forward with troubled reproach in her face, "you never complained about it."

A dull red rolled over Mrs. Burton's thin features again, and receded, leaving her face pinched and haggard-looking. She felt as if she were seeing visions. This couldn't be her own sister, all dressed up so, and yet speaking in the old sympathetic tone.

"Oh, I never complain, of course. It don't do any good."

The conversation was interrupted by another tap on the door. Donald opened it, and received a large express package. While he was giving some orders to the servant, Mrs. Burton leaned forward, and said in a low tone to her sister:

"For goodness' sake, Lucretia Ward, what does all this mean? How ever did you get decked out like that?"

Then Donald's clear voice broke in upon them as the door closed once more, and Luella watched him curiously cutting with eager, boyish haste the cords of the express package.

"Aunt Crete, your cloak has come. Now we'll all see if it's becoming."

"Bless the boy," said Aunt Crete, looking up with delighted eyes. "Cloak; what cloak? I'm sure I've got wraps enough now. There's the cloth coat, and the silk one, and that elegant black lace —"

"No, you haven't. I saw right off what you needed when we went out in the auto last night, and I telephoned to that Miss Brower up in the city this morning, and she's fixed it all up. I hope you'll like it."

With that he pulled the cover off the box, and brought to view a long, full evening cloak of pale pearl-colored broadcloth lined with white silk, and a touch about the neck of black velvet and handsome creamy lace.

He held it up at arm's length admiringly.

"It's all right, Aunt Crete. It looks just like you. I knew that woman would understand. Stand up, and let's see how you look in it, and then after dinner we'll take a little spin around the streets to try you in it."

Aunt Crete, blushing like a pretty girl, stood up, and he folded the soft garment about her in all its elegant richness. She stood just in front of the full-length mirror, and could not deny to herself that it was becoming. But she was getting used to seeing herself look well, and was not so much overpowered with the sight as she was with the tender thought of the boy that had got it for her. She forgot Carrie and Luella, and everything but that Donald had gone to great trouble and expense to please her, and she just turned around, and put her two hands, one on each of his cheeks, standing on her tiptoes to reach him, and kissed him.

He bent and returned the kiss laughingly.

"It's a lot of fun to get you things, Aunt Crete," he said; "you always like them so much."

"It is beautiful, beautiful," she said, looking down and smoothing the cloth tenderly as if it had been his cheek. "It's much too beautiful for me. Donald, you will spoil me."

"Yes, I should think so," sniffed Luella, as if offering an apology in some sort for her childish aunt.

"A little spoiling won't hurt you, dear Aunt," said Donald seriously. "I don't believe you've had your share of spoiling yet, and I mean to give it to you if I can. Doesn't she look pretty in it, Cousin Luella? Come now, Aunt Carrie, I suppose it's time to go down to dinner, or we shan't get through in time for the fun. Are you sure your ankle is quite well? Are you able to go to the Casino tonight? I've tickets for us all. Sousa's orchestra is to be there, and the program is an unusually fine one."

Luella was mortified and angry beyond words, but a chance to go to the Casino, in company with Clarence Grandon and his mother, was not to be lightly thrown away, and she crushed down her mortification, contenting herself with darting an angry glance and a hateful curl of her lip at Aunt Crete as they went out the door together. This, however, was altogether lost on that little woman, for she was watching her nephew's face, and wondering how it came that such joy had fallen to her lot.

There was no chance for the mortified mother and daughter to exchange a word as they went down in the elevator or followed in the wake of their relatives, before whom all porters and office boys and even headwaiters bowed, and jumped to offer assistance. They were having their wish, to be sure, entering the dining hall behind the handsome young man and the elegant, gray-clad, fashionably coiffured old lady, a part of the train, with the full consciousness of "belonging," yet in what a way! Both were having ample opportunity for reflection, for they could see at a glance that no one noticed them, and all attention was for those ahead of them.

Luella bit her lip angrily, and looked in wonder at Aunt Crete, who somehow had lost her dumpiness, and walked as gracefully beside her tall young nephew as if she had been accustomed to walk in the eyes of the world thus for years. The true secret of her grace, if Luella had but known it, was that she was not thinking in the least of herself. Her conscience was at rest now, for the meeting between the cousins was over, and Luella was to have a good time too. Aunt Crete was never the least bit selfish. It seemed to her that her good time was only blooming into yet larger things, after all.

Behind her walked her sister and niece in mortified humiliation. Luella was trying to recall just what she had said about "country cousins" over the telephone, and exactly what she had said to the girl in the pony cart the morning she left home. The memory did not serve to cool her already heated complexion. It was beginning to dawn upon her that she had made a mighty mistake in running away from such a cousin and in such a manner.

All her life, in such a case, Luella had been accustomed to lay the blame of her disappointments upon someone else, and vent, as it were, her spite upon that one. Now, in looking about to find such an object of blame her eyes naturally fell upon the one that had borne the greater part of all blame for her. But, try as she would to pour out blame and scorn from her large, bold eyes upon poor Aunt Crete, somehow the blame seemed to slip off from the sweet gray garments, and leave Aunt Crete as serene as ever, with her eyes turned trustingly toward her dear Donald. Luella was brought to the verge of vexation by this, and could scarcely eat any dinner.

The dessert was just being served when the waiter brought Aunt Crete a dainty note from which a faint perfume of violets stole across the table to the knowing nostrils of Luella.

With the happy abandonment of a child Aunt Crete opened it joyously.

"Who in the world can be writing to me?" she said wonderingly. "You'll have to read it for me, Donald; I've left my glasses up in my room."

Luella made haste to reach out her hand for the note, but Donald had it first, as if he had not seen her impatient hand claiming her right to read Aunt Crete's notes.

"It's from Mrs. Grandon, Auntie," he said.

"Dear Miss Ward," he read, "I am sorry that I am feeling too weary to go to the concert this evening as we had planned, and my son makes such a baby of me that he thinks he cannot leave me alone; but I do hope we can have the pleasure of the company of yourself and your nephew on a little auto trip tomorrow afternoon. My brother has a villa a few miles up the

shore, and he telephoned us this morning to dine with them tonight. When he heard of your being here, he said by all means to bring you with us. My brother knows of your nephew's friendship with Clarence, and is anxious to meet him, as are the rest of his family. I do hope you will feel able to go with us.

"With sincere regrets that I cannot go with you to the Casino this evening,

HELEN GRANDON."

For the moment Luella forgot everything else in her amazement at this letter. Aunt Crete receiving notes from Mrs. Grandon, from whom she and her mother could scarcely get a frigid bow! Aunt Crete invited on automobile trips and dinners in villas! Donald an intimate friend of Clarence Grandon's! Oh, fool and blind! What had she done! Or what had she undone? She studied the handsome, keen face of her cousin as he bent over the letter, and writhed to think of her own words, "I'm running away from a backwoods cousin"! She could hear it shouted from one end of the great dining hall to the other, and her face blazed redder and redder till she thought it would burst. Her mother turned from her in mortified silence, and wondered why Luella couldn't have had a good complexion.

Studied politeness was the part that Donald had set for himself this evening. He began to see that his victims were sufficiently unhappy. He had no wish to see them writhe under further tortures, though when he looked upon Aunt Crete's happy face, and thought how white it had turned at dread of them, he felt he must let the thorns he had planted in their hearts remain long enough to bring forth a true repentance. But he said nothing further to distress them, and they began to wonder whether, after all, he really had seen through their plan of running away from him.

It was all Aunt Crete's fault. She ought to have arranged it in some way to get them quietly home as soon as she found out what kind of cousin it was that had come to see them. It never occurred to Luella that nothing her poor, abused aunt could have said would have convinced her that her cousin was worthy of her homecoming.

As the concert drew near to its close, Luella and her mother began to prepare for a time of reckoning for Aunt Crete. When she was safely in her room what was to hinder them from going to her alone and having it out? The sister's face hardened, and the niece's eyes glittered as she stonily thought of the scornful sentences she would hurl after her aunt.

Donald looked at her menacing face, and read its thoughts. He resolved to protect Aunt Crete, whatever came; so at the door, when he saw a motion on his Aunt Crete's part to pause, he said gently: "Aunt Crete, I guess we'll have to say good-night now, for you've had a hard day of it, and I want you to be bright and fresh for morning. We want to take an early dip in the ocean. The bathing hours are early tomorrow, I see."

He bowed good-night in his pleasantest manner, and the ladies from the fourth floor reluctantly withdrew to the elevator, but fifteen minutes later surreptitiously tapped at the private door of the room they understood to be Aunt Crete's.

Chapter 7
Luella's Humiliation

The door was opened cautiously by the maid, who was doing Aunt Crete's hair, having just finished a most refreshing facial massage given at Donald's express orders.

Aunt Crete looked round upon her visitors with a rested, rosy countenance, which bloomed out under her fluff of soft, white hair, and quite startled her sister with its freshness and youth. Could it be possible that this was really her sister Crete, or had she made a terrible mistake, and entered the wrong apartment?

But a change came suddenly over the ruddy countenance of Aunt Crete as over the face of a child that in the midst of happy play sees a trouble descending upon it. A look almost of terror came over her, and she caught her breath, and waited to see what was coming.

"Why, Carrie, Luella!" she gasped weakly. "I thought you'd gone to bed. Marie's just doing up my hair for night. She's been giving me a face massage. You ought to try one. It makes you feel young again."

"H'm!" said her affronted sister. "I shouldn't care for one."

Marie looked over Luella and her mother, beginning with the painfully elaborate arrangement of hair, and going down to the tips of their boots. Luella's face burned with mortification as she read the withering disapproval in the French woman's countenance.

"Let's sit down till she's done," said Luella, dropping promptly on the foot of Aunt Crete's bed and gazing around in frank surprise over the spaciousness of the apartment.

Thereupon the maid ignored them, and went about her work, brushing out and deftly manipulating the wavy white hair, and chattering pleasantly meanwhile, just as if no one else were in the room. Aunt Crete tried to forget what was before her, or, rather, behind her; but her hands trembled a little as they lay in her lap in the folds of the pretty pink and gray challis kimono she wore; and all of a sudden she remembered the unwhitewashed cellar, and the uncooked jam, and the unmade shirtwaists, and the little hot brick house gazing at her reproachfully from the distant home, and she here in this fine array, forgetting it all and being waited upon by a maid — a lazy truant from her duty.

Did the heart of the maid divine the state of things, or was it only her natural instinct that made her turn to protect the pleasant little woman, in whose service she had always been well paid, against the two women that were so evidently of the common walks of life, and were trying to ape those that in the eyes of the maid were their betters? However it was, Marie prolonged her duties a good half hour, and Luella's impatience waxed furious, so that she lost her fear of the maid gradually, and yawned loudly, declaring that Aunt Crete had surely had enough fussing over for one evening.

They held in their more personal remarks until the door finally closed upon Marie, but burst forth so immediately that she heard the opening sentences through the transom, and thought it wise to step to the young gentleman's door and warn him that his elderly relative of whom he seemed so careful was likely to be disturbed beyond a reasonable hour for retiring. Then she discreetly withdrew, having not only added to her generous income by a good bit of silver, but also having followed out the dictates of her heart, which had taken kindly to the gentle woman of the handsome clothes and few pretensions.

"Well, upon my word! I should think you'd be ashamed, Aunt Crete!" burst forth Luella, arising from the bed in a majesty of wrath. "Sitting there, being waited on like a baby, when you ought to be at home this minute earning your living. What do you think of yourself, anyway, living in this kind of luxury when you haven't a cent in the world of your own, and your own sister, who has supported you for years, up in a little dark fourth-floor room? Such selfishness I never saw in all my life. I wouldn't have believed it of you, though we might have suspected it long ago from the foolish things you were always doing. Aunt Crete, have you any idea how much all this costs?"

She waved her hand tragically over the handsome room, including the trunk standing open, and the gleam of silver-gray silk that peeped through the half-open closet door. Aunt Crete fairly cringed under Luella's scornful eyes.

"And you, nothing in the world but a beggar, a *beggar!* That's what you are — a beggar depending upon *us;* and you swelling around as if you owned the earth, and daring to wear silk dresses and real lace collars and expensive jewelry, and even having a maid, and shaming your own relatives, and getting in ahead of us, who have always been good to you, and taking away our friends, and making us appear like two cents! It's just fierce, Aunt Crete! It's — it's *heathenish!*" Luella paused in her anger for a fitting word, and then took the first one that came.

Aunt Crete winced. She was devoted to the Woman's Missionary Society, and it was terrible to be likened to a heathen. She wished Luella had chosen some other word.

"I should think you'd be so ashamed you couldn't hold your head up before your honest relatives," went on the shameless girl. "Taking money from a stranger — that's what he is, a *stranger* — and you whining round and lowering yourself to let him buy you clothes and things, as if you didn't have proper clothes suited to your age and station. He's a young upstart coming along and daring to buy you any — and such clothes! Do you know you're a laughingstock? What would Mrs. Grandon say if she knew whom she was inviting to her automobile rides and dinners? Think of you in your old purple calico washing the dishes at home, and scrubbing the kitchen, and ask yourself what you would say if Mrs. Grandon should come to call on you, and find you that way. You're a hypocrite, Aunt Crete, an awful hypocrite!"

Luella towered over Aunt Crete, and the little old lady looked into her eyes with a horrible fascination, while her great grief and horror poured down her sweet face in tears of anguish that would not be stayed. Her kindly lips were quivering, and her eyes were wide with the tears.

Luella saw that she was making an impression, and she went on more wildly than before, her fury growing with every word, and not realizing how loud her voice was.

"And it isn't enough that you should do all that, but now you're going to spoil my prospects with Clarence Grandon. You can't keep up this masquerade long, and when they find out what you really are, what will they think of *me?* It'll be all over with me, and it'll be your fault, Aunt Crete, your fault, and you'll never have a happy moment afterwards, thinking of how you spoiled my life."

"Now, Luella," broke in Aunt Crete solemnly through her tears, "you're mistaken about one thing. It won't be my fault there, for it wouldn't have made a bit of difference, poor child. I'm real sorry for you, and I meant to tell you just as soon as we got home, for I couldn't bear to spoil your pleasure while we were here, but that Clarence Grandon belongs to someone else. He isn't for you, Luella, and there must have been some mistake about it. Perhaps he was just being kind to you. For Donald knows him real well, and he says he's engaged to a girl out west, and they're going to be married this fall, and Donald says she's real sweet and —"

But Aunt Crete's quavering voice stopped suddenly in mild affright, for Luella sprang toward her like some mad creature, shaking her finger in her aunt's face, and screaming at the top of her voice:

"It's a lie! I say it's a lie! Aunt Crete, you're a liar; that's what you are with all the rest."

And the high-strung, uncontrolled girl burst into angry sobs.

No one heard the gentle knock that had been twice repeated during the scene, and no one saw the door open until they all suddenly became aware that Donald stood in the room, looking from one face to another in angry surprise.

Donald had not retired at once after bidding Aunt Crete good-night. He found letters and telegrams awaiting his attention, and he had been busy writing a letter of great importance when the maid gave him the hint of Aunt Crete's late callers. Laying down his pen, he stepped quietly across the private parlor that separated his room from his aunt's, and stopped a moment before the door to make sure he heard voices. Then he had knocked, and knocked again, unable to keep from hearing the most of Luella's tirade.

His indignation knew no bounds, and he concluded his time had come to interfere, so he opened the door, and went in.

"What does all this mean?" he asked in a tone that frightened his Aunt Carrie, and made Luella stop her angry sobs in sudden awe.

No one spoke, and Aunt Crete looked a mute appeal through her tears. "What is it, dear Aunt?" he said, stepping over by her side, and placing his arm protectingly round the poor, shrinking little figure, who somehow in her sorrow and helplessness reminded him strongly of his own lost mother. He could not remember at that moment that the other woman, standing hard and cold and angry across the room, was also his mother's sister. She did not look like his mother, nor act like her.

Aunt Crete put her little curled white head in its crisping-pins down on Donald's coat sleeve, and shrank into her pink and gray kimono appealingly as she tried to speak.

"It's just as I told you, Donald, you dear boy," she sobbed out. "I — oughtn't to have come. I knew it, but it wasn't your fault. It was all mine. I ought to have stayed at home, and not dressed up and come off here. I've had a beautiful time, but it wasn't for me, and I oughtn't to have taken it. It's just spoiled Luella's nice time, and she's blaming me, just as I knew she would."

"What does my cousin mean by using that terrible word to you, which I heard as I entered the room?"

Donald's voice was keen and scathing, and his eyes fairly piercing as he asked the question and looked straight at Luella, who answered not a word.

"That wasn't just what she'd have meant, Donald," said Aunt Crete apologetically. "She was most out of her mind with trouble. You see I had to tell her what you told me about that Clarence Grandon being engaged to another girl —"

"Aunt Crete, don't say another word about that!" burst out Luella with flashing eyes and crimson face.

"For mercy's sake, Crete, can't you hold your tongue?" said Luella's mother sharply.

"Go on, Aunt Crete, did my cousin call you a liar for saying that? Yet it was entirely true. If she is not disposed to believe me either, I can call Mr. Grandon in to testify in the matter. He will come if I send for him. But I feel sure, after all, that that will not be necessary. It is probably true, as Aunt Crete says, that you were excited, Luella, and did not mean what you said; and after a good night's sleep you will be prepared to apologize to Aunt Crete, and be sorry enough for worrying her. I am going to ask you to leave Aunt Crete now, and let her rest. She has had a wearying day, and needs to be quiet at once. She is my mother's sister, you know, and I feel as if I must take care of her."

"You seem to forget that I am your mother's sister, too," said Aunt Carrie coldly, as she stood stiff and disapproving beside the door, ready to pass out.

"If I do, Aunt Carrie, forgive me," said Donald courteously. "It is not strange when you remember that you forgot that I was your sister's child, and ran away from me. But never mind, we will put that aside and try to forget it. Good-night, Aunt Carrie. Good-night, Cousin Luella. We will all feel better about it in the morning."

They bowed their diminished heads, and went with shame and confusion to the fourth floor back; and, when the door was closed upon them, they burst into angry talk, each blaming the other, until at last Luella sank in a piteous heap upon the bed, and gave herself over to helpless tears.

"Luella," said her mother in a businesslike tone, "you stop that bawling and sit up here and answer me some questions. Did you or did you not go riding with Mr. Clarence Grandon last winter in his automobile?"

Luella paused in her grief, and nodded assent hopelessly.

"Well, how'd it come about? There's no use sniffing. Tell me exactly."

"Why, it was a rainy day," sobbed out the girl, "and I met him on the street in front of the public library the day I'd been to take back *The Legacy of Earl Crafton,* and that other book by the same author —"

"Never mind what books; tell me what happened," said the exasperated mother.

"Well, if you're going to be cross, I shan't tell you anything," was the final reply; and for a moment nothing was heard in the room but sobs.

However, Luella recovered the thread of her story and went on to relate how in company with a lot of other girls she had met Mr. Grandon the day before at the golf links, where a championship game was being played. She did not explain the various maneuvers by which she had contrived to be introduced to him, nor that he had not seemed to know her at first when she bowed in front of the library building. She had called out, "It's a fine day for ducks, Mr. Grandon; isn't it good the game was yesterday instead of today?" and he had asked her to ride home with him.

That was her version. Her mother by dint of careful questioning finally arrived at the fact that the girl had more than hinted to be taken home, having loudly announced her lack of rubbers and umbrella, though she seldom wore rubbers, and had on a raincoat and an old hat.

"But how about that big box of chocolates he sent you, Luella? That was a very particular attention to show if he was engaged."

"Oh," pouted Luella, "I don't suppose that meant anything either, for I caught him in a philopena on the way home that day. We said the same words at the same time, something like 'It's going to clear off,' and I told him, when we girls did that, the one that spoke first had to give the other a box of chocolates; so the next day he sent them."

"Luella, I never brought you up to do things like that. I don't think that was very nice."

"Oh, now, Ma, don't you preach. I guess you weren't a saint when you were a girl. Besides, I don't think you're very sympathetic." She mopped her swollen eyes.

"Luella, didn't he ever pay you any more attention after that? I kind of thought you thought he liked you, by the way you talked."

"No, he never even looked at me," sobbed the girl, her grief breaking out afresh. "He didn't even know me the next time we met, but stared straight at me till I bowed, and then he gave me a cold little touch of his hat. And down here he hasn't even recognized me once. I suppose that lady mother of his didn't like my looks."

"Look here, Luella; I wish you'd act sensible. This has been pretty expensive trying to run around after the Grandons. Here's the hotel bills, and all that dress making, and now no telling how Aunt Crete will act after we get home. Like as not she'll think she's got to have a maid, and dress in silks and satins. There's one comfort, probably some of her clothes will fix over for you when she gets off her high horse and comes down to everyday living again. But I wish you'd brace up and forget these Grandons. It's no use trying to get up in the world higher than you belong. There's that nice

John Peters who would have been real devoted to you if you'd just let him; and he owns a house of his own already, and has the name of being the best plumber in Midvale.''

Luella sighed.

"He's only a plumber, Ma, and his hands are all red and rough.''

"Well, what's that?'' snapped her practical mother. "He may have his own automobile before long, for all that. Now dry up your eyes, and go to sleep; and in the morning you go down real early, and apologize to your silly Aunt Crete, and make her understand that she's not to disgrace us under any consideration by going bathing while she's here. My land! I expect to see her riding round on one of those saddle ponies on the beach next, or maybe driving that team of goats we saw today, with pink ribbon reins. Come now, Luella, don't you worry. Set out to show your cousin Donald how nice you can be, and maybe some of the silk dresses will come your way. Anyhow, this can't last forever, and John Peters is at home when we get there.''

So Luella, soothed in spirit, went to bed, and arose very early the next morning, descending upon poor Aunt Crete while yet the dreams of sailing alone with Donald on a moonlit sea were mingling with her waking thoughts.

Chapter 8
Aunt Crete's Partnership

Luella did her work quietly, firmly, and thoroughly. She vanished before Marie had thought of coming to her morning duties.

At breakfast-time Donald found a sad, cowed little woman waiting for him to go down to the dining room. He tried to cheer her up by telling her how nice a time they were to have in bathing that morning, for the water was sure to be delightful, but Aunt Crete shook her head sadly, and said she guessed she had better not go in bathing anymore. Then she sighed, and looked wistfully out on the blue waves dancing in the sunshine.

"Don't you feel well, Aunt Crete?" asked Donald anxiously.

"Oh, yes, real well," she answered.

"Did it hurt you to go in yesterday, do you think?"

"No, not a mite," she responded promptly.

"Then why in the name of common sense don't you want to go in to-day? Has Luella been trying to talk some of her nonsense?"

"Well, Luella thinks my figger looks so bad in a bathing suit. She says of course you want to be polite to me, but you don't really know how folks will laugh at me, and make her ashamed of belonging to me."

"Well, I like that!" said Donald. "You just tell Miss Luella we're not running this vacation for her sole benefit. Now, Aunt Crete, you're going in bathing, or else I won't go, and you wouldn't like to deprive me of that pleasure, would you? Well, I thought not. Now come on down to breakfast, and we'll have the best day yet. Don't you let Luella worry you. And, by the way, Aunt Crete, I'm thinking of taking a run up to Cape Cod, and perhaps getting a glimpse of the coast of Maine before I get through. How would you like to go with me?"

"Oh!" gasped Aunt Crete in a daze of delight. "Could I?" Then, mindful of Luella's mocking words the night before: "But I mustn't be an expense to you. I'd just be a burden. You know I haven't a cent of my own in the world, so I couldn't pay my way, and you've done a great deal more than I ought to have let you do."

"Now, Aunt Crete, once for all you must get that idea out of your head. You could never be a burden to me. I want you for a companion. If my mother were here, shouldn't I just love to take her on a journey with me, and spend every cent I had to make her happy? Well, I haven't Mother here; but you are the nearest to Mother I can find, and I somehow feel she'd like me to have you in her place. Will you come? Or is it asking too much to ask you to leave Aunt Carrie and Cousin Luella? They've got each other, and they never really needed you as I do. I've got plenty of money for us to do as we please, and I mean it with all my heart. Will you come and stay with me? I may have to take a flying trip to Europe before the summer's over, and, if I do, it would be dreadfully lonesome to go alone. I think you'd like a trip on the ocean, wouldn't you? and a peep at London, and perhaps Paris and Vienna and old Rome for a few days? And in the fall I'm booked for work in my old university. It's only an assistant professorship yet, but it means a big thing for a young fellow like me, and I want you to come with me and make a cozy little home for me between whiles and a place where I can bring my friends when they get homesick."

He paused and looked down for an answer, and was almost startled by the glory of joy in Aunt Crete's face.

"Oh, Donald, could I do that? Could I be that to you? Do you really think I could be of use enough to you to earn my living?"

He stooped and kissed her forehead reverently to hide the tears that had come unbidden to his eyes. It touched him beyond measure that this sweet life had been so empty of love and so full of drudgery that she should speak thus about so simple a matter. It filled him with indignation against those who had taken the sweetness from her and given her the dregs of life instead.

"Dear Aunt," he said, "you could be of great use to me, and more than earn anything I could do for you many times over, just by being yourself and mothering me; but as for work, there is not to be one stroke done except just what you want to do for amusement. We'll have servants to do all the work, and you shall manage them. I want you for an ornament in my home, and you are going to have a good rest and a continual vacation the rest of your life, if I know anything about it. Now come down to breakfast, so we can go in bathing early, and don't you worry another wrinkle about Luella. You don't belong to her anymore. We'll send her a parasol from New York and a party gown from Paris, and she won't bother her pompadour anymore about you, you may be sure."

In a maze of delight Aunt Crete went down to breakfast, and dawned upon the astonished vision of her sister and niece in all the beauty of her dainty white morning costume. They were fairly startled at the vision she was in white, with her pretty white hair to match it. Luella gasped and held her disapproving breath, but Aunt Crete was too absorbed in the vision of joy that had opened before her to know or care what they thought of her in a white dress.

No girl in the new joy of her first love was ever in a sweeter dream of bliss than was Aunt Crete as she beamed through her breakfast. Luella's looks of scorn and Luella's mother's sour visage had no effect upon her whatever. She smiled happily, and ate her breakfast in peace, for had she not been set free forever from the things that had made her life a burden heretofore, and shown into a large place of new joys where her heart might find rest?

After breakfast Donald made them all walk down the boardwalk to the various shops filled with curios, where he bought everything that Luella looked at, and lavished several gifts also upon her mother, including a small Oriental rug that she admired. They returned to the hotel in a good humor, and Luella began to have visions of luxurious days to come. She felt sure she could keep Aunt Crete down about where she wanted her, and her eyes gloated over the beautiful white dress that she hoped to claim for her own when they all went home and she had convinced Aunt Crete how unsuitable white was for old ladies.

She was quite astonished, after her morning talk with her aunt, to hear Donald say as he looked at his watch, "Come, Aunt Crete, it's time for our bath," and to see Aunt Crete walk smiling off toward the bathhouses, utterly regardless of her wrathful warning glances. It was rather disconcerting to have Aunt Crete become unmanageable right at the beginning this way. But in view of the fact that her hands were filled with pretty trifles bought by her cousin she did not feel like making any protest beyond threatening glances, which the dear soul whose mind was in Europe, and whose heart was in a cozy little home all her own and Donald's, did not see at all.

Aunt Crete was happy. She felt it in every nerve of her body as she stepped into the crisp waves and bounded out to meet them with the elasticity of a girl.

Luella, following a moment later in her flashy bathing suit of scarlet and white, watched her aunt in amazement, and somehow felt that Aunt Crete was drifting away from her, separated by something more than a few yards of blue salt water.

Donald kept up a continual flow of bright conversation during the noon meal, and managed to engage Luella and her mother on the long piazza in looking through the marine glass at a great ship that went lazily floating by, while Aunt Crete was getting ready to go on the ride; and before Luella and her mother were quite aware of what was happening they stood on the piazza watching Aunt Crete in her handsome black crepe de chine, which even boasted a modest train, and her black lace wrap and bonnet, being handed into the Grandon motorcar, while Donald carried her long new gray cloak on his arm. The gray car moved smoothly away out of sight, and Luella and her mother were left staring at the sea with their own bitter reflections.

The automobile party did not return until late that night, for the moon was full and the roads were fine, and Donald saw to it that Aunt Crete was guarded against any intrusion.

It was at breakfast next morning that Donald told them, and Aunt Crete was listening with the rapt smile that a slave might have worn as he listened to the reading of the proclamation of emancipation.

"Aunt Carrie," he began as pleasantly as if he were about to propose that they all go rowing, "Aunt Crete and I have decided to set up a permanent partnership. She has consented to come and mother me. I have accepted a position in my old university, and I am very tired of boarding. I think we shall have a cozy, pleasant home; and we'll be glad to have you and Luella come and visit us sometimes after we get settled and have some good servants so that Aunt Crete will have plenty of time to take you around and show you the sights. In the meantime, it is very likely that I may have to take a brief trip abroad for the university. If so, I shall probably start in about a week, and before that I want to get a glimpse of the New England coast. I have decided to take Aunt Crete, and run away from you today. We leave on the noon train; so there is time for a little frolic yet. Suppose we go down to the boardwalk, and eat an ice-cream cone. I saw some delicious ones last night that made my mouth water, and we haven't had that experience yet. We'll get some rolling chairs so that Aunt Crete won't be too tired for her journey. Come, Aunt Crete, you won't need to go upstairs again, shall you? I told Marie about the packing. It won't be necessary for you to go back until it's time for you to change to your traveling garb."

In a daze of anger and humiliation Luella and her mother climbed into their double rolling chair, and ate their ice-cream cones sullenly, propelled by a large boy; but Aunt Crete had a chair to herself, and was attended by Donald, who kept up a constant stream of delightfully funny conversation about the people and things they passed that made Aunt Crete laugh until the tears came into her happy eyes.

There was no opportunity for Luella and her mother to talk to Aunt Crete alone, even after they returned to the hotel, for Donald kept himself in evidence everywhere, until at last Luella made bold to declare that she didn't see why Donald thought he had a right to come and take Aunt Crete away from them, when they had always taken care of her; and her mother added in an injured tone:

"Yes, you don't seem to realize what a burden it's been all these years, having to support Crete, and her so childish and unreasonable in a great many ways, and not having any idea of the value of money. I've spent a good deal on Crete, take it all in all; and now, when Luella's going out, and has to have clothes and company, it's rather hard to have her leave us in the lurch this way, and me with all the work to do."

"That being the case, Aunt Carrie," said Donald pleasantly, "I should suppose you'd be very glad to have me relieve you of the burden of Aunt Crete's support, for it will be nothing but a pleasure to me to care for her the rest of her life. As for what you have spent for her, just run it over in your mind, and I shall be quite glad to reimburse you. Aunt Crete is really too frail and sweet to have to work any longer. I should think my cousin was almost old enough to be a help to you now, and she looks perfectly strong and able to work."

Luella flashed a vindictive glance at her cousin, and turned haughtily toward the window; then the porter came for the trunks, and the travelers said a hasty good-bye, and flitted.

As Donald shook hands with Luella in parting, he looked merrily into her angry eyes, and said:

"I do hope, Luella, that it hasn't been too much of a trial to have your 'backwoods cousin' spend a few days here. You'll find a box of bonbons up in your room, if the porter did his duty, which may sweeten your bitter thoughts of me; and we hope you'll have a delightful time the remainder of your stay here. Goodbye."

* * *

About three months after Donald had returned from Europe and settled into his western university life Aunt Crete received a letter from her sister. It was brief and to the point, and Aunt Crete could read between the lines. It read:

> *Dear Crete* — Aren't you about sick of that nonsense, and ready to come home? Luella has decided that she can't do better than take John Peters. He has promised to buy an auto next year, if the plumbing business keeps up. I think at least you might come home and help get her things ready, for there's a gread deal of sewing to do, and you know I can't afford to hire it; and Luella's out so much, now she's engaged. Do come soon.
>
> Your sister, CARRIE.

Aunt Crete looked sober, but Donald, looking over her shoulder, read, and then went to his desk for a moment. Coming back, he dropped a check for five hundred dollars into his aunt's lap.

"Send her that from me, Aunt Crete, and another from yourself, if you like, and let her hire the sewing done. They don't want you, and I do."

Aunt Crete had her own bank account now, thanks to her thoughtful nephew, and she smiled back a delighted, "I will," and went off to write the letter, for Aunt Crete was at last emancipated.

THE GIRL
FROM
MONTANA

Chapter 1
The Girl, and a Great Peril

The late afternoon sun was streaming in across the cabin floor as the girl stole around the corner and looked cautiously in at the door.

There was a kind of tremulous courage in her face. She had a duty to perform, and she was resolved to do it without delay. She shaded her eyes with her hand from the glare of the sun, set a firm foot upon the threshold, and, with one wild glance around to see whether all was as she had left it, entered her home and stood for a moment shuddering in the middle of the floor.

A long procession of funerals seemed to come out of the past and meet her eye as she looked about upon the signs of the primitive, unhallowed funeral which had just gone out from there a little while before.

The girl closed her eyes, and pressed their hot, dry lids hard with her cold fingers; but the vision was clearer even than with her eyes open.

She could see the tiny baby sister lying there in the middle of the room, so little and white and pitiful; and her handsome, careless father sitting at the head of the rude home-made coffin, sober for the moment; and her tired, disheartened mother, faded before her time, dry-eyed and haggard, beside him. But that was long ago, almost at the beginning of things for the girl.

There had been other funerals, the little brother who had been drowned while playing in a forbidden stream, and the older brother who had gone off in search of gold or his own way, and had crawled back parched with fever to die in his mother's arms. But those, too, seemed long ago to the girl as she stood in the empty cabin and looked fearfully about her. They seemed almost blotted out by the last three that had crowded so close within the year. The father, who even at his worst had a kind word for her and her mother, had been brought home mortally hurt — an encounter with wild cattle, a fall from his horse in a treacherous place — and had never roused to consciousness again.

At all these funerals there had been a solemn service, conducted by a travelling preacher when one happened to be within reach, and, when there was none, by the trembling, determined, untaught lips of the white-faced mother. The mother had always insisted upon it, especially upon a prayer. It had seemed like a charm to help the departed one into some kind of a pitiful heaven.

And when, a few months after the father, the mother had drooped and grown whiter and whiter, till one day she clutched at her heart and lay down gasping, and said: "Good-by, Bess! Mother's good girl! Don't forget!" and was gone from her life of burden and disappointment forever, the girl had prepared the funeral with the assistance of the one brother left. The girl's voice had uttered the prayer, "Our Father," just as her mother had taught her, because there was no one else to do it; and she was afraid to send the wild young brother off after a preacher, lest he should not return in time.

It was six months now since the sad funeral train had wound its way among sage-brush and greasewood; and the body of the mother had been laid to rest beside her husband. For six months the girl had kept the cabin in order, and held as far as possible the wayward brother to his work and home. But within the last few weeks he had more and more left her alone, for a day, and sometimes more, and had come home in a sad condition and with bold, merry companions who made her life a constant terror. And now, but two short days ago, they had brought home his body lying across his own faithful horse, with two shots through his heart. It was a drunken quarrel, they told her; and all were sorry, but no one seemed responsible.

They had been kind in their rough way, those companions of her brother. They had stayed and done all that was necessary, had dug the grave, and stood about their comrade in good-natured grimness, marching in order about him to give the last look; but, when the sister tried to utter the prayer she knew her mother would have spoken, her throat refused to make a sound, and her tongue cleaved to the roof of her mouth. She had taken sudden refuge in the little shed that was her own room, and there had stayed till the rough companions had taken away the still form of the only one left in the family circle.

In silence the funeral procession wound its way to the spot where the others were buried. They respected her tearless grief, these great, passionate, uncontrolled young men. They held in the rude jokes with which they would have taken the awesomeness from the occasion for themselves, and for the most part kept the way silently and gravely, now and then looking back with admiration to the slim girl with the stony face and unblinking eyes who followed them mechanically. They had felt that some one ought to do something; but no one knew exactly what, and so they walked silently.

Only one, the hardest and boldest, the ringleader of the company, ventured back to ask whether there was anything he could do for her, anything she would like to have done; but she answered him coldly with a "No!" that cut him to the quick. It had been a good deal for him to do, this touch of gentleness he had forced himself into. He turned from her with a wicked gleam of intent in his eyes, but she did not see it.

When the crude ceremony was over, the last clod was heaped upon the pitiful mound, and the relentless words, "dust to dust," had been murmured by one more daring than the rest, they turned and looked at the girl, who had all the time stood upon a mound of earth and watched them, as a statue of Misery might look down upon the world. They could not make her out, this silent, marble girl. They hoped now she would change. It was over. They felt an untold relief themselves from the fact that their reckless comrade was no longer lying cold and still among them. They were done with him. They had paid their last tribute, and wished to forget. He must settle his own account with the hereafter now; they had enough in their own lives without the burden of his.

Then there had swept up into the girl's face one gleam of life that made her beautiful for the instant, and she had bowed to them with a slow, almost haughty, inclination of her head, and spread out her hands like one who would like to bless but dared not, and said clearly, "I thank you — all!" There had been just a slight hesitation before the last word "all," as if she were not quite sure, as her eyes rested upon the ringleader with doubt and dislike; then her lips had hardened as if justice must be done, and she had spoken it, "all!" and, turning, sped away to her cabin alone.

They were taken by surprise, those men who feared nothing in the wild and primitive West, and for a moment they watched her go in silence. Then the words that broke upon the air were not all pleasant to hear; and, if the girl could have known, she would have sped far faster, and her cheeks would have burned a brighter red than they did.

But one, the boldest, the ringleader, said nothing. His brows darkened, and the wicked gleam came and sat in his hard eyes with a green light. He drew a little apart from the rest, and walked on more rapidly. When he came to the place where they had left their horses, he took his and went on toward the cabin with a look that did not invite the others to follow. As their voices died away in the distance, and he drew nearer to the cabin, his eyes gleamed with cunning.

The girl in the cabin worked rapidly. One by one she took the boxes on which the crude coffin of her brother had rested, and threw them far out the back door. She straightened the furniture around fiercely, as if by erasing every sign she could force from memory the thought of the scenes that had just passed. She took her brother's coat that hung against the wall, and an old pipe from the mantle, and hid them in the room that was hers. Then she looked about for something else to be done.

A shadow darkened the sunny doorway. Looking up, she saw the man she believed to be her brother's murderer.

"I came back, Bess, to see if I could do anything for you."

The tone was kind; but the girl involuntarily put her hand to her throat, and caught her breath. She would like to speak out and tell him what she thought, but she dared not. She did not even dare let her thought appear in her eyes. The dull, statue-like look came over her face that she had worn at the grave. The man thought it was the stupefaction of grief.

"I told you I didn't want any help," she said, trying to speak in the same tone she had used when she thanked the men.

"Yes, but you're all alone," said the man insinuatingly; she felt a menace in the thought, "and I am sorry for you!"

He came nearer, but her face was cold. Instinctively she glanced to the cupboard door behind which lay her brother's belt with two pistols.

"You're very kind," she forced herself to say; "but I'd rather be alone now." It was hard to speak so when she would have liked to dash on him, and call down curses for the death of her brother; but she looked into his evil face, and a fear of herself worse than death stole into her heart.

He took encouragement from her gentle dignity. Where did she get that manner so imperial, she, born in a mountain cabin and bred on the wilds? How could she speak with an accent so different from those about her? The brother was not so, not so much so; the mother had been plain and quiet. He had not known her father, for he had lately come to this State in hiding from another. He wondered, with his wide knowledge of the world, over her wild, haughty beauty, and gloated over it. He liked to think just what worth was within his easy grasp. A prize for the asking, and here alone, unprotected.

"But it ain't good for you to be alone, you know, and I've come to protect you. Besides, you need cheering up, little girl." He came closer. "I love you, Bess, you know, and I'm going to take care of you now. You're all alone. Poor little girl."

He was so near that she almost felt his breath against her cheek. She faced him desperately, growing white to the lips. Was there nothing on earth or in heaven to save her? Mother! Father! Brother! All gone! Ah! Could she but have known that the quarrel which ended her wild young brother's life had been about her, perhaps pride in him would have salved her grief, and choked her horror.

While she watched the green lights play in the evil eyes above her, she gathered all the strength of her young life into one effort, and schooled herself to be calm. She controlled her involuntary shrinking from the man, only drew herself back gently, as a woman with wider experience and gentler breeding might have done.

"Remember," she said, "that my brother just lay there dead!" and she pointed to the empty centre of the room. The dramatic attitude was almost a condemnation to the guilty man before her. He drew back as if the sheriff had entered the room, and looked instinctively to where the coffin had been but a short time before, then laughed nervously and drew himself together.

The girl caught her breath, and took courage. She had held him for a minute; could she not hold him longer?

"Think!" she said. "He is but just buried. It is not right to talk of such things as love in this room where he had just gone out. You must leave me alone for a little while. I cannot talk and think now. We must respect the dead, you know." She looked appealing at him, acting her part desperately, but well. It was as if she were trying to charm a lion or an insane man.

He stood admiring her. She argued well. He was half-minded to humor her, for somehow when she spoke of the dead he could see the gleam in her brother's eyes just before he shot him. Then there was promise in this wooing. She was no girl to be lightly won, after all. She could hold her own, and perhaps she would be the better for having her way for a little. At any rate, there was more excitement in such game.

She saw that she was gaining, and her breath came freer.

"Go!" she said with a flickering smile. "Go! For — a little while," and then she tried to smile again.

He made a motion to take her in his arms and kiss her; but she drew back suddenly, and spread her hands before her, motioning him back.

"I tell you you must not now. Go! Go! or I will never speak to you again."

He looked into her eyes, and seemed to feel a power that he must obey. Half sullenly he drew back toward the door.

"But, Bess, this ain't the way to treat a fellow," he whined. "I came way back here to take care of you. I tell you I love you, and I'm going to have you. There ain't any other fellow going to run off with you —"

"Stop!" she cried tragically. "Don't you see you're not doing right? My brother is just dead. I must have some time to mourn. It is only decent." She was standing now with her back to the little cupboard behind whose door lay the two pistols. Her hand was behind her on the wooden latch.

"You don't respect my trouble!" she said, catching her breath, and putting her hand to her eyes. "I don't believe you care for me when you don't do what I say."

The man was held at bay. He was almost conquered by her sign of tears. It was a new phase of her to see her melt into weakness so. He was charmed.

"How long must I stay away?" he faltered.

She could scarcely speak, so desperate she felt. O if she dared but say, "Forever," and shout it at him! She was desperate enough to try her chances at shooting him if she but had the pistols, and was sure they were loaded — a desperate chance indeed against the best shot on the Pacific coast, and a desperado at that.

She pressed her hands to her throbbing temples, and tried to think. At last she faltered out,

"Three days!"

He swore beneath his breath, and his brows drew down in heavy frowns that were not good to see. She shuddered at what it would be to be in his power forever. How he would play with her and toss her aside! Or kill her, perhaps, when he had tired of her! Her life on the mountain had made her familiar with evil characters.

He came a step nearer, and she felt she was losing ground.

Straightening up, she said coolly:

"You must go away at once, and not think of coming back at least until to-morrow night. Go!" With wonderful control she smiled at him, one frantic, brilliant smile; and to her great wonder he drew back. At the door he paused, a softening look upon his face.

"Mayn't I kiss you before I go?"

She shuddered involuntarily, but put out her hands in protest again. "Not to-night!" She shook her head, and tried to smile.

He thought he understood her, but turned away half satisfied. Then she heard his step coming back to the door again, and she went to meet him. He must not come in. She had gained in sending him out, if she could but close the door fast. It was in the doorway that she faced him as he stood with one foot ready to enter again. The crafty look was out upon his face plainly now, and in the sunlight she could see it.

"You will be all alone to-night."

"I am not afraid," calmly. "And no one will trouble me. Don't you know what they say about the spirit of a man —" she stopped; she had almost said "a man who has been murdered" — "coming back to his home the first night after he is buried?" It was her last frantic effort.

The man before her trembled, and looked around nervously.

"You better come away to-night with me," he said, edging away from the door.

"See, the sun is going down! You must go now," she said imperiously; and reluctantly the man mounted his restless horse, and rode away down the mountain.

She watched him silhouetted against the blood-red globe of the sun as it sank lower and lower. She could see every outline of his slouch-hat and muscular shoulders as he turned now and then and saw her standing still alone at her cabin door. Why he was going he could not tell; but he went, and he frowned as he rode away, with the wicked gleam still in his eye; for he meant to return.

At last he disappeared; and the girl, turning, looked up, and there rode the white ghost of the moon overhead. She was alone.

Chapter 2
The Flight

A great fear settled down upon the girl as she realized that she was alone and, for a few hours at least, free. It was a miraculous escape. Even now she could hear the echo of the man's last words, and see his hateful smile as he waved his good-by and promised to come back for her to-morrow.

She felt sure he would not wait until the night. It might be he would return even yet. She cast another reassuring look down the darkening road, and strained her ear; but she could no longer hear hoof-beats. Nevertheless, it behooved her to hasten. He had blanched at her suggestion of walking spirits; but, after all, his courage might arise. She shuddered to think of his returning later, in the night. She must fly somewhere at once.

Instantly her dormant senses seemed to become alert. Fully fledged plans flashed through her brain. She went into the cabin, and barred the door. She made every movement swiftly, as if she had not an instant to spare. Who could tell? He might return even before dark. He had been hard to deter, and she did not feel at all secure. It was her one chance of safety to get away speedily, whither it mattered little, only so she was away and hidden.

Her first act inside the cottage was to get the belt from the cupboard and buckle it around her waist. She examined and loaded the pistols. Her throat seemed seized with sudden constriction when she discovered that the barrels had been empty and the weapons would have done her no good even if she could have reached them.

She put into her belt the sharp little knife her brother used to carry, and then began to gather together everything eatable that she could carry with her. There was not much that could be easily carried — some dried beef, a piece of cheese, some corn-meal, a piece of pork, a handful of cheap coffee-berries, and some pieces of hard corn bread. She hesitated over a pan half full of baked beans, and finally added them to the store. They were bulky, but she ought to take them if she could. There was nothing else in the house that seemed advisable to take in the way of edibles. Their stores had been running low, and the trouble of the last day or two had put housekeeping entirely out of her mind. She had not cared to eat, and now it occurred to her that food had not passed her lips that day. With strong self-control she forced herself to eat a few of the dry pieces of corn bread, and to drink some cold coffee that stood in the little coffee-pot. This she did while she worked, wasting not one minute.

There were some old flour-sacks in the house. She put the food into two of them, with the pan of beans on the top, adding a tin cup, and tied them securely together. Then she went into her little shed room, and put on the few extra garments in her wardrobe. They were not many, and that was the easiest way to carry them. Her mother's wedding-ring, sacredly kept in a box since the mother's death, she slipped upon her finger. It seemed the closing act of her life in the cabin, and she paused and bent her head as if to ask the mother's permission that she might wear the ring. It seemed a kind of protection to her in her lonely situation.

There were a few papers and an old letter or two yellow with years, which the mother had always guarded sacredly. One was the certificate of her mother's marriage. The girl did not know what the others were. She had never looked into them closely, but she knew that her mother had counted them precious. These she pinned into the bosom of her calico gown. Then she was ready.

She gave one swift glance of farewell about the cabin where she had spent nearly all of her life that she could remember, gathered up the two flour-sacks and an old coat of her father's that hung on the wall, remembering at the last minute to put into its pocket the few matches and the single candle left in the house, and went out from the cabin, closing the door behind her.

She paused, looking down the road, and listened again; but no sound came to her save a distant howl of a wolf. The moon rode high and clear by this time; and it seemed not so lonely here, with everything bathed in soft silver, as it had in the darkening cabin with its flickering candle.

The girl stole out from the cabin and stealthily across the patch of moonlight into the shadow of the shackly barn where stamped the poor, ill-fed, faithful horse that her brother had ridden to his death upon. All her movements were stealthy as a cat's.

She laid the old coat over the horse's back, swung her brother's saddle into place — she had none of her own, and could ride his, or without any; it made no difference, for she was perfectly at home on horseback — and strapped the girths with trembling fingers that were icy cold with excitement. Across the saddle-bows she hung the two flour-sacks containing her provisions. Then with added caution she tied some old burlap about each of the horse's feet. She must make no sound and leave no track as she stole forth into the great world.

The horse looked curiously down and whinnied at her, as she tied his feet up clumsily. He did not seem to like his new habiliments, but he suffered anything at her hand.

"Hush!" she murmured softly, laying her cold hands across his nostrils; and he put his muzzle into her palm, and seemed to understand.

She led him out into the clear moonlight then, and paused a second, looking once more down the road that led away in front of the cabin; but no one was coming yet, though her heart beat high as she listened, fancying every falling bough or rolling stone was a horse's hoof-beat.

There were three trails leading away from the cabin, for they could hardly be dignified by the name of road. One led down the mountain toward the west, and was the way they took to the nearest clearing five or six miles beyond and to the supply store some three miles further. One led off to the east, and was less travelled, being the way to the great world; and the third led down behind the cabin, and was desolate and barren under the moon. It led down, back, and away to desolation, where five graves lay stark and ugly at the end. It was the way they had taken that afternoon.

She paused just an instant as if hesitating which way to take. Not the way to the west — ah, any but that! To the east? Yes, surely, that must be the trail she would eventually strike; but she had a duty yet to perform. That prayer was as yet unsaid, and before she was free to seek safety — if safety there were for her in the wide world — she must take her way down the lonely path. She walked, leading the horse, which followed her with muffled tread and arched neck as if he felt he were doing homage to the dead. Slowly, silently, she moved along into the river of moonlight and dreariness; for the moonlight here seemed cold, like the graves it shone upon, and the girl, as she walked with bowed head, almost fancied she saw strange misty forms flit past her in the night.

As they came in sight of the graves, something dark and wild with plumy tail slunk away into the shadows, and seemed a part of the place. The girl stopped a moment to gain courage in full sight of the graves, and the horse snorted, and stopped too, with his ears a-quiver, and a half-fright in his eyes.

She patted his neck and soothed him incoherently, as she buried her face in his mane for a moment, and let the first tears that had dimmed her eyes since the blow had fallen come smarting their way out. Then, leaving the horse to stand curiously watching her, she went down and stood at the head of the new-heaped mound. She tried to kneel, but a shudder passed through her. It was as if she were descending into the place of the dead herself; so she stood up and raised her eyes to the wide white night and the moon riding so high and far away.

"Our Father," she said in a voice that sounded miles away to herself. Was there any Father, and could He hear her? And did He care? "Which art in heaven —" but heaven was so far away and looked so cruelly serene to her in her desolateness and danger! "hallowed be thy name. Thy kingdom come —" whatever that might mean. "Thy will be done in earth, as it is in heaven." It was a long prayer to pray, alone with the pale moonrain and the graves, and a distant wolf, but it was her mother's wish. Her will being done here over the dead — was that anything like the will of the Father being done in heaven? Her untrained thoughts hovered on the verge of great questions, and then slipped back into her pathetic self and its fear, while her tongue hurried on through the words of the prayer.

Once the horse stirred and breathed a soft protest. He could not understand why they were stopping so long in this desolate place, for nothing apparently. He had looked and looked at the shapeless mound before which the girl was standing; but he saw no sign of his lost master, and his instincts warned him that there were wild animals about. Anyhow, this was no place for a horse and a maid to stop in the night.

A few loose stones rattled from the horse's motion. The girl started, and looked hastily about, listening for a possible pursuer; but everywhere in the white sea of moonlight there was empty, desolate space. On to the "Amen" she finished then, and with one last look at the lonely graves she turned to the horse. Now they might go, for the duty was done, and there was no time to be lost.

Somewhere over toward the east across the untravelled wilderness of white light was the trail that started to the great world from the little cabin she had left. She dared not go back to the cabin to take it, lest she find herself already followed. She did not know the way across this lonely plain, and neither did the horse. In fact, there was no way, for it was all one arid plain so situated that human travellers seldom came near it, so large and so barren that one might wander for hours and gain no goal, so dry that nothing would grow.

With another glance back on the way she had come, the girl mounted the horse and urged him down into the valley. He stepped cautiously into the sandy plain, as if he were going into a river and must try its depth. He did not like the going here, but he plodded on with his burdens. The girl was light; he did not mind her weight; but he felt this place uncanny, and now and then would start on a little spurt of haste, to get into a better way.

He liked the high mountain trails, where he could step firmly and hear the twigs crackle under his feet, not this muffled, velvet way where one made so little progress and had to work so hard.

The girl's heart sank as they went on, for the sand seemed deep and drifted in places. She felt she was losing time. The way ahead looked endless, as if they were but treading sand behind them which only returned in front to be trodden over again. It was to her like the valley of the dead, and she longed to get out of it. A great fear lest the moon should go down and leave her in this low valley alone in the dark took hold upon her. She felt she must get away, up higher. She turned the horse a little more to the right, and he paused, and seemed to survey the new direction and to like it. He stepped up more briskly, with a courage that could come only from an intelligent hope for better things. And at last they were rewarded by finding the sand shallower, and now and then a bit of rock cropping out for a firmer footing.

The young rider dismounted, and untied the burlap from the horse's feet. He seemed to understand, and to thank her as he nosed about her neck. He thought, perhaps, that this mission was over and they were going to strike out for home now.

The ground rose steadily before them now, and at times grew quite steep; but the horse was fresh as yet, and clambered upward with good heart; and the rider was used to rough places, and felt no discomfort from her position. The fear of being followed had succeeded to the fear of being lost, for the time being; and instead of straining her ears on the track behind she was straining her eyes to the wilderness before. The growth of sage-brush was dense now, and trees were ahead.

After that the way seemed steep, and the rider's heart stood still with fear lest she could never get up and over to the trail which she knew must be somewhere in that direction, though she had never been far out on its course herself. That it led straight east into all the great cities she never doubted, and she must find it before she was pursued. That man would be angry, *angry* if he came and found her gone! He was not beyond shooting her for giving him the slip in this way.

The more she thought over it, the more frightened she became, till every bit of rough way, and every barrier that kept her from going forward quickly, seemed terrible to her. A bob-cat shot across the way just ahead, and the green gleam of its eyes as it turned one swift glance at this strange intruder in its chosen haunts made her catch her breath and put her hand on the pistols.

They were climbing a long time — it seemed hours to the girl — when at last they came to a space where a better view of the land was possible. It was high, and sloped away on three sides. To her looking now in the clear night the outline of a mountain ahead of her became distinct, and the lay of the land was not what she had supposed. It brought her a curious sense of being lost. Over there ought to be the familiar way where the cabin stood, but there was no sign of anything she had ever seen before, though she searched eagerly for landmarks. The course she had chosen, and which had seemed the only one, would take her straight up, up over the mountain, a way well-nigh impossible, and terrible even if it were possible.

It was plain she must change her course, but which way should she go? She was completely turned around. After all, what mattered it? One way might be as good as another, so it led not home to the cabin which could never be home again. Why not give the horse his head, and let him pick out a safe path? Was there danger that he might carry her back to the cabin again, after all? Horses did that sometimes. But at least he could guide through this maze of perplexity till some surer place was reached. She gave him a sign, and he moved on, nimbly picking a way for his feet.

They entered a forest growth where weird branches let the pale moon through in splashes and patches, and grim moving figures seemed to chase them from every shadowy tree-trunk. It was a terrible experience to the girl. Sometimes she shut her eyes and held to the saddle, that she might not see and be filled with this frenzy of things, living or dead, following her. Sometimes a real black shadow crept across the path, and slipped into the engulfing darkness of the undergrowth to gleam with yellow-lighted eyes upon the intruders.

But the forest did not last forever, and the moon was not yet gone when they emerged presently upon the rough mountain-side. The girl studied the moon then, and saw by the way it was setting that after all they were going in the right general direction. That gave a little comfort until she made herself believe that in some way she might have made a mistake and gone the wrong way from the graves, and so be coming up to the cabin after all.

It was a terrible night. Every step of the way some new horror was presented to her imagination. Once she had to cross a wild little stream, rocky and uncertain in its bed, with slippery, precipitous banks; and twice in climbing a steep incline she came sharp upon sheer precipices down into a rocky gorge, where the moonlight seemed repelled by dark, bristling evergreen trees growing half-way up the sides. She could hear the rush and clamor of a tumbling mountain stream in the depths below. Once she fancied she heard a distant shot, and the horse pricked up his ears, and went forward excitedly.

But at last the dawn contended with the night, and in the east a faint pink flush crept up. Down in the valley a mist like a white feather rose gently into a white cloud, and obscured everything. She wished she might carry the wall of white with her to shield her. She had longed for the dawn; and now, as it came with sudden light and clear revealing of the things about her, it was almost worse than night, so dreadful were the dangers when clearly seen, so dangerous the chasms, so angry the mountain torrents.

With the dawn came the new terror of being followed. The man would have no fear to come to her in the morning, for murdered men were not supposed to haunt their homes after the sun was up, and murderers were always courageous in the day. He might the sooner come, and find her gone, and perhaps follow; for she felt that he was not one easily to give up an object he coveted, and she had seen in his evil face that which made her fear unspeakably.

As the day grew clearer, she began to study the surroundings. All seemed utter desolation. There was no sign that anyone had ever passed that way before; and yet, just as she had thought that, the horse stopped and snorted, and there in the rocks before them lay a man's hat riddled with shot. Peering fearfully around, the girl saw a sight which made her turn icy cold and begin to tremble; for there, below them, as if he had fallen from his horse and rolled down the incline, lay a man on his face.

For the instant fear held her riveted, with the horse, one figure like a statue, girl and beast; the next, sudden panic took hold upon her. Whether the man were dead or not, she must make haste. It might be he would come to himself and pursue her, though there was that in the rigid attitude of the figure down below that made her sure he had been dead some time. But how had he died? Scarcely by his own hand. Who had killed him? Were there fiends lurking in the fastnesses of the mountain growth above her?

With guarded motion she urged her horse forward, and for miles beyond the horse scrambled breathlessly, the girl holding on with shut eyes, not daring to look ahead for fear of seeing more terrible sights, not daring to look behind for fear of — what she did not know.

At last the way sloped downward, and they reached more level ground, with wide stretches of open plain, dotted here and there with sage-brush and greasewood.

She had been hungry back there before she came upon the dead man; but now the hunger had gone from her, and in its place was only faintness. Still, she dared not stop long enough to eat. She must make as much time as possible here in this open space, and now she was where she could be seen more easily if any one were in pursuit.

But the horse had decided that it was time for breakfast. He had had one or two drinks of water on the mountain, but there had been no time for him to eat. He was decidedly hungry, and the plain offered nothing in the shape of breakfast. He halted, lingered, and came to a neighing stop, looking around at his mistress. She roused from her lethargy of trouble, and realized that his wants — if not her own — must be attended to.

She must sacrifice some of her own store of eatables, for by and by they would come to a good grazing-place perhaps, but now there was nothing.

The corn-meal seemed the best for the horse. She had more of it than of anything else. She poured a scanty portion out on a paper, and the beast smacked his lips appreciatively over it, carefully licking every grain from the paper, as the girl guarded it lest his breath should blow any away. He snuffed hungrily at the empty paper, and she gave him a little more meal, while she ate some of the cold beans, and scanned the horizon anxiously. There was nothing but sage-brush in sight ahead of her, and more hills further on where dim outlines of trees could be seen. If she could but get up higher where she could see farther, and perhaps reach a bench where there would be grass and some shelter.

It was only a brief rest she allowed; and then, hastily packing up her stores, and retaining some dry corn bread and a few beans in her pocket, she mounted and rode on.

The morning grew hot, and the way was long. As the ground rose again, it was stony and overgrown with cactus. A great desolation took possession of the girl. She felt as if she were in an endless flight from an unseen pursuer, who would never give up until he had her.

It was high noon by the glaring sun when she suddenly saw another human being. At first she was not quite sure whether he were human. It was only a distant view of a moving speck; but it was coming toward her, though separated by a wide valley that had stretched already for miles. He was moving along against the sky-line on a high bench on one side of the valley, and she mounted as fast as her weary beast would go to the top of another, hoping to find a grassy stretch and a chance to rest.

But the sight of the moving speck startled her. She watched it breathlessly as they neared each other. Could it be a wild beast? No, it must be a horse and rider. A moment later there came a puff of smoke as from a rifle discharged, followed by the distant echo of the discharge. It was a man, and he was yet a great way off. Should she turn and flee before she was discovered? But where? Should she go back? No, a thousand times, no! Her enemy was there. This could not be the one from whom she fled. He was coming from the opposite direction, but he might be just as bad. Her experience taught her that men were to be shunned. Even fathers and brothers were terribly uncertain, sorrow-bringing creatures.

She could not go back to the place where the dead man lay. She must not go back. And forward she was taking the only course that seemed at all possible through the natural obstructions of the region. She shrank to her saddle, and urged the patient horse on. Perhaps she could reach the bench and get away out of sight before the newcomer saw her.

But the way was longer to the top, and steeper than it had seemed at first, and the horse was tired. Sometimes he stopped of his own accord, and snorted appealingly to her with his head turned inquiringly as if to know how long and how far this strange ride was to continue. Then the man in the distance seemed to ride faster. The valley between them was not so wide here. He was quite distinctly a man now, and his horse was going rapidly. Once it seemed as if he waved his arms; but she turned her head, and urged her horse with sudden fright. They were almost to the top now. She dismounted and clambered alongside of the animal up the steep incline, her breath coming in quick gasps, with the horse's breath hot upon her cheek as they climbed together.

At last! They were at the top! Ten feet more and they would be on a level, where they might disappear from view. She turned to look across the valley, and the man was directly opposite. He must have ridden hard to get there so soon. Oh, horror! He was waving his hands and calling. She could distinctly hear a cry! It chilled her senses, and brought a frantic, unreasoning fear. Somehow she felt he was connected with the one from whom she fled. Some emissary of his sent out to foil her in her attempt for safety, perhaps.

She clutched the bridle wildly, and urged the horse up with one last effort; and just as they reached high ground she heard the wild cry ring clear and distinct, "Hello! Hello!" and then something else. It sounded like "Help!" but she could not tell. Was he trying to deceive her? Pretending he would help her?

She flung herself into the saddle, giving the horse the signal to run; and, as the animal obeyed and broke into his prairie run, she cast one fearful glance behind her. The man was pursuing her at a gallop! He was crossing the valley. There was a stream to cross, but he would cross it. He had determination in every line of his flying figure. His voice was pursuing her, too. It seemed as if the sound reached out and clutched her heart, and tried to draw her back as she fled. And now her pursuers were three: her enemy, the dead man upon the mountain, and the voice.

Chapter 3
The Pursuit

Straight across the prairie she galloped, not daring to stop for an instant, with the voice pursuing her. For hours it seemed to ring in her ears, and even after she was far beyond any possibility of hearing it she could not be sure but there was now and then a faint echo of it ringing yet, "Hello!" — ringing like some strange bird amid the silence of the world.

There were cattle and sheep grazing on the bench, and the horse would fain have stopped to dine with them; but the girl urged him on, seeming to make him understand the danger that might be pursuing them.

It was hours before she dared stop for the much-needed rest. Her brain had grown confused with the fright and weariness. She felt that she could not much longer stay in the saddle. She might fall asleep. The afternoon sun would soon be slipping down behind the mountains. When and where dared she rest? Not in the night, for that would be almost certain death, with wild beasts about.

A little group of greasewood offered a scanty shelter. As if the beast understood her thoughts he stopped with a neigh, and looked around at her. She scanned the surroundings. There were cattle all about. They had looked up curiously from their grazing as the horse flew by, but were now going quietly about their business. They would serve as a screen if any should be still pursuing her. One horse among the other animals in a landscape would not be so noticeable as one alone against the sky. The greasewood was not far from sloping ground where she might easily flee for hiding if danger approached.

The horse had already begun to crop the tender grass at his feet as if his life depended upon a good meal. The girl took some more beans from the pack she carried, and mechanically ate them, though she felt no appetite, and her dry throat almost refused to swallow. She found her eyes shutting even against her will; and in desperation she folded the old coat into a pillow, and with the horse's bridle fastened in her belt she lay down.

The sun went away; the horse ate his supper; and the girl slept. By and by the horse drowsed off too, and the bleating sheep in the distance, the lowing of the cattle, the sound of night-birds, came now and again from the distance; but still the girl slept on. The moon rose full and round, shining with flickering light through the cottonwoods; and the girl stirred in a dream and thought some one was pursuing her, but slept on again. Then out through the night rang a vivid human voice, "Hello! Hello!" The horse roused from his sleep, and stamped his feet nervously, twitching at his bridle; but the relaxed hand that lay across the leather strap did not quicken, and the girl slept on. The horse listened, and thought he heard a sound good to his ear. He neighed, and neighed again; but the girl slept on.

The first ray of the rising sun at last shot through the gray of dawning, and touched the girl full in the face as it slid under the branches of her sheltering tree. The light brought her acutely to her senses. Before she opened her eyes she seemed to be keenly and painfully aware of much that had gone on during her sleep. With another flash her eyes flew open. Not because she willed it, but rather as if the springs that held the lids shut had unexpectedly been touched and they sprang back because they had to.

She shrank, as her eyes opened, from a new day, and the memory of the old one. Then before her she saw something which kept her motionless, and almost froze the blood in her veins. She could not stir nor breathe, and for a moment even thought was paralyzed. There before her but a few feet away stood a man! Beyond him, a few feet from her own horse, stood his horse. She could not see it without turning her head, and that she dared not do; but she knew it was there, felt it even before she noticed the double stamping and breathing of the animals. Her keen senses seemed to make the whole surrounding landscape visible to her without the moving of a muscle. She knew to a nicety exactly how her weapons lay, and what movement would bring her hand to the trigger of her pistol; yet she stirred not.

Gradually she grew calm enough to study the man before her. He stood almost with his back turned toward her, his face just half turned so that one cheek and a part of his brow were visible. He was broad-shouldered and well built. There was strength in every line of his body. She felt how powerless she would be in his grasp. Her only hope would be in taking him unaware. Yet she moved not one atom.

He wore a brown flannel shirt, open at the throat, brown leather belt and boots; in short, his whole costume was in harmonious shades of brown, and looked new as if it had been worn but a few days. His soft felt sombrero was rolled back from his face, and the young red sun tinged the short brown curls to a ruddy gold. He was looking toward the rising sun. The gleam of it shot across his brace of pistols in his belt, and flashed twin rays into her eyes. Then all at once the man turned and looked at her.

Instantly the girl sprang to her feet, her hands upon her pistol, her eyes meeting with calm, desperate defiance the blue ones that were turned to her.

She was braced against a tree, and her senses were measuring the distance between her horse and herself, and deciding whether escape were possible.

"Good morning," said the man politely. "I hope I haven't disturbed your nap."

The girl eyed him solemnly, and said nothing. This was a new kind of man. He was not like the one from whom she had fled, nor like any she had ever seen; but he might be a great deal worse. She had heard that the world was full of wickedness.

"You see," went on the man with an apologetic smile, which lit up his eyes in a wonderfully winning way, "you led me such a desperate race nearly all day yesterday that I was obliged to keep you in sight when I finally caught you."

He looked for an answering smile, but there was none. Instead, the girl's dark eyes grew wide and purple with fear. He was the same one, then, that she had seen in the afternoon, the voice who had cried to her; and he had been pursuing her. He was an enemy, perhaps, sent by the man from whom she fled. She grasped her pistol with trembling fingers, and tried to think what to say or do.

The young man wondered at the formalities of the plains. Were all these Western maidens so reticent?

"Why did you follow me? Who did you think I was?" she asked breathlessly at last.

"Well, I thought you were a man," he said, "at least, you appeared to be a human being, and not a wild animal. I hadn't seen anything but wild animals for six hours, and very few of those; so I followed you."

The girl was silent. She was not reassured. It did not seem to her that her question was directly answered. The young man was playing with her.

"What right had you to follow me?" she demanded fiercely.

"Well, now that you put it in that light, I'm not sure that I had any right at all, unless it may be the claim that every human being has upon all creation."

His arms were folded now across his broad brown flannel chest, and the pistols gleamed in his belt below like fine ornaments. He wore a philosophical expression, and looked at his companion as if she were a new specimen of the human kind, and he was studying her variety, quite impersonally, it is true, but interestingly. There was something in his look that angered the girl.

"What do you want?" She had never heard of the divine claims of all the human family. Her one instinct at present was fear.

An expression that was almost bitter flitted over the young man's face, as of an unpleasant memory forgotten for the instant.

"It really wasn't of much consequence when you think of it," he said with a shrug of his fine shoulders. "I was merely lost, and was wanting to inquire where I was — and possibly the way to somewhere. But I don't know as 'twas worth the trouble."

The girl was puzzled. She had never seen a man like this before. He was not like her wild, reckless brother, nor any of his associates.

"This is Montana," she said, "or was, when I started," she added with sudden thought.

"Yes? Well, it was Montana when I started, too; but it's as likely to be the Desert of Sahara as anything else. I'm sure I've come far enough, and found it barren enough."

"I never heard of that place," said the girl seriously; "is it in Canada?"

"I believe not," said the man with sudden gravity; "at least, not that I know of. When I went to school, it was generally located somewhere in Africa."

"I never went to school," said the girl wistfully; "but —" with a sudden resolve — "I'll go now."

"Do!" said the man. "I'll go with you. Let's start at once; for, now that I think of it, I haven't had anything to eat for over a day, and there might be something in that line near a schoolhouse. Do you know the way?"

"No," said the girl, slowly studying him — she began to feel he was making fun of her; "but I can give you something to eat."

"Thank you!" said the man. "I assure you I shall appreciate anything from hardtack to bisque ice-cream."

"I haven't any of those," said the girl, "but there are plenty of beans left; and, if you will get some wood for a fire, I'll make some coffee."

"Agreed," said the man. "That sounds better than anything I've heard for forty-eight hours."

The girl watched him as he strode away to find wood, and frowned for an instant; but his face was perfectly sober, and she turned to the business of getting breakfast. For a little her fears were allayed. At least, he would do her no immediate harm. Of course she might fly from him now while his back was turned; but then of course he would pursue her again, and she had little chance of getting away. Besides, he was hungry. She could not leave him without something to eat.

"We can't make coffee without water," she said as he came back with a bundle of sticks.

He whistled.

"Could you inform me where to look for water?" he asked.

She looked into his face, and saw how worn and gray he was about his eyes; and a sudden compassion came upon her.

"You'd better eat something first," she said, "and then we'll go and hunt for water. There's sure to be some in the valley. We'll cook some meat."

She took the sticks from him, and made the fire in a businesslike way. He watched her, and wondered at her grace. Who was she, and how had she wandered out into this waste place? Her face was both beautiful and interesting. She would make a fine study if he were not so weary of all human nature, and especially woman. He sighed as he thought again of himself.

The girl caught the sound, and, turning with the quickness of a wild creature, caught the sadness in his face. It seemed to drive away much of her fear and resentment. A half-flicker of a smile came to her as their eyes met. It seemed to recognize a comradeship in sorrow. But her face hardened again almost at once into disapproval as he answered her look.

The man felt a passing disappointment. After a minute, during which the girl had dropped her eyes to her work again, he said: "Now, why did you look at me in that way? Ought I to be helping you in some way? I'm awkward, I know, but I can obey if you'll just tell me how."

The girl seemed puzzled; then she replied almost sullenly:

"There's nothing more to do. It's ready to eat."

She gave him a piece of the meat and the last of the corn bread in the tin cup, and placed the pan of beans beside him; but she did not attempt to eat anything herself.

He took a hungry bite or two, and looked furtively at her.

"I insist upon knowing why you looked —" he paused and eyed her — "why you look at me in that way. I'm not a wolf if I am hungry, and I'm not going to eat you up."

The look of displeasure deepened on the girl's brow. In spite of his hunger the man was compelled to watch her. She seemed to be looking at a flock of birds in the sky. Her hand rested lightly at her belt. The birds were coming towards them, flying almost over their heads.

Suddenly the girl's hand was raised with a quick motion, and something gleamed in the sun across his sight. There was a loud report, and one of the birds fell almost at his feet, dead. It was a sage-hen. Then the girl turned and walked towards him with as haughty a carriage as ever a society belle could boast.

"You were laughing at me," she said quietly.

It had all happened so suddenly that the man had not time to think.

Several distinct sensations of surprise passed over his countenance. Then, as the meaning of the girl's act dawned upon him, and the full intention of her rebuke, the color mounted in his nice, tanned face. He set down the tin cup, and balanced the bit of corn bread on the rim, and arose.

"I beg your pardon," he said. "I never will do it again. I couldn't have shot that bird to save my life," and he touched it with the tip of his tan leather boot as if to make sure it was a real bird.

The girl was sitting on the ground, indifferently eating some of the cooked pork. She did not answer. Somehow the young man felt uncomfortable. He sat down, and took up his tin cup, and went at his breakfast again; but his appetite seemed in abeyance.

"I've been trying myself to learn to shoot during the last week," he began soberly. "I haven't been able yet to hit anything but the side of a barn. Say, I'm wondering, suppose I had tried to shoot at those birds just now and had missed, whether you wouldn't have laughed at me — quietly, all to yourself, you know. Are you quite sure?"

The girl looked up at him solemnly, without saying a word for a full minute.

"Was what I said as bad as that?" she asked slowly.

"I'm afraid it was," he answered thoughtfully; "but I was a blamed idiot for laughing at you. A girl that shoots like that may locate the Desert of Sahara in Canada if she likes, and Canada ought to be proud of the honor."

She looked into his face for an instant, and noted his earnestness; and all at once she broke into a clear ripple of laughter. The young man was astonished anew that she had understood him enough to laugh. She must be unusually keen-witted, this lady of the desert.

"If 'twas as bad as that," she said in quite another tone, "you c'n laugh."

They looked at each other then in mutual understanding, and each fell to eating his portion in silence. Suddenly the man spoke.

"I am eating your food that you had prepared for your journey, and I have not even said, 'Thank you' yet, nor asked if you have enough to carry you to a place where there is more. Where are you going?"

The girl did not answer at once; but, when she did, she spoke thoughtfully, as if the words were a newly made vow from an impulse just received.

"I am going to school," she said in her slow way, "to learn to 'sight' the Desert of Sahara."

He looked at her, and his eyes gave her the homage he felt was her due; but he said nothing. Here evidently was an indomitable spirit, but how did she get out into the wilderness? Where did she come from, and why was she alone? He had heard of the freedom of Western women, but surely such girls as this did not frequent so vast a waste of uninhabited territory as his experience led him to believe this was. He sat studying her.

The brow was sweet and thoughtful, with a certain keen inquisitiveness about the eyes. The mouth was firm; yet there were gentle lines of grace about it. In spite of her coarse, dark calico garb, made in no particular fashion except with an eye to covering with the least possible fuss and trouble, she was graceful. Every movement was alert and clean-cut. When she turned to look full in his face, he decided that she had almost beautiful eyes.

She had arisen while he was watching her, and seemed to be looking off with sudden apprehension. He followed her gaze, and saw several dark figures moving against the sky.

"It's a herd of antelope," she said with relief; "but it's time we hit the trail." She turned, and put her things together with incredible swiftness, giving him very little opportunity to help, and mounted her pony without more words.

For an hour he followed her at high speed as she rode full tilt over rough and smooth, casting furtive, anxious glances behind her now and then, which only half included him. She seemed to know that he was there and was following; that was all.

The young man felt rather amused and flattered. He reflected that most women he knew would have ridden by his side, and tried to make him talk. But this girl of the wilderness rode straight ahead as if her life depended upon it. She seemed to have nothing to say to him, and to be anxious neither to impart her own history nor to know his.

Well, that suited his mood. He had come out into the wilderness to think and to forget. Here was ample opportunity. There had been a little too much of it yesterday, when he wandered from the rest of his party who had come out to hunt; and for a time he had felt that he would rather be back in his native city with a good breakfast and all his troubles than to be alone in the vast waste forever. But now there was human company, and a possibility of getting somewhere sometime. He was content.

The lithe, slender figure of the girl ahead seemed one with the horse it rode. He tried to think what this ride would be if another woman he knew were riding on that horse ahead, but there was very small satisfaction in that. In the first place, it was highly improbable, and the young man was of an intensely practical turn of mind. It was impossible to imagine the haughty beauty in a brown calico riding a high-spirited horse of the wilds. There was but one parallel. If she had been there, she would, in her present state of mind, likely be riding imperiously and indifferently ahead instead of by his side where he wanted her. Besides, he came out to the plains to forget her. Why think of her?

The sky was exceedingly bright and wide. Why had he never noticed this wilderness in skies at home? There was another flock of birds. What if he should try to shoot one? Idle talk. He would probably hit anything but the birds. Why had that girl shot that bird, anyway? Was it entirely because she might need it for food? She had picked it up significantly with the other things, and fastened it to her saddle-bow without a word. He was too ignorant to know whether it was an edible bird or not, or she was merely carrying it to remind him of her skill.

And what sort of a girl was she? Perhaps she was escaping from justice. She ran from him yesterday, and apparently stopped only when utterly exhausted. She seemed startled and anxious when the antelopes came into sight. There was no knowing whether her company meant safety, after all. Yet his interest was so thoroughly aroused in her that he was willing to risk it.

Of course he might go more slowly and gradually, let her get ahead, and he slip out of sight. It was not likely he had wandered so many miles away from human habitation but that he would reach one sometime; and, now that he was re-enforced by food, perhaps it would be the better part of wisdom to part with this strange maiden. As he thought, he unconsciously slackened his horse's pace. The girl was several yards ahead, and just vanishing behind a clump of sage-brush. She vanished, and he stopped for an instant, and looked about him on the desolation; and a great loneliness settled upon him like a frenzy. He was glad to see the girl riding back toward him with a smile of good fellowship on her face.

"What's the matter?" she called. "Come on! There's water in the valley."

The sound of water was good; and life seemed suddenly good for no reason whatever but that the morning was bright, and the sky was wide, and there was water in the valley. He rode forward, keeping close beside her now, and in a moment there gleamed below in the hot sunshine the shining of a sparkling stream.

"You seem to be running away from someone," he explained. "I thought you wanted to get rid of me, and I would give you a chance."

She looked at him surprised.

"I am running away," she said, "but not from you."

"From whom, then, may I ask? It might be convenient to know, if we are to travel in the same company."

She looked at him keenly.

"Who are you, and where do you belong?"

Chapter 4
The Two Fibugitives

"I'm not anybody in particular," he answered, "and I'm not just sure where I belong. I live in Pennsylvania, but I didn't seem to belong there exactly, at least not just now, and so I came out here to see if I belonged anywhere else. I concluded yesterday that I didn't. At least, not until I came in sight of you. But I suspect I am running away myself. In fact, that is just what I am doing, running away from a woman!"

He looked at her with his honest hazel eyes, and she liked him. She felt he was telling her the truth, but it seemed to be a truth he was just finding out for himself as he talked.

"Why do you run away from a woman? How could a woman hurt you? Can she shoot?"

He flashed her a look of amusement and pain mingled.

"She uses other weapons," he said. "Her words are darts, and her looks are swords."

"What a queer woman! Does she ride well?"

"Yes, in an automobile!"

"What is that?" She asked the question shyly as if she feared he might laugh again; and he looked down, and perceived that he was talking far above her. In fact, he was talking to himself more than to the girl.

There was a bitter pleasure in speaking of his lost lady to this wild creature who almost seemed of another kind, more like an intelligent bird or flower.

"An automobile is a carriage that moves about without horses," he answered her gravely. "It moves by machinery."

"I should not like it," said the girl decidedly. "Horses are better than machines. I saw a machine once. It was to cut wheat. It made a noise, and did not go fast. It frightened me."

"But automobiles go very fast, faster than any horses. And they do not all make a noise."

The girl looked around apprehensively.

"My horse can go very fast. You do not know how fast. If you see her coming, I will change horses with you. You must ride to the nearest bench and over, and then turn backward on your tracks. She will never find you that way. And I am not afraid of a woman."

The man broke into a hearty laugh, loud and long. He laughed until the tears rolled down his cheeks; and the girl, offended, rode haughtily beside him. Then all in a moment he grew quite grave.

"Excuse me," he said. "I am not laughing at you now, though it looks that way. I am laughing out of the bitterness of my soul at the picture you put before me. Although I am running away from her, the lady will not come out in her automobile to look for me. She does not want me!"

"She does not want you! And yet you ran away from her?"

"That's exactly it," he said. "You see, *I* wanted *her!*"

"Oh!" She gave a sharp, quick gasp of intelligence, and was silent. After a full minute she rode quite close to his horse, and laid her small brown hand on the animal's mane.

"I am sorry," she said simply.

"Thank you," he answered. "I'm sure I don't know why I told you. I never told anyone before."

There was a long silence between them. The man seemed to have forgotten her as he rode with his eyes upon his horse's neck, and his thoughts apparently far away.

At last the girl said softly, as if she were rendering return for the confidence given her, "I ran away from a man."

The man lifted his eyes courteously, questioningly, and waited.

"He is big and dark and handsome. He shoots to kill. He killed my brother. I hate him. He wants me, and I ran away from him. But he is a coward. I frightened him away. He is afraid of dead men that he has killed."

The young man gave his attention now to the extraordinary story which the girl told as if it were a common occurrence.

"But where are your people, your family and friends? Why do they not send the man away?"

"They're all back there in the sand," she said with a sad little flicker of a smile and a gesture that told of tragedy. "I said the prayer over them. Mother always wanted it when we died. There wasn't anybody left but me. I said it, and then I came away. It was cold moonlight, and there were noises. The horse was afraid. But I said it. Do you suppose it will do any good?"

She fastened her eyes upon the young man with her last words as if demanding an answer. The color came up to his cheeks. He felt embarrassed at such a question before her trouble.

"Why, I should think it ought to," he stammered. "Of course it will," he added with more confident comfort.

"Did you ever say the prayer?"

"Why — I — yes, I believe I have," he answered somewhat uncertainly.

"Did it do any good?" She hung upon his words.

"Why, I — believe — yes, I suppose it did. That is, praying is always a good thing. The fact is, it's a long time since I've tried it. But of course it's all right."

A curious topic for conversation between a young man and woman on a ride through the wilderness. The man had never thought about prayer for so many minutes consecutively in the whole of his life; at least, not since the days when his nurse tried to teach him "Now I lay me."

"Why don't you try it about the lady?" asked the girl suddenly.

"Well, the fact is, I never thought of it."

"Don't you believe it will do any good?"

"Well, I suppose it might."

"Then let's try it. Let's get off now, quick, and both say it. Maybe it will help us both. Do you know it all through? Can't you say it?" This last anxiously, as he hesitated and looked doubtful.

The color came into the man's face. Somehow this girl put him in a very bad light. He couldn't shoot; and, if he couldn't pray, what would she think of him?

"Why, I think I could manage to say it with help," he answered uneasily. "But what if that man should suddenly appear on the scene?"

"You don't think the prayer is any good, or you wouldn't say that." She said it sadly, hopelessly.

"O, why certainly," he said, "only I thought there might be some better time to try it; but, if you say so, we'll stop right here." He sprang to the ground, and offered to assist her; but she was beside him before he could get around his horse's head.

Down she dropped, and clasped her hands as a little child might have done, and closed her eyes.

"Our Father," she repeated slowly, precisely, as if every word belonged to a charm and must be repeated just right or it would not work. The man's mumbling words halted after hers. He was reflecting upon the curious tableau they would make to the chance passer-by on the desert if there were any passers-by. It was strange, this aloneness. There was a wideness here that made praying seem more natural than it would have been at home in the open country.

The prayer, by reason of the unaccustomed lips, went slowly; but, when it was finished, the girl sprang to her saddle again with a businesslike expression.

"I feel better," she said with a winning smile. "Don't you? Don't you think He heard?"

"Who heard?"

"Why, 'our Father.' "

"O certainly! That is, I've always been taught to suppose He did. I haven't much experimental knowledge in this line, but I dare say it'll do some good somewhere. Now do you suppose we could get some of that very sparkling water? I feel exceedingly thirsty."

They spurred their horses, and were soon beside the stream, refreshing themselves.

"Did you ride all night?" asked the girl.

"Pretty much," answered the man. "I stopped once to rest a few minutes; but a sound in the distance stirred me up again, and I was afraid to lose my chance of catching you, lest I should be hopelessly lost. You see, I went out with a party hunting, and I sulked behind. They went off up a steep climb, and I said I'd wander around below till they got back, or perhaps ride back to camp; but, when I tried to find the camp, it wasn't where I had left it."

"Well, you've got to lie down and sleep awhile," said the girl decidedly. "You can't keep going like that. It'll kill you. You lie down, and I'll watch, and get dinner. I'm going to cook that bird."

He demurred, but in the end she had her way; for he was exceedingly weary, and she saw it. So he let her spread the old coat down for him while he gathered some wood for a fire, and then he lay down and watched her simple preparations for the meal. Before he knew it he was asleep.

When he came to himself, there was a curious blending of dream and reality. He thought his lady was coming to him across the rough plains in an automobile, with gray wings like those of the bird the girl had shot, and his prayer as he knelt in the sand was drawing her, while overhead the air was full of a wild, sweet music from strange birds that mocked and called and trilled. But, when the automobile reached him and stopped, the lady withered into a little, old, dried-up creature of ashes; and the girl of the plains was sitting in her place radiant and beautiful.

He opened his eyes, and saw the rude little dinner set, and smelt the delicious odor of the roasted bird. The girl was standing on the other side of the fire, gravely whistling a most extraordinary song, like unto all the birds of the air at once.

She had made a little cake out of the corn-meal, and they feasted royally.

"I caught two fishes in the brook. We'll take them along for supper," she said as they packed the things again for starting. He tried to get her to take a rest also, and let him watch; but she insisted that they must go on, and promised to rest just before dark. "For we must travel hard at night, you know," she added fearfully.

He questioned her more about the man who might be pursuing, and came to understand her fears.

"The scoundrel!" he muttered, looking at the delicate features and clear, lovely profile of the girl. He felt a strong desire to throttle the evil man.

He asked a good many questions about her life, and was filled with wonder over the flower-like girl who seemed to have blossomed in the wilderness with no hand to cultivate her save a lazy, clever, drunken father, and a kind but ignorant mother. How could she have escaped being coarsened amid such surroundings? How was it, with such brothers as she had, that she had come forth as lovely and unhurt as she seemed? He somehow began to feel a great anxiety for her lonely future and a desire to put her in the way of protection. But at present they were still in the wilderness; and he began to be glad that he was here too, and might have the privilege of protecting her now, if there should be need.

As it grew toward evening, they came upon a little grassy spot in a coulee where the horses might rest and eat. Here they stopped, and the girl threw herself under a shelter of trees, with the old coat for a pillow, and rested, while the man paced up and down at a distance, gathering wood for a fire, and watching the horizon. As night came on, the city-bred man longed for shelter. He was by no means a coward where known quantities were concerned, but to face wild animals and drunken brigands in a strange, wild plain with no help near was anything but an enlivening prospect. He could not understand why they had not come upon some human habitation by this time. He had never realized how vast this country was before. When he came westward on the train he did not remember to have traversed such long stretches of country without a sign of civilization, though of course a train went so much faster than a horse that he had no adequate means of judging. Then, besides, they were on no trail now, and had probably gone in a most round-about way to anywhere. In reality they had twice come within five miles of little homesteads, tucked away beside a stream in a fertile spot; but they had not known it. A mile further to the right at one spot would have put them on the trail and made their way easier and shorter, but that they could not know.

The girl did not rest long. She seemed to feel her pursuit more as the darkness crept on, and kept anxiously looking for the moon.

"We must go toward the moon," she said as she watched the bright spot coming in the east.

They ate their supper of fish and cornbread with the appetite that grows on horseback, and by the time they had started on their way again the moon spread a path of silver before them, and they went forward feeling as if they had known each other a long time. For a while their fears and hopes were blended in one.

Meantime, as the sun sank and the moon rose, a traveller rode up the steep ascent to the little lonely cabin which the girl had left. He was handsome and dark and strong, with a scarlet kerchief knotted at his throat; and he rode slowly, cautiously, looking furtively about and ahead of him. He was doubly armed, and his pistols gleamed in the moonlight, while an ugly knife nestled keenly in a secret sheath.

He was wicked, for the look upon his face was not good to see; and he was a coward, for he started at the flutter of a night-bird hurrying late to its home in a rock by the wayside. The mist rising from the valley in wreaths of silver gauze startled him as he rounded the trail to the cabin, and for an instant he stopped and drew his dagger, thinking the ghost he feared was walking thus early. A draught from the bottle he carried in his pocket steadied his nerves, and he went on, but stopped again in front of the cabin; for there stood another horse, and there in the doorway stood a figure in the darkness! His curses rang through the still air and smote the moonlight. His pistol flashed forth a volley of fire to second him.

In answer to his demand who was there came another torrent of profanity. It was one of the comrades of the day before. He explained that he and two others had come up to pay a visit to the pretty girl. They had had a wager as to who could win her, and they had come to try; but she was not here. The door was fastened. They had forced it. There was no sign of her about. The other two had gone down to the place where her brother was buried to see whether she was there. Women were known to be sentimental. She might be that kind. He had agreed to wait here, but he was getting uneasy. Perhaps, if the other two found her, they might not be fair.

The last comer with a mighty oath explained that the girl belonged to him, and that no one had a right to her. He demanded that the other come with him to the grave, and see what had become of the girl; and then they would all go and drink together — but the girl belonged to him.

They rode to the place of the graves, and met the two others returning; but there was no sign of the girl, and the three taunted the one, saying that the girl had given him the slip. Amid much argument as to whose she was and where she was, they rode on cursing through God's beauty. They passed the bottle continually, that their nerves might be the steadier; and, when they came to the deserted cabin once more, they paused and discussed what to do.

At last it was agreed that they should start on a quest after her, and with oaths, and coarse jests, and drinking, they started down the trail of which the girl had gone in search by her roundabout way.

Chapter 5

A Night Ride

It was a wonderful night that the two spent wading the sea of moonlight together on the plain. The almost unearthly beauty of the scene grew upon them. They had none of the loneliness that had possessed each the night before, and might now discover all the wonders of the way.

Early in the way they came upon a prairie-dogs' village, and the man would have lingered watching with curiosity, had not the girl urged him on. It was the time of night when she had started to run away, and the same apprehension that filled her then came upon her with the evening. She longed to be out of the land which held the man she feared. She would rather bury herself in the earth and smother to death than be caught by him. But, as they rode on, she told her companion much of the habits of the curious little creatures they had seen; and then, as the night settled down upon them, she pointed out the dark, stealing creatures that slipped from their way now and then, or gleamed with a fearsome green eye from some temporary refuge.

At first the cold shivers kept running up and down the young man as he realized that here before him in the sage-brush was a real live animal about which he had read so much, and which he had come out bravely to hunt. He kept his hand upon his revolver, and was constantly on the alert, nervously looking behind lest a troop of coyotes or wolves should be quietly stealing upon him. But, as the girl talked fearlessly of them in much the same way as we talk of a neighbor's fierce dog, he grew gradually calmer, and was able to watch a dark, velvet-footed moving object ahead without starting.

By and by he pointed to the heavens, and talked of the stars. Did she know that constellation? No? Then he explained. Such and such stars were so many miles from the earth. He told their names, and a bit of mythology connected with the name, and then went on to speak of the moon, and the possibility of its once having been inhabited.

The girl listened amazed. She knew certain stars as landmarks, telling east from west and north from south; and she had often watched them one by one coming out, and counted them her friends; but that they were worlds, and that the inhabitants of this earth knew anything whatever about the heavenly bodies, she had never heard. Question after question she plied him with, some of them showing extraordinary intelligence and thought, and others showing deeper ignorance than a little child in our kindergartens would show.

He wondered more and more as their talk went on. He grew deeply interested in unfolding the wonders of the heavens to her; and, as he studied her pure profile in the moonlight with eager, searching, wistful gaze, her beauty impressed him more and more. In the East the man had a friend, an artist. He thought how wonderful a theme for a painting this scene would make. The girl in picturesque hat of soft felt, riding with careless ease and grace; horse, maiden, plain, bathed in a sea of silver.

More and more as she talked the man wondered how this girl reared in the wilds had acquired a speech so free from grammatical errors. She was apparently deeply ignorant, and yet with a very few exceptions she made no serious errors in English. How was it to be accounted for?

He began to ply her with questions about herself, but could not find that she had ever come into contact with people who were educated. She had not even lived in any of the miserable little towns that flourish in the wildest of the West, and not within several hundred miles of a city. Their nearest neighbors in one direction had been forty miles away, she said, and said it as if that were an everyday distance for a neighbor to live.

Mail? They had had a letter once that she could remember, when she was a little girl. It was just a few lines in pencil to say that her mother's father had died. He had been killed in an accident of some sort, working in the city where he lived. Her mother had kept the letter and cried over it till almost all the pencil marks were gone.

No, they had no mail on the mountain where their homestead was.

Yes, her father went there first because he thought he had discovered gold, but it turned out to be a mistake; so, as they had no other place to go to, and no money to go with, they had just stayed there; and her father and brothers had been cow-punchers, but she and her mother had scarcely ever gone away from home. There were the little children to care for; and, when they died, her mother did not care to go, and would not let her go far alone.

O, yes, she had ridden a great deal, sometimes with her brothers, but not often. They went with rough men, and her mother felt afraid to have her go. The men all drank. Her brothers drank. Her father drank too. She stated it as if it were a sad fact common to all mankind, and ended with the statement which was almost, not quite, a question, "I guess you drink too."

"Well," said the young man hesitatingly, "not that way. I take a glass of wine now and then in company, you know —"

"Yes, I know," sighed the girl. "Men are all alike. Mother used to say so. She said men were different from women. They had to drink. She said they all did it. Only she said her father never did; but he was very good, though he had to work hard."

"Indeed," said the young man, his color rising in the moonlight, "indeed, you make a mistake. I don't drink at all, not that way. I'm not like them. I — why, I only — well, the fact is, I don't care a red cent about the stuff anyway; and I don't want you to think I'm like them. If it will do you any good, I'll never touch it again, not a drop."

He said it earnestly. He was trying to vindicate himself. Just why he should care to do so he did not know, only that all at once it was very necessary that he should appear different in the eyes of this girl from the other men she had known.

"Will you really?" she asked, turning to look in his face. "Will you promise that?"

"Why, certainly I will," he said, a trifle embarrassed that she had taken him at his word. "Of course I will. I tell you it's nothing to me. I only took a glass at the club occasionally when the other men were drinking, and sometimes when I went to banquets, class banquets, you know, and dinners —"

Now the girl had never heard of class banquets, but to take a glass occasionally when the other men were drinking was what her brothers did; and so she sighed, and said: "Yes, you may promise, but I know you won't keep it. Father promised too; but, when he got with the other men, it did no good. Men are all alike."

"But I'm not," he insisted stoutly. "I tell you I'm not. I don't drink, and I won't drink. I promise you solemnly here under God's sky that I'll never drink another drop of intoxicating liquor again if I know it as long as I live."

He put out his hand toward her, and she put her own into it with a quick grasp for just an instant.

"Then you're not like other men, after all," she said with a glad ring in her voice. "That must be why I wasn't so very much afraid of you when I woke up and found you standing there."

A distinct sense of pleasure came over him at her words. Why it should make him glad that she had not been afraid of him when she had first seen him in the wilderness he did not know. He forgot all about his own troubles. He forgot the lady in the automobile. Right then and there he dropped her out of his thoughts. He did not know it; but she was forgotten, and he did not think about her any more during that journey. Something had erased her. He had run away from her, and he had succeeded most effectually, more so than he knew.

There in the desert the man took his first temperance pledge, urged thereto by a girl who had never heard of a temperance pledge in her life, had never joined a woman's temperance society, and knew nothing about women's crusades. Her own heart had taught her out of a bitter experience just how to use her God-given influence.

They came to a long stretch of level ground then, smooth and hard; and the horses as with common consent set out to gallop shoulder to shoulder in a wild, exhilarating skim across the plain. Talking was impossible. The man reflected that he was making great strides in experience, first a prayer and then a pledge, all in the wilderness. If anyone had told him he was going into the West for this, he would have laughed him to scorn.

Towards morning they rode more slowly. Their horses were growing jaded. They talked in lower tones as they looked toward the east. It was as if they feared they might waken someone too soon. There is something awesome about the dawning of a new day, and especially when one has been sailing a sea of silver all night. It is like coming back from an unreal world into a sad, real one. Each was almost sorry that the night was over. The new day might hold so much of hardship or relief, so much of trouble or surprise; and this night had been perfect, a jewel cut to set in memory with every facet flashing to the light. They did not like to get back to reality from the converse they had held together. It was an experience for each which would never be forgotten.

Once there came the distant sound of shots and shouts. The two shrank nearer each other, and the man laid his strong hand protectingly on the mane of the girl's horse; but he did not touch her hand. The lady of his thoughts had sometimes let him hold her jewelled hand, and smiled with drooping lashes when he fondled it; and, when she had tired of him, other admirers might claim the same privilege. But this woman of the wilderness — he would not even in his thoughts presume to touch her little brown, firm hand. Somehow she had commanded his honor and respect from the first minute, even before she shot the bird.

Once a bob-cat shot across their path but a few feet in front of them, and later a kit-fox ran growling up with ruffled fur; but the girl's quick shot soon put it to flight, and they passed on through the dawning morning of the first real Sabbath day the girl had ever known.

"It is Sunday morning at home," said the man gravely as he watched the sun lift its rosy head from the mist of mountain and valley outspread before them. "Do you have such an institution out here?"

The girl grew white about the lips. "Awful things happen on Sunday," she said with a shudder.

He felt a great pity rising in his heart for her, and strove to turn her thoughts in other directions. Evidently there was a recent sorrow connected with the Sabbath.

"You are tired," said he, "and the horses are tired. See! We ought to stop and rest. The daylight has come, and nothing can hurt us. Here is a good place, and sheltered. We can fasten the horses behind these bushes, and no one will guess we are here."

She assented, and they dismounted. The man cut an opening into a clump of thick growth with his knife, and there they fastened the weary horses, well hidden from sight if anyone chanced that way. The girl lay down a few feet away in a spot almost entirely surrounded by sage-brush which had reached an unusual height and made a fine hiding-place. Just outside the entrance of this natural chamber the man lay down on a fragrant bed of sage-brush. He had gathered enough for the girl first, and spread out the old coat over it; and she had dropped asleep almost as soon as she lay down. But, although his own bed of sage-brush was tolerably comfortable, even to one accustomed all his life to the finest springs and hair mattress that money could buy, and although the girl had insisted that he must rest too, for he was weary and there was no need to watch, sleep would not come to his eyelids.

He lay there resting and thinking. How strange was the experience through which he was passing! Came ever a wealthy, college-bred, society man into the like before? What did it all mean? His being lost, his wandering for a day, the sight of this girl and his pursuit, the prayer under the open sky, and that night of splendor under the moonlight riding side by side. It was like some marvellous tale.

And this girl! Where was she going? What was to become of her? Out in the world where he came from, were they ever to reach it, she would be nothing. Her station in life was beneath his so far that the only recognition she could have would be one which would degrade her. This solitary journey they were taking, how the world would lift up its hands in horror at it! A girl without a chaperon! She was impossible! And yet it all seemed right and good, and the girl was evidently recognized by the angels; else how had she escaped from degradation thus far?

Ah! How did he know she had? But he smiled at that. No one could look into that pure, sweet face, and doubt that she was as good as she was beautiful. If it was not so, he hoped he would never find it out. She seemed to him a woman yet unspoiled, and he shrank from the thought of what the world might do to her — the world and its cultivation, which would not be for her, because she was friendless and without money or home. The world would have nothing but toil to give her, with a meagre living.

Where was she going, and what was she proposing to do? Must he not try to help her in some way? Did not the fact that she had saved his life demand so much from him? If he had not found her, he must surely have starved before he got out of this wild place. Even yet starvation was not an impossibility; for they had not reached any signs of habitation yet, and there was but one more portion of corn-meal and a little coffee left. They had but two matches now, and there had been no more flights of birds, nor brooks with fishes.

In fact, the man found a great deal to worry about as he lay there, too weary with the unaccustomed exercise and experiences to sleep.

He reflected that the girl had told him very little, after all, about her plans. He must ask her. He wished he knew more of her family. If he were only older and she younger, or if he had the right kind of a woman friend to whom he might take her, or send her! How horrible that that scoundrel was after her! Such men were not men, but beasts, and should be shot down.

Far off in the distance, it might have been in the air or in his imagination, there sometimes floated a sound as of faint voices or shouts; but they came and went, and he listened, and by and by heard no more. The horses breathed heavily behind their sage-brush stable, and the sun rose higher and hotter. At last sleep came, troubled, fitful, but sleep, oblivion. This time there was no lady in an automobile.

It was high noon when he awoke, for the sun had reached around the sage-brush, and was pouring full into his face. He was very uncomfortable, and moreover an uneasy sense of something wrong pervaded his mind. Had he or had he not, heard a strange, low, sibilant, writhing sound just as he came to consciousness? Why did he feel that something, someone, had passed him but a moment before?

He rubbed his eyes open, and fanned himself with his hat. There was not a sound to be heard save a distant hawk in the heavens, and the breathing of the horses. He stepped over, and made sure that they were all right, and then came back. Was the girl still sleeping? Should he call her? But what should he call her? She had no name to him as yet. He could not say, "My dear madam" in the wilderness, nor yet "mademoiselle."

Perhaps it was she who had passed him. Perhaps she was looking about for water, or for fire-wood. He cast his eyes about, but the thick growth of sage-brush everywhere prevented his seeing much. He stepped to the right and then to the left of the little enclosure where she had gone to sleep, but there was no sign of life.

At last the sense of uneasiness grew upon him until he spoke.

"Are you awake yet?" he ventured; but the words somehow stuck in his throat, and would not sound out clearly. He ventured the question again, but it seemed to go no further than the gray-green foliage in front of him. Did he catch an alert movement, the sound of attention, alarm? Had he perhaps frightened her?

His flesh grew creepy, and he was angry with himself that he stood here actually trembling and for no reason. He felt that there was danger in the air. What could it mean? He had never been a believer in premonitions or superstitions of any kind. But the thought came to him that perhaps that evil man had come softly while he slept, and had stolen the girl away. Then all at once a horror seized him, and he made up his mind to end this suspense and venture in to see whether she were safe.

Chapter 6
A Christian Endeavor Meeting in the Wilderness

He stepped boldly around the green barrier, and his first glance told him she was lying there still asleep; but the consciousness of another presence held him from going away. There, coiled on the ground with venomous fangs extended and eyes glittering like slimy jewels, was a rattlesnake, close beside her.

For a second he gazed with a kind of fascinated horror, and his brain refused to act. Then he knew he must do something, and at once. He had read of serpents and travellers' encounters with them, but no memory of what was to be done under such circumstances came. Shoot? He dared not. He would be more likely to kill the girl than the serpent, and in any event would precipitate the calamity. Neither was there any way to awaken the girl and drag her from peril, for the slightest movement upon her part would bring the poisoned fangs upon her.

He cast his eyes about for some weapon, but there was not a stick or a stone in sight. He was a good golf-player; if he had a loaded stick, he could easily take the serpent's head off, he thought; but there was no stick. There was only one hope, he felt, and that would be to attract the creature to himself; and he hardly dared move lest the fascinated gaze should close upon the victim as she lay there sweetly sleeping, unaware of her new peril.

Suddenly he knew what to do. Silently he stepped back out of sight, tore off his coat, and then cautiously approached the snake again, holding the coat up before him. There was an instant's pause when he calculated whether the coat could drop between the snake and the smooth brown arm in front before the terrible fangs would get there; and then the coat dropped, the man bravely holding one end of it as a wall between the serpent and the girl, crying to her in an agony of frenzy to awaken and run.

There was a terrible moment in which he realized that the girl was saved and he himself was in peril of death, while he held to the coat till the girl was on her feet in safety. Then he saw the writhing coil at his feet turn and fasten its eyes of fury upon him. He was conscious of being uncertain whether his fingers could let go the coat, and whether his trembling knees could carry him away before the serpent struck; then it was all over, and he and the girl were standing outside the sage-brush, with the sound of the pistol dying away among the echoes, and the fine ache of his arm where her fingers had grasped him to drag him from danger.

The serpent was dead. She had shot it. She took that as coolly as she had taken the bird in its flight. But she stood looking at him with great eyes of gratitude, and he looked at her amazed that they were both alive, and scarcely understanding all that had happened.

The girl broke the stillness.

"You are what they call a 'tenderfoot,' " she said significantly.

"Yes," he assented humbly, "I guess I am. I couldn't have shot it to save anybody's life."

"You are a tenderfoot, and you couldn't shoot," she continued eulogistically, as if it were necessary to have it all stated plainly, "but you — you are what my brother used to call 'a white man.' You couldn't shoot; but you could risk your life, and hold that coat, and look death in the face. *You* are no tenderfoot."

There was eloquence in her eyes, and in her voice there were tears. She turned away to hide if any were in her eyes. But the man put out his hand on her sure little brown one, and took it firmly in his own, looking down upon her with his own eyes filled with tears of which he was not ashamed.

"And what am I to say to you for saving my life?" he said.

"I? O, that was easy," said the girl, rousing to the commonplace. "I can always shoot. Only you were hard to drag away. You seemed to want to stay there and die with your coat."

"They laughed at me for wearing that coat when we started away. They said a hunter never bothered himself with extra clothing," he mused as they walked away from the terrible spot.

"Do you think it was the prayer?" asked the girl suddenly.

"It may be!" said the man with wondering accent.

Then quietly, thoughtfully, they mounted and rode onward.

Their way, due east, led them around the shoulder of a hill. It was tolerably smooth, but they were obliged to go single file, so there was very little talking done.

It was nearly the middle of the afternoon when all at once a sound reached them from below, a sound so new that it was startling. They stopped their horses, and looked at each other. It was the faint sound of singing wafted on the light breeze, singing that came in whiffs like a perfume, and then died out. Cautiously they guided their horses on around the hill, keeping close together now. It was plain they were approaching some human being or beings. No bird could sing like that. There were indistinct words to the music.

They rounded the hillside, and stopped again side by side. There below them lay the trail for which they had been searching, and just beneath them, nestled against the hill, was a little schoolhouse of logs, weatherboarded, its windows open; and behind it and around it were horses tied, some of them tied, some of them hitched to wagons, but most of them with saddles.

The singing was clear and distinct now. They could hear the words. "O, that will be glory for me, glory for me, glory for me —"

"What is it?" she whispered.

"Why, I suspect it is a Sunday school or something of the kind."

"O! A school! Could we go in?"

"If you like," said the man, enjoying her simplicity. "We can tie our horses here behind the building, and they can rest. There is fresh grass in this sheltered place; see?"

He led her down behind the schoolhouse to a spot where the horses could not be seen from the trail. The girl peered curiously around the corner into the window. There sat two young girls about her own age, and one of them smiled at her. It seemed an invitation. She smiled back, and went on to the doorway reassured. When she entered the room, she found them pointing to a seat near a window, behind a small desk.

There were desks all over the room at regular intervals, and a larger desk up in front. Almost all the people sat at desks.

There was a curious wooden box in front at one side of the big desk, and a girl sat before it pushing down some black and white strips that looked like sticks, and making her feet go, and singing with all her might. The curious box made music, the same music the people were singing. Was it a piano? she wondered. She had heard of pianos. Her father used to talk about them. O, and what was that her mother used to want? A "cab'net-organ." Perhaps this was a cab'net-organ. At any rate, she was entranced with the music.

Up behind the man who sat at the big desk was a large board painted black with some white marks on it. The sunlight glinted across it, and she could not tell what they were; but, when she moved a little, she saw quite clearly it was a large cross with words beneath it — "He will hide me."

It was a strange place. The girl looked around shyly, and felt submerged in the volume of song that rolled around her, from voices untrained, perhaps, but hearts that knew whereof they sang. To her it was heavenly music, if she had the least conception of what such music was like. "Glory," "glory," "glory!" The words seemed to fit the day, and the sunshine, and the deliverance that had come to her so recently. She looked around for her companion and deliverer to enjoy it with him, but he had not come in yet.

The two girls were handing her a book now and pointing to the place. She could read. Her mother had taught her just a little before the other children were born, but not much in the way of literature had ever come in her way. She grasped the book eagerly, hungrily, and looked where the finger pointed. Yes, there were the words. "Glory for me!" "Glory for me!" Did that mean her? Was there glory for her anywhere in the world? She sighed with the joy of the possibility, as the "Glory Song" rolled along, led by the enthusiasm of one who had recently come from a big city where it had been sung in a great revival service. Some kind friend had given some copies of a leaflet containing it and a few other new songs to this little handful of Christians, and they were singing them as if they had been a thousand strong.

The singing ceased and the man at the big desk said, "Let us have the verses."

" 'The eternal God is thy refuge, and underneath are the everlasting arms,' " said a careworn woman in the front seat.

" 'He shall cover thee with his feathers, and under his wings shalt thou trust,' " said a young man next.

" 'In the time of trouble he shall hide me in his pavilion; in the secret of his tabernacle shall he hide me,' " read the girl who had handed the book. The slip of paper she had written it on fluttered to the floor at the feet of the stranger, and the stranger stooped and picked it up, offering it back; but the other girl shook her head, and the stranger kept it, looking wonderingly at the words, trying to puzzle out a meaning.

There were other verses repeated, but just then a sound smote upon the girl's ear which deadened all others. In spite of herself she began to tremble. Even her lips seemed to her to move with the weakness of her fear. She looked up, and the man was just coming toward the door; but her eyes grew dizzy, and a faintness seemed to come over her.

Up the trail on horseback, with shouts and ribald songs, rode four rough men, too drunk to know where they were going. The little schoolhouse seemed to attract their attention as they passed, and just for deviltry they shouted out a volley of oaths and vile talk to the worshippers within. One in particular, the leader, looked straight into the face of the young man as he returned from fastening the horses and was about to enter the schoolhouse, and pretended to point his pistol at him, discharging it immediately into the air. This was the signal for some wild firing as the men rode on past the schoolhouse, leaving a train of curses behind them to haunt the air and struggle with the "Glory Song" in the memories of those who heard.

The girl looked out from her seat beside the window, and saw the evil face of the man from whom she had fled. She thought for a terrible minute, which seemed ages long to her, that she was cornered now. She began to look about on the people there helplessly, and wonder whether they would save her, would help her, in her time of need. Would they be able to fight and prevail against those four terrible men mad with liquor?

Suppose he said she was his — his wife, perhaps, or sister, who had run away. What could they do? Would they believe her? Would the man who had saved her life a few minutes ago believe her? Would anybody help her?

The party passed, and the man came in and sat down beside her quietly enough; but without a word or a look he knew at once who the man was he had just seen. His soul trembled for the girl, and his anger rose hot. He felt that a man like that ought to be wiped off the face of the earth in some way, or placed in solitary confinement the rest of his life.

He looked down at the girl, trembling, brave, white, beside him; and he felt like gathering her in his arms and hiding her himself, such a frail, brave, courageous little soul she seemed. But the calm nerve with which she had shot the serpent was gone now. He saw she was trembling and ready to cry. Then he smiled upon her, a smile the like of which he had never given to a human being before; at least, not since he was a tiny baby and smiled confidingly into his mother's face. Something in that smile was like sunshine to a nervous chill.

The girl felt the comfort of it, though she still trembled. Down her eyes drooped to the paper in her shaking hands. Then gradually, letter by letter, word by word, the verse spoke to her. Not all the meaning she gathered, for "pavilion" and "tabernacle" were unknown words to her, but the hiding she could understand. She had been hidden in her time of trouble. Someone had done it. "He" — the word would fit the man by her side, for he had helped to hide her, and to save her more than once; but just now there came a dim perception that it was some other He, some One greater who had worked this miracle and saved her once more to go on perhaps to better things.

There were many things said in that meeting, good and wise and true. They might have been helpful to the girl if she had understood, but her thoughts had much to do. One grain of truth she had gathered for her future use. There was a "hiding" somewhere in this world, and she had had it in a time of trouble. One moment more out upon the open, and the terrible man might have seen her.

There came a time of prayer in which all heads were bowed, and a voice here and there murmured a few soft little words which she did not comprehend; but at the close they all joined in "the prayer"; and, when she heard the words, "Our Father," she closed her eyes, which had been curiously open and watching, and joined her voice softly with the rest. Somehow it seemed to connect her safety with "our Father," and she felt a stronger faith than ever in her prayer.

The young man listened intently to all he heard. There was something strangely impressive to him in this simple worship out in what to him was a vast wilderness. He felt more of the true spirit of worship than he had ever felt at home sitting in the handsomely upholstered pew beside his mother and sister while the choir-boys chanted the processional and the light filtered though costly windows of many colors over the large and cultivated congregation. There was something about the words of these people that went straight to the heart more than all the intonings of the cultured voices he had ever heard. Truly they meant what they said, and God had been a reality to them in many a time of trouble. That seemed to be the theme of the afternoon, the saving power of the eternal God, made perfect through the need and the trust of His people. He was reminded more than once of the incident of the morning and the miraculous saving of his own and his companion's life.

When the meeting was over, the people gathered in groups and talked with one another. The girl who had handed the book came over and spoke to the strangers, putting out her hand pleasantly. She was the missionary's daughter.

"What is this? School?" asked the stranger eagerly.

"Yes, this is the schoolhouse," said the missionary's daughter; "but this meeting is Christian Endeavor. Do you live near here? Can't you come every time?"

"No, I live a long way off," said the girl sadly. "That is, I did. I don't live anywhere now. I'm going away."

"I wish you lived here. Then you could come to our meeting. Did you have a Christian Endeavor where you lived?"

"No. I never saw one before. It's nice. I like it."

Another girl came up now, and put out her hand in greeting. "You must come again," she said politely.

"I don't know," said the visitor. "I sha'n't be coming back soon."

"Are you going far?"

"As far as I can. I'm going East."

"O," said the inquisitor; and then, seeing the missionary's daughter was talking to someone else, she whispered, nodding toward the man, "Is he your husband?"

The girl looked startled, while a slow color mounted into her cheeks.

"No," said she gravely, thoughtfully. "But — he saved my life a little while ago."

"Oh!" said the other, awestruck. "My! And ain't he handsome? How did he do it?"

But the girl could not talk about it. She shuddered.

"It was a dreadful snake," she said, "and I was — I didn't see it. It was awful! I can't tell you about it."

"My!" said the girl. "How terrible!"

The people were passing out now. The man was talking with the missionary, asking the road to somewhere. The girl suddenly realized that this hour of preciousness was over, and life was to be faced again. Those men, those terrible men! She had recognized the others as having been among her brother's funeral train. Where were they, and why had they gone that way? Were they on her track? Had they any clue to her whereabouts? Would they turn back pretty soon, and catch her when the people were gone home?

It appeared that the nearest town was Malta, sixteen miles away, down in the direction where the party of men had passed. There were only four houses near the schoolhouse, and they were scattered in different directions along the stream in the valley. The two stood still near the door after the congregation had scattered. The girl suddenly shivered. As she looked down the road, she seemed again to see the coarse face of the man she feared, and to hear his loud laughter and oaths. What if he should come back again? "I cannot go that way!" she said, pointing down the trail toward Malta. "I would rather die with wild beasts."

"No!" said the man with decision. "On no account can we go that way. Was that the man you ran away from?"

"Yes." She looked up at him, her eyes filled with wonder over the way in which he had coupled his lot with hers.

"Poor little girl!" he said with deep feeling. "You would be better off with the beasts. Come, let us hurry away from here!"

They turned sharply away from the trail, and followed down behind a family who were almost out of sight around the hill. There would be a chance of getting some provisions, the man thought. The girl thought of nothing except to get away. They rode hard, and soon came within hailing-distance of the people ahead of them, and asked a few questions.

No, there were no houses to the north until you were over the Canadian line, and the trail was hard to follow. Few people went that way. Most went down to Malta. Why didn't they go to Malta? There was a road there, and stores. It was by all means the best way. Yes, there was another house about twenty miles away on this trail. It was a large ranch, and was near to another town that had a railroad. The people seldom came this way, as there were other places more accessible to them. The trail was little used, and might be hard to find in some places; but, if they kept the Cottonwood Creek in sight, and followed on to the end of the valley, and then crossed the bench to the right, they would be in sight of it, and couldn't miss it. It was a good twenty miles beyond their house; but, if the travellers didn't miss the way, they might reach it before dark. Yes, the people could supply a few provisions at their house if the strangers didn't mind taking what was at hand.

The man in the wagon tried his best to find out where the two were going and what they were going for; but the man from the East baffled his curiosity in a most dexterous manner, so that, when the two rode away from the two-roomed log house where the kind-hearted people lived, they left no clue to their identity or mission beyond the fact that they were going quite a journey, and had got a little off their trail and run out of provisions.

They felt comparatively safe from pursuit for a few hours at least, for the men could scarcely return and trace them very soon. They had not stopped to eat anything; but all the milk they could drink had been given to them, and its refreshing strength was racing through their veins. They started upon their long ride with the pleasure of their companionship strong upon them.

"What was it all about?" asked the girl as they settled into a steady gait after a long gallop across a smooth level place.

He looked at her questioningly.

"The school. What did it mean? She said it was a Christian Endeavor. What is that?"

"Why, some sort of a religious meeting, or something of that kind, I suppose," he answered lamely. "Did you enjoy it?"

"Yes," she answered solemnly, "I liked it. I never went to such a thing before. The girl said they had one everywhere all over the world. What do you think she meant?"

"Why, I don't know, I'm sure, unless it's some kind of a society. But it looked to me like a prayer meeting. I've heard about prayer meetings, but I never went to one, though I never supposed they were so interesting. That was a remarkable story that old man told of how he was taken care of that night among the Indians. He evidently believes that prayer helps people.''

"Don't you?" she asked quickly.

"O, certainly!" he said, "but there was something so genuine about the way the old man told it that it made you feel it in a new way.''

"It is all new to me," said the girl. "But mother used to go to Sunday school and church and prayer meeting. She's often told me about it. She used to sing sometimes. One song was 'Rock of Ages.' Did you ever hear that?

'Rock of Ages, cleft for me,
Let me hide myself in Thee.' ''

She said it slowly and in a singsong voice, as if she were measuring the words off to imaginary notes. "I thought about that the night I started. I wished I knew where that rock was. Is there a rock anywhere that they call the Rock of Ages?''

The young man was visibly embarrassed. He wanted to laugh, but he would not hurt her in that way again. He was not accustomed to talking religion; yet here by this strange girl's side it seemed perfectly natural that he, who knew so very little experimentally himself about it, should be trying to explain the Rock of Ages to a soul in need. All at once it flashed upon him that it was for just such souls in need as this one that the Rock of Ages came into the world.

"I've heard the song. Yes, I think they sing it in all churches. It's quite common. No, there isn't any place called Rock of Ages. It refers — that is, I believe — why, you see the thing is figurative — that is, a kind of picture of things. It refers to the Deity.''

"O! Who is that?" asked the girl.

"Why — God." He tried to say it as if he had been telling her it was Mr. Smith or Mr. Jones, but somehow the sound of the word on his lips thus shocked him. He did not know how to go on. "It just means God will take care of people.''

"Oh!" she said, and this time a light of understanding broke over her face. "But," she added, "I wish I knew what it meant, the meeting, and why they did it. There must be some reason. They wouldn't do it for nothing. And how do you know it's all so? Where did they find it out?''

The man felt he was beyond his depth; so he sought to change the subject. "I wish you would tell me about yourself," he said gently. "I should like to understand you better. We have travelled together for a good many hours now, and we ought to know more about each other.''

"What do you want to know?" She asked it gravely. "There isn't much to tell but what I've told you. I've lived on a mountain all my life, and helped mother. The rest all died. The baby first, and my two brothers, and father, and mother, and then John. I said the prayer for John, and ran away."

"Yes, but I want to know about your life. You know I live in the East where everything is different. It's all new to me out here. I want to know, for instance, how you come to talk so well. You don't talk like a girl that never went to school. You speak as if you had read and studied. You make so few mistakes in your English. You speak quite correctly. That is not usual, I believe, when people have lived all their lives away from school, you know. You don't talk like the girls I have met since I came out here."

"Father always made me speak right. He kept at every one of us children when we said a word wrong, and made us say it over again. It made him angry to hear words said wrong. He made mother cry once when she said 'done' when she ought to have said 'did.' Father went to school once, but mother only went a little while. Father knew a great deal, and when he was sober he used to teach us things once in a while. He taught me to read. I can read anything I ever saw."

"Did you have many books and magazines?" he asked innocently.

"We had three books!" she answered proudly, as if that were a great many. "One was a grammar. Father bought it for mother before they were married, and she always kept it wrapped up in paper carefully. She used to get it out for me to read in sometimes; but she was very careful with it, and when she died I put it in her hands. I thought she would like to have it close to her, because it always seemed so much to her. You see father bought it. Then there was an almanac, and a book about stones and earth. A man who was hunting for gold left that. He stopped over night at our house, and asked for something to eat. He hadn't any money to pay for it; so he left that book with us, and said when he found the gold he would come and buy it back again. But he never came back."

"Is that all that you have ever read?" he asked compassionately.

"O, no! We got papers sometimes. Father would come home with a whole paper wrapped around some bundle. Once there was a beautiful story about a girl; but the paper was torn in the middle, and I never knew how it came out."

There was great wistfulness in her voice. It seemed to be one of the regrets of her girlhood that she did not know how that other girl in the story fared. All at once she turned to him.

"Now tell me about your life," she said. "I'm sure you have a great deal to tell."

His face darkened in a way that made her sorry.

"O, well," said he as if it mattered very little about his life, "I had a nice home — have yet, for the matter of that. Father died when I was little, and mother let me do just about as I pleased. I went to school because the other fellows did, and because that was the thing to do. After I grew up I liked it. That is, I liked some studies; so I went to a university."

"What is that?"

"O, just a higher school where you learn grown-up things. Then I travelled. When I came home, I went into society a good deal. But" — and his face darkened again — "I got tired of it all, and thought I would come out here for a while and hunt, and I got lost, and I found you!" He smiled into her face. "Now you know the rest."

Something passed between them in that smile and glance, a flash of the recognition of souls, and a gladness in each other's company, that made the heart warm. They said no more for some time, but rode quietly side by side.

They had come to the end of the valley, and were crossing the bench. The distant ranch could quite distinctly be seen. The silver moon had come up, for they had not been hurrying, and a great beauty pervaded everything. They almost shrank from approaching the buildings and people. They had enjoyed the ride and the companionship. Every step brought them nearer to what they had known all the time was an indistinct future from which they had been joyously shut away for a little time till they might know each other.

Chapter 7

Bad News

They found rest for the night at the ranch house. The place was wide and hospitable. The girl looked about her with wonder on the comfortable arrangements for work. If only her mother had had such a kitchen to work in, and such a pleasant, happy home, she might have been living yet. There was a pleasant-faced, sweet-voiced woman with gray hair whom the men called "mother." She gave the girl a kindly welcome, and made her sit down to a nice warm supper, and, when it was over, led her to a little room where her own bed was, and told her she might sleep with her. The girl lay down in a maze of wonder, but was too weary with the long ride to keep awake and think about it.

They slept, the two travellers, a sound and dreamless sleep, wherein seemed peace and moonlight, and a forgetting of sorrows.

Early the next morning the girl awoke. The woman by her side was already stirring. There was breakfast to get for the men. The woman asked her a few questions about her journey.

"He's your brother, ain't he, dearie?" asked the woman as she was about to leave the room.

"No," said the girl.

"O," said the woman, puzzled, "then you and he's goin' to be married in the town."

"O, no!" said the girl with scarlet cheeks, thinking of the lady in the automobile.

"Not goin' to be married, dearie? Now that's too bad. Ain't he any kind of relation to you? Not an uncle nor cousin nor nothin?"

"No."

"Then how be's you travellin' 'lone with him? It don't seem just right. You's a sweet, good girl; an' he's a fine man. But harm's come to more'n one. Where'd you take up with each other? Be he a neighbor? He looks like a man from way off, not hereabouts. You sure he ain't deceivin' you, dearie?"

The girl flashed her eyes in answer.

"Yes, I'm sure. He's a good man. He prays to our Father. No, he's not a neighbor, nor an uncle, nor a cousin. He's just a man that got lost. We were both lost on the prairie in the night; and he's from the East, and got lost from his party of hunters. He had nothing to eat, but I had; so I gave him some. Then he saved my life when a snake almost stung me. He's been good to me."

The woman looked relieved.

"And where you goin', dearie, all 'lone? What your folks thinkin' 'bout to let you go 'lone this way?"

"They're dead," said the girl with great tears in her eyes.

"Dearie me! And you so young! Say, dearie, s'pose you stay here with me. I'm lonesome, an' there's no women near by here. You could help me and be comp'ny. The men would like to have a girl round. There's plenty likely men on this ranch could make a good home for a girl sometime. Stay here with me, dearie."

Had this refuge been offered the girl during her first night in the wilderness, with what joy and thankfulness she would have accepted! Now it suddenly seemed a great impossibility for her to stay. She must go on. She had a pleasant ride before her, and delightful companionship; and she was going to school. The world was wide, and she had entered it. She had no mind to pause thus on the threshold, and never see further than Montana. Moreover, the closing words of the woman did not please her.

"I cannot stay," she said decidedly. "I'm going to school. And I do not want a man. I have just run away from a man, a dreadful one. I am going to school in the East. I have some relations there, and perhaps I can find them."

"You don't say so!" said the woman, looking disappointed. She had taken a great fancy to the sweet young face. "Well, dearie, why not stay here a little while, and write to your folks, and then go on with someone who is going your way? I don't like to see you go off with that man. It ain't the proper thing. He knows it himself. I'm afraid he's deceivin' you. I can see by his clo'es he's one of the fine young fellows that does as they please. He won't think any good of you if you keep travellin' 'lone with him. It's all well 'nough when you get lost, an' he was nice to help you out and save you from snakes; but he knows he ain't no business travellin' 'lone with you, you pretty little creature."

"You must not talk so!" said the girl, rising and flashing her eyes again. "He's a good man. He's what my brother called 'a white man all through.' Besides, he's got a lady, a beautiful lady, in the East. She rides in some kind of a grand carriage that goes of itself, and he thinks a great deal of her."

The woman looked as if she were but half convinced.

"It may seem all right to you, dearie," she said sadly; "but I'm old, and I've seen things happen. You'd find his fine lady wouldn't go jantin' round the world 'lone with him unless she's married. I've lived East, and I know; and what's more, he knows it too. He may mean all right, but you never can trust folks."

The woman went away to prepare breakfast then, and left the girl feeling as if the whole world was against her, trying to hold her. She was glad when the man suggested that they hurry their breakfast and get away as quickly as possible. She did not smile when the old woman came out to bid her good-by, and put a detaining hand on the horse's bridle, saying "You better stay with me, after all, hadn't you, dearie?"

The man looked inquiringly at the two women, and saw like a flash the suspicion of the older woman, read the trust and haughty anger in the beautiful younger face, and then smiled down on the old woman whose kindly hospitality had saved them for a while from the terrors of the open night, and said:

"Don't you worry about her, auntie. I'm going to take good care of her, and perhaps she'll write you a letter some day, and tell you where she is and what she's doing."

Half reassured, the old woman gave him her name and address; and he wrote them down in a little red notebook.

When they were well started on their way, the man explained that he had hurried because from conversation with the men he had learned that this ranch where they had spent the night was on the direct trail from Malta to another small town. It might be that the pursuers would go further than Malta. Did she think they would go so far? They must have come almost a hundred miles already. Would they not be discouraged?

But the girl looked surprised. A hundred miles on horseback was not far. Her brother often used to ride a hundred miles just to see a fight or have a good time. She felt sure the men would not hesitate to follow a long distance if something else did not turn them aside.

The man's face looked sternly out from under his wide hat. He felt a great responsibility for the girl since he had seen the face of the man who was pursuing her.

Their horses were fresh, and the day was fine. They rode hard as long as the road was smooth, and did little talking. The girl was turning over in her mind the words the woman had spoken to her. But the thing that stuck there and troubled her was, "And he knows it is so."

Was she doing something for which this man by her side would not respect her? Was she overstepping some unwritten law of which she had never heard, and did he know it, and yet encourage her in it?

That she need fear him in the least she would not believe. Had she not watched the look of utmost respect on his face as he stood quietly waiting for her to awake the first morning they had met? Had he not had opportunity again and again to show her dishonor by word or look? Yet he had never been anything but gentle and courteous to her. She did not call things by these names, but she felt the gentleman in him.

Besides, there was the lady. He had told about her at the beginning. He evidently honored the lady. The woman had said that the lady would not ride with him alone. Was it true? Would he not like to have the lady ride alone with him when she was not his relative in any way? Then was there a difference between his thought of the lady and of herself? Of course, there was some; he loved the lady, but he should not think less honorably of her than of any lady in the land.

She sat straight and proudly in her man's saddle, and tried to make him feel that she was worthy of respect. She had tried to show him this when she had shot the bird. Now she recognized that there was a fine something, higher than shooting or prowess of any kind, which would command respect. It was something she felt belonged to her, yet she was not sure she commanded it. What did she lack, and how could she secure it?

He watched her quiet, thoughtful face, and the lady of his former troubled thoughts was as utterly forgotten by him as if she had never existed. He was unconsciously absorbed in the study of eye and lip and brow. His eyes were growing accustomed to the form and feature of this girl beside him, and he took pleasure in watching her.

They stopped for lunch in a coulee under a pretty cluster of cedar-trees a little back from the trail, where they might look over the way they had come and be warned against pursuers. About three o'clock they reached a town. Here the railroad came directly from Malta, but there was but one train a day each way.

The man went to the public stopping-place and asked for a room, and boldly demanded a private place for his "sister" to rest for a while. "She is my little sister," he told himself in excuse for the word. "She is my sister to care for. That is, if she were my sister, this is what I should want some good man to do for her."

He smiled as he went on his way after leaving the girl to rest. The thought of a sister pleased him. The old woman at the ranch had made him careful for the girl who was thus thrown in his company.

He rode down through the rough town to the railway station, but a short distance from the rude stopping-place; and there he made inquiries concerning roads, towns, etc., in the neighboring locality, and sent a telegram to the friends with whom he had been hunting when he got lost. He said he would be at the next town about twenty miles away. He knew that by this time they would be back home and anxious about him, if they were not already sending out searching parties for him. His message read:

"Hit the trail all right. Am taking a trip for my health. Send mail to me at —"

Then after careful inquiry as to directions, and learning that there was more than one route to the town he had mentioned in his telegram, he went back to his companion. She was ready to go, for the presence of other people about her made her uneasy. She feared again there would be objection to their further progress together. Somehow the old woman's words had grown into a shadow which hovered over her. She mounted her horse gladly, and they went forward. He told her what he had just done, and how he expected to get his mail the next morning when they reached the next town. He explained that there was a ranch half-way there where they might stop all night.

She was troubled at the thought of another ranch. She knew there would be more questions, and perhaps other disagreeable words said; but she held her peace, listening to his plans. Her wonder was great over the telegram. She knew little or nothing about modern discoveries. It was a mystery to her how he could receive word by morning from a place that it had taken them nearly two days to leave behind, and how had he sent a message over a wire? Yes, she had heard of telegrams, but had never been quite sure they were true. When he saw that she was interested, he went on to tell her of other wonderful triumphs of science, the telephone, the electric light, gas, and the modern system of waterworks. She listened as if it were all a fairy tale. Sometimes she looked at him, and wondered whether it could be true, or whether he were not making fun of her; but his earnest, honest eyes forbade doubt.

At the ranch they found two women, a mother and her daughter. The man asked frankly whether they could take care of this young friend of his overnight, saying that she was going on to the town in the morning, and was in his care for the journey. This seemed to relieve all suspicion. The two girls eyed each other, and then smiled.

"I'm Myrtle Baker," said the ranch-owner's daughter. "Come; I'll take you where you can wash your hands and face, and then we'll have some supper."

Myrtle Baker was a chatterer by nature. She talked incessantly; and, though she asked many questions, she did not wait for half of them to be answered. Besides, the traveller had grown wary. She did not intend to talk about the relationship between herself and her travelling companion. There was a charm in Myrtle's company which made the girl half regret leaving the next morning, as they did quite early, amid protests from Myrtle and her mother, who enjoyed a visitor in their isolated home.

But the ride that morning was constrained. Each felt in some subtle way that their pleasant companionship was coming to a crisis. Ahead in that town would be letters, communications from the outside world of friends, people who did not know or care what these two had been through together, and who would not hesitate to separate them with a firm hand. Neither put this thought into words, but it was there in their hearts, in the form of a vague fear. They talked very little, but each was feeling how pleasant the journey had been, and dreading what might be before.

They wanted to stay in this Utopia of the plains, forever journeying together, and never reaching any troublesome futures where were laws and opinions by which they must abide.

But the morning grew bright, and the road was not half long enough. Though at the last they walked their horses, they reached the town before the daily train had passed through. They went straight to the station, and found that the train was an hour late; but a telegram had arrived for the man. He took it nervously, his fingers trembling. He felt a premonition that it contained something unpleasant.

The girl sat on her horse by the platform, watching him through the open station door where he was standing as he tore open the envelope. She saw a deathly pallor overspread his face, and a look of anguish as if an arrow had pierced his heart. She felt as if the arrow had gone on into her own heart, and then she sat and waited. It seemed hours before he glanced up, with an old, weary look in his eyes. The message read:

"Your mother seriously ill. Wants you immediately. Will send your baggage on morning train. Have wired you are coming."

It was signed by his cousin with whom he had been taking his hunting-trip, and who was bound by business to go further West within a few days more.

The strong young man was almost bowed under this sudden shock. His mother was very dear to him. He had left her well and happy. He must go to her at once, of course; but what should he do with the girl who had within the last two days taken so strong a hold upon his — he hesitated, and called it "protection." That word would do in the present emergency.

Then he looked, and saw her own face pale under the tan, and stepped out to the platform to tell her.

Chapter 8
The Parting

She took the news like a Spartan. Her gentle pity was simply expressed, and then she had held her peace. He must go. He must leave her. She knew that the train would carry him to his mother's bedside quicker than a horse could go. She felt by the look in his eyes and the set of his mouth that he had already decided that. Of course he must go. And the lady was there too! His mother and the lady! The lady would be sorry by this time, and would love him. Well, it was all right. He had been good to her. He had been a strong, bright angel God had sent to help her out of the wilderness; and now that she was safe the angel must return to his heaven. This was what she thought.

He had gone into the station to inquire about the train. It was an hour late. He had one short hour in which to do a great deal. He had very little money with him. Naturally men do not carry a fortune when they go into the wilderness for a day's shooting. Fortunately he had his railroad return ticket to Philadelphia. That would carry him safely. But the girl. She of course had no money. And where was she going? He realized that he had failed to ask her many important questions. He hurried out, and explained to her.

"The train is an hour late. We must sell our horses, and try to get money enough to take us East. It is the only way. Where do you intend going?"

But the girl stiffened in her seat. She knew it was her opportunity to show that she was worthy of his honor and respect.

"I cannot go with you," she said very quietly.

"But you must," said he impatiently. "Don't you see there is no other way? I must take this train and get to my mother as soon as possible. She may not be living when I reach her if I don't." Something caught in his throat as he uttered the horrible thought that kept coming to his mind.

"I know," said the girl quietly. "You must go, but I must ride on."

"And why? I should like to know. Don't you see that I cannot leave you here alone? Those villains may be upon us at any minute. In fact, it is a good thing for us to board the train and get out of their miserable country as fast as steam can carry us. I am sorry you must part with your horse, for I know you are attached to it; but perhaps we can arrange to sell it to someone who will let us redeem it when we send the money out. You see I have not money enough with me to buy you a ticket. I couldn't get home myself if I hadn't my return ticket with me in my pocket. But surely the sale of both horses will bring enough to pay your way.''

"You are very kind, but I must not go.'' The red lips were firm, and the girl was sitting very erect. She looked as she had done after she had shot the bird.

"But why?''

"I cannot travel alone with you. It is not your custom where you come from. The woman on the ranch told me. She said you knew girls did not do that, and that you did not respect me for going alone with you. She said it was not right, and that you knew it.''

He looked at her impatient, angry, half ashamed that she should face him with these words.

"Nonsense!'' said he. "This is a case of necessity. You are to be taken care of, and I am the one to do it.''

"But it is not the custom among people where you live, is it?''

The clear eyes faced him down, and he had to admit that it was not.

"Then I can't go,'' she said decidedly.

"But you must. If you don't, I won't go.''

"But you must,'' said the girl, "and I mustn't. If you talk that way, I'll run away from you. I've run away from one man, and I guess I can from another. Besides, you're forgetting the lady.''

"What lady?''

"Your lady. The lady who rides in a carriage without horses.''

"Hang the lady!'' he said inelegantly. "Do you know that the train will be along here in less than an hour, and we have a great deal to do before we can get on board? There's no use stopping to talk about this matter. We haven't time. If you will just trust things to me, I'll attend to them all, and I'll answer your questions when we get safely on the train. Every instant is precious. Those men might come around that corner over there any minute. That's all bosh about respect. I respect you more than any woman I ever met. And it's my business to take care of you.''

"No, it's not your business,'' said the girl bravely, "and I can't let you. I'm nothing to you, you know.''

"You're every — that is — why, you surely know you're a great deal to me. Why, you saved my life, you know!''

"Yes, and you saved mine. That was beautiful, but that's all.''

"Isn't that enough? What are you made of, anyway, to sit there when there's so much to be done, and those villains on our track, and insist that you won't be saved? Respect you! Why a lion in the wilderness would have to respect you. You're made of iron and steel and precious stones. You've the courage of a — a — I was going to say a man, but I mean an angel. You're pure as snow, and true as the heavenly blue, and firm as a rock; and, if I had never respected you before, I would have to now. I respect, I honor, I — I — I pray for you!'' he finished fiercely.

He turned his back to hide his emotions.

She lifted her eyes to his when he turned again, and her own were full of tears.

"Thank you!" She said it very simply. "That makes me — very — glad! But I cannot go with you."

"Do you mean that?" he asked her desperately.

"Yes," steadily.

"Then I shall have to stay too."

"But you can't! You must go to your mother. I won't be stayed with. And what would she think? Mothers are — everything!" she finished. "You must go quick and get ready. What can I do to help?"

He gave her a look which she remembered long years afterward. It seemed to burn and sear its way into her soul. How was it that a stranger had the power to scorch her with anguish this way? And she him?

He turned, still with that desperate, half-frantic look in his face, and accosted two men who stood at the other end of the platform. They were not in particular need of a horse at present; but they were always ready to look at a bargain, and they walked speculatively down the uneven boards of the platform with him to where his horse stood, and inspected it.

The girl watched the whole proceeding with eyes that saw not but into the future. She put in a word about the worth of the saddle once when she saw it was going lower than it should. Three other men gathered about before the bargain was concluded, and the horse and its equipment sold for about half its value.

That done, the man turned toward the girl and motioned to her to lead her horse away to a more quiet place, and set him down to plead steadily against her decision. But the talk and the horse-selling had taken more time than he realized. The girl was more decided than ever in her determination not to go with him. She spoke of the lady again. She spoke of his mother, and mothers in general, and finished by reminding him that God would take care of her, and of him, too.

Then they heard the whistle of the train, and saw it growing from a speck to a large black object across the plain. To the girl the sight of this strange machine, that seemed more like a creature rushing toward her to snatch all beauty and hope and safety from her, sent a thrill of horror. To the man it seemed like a dreaded fate that was tearing him asunder. He had barely time to divest himself of his powder-horn, and a few little things that might be helpful to the girl in her journey, before the train was halted at the station. Then he took from his pocket the money that had been paid him for his horse; and, selecting a five-dollar bill for himself, he wrapped the rest in an envelope bearing his own name and address. The envelope was one addressed by the lady at home. It had contained some gracefully worded refusal of a request. But he did not notice now what envelope he gave her.

"Take this," he said. "It will help a little. Yes, you must! I cannot leave you — I *will* not — unless you do," when he saw that she hesitated and looked doubtful. "I owe you all and more for saving my life. I can never repay you. Take it. You may return it sometime when you get plenty more of your own, if it hurts your pride to keep it. Take it, please. Yes, I have plenty for myself. You will need it, and you must stop at nice places overnight. You will be very careful, won't you? My name is on that envelope. You must write to me and let me know that you are safe."

"Someone is calling you, and that thing is beginning to move again," said the girl, an awesome wonder in her face. "You will be left behind! O, hurry! Quick! Your mother!"

He half turned toward the train, and then came back.

"You haven't told me your name!" he gasped. "Tell me quick!"

She caught her breath.

"Elizabeth!" she answered, and waved him from her.

The conductor of the train was shouting to him, and two men shoved him toward the platform. He swung himself aboard with the accustomed ease of a man who has travelled; but he stood on the platform, and shouted, "Where are you going!" as the train swung noisily off.

She did not hear him, but waved her hand, and gave him a bright smile that was brimming with unshed tears. It seemed like instant, daring suicide in him to stand on that swaying, clattering house as it moved off irresponsibly down the plane of vision. She watched him till he was out of sight, a mere speck on the horizon of the prairie; and then she turned her horse slowly into the road, and went her way into the world alone.

The man stood on the platform, and watched her as he whirled away — a little brown girl on a little brown horse, so stanch and firm and stubborn and good. Her eyes were dear, and her lips as she smiled; and her hand was beautiful as it waved him good-by. She was dear, dear, dear! Why had he not known it? Why had he left her? Yet how could he stay? His mother was dying perhaps. He must not fail her in what might be her last summons. Life and death were pulling at his heart, tearing him asunder.

The vision of the little brown girl and the little brown horse blurred and faded. He tried to look, but could not see. He brought his eyes to nearer vision to fix their focus for another look, and straight before him whirled a shackly old saloon, rough and tumble, its character apparent from the men who were grouped about its doorway and from the barrels and kegs in profusion outside. From the doorway issued four men, wiping their mouths and shouting hilariously. Four horses stood tied to a fence nearby. They were so instantly passed, and so vaguely seen, that he could not be sure in the least, but those four men reminded him strongly of the four who had passed the schoolhouse on Sunday.

He shuddered, and looked back. The little brown horse and the little brown girl were one with the little brown station so far away, and presently the saloon and men were blotted out in one blur of green and brown and yellow.

He looked to the ground in his despair. He *must* go back. He could not leave her in such peril. She was his to care for by all the rights of manhood and womanhood. She had been put in his way. It was his duty.

But the ground whirled by under his madness, and showed him plainly that to jump off would be instant death. Then the thought of his mother came again, and the girl's words, "I am nothing to you, you know."

The train whirled its way between two mountains and the valley, and the green and brown and yellow blur was gone from sight. He felt as if he had just seen the coffin close over the girl's sweet face, and he had done it.

By and by he crawled into the car, pulled his slouch-hat down over his eyes, and settled down in a seat; but all the time he was trying to see over again that old saloon and those four men, and to make out their passing identity. Sometimes the agony of thinking it all over, and trying to make out whether those men had been the pursuers, made him feel frantic; and it seemed as if he must pull the bell-cord, and make the train stop, and get off to walk back. Then the utter hopelessness of ever finding her would come over him, and he would settle back in his seat again and try to sleep. But the least drowsiness would bring a vision of the girl galloping alone over the prairie with the four men in full pursuit behind. "Elizabeth, Elizabeth!" the car-wheels seemed to say.

Elizabeth — that was all he had of her. He did not know the rest of her name, nor where she was going. He did not even know where she had come from, just "Elizabeth" and "Montana." If anything happened to her, he would never know. Oh! why had he left her? Why had he not *made* her go with him? In a case like that a man should assert his authority. But, then, it was true he had none, and she had said she would run away. She would have done it too. O, if it had been anything but sickness and possible death at the other end — and his mother, his own little mother! Nothing else would have kept him from staying to protect Elizabeth.

What a fool he had been! There were questions he might have asked, and plans they might have made, all those beautiful days and those moon-silvered nights. If any other man had done the same, he would have thought him lacking mentally. But here he had maundered on, and never found out the all-important things about her. Yet how did he know then how important they were to be? It had seemed as if they had all the world before them in the brilliant sunlight. How could he know that modern improvements were to seize him in the midst of a prairie waste, and whirl him off from her when he had just begun to know what she was, and to prize her company as a most precious gift dropped down from heaven at his feet?

By degrees he came out of his hysterical frenzy, and returned to a somewhat normal state of mind. He reasoned himself several times into the belief that those men were not in the least like the men he had seen Sunday. He knew that one could not recognize one's own brother at that distance and that rate of passing speed. He tried to think that Elizabeth would be cared for. She had come through many a danger, and was it likely that the God in whom she trusted, who had guarded her so many times in her great peril, would desert her now in her dire need? Would He not raise up help for her somewhere? Perhaps another man as good as he, and as trustworthy as he had tried to be, would find her and help her.

But that thought was not pleasant. He put it away impatiently. It cut him. Why had she talked so much about the lady? The lady! Ah! How was it the lady came no more into his thoughts? The memory of her haughty face no more quickened his heart-beats. Was he fickle that he could lose what he had supposed was a lifelong passion in a few days?

The darkness was creeping on. Where was Elizabeth? Had she found a refuge for the night? Or was she wandering on an unknown trail, hearing voices and oaths through the darkness, and seeing the gleaming of wild eyes low in the bushes ahead? How could he have left her? How could he? He must go back even yet. He must, he must, *he must!*

And so it went on through the long night.

The train stopped at several places to take on water; but there seemed to be no human habitation near, or else his eyes were dim with his trouble.

Once, when they stopped longer than the other times, he got up and walked the length of the car and down the steps to the ground. He even stood there, and let the train start jerkily on till his car had passed him, and the steps were just sliding by, and tried to think whether he would not stay, and go back in some way to find her. Then the impossibility of the search, and of his getting back in time to do any good, helped him to spring on board just before it was too late. He walked back to his seat saying to himself, "Fool! Fool!"

It was not till morning that he remembered his baggage and went in search for it. There he found a letter from his cousin, with other letters and telegrams explaining the state of affairs at home. He came back to his seat laden with a large leather grip and a suitcase. He sat down to read his letters, and these took his mind away from his troubled thoughts for a little while. There was a letter from his mother, sweet, graceful, half wistfully offering her sympathy. He saw she guessed the reason why he had left her and gone to this far place. Dear little mother! What would she say if she knew his trouble now? And then would return his heart-frenzy over Elizabeth's peril. O to know that she was protected, hidden!

Fumbling in his pocket, he came upon a slip of paper, the slip the girl had given Elizabeth in the schoolhouse on Sunday afternoon. "For in the time of trouble he shall hide me in his pavilion; in the secret of his tabernacle shall he hide me."

Ah! God had hidden her then. Why not again? And what was that he had said to her himself, when searching for a word to cover his emotion? "I pray for you!" Why could he not pray? She had made him pray in the wilderness. Should he not pray for her who was in peril now? He leaned back in the hot, uncomfortable car-seat, pulling his hat down closer over his eyes, and prayed as he had never prayed before. "Our Father" he stumbled through as far as he could remember, and tried to think how her sweet voice had filled in the places where he had not known it the other time. Then, when he was done, he waited and prayed, "Our Father, care for Elizabeth," and added, "For Jesus' sake. Amen." Thereafter through the rest of his journey, and for days and weeks stretching ahead, he prayed that prayer, and sometimes found in it his only solace from the terrible fear that possessed him lest some harm had come to the girl, whom it seemed to him now he had deserted in cold blood.

Chapter 9
In a Trap

Elizabeth rode straight out to the east, crossing the town as rapidly as possible, going full gallop where the streets were empty. On the edge of the town she crossed another trail running back the way that they had come; but without swerving she turned out toward the world, and soon passed into a thick growth of trees, around a hill.

Not three minutes elapsed after she had passed the crossing of the trails before the four men rode across from the other direction, and, pausing, called to one another, looking this way and that:

"What d'ye think, Bill? Shall we risk the right hand 'r the left?"

"Take the left hand fer luck," answered Bill. "Let's go over to the ranch and ask. Ef she's been hereabouts, she's likely there. The old woman 'll know. Come on, boys!"

And who shall say that the angel of the Lord did not stand within the crossing of the ways and turn aside the evil men?

Elizabeth did not stop her fierce ride until about noon. The frenzy of her fear of pursuit had come upon her with renewed force. Now that she was alone and desolate she dared not look behind her. She had been strong enough as she smiled her farewell; but, when the train had dwindled into a mere speck in the distance, her eyes were dropping tears thick and fast upon the horse's mane. So in the first heaviness of her loneliness she rode as if pursued by enemies close at hand.

But the horse must rest if she did not, for he was her only dependence now. So she sat her down in the shade of a tree, and tried to eat some dinner. The tears came again as she opened the pack which the man's strong hands had bound together for her. How little she had thought at breakfast-time that she would eat the next meal alone!

It was all well enough to tell him he must go, and say she was nothing to him; but it was different now to face the world without a single friend when one had learned to know how good a friend could be. Almost it would have been better if he had never found her, never saved her from the serpent, never ridden beside her and talked of wonderful new things to her; for now that he was gone the emptiness and loneliness were so much harder to bear; and now she was filled with a longing for things that could not be hers.

It was well he had gone so soon, well she had no longer to grow into the charm of his society; for he belonged to the lady, and was not hers. Thus she ate her dinner with the indifference of sorrow.

Then she took out the envelope, and counted over the money. Forty dollars he had given her. She knew he had kept but five for himself. How wonderful that he should have done all that for her! It seemed a very great wealth in her possession. Well, she would use it as sparingly as possible, and thus be able the sooner to return it all to him. Some she must use, she supposed, to buy food; but she would do with as little as she could. She might sometimes shoot a bird, or catch a fish; or there might be berries fit for food by the way. Nights she must stop by the way at a respectable house. That she had promised. He had told her of awful things that might happen to her if she lay down in the wilderness alone. Her lodging would sometimes cost her something. Yet often they would take her in for nothing. She would be careful of the money.

She studied the name on the envelope. George Trescott Benedict, 2 — Walnut Street, Philadelphia, Penn. The letters were large and angular, not easy to read; but she puzzled them out. It did not look like his writing. She had watched him as he wrote the old woman's address in his little red book. He wrote small, round letters, slanting backwards, plain as print, pleasant writing to read. Now the old woman's address would never be of any use, and her wish that Elizabeth should travel alone was fulfilled.

There was a faint perfume from the envelope like wildwood flowers. She breathed it in, and wondered at it. Was it perfume from something he carried in his pocket, some flower his lady had once given him? But this was not a pleasant thought. She put the envelope into her bosom after studying it again carefully until she knew the words by heart.

Then she drew forth the papers of her mother's that she had brought from home, and for the first time read them over.

The first was the marriage certificate. That she had seen before, and had studied with awe; but the others had been kept in a box that was never opened by the children. The mother kept them sacredly, always with the certificate on the top.

The largest paper she could not understand. It was something about a mine. There were a great many "herebys" and "whereases" and "agreements" in it. She put it back into the wrapper as of little account, probably something belonging to her father, which her mother had treasured for old time's sake.

Then came a paper which related to the claim where their little log home had stood, and upon the extreme edge of which the graves were. That, too, she laid reverently within its wrapper.

Next came a bit of pasteboard whereon was inscribed, "Mrs. Merrill Wilton Bailey, Rittenhouse Square, Tuesdays." That she knew was her grandmother's name, though she had never seen the card before — her father's mother. She looked at the card in wonder. It was almost like a distant view of the lady in question. What kind of a place might Rittenhouse Square be, and where was it? There was no telling. It might be near that wonderful Desert of Sahara that the man had talked about. She laid it down with a sigh.

There was only one paper left, and that was a letter written in pale pencil lines. It said:

"My dear Bessie: Your pa died last week. He was killed falling from a scaffold. He was buried on Monday with five carriages and everything nice. We all got new black dresses, and have enough for a stone. If it don't cost too much, we'll have an angel on the top. I always thought an angel pointing to heaven was nice. We wish you was here. We miss you very much. I hope your husband is good to you. Why don't you write to us? You haven't wrote since your little girl was born. I s'pose you call her Bessie like you. If anything ever happens to you, you can send her to me. I'd kind of like her to fill your place. Your sister has got a baby girl too. She calls her Lizzie. We couldn't somehow have it natural to call her 'Lizabeth, and Nan wanted her called for me. I was always Lizzie, you know. Now you must write soon.

"Your loving mother,

"ELIZABETH BRADY."

There was no date nor address to the letter, but an address had been pencilled on the outside in her mother's cramped school-girl hand. It was dim but still readable, "Mrs. Elizabeth Brady, 18 — Flora Street, Philadelphia."

Elizabeth studied the last word, then drew out the envelope again, and looked at that. Yes, the two names were the same. How wonderful! Perhaps she would sometime, sometime, see him again, though of course he belonged to the lady. But perhaps, if she went to school and learned very fast, she might sometime meet him at church — he went to church, she was sure — and then he might smile, and not be ashamed of his friend who had saved his life. Saved his life! Nonsense! She had not done much. He would not feel any such ridiculous indebtedness to her when he got back to home and friends and safety. He had saved her much more than she had saved him.

She put the papers all back in safety, and after having prepared her few belongings for taking up the journey, she knelt down. She would say the prayer before she went on. It might be that would keep the terrible pursuers away.

She said it once, and then with eyes still closed she waited a moment. Might she say it for him, who was gone away from her? Perhaps it would help him, and keep him from falling from that terrible machine he was riding on. Hitherto in her mind prayers had been only for the dead, but now they seemed also to belong to all who were in danger or trouble. She said the prayer over once more, slowly, then paused a moment, and added: "Our Father, hide him from trouble. Hide George Trescott Benedict. And hide me, please, too."

Then she mounted her horse, and went on her way.

It was a long and weary way. It reached over mountains and through valleys, across winding, turbulent streams and broad rivers that had few bridges. The rivers twice led her further south than she meant to go, in her ignorance. She had always felt that Philadelphia was straight ahead east, as straight as one could go to the heart of the sun.

Night after night she lay down in strange homes, some poorer and more forlorn than others; and day after day she took up her lonely travel again.

Gradually, as the days lengthened, and mountains piled themselves behind her, and rivers stretched like barriers between, she grew less and less to dread her pursuers, and more and more to look forward to the future. It seemed so long a way! Would it never end?

Once she asked a man whether he knew where Philadelphia was. She had been travelling then for weeks, and thought she must be almost there. But he said "Philadelphia? O, Philadelphia is in the East. That's a long way off. I saw a man once who came from there."

She set her firm little chin then, and travelled on. Her clothes were much worn, and her skin was brown as a berry. The horse plodded on with a dejected air. He would have liked to stop at a number of places they passed, and remain for life, what there was left of it; but he obediently walked on over any kind of an old road that came in his way, and solaced himself with whatever kind of a bite the roadside afforded. He was becoming a much-travelled horse. He knew a threshing-machine by sight now, and considered it no more than a prairie bobcat.

At one stopping-place a good woman advised Elizabeth to rest on Sundays. She told her God didn't like people to do the same on His day as on other days, and it would bring her bad luck if she kept up her incessant riding. It was bad for the horse too. So, the night being Saturday, Elizabeth remained with the woman over the Sabbath, and heard read aloud the fourteenth chaper of John. It was a wonderful revelation to her. She did not altogether understand it. In fact, the Bible was an unknown book. She had never known that it was different from other books. She had heard it spoken of by her mother, but only as a book. She did not know it was a book of books.

She carried the beautiful thoughts with her on the way, and pondered them. She wished she might have the book. She remembered the name of it, Bible, the Book of God. Then God had written a book! Some day she would try to find it and read it.

"Let not your heart be troubled"; so much of the message drifted into her lonesome, ignorant soul, and settled down to stay. She said it over nights when she found a shelter in some unpleasant place, or days when the road was rough or a storm came up and she was compelled to seek shelter by the roadside under a haystack or in a friendly but deserted shack. She thought of it the day there was no shelter and she was drenched to the skin. She wondered afterward when the sun came out and dried her nicely whether God had really been speaking the words to her troubled heart, "Let not your heart be troubled."

Every night and every morning she said "Our Father" twice, once for herself and once for the friend who had gone out into the world, it seemed about a hundred years ago.

But one day she came across a railroad track. It made her heart beat wildly. It seemed now that she must be almost there. Railroads were things belonging to the East and civilization. But the way was lonely still for days, and then she crossed more railroads, becoming more and more frequent, and came into the line of towns that stretched along beside the snake-like tracks.

She fell into the habit of staying overnight in a town, and then riding on to the next in the morning; but now her clothes were becoming so dirty and ragged that she felt ashamed to go to nice-looking places lest they should turn her out; so she sought shelter in barns and small, mean houses. But the people in these houses were distressingly dirty, and she found no place to wash.

She had lost track of the weeks or the months when she reached her first great city, the only one she had come near in her uncharted wanderings.

Into the outskirts of Chicago she rode undaunted, her head erect, with the carriage of a queen. She had passed Indians and cowboys in her journeying; why should she mind Chicago? Miles and miles of houses and people. There seemed to be no end to it. Nothing but houses everywhere and hurried-looking people, many of them working hard. Surely this must be Philadelphia.

A large, beautiful building attracted her attention. There were handsome grounds about it, and girls playing some game with a ball and curious webbed implements across a net of cords. Elizabeth drew her horse to the side of the road, and watched a few minutes. One girl was skillful, and hit the ball back every time. Elizabeth almost exclaimed out loud once when a particularly fine ball was played. She rode reluctantly on when the game was finished, and saw over the arched gateway the words, "Janeway School for Girls."

Ah! This was Philadelphia at last, and here was her school. She would go in at once before she went to her grandmother's. It might be better.

She dismounted, and tied the horse to an iron ring in a post by the sidewalk. Then she went slowly, shyly up the steps into the charmed circles of learning. She knew she was shabby, but her long journey would explain that. Would they be kind to her, and let her study?

She stood some time before the door, with a group of laughing girls not far away whispering about her. She smiled at them; but they did not return the salutation, and their actions made her more shy. At last she stepped into the open door, and a maid in cap and apron came forward. "You must not come in here, miss," she said imperiously. "This is a school."

"Yes," said Elizabeth gravely, smiling. "I want to see the teacher."

"She's busy. You can't see her," snapped the maid.

"Then I will wait till she is ready. I've come a great many miles, and I must see her."

The maid retreated at this, and an elegant woman in trailing black silk and gold-rimmed glasses approached threateningly. This was a new kind of beggar, of course, and must be dealt with at once.

"What do you want?" she asked frigidly.

"I've come to school," said Elizabeth confidingly. "I know I don't look very nice, but I've had to come all the way from Montana on horseback. If you could let me go where I can have some water and a thread and needle, I can make myself look better."

The woman eyed the girl incredulously.

"You have come to school!" she said; and her voice was large, and frightened Elizabeth. "You have come all the way from Montana! Impossible! You must be crazy."

"No, ma'am, I'm not crazy," said Elizabeth. "I just want to go to school."

The woman perceived that this might be an interesting case for benevolently inclined people. It was nothing but an annoyance to herself. "My dear girl," — her tone was bland and disagreeable now — "are you aware that it takes money to come to school?"

"Does it?" said Elizabeth. "No, I didn't know it, but I have some money. I could give you ten dollars right now; and, if that is not enough, I might work some way, and earn more."

The woman laughed disagreeably.

"It is impossible," she said. "The yearly tuition here is five hundred dollars. Besides, we do not take girls of your class. This is a finishing school for young ladies. You will have to inquire further," and the woman swept away to laugh with her colleagues over the queer character, the new kind of tramp, she had just been called to interview. The maid came pertly forward, and said that Elizabeth could no longer stand where she was.

Bewilderment and bitter disappointment in her face, Elizabeth went slowly down to her horse, the great tears welling up into her eyes. As she rode away, she kept turning back to the school grounds wistfully. She did not notice the passers-by, nor know that they were commenting upon her appearance. She made a striking picture in her rough garments, with her wealth of hair, her tanned skin, and tear-filled eyes. An artist noticed it, and watched her down the street, half thinking he would follow and secure her as a model for his next picture.

A woman, gaudily bedecked in soiled finery, her face giving evidence of the frequent use of rouge and powder, watched her, and followed, pondering. At last she called, "My dear, my dear, wait a minute." She had to speak several times before Elizabeth saw that she was talking to her. Then the horse was halted by the sidewalk.

"My dear," said the woman, "you look tired and disappointed. Don't you want to come home with me for a while, and rest?"

"Thank you," said Elizabeth, "but I am afraid I must go on. I only stop on Sundays."

"But just come home with me for a little while," coaxed the wheedling tones. "You look so tired, and I've some girls of my own. I know you would enjoy resting and talking with them."

The kindness in her tones touched the weary girl. Her pride had been stung to the quick by the haughty woman in the school. This woman would soothe her with kindness.

"Do you live far from here?" asked Elizabeth.

"Only two or three blocks," said the woman. "You ride along by the sidewalk, and we can talk. Where are you going? You look as if you had come a long distance."

"Yes," said the girl wearily, "from Montana. I am going to school. Is this Philadelphia?"

"This is Chicago," said the woman. "There are finer schools here than in Philadelphia. If you'd like to come and stay at my house awhile, I will see about getting you into a school."

"Is it hard work to get people into schools?" asked the girl wonderingly. "I thought they would want people to teach."

"No, it's very hard," said the lying woman; "but I think I know a school where I can get you in. Where are your folks? Are they in Montana?"

"They are all dead," said Elizabeth, "and I have come away to school."

"Poor child!" said the woman glibly. "Come right home with me, and I'll take care of you. I know a nice way you can earn your living, and then you can study if you like. But you're quite big to go to school. It seems to me you could have a good time without that. You are a pretty girl; do you know it? You only need pretty clothes to make you a beauty. If you come with me, I will let you earn some beautiful new clothes."

"You are very kind," said the girl gravely. "I do need new clothes; and, if I could earn them, that would be all the better." She did not quite like the woman; yet of course that was foolish.

After a few more turns they stopped in front of a tall brick building with a number of windows. It seemed to be a good deal like other buildings; in fact, as she looked up the street, Elizabeth thought there were miles of them just alike. She tied her horse in front of the door and went in with the woman. The woman told her to sit down a minute until she called the lady of the house, who would tell her more about the school. There were a number of pretty girls in the room, and they made very free to speak to her. They twitted her about her clothes, and in a way reminded Elizabeth of the girls in the school she had just interviewed.

Suddenly she spoke up to the group. An idea had occurred to her. This was the school, and the woman had not liked to say so until she spoke to the leader about her.

"Is this a school?" she asked shyly.

Her question was met with a shout of derisive laughter.

"School!" cried the boldest, prettiest one. "School for scandal! School for morals!"

There was one, a thin, pale girl with dark circles under her eyes, a sad droop to her mouth, and bright scarlet spots in her cheeks. She came over to Elizabeth, and whispered something to her. Elizabeth started forward, unspeakable horror in her face.

She fled to the door where she had come in, but found it fastened. Then she turned as if she had been brought to bay by a pack of lions.

Chapter 10
Philadelphia at Last

"Open this door!" she commanded. "Let me out of here at once."

The pale girl started to do so, but the pretty one held her back. "No, Nellie; Madam will be angry with us all if you open that door." Then she turned to Elizabeth, and said:

"Whoever enters that door never goes out again. You are nicely caught, my dear."

There was a sting of bitterness and self-pity in the taunt at the end of the words. Elizabeth felt it, as she seized her pistol from her belt, and pointed it at the astonished group. They were not accustomed to girls with pistols. "Open that door, or I will shoot you all!" she cried.

Then, as she heard someone descending the stairs, she rushed again into the room where she remembered the windows were open. They were guarded by wire screens; but she caught up a chair, and dashed it through one, plunging out into the street in spite of detaining hands that reached for her, hands much hindered by the gleam of the pistol and the fear that it might go off in their midst.

It took but an instant to wrench the bridle from its fastening and mount her horse; then she rode forward through the city at a pace that only millionaires and automobiles were allowed to take. She met and passed her first automobile without a quiver. Her eyes were dilated, her lips set; angry, frightened tears were streaming down her cheeks, and she urged her poor horse forward until a policeman here and there thought it his duty to make a feeble effort to detain her. But nothing impeded her way. She fled through a maze of wagons, carriages, automobiles, and trolley-cars, until she passed the whirl of the great city, and at last was free again and out in the open country.

She came toward evening to a little cottage on the edge of a pretty suburb. The cottage was covered with roses, and the front yard was full of great old-fashioned flowers. On the porch sat a plain little old lady in a rocking-chair, knitting. There was a little gate with a path leading up to the door, and at the side another open gate with a road leading around to the back of the cottage.

Elizabeth saw, and murmering, "O 'our Father,' please hide me!" she dashed into the driveway, and tore up to the side of the piazza at a full gallop. She jumped from the horse; and, leaving him standing panting with his nose to the fence, and a tempting strip of clover in front of him where he could graze when he should get his breath, she ran up the steps, and flung herself in a miserable little heap at the feet of the astonished old lady.

"O, please, please, won't you let me stay here a few minutes, and tell me what to do? I am so tired, and I have had such a dreadful, awful time!"

"Why, dearie me!" said the old lady. "Of course I will. Poor child; sit right down in this rocking-chair, and have a good cry. I'll get you a glass of water and something to eat, and then you shall tell me all about it."

She brought the water, and a tray with nice broad slices of brown bread and butter, a generous piece of apple pie, some cheese, and a glass pitcher of creamy milk.

Elizabeth drank the water, but before she could eat she told the terrible tale of her last adventure. It seemed awful for her to believe, and she felt she must have help somewhere. She had heard there were bad people in the world. In fact, she had seen men who were bad, and once a woman had passed their ranch whose character was said to be questionable. She wore a hard face, and could drink and swear like the men. But that sin should be in this form, with pretty girls and pleasant, wheedling women for agents, she had never dreamed; and this in the great, civilized East! Almost better would it have been to remain in the desert alone, and risk the pursuit of that awful man, than to come all this way to find the world gone wrong.

The old lady was horrified, too. She had heard more than the girl of licensed evil; but she had read it in the paper as she had read about the evils of the slave-traffic in Africa, and it had never really seemed true to her. Now she lifted up her hands in horror, and looked at the beautiful girl before her with something akin to awe that she had been in one of those dens of iniquity and escaped. Over and over she made the girl tell what was said, and how it looked, and how she pointed her pistol, and how she got out; and then she exclaimed in wonder, and called her escape a miracle.

They were both weary from excitement when the tale was told. Elizabeth ate her lunch; then the old lady showed her where to put the horse, and made her go to bed. It was only a wee little room with a cot-bed white as snow where she put her; but the roses peeped in at the window, and the box covered with an old white curtain contained a large pitcher of fresh water and a bowl and soap and towels. The old lady brought her a clean white nightgown, coarse and mended in many places, but smelling of rose leaves; and in the morning she tapped at the door quite early before the girl was up, and came in with an armful of clothes.

"I had some boarders last summer," she explained, "and, when they went away, they left these things and said I might put them into the home-mission box. But I was sick when they sent it off this winter; and, if you ain't a home mission, then I never saw one. You put 'em on. I guess they'll fit. They may be a mite large, but she was about your size. I guess your clothes are about worn out; so you just leave 'em here fer the next one, and use these. There's a couple of extra shirt-waists you can put in a bundle for a change. I guess folks won't dare fool with you if you have some clean, nice clothes on."

Elizabeth looked at her gratefully, and wrote her down in the list of saints with the woman who read the fourteenth chapter of John. The old lady had neglected to mention that from her own meagre wardrobe she had supplied some under-garments, which were not included in those the boarders had left.

Bathed and clothed in clean, sweet garments, with a white shirt-waist and a dark-blue serge skirt and coat, Elizabeth looked a different girl. She surveyed herself in the little glass over the box-washstand and wondered. All at once vanity was born within her, and an ambition to be always thus clothed, with a horrible remembrance of the woman of the day before, who had promised to show her how to earn some pretty clothes. It flashed across her mind that pretty clothes might be a snare. Perhaps they had been to those girls she had seen in that house.

With much good advice and kindly blessings from the old lady, Elizabeth fared forth upon her journey once more, sadly wise in the wisdom of the world, and less sweetly credulous than she had been, but better fitted to fight her way.

The story of her journey from Chicago to Philadelphia would fill a volume if it were written, but it might pall upon the reader from the very variety of its experiences. It was made slowly and painfully, with many haltings and much lessening of the scanty store of money that had seemed so much when she received it in the wilderness. The horse went lame, and had to be watched over and petted, and finally, by the advice of a kindly farmer, taken to a veterinary surgeon, who doctored him for a week before he finally said it was safe to let him hobble on again. After that the girl was more careful of the horse. If he should die, what would she do?

One dismal morning, late in November, Elizabeth, wearing the old overcoat to keep her from freezing, rode into Philadelphia.

Armed with instructions from the old lady in Chicago, she rode boldly up to a policeman, and showed him the address of the grandmother to whom she had decided to go first, her mother's mother. He sent her on in the right direction, and in due time with the help of other policemen she reached the right number on Flora Street.

It was a narrow street, banked on either side by small, narrow brick houses of the older type. Here and there gleamed out a scrap of a white marble door-step, but most of the houses were approached by steps of dull stone or of painted wood. There was a dejected and dreary air about the place. The street was swarming with children in various stages of the soiled condition.

Elizabeth timidly knocked at the door after being assured by the interested urchins who surrounded her that Mrs. Brady really lived there, and had not moved away or anything. It did not seem wonderful to the girl, who had lived her life thus far in a mountain shack, to find her grandmother still in the place from which she had written fifteen years before. She did not yet know what a floating population most cities contain.

Mrs. Brady was washing when the knock sounded through the house. She was a broad woman, with a face on which the cares and sorrows of the years had left a not too heavy impress. She still enjoyed life, even though a good part of it was spent at the wash-tub, washing other people's fine clothes. She had some fine ones of her own up-stairs in her clothes-press; and, when she went out, it was in shiny satin, with a bonnet bobbing with jet and a red rose, though of late years, strictly speaking, the bonnet had become a hat again, and Mrs. Brady was in style with the other old ladies.

The perspiration was in little beads on her forehead and trickling down the creases in her well-cushioned neck toward her ample bosom. Her gray hair was neatly combed, and her calico wrapper was open at the throat even on this cold day. She wiped on her apron the soapsuds from her plump arms steaming pink from the hot suds, and went to the door.

She looked with disfavor upon the peculiar person on the door-step attired in a man's overcoat. She was prepared to refuse the demands of the Salvation Army for a nickel for Christmas dinners; or to silence the bananaman, or the fish-man, or the man with shoe-strings and pins and pencils for sale; or to send the photograph-agent on his way; yes, even the man who sold albums for postcards. She had no time to bother with anybody this morning.

But the young person in the rusty overcoat, with the dark-blue serge Eton jacket under it, which might have come from Wanamaker's two years ago, who yet wore a leather belt with gleaming pistols under the Eton jacket, was a new species. Mrs. Brady was taken off her guard; else Elizabeth might have found entrance to her grandmother's home as difficult as she had found entrance to the finishing school of Madame Janeway.

"Are you Mrs. Brady?" asked the girl. She was searching the forbidding face before her for some sign of likeness to her mother, but found none. The cares of Elizabeth Brady's daughter had outweighed those of the mother, or else they sat upon a nature more sensitive.

"I am," said Mrs. Brady, imposingly.

"Grandmother, I am the baby you talked about in that letter," she announced, handing Mrs. Brady the letter she had written nearly eighteen years before.

The woman took the envelope gingerly in the wet thumb and finger that still grasped a bit of the gingham apron. She held it at arm's length, and squinted up her eyes, trying to read it without her glasses. It was some new kind of beggar, of course. She hated to touch these dirty envelopes, and this one looked old and worn. She stepped back to the parlor table where her glasses were lying, and, adjusting them, began to read the letter.

"For the land sakes! Where'd you find this?" she said, looking up suspiciously. "It's against the law to open letters that ain't your own. Didn't me daughter ever get it? I wrote it to her meself. How come you by it?"

"Mother read it to me long ago when I was little," answered the girl, the slow hope fading from her lips as she spoke. Was every one, was even her grandmother, going to be cold and harsh with her? "Our Father, hide me!" her heart murmured, because it had become a habit; and her listening thought caught the answer, "Let not your heart be troubled."

"Well, who are you?" said the uncordial grandmother, still puzzled. "You ain't Bessie, me Bessie. Fer one thing, you're 'bout as young as she was when she went off 'n' got married, against me 'dvice, to that drunken, lazy dude." Her brow was lowering, and she proceeded to finish her letter.

"I am Elizabeth," said the girl with a trembling voice, "the baby you talked about in that letter. But please don't call father that. He wasn't ever bad to us. He was always good to mother, even when he was drunk. If you talk like that about him, I shall have to go away."

"Fer the land sakes! You don't say," said Mrs. Brady, sitting down hard in astonishment on the biscuit upholstery of her best parlor chair. "Now you ain't Bessie's child! Well, I *am clear* beat. And growed up so big! You look strong, but you're kind of thin. What makes your skin so black? Your ma never was dark, ner your pa, neither."

"I've been riding a long way in the wind and sun and rain."

"Fer the land sakes!" as she looked through the window to the street. "Not on a horse?"

"Yes."

"H'm! What was your ma thinkin' about to let you do that?"

"My mother is dead. There was no one left to care what I did. I had to come. There were dreadful people out there, and I was afraid."

"Fer the land sakes!" That seemed the only remark that the capable Mrs. Brady could make. She looked at her new granddaughter in bewilderment, as if a strange sort of creature had suddenly laid claim to relationship.

"Well, I'm right glad to see you," she said stiffly, wiping her hand again on her apron and putting it out formally for a greeting.

Elizabeth accepted her reception gravely, and sat down. She sat down suddenly, as if her strength had given way and a great strain was at an end. As she sat down, she drooped her head back against the wall; and a gray look spread about her lips.

"You're tired," said the grandmother, energetically. "Come far this morning?"

"No," said Elizabeth, weakly, "not many miles; but I hadn't any more bread. I used it all up yesterday, and there wasn't much money left. I thought I could wait till I got here, but I guess I'm hungry."

"Fer the land sakes!" ejaculated Mrs. Brady as she hustled out to the kitchen, and clattered the frying-pan onto the stove, shoving the boiler hastily aside. She came in presently with a steaming cup of tea, and made the girl drink it hot and strong. Then she established her in the big rocking-chair in the kitchen with a plate of appetizing things to eat, and went on with her washing, punctuating every rub with a question.

Elizabeth felt better after her meal, and offered to help, but the grandmother would not hear to her lifting a finger.

"You must rest first," she said. "It beats me how you ever got here. I'd sooner crawl on me hands and knees than ride a great, scary horse."

Elizabeth sprang to her feet.

"The horse!" she said. "Poor fellow! He needs something to eat worse than I did. He hasn't had a bite of grass all this morning. There was nothing but hard roads and pavements. The grass is all brown, anyway, now. I found some cornstalks by the road, and once a man dropped a big bundle of hay out of his load. If it hadn't been for Robin, I'd never have got here; and here I've sat enjoying my breakfast, and Robin out there hungry!"

"Fer the land sakes!" said the grandmother, taking her arms out of the suds and looked troubled. "Poor fellow! What would he like? I haven't got any hay, but there's some mashed potatoes left, and what is there? Why, there's some excelsior the lamp-shade came packed in. You don't suppose he'd think it was hay, do you? No, I guess it wouldn't taste very good."

"Where can I put him, Grandmother?"

"Fer the land sakes! I don't know," said the grandmother, looking around the room in alarm. "We haven't any place fer horses. Perhaps you might get him into the back yard fer a while till we think what to do. There's a stable, but they charge high to board horses. Lizzie knows one of the fellers that works there. Mabbe he'll tell us what to do. Anyway, you lead him round to the alleyway, and we'll see if we can't get him in the little ash-gate. You don't suppose he'd try to get in the house, do you? I shouldn't like him to come in the kitchen when I was getting supper."

"O no!" said Elizabeth. "He's very good. Where is the back yard?"

This arrangement was finally made, and the two women stood in the kitchen door, watching Robin drink a bucketful of water and eat heartily of the various viands that Mrs. Brady set forth for him, with the exception of the excelsior, which he sniffed at in disgust.

"Now, ain't he smart?" said Mrs. Brady, watching fearfully from the door-step, where she might retreat if the animal showed any tendency to step nearer to the kitchen. "But don't you think he's cold? Wouldn't he like a — a — shawl or something?"

The girl drew the old coat from her shoulders, and threw it over him, her grandmother watching her fearless handling of the horse with pride and awe.

"We're used to sharing this together," said the girl simply.

"Nan sews in an up-town dressmaker's place," explained Mrs. Brady by and by, when the wash was hung out in fearsome proximity to the weary horse's heels, and the two had returned to the warm kitchen to clean up and get supper. "Nan's your ma's sister, you know, older'n her by two years; and Lizzie, that's her girl, she's about 's old 's you. She's got a good place in the ten-cent store. Nan's husband died four years ago, and her and me've been livin' together ever since. It'll be nice fer you and Lizzie to be together. She'll make it lively fer you right away. Prob'ly she can get you a place at the same store. She'll be here at half past six to-night. This is her week to get out early."

The aunt came in first. She was a tall, thin woman with faded brown hair and a faint resemblance to Elizabeth's mother. Her shoulders stooped slightly, and her voice was nasal. Her mouth looked as if it was used to holding pins in one corner and gossiping out of the other. She was one of the kind who always gets into a rocking-chair to sew if they can, and rock as they sew. Nevertheless, she was skillful in her way, and commanded good wages. She welcomed the new niece reluctantly, more excited over her remarkable appearance among her relatives after so long a silence than pleased, Elizabeth felt. But after she had satisfied her curiosity she was kind, beginning to talk about Lizzie, and mentally compared this thin, brown girl with rough hair and dowdy clothes to her own stylish daughter. Then Lizzie burst in. They could hear her calling to a young man who had walked home with her, even before she entered the house.

"It's just fierce out, Ma!" she exclaimed. "Grandma, ain't supper ready yet? I never was so hungry in all my life. I could eat a house afire."

She stopped short at sight of Elizabeth. She had been chewing gum— Lizzie was always chewing gum—but her jaws ceased action in sheer astonishment.

"This is your cousin Bessie, come all the way from Montana on horseback, Lizzie. She's your aunt Bessie's child. Her folks is dead now, · and she's come to live with us. You must see if you can't get her a place in the ten-cent store 'long with you," said grandmother.

Lizzie came airily forward, and grasped her cousin's hand in mid-air, giving it a lateral shake that bewildered Elizabeth.

"Pleased to meet you," she chattered glibly, and set her jaws to work again. One could not embarrass Lizzie long. But she kept her eyes on the stranger, and let them wander disapprovingly over her apparel in a pointed way as she took out the long hat-pins from the cumbersome hat she wore and adjusted her ponderous pompadour.

"Lizzie 'll have to help fix you up," said the aunt, noting Lizzie's glance. "You're all out of style. I suppose they get behind times out in Montana. Lizzie, can't you show her how to fix her hair pompadour?"

Lizzie brightened. If there was a prospect of changing things, she was not averse to a cousin of her own age; but she never could take such a dowdy-looking girl into society, not the society of the ten-cent store.

"O, cert!" answered Lizzie affably. "I'll fix you fine. Don't you worry. How'd you get so awful tanned? I s'pose riding. You look like you'd been to the seashore, and lay out on the beach in the sun. But 'tain't the right time o'year quite. It must be great to ride horseback!"

"I'll teach you how if you want to learn," and Elizabeth, endeavoring to show a return of the kindly offer.

"Me? What would I ride? Have to ride a counter, I guess. I guess you won't find much to ride here in the city, 'cept trolley-cars."

"Bessie's got a horse. He's out in the yard now," said the grandmother with pride.

"A horse! All your own? Gee whiz! Won't the girls stare when I tell them? Say, we can borrow a rig at the livery some night, and take a ride. Dan'll go with us, and get the rig for us. Won't that be great?"

Elizabeth smiled. She felt the glow of at last contributing something to the family pleasure. She did not wish her coming to be so entirely a wet blanket as it had seemed at first; for, to tell the truth, she had seen blank dismay on the face of each separate relative as her identity had been made known. Her heart was lonely, and she hungered for someone who "belonged" and loved her.

Supper was put on the table, and the two girls began to get a little acquainted, chattering over clothes and the arrangement of hair.

"Do you know whether there is anything in Philadelphia called 'Christian Endeavor'?" asked Elizabeth after the supper-table was cleared off.

"O, Chrishun 'deavor! Yes, I used t'b'long," answered Lizzie. She had removed the gum from her mouth while she ate her supper, but now it was busy again between sentences. "Yes, we have one down to our church. It was real interesting, too; but I got mad at one of the members, and quit. She was a stuck-up old maid, anyway. She was always turning round and scowling at us girls if we just whispered the least little bit, or smiled; and one night she was leading the meeting, and Jim Forbes got in a corner behind a post, and made mouths at her behind his book. He looked awful funny. It was something fierce the way she always screwed her face up when she sang, and he looked just like her. We girls, Hetty and Em'line and I, got to laughing, and we just couldn't stop; and didn't that old thing stop the singing after one verse, and look right at us, and say she thought Christian Endeavor members should remember whose house they were in, and that the owner was there, and all that rot. I nearly died, I was so mad. Everybody look around, and we girls choked, and got up and went out. I haven't been down since. The lookout committee came to see us 'bout it; but I said I wouldn't go back where I'd been insulted, and I've never been inside the doors since. But she's moved away now. I wouldn't mind going back if you want to go."

"Whose house did she mean it was? Was it her house?"

"O, no, it wasn't her house," laughed Lizzie. "It was the church. She meant it was God's house, I s'pose, but she needn't have been so pernickety. We weren't doing any harm."

"Does God have a house?"

"Why, yes; didn't you know that? Why, you talk like a heathen, Bessie. Didn't you have churches in Montana?"

"Yes, there was a church fifty miles away. I heard about it once, but I never saw it," answered Elizabeth. "But what did the woman mean? Who did she say was there? God? Was God in the church? Did you see Him, and know He was there when you laughed?"

"O, you silly!" giggled Lizzie. "Wouldn't the girls laugh at you, though, if they could hear you talk? Why, of course God was there. He's everywhere, you know," with superior knowledge; "but I didn't see Him. You can't see God."

"Why not?"

"Why, because you can't!" answered her cousin with final logic. "Say, haven't you got any other clothes with you at all? I'd take you down with me in the morning if you was fixed up."

Chapter 11
In Flight Again

When Elizabeth lay down to rest that night, with Lizzie still chattering by her side, she found that there was one source of intense pleasure in anticipation, and that was the prospect of going to God's house to Christian Endeavor. Now perhaps she would be able to find out what it all had meant, and whether it were true that God took care of people and hid them in time of trouble. She felt almost certain in her own little experience that He had cared for her, and she wanted to be quite sure, so that she might grasp this precious truth to her heart and keep it forever. No one could be quite alone in the world if there was a God who cared and loved and hid.

The aunt and the grandmother were up betimes the next morning, looking over some meagre stores of old clothing, and there was found an old dress which it was thought could be furbished over for Elizabeth. They were hard-working people with little money to spare, and everything had to be utilized; but they made a great deal of appearance, and Lizzie was proud as a young peacock. She would not take Elizabeth to the store to face the head man without having her fixed up according to the most approved style.

So the aunt cut and fitted before she went off for the day, and Elizabeth was ordered to sew while she was gone. The grandmother presided at the rattling old sewing-machine, and in two or three days Elizabeth was pronounced to be fixed up enough to do for the present till she could earn some new clothes. With her fine hair snarled into a cushion and puffed out into an enormous pompadour that did not suit her face in the least, and with an old hat and jacket of Lizzie's which did not become her nor fit her exactly, she started out to make her way in the world as a saleswoman. Lizzie had already secured her a place if she suited.

The store was a maze of wonder to the girl from the mountains — so many bright, bewildering things, ribbons and tin pans, glassware and toys, cheap jewelry and candies. She looked about with the dazed eyes of a creature from another world.

But the manager looked upon her with eyes of favor. He saw that her eyes were bright and keen. He was used to judging faces. He saw that she was as yet unspoiled, with a face of refinement far beyond the general run of the girls who applied to him for positions. And he was not beyond a friendly flirtation with a pretty new girl himself; so she was engaged at once, and put on duty at the notion-counter.

The girls flocked around her during the intervals of custom. Lizzie had told of her cousin's long ride, embellished, wherever her knowledge failed, by her extremely wild notions of Western life. She had told how Elizabeth arrived wearing a belt with two pistols, and this gave Elizabeth standing at once among all the people in the store. A girl who could shoot, and who wore pistols in a belt like a real cowboy, had a social distinction all her own.

The novel-reading, theatre-going girls rallied around her to a girl; and the young men in the store were not far behind. Elizabeth was popular from the first. Moreover, as she settled down into the routine of life, and had three meals every day, her cheeks began to round out just a little; and it became apparent that she was unusually beautiful in spite of her dark skin, which whitened gradually under the electric light and high-pressure life of the store.

They went to Christian Endeavor, Elizabeth and her cousin; and Elizabeth felt as if heaven had suddenly dropped down about her. She lived from week to week for that Christian Endeavor.

The store, which had been a surprise and a novelty at first, began to be a trial to her. It wore upon her nerves. The air was bad, and the crowds were great. It was coming on toward Christmas time, and the store was crammed to bursting day after day and night after night, for they kept open evenings now until Christmas. Elizabeth longed for a breath from the mountains, and grew whiter and thinner. Sometimes she felt as if she must break away from it all, and take Robin, and ride into the wilderness again. If it were not for the Christian Endeavor, she would have done so, perhaps.

Robin, poor beast, was well housed and well fed; but he worked for his living as did his mistress. He was a grocer's delivery horse, worked from Monday morning early till Saturday night at ten o'clock, subject to curses and kicks from the grocery boy, expected to stand meekly at the curb-stones, snuffing the dusty brick pavements while the boy delivered a box of goods, and while trolleys and beer-wagons and automobiles slammed and rumbled and tooted by him, and then to start on the double-quick to the next stopping-place.

He to be thus under the rod who had trod the plains with a free foot and snuffed the mountain air! It was a great come-down, and his life became a weariness to him. But he earned his mistress a dollar a week besides his board. There would have been some consolation in that to his faithful heart if he only could have known it. Albeit she would have gladly gone without the dollar if Robin could have been free and happy.

One day, one dreadful day, the manager of the ten-cent store came to Elizabeth with a look in his eyes that reminded her of the man in Montana from whom she had fled. He was smiling, and his words were unduly pleasant. He wanted her to go with him to the theatre that evening, and he complimented her on her appearance. He stated that he admired her exceedingly, and wanted to give her pleasure. But somehow Elizabeth had fallen into the habit ever since she left the prairies of comparing all men with George Trescott Benedict; and this man, although he dressed well, and was every bit as handsome, did not compare well. There was a sinister, selfish glitter in his eyes that made Elizabeth think of the serpent on the plain just before she shot it. Therefore Elizabeth declined the invitation.

It happened that there was a missionary meeting at the church that evening. All the Christian endeavorers had been urged to attend. Elizabeth gave this as an excuse; but the manager quickly swept that away, saying she could go to church any night, but she could not go to this particular play with him always. The girl eyed him calmly with much the same attitude with which she might have pointed her pistol at his head, and said gravely,

"But I do not want to go with you."

After that the manager hated her. He always hated girls who resisted him. He hated her, and wanted to do her harm. But he fairly persecuted her to receive his attentions. He was a young fellow, extremely young to be occupying so responsible a position. He undoubtedly had business ability. He showed it in his management of Elizabeth. The girl's life became a torment to her. In proportion as she appeared to be the manager's favorite the other girls became jealous of her. They taunted her with the manager's attentions on every possible occasion. When they found anything wrong, they charged it upon her; and so she was kept constantly going to the manager, which was perhaps just what he wanted.

She grew paler and paler, and more and more desperate. She had run away from one man; she had run away from a woman; but here was a man from whom she could not run away unless she gave up her position. If it had not been for her grandmother, she would have done so at once; but, if she gave up her position, she would be thrown upon her grandmother for support, and that must not be. She understood from the family talk that they were having just as much as they could do already to make both ends meet and keep the all-important god of Fashion satisfied. This god of Fashion had come to seem to Elizabeth an enemy of the living God. It seemed to occupy all people's thoughts, and everything else had to be sacrificed to meet its demands.

She had broached the subject of school one evening soon after she arrived, but was completely squelched by her aunt and cousin.

"You're too old!" sneered Lizzie. "School is for children."

"Lizzie went through grammar school, and we talked about high for her," said the grandmother proudly.

"But I just hated school," grinned Lizzie. "It ain't so nice as it's cracked up to be. Just sit and study all day long. Why, they were always keeping me after school for talking or laughing. I was glad enough when I got through. You may thank your stars you didn't have to go, Bess."

"People who have to earn their bread can't lie around and go to school," remarked Aunt Nan dryly, and Elizabeth said no more.

But later she heard of a night-school, and then she took up the subject once more. Lizzie scoffed at this. She said night-school was only for very poor people, and it was a sort of disgrace to go. But Elizabeth stuck to her point, until one day Lizzie came home with a tale about Temple College. She had heard it was very cheap. You could go for ten cents a night, or something like that. Things that were ten cents appealed to her. She was used to bargain-counters.

She heard it was quite respectable to go there, and they had classes in the evening. You could study gymnastics, and it would make you graceful. She wanted to be graceful. And she heard they had a course in millinery. If it was so, she believed she would go herself, and learn to make the new kinds of bows they were having on hats this winter. She could not seem to get the right twist to the ribbon.

Elizabeth wanted to study geography. At least, that was the study Lizzie said would tell her where the Desert of Sahara was. She wanted to know things, all kinds of things; but Lizzie said such things were only for children, and she didn't believe they taught such baby studies in a college. But she would inquire. It was silly of Bessie to want to know, she thought, and she was half ashamed to ask. But she would find out.

It was about this time that Elizabeth's life at the store grew intolerable.

One morning — it was little more than a week before Christmas — Elizabeth had been sent to the cellar to get seven little red tin pails and shovels for a woman who wanted them for Christmas gifts for some Sunday-school class. She had just counted out the requisite number and turned to go up-stairs when she heard someone step near her, and, as she looked up in the dim light, there stood the manager.

"At last I've got you alone, Bessie, my dear!" He said it with suave triumph in his tones. He caught Elizabeth by the wrists, and before she could wrench herself away he had kissed her.

With a scream Elizabeth dropped the seven tin pails and the seven tin shovels, and with one mighty wrench took her hands from his grasp. Instinctively her hand went to her belt, where were now no pistols. If one had been there she certainly would have shot him in her horror and fury. But, as she had no other weapon, she seized a little shovel, and struck him in the face. Then with the frenzy of the desert back upon her she rushed up the stairs, out through the crowded store, and into the street, hatless and coatless in the cold December air. The passers-by made way for her, thinking she had been sent out on some hurried errand.

She had left her pocketbook, with its pitifully few nickels for car-fare and lunch, in the cloak-room with her coat and hat. But she did not stop to think of that. She was fleeing again, this time on foot, from a man. She half expected he might pursue her, and make her come back to the hated work in the stifling store with his wicked face moving everywhere above the crowds. But she turned not to look back. On over the slushy pavements, under the leaden sky, with a few busy flakes floating above her.

The day seemed pitiless as the world. Where could she go and what should she do? There seemed no refuge for her in the wide world. Instinctively she felt her grandmother would feel that a calamity had befallen them in losing the patronage of the manager of the ten-cent store. Perhaps Lizzie would get into trouble. What should she do?

She had reached the corner where she and Lizzie usually took the car for home. The car was coming now; but she had no hat nor coat, and no money to pay for a ride. She must walk. She paused not, but fled on in a steady run, for which her years on the mountain had given her breath. Three miles it was to Flora Street, and she scarcely slackened her pace after she had settled into the steady half-run, half-walk. Only at the corner of Flora Street she paused, and allowed herself to glance back once. No, the manager had not pursued her. She was safe. She might go in and tell her grandmother without fearing he would come behind her as soon as her back was turned.

Chapter 12

Elizabeth's Declaration of Independence

Mrs. Brady was at the wash-tub again when her most uncommon and unexpected grandchild burst into the room.

She wiped her hands on her apron, and sat down with her usual exclamation. "Fer the land sakes! What's happened? Bessie, tell me quick. Is anything the matter with Lizzie? Where is she?"

But Elizabeth was on the floor at her feet in tears. She was shaking with sobs, and could scarcely manage to stammer out that Lizzie was all right. Mrs. Brady settled back with a relieved sigh. Lizzie was the first grandchild, and therefore the idol of her heart. If Lizzie was all right, she could afford to be patient and find out by degrees.

"It's that awful man, grandmother!" Elizabeth sobbed out.

"What man? That feller in Montana you run away from?" The grandmother sat up with snapping eyes. She was not afraid of a man, even if he did shoot people. She would call in the police and protect her own flesh and blood. Let him come. Mrs. Brady was ready for him.

"No, no, grandmother, the man-man-manager at the ten-cent store," sobbed the girl; "he kissed me! Oh!" and she shuddered as if the memory was the most terrible thing that ever came to her.

"Fer the land sakes! Is that all?" said the woman with much relief and a degree of satisfaction. "Why, that's nothing. You ought to be proud. Many a girl would go boasting round about that. What are you crying for? He didn't hurt you, did he? Why, Lizzie seems to think he's fine. I tell you Lizzie wouldn't cry if he was to kiss her, I'm sure. She'd just laugh, and ask him fer a holiday. Here, sit up, child, and wash your face, and go back to your work. You've evidently struck the manager on the right side, and you're bound to get a rise in your wages. Every girl he takes a notion to gets up and does well. Perhaps you'll get money enough to go to school. Goodness knows what you want to go for. I s'pose it's in the blood, though Bess used to say our pa wa'n't any good at study. But, if you've struck the manager the right way, no telling what he might do. He might even want to marry you."

"Grandmother!"

Mrs. Brady was favored with the flashing of the Bailey eyes. She viewed it in astonishment not unmixed with admiration.

"Well, you certainly have got spirit," she ejaculated. "I don't wonder he liked you. I didn't know you was so pretty, Bessie; you look like your mother when she was eighteen; you really do. I never saw the resemblance before. I believe you'll get on all right. Don't you be afraid. I wish you had your chance if you're so anxious to go to school. I shouldn't wonder ef you'd turn out to be something and marry rich. Well, I must be getting back to me tub. Land sakes, but you did give me a turn. I thought Lizzie had been run over. I couldn't think what else'd make you run off way here without your coat. Come, get up, child, and go back to your work. It's too bad you don't like to be kissed, but don't let that worry you. You'll have lots worse than that to come up against. When you've lived as long as I have and worked as hard, you'll be pleased to have someone admire you. You better wash your face, and eat a bite of lunch, and hustle back. You needn't be afraid. If he's fond of you, he won't bother about your running away a little. He'll excuse you ef 'tis busy times, and not dock your pay neither."

"Grandmother!" said Elizabeth. "Don't! I can never go back to that awful place and that man. I would rather go back to Montana. I would rather be dead."

"Hoity-toity!" said the easy-going grandmother, sitting down to her task, for she perceived some wholesome discipline was necessary. "You can't talk that way, Bess. You got to go to your work. We ain't got money to keep you in idleness, and land knows where you'd get another place as good's this one. Ef you stay home all day, you might make him awful mad; and then it would be no use goin' back, and you might lose Lizzie her place too."

But, though the grandmother talked and argued and soothed by turns, Elizabeth was firm. She would not go back. She would never go back. She would go to Montana if her grandmother said any more about it.

With a sigh at last Mrs. Brady gave up. She had given up once before nearly twenty years ago. Bessie, her oldest daughter, had a will like that, and tastes far above her station. Mrs. Brady wondered where she got them.

"You're fer all the world like yer ma," she said as she thumped the clothes in the wash-tub. "She was jest that way, when she would marry your pa. She could 'a' had Jim Stokes, the groceryman, er Lodge, the milkman, er her choice of three railroad men, all of 'em doing well, and ready to let her walk over 'em; but she *would have* your pa, the drunken, good-for-nothing, slippery dude. The only thing I'm surprised at was that he ever married her. I never expected it. I s'posed they'd run off, and he'd leave her when he got tired of her; but it seems he stuck to her. It's the only good thing he ever done, and I'm not sure but she'd 'a' been better off ef he hadn't 'a' done that."

"Grandmother!" Elizabeth's face blazed.

"Yes, *gran*'mother!" snapped Mrs. Brady. "It's all true, and you might's well face it. He met her in church. She used to go reg'lar. Some boys used to come and set in the back seat behind the girls, and then go home with them. They was all nice enough boys 'cept him. I never had a bit a use for him. He belonged to the swells and the stuck-ups; and he knowed it, and presumed upon it. He jest thought he could wind Bessie round his finger, and he did. If he said, 'Go,' she went, no matter what I'd do. So, when his ma found it out, she was hoppin' mad. She jest came driving round here to me house, and presumed to talk to me. She said Bessie was a designing snip, and a bad girl, and a whole lot of things. Said she was leading her son astray, and would come to no good end, and a whole lot of stuff; and told me to look after her. It wasn't so. Bess got John Bailey to quit smoking for a whole week at a time, and he said if she'd marry him he'd quit drinking too. His ma couldn't 'a' got him to promise that. She wouldn't even believe he got drunk. I told her a few things about her precious son, but she curled her fine, aristocratic lip up, and said, 'Gentlemen never get drunk.' Humph! Gentlemen! That's all she knowed about it. He got drunk all right, and stayed drunk, too. So after that, when I tried to keep Bess at home, she slipped away one night; said she was going to church; and she did too; went to the minister's study in a strange church, and got married, her and John; and then they up and off West. John, he'd sold his watch and his fine diamond stud his ma had give him; and he borrowed some money from some friends of his father's, and he off with three hundred dollars and Bess; and that's all I ever saw more of me Bessie."

The poor woman sat down in her chair, and wept into her apron regardless for once of the soap-suds that rolled down her red, wet arms.

"Is my grandmother living yet?" asked Elizabeth. She was sorry for this grandmother, but did not know what to say. She was afraid to comfort her lest she take it for yielding.

"Yes, they say she is," said Mrs. Brady, sitting up with a show of interest. She was always ready for a bit of gossip. "Her husband's dead, and her other son's dead, and she's all alone. She lives in a big house on Rittenhouse Square. If she was any 'count, she'd ought to provide for you. I never thought about it. But I don't suppose it would be any use to try. You might ask her. Perhaps she'd help you to go to school. You've got a claim on her. She ought to give you her son's share of his father's property, though I've heard she disowned him when he married our Bess. You might fix up in some of Lizzie's best things, and go up there and try. She might give you some money."

"I don't want her money," said Elizabeth stiffly. "I guess there's work somewhere in the world I can do without begging even of grandmothers. But I think I ought to go and see her. She might want to know about father."

Mrs. Brady looked at her granddaughter wonderingly. This was a view of things she had never taken.

"Well," said she resignedly, "go your own gait. I don't know where you'll come up at. All I say is, ef you're going through the world with such high and mighty fine notions, you'll have a hard time. You can't pick out roses and cream and a bed of down every day. You have to put up with life as you find it."

Elizabeth went to her room, the room she shared with Lizzie. She wanted to get away from her grandmother's disapproval. It lay on her heart like lead. Was there no refuge in the world? If grandmothers were not refuges, where should one flee? The old lady in Chicago had understood; why had not Grandmother Brady?

Then came the sweet old words, "Let not your heart be troubled." "In the time of trouble he shall hide me in his pavilion; in the secret of his tabernacle shall he hide me." She knelt down by the bed and said "Our Father." She was beginning to add some words of her own now. She had heard them pray so in Christian Endeavor in the sentence prayers. She wished she knew more about God, and His Book. She had had so little time to ask or think about it. Life seemed all one rush for clothes and position.

At supper-time Lizzie came home much excited. She had been in hot water all the afternoon. The girls had said at lunch-time that the manager was angry with Bessie, and had discharged her. She found her coat and hat, and had brought them home. The pocketbook was missing. There was only fifteen cents in it; but Lizzie was much disturbed, and so was the grandmother. They had a quiet consultation in the kitchen; and, when the aunt came, there was another whispered conversation among the three.

Elizabeth felt disapproval in the air. Aunt Nan came, and sat down beside her, and talked very coldly about expenses and being dependent upon one's relatives, and let her understand thoroughly that she could not sit around and do nothing; but Elizabeth answered by telling her how the manager had been treating her. The aunt then gave her a dose of worldly wisdom, which made the girl shrink into herself. It needed only Lizzie's loud-voiced exhortations to add to her misery and make her feel ready to do anything. Supper was a most unpleasant meal. At last the grandmother spoke up.

"Well, Bessie," she said firmly, "we've decided, all of us, that, if you are going to be stubborn about this, something will have to be done; and I think the best thing is for you to go to Mrs. Bailey and see what she'll do for you. It's her business, anyway."

Elizabeth's cheeks were very red. She said nothing. She let them go on with the arrangements. Lizzie went and got her best hat, and tried it on Elizabeth to see how she would look, and produced a silk waist from her store of garments, and a spring jacket. It wasn't very warm, it is true; but Lizzie explained that the occasion demanded strenuous measures, and the jacket was undoubtedly stylish, which was the main thing to be considered. One could afford to be cold if one was stylish.

Lizzie was up early the next morning. She had agreed to put Elizabeth in battle-array for her visit to Rittenhouse Square. Elizabeth submitted meekly to her borrowed adornings. Her hair was brushed over her face, and curled on a hot iron, and brushed backward in a perfect mat, and then puffed out in a bigger pompadour than usual. The silk waist was put on with Lizzie's best skirt, and she was adjured not to let that drag. Then the best hat with the cheap pink plumes was set atop the elaborate coiffure; the jacket was put on; and a pair of Lizzie's long silk gloves were struggled into. They were a trifle large when on, but to the hands unaccustomed to gloves they were like being run into a mould.

Elizabeth stood it all until she was pronounced complete. Then she came and stood in front of the cheap little glass, and surveyed herself. There were blisters in the glass that twisted her head into a grotesque shape. The hairpins stuck into her head. Lizzie had tied a spotted veil tight over her nose and eyes. The collar of the silk waist was frayed, and cut her neck. The shirt-band was too tight, and the gloves were torture. Elizabeth turned slowly, and went down-stairs, past the admiring aunt and grandmother, who exclaimed at the girl's beauty, now that she was attired to their mind, and encouraging her by saying they were sure her grandmother would want to do something for so pretty a girl.

Lizzie called out to her not to worry, as she flew for her car. She said she had heard there was a variety show in town where they wanted a girl who could shoot. If she didn't succeed with her grandmother, they would try and get her in at the show. The girls at the store knew a man who had charge of it. They said he liked pretty girls, and they thought would be glad to get her. Indeed, Mary James had promised to speak to him last night, and would let her know to-day about it. It would likely be a job more suited to her cousin's liking.

Elizabeth shuddered. Another man! Would he be like all the rest? — all the rest save one!

She walked a few steps in the direction she had been told to go, and then turned resolutely around, and came back. The watching grandmother felt her heart sink. What was this headstrong girl going to do next? Rebel again?

"What's the matter, Bessie?" she asked, meeting her anxiously at the door. "It's bad luck to turn back when you've started."

"I can't go this way," said the girl excitedly. "It's all a cheat. I'm not like this. It isn't mine, and I'm not going in it. I must have my own clothes and be myself when I go to see her. If she doesn't like me and want me, then I can take Robin and go back." And like another David burdened with Saul's armor she came back to get her little sling and stones.

She tore off the veil, and the sticky gloves from her cold hands, and all the finery of silk waist and belt, and donned her old plain blue coat and skirt in which she had arrived in Philadelphia. They had been frugally brushed and sponged, and made neat for a working dress. Elizabeth felt that they belonged to her. Under the jacket, which fortunately was long enough to hide her waist, she buckled her belt with the two pistols. Then she took the battered old felt hat from the closet, and tried to fasten it on; but the pompadour interfered. Relentlessly she pulled down the work of art that Lizzie had created, and brushed and combed her long, thick hair into subjection again, and put it in its long braid down her back. Her grandmother should see her just as she was. She should know what kind of a girl belonged to her. Then, if she chose to be a real grandmother, well and good.

Mrs. Brady was much disturbed in mind when Elizabeth came downstairs. She exclaimed in horror, and tried to force the girl to go back, telling her it was a shame and a disgrace to go in such garments into the sacred precincts of Rittenhouse Square; but the girl was not to be turned back. She would not even wait till her aunt and Lizzie came home. She would go now, at once.

Mrs. Brady sat down in her rocking-chair in despair for full five minutes after she had watched the reprehensible girl go down the street. She had not been so completely beaten since the day when her own Bessie left the house and went away to a wild West to die in her own time and way. The grandmother shed a few tears. The girl was like her own Bessie, and she could not help loving her, though there was a streak of something else about her that made her seem above them all; and that was hard to bear. It must be the Bailey streak, of course. Mrs. Brady did not admire the Baileys, but she was obliged to reverence them.

If she had watched or followed Elizabeth, she would have been still more horrified. The girl went straight to the corner grocery, and demanded her own horse, handing back to the man the dollar he had paid her last Saturday night, and saying she had need of the horse at once. After some parley, in which she showed her ability to stand her own ground, the boy unhitched the horse from the wagon, and got her own old saddle from the stable. Then Elizabeth mounted her horse and rode away to Rittenhouse Square.

Chapter 13
Another Grandmother

Elizabeth's idea in taking the horse along with her was to have all her armor on, as a warrior goes out to meet the foe. If this grandmother proved impossible, why, then so long as she had life and breath and a horse she could flee. The world was wide, and the West was still open to her. She could flee back to the wilderness that gave her breath.

The old horse stopped gravely and disappointedly before the tall, aristocratic house in Rittenhouse Square. He had hoped that city life was now to end, and that he and his dear mistress were to travel back to their beloved prairies. No amount of oats could ever make up to him for his freedom, and the quiet, and the hills. He had a feeling that he should like to go back home and die. He had seen enough of the world.

She fastened the halter to a ring in the sidewalk, which surprised him. The grocer's boy never fastened him. He looked up questioningly at the house, but saw no reason why his mistress should go in there. It was not familiar ground. Coffee and Sons never came up this way.

Elizabeth, as she crossed the sidewalk and mounted the steps before the formidable carved doors, felt that here was the last hope of finding an earthly habitation. If this failed her, then there was the desert, and starvation, and a long, long sleep. But while the echo of the bell still sounded through the high-ceiled hall there came to her the words: "Let not your heart be troubled. . . . In my Father's house are many mansions; if it were not so, I would have told you. I go to prepare a place for you. . . . I will come again and receive you." How sweet that was! Then, even if she died on the desert, there was a home prepared for her. So much she had learned in Christian Endeavor meeting.

The stately butler let her in. He eyed her questioningly at first, and said madam was not up yet; but Elizabeth told him she would wait.

"Is she sick?" asked Elizabeth with a strange constriction about her heart.

"O no, she is not up yet, miss," said the kind old butler, "she never gets up before this. You're from Mrs. Sands, I suppose." Poor soul, for once his butler eyes had been mistaken. He thought she was the little errand-girl from Madam Bailey's modiste.

"No, I'm just Elizabeth," said the girl, smiling. She felt that this man, whoever he was, was not against her. He was old, and he had a kind look.

He still thought she meant she was not the modiste, just her errand-girl. Her quaint dress and the long braid down her back made her look like a child.

"I'll tell her you've come. Be seated," said the butler, and gave her a chair in the dim hall just opposite the parlor door, where she had a glimpse of elegance such as she had never dreamed existed. She tried to think how it must be to live in such a room and walk on velvet. The carpet was deep and rich. She did not know it was a rug, nor that it was woven in some poor peasant's home and then was brought here years afterward at a fabulous price. She only knew it was beautiful in its silvery sheen, with gleaming colors through it like jewels in the dew.

On through another open doorway she caught a glimpse of a painting on the wall. It was a man as large as life, sitting in a chair; and the face and attitude were her father's — her father at his best. She was fairly startled. Who was it? Could it be her father? And how had they made this picture of him? He must be changed in those twenty years he had been gone from home.

Then the butler came back, and before he could speak she pointed toward the picture. "Who is it?" she asked.

"That, miss? That's Mr. John, Madam's husband that's dead a good many years now. But I remember him well."

"Could I look at it? He is so much like my father." She walked rapidly over the ancient rug, unheeding its beauties, while the wondering butler followed a trifle anxiously. This was unprecedented. Mrs. Sands's errand-girls usually knew their place.

"Madam said you was to come right up to her room," said the butler pointedly. But Elizabeth stood rooted to the ground, studying the picture. The butler had to repeat his message. She smiled and turned to follow him, and as she did so saw on a side wall the portraits of two boys.

"Who are they?" she pointed swiftly. They were much like her own two brothers.

"Them are Mr. John and Mr. James, Madam's two sons. They's both of them dead now," said the butler. "At least, Mr. James is, I'm sure. He died two years ago. But you better come right up. Madam will be wondering."

She followed the old man up the velvet-shod stairs that gave back no sound from footfall, and pondered as she went. Then that was her father, that boy with the beautiful face and the heavy wavy hair tossed back from his forehead, and the haughty, imperious, don't-care look. And here was where he had lived. Here amid all this luxury.

Like a flash came the quick contrast of the home in which he had died, and a great wave of reverence for her father rolled over her. From such a home and such surroundings it would not have been strange if he had grown weary of the rough life out West, and deserted his wife, who was beneath him in station. True, he had not been of much use to her, and much of the time had been but a burden and anxiety; but he had stayed and loved her — when he was sober. She forgave him his many trying ways, his faultfindings with her mother's many little blunders — no wonder, when he came from this place.

The butler tapped on a door at the head of the stairs, and a maid swung it open.

"Why, you're not the girl Mrs. Sands sent the other day," said a querulous voice from a mass of lace-ruffled pillows on the great bed.

"I am Elizabeth," said the girl, as if that were full explanation.

"Elizabeth? Elizabeth who? I don't see why she sent another girl. Are you sure you will understand the directions? They're very particular, for I want my frock ready for to-night without fail." The woman sat up, leaning on one elbow. Her lace nightgown and pale-blue silk dressing-sack fell away from a round white arm that did not look as if it belonged to a very old lady. Her gray hair was becomingly arranged, and she was extremely pretty, with small features. Elizabeth looked and marvelled. Like a flash came the vision of the other grandmother at the wash-tub. The contrast was startling.

"I am Elizabeth Bailey," said the girl quietly, as if she would break a piece of hard news gently. "My father was your son John."

"The idea!" said the new grandmother, and promptly fell back upon her pillows with her hand upon her heart. "John, John, my little John. No one has mentioned his name to me for years and years. He never writes to me." She put up a lace-trimmed handkerchief, and sobbed.

"Father died five years ago," said Elizabeth.

"You wicked girl!" said the maid. "Can't you see that Madam can't bear such talk? Go right out of the room!" The maid rushed up with smelling-salts and a glass of water, and Elizabeth in distress came and stood by the bed.

"I'm sorry I made you feel bad, Grandmother," she said when she saw that the fragile, childish creature on the bed was recovering somewhat.

"What right have you to call me that? Grandmother, indeed! I'm not so old as that. Besides, how do I know you belong to me? If John is dead, your mother better look after you. I'm sure I'm not responsible for you. It's her business. She wheedled John away from his home, and carried him off to that awful West, and never let him write to me. She has done it all, and now she may bear the consequences. I suppose she has sent you here to beg, but she has made a mistake. I shall not have a thing to do with her or her children."

"Grandmother!" Elizabeth's eyes flashed as they had done to the other grandmother a few hours before. "You must not talk so. I won't hear it. I wouldn't let Grandmother Brady talk about my father, and you can't talk so about mother. She was my mother, and I loved her, and so did father love her; and she worked hard to keep him and take care of him when he drank years and years, and didn't have any money to help her. Mother was only eighteen when she married father, and you ought not to blame her. She didn't have a nice home like this. But she was good and dear, and now she is dead. Father and mother are both dead, and all the other children. A man killed my brother, and then as soon as he was buried he came and wanted me to go with him. He was an awful man, and I was afraid, and took my brother's horse and ran away. I rode all this long way because I was afraid of that man, and I wanted to get to some of my own folks, who would love me, and let me work for them, and let me go to school and learn something. But I wish now I had stayed out there and died. I could have lain down in the sage-brush, and a wild beast would have killed me perhaps, and that would be a great deal better than this; for Grandmother Brady does not understand, and you do not want me; but in my Father's house in heaven there are many mansions, and He went to prepare a place for me; so I guess I will go back to the desert, and perhaps He will send for me. Good-by, Grandmother."

Then before the astonished woman in the bed could recover her senses from this remarkable speech Elizabeth turned and walked majestically from the room. She was slight and not very tall, but in the strength of her pride and purity she looked almost majestic to the awe-struck maid and the bewildered woman.

Down the stairs walked the girl, feeling that all the wide world was against her. She would never again try to get a friend. She had not met a friend except in the desert. One man had been good to her, and she had let him go away; but he belonged to another woman, and she might not let him stay. There was just one thing to be thankful for. She had knowledge of her Father in heaven, and she knew what Christian Endeavor meant. She could take that with her out into the desert, and no one could take it from her. One wish she had, but maybe that was too much to hope for. If she could have had a Bible of her own! She had no money left. Nothing but her mother's wedding-ring, the papers, and the envelope that had contained the money the man had given her when he left. She could not part with them, unless perhaps someone would take the ring and keep it until she could buy it back. But she would wait and hope.

She walked by the old butler with her hand on her pistol. She did not intend to let anyone detain her now. He bowed pleasantly, and opened the door for her, however; and she marched down the steps to her horse. But just as she was about to mount and ride away into the unknown where no grandmother, be she Brady or Bailey, would ever be able to search her out, no matter how hard she tried, the door suddenly opened again, and there was a great commotion. The maid and the old butler both flew out, and laid hands upon her. She dropped the bridle, and seized her pistol, covering them both with its black, forbidding nozzle.

They stopped, trembling, but the butler bravely stood his ground. He did not know why he was to detain this extraordinary young person, but he felt sure something was wrong. Probably she was a thief, and had taken some of Madam's jewels. He could call the police. He opened his mouth to do so when the maid explained.

"Madam wants you to come back. She didn't understand. She wants to see you and ask about her son. You must come, or you will kill her. She has heart-trouble, and you must not excite her."

Elizabeth put the pistol back into its holster, and, picking up the bridle again, fastened it in the ring, saying simply, "I will come back."

"What do you want?" she asked abruptly when she returned to the bedroom.

"Don't you know that's a disrespectful way to speak?" asked the woman querulously. "What did you have to get into a temper for, and go off like that without telling me anything about my son? Sit down, and tell me all about it."

"I'm sorry, Grandmother," said Elizabeth, sitting down. "I thought you didn't want me and I better go."

"Well, the next time wait until I send you. What kind of a thing have you got on, anyway? That's a queer sort of a hat for a girl to wear. Take it off. You look like a rough boy with that on. You make me think of John when he had been out disobeying me."

Elizabeth took off the offending headgear, and revealed her smoothly parted, thick brown hair in its long braid down her back.

"Why, you're rather a pretty girl if you were fixed up," said the old lady, sitting up with interest now. "I can't remember your mother, but I don't think she had fine features like that."

"They said I looked like Father," said Elizabeth.

"Did they? Well, I believe it's true," with satisfaction. "I couldn't bear if you looked like those low-down —"

"Grandmother!" Elizabeth stood up, and flashed her Bailey eyes.

"You needn't 'grandmother' me all the time," said the lady petulantly. "But you look quite handsome when you say it. Take off that ill-fitted coat. It isn't thick enough for winter, anyway. What in the world have you got round your waist? A belt? Why, that's a man's belt! And what have you got on it? Pistols? Horrors! Marie, take them away quick! I shall faint! I never could bear to be in a room with one. My husband used to have one on his closet shelf, and I never went near it, and always locked the room when he was out. You must put them out in the hall. I cannot breathe where pistols are. Now sit down and tell me all about it, how old you are, and how you got here."

Elizabeth surrendered her pistols with hesitation. She felt that she must obey her grandmother, but was not altogether certain whether it was safe for her to be weaponless until she was sure this was friendly ground.

At the demand she began back as far as she could remember, and told the story of her life, pathetically, simply, without a single claim to pity, yet so earnestly and vividly that the grandmother, lying with her eyes closed, forgot herself completely, and let the tears trickle unbidden and unheeded down her well-preserved cheeks.

When Elizabeth came to the graves in the moonlight, she gasped, and sobbed: "O Johnny, Johnny, my little Johnny! Why did you always be such a bad, bad boy?" and when the ride in the desert was described, and the man from whom she fled, the grandmother held her breath, and said, "O, how fearful!" Her interest in the girl was growing, and kept at white heat during the whole of the story.

There was one part of her experience, however, that Elizabeth passed over lightly, and that was the meeting with George Trescott Benedict. Instinctively she felt that this experience would not find a sympathetic listener. She passed it over by merely saying that she had met a kind gentleman from the East who was lost, and that they had ridden together for a few miles until they reached a town; and he had telegraphed to his friends, and gone on his way. She said nothing about the money he had lent to her, for she shrank from speaking about him more than was necessary. She felt that her grandmother might feel as the old woman of the ranch had felt about their travelling together. She left it to be inferred that she might have had a little money with her from home. At least, the older woman asked no questions about how she secured provisions for the way.

When Elizabeth came to her Chicago experience, her grandmother clasped her hands as if a serpent had been mentioned, and said: "How degrading! You certainly would have been justified in shooting the whole company. I wonder such places are allowed to exist!" But Marie sat with large eyes of wonder, and retailed the story over again in the kitchen afterwards for the benefit of the cook and the butler, so that Elizabeth became henceforth a heroine among them.

Elizabeth passed on to her Philadelphia experience, and found that here her grandmother was roused to blazing indignation, but the thing that roused her was the fact that a Bailey should serve behind a counter in a ten-cent store. She lifted her hands, and uttered a moan of real pain, and went on at such a rate that the smelling-salts had to be brought into requisition again.

When Elizabeth told of her encounter with the manager in the cellar, the grandmother said: "How disgusting! The impertinent creature! He ought to be sued. I will consult the lawyer about the matter. What did you say his name was? Marie, write that down. And so, dear, you did quite right to come to me. I've been looking at you while you talked, and I believe you'll be a pretty girl if you are fixed up. Marie, go to the telephone, and call up Blandeaux, and tell him to send up a hair-dresser at once. I want to see how Miss Elizabeth will look with her hair done low in one of those new coils. I believe it will becoming. I shall have tried it long ago myself; only it seems a trifle too youthful for hair that is beginning to turn gray."

Elizabeth watched her grandmother in wonder. Here truly was a new phase of woman. She did not care about great facts, but only about little things. Her life was made up of the great pursuit of fashion, just like Lizzie's. Were people in cities all alike? No, for he, the one man she had met in the wilderness, had not seemed to care. Maybe, though, when he got back to the city he did care. She sighed and turned toward the new grandmother.

"Now I have told you everything, Grandmother. Shall I go away? I wanted to go to school; but I see that it costs a great deal of money, and I don't want to be a burden on anyone. I came here, not to ask you to take me in, because I did not want to trouble you; but I thought before I went away I ought to see you once because—because you are my grandmother."

"I've never been a grandmother," said the little woman of the world reflectively, "but I don't know but it would be rather nice. I'd like to make you into a pretty girl, and take you out into society. That would be something new to live for. I'm not very pretty myself any more, but I can see that you will be. Do you wear blue or pink? I used to wear pink myself, but I believe you could wear either when you get your complexion in shape. You've tanned it horribly, but it may come out all right. I think you'll take. You say you want to go to school. Why, certainly, I suppose that will be necessary; living out in that barbarous, uncivilized region, of course you don't know much. You seem to speak correctly, but John always was particular about his speech. He had a tutor when he was little who tripped him up every mistake he made. That was the only thing that tutor was good for; he was a linguist. We found out afterwards he was terribly wild, and drank. He did John more harm than good. Marie, I shall want Elizabeth to have the rooms next mine. Ring for Martha to see that everything is in order. Elizabeth, did you ever have your hands manicured? You have a pretty-shaped hand. I'll have the woman attend to it when she comes to shampoo your hair and put it up. Did you bring any clothes along? Of course not. You couldn't on horseback. I suppose you had your trunk sent by express. No trunk? No express? No railroad? How barbarous! How John must have suffered, poor fellow! He, so used to every luxury! Well, I don't see that it was my fault. I gave him everything he wanted except his wife, and he took her without my leave. Poor fellow, poor fellow!''

Mrs. Bailey in due time sent Elizabeth off to the suite of rooms that she said were to be hers exclusively, and arose to bedeck herself for another day. Elizabeth was a new toy, and she anticipated playing with her. It put new zest into a life that had grown monotonous.

Elizabeth, meanwhile, was surveying her quarters, and wondering what Lizzie would think if she could see her. According to orders, the coachman had taken Robin to the stable, and he was already rolling in all the luxuries of a horse of the aristocracy, and congratulating himself on the good taste of his mistress to select such a stopping-place. For his part he was now satisfied not to move further. This was better than the wilderness any day. Oats like these, and hay such as this, were not to be found on the plains.

Toward evening the grave butler, with many a deprecatory glance at the neighborhood, arrived at the door of Mrs. Brady, and delivered himself of the following message to that astonished lady, backed by her daughter and her granddaughter, with their ears stretched to the utmost to hear every syllable:

"Mrs. Merrill Wilton Bailey sends word that her granddaughter, Miss Elizabeth, has reached her home safely, and will remain with her. Miss Elizabeth will come sometime to see Mrs. Brady, and thank her for her kindness during her stay with her."

The butler bowed, and turned away with relief. His dignity and social standing had not been so taxed by the family demands in years. He was glad he might shake off the dust of Flora Street forever. He felt for the coachman. He would probably have to drive the young lady down here sometime, according to that message.

Mrs. Brady, her daughter, and Lizzie stuck their heads out into the lamplighted street, and watched the dignified butler out of sight. Then they went in and sat down in three separate stages of relief and astonishment.

"Fer the land sakes!" ejaculated the grandmother. "Well, now, if that don't beat all!" then after a minute: "The impertinent fellow! And the impidence of the woman! Thank me fer my kindness to me own grandchild! I'd thank her to mind her business, but then that's just like her."

"Her nest is certainly well feathered," said Aunt Nan enviously. "I only wish Lizzie had such a chance."

Said Lizzie: "It's awful queer, her looking like that, too, in that crazy rig! Well, I'm glad she's gone, fer she was so awful queer it was jest fierce. She talked religion a lot to the girls, and then they laughed at her behind her back; and they kep' a telling me I'd be a missionary 'fore long if she stayed with us. I went to Mr. Wray, the manager, and told him my cousin was awfully shy, and she sent word she wanted to be excused fer running away like that. He kind of colored up, and said 'twas all right, and she might come back and have her old place if she wanted, and he'd say no more about it. I told him I'd tell her. But I guess her acting up won't do me a bit of harm. The girls say he'll make up to *me* now. Wish he would. I'd have a fine time. It's me turn to have me wages raised, anyway. He said if Bess and I would come to-morrow ready to stay in the evening, he'd take us to a show that beat everything he ever saw in Philadelphia. I mean to make him take me, anyway. I'm just glad she's out of the way. She wasn't like the rest of us."

Said Mrs. Brady: "It's the Bailey in her. But she said she'd come back and see me, didn't she?" and the grandmother in her meditated over that fact for several minutes.

Chapter 14
In a New World

Meantime the panorama of Elizabeth's life passed on into more peaceful scenes. By means of the telephone and the maid a lot of new and beautiful garments were provided for her, which fitted perfectly, and which bewildered her not a little until they were explained by Marie. Elizabeth had her meals up-stairs until these things had arrived and she had put them on. The texture of the garments was fine and soft, and they were rich with embroidery and lace. The flannels were as soft as the down in a milkweed pod, and everything was of the best. Elizabeth found herself wishing she might share them with Lizzie, — Lizzie who adored rich and beautiful things, and who had shared her meagre outfit with her. She mentioned this wistfully to her grandmother, and in a fit of childish generosity that lady said: "Certainly, get her what you wish. I'll take you downtown some day, and you can pick out some nice things for them all. I hate to be under obligations."

A dozen ready-made dresses had been sent out before the first afternoon was over, and Elizabeth spent the rest of the day in trying on and walking back and forth in front of her grandmother. At last two or three were selected which it was thought would "do" until the dressmaker could be called in to help, and Elizabeth was clothed and allowed to come down into the life of the household.

It was not a large household. It consisted of the grandmother, her dog, and the servants. Elizabeth fitted into it better than she had feared. It seemed pleasanter to her than the house on Flora Street. There was more room, and more air, and more quiet. With her mountain breeding she could not get her breath in a crowd.

She was presently taken in a luxurious carriage, drawn by two beautiful horses, to a large department store, where she sat by the hour and watched her grandmother choose things for her. Another girl might have gone half wild over the delightful experience of being able to have anything in the shops. No so Elizabeth. She watched it all apathetically, as if the goods displayed about had been the leaves upon the trees set forth for her admiration. She could wear but one dress at once, and one hat. Why were so many necessary? Her main hope lay in the words her grandmother had spoken about sending her to school.

The third day of her stay in Rittenhouse Square, Elizabeth had reminded her of it, and the grandmother had said half impatiently: "Yes, yes, child; you shall go of course to a finishing school. That will be necessary. But first I must get you fixed up. You have scarcely anything to put on." So Elizabeth subsided.

At last there dawned a beautiful Sabbath when, the wardrobe seemingly complete, Elizabeth was told to array herself for church, as they were going that morning. With great delight and thanksgiving she put on what she was told; and, when she looked into the great French plate mirror after Marie had put on the finishing touches, she was astonished at herself. It was all true, after all. She was a pretty girl.

She looked down at the beautiful gown of finest broadcloth, with the exquisite finish that only the best tailors can put on a garment, and wondered at herself. The very folds of dark-green cloth seemed to bring a grace into her movements. The green velvet hat with its long curling plumes of green and cream-color seemed to be resting lovingly above the beautiful hair that was arranged so naturally and becomingly.

Elizabeth wore her lovely ermine collar and muff without ever knowing they were costly. They all seemed so fitting and quiet and simple, so much less obtrusive than Lizzie's pink silk waist and cheap pink plumes. Elizabeth liked it, and walked to church beside her grandmother with a happy feeling in her heart.

The church was just across the Square. Its tall brown stone spire and arched doorways attracted Elizabeth when she first came to the place. Now she entered with a kind of delight.

It was the first time she had ever been to a Sabbath morning regular service in church. The Christian Endeavor had been as much as Lizzie had been able to stand. She said she had to work too hard during the week to waste so much time on Sunday in church. "The Sabbath was made for man" and "for rest," she had quoted glibly. For the first time in her life since she left Montana Elizabeth felt as if she had a real home and was like other people. She looked around shyly to see whether perchance her friend of the desert might be sitting near, but no familiar face met her gaze. Then she settled back, and gave herself up to delight in the service.

The organ was playing softly, low, tender music. She learned afterward that the music was Handel's "Largo." She did not know that the organ was one of the finest in the city, nor that the organist was one of the most skillful to be had; she knew only that the music seemed to take her soul and lift it up above the earth so that heaven was all around her, and the very clouds seemed singing to her. Then came the processional, with the wonderful voices of the choir-boys sounding far off, and then nearer. It would be impossible for anyone who had been accustomed all his life to these things to know how it affected Elizabeth.

It seemed as though the Lord Himself was leading the girl in a very special way. At scarcely any other church in a fashionable quarter of the great city would Elizabeth have heard preaching so exactly suited to her needs. The minister was one of those rare men who lived with God, and talked with Him daily. He had one peculiarity which marked him from all other preachers, Elizabeth heard afterward. He would turn and talk with God in a gentle, sweet, conversational tone right in the midst of his sermon. It made the Lord seem very real and very near.

If he had not been the great and brilliant preacher of an old established church, and revered by all denominations as well as his own, the minister would have been called eccentric and have been asked to resign, because his religion was so very personal that it became embarrassing to some. However, his rare gifts, and his remarkable consecration and independence in doing what he thought right, had produced a most unusual church for a fashionable neighborhood.

Most of his church-members were in sympathy with him, and a wonderful work was going forward right in the heart of Sodom, unhampered by fashion or form or class distinctions. It is true there were some who, like Madam Bailey sat calmly in their seats, and let the minister attend to the preaching end of the service without ever bothering their thoughts as to what he was saying. It was all one to them whether he prayed three times or once, so the service got done at the usual hour. But the majority were being led to see that there is such a thing as a close and intimate walk with God upon this earth.

Into this church came Elizabeth, the sweet heathen, eager to learn all that could be learned about the things of the soul. She sat beside her grandmother, and drank in the sermon, and bowed her lovely, reverent head when she became aware that God was in the room and was being spoken to by His servant. After the last echo of the recessional had died away, and the bowed hush of the congregation had grown into a quiet, well-bred commotion of the putting on of wraps and the low Sabbath greetings, Elizabeth turned to her grandmother.

"Grandmother, may I please go and ask that man some questions? He said just what I have been longing and longing to know, and I must ask him more. Nobody else ever told me these things. Who is he? How does he know it is all true?"

The elder woman watched the eager, flushed face of the girl; and her heart throbbed with pride that this beautiful young thing belonged to her. She smiled indulgently.

"The rector, you mean? Why, I'll invite him to dinner if you wish to talk with him. It's perfectly proper that a young girl should understand about religion. It has a most refining influence, and the Doctor is a charming man. I'll invite his wife and daughter too. They move in the best circles, and I have been meaning to ask them for a long time. You might like to be confirmed. Some do. It's a very pretty service. I was confirmed myself when I was about your age. My mother thought it a good thing for a girl before she went into society. Now, just as you are a schoolgirl, is the proper time. I'll send for him this week. He'll be pleased to know you are interested in these things. He has some kind of a young people's club that meets on Sunday. 'Christian Something' he calls it; I don't know just what, but he talks a great deal about it, and wants every young person to join. You might pay the dues, whatever they are, anyway. I suppose it's for charity. It wouldn't be necessary for you to attend the meetings, but it would please the Doctor."

"Is it Christian Endeavor?" asked Elizabeth, with her eyes sparkling.

"Something like that, I believe. Good morning, Mrs. Schuyler. Lovely day, isn't it? for December. No, I haven't been very well. No, I haven't been out for several weeks. Charming service, wasn't it? The Doctor grows more and more brilliant, I think. Mrs. Schuyler, this is my granddaughter, Elizabeth. She has just come from the West to live with me and complete her education. I want her to know your daughter."

Elizabeth passed through the introduction as a necessary interruption to her train of thought. As soon as they were out upon the street again she began.

"Grandmother, was God in that church?"

"Dear me, child! What strange questions you do ask! Why, yes, I suppose He was, in a way. God is everywhere, they say. Elizabeth, you had better wait until you can talk these things over with a person whose business it is. I never understood much about such questions. You look very nice in that shade of green, and your hat is most becoming."

So was the question closed for the time, but not put out of the girl's thoughts.

The Christmas time had come and passed without much notice on the part of Elizabeth, to whom it was an unfamiliar festival. Mrs. Bailey had suggested that she select some gifts for her "relatives on her mother's side," as she always spoke of the Bradys; and Elizabeth had done so with alacrity, showing good sense and good taste in her choice of gifts, as well as deference to the wishes of the one to whom they were to be given. Lizzie, it is true, was a trifle disappointed that her present was not a gold watch or a diamond ring; but on the whole she was pleased.

A new world opened before the feet of Elizabeth. School was filled with wonder and delight. She absorbed knowledge like a sponge in the water, and rushed eagerly from one study to another, showing marvellous aptitude, and bringing to every task the enthusiasm of a pleasure-seeker.

Her growing intimacy with Jesus Christ through the influence of the pastor who knew Him so well caused her joy in life to blossom into loveliness.

The Bible she studied with the zest of a novel-reader, for it was a novel to her; and daily, as she took her rides in the park on Robin, now groomed into self-respecting sleekness, and wearing a saddle of the latest approved style, she marvelled over God's wonderful goodness to her, just a maid of the wilderness.

So passed three beautiful years in peace and quietness. Every month Elizabeth went to see her Grandmother Brady, and to take some charming little gifts; and every summer she and her Grandmother Bailey spent at some of the fashionable watering-places or in the Catskills, the girl always dressed in most exquisite taste, and as sweetly indifferent in her clothes as a bird of the air or a flower of the field.

The first pocket-money she had been given she saved up, and before long had enough to send the forty dollars to the address the man in the wilderness had given her. But with it she sent no word. It was like her to think she had no right.

She went out more and more with her grandmother among the fashionable old families in Philadelphia society, though as yet she was not supposed to be "out," being still in school; but in all her goings she neither saw nor heard of George Trescott Benedict.

Often she looked about upon the beautiful women that came to her grandmother's house, who smiled and talked to her, and wondered which of them might be the lady to whom his heart was bound. She fancied she must be most sweet and lovely in every way, else such as he could not care for her; so she would pick out this one and that one; and then, as some disagreeableness or glaring fault would appear, she would drop that one for another. There were only a few, after all, that she felt were good enough for the man who had become her ideal.

But sometimes in her dreams he would come and talk with her, and smile as he used to do when they rode together; and he would lay his hand on the mane of her horse — there were always the horses in her dreams. She liked to think of it when she rode in the park, and to think how pleasant it would be if he could be riding there beside her, and they might talk of a great many things that had happened since he left her alone. She felt she would like to tell him of how she had found a friend in Jesus Christ. He would be glad to know about it, she was sure. He seemed to be one who was interested in such things, not like other people who were all engaged in the world.

Sometimes she felt afraid something had happened to him. He might have been thrown from that terrible train and killed, perhaps; and no one know anything about it. But as her experience grew wider, and she travelled on the trains herself, of course this fear grew less. She came to understand that the world was wide, and many things might have taken him away from his home.

Perhaps the money she had sent reached him safely, but she had put in no address. It had not seemed right that she should. It would seem to draw his attention to her, and she felt "the lady" would not like that. Perhaps they were married by this time, and had gone far away to some charmed land to live. Perhaps — a great many things. Only this fact remained; he never came any more into the horizon of her life; and therefore she must try to forget him, and be glad that God had given her a friend in him for her time of need. Some day in the eternal home perhaps she would meet him and thank him for his kindness to her, and then they might tell each other all about the journey through the great wilderness of earth after they had parted. The links in Elizabeth's theology had been well supplied by this time, and her belief in the hereafter was strong and simple like a child's.

She had one great longing, however, that he, her friend, who had in a way been the first to help her toward higher things, and to save her from the wilderness, might know Jesus Christ as he had not known Him when they were together. And so in her daily prayer she often talked to her heavenly Father about him, until she came to have an abiding faith that some day, somehow, he would learn the truth about his Christ.

During the third season of Elizabeth's life in Philadelphia her grandmother decided that it was high time to bring out this bud of promise, who was by this time developing into a more beautiful girl than even her fondest hopes had pictured.

So Elizabeth "came out," and Grandmother Brady read her doings and sayings in the society columns with her morning coffee and an air of deep satisfaction. Aunt Nan listened with her nose in the air. She could never understand why Elizabeth should have privileges beyond her Lizzie. It was the Bailey in her, of course, and mother ought not to think well of it. But Grandmother Brady felt that, while Elizabeth's success was doubtless due in large part to the Bailey in her, still, she was a Brady, and the Brady had not hindered her. It was a step upward for the Bradys.

Lizzie listened, and with pride retailed at the ten-cent store the doings of "my cousin, Elizabeth Bailey," and the other girls listened with awe.

And so it came on to be the springtime of the third year that Elizabeth had spent in Philadelphia.

Chapter 15
An Eventful Picnic

It was summer and it was June. There was to be a picnic, and Elizabeth was going.

Grandmother Brady had managed it. It seemed to her that, if Elizabeth could go, her cup of pride would be full to overflowing; so after much argument, pro and con, with her daughter and Lizzie, she set herself down to pen the invitation. Aunt Nan was decidedly against it. She did not wish to have Lizzie outshone. She had been working nights for two weeks on an elaborate organdie, with pink roses all over it, for Lizzie to wear. It had yards and yards of cheap lace and insertion, and a whole bolt of pink ribbons of various widths. The hat was a marvel of impossible roses, just calculated for the worst kind of a wreck if a thunder-shower should come up at a Sunday-school picnic. Lizzie's mother was even thinking of getting her a pink chiffon parasol to carry; but the family treasury was well-nigh depleted, and it was doubtful whether that would be possible. After all that, it did not seem pleasant to have Lizzie put in the shade by a fine-lady cousin in silks and jewels.

But Grandmother Brady had waited long for her triumph. She desired above all things to walk among her friends and introduce her granddaughter, Elizabeth Bailey, and inadvertently remark: "You must have seen me granddaughter's name in the paper often, Mrs. Babcock. She was giving a party in Rittenhouse Square the other day."

Elizabeth would likely be married soon, and perhaps go off somewhere away from Philadelphia — New York or Europe, there was no telling what great fortune might come to her. Now the time was ripe for triumph if ever, and when things are ripe they must be picked. Mrs. Brady proceeded to pick.

She gathered together at great pains pen, paper, and ink. A pencil would be inadequate when the note was going to Rittenhouse Square. She sat down when Nan and Lizzie had left for their day's work, and constructed her sentences with great care.

"Dear Bessie —" Elizabeth had never asked her not to call her that, although she fairly detested the name. But still it had been her mother's name, and was likely dear to her grandmother. It seemed disloyalty to her

mother to suggest that she be called "Elizabeth." So Grandmother Brady serenely continued to call her "Bessie" to the end of her days. Elizabeth decided that to care much about such little things, in a world where there were so many great things, would be as bad as to give one's mind entirely over to the pursuit of fashion.

The letter proceeded laboriously:

"Our Sunday school is going to have a picnic out to Willow Grove. It's on Tuesday. We're going in the trolley. I'd be pleased if you would go 'long with us. We will spend the day, and take our dinner and supper along, and wouldn't get home till late; so you could stay overnight here with us, and not go back home till after breakfast. You needn't bring no lunch; fer we've got a lot of things planned, and it ain't worth while. But if you wanted to bring some candy, you might. I ain't got time to make any, and what you buy at our grocery might not be fine enough for you. I want you to go real bad. I've never took my two granddaughters off to anything yet, and your Grandmother Bailey has you to things all the time. I hope you can manage to come. I am going to pay all the expenses. Your old Christian Deaver you used to 'tend is going to be there; so you'll have a good time. Lizzie has a new pink organdie, with roses on her hat; and we're thinking of getting her a pink umbreller if it don't cost too much. The kind with chiffon flounces on it. You'll have a good time, fer there's lots of side-shows out to Willow Grove, and we're going to see everything there is to see. There's going to be some music too. A man with a name that sounds like swearing is going to make it. I don't remember it just now, but you can see it advertised round on the trolley-cars. He comes to Willow Grove every year. Now please let me hear if you will go at once, as I want to know how much cake to make.

"Your loving grandmother,
"ELIZABETH BRADY."

Elizabeth laughed and cried over this note. It pleased her to have her grandmother show kindness to her. She felt that whatever she did for Grandmother Brady was in a sense showing her love to her own mother; so she brushed aside several engagements, much to the annoyance of her Grandmother Bailey, who could not understand why she wanted to go down to Flora Street for two days and a night just in the beginning of warm weather. True, there was not much going on just now between seasons, and Elizabeth could do as she pleased; but she might get a fever in such a crowded neighborhood. It wasn't in the least wise. However, if she must, she must. Grandmother Bailey was on the whole lenient. Elizabeth was too much of a success, and too willing to please her in all things, for her to care to cross her wishes.

So Elizabeth wrote on her fine note-paper bearing the Bailey crest in silver:

"Dear Grandmother: I shall be delighted to go to the picnic with you, and I'll bring a nice box of candy, Huyler's best. I'm sure you'll think it's the best you ever tasted. Don't get Lizzie a parasol; I'm going to bring her one to surprise her. I'll be at the house by eight o'clock.

"Your loving granddaughter,

"ELIZABETH."

Mrs. Brady read this note with satisfaction and handed it over to her daughter to read with a gleam of triumph in her eyes at the suppertable. She knew the gift of the pink parasol would go far toward reconciling Aunt Nan to the addition to their party. Elizabeth never did things by halves, and the parasol would be all that could possibly be desired without straining the family pocketbook any further.

So Elizabeth went to the picnic in a cool white dimity, plainly made, with tiny frills of itself, edged with narrow lace that did not shout to the unknowing multitude, "I am real!" but was content with being so; and with a white Panama hat adorned with only a white silken scarf, but whose texture was possible only at a fabulous price. The shape reminded Elizabeth of the old felt hat belonging to her brother, which she had worn on her long trip across the continent. She had put it on in the hat-store one day; and her grandmother, when she found how exquisite a piece of weaving the hat was, at once purchased it for her. It was stylish to wear those soft hats in all sorts of odd shapes. Madam Bailey thought it would be just the thing for the seashore.

Her hair was worn in a low coil on her neck, making the general appearance and contour of her head much as it had been three years before. She wore no jewelry, save the unobtrusive gold buckle at her belt and the plain gold hatpin which fastened her hat. There was nothing about her which marked her as one of the "four hundred." She did not even wear the gloves, but carried them in her hand, and threw them carelessly upon the table when she arrived in Flora Street. Long, soft white ones, they lay there in their costly elegance beside Lizzie's postcard album that the livery-stable man gave her on her birthday, all the long day while Elizabeth was at Willow Grove, and Lizzie sweltered around under her pink parasol in long white silk gloves.

Grandmother Brady surveyed Elizabeth with decided disapproval. It seemed too bad on this her day of triumph, and after she had given a hint, as it were, about Lizzie's fine clothes, that the girl should be so blind or stubborn or both as to come around in that plain rig. Just a common white dress, and an old hat that might have been worn about a livery-stable. It was mortifying in the extreme. She expected a light silk, and kid gloves, and a beflowered hat. Why, Lizzie looked a great deal finer. Did Mrs. Bailey rig her out this way for spite? she wondered.

But, as it was too late to send Elizabeth back for more fitting garments, the old lady resigned herself to her disappointment. The pink parasol was lovely, and Lizzie was wild over it. Even Aunt Nan seemed mollified. It gave her great satisfaction to look the two girls over. Her own outshone the one from Rittenhouse Square by many counts, so thought the mother; but all day long, as she walked behind them or viewed them from afar, she could not understand why it was that the people who passed them always looked twice at Elizabeth and only once at Lizzie. It seemed, after all, that clothes did not make the girl. It was disappointing.

The box of candy was all that could possibly be desired. It was ample for the needs of them all, including the two youths from the livery-stable who had attached themselves to their party from the early morning. In fact, it was two boxes, one of the most delectable chocolates of all imaginable kinds, and the other of mixed candies and candied fruit. Both boxes bore the magic name "Huyler's" on the covers. Lizzie had often passed Huyler's, taking her noon walk on Chestnut Street, and looked enviously at the girls who walked in and out with white square bundles tied with gold cord as if it were an everyday affair. And now she was actually eating all she pleased of those renowned candies. It was almost like belonging to the great elite.

It was a long day and a pleasant one even to Elizabeth. She had never been to Willow Grove before, and the strange blending of sweet nature and Vanity Fair charmed her. It was a rest after the winter's round of monotonous engagements. Even the loud-voiced awkward youths from the livery-stable did not annoy her extremely. She took them as a part of the whole, and did not pay much attention to them. They were rather shy of her, giving the most of their attention to Lizzie, much to the satisfaction of Aunt Nan.

They mounted the horses in the merry-go-rounds, and tried each one several times. Elizabeth wondered why anybody desired this sort of amusement, and after her first trip would have been glad to sit with her grandmother and watch the others, only that the old lady seemed so much to desire to have her get on with the rest. She would not do anything to spoil the pleasure of the others if she could help it; so she obediently seated herself in a great sea-shell drawn by a soiled plaster nymph, and whirled on till Lizzie declared it was time to go to something else.

They went into the Old Mill, and down into the Mimic Mine, and sailed through the painted Venice, eating candy and chewing gum and shouting. All but Elizabeth. Elizabeth would not chew gum nor talk loud. It was not her way. But she smiled serenely on the rest, and did not let it worry her that someone might recognize the popular Miss Bailey in so ill-bred a crowd. She knew that it was their way, and they could have no other. They were having a good time, and she was a part of it for to-day. They weighed one another on the scales with many jokes and much laughter, and went to see all the moving pictures in the place. They ate their lunch under the trees, and then at last the music began.

They seated themselves on the outskirts of the company, for Lizzie declared that was the only pleasant place to be. She did not want to go "way up front." She had a boy on either side of her, and she kept the seat shaking with laughter. Now and then a weary guard would look distressedly down the line, and motion for less noise; but they giggled on. Elizabeth was glad they were so far back that they might not annoy more people than was necessary.

But the music was good, and she watched the leader with great satisfaction. She noticed that there were many people given up to the pleasure of it. The melody went to her soul, and thrilled through it. She had not had much good music in her life. The last three years, of course, she had been occasionally to the Academy of Music; but, though her grandmother had a box there, she very seldom had time or cared to attend concerts. Sometimes, when Melba, or Caruso, or some world-renowned favorite was there, she would take Elizabeth for an hour, usually slipping out just after the favorite solo with noticeable loftiness, as if the orchestra were the common dust of the earth, and she only condescended to come for the soloist. So Elizabeth had scarcely known the delight of a whole concert of fine orchestral music.

She heard Lizzie talking.

"Yes, that's Walter Damrosh! Ain't that name fierce? Grandma thinks it's kind of wicked to pernounce it that way. They say he's fine, but I must say I liked the band they had last year better. It played a whole lot of lively things, and once they had a rattle-box and a squeaking thing that cried like a baby right out in the music, and everybody just roared laughing. I tell you that was great. I don't care much for this here kind of music myself. Do you?" And Jim and Joe both agreed that they didn't, either. Elizabeth smiled, and kept on enjoying it.

Peanuts were the order of the day, and their assertive crackle broke in upon the finest passages. Elizabeth wished her cousin would take a walk;

and by and by she did, politely inviting Elizabeth to go along; but she declined, and they were left to sit through the remainder of the afternoon concert.

After supper they watched the lights come out, Elizabeth thinking about the description of the heavenly city as one after another the buildings blazed out against the darkening blue of the June night. The music was about to begin. Indeed, it could be heard already in the distance, and drew the girl irresistibly. For the first time that day she made a move, and the others followed, half wearied of their dissipations, and not knowing exactly what do to next.

They stood the first half of the concert very well, but at the intermission they wandered out to view the electric fountain with its many-colored fluctuations, and to take a row on the tiny sheet of water. Elizabeth remained sitting where she was, and watched the fountain. Even her grandmother and aunt grew restless, and wanted to walk again. They said they had had enough music, and did not want to hear any more. They could hear it well enough, anyway, from further off. They believed they would have some ice-cream. Didn't Elizabeth want some?

She smiled sweetly. Would Grandmother mind if she sat right there and heard the second part of the concert? She loved music, and this was fine. She didn't feel like eating another thing to-night. So the two ladies, thinking the girl queer that she didn't want ice-cream, went off to enjoy theirs with a clear conscience; and Elizabeth drew a long breath, and sat back with her eyes closed, to rest and breathe in the sweet sounds that were beginning to float out delicately as if to feel whether the atmosphere were right for what was to come after.

It was just at the close of this wonderful music, which the programme said was Mendelssohn's "Spring Song," when Elizabeth looked up to meet the eyes of someone who stood near in the aisle watching her, and there beside her stood the man of the wilderness!

He was looking at her face, drinking in the beauty of the profile and wondering whether he was right. Could it be that this was his little brown friend, the maid of the wilderness? This girl with the lovely, refined face, the intellectual brow, the dainty fineness of manner? She looked like some white angel dropped down into that motley company of Sunday-school picknickers and city pleasure-seekers. The noise and clatter of the place seemed far away from her. She was absorbed utterly in the sweet sounds.

When she looked up and saw him, the smile that flashed out upon her face was like the sunshine upon a day that has hitherto been still and almost sad. The eyes said, "You are come at last!" The curve of the lips said, "I am glad you are here!"

He went to her like one who had been hungry for the sight of her for a long time, and after he had grasped her hand they stood so for a moment while the hum and gentle clatter of talk that always starts between numbers seethed around them and hid the few words they spoke at first.

"O, I have so longed to know if you were safe!" said the man as soon as he could speak.

Then straightway the girl forgot all her three years of training, and her success as a débutante, and became the grave, shy thing she had been to him when he first saw her, looking up with awed delight into the face she had seen in her dreams for so long, and yet might not long for.

The orchestra began again, and they sat in silence listening. But yet their souls seemed to speak to each other through the medium of the music, as if the intervening years were being bridged and brought together in the space of those few waves of melody.

"I have found out," said Elizabeth, looking up shyly with a great light in her eyes. "I have found what it all means. Have you? O, I have wanted so much to know whether you had found out too!"

"Found out what?" he asked half sadly that he did not understand.

"Found out how God hides us. Found what a friend Jesus Christ can be."

"You are just the same," said the man with satisfaction in his eyes. "You have not been changed nor spoiled. They could not spoil you."

"Have you found out too?" she asked softly. She looked up into his eyes with wistful longing. She wanted this thing so very much. It had been in her prayers for so long.

He could not withdraw his own glance. He did not wish to. He longed to be able to answer what she wished.

"A little, perhaps," he said doubtfully. "Not so much as I would like to. Will you help me?"

"*He* will help you. You will find Him if you search for Him with all your heart," she said earnestly. "It says so in His book."

Then came more music, wistful, searching, tender. Did it speak of the things of heaven to other souls there than those two?

He stooped down, and said in a low tone that somehow seemed to blend with the music like the words that fitted it:

"I will try with all my heart if you will help me."

She smiled her answer, brimming back with deep delight.

Into the final lingering notes of an andante from one of Beethoven's sublime symphonies clashed the loud voice of Lizzie:

"O Bess! Bess! B-es-see! I say, Bessie! Ma says we'll have to go over by the cars now if we want to get a seat. The concert's most out, and there'll be a fierce rush. Come on! And Grandma says, bring your friend along with you if you want." This last with a smirking recognition of the man, who had turned around wonderingly to see who was speaking.

With a quick, searching glance that took in bedraggled organdie, rose hat, and pink parasol, and set them aside for what they were worth, George Benedict observed and classified Lizzie.

"Will you excuse yourself, and let me take you home a little later?" he asked in a low tone. "The crowd will be very great, and I have my automobile here."

She looked at him gratefully, and assented. She had much to tell him. She leaned across the seats, and spoke in a clear tone to her cousin.

"I will come a little later," she said, smiling with her Rittenhouse Square look that always made Lizzie a little afraid of her. "Tell Grandmother I have found an old friend I have not seen for a long time. I will be there almost as soon as you are."

They waited while Lizzie explained, and the grandmother and aunt nodded a reluctant assent. Aunt Nan frowned. Elizabeth might have brought her friend along, and introduced him to Lizzie. Did Elizabeth think Lizzie wasn't good enough to be introduced?

He wrapped her in a great soft rug that was in the automobile, and tucked her in beside him; and she felt as if the long, hard days that had passed since they had met were all forgotten and obliterated in this night of delight. Not all the attentions of all the fine men she had met in society had ever been like his, so gentle, so perfect. She had forgotten the lady as completely as if she had never heard of her. She wanted now to tell her friend about her heavenly Father.

He let her talk, and watched her glowing, earnest face by the dim light of the sky; for the moon had come out to crown the night with beauty, and the unnatural brilliance of electric blaze, with all the glitter and noise of Willow Grove, died into the dim, sweet night as those two sped onward toward the city. The heart of the man kept singing, singing, singing: "I have found her at last! She is safe!"

"I have prayed for you always," he said in one of the pauses. It was just as they were coming into Flora Street. The urchins were all out on the sidewalk yet, for the night was hot; and they gathered about, and ran hooting after the car as it slowed up at the door. "I am sure He did hide you safely, and I shall thank Him for answering my prayer. And now I am coming to see you. May I come to-morrow?"

There was a great gladness in her eyes. "Yes," she said.

The Bradys had arrived from the corner trolley, and were hovering about the door self-assertively. It was almost apparent to an onlooker that this was a good opportunity for an introduction, but the two young people were entirely oblivious. The man touched his hat gravely, a look of great admiration in his eye, and said, "Good night" like a benediction. Then the girl turned and went into the plain little home and to her belligerent relatives with a light in her eyes and a joy in her steps that had not been there earlier in the day. The dreams that visited her hard pillow that night were heavenly and sweet.

Chapter 16
Alone Again

"Now we're goin' to see ef the paper says anythin' about our Bessie," said Grandmother Brady the next morning, settling her spectacles over her nose comfortably and crossing one fat gingham knee over the other. "I always read the society notes, Bess."

Elizabeth smiled, and her grandmother read down the column:

"Mr. George Trescott Benedict and his mother, Mrs. Vincent Benedict, have arrived home after an extended tour of Europe," read Mrs. Brady. "Mrs. Benedict is much improved in health. It is rumored they will spend the summer in their country seat on Wissahickon Heights."

"My!" interrupted Lizzie with her mouth full of fried potatoes. "That's the fellow that was engaged to that Miss What's-her-Name Loring. Don't you 'member? They had his picture in the papers, and her; and then all at once she threw him over for some dook or something, and this feller went off. I heard about it from Mame. Her sister works in a department-store, and she knows Miss Loring. She says she's an awfully handsome girl, and George Benedict was just gone on her. He had a fearful case. Mame says Miss Loring — what *is* her name? — O, Geraldine — Geraldine Loring bought some lace of her. She heard her say it was for the gown she was going to wear at the horse-show. They had her picture in the paper just after the horse-show, and it was all over lace. I saw it. It cost a whole lot. I forget how many dollars a yard. But there was something the matter with the dook. She didn't marry him, after all. In her picture she was driving four horses. Don't you remember it, Grandma? She sat up tall and high on a seat, holding a whole lot of ribbons and whips and things. She has an elegant figger. I guess mebbe the dook wasn't rich enough. She hasn't been engaged to anybody else, and I shouldn't wonder now but she'd take George Benedict back. He was so awful stuck on her!"

Lizzie rattled on, and the grandmother read more society notes, but Elizabeth heard no more. Her heart had suddenly frozen, and dropped down like lead into her being. She felt as if she never would be able to raise it again. The lady! Surely she had forgotten the lady. But Geraldine Loring! Of all women! Could it be possible! Geraldine Loring was almost—well, fast, at least, as nearly so as one who was really of a fine old family, and still held her own in society, could be. She was beautiful as a picture; but her face, to Elizabeth's mind, was lacking in fine feeling and intellect. A great pity went out from her heart to the man whose fate was in the doll-girl's hands. True, she had heard that Miss Loring's family were unquestionable, and she knew her mother was a most charming woman. Perhaps she had misjudged her, for it could not be otherwise.

The joy had gone out of the morning when Elizabeth went home. She went up to her Grandmother Bailey at once, and after she had read her letters for her, and performed the little services that were her habit, she said; "Grandmother, I'm expecting a man to call upon me to-day. I thought I had better tell you."

"A man!" said Madam Bailey, alarmed at once. She wanted to look over and portion out the right man when the time came. "What man?"

"Why, a man I met in Montana, " said Elizabeth, wondering how much she ought to tell.

"A man you met in Montana! Horrors!" exclaimed the now thoroughly aroused grandmother. "Not that dreadful creature you ran away from?"

"O no!" said Elizabeth, smiling. "Not that man. A man who was very kind to me, and whom I like very much."

So much the worse. Immediate action was necessary.

"Well, Elizabeth," said Madam Bailey in her stiffest tones, "I really do not care to have any of your Montana friends visit you. You will have to excuse yourself. It will lead to embarrassing entanglements. You do not in the least realize your position in society. It is all well enough to please relatives, although I think you often overdo that. You could just as well send them a present now and then, and please them more that to go yourself. But as for any outsiders, it is impossible. I draw the line there."

"But Grandmother—"

"Don't interrupt me, Elizabeth; I have something more to say. I had word this morning from the steamship company. They can give us our staterooms on the Deutschland on Saturday, and I have decided to take them. I have telegraphed, and we shall leave here to-day for New York. We shall go to the Waldorf for a few days, and you will have more opportunity to see New York than you have yet. It will not be too warm to enjoy going about a little, I fancy; and a number of our friends are going to be at the Waldorf, too. The Craigs sail on Saturday with us. You will have young company on the voyage."

Elizabeth's heart sank lower than she had known it could go, and she grew white to the lips. The observant grandmother decided that she had done well to be so prompt. The man from Montana was by no means to be admitted. She gave orders to that effect, unknown to Elizabeth.

The girl went slowly to her room. All at once it had dawned upon her that she had not given her address to the man the night before, nor told him by so much as a word what were her circumstances. An hour's meditation brought her to the unpleasant decision that perhaps even now in this hard spot God was only hiding her from worse trouble. Mr. George Benedict belonged to Geraldine Loring. He had declared as much when he was in Montana. It would not be well for her to renew the acquaintance. Her heart told her by its great ache that she would be crushed under a friendship that could not be lasting.

Very sadly she sat down to write a note.

"My dear Friend," she wrote on plain paper with no crest. It was like her to choose that. She would not flaunt her good fortune to his face. She was a plain Montana girl to him, and so she would remain.

"My grandmother has been very ill, and is obliged to go away for her health. Unexpectedly I find that we are to go to-day. I supposed it would not be for a week yet. I am so sorry not to see you again, but I send you a little book that has helped me to get acquainted with Jesus Christ. Perhaps it will help you too. It is called 'My Best Friend.' I shall not forget to pray always that you may find Him. He is so precious to me! I must thank you in words, though I never can say it as it should be said, for your very great kindness to me when I was in trouble. God sent you to me, I am sure. Always gratefully your friend,

"ELIZABETH."

That was all, no date, no address. He was not hers, and she would hang out no clues for him to find her, even if he wished. It was better so.

She sent the note and the little book to his address on Walnut Street; and then after writing a note to her Grandmother Brady, saying that she was going away for a long trip with Grandmother Bailey, she gave herself into the hands of the future like a submissive but weary child.

The noon train to New York carried in its drawing-room-car Madam Bailey, her granddaughter, her maid, and her dog, bound for Europe. The society columns so stated; and so read Grandmother Brady a few days afterward. So also read George Benedict, but it meant nothing to him.

When he received the note, his mind was almost as much excited as when he saw the little brown girl and the little brown horse vanishing behind the little brown station on the prairie. He went to the telephone, and reflected that he knew no names. He called up his automobile, and tore up to Flora Street; but in his bewilderment of the night before he had not noticed which block the house was in, nor which number. He thought he knew where to find it, but in broad daylight the houses were all alike for three blocks, and for the life of him he could not remember whether he had turned up to the right or the left when he came to Flora Street. He tried both, but saw no sign of the people he had but casually noticed at Willow Grove.

He could not ask where she lived, for he did not know her name. Nothing but Elizabeth, and they had called her Bessie. He could not go from house to house asking for a girl named Bessie. They would think him a fool, as he was, for not finding out her name, her precious name, at once. How could he let her slip from him again when he had just found her?

At last he hit upon a bright idea. He asked some children along the street whether they knew of any young woman named Bessie or Elizabeth living there, but they all with one accord shook their heads, though one volunteered the information that "Lizzie Smith lives there." It was most distracting and unsatisfying. There was nothing for it but for him to go home and wait in patience for her return. She would come back sometime probably. She had not said so, but she had not said she would not. He had found her once; he might find her again. And he could pray. She had found comfort in that; so would he. He would learn what her secret was. He would get acquainted with her "best Friend." Diligently did he study that little book, and then he went and hunted up the man of God who had written it, and who had been the one to lead Elizabeth into the path of light by his earnest preaching every Sabbath, though this fact he did not know.

The days passed, and the Saturday came. Elizabeth, heavy-hearted, stood on the deck of the Deutschland, and watched her native land disappear from view. So again George Benedict had lost her from sight.

It struck Elizabeth, as she stood straining her eyes to see the last of the shore through tears that would burn to the surface and fall down her white cheeks, that again she was running away from a man, only this time not of her own free will. She was being taken away. But perhaps it was better.

And it never once entered her mind that, if she had told her grandmother who the friend in Montana was, and where he lived in Philadelphia, it would have made all the difference in the world.

From the first of the voyage Grandmother Bailey grew steadily worse, and when they landed on the other side they went from one place to another seeking health. Carlsbad waters did not agree with her, and they went to the south of France to try the climate. At each move the little old lady grew weaker and more querulous. She finally made no further resistance, and gave up to the role of invalid. Then Elizabeth must be in constant attendance. Madam Bailey demanded reading, and no voice was so soothing as Elizabeth's.

Gradually Elizabeth substituted books of her own choice as her grandmother seemed not to mind, and now and then she would read a page of some book that told of the best Friend. At first because it was written by the dear pastor at home it commanded her attention, and finally because some dormant chord in her heart had been touched, she allowed Elizabeth to speak of these things. But it was not until they had been away from home for three months, and she had been growing daily weaker and weaker, that she allowed Elizabeth to read in the Bible.

The girl chose the fourteenth chapter of John, and over and over again, whenever the restless nerves tormented their victim, she would read those words, "Let not your heart be troubled" until the selfish soul, who had lived all her life to please the world and do her own pleasure, came at last to hear the words, and feel that perhaps she did believe in God, and might accept that invitation, "Believe also in me."

One day Elizabeth had been reading a psalm, and thought her grandmother was asleep. She was sitting back with weary heart, thinking what would happen if her grandmother should not get well. The old lady opened her eyes.

"Elizabeth," she said abruptly, just as when she was well, "you've been a good girl. I'm glad you came. I couldn't have died right without you. I never thought much about these things before, but it really is worth while. In my Father's house. He is my Father, Elizabeth."

She went to sleep then, and Elizabeth tiptoed out and left her with the nurse. By and by Marie came crying in, and told her that the Madam was dead.

Elizabeth was used to having people die. She was not shocked; only it seemed lonely again to find herself facing the world, in a foreign land. And when she came to face the arrangements that had to be made, which, after all, money and servants made easy, she found herself dreading her own land. What must she do after her grandmother was laid to rest? She could not live in the great house in Rittenhouse Square, and neither could she very well go and live in Flora Street. O, well, her Father would hide her. She need not plan; He would plan for her. The mansions on the earth were His too, as well as those in heaven.

And so resting she passed through the weary voyage and the day when the body was laid to rest in the Bailey lot in the cemetery, and she went back to the empty house alone. It was not until after the funeral that she went to see Grandmother Brady. She had not thought it wise or fitting to invite the hostile grandmother to the other one's funeral. She had thought Grandmother Bailey would not like it.

She rode to Flora Street in the carriage. She felt too weary to walk or go in the trolley. She was taking account of stock in the way of friends, thinking over whom she cared to see. One of the first bits of news she had heard on arriving in this country had been that Miss Loring's wedding was to come off in a few days. It seemed to strike her like a thunderbolt, and she was trying to arraign herself for this as she rode along. It was therefore not helpful to her state of mind to have her grandmother remark grimly:

"That feller o' yurs 'n his aughtymobble has been goin' up an' down this street, day in, day out, this whole blessed summer. Ain't been a day he didn't pass, sometimes once, sometimes twicet. I felt sorry fer him sometimes. Ef he hadn't been so high an' mighty stuck up that he couldn't recognize me, I'd 'a' spoke to him. It was plain ez the nose on your face he was lookin' fer you. Don't he know where you live?"

"I don't believe he does," said Elizabeth languidly. "Say, Grandmother, would you care to come up to Rittenhouse Square and live?"

"Me? In Rittenhouse Square? Fer the land sakes, child, no. That's flat. I've lived me days out in me own sp'ere, and I don't intend to change now at me time o' life. Ef you want to do somethin' nice for me, child, now you've got all that money, I'd like real well to live in a house that hed white marble steps. It's been me one aim all me life. There's some round on the next street that don't come high. There'd be plenty room for us all, an' a nice place fer Lizzie to get married when the time comes. The parlor's real big, and you could send her some roses, couldn't you?"

"All right, Grandmother. You shall have it," said Elizabeth with a relieved sigh, and in a few minutes she went home. Some day pretty soon she must think what to do, but there was no immediate hurry. She was glad that Grandmother Brady did not want to come to Rittenhouse Square. Things would be more congenial without her.

But the house seemed great and empty when she entered, and she was glad to hear the friendly telephone bell ringing. It was the wife of her pastor, asking her to come to them for a quiet dinner.

This was the one home in the great city where she felt like going in her loneliness. There would be no form nor ceremony. Just a friend with them. It was good. The doctor would give her some helpful words. She was glad they had asked her.

Chapter 17

A Final Flight and Pursuit

"George," said Mrs. Vincent Benedict, "I want you to do something for me."

"Certainly, Mother, anything I can."

"Well, it's only to go to dinner with me to-night. Our pastor's wife has telephoned me that she wants us very much. She especially emphasized you. She said she absolutely needed you. It was a case of charity, and she would be so grateful to you if you would come. She has a young friend with her who is very sad, and she wants to cheer her up. Now don't frown. I won't bother you again this week. I know you hate dinners and girls. But really, George, this is an unusual case. The girl is just home from Europe, and buried her grandmother yesterday. She hasn't a soul in the world belonging to her that can be with her, and the pastor's wife has asked her over to dinner quietly. Of course she isn't going out. She must be in mourning. And you know you're fond of the doctor."

"Yes, I'm fond of the doctor," said George, frowning discouragedly; "but I'd rather take him alone, and not with a girl flung at me everlastingly. I'm tired of it. I didn't think it of Christian people, though; I thought she was above such things."

"Now, George," said his mother severely, "that's a real insult to the girl, and to our friend too. She hasn't an idea of doing any such thing. It seems this girl is quite unusual, very religious, and our friend thought you would be just the one to cheer her. She apologized several times for presuming to ask you to help her. You really will have to go."

"Well, who is this paragon, anyway? Anyone I know? I suppose I've got to go."

"Why, she's a Miss Bailey," said the mother, relieved. "Mrs. Wilton Merrill Bailey's granddaughter. Did you ever happen to meet her? I never did."

"Never heard of her," growled George. "Wish I hadn't now."

"George!"

"Well, Mother, go on. I'll be good. What does she do? Dance, and play bridge, and sing?"

"I haven't heard anything that she does," said his mother, laughing.

"Well, of course she's a paragon; they all are, Mother. I'll be ready in half an hour. Let's go and get it done. We can come home early, can't we?"

Mrs. Benedict sighed. If only George would settle down on some suitable girl of good family! But he was so queer and restless. She was afraid for him. Ever since she had taken him away to Europe, when she was so ill, she had been afraid for him. He seemed so moody and absent-minded then and afterwards. Now this Miss Bailey was said to be as beautiful as she was good. If only George would take a notion to her!

Elizabeth was sitting in a great arm-chair by the open fire when he entered the room. He had not expected to find anyone there. He heard voices up-stairs, and supposed Miss Bailey was talking with her hostess. His mother followed the servant to remove her wraps, and he entered the drawing-room alone. She stirred, looked up, and saw him.

"Elizabeth!" he said, and came forward to grasp her hand. "I have found you again. How came you here?"

But she had no opportunity to answer, for the ladies entered almost at once, and there stood the two smiling at each other.

"Why, you have met before!" exclaimed the hostess. "How delighted I am! I knew you two would enjoy meeting. Elizabeth, child, you never told me you knew George."

George Benedict kept looking around for Miss Bailey to enter the room; but to his relief she did not come, and, when they went out to the dining-room, there was no place set for her. She must have preferred to remain at home. He forgot her, and settled down to the joy of having Elizabeth by his side. His mother, opposite, watched his face blossom into the old-time joy as he handed this new girl the olives, and had eyes for no one else.

It was to Elizabeth a blessed evening. They held sweet converse one with another as children of the King. For a little time under the old influence of the restful, helpful talk she forgot "the lady," and all the perplexing questions that had vexed her soul. She knew only that she had entered into an atmosphere of peace and love and joy.

It was not until the evening was over, and the guests were about to leave, that Mrs. Benedict addressed Elizabeth as Miss Bailey. Up to that moment it had not entered her son's mind that Miss Bailey was present at all. He turned with a start, and looked into Elizabeth's eyes; and she smiled back to him as if to acknowledge the name. Could she read his thoughts? he wondered.

It was only a few steps across the Square, and Mrs. Benedict and her son walked to Elizabeth's door with her. He had no opportunity to speak to

Elizabeth alone, but he said as he bade her good-night, "I shall see you tomorrow, then, in the morning."

The inflection was almost a question; but Elizabeth only said, "Good night," and vanished into the house.

"Then you have met her before, George?" asked his mother wonderingly.

"Yes," he answered hurriedly, as if to stop her further question. "Yes, I have met her before. She is very beautiful, Mother."

And because the mother was afraid she might say too much she assented, and held her peace. It was the first time in years that George had called a girl beautiful.

Meantime Elizabeth had gone to her own room and locked the door. She hardly knew what to think, her heart was so happy. Yet beneath it all was the troubled thought of the lady, the haunting lady for whom they had prayed together on the prairie. And as if to add to the thought she found a bit of newspaper lying on the floor beside her dressing-table. Marie must have dropped it as she came in to turn up the lights. It was nothing but the corner torn from a newspaper, and should be consigned to the waste-basket; yet her eye caught the words in large head-lines as she picked it up idly, "Miss Geraldine Loring's Wedding to Be an Elaborate Affair." There was nothing more readable. The paper was torn in a zigzag line just beneath. Yet that was enough. It reminded her of her duty.

Down beside the bed she knelt, and prayed: "O my Father, hide me now; hide me! I am in trouble; hide me!" Over and over she prayed till her heart grew calm and she could think.

Then she sat down quietly, and put the matter before her.

This man whom she loved with her whole soul was to be married in a few days. The world of society would be at the wedding. He was pledged to another, and he was not hers. Yet he was her old friend, and was coming to see her. If he came and looked into her face with those clear eyes of his, he might read in hers that she loved him. How dreadful that would be!

Yes, she must search yet deeper. She had heard the glad ring in his voice when he met her, and said, "Elizabeth!" She had seen his eyes. He was in danger himself. She knew it; she might not hide it from herself. She must help him to be true to the woman to whom he was pledged, whom now he would have to marry.

She must go away from it all. She would run away, now at once. It seemed that she was always running away from someone. She could go back to the mountains where she had started. She was not afraid now of the man from whom she had fled. Culture and education had done their work. Religion had set her upon a rock. She could go back with the protection that her money would put about her, with the companionship of some good, elderly woman, and be safe from harm in that way; but she could not stay here and meet George Benedict in the morning, nor face Geraldine Loring on her wedding-day. It would be all the same the facing whether she were in the wedding-party or not. Her days of mourning for her grandmother would of course protect her from this public facing. It was the thought she could not bear. She must get away from it all forever.

Her lawyers should arrange the business. They would purchase the house that Grandmother Brady desired, and then give her her money to build a church. She would go back, and teach among the lonely wastes of mountain and prairie what Jesus Christ longed to be to the people made in His image. She would go back and place above the graves of her father and mother and brothers stones that should bear the words of life to all who should pass by in that desolate region. And that should be her excuse to the world for going, if she needed any excuse — she had gone to see about placing a monument over her father's grave. But the monument should be a church somewhere where it was most needed. She was resolved about that.

That was a busy night. Marie was called upon to pack a few things for a hurried journey. The telephone rang, and the sleepy night-operator answered crossly. But Elizabeth found out all she wanted to know about the early Chicago trains, and then lay down to rest.

Early the next morning George Benedict telephoned for some flowers from the florist; and, when they arrived, he pleased himself by taking them to Elizabeth's door.

He did not expect to find her up, but it would be a pleasure to have them reach her by his own hand. They would be sent up to her room, and she would know in her first waking thought that he remembered her. He smiled as he touched the bell and stood waiting.

The old butler opened the door. He looked as if he had not fully finished his night's sleep. He listened mechanically to the message, "For Miss Bailey with Mr. Benedict's good-morning," and then his face took on a deprecatory expression.

"I'm sorry, Mr. Benedict," he said, as if in the matter he were personally to blame; "but she's just gone. Miss Elizabeth's mighty quick in her ways, and last night after she come home she decided to go to Chicago on the early train. She's just gone to the station not ten minutes ago. They was late, and had to hurry. I'm expecting the footman back every minute."

"Gone?" said George Benedict, standing blankly on the door-step and looking down the street as if that should bring her. "Gone? To Chicago, did you say?"

"Yes, sir, she's gone to Chicago. That is, she's going further, but she took the Chicago Limited. She's gone to see about a monument for Madam's son John, Miss 'Lizabuth's father. She said she must go at once, and she went."

"What time does that train leave?" asked the young man. It was a thread of hope. He was stung into a superhuman effort as he had been on the prairie when he had caught the flying vision of the girl and horse, and he had shouted, and she would not stop for him.

"Nine-fifty, sir," said the butler. He wished this excited young man would go after her. She needed someone. His heart had often stirred against fate that this pearl among young mistresses should have no intimate friend or lover now in her loneliness.

"Nine-fifty!" He looked at his watch. No chance! "Broad Street?" he asked sharply.

"Yes, sir."

Would there be a chance if he had his automobile? Possibly, but hardly unless the train was late. There would be a trifle more chance of catching the train at West Philadelphia. O for his automobile! He turned to the butler in despair.

"Telephone her!" he said. "Stop her if you possibly can on board the train, and I will try to get there. I must see her. It is important." He started down the steps, his mind in a whirl of trouble. How should he go? The trolley would be the only available way, and yet the trolley would be useless; it would take too long. Nevertheless, he sped down toward Chestnut Street blindly, and now in his despair his new habit came to him. "O my Father, help me! Help me! Save her for me!"

Up Walnut Street at a breakneck pace came a flaming red automobile, sounding its taunting menace, "Honk-honk! Honk-honk!" but George Benedict stopped not for automobiles. Straight into the jaws of death he rushed, and was saved only by the timely grasp of a policeman, who rolled him over on the ground. The machine came to a halt, and a familiar voice shouted: "Conscience alive, George, is that you? What are you trying to do? Say, but that was a close shave! Where you going in such a hurry, anyway? Hustle in, and I'll take you there."

The young man sprang into the seat, and gasped: "West Philadelphia station, Chicago Limited! Hurry! Train leaves Broad Street station at nine-fifty. Get me there if you can, Billy. I'll be your friend forever."

By this time they were speeding fast. Neither of the two had time to consider which station was the easier to make; and, as the machine was headed toward West Philadelphia, on they went, regardless of laws or vainly shouting policemen.

George Benedict sprang from the car before it had stopped, and nearly fell again. His nerves were not steady from his other fall yet. He tore into the station and out through the passageway past the beckoning hand of the ticket-man who sat in the booth at the staircase, and strode up three steps at a time. The guard shouted: "Hurry! You may get it; she's just starting!" and a friendly hand reached out, and hauled him up on the platform of the last car.

For an instant after he was safely in the car he was too dazed to think. It seemed as if he must keep on blindly rushing through that train all the way to Chicago, or she would get away from him. He sat down in an empty seat for a minute to get his senses. He was actually on the train! It had not gone without him!

Now the next question was, Was she on it herself, or had she in some way slipped from his grasp even yet? The old butler might have caught her by telephone. He doubted it. He knew her stubborn determination, and all at once he began to suspect that she was with intention running away from him, and perhaps had been doing so before! It was an astonishing thought and a grave one, yet, if it were true, what had meant that welcoming smile in her eyes that had been like dear sunshine to his heart?

But there was no time to consider such questions now. He had started on this quest, and he must continue it until he found her. Then she should be made to explain once and for all most fully. He would live through no more torturing agonies of separation without a full understanding of the matter. He got upon his shaking feet, and started to hunt for Elizabeth.

Then all at once he became aware that he was still carrying the box of flowers. Battered and out of shape it was, but he was holding it as if it held the very hope of life for him. He smiled grimly as he tottered shakily down the aisle, grasping his floral offering with determination. This was not exactly the morning call he had planned, nor the way he had expected to present his flowers; but it seemed to be the best he could do. Then, at last, in the very furthest car from the end, in the drawing-room he found her, sitting gray and sorrowful, looking at the fast-flying landscape.

"Elizabeth!" He stood in the open door and called to her; and she started as from a deep sleep, her face blazing into glad sunshine at sight of him. She put her hand to her heart, and smiled.

"I have brought you some flowers," he said grimly. "I am afraid there isn't much left of them now; but, such as they are, they are here. I hope you will accept them."

"Oh!" gasped Elizabeth, reaching out for the poor crushed roses as if they had been a little child in danger. She drew them from the battered box and to her arms with a delicious movement of caressing, as if she would make up to them for all they had come through. He watched her, half pleased, half savagely. Why should all that tenderness be wasted on mere fading flowers?

At last he spoke, interrupting her brooding over his roses.

"You are running away from me!" he charged.

"Well, and what if I am?" She looked at him with a loving defiance in her eye.

"Don't you know I love you?" he asked, sitting down beside her and talking low and almost fiercely. "Don't you know I've been torn away from you, or you from me, twice before now, and that I cannot stand it any more? Say, don't you know it? Answer, please!" The demand was kind, but peremptory.

"I was afraid so," she murmured with drooping eyes, and cheeks from which all color had fled.

"Well, why do you do it? Why did you run away? Don't you care for me? Tell me that. If you can't ever love me, you are excusable; but I must know it all now."

"Yes, I care as much as you," she faltered, "but —"

"But what?" sharply.

"But you are going to be married this week," she said in desperation, raising her miserable eyes to his.

He looked at her in astonishment.

"Am I?" said he. "Well, that's news to me; but it's the best news I've heard in a long time. When does the ceremony come off? I wish it was this morning. Make it this morning, will you? Let's stop this blessed old train and go back to the Doctor. He'll fix it so we can't ever run away from each other again. Elizabeth, look at me!"

But Elizabeth hid her eyes now. They were full of tears.

"But the lady —" she gasped out, struggling with the sobs. She was so weary, and the thought of what he had suggested was so precious.

"What lady? There is no lady but you, Elizabeth, and never has been. Haven't you known that for a long time? I have. That was all a hallucination of my foolish brain. I had to go out on the plains to get rid of it, but I left it there forever. She was nothing to me after I saw you."

"But — but people said — and it was in the paper. I saw it. You cannot desert her now; it would be dishonorable."

"Thunder!" ejaculated the distracted young man. "In the paper! What lady?"

"Why, Miss Loring! Geraldine Loring. I saw that the preparations were all made for her wedding, and I was told she was to marry you."

In sheer relief he began to laugh.

At last he stopped, as the old hurt look spread over her face.

"Excuse me, dear," he said gently. "There was a little acquaintance between Miss Loring and myself. It only amounted to a flirtation on her part, one of many. It was a great distress to my mother, and I went out West, as you know, to get away from her. I knew she would only bring me unhappiness, and she was not willing to give up some of her ways that were impossible. I am glad and thankful that God saved me from her. I believe she is going to marry a distant relative of mine by the name of Benedict, but I thank the kind Father that *I* am not going to marry *her*. There is only one woman in the whole wide world that I am willing to marry, or ever will be; and she is sitting beside me now."

The train was going rapidly now. It would not be long before the conductor would reach them. The man leaned over, and clasped the little gloved hand that lay in the girl's lap; and Elizabeth felt the great joy that had tantalized her for these three years in dreams and visions settle down about her in beautiful reality. She was his now forever. She need never run away again.

The conductor was not long in coming to them, and the matter-of-fact world had to be faced once more. The young man produced his card, and said a few words to the conductor, mentioning the name of his uncle, who, by the way, happened to be a director of the road; and then he explained the situation. It was very necessary that the young lady be recalled at once to her home because of a change in the circumstances. He had caught the train at West Philadelphia by automobile, coming as he was in his morning clothes, without baggage and with little money. Would the conductor be so kind as to put them off that they might return to the city by the shortest possible route?

The conductor glared and scolded, and said people "didn't know their own minds," and "wanted to move the earth." Then he eyed Elizabeth, and she smiled. He let a grim glimmer of what might have been a sour smile years ago peep out for an instant, and — he let them off.

They wandered delightedly about from one trolley to another until they found an automobile garage, and soon were speeding back to Philadelphia.

They waited for no ceremony, those two who had met and loved by the way in the wilderness. They went straight to Mrs. Benedict for her blessing, and then to the minister to arrange for his services; and within the week a quiet wedding-party entered the arched doors of the placid brown church with the lofty spire, and Elizabeth Bailey and George Benedict were united in the sacred bonds of matrimony.

There were present Mrs. Benedict, and one or two intimate friends of the family, besides Grandmother Brady, Aunt Nan, and Lizzie.

Lizzie brought a dozen bread-and-butter plates from the ten-cent store. They were adorned with cupids and roses and much gilt. But Lizzie was disappointed. No display, no pomp and ceremony. Just a simple white dress and white veil. Lizzie did not understand that the veil had been in the Bailey family for generations, and that the dress was an heirloom also. It was worn because Grandmother Bailey had given it to her, and told her she wanted her to wear it on her wedding-day. Sweet and beautiful she looked as she turned to walk down the aisle on her husband's arm, and she smiled at Grandmother Brady in a way that filled the grandmother's heart with pride and triumph. Elizabeth was not ashamed of the Bradys even among her fine friends. But Lizzie grumbled all the way home at the plainness of the ceremony, and the lack of bridesmaids and fuss and feathers.

The social column of the daily papers stated that young Mr. and Mrs. George Benedict were spending their honeymoon in an extended tour of the West, and Grandmother Brady so read it aloud at the breakfast table to the admiring family. Only Lizzie looked discontented:

"She just wore a dark blue tricotine one-piece dress and a little plain dark hat. She ain't got a bit of taste. Oh *Boy!* If I just had her pocket book wouldn't I show the world? But anyhow I'm glad she went in a private car. There was a *little* class to her, though if t'had been mine I'd uv preferred ridin' in the parlor coach an' havin' folks see me and my fine husband. He's some looker, George Benedict is! Everybody turns to watch 'em as they go by, and they sail along and never seem to notice. It's all perfectly throwed away on 'em. Gosh! I'd hate to be such a nut!"

"Now, Lizzie, you know you hadn't oughtta talk like that!" reproved her grandmother. "After her giving you all that money fer your own wedding. A thousand dollars just to spend as you please on your cloes and a blowout, and house linens. Jest because she don't care for gewgaws like you do, you think she's a fool. But she's no fool. She's got a good head on her, and she'll get more in the long run out of life than you will. She's been real loving and kind to us all, and she didn't have any reason to neither. We never did much fer her. And look at how nice and common she's been with us all, not a bit high headed. I declare, Lizzie, I should think you'd be ashamed!"

"Oh, well," said Lizzie shrugging her shoulders indifferently. "She's all right in her way, only 'taint my way. And I'm thankful t'goodness that I had the nerve to speak up when she offered to give me my trousseau. She askt me would I druther hav her buy it for me, or have the money to pick it out m'self, and I spoke up right quick and says, 'Oh, cousin Bessie, I wouldn't *think* of givin' ya all that trouble. I'd take the *money* ef it's all the same t'you,' and she jest smiled and said all right, she expected I knew what I wanted better'n she did. So yes'teddy when I went down to the station to see her off she handed me a bank book. And — Oh, say, I fergot! She said there was a good-bye note inside. I ain't had time to look at it since. I went right to the movies on the dead run to get there 'fore the first show begun, and it's in my coat pocket. Wait 'till I get it. I s'pose it's some of her old *religion!* She's always preaching at me. It ain't that she says so much as that she's always *meanin'* it underneath everything, that gets my goat! It's sorta like having a piece of God round with you all the time watching you. You kinda hate to be enjoyin' yerself fer fear she won't think yer doin' it accordin' to the Bible.''

Lizzie hurtled into the hall and brought back her coat, fumbling in the pocket.

"Yes, here 'tis Ma! Wanta see the figgers? You never had a whole thousand dollars in the bank t'woncet yerself, did ya?''

Mrs. Brady put on her spectacles and reached for the book, while Lizzie's mother got up and came behind her mother's chair to look over at the magic figures. Lizzie stooped for the little white note that had fluttered to her feet as she opened the book, but she had little interest to see what it said. She was more intent upon the new bank book.

It was Grandmother Brady that discovered it:

"Why, Lizzie! It ain't *one* thousand, it's *five* thousand, the book says! You don't s'pose she's made a mistake, do you?''

Lizzie seized the book and gazed, her jaw dropping open in amaze. "Let me have it!'' demanded Lizzie's mother, reaching for the book.

"Where's yer note, Lizzie, mebbe it'll explain,'' said the excited grandmother.

Lizzie recovered the note which again had fluttered to the floor in the confusion and opening it began to read:

"Dear Lizzie," it read,

"I've made it five thousand so you will have some over for furnishing your home, and if you still think you want the little bungalow out on the Pike you will find the deed at my lawyer's, all made out in your name. It's my wedding gift to you, so you can go to work and buy your furniture at once, and not wait till Dan gets a raise. And here's wishing you a great deal of happiness,

"Your loving cousin,

"ELIZABETH.''

"There!" said Grandmother Brady sitting back with satisfaction and holding her hands composedly, "Whadd' I tell ya?"

"Mercy!" said Lizzie's mother. "Let me see that note! The idea of her *giving* all that money when she didn't have to!"

But Lizzie's face was a picture of joy. For once she lost her hard little worldly screwed-up expression and was wreathed in smiles of genuine eagerness:

"Oh *Boy!*" she exclaimed delightedly, dancing around the room. "Now we can have a victrola, an' a player-piano, and Dan'll get a Ford, one o' those limousine-kind! Won't I be some swell? What'll the girls at the store think now?"

"H'm! You'd much better get a washing machine and a 'lectric iron!" grumbled Grandmother Brady practically.

"Well, all I got to say about it is, she was an awful fool to trust *you* with so much money," said Lizzie's mother discontentedly, albeit with a pleased pride as she watched her giddy daughter fling on hat and coat to go down and tell Dan.

"I sh'll work in the store fer the rest of the week, jest to 'commode 'em," she announced putting her head back in the door as she went out, "but not a day longer. I got a lot t'do. Say, won't I be some lady in the five-an'-ten the rest o' the week? Oh *Boy! I'll tell the world!*"

Meantime in their own private car the bride and groom were whirling on their way to the west, but they saw little of the scenery, being engaged in the all-absorbing story of each other's lives since they had parted.

And one bright morning, they stepped down from the train at Malta and gazed about them.

The sun was shining clear and wonderful, and the little brown station stood drearily against the brightness of the day like a picture that has long hung on the wall of one's memory and is suddenly brought out and the dust wiped away.

They purchased a couple of horses, and with camp accoutrements following began their real wedding trip, over the road they had come together when they first met. Elizabeth had to show her husband where she had hidden while the men went by, and he drew her close in his arms and thanked God that she had escaped so miraculously.

It seemed so wonderful to be in the same places again, for nothing out here in the wilderness seemed much to have changed, and yet they two were so changed that the people they met did not seem to recognize them as ever having been that way before.

They dined sumptuously in the same coulee, and recalled little things they had said and done, and Elizabeth now worldly wise, laughed at her own former ignorance as her husband reminded her of some questions she had asked him on that memorable journey. And ever through the beautiful journey he was telling her how wonderful she seemed to him, both then and now.

Not however, till they reached the old ranchhouse, where the woman had tried to persuade her to stay, did they stop for long.

Elizabeth had a tender feeling in her heart for that motherly woman who had sought to protect her, and felt a longing to let her know how safely she had been kept through the long journey and how good the Lord had been to her through the years. Also they both desired to reward these kind people for their hospitality in the time of need. So, in the early evening they rode up just as they did before to the little old log house. But no friendly door flung open wide as they came near, and at first they thought the cabin deserted, till a candle flare suddenly shone forth in the bedroom, and then Benedict dismounted and knocked.

After some waiting the old man came to the door holding a candle high above his head. His face was haggard and worn, and the whole place looked dishevelled. His eyes had a weary look as he peered into the night and it was evident that he had no thought of ever having seen them before:

"I can't do much fer ya, strangers," he said, his voice sounding tired and discouraged. "If it's a woman ye have with ye, ye better ride on to the next ranch. My woman is sick. Very sick. There's nobody here with her but me, and I have all I can tend to. The house ain't kept very tidy. It's six weeks since she took to bed."

Elizabeth had sprung lightly to the ground and was now at the threshold:

"Oh, is she sick? I'm so sorry? Couldn't I do something for her? She was good to me once several years ago!"

The old man peered at her blinkingly, noting her slender beauty, the exquisite eager face, the dress that showed her of another world — and shook his head:

"I guess you made a mistake, lady. I don't remember ever seeing you before —"

"But I remember you," she said eagerly stepping into the room. "Won't you please let me go to her?"

"Why, shore, lady, go right in ef you want to. She's layin' there in the bed. She ain't likely to get out of it again I'm feared. The doctor says nothin' but a 'noperation will ever get her up, and we can't pay fer 'noperations. It's a long ways to the hospital in Chicago where he wants her sent, and M'ria and I, we ain't allowin' to part. It can't be many years —"

But Elizabeth was not waiting to hear. She had slipped into the old bedroom that she remembered now so well and was kneeling beside the bed talking to the white faced woman on the thin pillow:

"Don't you remember me?" she asked. "I'm the girl you tried to get to stay with you once. The girl that came here with a man she had met in the wilderness. You told me things that I didn't know, and you were kind and wanted me to stay here with you? Don't you remember me? I'm Elizabeth!"

The woman reached out a bony hand and touched the fair young face that she could see but dimly in the flare of the candle that the old man now brought into the room:

"Why, yes, I remember," the woman said, her voice sounded alive yet in spite of her illness. "Yes, I remember you. You were a dear little girl, and I was so worried about you. I would have kept you for my own — but you wouldn't stay. And he was a nice looking young man, but I was afraid for you — You can't always tell about them — You *mostly* can't —!"

"But he was all right, Mother!" Elizabeth's voice rang joyously through the cabin. "He took care of me and got me safely started toward my people, and now he's my husband. I want you to see him. George come here!"

The old woman half raised herself from the pillow and looked toward the young man in the doorway:

"You don't say! He's your *husband!* Well, now isn't that grand! Well, I certainly am glad! I was that worried —!"

They sat around the bed talking, Elizabeth telling briefly of her own experiences and her wedding trip which they were taking back over the old trail, and the old man and woman speaking of their trouble, the woman's break-down and how the doctor at Malta said there was a chance she could get well if she went to a great doctor in Chicago, but how they had no money unless they sold the ranch and that nobody wanted to buy it.

"Oh, but we have money," laughed Elizabeth joyously, "and it is our turn now to help you. You helped us when we were in trouble. How soon can you start? I'm going to play you are my own father and mother. We can send them both, can't we George?"

It was a long time before they settled themselves to sleep that night because there was so much planning to be done, and then Elizabeth and her husband had to get out their stores and cook a good supper for the two old people who had been living mostly on corn meal mush for several weeks.

And after the others were all asleep the old woman lay praying and thanking God for the two angels who had dropped down to help them in their distress.

The next morning George Benedict with one of the men who looked after their camping outfit went to Malta and got in touch with the Chicago doctor and hospital, and before he came back to the ranch that night everything was arranged for the immediate start of the two old people. He had even planned for an automobile and the Malta doctor to be in attendance in a couple of days to get the invalid to the station.

Meantime Elizabeth had been going over the old woman's wardrobe which was scanty and coarse, and selecting garments from her own baggage that would do for the journey.

The old woman looked glorified as she touched the delicate white garments with their embroidery and ribbons:

"Oh, dear child! Why, I couldn't wear a thing like that on my old worn-out body. Those look like angels' clothes." She put a work-worn finger on the delicate tracery of embroidery and smoothed a pink satin ribbon bow.

But Elizabeth overruled her. It was nothing but a plain little garment she had bought for the trip. If the friend thought it was pretty she was glad, but nothing was too pretty for the woman who had taken her in in her distress and tried to help her and keep her safe.

The invalid was thin with her illness, and it was found that she could easily wear the girl's simple dress of dark blue with a white collar, and little dark hat, and Elizabeth donned a khaki shirt and brown cap and sweater herself and gladly arrayed her old friend in her own bridal travelling gown for her journey. She had not brought a lot of things for her journey because she did not want to be bothered, but she could easily get more when she got to a large city, and what was money for but to clothe the naked and feed the hungry? She rejoiced in her ability to help this woman of the wilderness.

On the third day, garbed in Elizabeth's clothes, her husband fitted out for the East in some of George Benedict's extra things, they started. They carried a bag containing some necessary changes, and some wonderful toilet accessories with silver monograms, enough to puzzle the most snobbish nurse, also there was a luscious silk kimona of Elizabeth's in the bag. The two old people were settled in the Benedict private car, and in due time hitched onto the Chicago Express and hurried on their way. Before the younger pair went back to their pilgrimage they sent a series of telegrams arranging for every detail of the journey for the old couple, so that they would be met with cars and nurses and looked after most carefully.

And the thanksgiving and praise of the old people seemed to follow them like music as they rode happily on their way.

They paused at the little old schoolhouse where they had attended the Christian Endeavor meeting, and Elizabeth looked half fearfully up the road where her evil pursuers had ridden by, and rode closer to her husband's side. So they passed on the way as nearly as Elizabeth could remember every step back as she had come, telling her husband all the details of the journey.

That night they camped in the little shelter where Benedict had come upon the girl that first time they met, and under the clear stars that seemed so near they knelt together and thanked God for His leading.

They went to the lonely cabin on the mountain, shut up and going to ruin now, and Benedict gazing at the surroundings and then looking at the delicate face of his lovely wife was reminded of a white flower he had once seen growing out of the blackness down in a coal mine, pure and clean without a smirch of soil.

They visited the seven graves in the wilderness, and standing reverently beside the sand-blown mounds she told him much of her early life that she had not told him before, and introduced him to her family, telling a bit about each that would make him see the loveable side of them. And then they planned for seven simple white stones to be set up, bearing words from the book they both loved. Over the care worn mother was to be written "Come unto me all ye that labor and are heavy laden and I will give you rest."

It was on that trip that they planned what came to pass in due time. The little cabin was made over into a simple, pretty home, with vines planted about the garden, and a garage with a sturdy little car; and not far away a church nestled into the side of the hill, built out of the stones that were native, with many sunny windows and a belfry in which bells rang out to the whole region round.

At first it had seemed impractical to put a church out there away from the town, but Elizabeth said that it was centrally located, and high up where it could be seen from the settlements in the valleys, and was moreover on a main trail that was much travelled. She longed to have some such spot in the wilderness that could be a refuge for any who longed for better things.

When they went back they sent out two consecrated missionaries to occupy the new house and use the sturdy little car. They were to ring the bells, preach the gospel and play the organ and piano in the little church.

Over the pulpit there was a beautiful window bearing a picture of Christ, the Good Shepherd, and in clear letters above were the words: "And thou shalt remember all the way which the Lord thy God led thee these forty years in the wilderness, to humble thee, and to prove thee, to know what was in thine heart, whether thou wouldst keep his commandments, or no."

And underneath the picture were the words:

" 'In the time of trouble He shall hide me in His pavilion; in the secret of His tabernacle shall He hide me.' In memory of His hidings,

"George and Elizabeth Benedict."

But in the beautiful home in Philadelphia, in an inner intimate room these words are exquisitely graven on the wall, "Let not your heart be troubled."

THE STORY

OF A

WHIM

Chapter 1

Five Girls, an Organ, and the Whim

"How cold it is! Let's walk up and down the platform, girls. Why doesn't that train come?"

"I'm going in to see if the agent knows anything about it," said one with determined mouth and big brown eyes.

They waited shivering in a group until she returned, five girls just entering womanhood. They were part of a small house-party, spending Thanksgiving week at the old stone house on the hill above the station, and they had come down to meet another girl who was expected on the train.

"He says the train is half an hour late," said Hazel Winship, the hostess, coming down the stone steps of the station.

"What shall we do? There is not time to make it worth while to go back to the house. Shall we go inside, or walk?"

"O, walk by all means," said Victoria Landis. "It is so stuffy and hot in there I feel as if I was a turkey half-roasted now from the little time we stayed there."

"Let us walk up this long platform to that freight-house and see the men unload that car," proposed Esther Wakefield. And so it was agreed.

"Tra la la!" hummed Victoria. "O girls, why didn't we stay and finish singing that glee? It was so pretty! Listen. Is this right?" and she hummed it over again.

"Yes, it was too bad to have to tear ourselves away from that dear piano," said Ruth Summers. "Say, Hazel, what are you going to do with your poor despised organ? Send it to a home missionary?"

"I'll send it somewhere, I suppose. I don't know anyone around here to give it to. I wish I could send it where it would give pleasure to someone."

"There are probably plenty of people who would be delighted with it if you only knew them. The owner of this forlorn furniture, for instance," said Victoria as they separated to thread their way between boxes and chairs that had been shoved out on the platform from a half-emptied freight-car. "Girls, just look at that funny old stove and those uncomfortable chairs! How would you like to set up housekeeping with that?"

"The couch isn't so bad if it were covered," said Hazel, poking it in a gingerly way with her gloved finger. "It looks as though it might have been comfortable once."

"That's Hazel all over!" said Esther. "If it were possible, she would just enjoy having that couch stay over a train or two while she re-covered it with some bright denim, and make a pillow for it;" and clear girlish laughter rang out, while Hazel's cheeks grew pink as she joined in.

"Well, girls, wouldn't that be interesting? Just think how pleased the dear old lady who owns it would be when she found the new cover, and how entirely mystified."

"You might send her your organ," suggested Ruth Summers. "Perhaps she would like that just as well."

"What a lovely idea!" said Hazel, her eyes shining with enthusiasm. "I'll just do it. Come, let's look for the address."

"You romantic little goose!" exclaimed her friends. "Take her away! The perfect idea! I just believe she would!"

"Of course I would," said Hazel; "why shouldn't I? Papa said I might do as I please with it. Here; this is a card behind here. Read it. 'Christie W. Bailey, Pine Ridge, Fla.' Girls, I shall *do* it. Who has a pencil? I want to write it down. Do all these things belong to the same person? Look on their cards. She must be very poor."

"Poor as a church mouse," said Victoria, "if this is all she has."

"I should like to inquire how you are so sure it is a 'she,' " said Emily Whitten; " 'Christie' sounds as though it might belong to a man or a boy. Don't you think so, Victoria?"

"It's an old colored mammy, I'm positive," said Victoria.

"I don't care," said Hazel of the firm mouth. "If they are black people they will enjoy it all the more. Black people are fond of music, and it will be a real help for the little children. But I don't believe Christie is an old mammy at all. She is a girl about our own age. She has had to go to Florida on account of her health, and she is poor, too poor to board; so she will keep house in a room or two," — waving her hand toward the unpretentious huddling of furniture about them, — "and perhaps she teaches school. She will put the organ in the schoolroom, or have a Sunday school in her own home, and I shall write her a note and send some music for the children to learn. She can do lots of nice things with that organ."

"Now, Hazel," protested five voices, but just then the shriek of a whistle brought them all about face and flying down the platform to reach the station before the train drew up. In the bustle of welcoming the newcomer Hazel's scheme was forgotten, and not until when in the evening they were seated about the great open fire did it again come into the conversation. It was Victoria Landis who told the newcomer about it, beginning with: "O Marion, you can't think what Hazel's latest wild scheme of philanthropy is."

But Marion, a girl after Hazel's own heart, listened with glowing eyes. "Really, Hazel?" she said when the tale was finished, looking at her hostess with sympathy. "Won't that be just lovely! You must send it in time for Christmas, you know; and why not pack a box to go with it? We could all help. It would be great fun, and give us something to do not entirely selfish while we are enjoying ourselves here."

"Do you mean it?" said Victoria. "Well, I will not be outdone. I will give a covering for that old couch, and Ruth shall make a most bewildering sofa pillow for it, the like of which was never seen in any house in Florida. What color shall it be, blue or red? And will denim be fine enough, or do you prefer tapestry or brocatelle? Speak out, Hazel; we're with you hand and heart, no matter how wildly you soar this time."

And so amid laughter and jokes the plan grew.

"I have a lot of singing-books, if you think there is really a chance of a Sunday school," said Esther.

"There must be something pretty for the house, a good picture perhaps," mused Ruth Summers; and Hazel's eyes grew bright with joy as she looked from one face to another and saw that they really meant what they said.

Six pairs of hands can do much in four days; and, when the guests left for their various homes or schools, there stood on the back porch of the old stone house on the hill a well-packed box marked and labelled, an organ securely boxed, and a large roll, all bearing the magic sentence, "Christie W. Bailey, Pine Ridge, Fla."

There had been much discussion and argument on the part of Mrs. Winship and her husband. They were inclined to think Hazel had outdone herself in romance this time, though they were well used to such unprecedented escapades from her babyhood; but she had finally won them all over, had explained how the goods had been put off at that particular freight-station from up the branch road, to be put on the through freight at the Junction, had enlarged upon the desolateness of the life of that young girl who was moving to Florida alone, until every member of the party became infected with pity for her, and vied with the others to make that Christmas box the nicest ever sent to a girl.

They began to believe in "Christie," and to wonder whether her name was Christine or Christiana, or simply Christie after some family name;

and gradually all thought of her being other than a young girl faded from their minds.

Mother Winship had so far forgotten her doubts as to contribute a good Smyrna rug no more in use in the stone house, after the party had gone down to the freight-house and watched the goods repacked in another freight-car for the Junction, and come back with the report that there was not a sign of a carpet in the lot. They also told how they had peeked through the crack of a box of books and distinctly seen the worn cover of an arithmetic, which proved the "school-ma'am theory," while an old blue-checked apron, visible through another crack, settled the sex of Christie irrevocably.

Hazel Winship had written a long letter in her delicate tracery on her finest paper, and sealed it with a prayer, and had gone back to her college duties a hundred miles away, and Christmas was fast coming on as the three freight pieces started on their way.

On the edge of a clearing, where the tall pines thinned against the sky, and tossed their garlands of gray moss from bough to bough, there stood a little cabin built of logs. It was set up on stilts out of the hot white sand, and, underneath, a few chickens wandered aimlessly, as unaware of the home over their heads as mortals are of the heaven above them. Some sickly orange-trees, apparently just set out, gave the excuse for the clearing, and beyond the distance stretched away into desolateness and black-jack oaks.

A touch of whitewash here and there and a bit of grass — which in that part of the world is so scarce that it is usually used for a path instead of being a setting for that path — would have done wonders for the place, but there was nothing but the white, neglected, "mushy" sand, discouraging alike to wheel and foot.

Inside the cabin there was a rusty cook-stove, and a sulky tea-kettle at the back and the remains of a meal in a greasy frying-pan still over the dead fire. An old table was drawn out with one leaf up and piled with un-washed dishes, boxes of crackers, and papers of various eatables. The couch in the corner was evidently the only bed, and the red and gray blankets still lay in the heap where they had been tossed when the occupant arose that morning. From some nails in the corner hung several articles of clothing and a hat. The corner by the door was given over to tools and a few garden implements which were considered too good to leave out-of-doors. Every chair but one was occupied by books or papers or clothing.

Outside the back door a dry-goods box by the pump with a tin basin and a cake of soap did duty as a wash-stand. On the whole, it was not an attractive home, even though sky and air were more than perfect.

The occupant of this residence was driving dully along the sand road at the will of a stubborn little Florida pony, which wriggled his whole body with a motion intended to convey to his driver the idea that he was trotting as fast as any reasonable being could expect a horse to go, while in reality the monotonous sand and scrub-oaks were moving past as slowly as was possible.

It was the day before Christmas, but the driver did not care. What was Christmas to one whose friends were all gone, and who never gave or received a Christmas gift?

The pony, like all slow things, got there at last, and came trotting up to the post-office in good style. The driver got out of the shackly wagon, and went into the post-office, which served also as general store.

"Hollo Chris!" called a sickly looking man from the group on the counter. "Bin a-wonderin' when you was comin.' Got some moh freight fer yoh oveh to the station."

The newcomer turned his broad shoulders about, and faced the speaker.

"I haven't any more freight coming," he said. "It's all come three weeks ago."

"Well, but it's oveh theh," insisted the other, "three pieces. Your name mahked plain same like the otheh."

"Somebody sent you a Christmas gift, Chris," said a tall young fellow, slapping him on the shoulder, "better go and get it."

Chapter 2

A Christmas Box That Didn't Match

The young man, still insisting that the freight was not his, followed the agent reluctantly over to the station, accompanied by several of his companions, who had nothing better to do than to see the joke out.

There it was, a box, a bundle, and a packing-case, all labelled plainly and most mysteriously, "Christie W. Bailey, Pine Ridge, Fla."

The man who owned the name could scarcely believe his eyes. He knew of no one who would send him anything. An old neighbor had forwarded the few things he had saved from the sale of the old farm after his father and mother died, and the neighbor had since died himself; so this could not be something forgotten.

He felt annoyed at the arrival of the mystery, and did not know what to do with the things, but at last brought over the wagon and reluctant pony, and with the help of the other men got them loaded on, the pony meanwhile eying his load with dislike and meditating how slow he could make his gait on account of his burden.

Christie Bailey did not wait at the store that night as long as he usually did. He had intended going home by moonlight, but decided to try to make it before the sun went down. He wanted to understand about the freight at once. He found when he went back to the post-office that he could not sit with the same pleasure on a nail-keg and talk as usual. His mind was on the wagon-load. He bought a few things, and started home.

The sun had brought the short winter day suddenly to a close, as it has a habit of doing in Florida, by dropping out of sight and leaving utter darkness with no twilight.

Christie lighted an old lantern, and got the things into the cabin at once. Then he took his hatchet and screw-driver, and set to work.

First the packing-case, for he instinctively felt that herein lay the heart of the matter. But not until he had taken the entire front off the case and taken out the handsome organ did he fully realize what had come to him.

More puzzled than ever, he stood back with his arms folded, and whistled. He saw the key attached to a card, and, unlocking the organ, touched gently one of the ivory keys with his rough finger, as one might touch a being from another world.

Then he glanced about to see where he should put it; and suddenly, even in the dull, smoky lamplight, the utter gloom and neglect of the place burst upon him. Without more ado he selected the freest side of the room, and shoved everything out of the way.

Then he brought a broom and swept it clean. After that he set the organ against the wall, and stood back to survey the effect. The disorderly table and the rusty stove were behind him, and the organ gave the spot a strange, cleared-up appearance.

He did not feel at home. He turned to the confusion behind him. Something must be done before he opened anything more. He felt somehow as if the organ was a visitor, and must not see his poor housekeeping.

He seized the frying-pan, scraped the contents into the yard, and called the dog. The dishes he put into a wooden tub outside the door, and pumped water over them. Then the mass of papers and boxes on table and chairs he piled into the darkest corner on the floor, straightened the row of boots and shoes, and, having done all that he could, he came back to the roll and box still unopened.

The roll came first. He undid the strings with awkward fingers, and stood back in admiration once more when he brought to light a thick, bright rug and a Japanese screen.

He spread the rug down, and puzzled some time over the screen, as to its use, but finally stood it up in front of the worst end of the room and began on his box.

There, at last, on the top was a letter in a fine, unknown hand. He opened it slowly, the blood mounting into his face, he knew not why, and read:

"Dear Christie: — You see I am so sure you are a girl of my own age that I have concluded to begin my letter informally, and wish you a very merry Christmas and a glad, bright New Year. Of course you may be an old lady or a nice, comfortable, middle-aged one; and then perhaps you will think we are very silly; but we hope and believe you are a girl like ourselves, and so our hearts have opened to you, and we are sending you some things for Christmas."

There followed an account of the afternoon at the freight-station, written in Hazel's most winning way, in which the words and ways and almost the voices and faces of Victoria Landis and Ruth and Esther and Marion and all the rest were shadowed forth.

The color on the young man's face deepened as he read, and he glanced up uneasily at his few poor chairs and miserable couch; then before he read further he went and pulled the screen along to hide more of the confusion.

He read the letter through, his heart waking up to the world and to long-ings he had never known he possessed before, — to the world in which Christmas has a place and in which young, bright life gives forth glad im-pulses; read to the end even, where Hazel inscribed her bit of a sermon full of good wishes and a little tender prayer that the spirit of Christmas might reign in that home and that the organ might be a help and a blessing to all around.

There was a pitiful look of almost helpless misery on the young man's face when he had finished. The good old times when God had been a re-ality were suddenly brought into his reckless, isolated life, and he knew that God was God, even though he had neglected Him so long, and that to-morrow was Christmas Day.

As a refuge from his own thoughts he turned back to the brimming box.

The first article he took out was a pair of dainty knit lavender bedroom slippers with black and white ermine edges and delicate satin bows. Emily Whitten's aunt had knit them for her to take to college with her; and, Emily's feet being many sizes smaller than her aunt supposed, she had never worn them, and had tucked them in at the last minute to make a safe resting-place for a delicate glass vase, which she said would be lovely to hold flowers, on the organ, Sundays.

They had written their nonsense thoughts on bits of labels all over the things, these gay young girls; and the young man read and smiled, and finally laughed aloud. He felt like a little boy just opening his first Christmas stocking.

He unpinned the paper on the couch-cover, and read in Victoria's large, stylish, angular hand full directions for putting it on the couch. He glanced with a twinge of shame at the old lounge, and realized that these gay girls had seen all his shabby belongings and pitied him, and he half-resented the whole thing, until the delight of being pitied and cared for overcame his bitterness, and he laughed again.

Green, soft and restful, had been chosen for the couch-cover; and it could not have fitted better if Victoria Landis had secretly had a tape-measure in her pocket and measured the couch, which perhaps she did on her second trip to the freight-house.

Ruth Summers had made the pillows — there were two of them, and they were large and comfortable and sensible, of harmonizing greens and browns and a gleam of gold here and there.

With careful attention to the directions, the new owner arrayed his old lounge, and placed the pillows as directed, "with a throw and a pat, not *laid* stiffly," from a postscript in Ruth's clear feminine hand. Then he stood back in awe that a thing so familiar and so ugly could suddenly assume such an air of ease and elegance. Would he ever be able to bring the rest of the room up to the same standard?

But the box invited further investigation. There was a bureau set of dainty blue and white, a cover for the top and a pincushion to match. There were also a few yards of the material and a rough sketch with directions for a possible dressing-table, to be made of a wooden box in case Christie had no bureau.

It was from Emily Whitten, and she said she could not remember seeing a bureau among the things, but she was sure any girl would know how to fix one up, and perhaps be glad of some new fixings for it.

At these things the young man looked helplessly, and finally went out into the moonlight, and hunted up an old box which he brushed off with the broom and brought inside, where he clumsily spread out the blue and white frills over its splintery top, and then solemnly tried to stick a pin into the cushion, fumbling in the lapel of his coat for one.

He was growing more and more bewildered with his new possessions, and as each came to light he began to wonder how he was going to be able to entertain and keep up to such a lot of fineries.

Mother Winship had put in a gay knit afghan which looked well over the couch, and next came a layer of Sunday-school singing-books, a Bible, and some lesson leaves. A card said that Esther Wakefield had sent these and she hoped they would be a help in the new Sunday school.

There followed a roll of blackboard cloth, a large cloth map of Palestine, and a box of chalk; and the young man grew more and more helpless. This was worse than the bureau set and the slippers. What was he to do with them all? *He* start a Sunday school! He would be much more likely to start children in the opposite way from heaven if he went on as he had been going the last two years.

His face hardened, and he was almost ready to sweep the whole lot back into the box, nail them up, and send them back where they came from. What did he want of a lot of trash with a set of such burdensome obligations attached?

But curiosity made him go back to see what there was left in the box, and a glance around his room made him unwilling to give up all this luxury.

He looked curiously at the box of fluffy lace things with Marion Halstead's card lying atop. He could only guess that they were some girl's fixings, and he wondered vaguely what he should do with them. Then he unwrapped a photograph of the six girls which had been hurriedly taken and was inscribed, "Guess which is which," with a list of their names written on a circle of paper like spokes to a wheel.

He studied each face with interest, and somehow it was for the writer of the letter that he sought, Hazel Winship. And he thought he should know her at once.

This was going to be very interesting. It would while away some of the long hours when there was nothing worth while to do, and keep him from thinking how long it took orange groves to pay, and what hard luck he had always had.

He decided at first glance that the one in the centre with the clear eyes and firm, sweet mouth was the instigator of all this bounty; and, as his eyes travelled from one face to another and came back to hers each time, he felt more sure of it. There was something frank and pleasant in her gaze. Somehow it would not do to send that girl back her things and tell her he was in no need of her charity. He liked to think she had thought of him, even though she did think of him as a poor discouraged girl or an old mammy.

He stood the picture up against the lace of the pincushion, and forever gave up the idea of trying to send those things back.

There seemed to be one thing more in the bottom of the box, and it was fastened inside another protecting board. He took it at last from its wrappings — a large picture, Hofmann's head of Christ, framed in broad dark Flemish oak to match the tint of the etching.

Dimly he understood who was the subject of the picture, although he had never seen it before. Silently he found a nail and drove it deep into the log of the wall. Just over the organ he hung it, without the slightest hesitation. He had recognized at once where this picture belonged, and knew that it, and not the bright rug, nor the restful couch, nor the gilded screen, nor even the organ itself, was to set the standard henceforth for his home and his life.

He knew this all in an undertone, without its quite coming to the surface of his consciousness. He was weary by this time, with the unusual excitement of the occasion, and much bewildered. He felt like a person suddenly lifted up a little way from the earth and obliged against his will to walk along unsupported in the air.

His mind was in a perfect whirl. He looked from one new thing to another, wondering more and more what they expected of him. The ribbons and lace of the bureau fixings worried him, and the lace collars and pincushion. What had he to do with such? Those foolish little slippers mocked him with a something that was not in his life, a something for which he was not even trying to fit himself. The organ and the books and, above all, the picture seemed to dominate him and demanded of him things which he could never give. A Sunday school! What an absurdity! He!

And the eyes in the picture seemed to look into his soul, and to say, all quietly enough, that He had come here now to live, to take command of his home and its occupant.

He rebelled against it, and turned away from the picture. He seemed to hate all the things, and yet the comfort of them drew him irresistibly.

In sheer weariness at last he put out his light, and, wrapping his old blankets about him, lay down upon the rug; for he would not disturb the couch lest the morning should dawn and his new dream of comfort look as if it had fled away. Besides, how was he ever to get it together again? And, when the morning broke and Christie awoke to the splendor of his things by daylight, the wonder of it all dawned, too, and he went about his work with the same spell still upon him.

Now and again he would raise his eyes to the pictured Christ and drop them again, reverently. It seemed to him this morning as if that Presence were living and had come to him in spite of all his railings at fate, his bitterness and scoffing, and his feckless life. It seemed to say with that steady gaze: "What will you do with me? I am here, and you cannot get away from my drawing."

It was not as if his life had been filled formerly with tradition and teaching; for his mother had died when he was a little fellow, and the thinlipped, hard-working maiden aunt who had cared for him in her place, whatever religion she might have had in her heart, never thought it necessary to speak it out beyond requiring a certain amount of decorum on Sunday and regular attendance at Sunday school.

In Sunday school it had been his lot to be under a good elder who read the questions from a lesson leaf and looked helplessly at the boys who were employing their time in more pleasurable things the while. The very small amount of holy things he had absorbed from his days at Sunday schools had failed to leave him with a strong idea of the love of God or any adequate knowledge of the way to be saved.

In later years, of course, he had listened listlessly to preaching; and, when he went to college—a small, insignificant one, — he had come in contact with religious people; but here, too, he had heard as one hears a thing in which one has not the slightest interest.

He had gathered and held this much, that the God in whom the Christian world believed was holy and powerful, and that most of the world were culprits. Heretofore God's love had passed him by unaware.

Now the pictured eyes of the Son of God seemed to breathe out tenderness and yearning. For the first time in his life a thought of the possibility of love between his soul and God came to him.

His work that morning was much more complicated than usual. He wasted little time in getting breakfast. He had to clean house. He could not bear the idea that the old regime and the new should touch shoulders as they did behind that screen. So with broom and scrubbing-brush he went to work.

He had things in pretty good shape at last, and was just coming in from giving the horse a belated breakfast when a strange impulse seized him.

At his feet, creeping all over the white sand in delicate tracery, were wild pea blossoms, crimson, white, and pink. He had never noticed them before. What were they but weeds? But with a new insight into possibilities in art, he stooped and gathered a few of them, and, holding them awkwardly, went into the house to put them into his new vase. He felt half-ashamed of them, and held them behind him as he entered; but with the shame there mingled an eagerness to see how they would look in the vase on the "blue bureau thing."

" 'Will you walk into my parlor?'
Said the spider to the fly,
'Tis the prettiest little parlor
That ever you did spy,' "

sang out a rich tenor voice in greeting.

"I say, Chris! What are you setting up for? What does it all mean? Ain't going to get married or nothing, are you, man? because I'll be obliged to go to town and get my best coat out of pawn if you are."

"Aw, now that is gweat!" drawled another voice, English in its accents. "Got anything good to dwink? Twot it out, and we'll be better able to appweciate all this lugshuwy!"

Chapter 3
"And What Are You Going to Say to Her?"

The young man felt a rising tendency to swear. He had forgotten all about the fellows and their agreement to meet and have the day out in jollification. So great had been the spell upon him that he had forgotten to put the little feminine things away from curious eyes.

There he stood foolishly in the middle of his own floor, a bunch of "weeds" in his hand which he had not the sense to drop, while afar the sound of a cracked church bell gave a soft reminder, which the distant popping of firecrackers at a cabin down the road confirmed, that this was Christmas Day. Christmas Day, and the face of the Christ looking down at him tenderly from his own wall.

The oath that was rising to his lips at his foolish plight was stayed. He could not take that name in vain with those eyes upon him. The spell was not broken even yet.

With a sudden quick settling of his lips, he threw back his head, daring in his eyes, and walked over to the glass vase to fill it with water. It was like him to brave it out and tell the whole story now that he was caught.

He was a broad-shouldered young man, firmly knit, with a head well set on his shoulders, and but for a certain careless slouch in his gait might have been fine to look upon. His face was not handsome, but he had good brown eyes with deep hazel lights in them that kindled when he looked at you.

His hair was red, deep and rich, and decidedly curly. His gestures were strong and regular. If there had not been a certain hardness about his face he would have been interesting, but that look made one turn away disappointed.

His companions were both big men like himself. The Englishman — one of that large class of second or third sons with a good education and a poor fortune, and very little practical knowledge how to better it, so many of whom come to Florida to try orange-growing — was loose-jointed and awkward, with pale blue eyes, hay-colored hair, and a large jaw with loose lips. The other was handsome and dark, with a weak mouth and daring black eyes which continually warred with one another.

Both were dressed in rough clothes, trousers tucked into boots with spurs, dark flannel shirts, and soft riding-hats. The Englishman wore gloves and affected a certain loud style in dress. They carried their riding-whips, and walked undismayed upon the bright colors of the rug.

"O, I say now, get off there with those great clods of boots, can't you?" exclaimed Christie, with a sudden descent of housewifely carefulness. "Anybody'd think you'd been brought up in a barn, Armstrong."

Armstrong put on his eye-glasses, — he always wore them as if they were a monocle, — and examined the rug carefully.

"Aw, I beg pawdon! Awfully nice, ain't it? Sorry I didn't bwing my patent leathers along. Wemind me next time, please, Maw-timer."

Christie told the story of his Christmas gifts in as few words as possible. Somehow he did not feel like elaborating it.

The guests seized upon the photograph of the girls, and became hilarious over it.

"Takes you for a girl, does she?" said Mortimer. "That's great! Which one is she? I choose that fine one with snapping black eyes and handsome teeth. She knew her best point, or she wouldn't have laughed when her picture was taken."

Victoria Landis's eyes would have snapped indeed, could she have heard the comments upon herself and the others; but she was safe out of hearing, far up in the North.

The comments went on most freely. Christie found himself disgusted with his friends. Only yesterday he would have laughed at all they said, and now what made the difference? Was it that letter? Would the other fellows feel the same if he should read it to them?

But he never would! The red blood stole up in his face. He could hear their shouts of laughter now over the tender little girlish phrases. It should not be desecrated. He was glad indeed that he had put it in his coat pocket the night before.

There seemed to be a sacredness about the letter and the pictures and all the things, and it went against the grain to hear the coarse laughter of his friends.

At last they began to speak about the girl in the centre of the group, the clear-eyed, firm-mouthed one whom he had selected for Hazel. His blood boiled. He could stand it no longer. With one sweep of his long, strong arm he struck the picture from them with "Aw, shut up! You make me tired!" and, picking it up, put it in his pocket.

Whereat the fun of his companions took a new turn. It suited their fancy to examine the toilet-table decked out in blue and lace. The man named

Mortimer knew the lace collars and handkerchiefs for woman's attire, and they turned upon their most unwilling host and decked him in fine array.

He sat helpless and mad, with a large lace collar over his shoulders, and another hanging down in front arranged over the bureau-cover, which was spread across him as a background, while a couple of lace-bordered handkerchiefs adorned his head.

"And what are you going to say to her for all these pretty presents, Christie, my girl?" laughed Mortimer.

"Say to her!" gasped Christie.

It had not occurred to him before that it would be necessary to say anything. A horrible oppression seemed to be settling down upon his chest. He wished that the whole array of things were back in their boxes and on their way to their ridiculous owners. He got up, and kicked at the rug, and tore the lace finery from his neck, stumbling on the lavender bedroom slippers which his tormentors had stuck on the toes of his shoes.

"Why, certainly, man, — I beg your pardon, — *my dear girl* —" went on Mortimer. "You don't intend to be so rude as not to reply, or say, 'I thank you very kindly'!"

Christie's thick auburn brows settled into a scowl, and the attention of the others was drawn to the side of the room where the organ stood.

"That's awfully fine, don't you know?" remarked Armstrong, levelling his eye-glasses at the picture. "It's by somebody gweat, I dawn just wemembah who."

"Fine frame," said Mortimer tersely as he opened the organ and sat down before it.

And the new owner of the picture felt for the first time in his acquaintance with those two men that they were somehow out of harmony with him.

He glanced up at the picture with the color mounting in his face, half pained for the friendly gaze that had been so lightly treated. He did not in the least understand himself.

But the fingers touching the keys now were not altogether unaccustomed. A soft, sweet strain broke through the room, and swelled louder and fuller until it seemed to fill the little log house and be wafted through the open windows to the world outside.

Christie stopped in his walk across the room, held by the music. It seemed the full expression of all he had thought and felt during the last few hours.

A few chords, and the player abruptly reached out to the pile of singing-books above him, and, dashing the book open at random, began playing, and in a moment in a rich, sweet tenor sang. The others drew near, and each took a book and joined in.

> "He holds the key of all unknown,
>   And I am glad;
>   If other hands should hold the key,
>   Or if He trusted it to me,
>   I might be sad."

The song was a new creed spoken to Christie's soul by a voice that seemed to fit the eyes in the picture. What was the matter with him? He did not at all know. His whole life seemed suddenly shaken.

It may be that the fact of his long residence alone in that desolate land, with but few acquaintances, had made him more ready to be swayed by this sudden stirring of new thoughts and feelings. Certain it was that Christie Bailey was not acting like himself.

But the others were interested in the singing. It had been long since they had had an instrument to accompany them, and they enjoyed the sound of their own voices. They would have preferred, perhaps, a book of college songs, or, better still, the latest street songs; but, as they were not at hand, and "Gospel Hymns" were, they found pleasure even in these.

On and on they sang, through hymn after hymn, their voices growing stronger as they found pieces which had in them some hint of familiarity.

The music filled the house, and floated out into the bright summer Christmas world outside; and presently Christie felt rather than saw a movement at the window, and, looking up, beheld it dark with little, eager faces of the black children. Their supply of firecrackers having given out, they had sought for further celebration, and had been drawn with delight by the unusual sounds. Christie dropped into a chair and gazed at them in wonder, his eyes growing troubled and the frown deepening. He could not make it out. Here he had been for some time, and these little children had never ventured to his premises. Now here they were in full force, their faces fairly shining with delight, their eyes rolling with wonder and joy over the music.

It seemed a fulfilment of the prophecy of the letter that had come with the organ. He began to tremble at the thought of the possibilities that might be entailed upon him with his newly acquired and unsought-for property. And yet he could not help a feeling of pride that all these things were his and that a girl of such evident refinement and cultivation had taken the trouble to send them. To be sure, she wouldn't have done it at all if she had had any idea who or what he was, but that did not matter. She did not know, and she never would know.

He saw the children's curious eyes wander over the room and rest here and there delighted, and his own eyes followed theirs. How altogether nice it was! What a desolate hole it had been before! How was it he had not noticed?

Amid all these thoughts the concert came suddenly to a close. The organist turned upon his stool, and, addressing the audience in the window, remarked, with a good many flourishes: "That finishes the programme for to-day, dear friends. Allow me to announce that a Sunday school will be held in this place on next Sunday afternoon at half-past two o'clock, at which you are all invited to be present. Do you understand? Half-past two. And bring your friends. Now will you all come?"

Amid many a giggle and a bobbing of round black heads they answered as one boy and one girl, "Yes, sah!" and went rollicking down the road in haste to spread the news, their bare feet flying through the sand, and vanished as they had come.

Chapter 4
"A Letter That Wrote Itself"

"What did you do that for?" thundered Christie, suddenly realizing what would be the outcome of this performance.

"Don't speak so loud, Christie, dear; it isn't ladylike, you know. I was merely saving you the trouble of announcing the services. You'll have a good attendance, I'm sure, and we'll come and help you out with the music," said Mortimer in a sweetly unconscious tone.

Christie came at him with clenched fist, which he laughingly dodged, and went on bantering. But the two young men soon left, for Christie was angry and was not good company. They tried to coax him off to meet some of their other boon companions, but he answered shortly, "No," and they left him to himself.

Left alone, he was in no happy frame of mind. He had intended to go with them. There would be something good to eat, and of course something to drink, and cards, and a jolly good time all around. He could forget for a little while his hard luck, and the slowness of the oranges, and his own wasted life, and feel some of the joy of living. But he had the temper that went with his hair, and now nothing would induce him to go.

Was it possible there was something else, too, holding him back? A subtle something which he did not understand, somehow connected with the letter and the picture and the organ?

Well, if there was, he did not stop to puzzle it out. Instead, he threw himself down on the newly arrayed couch, and let his head sink on one of those delightfully soft pillows, and tried to think.

He took out the letter, and read it over again.

When he read the sentences about praying for him, there came a choking sensation in his throat such as he had not felt since the time he nearly drowned, and realized that there was no mother any more to go to. This girl wrote as a mother might perhaps talk, if one had a mother.

He folded the letter, and put it back in his pocket; and then, closing and locking the door, he sat down at the organ and tried to play it.

As he knew nothing whatever about music, he did not succeed very well, and he turned from it with a sigh to look up at those pictured eyes once more and find them following his every movement. Some pictures have that power of seeming to follow one around the room.

Christie got up and walked away, still looking at the picture, and turned and came back again.

Still the eyes seemed to remain upon his face with that strong, compelling gaze. He wondered what it meant, and yet he was glad it had come. It seemed like a new friend.

Finally he sat down and faced the question that was troubling him. He must write a letter to that girl — to those girls, and he might as well have done with it at once and get it out of the way. After that he could feel he had paid the required amount, and could enjoy his things. But it simply was not decent not to acknowledge their receipt. But the tug of war was to know how to do it.

Should he confess that he was a young man and not the Christie they had thought, and offer to send back the things for them to confer upon a more worthy subject?

He glanced hastily about on his new belongings with sudden dismay. Could he give up all this? No. He would not.

His eyes caught the pictured eyes once more. He had found a friend and a little comfort. It had come to him unbidden. He would not bid it depart.

Besides, it would only make those kind people most uncomfortable. They would think they had been doing something dreadful to send a young man presents, especially one whom they had never seen. He knew the ways of the world, a little. And that Hazel Winship who had written the letter, she was a charming person. He would not like to spoil her pretty dream of his being a friendless girl. Let her keep her fancies; they could do no harm.

He would write and thank her as if he were the girl they all supposed him. He had always been good at playing a part or imitating any one; he would just write the letter in a girlish hand — it would not be hard to do — and thank them as they expected to be thanked by another girl. That would be the end of it. Then, when his oranges came into bearing, — if they ever did, — he would send them each a box of oranges anonymously, and all would be right.

As for that miserable business Mortimer had got him into, he would fix that up by shutting up the house and riding away early Sunday morning, and the children might come to Sunday school to their hearts' content. He would not be there to be bothered or bantered.

In something like a good humor he settled to his task.

He wrote one or two formal notes, and tore them up. As he looked about on the glories of his room, he began to feel that such thanks were inadequate to express his feelings. Then he settled to work once more, and began to be interested.

"My dear unknown Friend," he wrote, "I scarcely know how to begin to thank you for the kindness you have showered upon me."

He read the sentence over, and decided it sounded very well and not at all as if a man had written it. The spirit of fun took possession of him, and he made up his mind to write those girls a good long letter, and tell them all about his life, only tell it just as if he were a girl. It would while away this long, unoccupied day. He wrote on:

"You wanted to know all about me; so I am going to tell you. I do not, as you suppose, teach school. I had a little money from the sale of father's farm after he died, and I put it into some land down here planted to young orange-trees. I had heard a great deal about how much money was to be made in orange-growing, and thought I would like to try it. I am all alone in the world — not a soul who cares in the least about me, and so there was no one to advise me against it.

"I came down here and boarded at first, but found it would be a good thing for me to live among my trees, so I could look after things better; so I had a little cabin built of logs right in the grove, and sent for all the old furniture that had been saved from the old home, which was not much, as most things had been sold with the house. You saw how few and poor they were.

"It seems so strange to think that you, who evidently have all the good things of the world to make you happy, should have stopped to think and take notice of poor, insignificant me. It is wonderful, more wonderful than anything that ever happened to me in all my life. I look about on my beautified room, and cannot believe it is I.

"I live all alone in my log cabin, surrounded by a lot of young trees which seem to me very slow in doing anything to make me rich. If I had known all I know now, I never would have come here; but one has to learn by experience, and I'll just have to stick now until something comes of it.

"I am not exactly a girl just like yourselves as you say; for I am twenty-eight years old, and, to judge by your pictures, there isn't one of you as old as that. You are none of you over twenty-two, I am sure, if you are that.

"Besides, you are all beautiful girls, while I most certainly am not. To begin with, my hair is red, and I am brown and freckled from the sun and wind and rain; and, in fact, I am what is called homely. So you see it is not as serious a matter for me to live all alone down here in an orange-grove as it would be for one of you. I have a strong little pony who carries me on his back or in my old buckboard, and does the ploughing. What work I cannot do myself about the grove, I hire done, of course. I also have a few chickens and a dog.

"If you could have seen my little house the night your boxes arrived and were unpacked, you would appreciate the difference the things you have sent make in my surroundings. But you can never know what a difference they will make in my life."

Here the rapid pen halted, and the writer wondered whether that might be a prophecy. So far, he reflected, he had written nothing but what was strictly true; and yet he had not made known his identity.

This last sentence seemed to be writing itself, for he really had no idea that the change in his room would make much difference in his life, except to add a little comfort. He raised his eyes; and, as they met those in the picture, it seemed to be forced upon him that there was to be a difference, and somehow he was not sorry. The old life was not attractive, but he wondered what it would be. He felt as if he were standing off watching the developments in his own life as one might watch the life of the hero in a story.

There was one more theme in Hazel Winship's letter which he had not touched upon, he found, after he had gone over each article by name and said nice things about them all and what a lot of comfort he would have from them.

He was especially pleased with his sentence about the bedroom slippers and lace collars. "They are much too fine and pretty to be worn," he had written, "especially by such a large, awkward person as I am; but I like to feel them and see them, and think how pretty they would look on some of the dainty, pretty girls who sent them to me."

But all the time he was reading his letter over he felt that something would have to be said on that other subject. At last he started it again:

"There is a cabin down the road a little way, and this morning a friend of mine came in and played a little while on the organ — I can't play myself, but I am going to learn" — he had not thought about learning before, but now he knew he should — "and we all got to singing out of the books you sent. By and by I looked up, and saw the doorway full of little ragamuffins listening for all they were worth. I presume I shall be able to give them a good deal of pleasure listening to that organ sometimes, though I am afraid I wouldn't be much of a hand at starting a Sunday school" — that sentence sounded rather mannish for a girl of twenty-eight; but he had to let it stand, as he could think of nothing better to say — "as I never knew much about such things. Though I'm obliged for your praying, I'm sure. It will give me a pleasant feeling at night when I'm all alone to know some one in the world is thinking about me, and I'm sure if prayers can do any good yours ought to.

"But about the Sunday school, I don't want to disappoint you after you've been so kind to send all the papers and books. Maybe I could give the black children some of the papers, and let them study the lessons out for themselves; and I used to be quite a hand at drawing once. I might practise up and draw them some pictures to amuse them sometime when they come around again. I'll do my best.

"I like to think of you all at college having a good time. My school days were the best of my life. I wish I could go over them again. I have a lot of books; but, when I come in tired at night, it seems so lonely here, and I'm so tired I just go to sleep. It doesn't seem to make much difference about my reading any more, anyway. The oranges won't know it. They grow just as soon for me as if I kept up with the procession.

"I appreciate your kindness, though I don't know how to tell you how deeply it has touched me. I have picked out the one in the middle, the girl with the laughing eyes, and a sweet, firm mouth, and the loveliest expression I ever saw on any face, to be Miss Hazel Winship, the one who thought of this whole beautiful plan. Am I right? I'll study the others up later.

"Yours very truly —" here he paused, and, carefully erasing the last word, wrote "lovingly,"

                                        "Christie W. Bailey."

He sat back, and covered his face with his hands. A queer, glad feeling had come over him while he was writing those things about Hazel Winship. He wondered what it was. He actually enjoyed saying those things to her and knowing she would be pleased to read them, and not think him impertinent.

And he had written a good many promises, after all. What led him on to that? Did he mean to keep them? Yes, he believed he did; only those fellows, Armstrong and Mortimer, should not know anything about it. He would carry out his plan of going away Sundays until those ridiculous fellows forgot their nonsense. And, so thinking, he folded and addressed his letter.

A little more than a week later six girls gathered in a cosy college room — Hazel's — to hear the letter read.

"You see," said Hazel, with triumphant light in her eyes, "I was right; she is a girl like us. It doesn't matter in the least little bit that she is twenty-eight. That isn't old. And for once I am glad you see that my impulses are not always crazy. I am going to send this letter home at once to father and mother. They were really quite troublesome about this. They thought it was the wildest thing I ever did, and I've been hearing from it all vacation. Now listen!"

And Hazel read the letter amid many interruptions.

"I'll tell you what it is, girls," she said, as she finished the letter; "we must keep track of her now we've found her. I'm so glad we did it. She isn't a Christian, that's evident; and we must try to make her into one, and work through her a Sunday school. That would be a work worth while. Then maybe sometime we can have her up here for a winter, and give her a change. Wouldn't she enjoy it? It can't be this winter, because we'll have to work so hard here in college we'd have no time for anything else; but after we have all graduated wouldn't it be nice? I'll tell you what I'd like to do; I'd like the pleasure of taking Christie Bailey to Europe. I know she would enjoy it. Just think what fun it would be to watch her eyes shine over new things. I don't mind her red hair one bit. Red-haired people are lovely if they know how to dress to harmonize with their complexions."

"How fortunate we used green for that couch-cover! Christie's hair will be lovely against it," murmured Victoria, in a serio-comic tone, while all the girls set up a shout at Hazel's wild flights of fancy.

"Take Christie Bailey to Europe! O, Hazel! I'm afraid you will be simply dreadful, now you have succeeded in one wild scheme. You will make us do all sorts of things, and never stop at reason."

Hazel's cheeks flushed. It always hurt her a little that these girls did not go quite as far in her philanthropic ideas as she did herself. She had quite taken this Christie girl into her heart, and she wanted them all to do the same.

"Well, girls, you must all write to her, anyway, and encourage her. Think what it would be to be down there, a girl, all alone, and raising oranges. I think she is a hero!"

"O, we'll all write, of course," said Victoria, with mischief in her eye; "but call her a heroine, do, Hazel."

And they all did write, letters full of bright nonsense, and sweet, tender, chatty letters, and letters full of girlish pity, attempts to make life more bearable to the poor girl all alone down in Florida. But a girl who confesses to being homely and red-haired and twenty-eight cannot long hold a prominent place in the life of any but an enthusiast such as Hazel was, and very soon the other five letters dropped off, and Christie Bailey was favored with but one correspondent from that Northern college.

But to return to Florida. That first Sunday morning after Christmas, everything did not go just as was planned by Christie.

In the first place, he overslept. He had discovered some miserable scales on some of his most cherished trees, and he had had to trudge to town Saturday morning, — the man was using the pony ploughing, — and get some whale-oil soap, and then spend the rest of the day until dark spraying his trees. It was no wonder that he was too tired to wake early the next day.

Then, when he finally went out to the pony, he discovered that he was suffering from a badly cut foot, probably the result of the careless hired man and a barbed-wire fence. The swollen foot needed attention.

The pony made comfortable, he reflected on what he would do next. To ride on that pony away anywhere was impossible. To walk he was not inclined. The sun was warm for that time of year, and he still felt stiff from his exertions of the day before. He concluded he would shut up the house, and lie down, and keep still when any one came to call, and they would think him away.

With this purpose in view he gave the pony and the chickens a liberal supply of food, that he need not come out again till evening, and went into the house; but he had no more than reached there when he heard a loud knocking at the front door, evidently with the butt end of a whip; and before he could decide what to do it was thrown open, and Mortimer and Armstrong entered, another young Englishman following close behind. Armstrong wore shiny patent-leather shoes, and seemed anxious to make them apparent.

"Good mawning, Miss Bailey," he said, affably. "Glad to see you looking so fresh and sweet. We just called round to help you pwepare for your little Sunday school."

Chapter 5
A Sunday School in Spite of Itself

Christie was angry. He stood still, looking from one to another of his three guests like a wild animal at bay. They knew he was angry, and that fact contributed not a little to their enjoyment. They meant to carry out the joke to the end.

The third man, Rushforth by name, stood grinning at the rear of the other two. The joke had been so thoroughly explained to him that he could fully appreciate it. He was not noted for being quick at a joke. Armstrong, however, seemed to have a full sense of the ridiculous.

Firmly and cheerfully they took their way with Christie; and he, knowing that resistance was futile, sat down upon his couch in glum silence, and let them work their will.

"I stopped on the way over, and reminded our friends in the cabin below that the hour was two-thirty," remarked Mortimer, as he took a large dinner-bell from his side pocket and rang a note or two. "That's to let them know the time when we are ready to 'take up.' "

Christie scowled, and the others laughed uproariously.

"Now, Armstrong, you and I will go out and reconnoitre for seats, while Rushforth stays here and helps this dear girl dust her parlor ornaments and brickbats. We'll need plenty of seats, for we'll have quite a congregation if all I've asked turn out."

They came back in a few minutes laden with boxes and boards which they ranged in three rows across the end of the cabin facing the organ.

Christie sat and glared at them.

He was very angry, and was trying to think whether to bear it out and see what they would do next, or run away to the woods. He had little doubt that if he should attempt the latter they would all three follow him, and perhaps bind him to a seat to witness the performances they had planned; for they were evidently "taking it out of him" for having all this luxury and not taking them into the innermost confidences of his heart about it.

He shut his teeth and wondered what Hazel would say if she knew how outrageously her idea of a Sunday school was going to be burlesqued.

Armstrong tacked up the blackboard, and got out the chalk. Then, discovering the folded cloth map of the Holy Land, he tacked that up at the end wall where all could see it. Mortimer mapped out the programme.

"Now, Rushforth, you pass the books and the lesson leaves, and I'll stay at the organ and preside. Miss Christie's a little shy about speaking out to-day, you see, and we'll have to help her along before we put her in the superintendent's place. Christie, you can make some pictures on the blackboard. Anything'll do. This is near Christmas — you can make Santa Claus coming down the chimney if you like. I'll run the music, and we'll have quite a time of it. We'll be able to tell the fellows all about it down at the lake next week, and I shouldn't wonder if we'd have a delegation over from Mulberry Creek next Sunday to hear Elder Bailey speak — I beg pardon; I mean Miss Bailey. You must excuse me, dear; on account of your freckles I sometimes take you for a man."

Mortimer spread open a Bible that had come with the singing-books, and actually found the place in the lesson leaf, and made them listen while he read, and declared that Christie ought to give a talk on the lesson. And thus they carried on their banter the whole morning long.

Christie sat glowering in the corner.

He could not make up his mind what to do. For some strange reason he did not want a Sunday school caricatured in his house and with that picture looking down upon it all, and yet he did not know why he didn't want it. He had never been squeamish before about such things. The fellows would not understand it, and he did not understand it himself. But it went against the grain.

Now as it came on about dinner-time he thought they would perhaps go if he offered no refreshments; but no; they seemed to have no such idea. Instead, they sent Armstrong outside to their light wagon they had tied at the tree by the roadside, and he came back laden with a large basket which they proceeded to unpack.

There were canned meats and jellies and pickles and baked beans and all sorts of canned goods that have to be substituted for the genuine article in Florida, where fresh meat and vegetables are not always to be had.

Armstrong went out again, and this time came back with a large case of bottles.

He set it down with a thump on the floor just opposite the picture, while he shut the door. The clink of the bottles bespoke a hilarious hour, and carried memories of many a time of feasting in which Christie had participated before.

His face crimsoned as if some honored friend had suddenly been brought to look upon the worst of his hard, careless life, and he suddenly rose with determination. Here was something which he could not stand.

He drank sometimes, it is true. The fellows all knew it. But both he and they knew that the worst things they had ever done in their lives had been done and said under the influence of liquor. They all had memories of wild debauches of several days' duration, when they had been off together and had not restrained themselves. Each one knew his own heart's shame after such a spree as this. Each knew the other's shame. They never spoke about it, but it was one of the bonds that bound them together, these drunken riots of theirs, when they put their senses at the service of cards and wine, and never stopped until the liquor had given out. At such times each knew that he would have sold his soul for one more penny to stake at the game, or one more drink, had the devil been about in human form to bid for it.

They were none of them drunkards, few of them even constant drinkers, partly because they had little money to spend in such a habit. They all had strong bodies able to endure much, and their life out-of-doors did not tend to create unnatural cravings of appetite. Rather had they forced themselves into these revelries as a means of amusing themselves in a land where there was little but work to fill up the long months and years of waiting.

This case of liquor was not the first that had been in Christie's cabin. He had never felt before that it was out of place in entering there; but now the picture hung there, and the case of liquor, representing the denial of God, seemed to Christie a direct insult to the One whose presence had in a mysterious way crept into the cabin with the picture.

Also he saw in a flash what the fellows were planning to do. They knew his weakness. They remembered how skilled his tongue was in turning phrases when loosened by intoxicants. They were planning to get him drunk — perhaps had even drugged some of the bottles slightly — and then to make him talk, and even pray, it might be!

At another time this might have seemed funny to him. He had not realized before how far he had been going in the way from truth and righteousness. But now his whole soul rose up in loathing of himself, his ways, and his companions.

A sentence of his mother's prayer for him when he was but a little child that had not been in his mind for years now came as clear as if a voice had spoken in his ear, "God make my little Chris a good man!"

And this was how it had been answered. Poor mother!

What Hazel Winship would think of the scene also flashed into his mind. He strode across that room in his angry strength before his astonished companions could stop him; and, taking that case of liquor in his muscular arms, he dashed it far out the open door across the road and into the woods. Then he turned back to the three amazed men.

"You won't have any of that stuff in here!" he said firmly. "If you're bound to have a Sunday school, a Sunday school we'll have; but we won't have any drunken men at it. Perhaps you enjoy mixing things up that way, but I'm not quite a devil yet."

They had not known there was such strength in him. He looked fairly splendid as he stood there in the might of right, his deep eyes glowing darker brown and every mahogany curl a-tremble with determination.

"Aw! Certainly! Beg pawdon!" said Armstrong, settling his eye-glasses that he might observe his former friend more closely. "I meant no hawm, I'm suah." Armstrong was always polite. If an earthquake had thrown him to the ground, he would have arisen and said, "Aw! I beg pawdon!"

But Christie was master in his own house. The others exclaimed a little, and tried to joke him upon his newly acquired temperance principles; but he would not open his lips further on the subject, and they ate their canned meats and jellies and bread moistened only by water from Christie's pump in the yard.

They had scarcely finished when the first instalment of the Sunday school arrived in faded but freshly starched calicoes laundered especially for the occasion. They pattered to the door barefooted, clean, and shining, followed by some of their elders, who lingered smiling and shy at the gateway, uncertain whether to credit the invitation to "Mr. Christie's" cabin. Mr. Christie had never been so hospitable before. But the children, spying the rudely improvised benches, crept in, and the others followed.

Christie stood scowling in the back end of the cabin. Sunday school was on his hands. He could not help it any more than he could help the coming of the organ and the picture. It was a part of his new possessions.

He felt determined that it should not be a farce. How he was going to prevent it he did not know, but he meant to do it.

He looked up at the picture again. It seemed to give him strength. Of course it was but fancy that it had seemed to smile approval after he had flung that liquor out the door; but in spite of his own reason he could not but feel that the Man of the picture was enduring insult here in his house, and that he must fight for His sake.

Added to that was Hazel Winship's faith in him and her desire for a Sunday school. His honor was at stake. He would never have gone out and gathered up a Sunday school to nurse into life, even for Hazel Winship. Neither would he have consented to help in one if his permission had been asked; but now, when it was, as it were, thrust upon him, like a little foundling child all smiling and innocent of possible danger to it, what could he do but help it out?

They were all seated now, and a hush of expectancy pervaded the room.

The three conspirators over by the organ were consulting and laughing in low tones.

Christie knew that the time had come for action. He raised his eyes to the picture once more. To his fancy the eyes seemed to smile assurance to him as he went forward to the organ.

Christie quietly took up a singing-book, and, opening at random, said, "Let us sing number one hundred and thirty-four." He was surprised when they began to sing to find it was the same song that Mortimer had sung first on Christmas morning.

His three friends turned in astonishment toward him. They began to think he was entering into the joke like his own old self, but instead there was a grave, earnest look on his face they had never seen there before.

Mortimer put his fingers on the keys, and began at once. Christie seemed to have taken the play out of their hands and turned the tables upon them. They began to wonder what he would do next. This was fine acting on his part, they felt, for him to take the predicament in which they had placed him and work it out in earnest.

The song was almost finished, and still Christie did not know what to do next.

He announced another hymn at random, and watched old Aunt Tildy settle her steel-bowed spectacles over her nose and fumble among the numbers. The Sunday school was entering into the music with zest. The male trio who led were singing with might and main, but with an amused smile on their faces as if they expected developments soon.

Just then an aged black man came hobbling in. His hair and whiskers were white, and his worn Prince Albert coat ill fitted his bent figure; but there was a clerical manner which clung to the old coat and gave Christie hope. When the song was finished, he raised his eyes without any hesitation and spoke clearly.

"Uncle Moses," he said, "we want to begin right, and you know all about Sunday schools; can't you give us a start?"

Uncle Moses slowly took off his spectacles, and put them carefully away in his pocket while he cleared his throat.

"I ain't much on speechifyin', Mistah Bailey," said he; "but I kin pray. 'Kase you see when I's talkin' to God den I ain't thinkin' of my own sinful, stumblin' speech."

The choir did not attempt to restrain their risibles, but Christie was all gravity.

"That's it, Uncle. That's what we need. You pray." It came to him to wonder for an instant whether Hazel Winship was praying for her Sunday school then, too.

All during the prayer Christie wondered at himself. He conducting a religious service in his own house and asking somebody to pray! And yet, as the trembling, pathetic sentences rolled out, he felt glad that homage was being rendered to the Presence that seemed to have been in the room ever since the picture came.

"O our Father in heaven, we is all poh sinnahs!" said Uncle Moses, earnestly, and Christie felt it was true, himself among the number. It was the first prayer that the young man ever remembered to have felt all the way through. "We is all sick and miserable with the disease of sin. We's got it *bad*, Lord" — here Christie felt the seat behind him shake. Mortimer was behaving very badly. "But, Lord," went on the quavering old voice, "we know dere's a remedy. Away down in Palestine, in de Holy Land, in an Irish shanty, was where de fust medicine-shop of de world was set up, an' we been gettin' de good ob it eber sence. O Lord, we praise thee to-day for de little chile dat lay in dat manger a long time ago, dat brung de fust chance of healing to us poh sinners —"

Mortimer could scarcely contain himself, and the two Englishmen were laughing on general principles. Christie raised his bowed head, and gave Mortimer a warning shove, and they subsided somewhat; but the remarkable prayer went on to its close, and to Christie it seemed to speak a new gospel, familiar, and yet never comprehended before. Could it be that these poor, ignorant people were to teach him a new way?

By the time the prayer was over, he had lost his trepidation. The spirit of it had put a determination into him to make this gathering a success, not merely for the sake of foiling his tormentors, but for the sake of the trusting, childlike children who had come there in good faith.

He felt a little exultant thrill as he thought of Hazel Winship and her commission. He would try to do his best for her sake to-day at least, whatever came of it in future. Neither should those idiots behind him have a grand tale of his breaking down in embarrassment to take away to the fellows over at the lake.

Summoning all his daring, he gave out another hymn, which happened fortunately to be familiar to the audience, and to have many verses; and he reached for a lesson leaf.

O, if his curiosity had but led him to examine the lesson for to-day, or any lesson, in fact! He must say something to carry things off, and he must have a moment to consider. The words swam before his eyes.

He could make nothing out of it all.

Dared he ask one of the fellows to read the Scripture lesson while he prepared his next line of action?

He looked at them. They were an uncertain quantity, but he must have time to think a minute. Armstrong was the safest. His politeness would hold him within bounds.

When the song finished, he handed the leaflet to Armstrong, saying, briefly, "You read the verses, Armstrong."

Armstrong in surprise answered, "Aw, certainly," and adjusting his eye-glasses, began, "Now when Jesus was bawn in Bethlehem —"

"Hallelujah!" interjected Uncle Moses, with his head thrown back and his eyes closed. He was so happy to be in a meeting once more.

"Aw! I beg pahdon, suh! What did you say?" said Armstrong, looking up innocently.

This came near to breaking up the meeting, at least, the white portion of it; but Christie, a gleam of determination in his eye because he had caught a little thread of a thought, said gruffly: "Go on, Armstrong. Don't mind Uncle Moses."

When the reading was over, Christie, annoyed by the actions of his supposed helpers, seized a riding-whip from the corner of the room and came forward to where the map of Palestine hung. As he passed his three friends, he gave them such a glare that instinctively they crouched away from the whip, wondering whether he were going to inflict instant punishment upon them. But Christie was only bent on teaching the lesson.

"This is a map," he said. "How many of you have ever seen a map of Florida?"

Several children raised their hands.

"Well, this isn't a map of Florida; it's a map of Palestine, that place that Uncle Moses spoke about when he prayed. And Bethlehem is on it somewhere. See if you can find it anywhere. Because that's the place that the verses that were just read tell about."

Rushforth suddenly roused to helpfulness. He espied Bethlehem, and at the risk of a cut with the whip from the angry Sunday-school superintendent he came forward and put his finger on Bethlehem.

Christie's face cleared. He felt that the waters were not quite so deep, after all. With Bethlehem in sight and Aunt Tildy putting on her spectacles, he felt he had his audience. He turned to the blackboard.

"Now," said he, taking up a piece of yellow chalk, "I'm going to draw a star. That was one of the first Christmas things that happened about that time. While I'm drawing it, I want you to think of some of the other things the lesson tells about; and, if I can, I'll draw them.''

The little heads bobbed eagerly this side and that to see the wonder of a star appear on the smooth black surface with those few quick strokes.

"I reckon you bettah put a rainbow up 'bove de stah, fer a promise,'' put in old Uncle Moses, " 'cause the Scripture say somewhere, 'Where is de promise of His comin'?' An' de rainbow is His promise in de heavens.''

"All right,'' said Christie, breathing more freely, though he did not quite see the connection. And soon a rainbow arch glowed at the top over the star. Then began to grow desire to see this and that thing drawn, and the scholars, interested beyond their leader's wildest expectations, called out: "Manger, wise men! King!''

Christie stopped at nothing from a sheep to an angel. He made some attempt to draw everything they asked for.

And his audience did not laugh. They were hushed into silence. Part of them were held in thrall by overwhelming admiration for his genius, and the other part by sheer astonishment. The young men, his companions, looked at Christie with a new respect, and gazed gravely from him to a shackly cow, which was intended to represent the oxen that usually fed from the Bethlehem manger, and wondered. A new Christie Bailey was before them, and they knew not what to make of him.

For Christie was getting interested in his work. The blackboard was almost full, and the perspiration was standing out on his brow and making little damp, dark rings of the curls about his forehead.

"There's just room for one more thing. What shall it be, Uncle Moses?'' he said as he paused. His face was eager and his voice was interested.

"Better write a cross down, sah, 'cause dat's de reason for dat baby's comin' into dis world. He came to die to save us all.''

"Amen!'' said Aunt Tildy, wiping her eyes and settling her spectacles for the last picture, and Christie turned with relief back to his almost finished task. A cross was an easy thing to make.

He built it of stone, massive and strong; and, as its arms grew, stretched out to save, something of its grandeur and purpose seemed to enter his mind and stay.

"Now let's sing 'Rock of Ages,' " said Uncle Moses, closing his eyes in a happy smile, and the choir hastily found it and began.

As the Sunday school rose to depart, and shuffled out with many a scrape and bow and admiring glance backward at the glowing blackboard, Christie felt a hand touch his arm; and, glancing down, he saw a small girl with great, dark eyes set in black fringes gazing up at the picture above the organ, her little bony hand on his sleeve.

"Is dat man yoh all's fader?" she asked him, timidly.

A great wave of color stole up into Christie's face.

"No," he answered. "That is a picture of Jesus when He grew up to be a man."

"O!" gasped the little girl, in admiration, "did you done draw dat? Did you all evah see Jesus?"

The color deepened.

"No, I did not draw that picture," said Christie; "it was sent a present to me."

"O," said the child, disappointed, "I thought you'd maybe seed Him sometime. But He look like you, He do. I thought He was you all's fader."

The little girl turned away, but her words lingered in Christie's heart. His Father! How that stirred some memory! His Father in heaven! Had he perhaps spoken wrong when he claimed no relationship with Jesus, the Christ?

Chapter 6
"My Father!"

The three young men who had come to play a practical joke had stayed to clear up. Gravely and courteously they had gone about the work, had piled the hymn-books neatly on top of the organ, and placed the boards and boxes away under the house for further use if needed, for the entire Sunday school had declared, upon leaving the house with a bow and a smile, "I'll come again next Sunday, Mistah Christie; I'll come every Sunday." And Christie had not said them nay.

The young men had bade a good evening to their host, not once calling him "Miss Christie," had voted the afternoon and genuine success, and were actually gone.

Christie sank to the couch, and looked into the eyes looking down upon him.

He was tired. O, he was more tired than he had ever been in his life before! He was so tired he would like to cry. And the pictured eyes seemed yearning to comfort him.

He thought of the words of the little black girl. "Is dat man you's fader?"

"My Father!" he said aloud. "My Father!" The words echoed with a pleasant ring in the little silent, lonely room. He did not know why he said it, but he repeated it again.

And now if the traditions of his childhood had been filled with the Bible, a host of verses would have flocked about him; but, as his mind had not been filled with holy things, he had it all to learn, and his ideas of the Man, Christ Jesus, were of the vaguest and crudest. And perhaps, as to the children of old, God was speaking directly to his heart.

Christie lay still and thought. Went over all his useless life, and hated it; went over the past week with its surprises, and then over the strange afternoon. His own conduct seemed to him the most surprising, after all. Now why, just why, had he thrown that case of liquor out of the door, and why had he gone ahead with that Sunday school? There was a mysterious power at work within him. Was the secret the presence of the Man of the picture?

The sun dropped over the rim of the flat, low horizon, and left the pines looming dark against a starry sky. All the earth went dark with night. And Christie lay there in the quiet darkness, yet not alone. He kept thinking over what the little girl had said to him, and once again he said it out loud in the hush of the room, "My Father!"

But, as the darkness grew deeper, there seemed to be a luminous halo up where he knew the picture hung, and while he rested there with closed eyes he felt that presence growing brighter. Those kind eyes were looking down upon him out of the dark of the room.

This time he called, "My Father!" with recognition in his voice, and out from the shadows of his life the Christ stepped nearer till He stood beside the couch, and, stooping, blessed him, breathed His love upon him, while he looked up in wonder and joy. And, perhaps because he was not familiar with the words of Christ, the young man was unable to recall in what form those precious words of blessing had fallen upon his ear during the dream, or trance, or whatever it might be, that had come upon him.

When the morning broke about him, Christie, waking, sat up and remembered, and decided that it must have been a dream induced by the unusual excitement of the day before; yet there lingered with him a wondrous joy for which he could not account.

Again and again he looked at the picture reverently, and said under his breath, "My Father."

He began to wonder whether he was growing daft. Perhaps his long loneliness was enfeebling his mind that he was so susceptible to what he had always considered superstition; nevertheless, it gave him joy, and he finally decided to humor himself in this fancy. This was the permission of his old self toward the new self that was being born within him.

He went about his work singing.

"He holds the key of all unknown,
And I am glad —"

"Well, I *am* glad!" he announced aloud, as if some one had disputed the fact he had just stated. "About the safest person to hold the key, after all, I guess;" and even as a maiden might steal a glance to the eyes of her lover, so the soul in him glanced up to the eyes of the picture.

The dog and the pony rejoiced as they heard their master's cheery whistle, and Christie felt happier that day than he had since he was a little boy.

Towards night he grew quieter. He was revolving a scheme. It would be rather interesting to write out an account of the Sunday school, not, of course, the part the fellows had in it, for that must not be known, but just the pleasant part, about Uncle Moses and Aunt Tildy. He would write it to Hazel Winship, — not that it was likely he would ever send it, but it would be pleasant work to pretend to himself he was writing her another letter. He had not enjoyed anything for a long time as much as he enjoyed writing that letter to her the other day.

Perhaps after a long time, if she ever answered his letter, — and here he suddenly realized he was cherishing a faint hope in his heart that she would answer it, — he might revise this letter and send it to her. It would please her to know he was trying to do his best with a Sunday school for her, and she would be likely to appreciate some of the things that had happened. He would do it; he would do it this very evening.

He hurried through his day's work with a zest. There was something to look forward to in the evening. It was foolish, perhaps, but surely no more foolish than his amusements the last four years had been. It was innocent, at least, and could do no one any harm.

Then, as he sat down to write, he glanced instinctively to the picture. It still wove its spell of the eyes about him, and he had not lost the feeling that Christ had come to him, though he had never made the slightest attempt or desired to come to Christ. And under the new influence he wrote his thoughts, as one might wing a prayer, scarce believing it would ever reach a listening ear, yet taking comfort in the sending. And so he wrote:

"*My dear new Friend:* — I did not expect to write to you again; at least, not so soon; for it seems impossible that one so blessed with this world's good things should have time to care to think twice of one like me. I do not even know now whether I shall ever send this when it is written, but it will while away my lonely evening to write, and give me the pleasure of a little talk with a companion whom I much appreciate, and if I never send it, it can do no harm.

"It is about the Sunday school. You know I told you I could never do anything like that; I did not know how; and I never dreamed that I could — or would, perhaps I ought to say — more than to give the negroes the papers you sent and let them hear the organ sometimes. But a very strange thing has happened. A Sunday school has come to me in spite of myself.

"The friend who was playing the organ this Christmas morning, when the black children stood at the door listening, in jest invited them to a Sunday school, and they came. I was vexed because I did not know what to do with them. Then, too, the friend came, bringing two others; and they all thought it was a huge joke. I saw they were going to act out a farce; and, while I never had much conscience about these things before, I seemed to know that it would not be what you would like. Then, too, that wonderful picture that you sent disturbed me. I did not like to laugh at religion with that picture looking on.

"You may perhaps wonder at me. I do not understand myself, but that picture has had a strange effect upon me. It made me do a lot of things Sunday that I did not want to do. It made me take hold and do something to make that Sunday school go right. I didn't know how in the least. Of course I've been to Sunday school; I did not mean that; but I never took much notice of things, how they were done; and I was not one to do it, anyway. I felt my unfitness dreadfully, and all the more because those friends of mine were here, and I knew they were making fun. I made them sing a lot, and then I asked old Uncle Moses to help us out. I wish I could show you Uncle Moses."

Here the writer paused, and seemed to be debating a point a moment, and then rapidly wrote:

"I'll try to sketch him roughly."

There followed a spirited sketch of Uncle Moses with both hands crossed atop his heavy cane, his benign chin leaning forward interestedly. One could fairly see how yellow with age were his whitened locks, how green with age his ancient coat. Christie had his talents, though there were few outlets for them.

It is of interest to note just here that, when this letter reached the Northern college, as it did one day, those six girls clubbed together, and laughed and cried over the pictures, and finally, after due council, Christie Bailey was offered a full course in a famous woman's college of art. This he smiled over and quitely declined, saying he was much too old to begin anything like that, which required that one should begin at babyhood to accomplish anything by it. This the girls sighed over and argued over, but finally gave up, as they found Christie wouldn't.

But to return to the letter. Christie gave a full account of the prayer, which had touched his own heart deeply. Then he described and sketched Aunt Tildy with her spectacles. He had a secret longing to put in Armstrong with his glasses and the incident of his interruption with the Bible-reading; but, as that would reflect somewhat upon his character as an elderly maiden, to be found consorting with three such young men, he restrained himself. But he put an extra vigor into the front row of little black heads, bobbing this way and that, singing with might and main.

"I knew they ought to have a lesson next, but I didn't know how to teach it any better than I know how to make an orange-tree bear in a hurry. However, I determined to do my best. I happened to remember there had been something said in what was read about a star; so I made one, and told them each to think of something they had heard about in that lesson that they wanted me to draw. That worked first-rate. They tried everything, pretty near, in the encyclopaedia, and I did my best at each till the whole big blackboard was full. I wish you could see it. It looks like a Noah's ark hanging up there on the wall now, for I have not cleaned it off yet. I keep it there to remind me that I really did teach a Sunday-school class once.

"When they went away, they all said they were coming again, and I don't doubt they'll do it. I'm sure I don't know what to do with them if they do, for I've drawn all there is to draw; and, as for teaching them anything, they can teach me more in a minute than I could teach them in a century. Why, one little child looked up at me with her big, round, soft eyes, for all the world like my faithful dog's eyes, so wistful and pretty, and asked me if that picture on the wall was my father.

"I wish I knew more about that picture. I know it must be meant for Jesus Christ. I am not quite so ignorant of all religion as not to see that. There is the halo with the shadow of the cross above His head. And, when the sun has almost set, it touches there, and the halo seems to glow and glow almost with phosphorescent light until the sun is gone and leaves us all in darkness; and then I fancy I can see it yet glow out between the three arms of the cross.

"And now I do not know why I am writing this. I did not mean to do so when I began, but I feel as if I must tell of the strange experience I had last night."

And then Christie told his dream. Told it till one reading could but feel as he felt, see the vision with him, yearn for the blessing, and be glad and wonder always after.

"Tell me what it means," he wrote. "It seems as if there was something in this presence for me. I cannot believe that it is all imagination, for it would leave me when day comes. It has set me longing for something, I know not what. I never longed before, except for my oranges to bring me money. When I wanted something I could not have, heretofore, I went and did something I knew I ought not, just for pleasure of doing wrong, a sort of defiant pleasure. Now I feel as if I wanted to do right, to be good, like a little child coming to its father. I feel as if I wanted to ask you, as that little soul asked me yesterday, 'Do you all's know that Man?' "

Christie folded his letter, and flung it down upon the table with his head upon his hands. With the writing of that experience the strength seemed to have gone out of him. He felt abashed in its presence. He seemed to have avowed something, to have made a declaration of desire and intention for which he was hardly ready yet; and still he did not want to go back. He was like a man groping in the dark, not knowing where he was, or whether there was light, or whether indeed he wanted the light if there was any to be had.

But before he retired that night he dropped upon his knees beside his couch, with bowed and reverent head, and after waiting silently awhile he said aloud, "My Father!" as if he were testing a call. He repeated it again, more eagerly, and a third time, with a ring in his voice, "My Father!"

That was all. He did not know how to pray. His soul had grown no farther than just to know how to call to his Father, but it was enough. A kind of peace seemed to settle down upon him, a feeling that he had been heard.

Once more there came to him a knowledge that he was acting out of all reason, and he wondered whether he could be losing his mind. He, a red-haired, hard-featured orange-grower, who but yesterday had carried curses so easily upon his lips, and might again to-morrow, to be allowing his emotions thus to carry him away! It was simply childish!

But so deep was the feeling that a Friend was near, that he might really say, "My Father," if only to the dark, that he determined to keep up the hallucination, if indeed hallucination it was, as long as it would last. And so he fell asleep again to dream of benediction.

And on the morrow a sudden desire took him to mail that letter he had written the night before. And what harm, since he would never see the girl, and since she thought him a poor, forlorn creature — half daft this letter might prove him; but even so she might write him again, which result he found he wanted very much when he came to think about it; and so without giving himself a chance to repent by rereading it he drove the limping pony to town and mailed it.

Now, as it came on toward the middle of the week, a conviction suddenly seized Superintendent Christie Bailey that another Sunday was about to dawn and another time of trial would perhaps be his. He had virtually bound himself to that Sunday school by the mailing of that foolish letter. He could have run away if it had not been for that, and those girls up North would never have bothered their heads any more about their old Sunday school. What if Mortimer should bring the fellows over from the lake? What if! Oh, horror! His blood froze in his veins.

Chapter 7
"I Love You"

After his supper that night he doggedly seized the lesson leaf, and began to study. He read the whole thing through, hints and suggestions and elucidations and illustrations and all, and then began over again.

At last it struck him that the hints for the infant class would about suit his needs, and without further ado he set himself to master them. Before long he was interested as a child in his plans, and the next evening was spent in cutting out paper crosses as suggested in the lesson, one for every scholar he expected to be present, and lettering them with the golden text.

He spent another evening still in making an elaborate picture on the reverse side of the blackboard, to be used at the close of his lesson after he had led up to it by more simple work on the other side.

He even went so far as to take the hymn-book and select the hymns, and to write out a regular programme. No one should catch him napping this time. Neither should the prayer be forgotten. Uncle Moses would be there, and they could trust him to pray.

Christie was a little anxious about his music, for upon that he depended principally for success. He felt surprised over himself that he so much wished to succeed, when a week ago he had not cared. What would he do, though, if Mortimer did not turn up, or, worse still, if he had planned more mischief?

But the three friends appeared promptly on the hour, gravity on their faces and helpfulness in the very atmosphere that surrounded them. They had no more practical jokes to play. They had recognized that for some hidden reason Christie meant to play this thing out in earnest, and their liking and respect for him were such that they wanted to assist in the same spirit.

They liked him none the less for his prompt handling of the case of liquors. They carried a code of honor in that colony that respected moral courage when they saw it. Besides, everybody liked Christie.

They listened gravely to Christie's lesson, even with interest. They took their little paper crosses, and studied them curiously, and folded them away in their breast pockets, — Armstrong had passed them about, being careful to reserve three for himself, Mortimer, and Rushforth, — and they sang with a right good will.

And, when the time came to leave, they shook hands with Christie like the rest, and without the least mocking in their voices said they had had a pleasant time and they would come again. Then each man took up a box and a board, and stowed them away as he passed out.

And thus was Christie set up above the rest to a position of honor and respect. This work that he had taken up — that they had partly forced him to take up — separated him from them somewhat, and perhaps it was this fact that Christie had to thank afterward for his freedom from temptation during those first few weeks of the young man's acquaintance with his heavenly Father.

For how would it have been possible for him to grow into the life of Christ if he had been constantly meeting and drinking liquor with these boon companions?

The new life could not have grown with the old.

Christie's action that first Sunday afternoon had made a difference between him and the rest. They could but recognize it, and they admired it in him; therefore they set him up. What was there for Christie but to try to act up to his position?

Before the end of another week there arrived from the North a package of books and papers and Sunday-school cards and helps such as would have delighted the heart of the most advanced Sunday-school teacher of the day. What those girls could not think of, the head of the large religious bookstore to which they had gone thought of for them, and Christie had food for thought and action during many a long, lonely evening.

And always these evenings ended in his kneeling in the dark, where he fancied the light of Christ's halo in the picture could send its glow upon him, and saying aloud in a clear voice, "My Father," while outside in the summer-winter night was only the wailing of the tall pines as they waved weird fingers dripping with gray moss, or the plaintive call of the tit-willow, through the night.

There had come with the package, too, a letter for Christie. He put it in his breast pocket with glad anticipation, and hustled that pony home at a most unmerciful trot; at least, so thought the pony.

When Hazel Winship read that second letter aloud to the other girls, she did not read the whole of it. The pages which contained the sketches she passed about freely, and they read and laughed over the Sunday school, and talked enthusiastically of its future; but the pages which told of the Sabbath-evening vision and of Christie's feeling toward the picture Hazel kept to herself.

She felt instinctively that Christie would rather not have it shown. It seemed so sacred to her and so wonderful. Her heart went out to the other soul seeking its Father.

When they were all gone out of her room that night, she locked her door and knelt a long time praying, praying for the soul of Christie Bailey. Something in the longing of that letter from the South had reproached her, that she, with all her helps to enlightenment, was not appreciating to its full the love and care of her heavenly Father. And so Christie unknowingly helped Hazel Winship nearer to her Master.

And then Hazel wrote the letter, in spite of a Greek thesis, THE thesis in fact, that was waiting and calling to her with urgency — the letter that Christie carried home in his breast pocket.

He did not wait to eat his supper, though he gave the pony his. Indeed, it was not a very attractive function at its best.

Christie was really handsome that night, with the lamplight bringing out all the copper tints and garnet shadows in his hair. His finely cut lips curled in a pleasant smile of anticipation. He had not realized before how much, how very much, he wanted to hear from Hazel Winship again.

His heart was thumping like a girl's as he tore open the delicately perfumed envelope and took out the many closely written pages of the letter; and his heart rejoiced that it was long and closely written. He resolved to read it slowly and make it last a good while.

"My dear, dear Christie," it began, "your second letter has come, and first I want to tell you that I *love* you."

Christie gasped, and dropped the sheets upon the table, his arms and face upon them. His heart was throbbing painfully, and his breath felt like great sobs.

When he raised his eyes by and by, as he was growing to have a habit of doing, to the picture, they were full of tears; and they fell and blurred the delicate writing of the pages on the table, and the Christ knew and pitied him, and seemed almost to smile.

No one had ever told Christie Bailey of loving him, not since his mother those long years ago had held him to her breast and whispered to God to make her little Chris a good man.

He had grown up without expecting love. He scarcely thought he knew the meaning of the word. He scorned it in the only sense he ever heard it spoken of. And now, in all his loneliness, when he had almost ceased to care what the world gave him, to have this free, sweet love of a pure-hearted girl rushed upon him without stint and without cause overpowered him.

Of course he knew it was not his, this love she gave so freely and so frankly. It was meant for a person who never existed, a nice, homely old maid, whose throne in Hazel's imagination had come to be located in his cabin for some strange wonderful reason; but yet it was his, too, his to enjoy, for it certainly belonged to no one else. He was robbing no one else to let his hungry heart be filled a little while with the fulness of it.

One resolve he made instantly, without hesitation, and that was that he would be worthy of such love if so be in him it lay to be. He would cherish it as a tender flower that had been meant for another, but had fallen instead into his rough keeping; and no thought or word or action of his should ever stain it.

Then with true knighthood in his heart to help him onward he raised his head and read on, a great joy upon him which almost engulfed him.

"And I believe you love me a little, too."

Christie caught his breath again. He saw that it was true, although he had not known it before.

"Shall I tell you why I think so? Because you have written me this little piece out of your heart-life, this story of your vision of Jesus Christ, for I believe it was such.

"I have not read that part of your letter to the other girls. I could not. It seemed sacred; and, while I know they would have sympathized and understood, yet I felt perhaps you wrote it just to me, and I would keep it sacred for you.

"And so I am sending you this little letter just to speak of that to you. I shall write in my other letter with the rest of the girls, all about the Sunday school, how glad we are, and all about the pictures how fine they are; and you will understand. But this letter is all about your own self.

"I have stopped most urgent work upon my thesis to write this, too; so you may know how important I consider you, Christie. I could not sleep last night, for praying about you."

It was a wonderful revelation to Christie, that story of the longing of another soul that his might be saved. To the lonely young fellow, grown used as he was to thinking that not another one in all the world cared for him, it seemed almost unbelievable.

He forgot for the time that she considered him another girl like herself. He forgot everything save her pleading that he would give himself to Jesus. She wrote of Jesus Christ as one would write of a much-loved friend, met often face to face, consulted about everything in life, and trusted beyond all others.

A few weeks ago this would indeed have been wonderful to the young man, but that it could have any relation to himself — impossible! Now, with the remembrance of his dream, and the joy his heart had felt from the presence of a picture in his room, it seemed it might be true that Christ would love even him, and with so great a love.

The pleading took hold upon him. Jesus was real to this one girl; He might become real to him.

The thought of that girlish figure kneeling beside her bed in the solemn night hours praying for him was almost more than he could bear. It filled him with awe and a great joy. He drew his breath in sobs, and did not try to keep the tears from flowing. It seemed that the fountains of the years were broken up in him, and he was weeping out his cry for the lonely, unloved childhood he had lost, and the bitter years of mistakes that had followed.

It appeared that the Bible had a great part to play in this new life put before him. Verses which he recognized as from the Scripture abounded in the letter, which he did not remember ever to have heard before, but which came to him with a rich sweetness as if spoken just for him.

Did the Bible contain all that? And why had he not known it before? He had gone to other books for respite from his loneliness. Why had he never known that here was deeper comfort than all else could give?

"Think of it, Christie," the letter said; "Jesus Christ would have come to this earth and lived and died to save you if you had been the only one out of the whole earth that was going to accept Him."

He turned his longing eyes to the picture. Was that true? And the eyes seemed to answer, "Yes, Christie, I would."

Before he turned out his light that night he took the Bible from the organ, and, opening at random, read, "For I have loved thee with an everlasting love; therefore with loving-kindness have I drawn thee." And a light of belief overspread his face. He could not sleep for many hours, for thinking of it all.

There was no question in his mind of whether he would or not. He felt he was the Lord's in spite of everything else. The loving-kindness that had drawn him had been too great for any human resistance.

Then with the realization of the loving-kindness had come self-reproach for his so long denial and worse than indifference. He did not understand the meaning of repentance and faith, but he was learning them in his life.

Christie was never the same after that night. Something had changed in him. It may have been growing all those days since the things first came, but that letter from Hazel Winship marked a decided epoch in his life. All his manhood rose to meet the sweetness of the girl's unasked prayer for him.

It mattered not that she thought not of him as a man. She had prayed, and the prayer had reached up to heaven and back to him again.

The only touch of sadness about it was that he should never be able to see her and thank her face to face for the good she had done to him. He thought of her as some far-away angel who had stooped to earth for a little while, and in some of his reveries dreamed that perhaps in heaven, where all things were made right, he should know her. For the present it was enough that he had her sweet friendship, and her companionship in writing.

Not for worlds now would he reveal his identity. And the thought that this might be wrong did not enter his mind. What harm could it possibly do? and what infinite good to himself! — and perhaps through himself to a few of those little black children. He let this thought come timidly to the front.

This was the beginning of the friendship that made life a new thing to Christie Bailey. Long letters he wrote, telling the thoughts of his inmost heart as he had never told them to any one on earth, as he would never have been able to tell them to one whom he hoped to meet sometime, as he would have told them to God.

And the college student found time amid her essays and her fraternities to answer them promptly.

Her companions wondered why she wasted so much valuable time on that poor "cracker" girl, as they sometimes spoke of Christie, and how she could have patience to write so long letters; but their curiosity did not go so far as to wonder what she found to say; else they might have noticed that less and less often did Hazel offer to read aloud her letters from the Southland. But they were busy, and only occasionally inquired about Christie now, or sent a message.

Hazel herself sometimes wondered why this stranger girl had taken so deep a hold upon her; but the days went by and the letters came frequently, and she never found herself willing to put one by unanswered. There was always some question that needed answering, some point on which her young convert to Jesus Christ needed enlightenment.

Then, too, she found herself growing nearer to Jesus because of this friendship with one who was just learning to trust Him in so childlike and earnest a way.

"Do you know," she said confidingly to Ruth Summers one day, "I cannot make myself see Christie Bailey as homely? It doesn't seem possible to me. I think she is mistaken. I know I shall find something handsome about her when I see her, which I shall some day."

And Ruth smiled mockingly. "O Hazel, Hazel, it will be better, then, for you never to see poor Christie, I am sure; for you will surely find your ideal different from the reality."

But Hazel's eyes grew dreamy, and she shook her head.

"No, Ruth, I'm sure, sure. A girl couldn't have all the beautiful thoughts Christie has, and not be fine in expression. There will be some beauty in her, I am sure. Her eyes, now, I know are magnificent. I wish she would send me a picture; but she won't have one taken, though I've coaxed and coaxed."

Chapter 8
Sad News From the North

In his own heart-life Christie was changing day by day. The picture of Christ was his constant companion. At first shyly and then openly he grew to make a confidant of it. He studied the lines of the face, and fitted them to the lines of the life depicted in the New Testament, and without his knowing it his own face was changing. The lines of recklessness and hardness about his mouth were gone. The dullness of discontent was gone from his eyes. They could light now from within in a flash with a joy that no discouragement could quite quench.

By common consent Christie's companions respected his new way of life, and perhaps after the first few weeks if he had shown a disposition to go back to the old way of doing might have even attempted to keep him to his new course.

They every one knew that their way was a bad way. Each man was glad at heart when Christie made an innovation. They came to the Sunday school and helped, controlling their laughter admirably whenever Uncle Moses gave occasion; and they listened to Christie's lessons, which, to say the least, were original, with a courteous deference, mingled with a kind of pride that one of their number could do this.

They also refrained from urging him to go with them on any more revellings. Always he was asked, but in a tone that he came to feel meant that they did not expect him to accept, and would perhaps have been disappointed if he had done so.

Once, when Christie, unthinkingly, half-assented to go on an all-day's ride with some of them, Mortimer put his hand kindly on Christie's shoulder, and said in a tone Christie had never heard him use before: "I wouldn't, Chris. It might be a bore."

Christie turned, and looked earnestly into his eyes for a minute, and then said, "Thank you, Mort!"

As he stood watching them ride away, a sudden instinct made him reach his hand to Mortimer, and say, "Stay with me this time, old fellow"; but the other shook his head, smiling somewhat sadly, Christie thought, and said as he rode off after the others, "Too late, Chris; it isn't any use."

Christie thought about it a good deal that day as he went about his grove without his customary whistle, and at night, before he began his evening's reading and writing, he knelt and breathed his first prayer for the soul of another.

The winter blossomed into spring, and the soft wind blew the breath of yellow jessamine and bay blossoms from the swamps. Christie's wire fence bloomed out into a mass of Cherokee roses, and among the glossy orange-leaves there gleamed many a white, starry blossom, earnest of the golden fruit to come.

Christie with throbbing heart and shining eyes picked his first orange-blossoms, a goodly handful, and, packing them after the most approved methods for long journeys, sent them to Hazel Winship.

Never any oranges, be they numbered by thousands of boxes, could give him the pleasure that those first white waxen blossoms gave as he laid his face gently among them and breathed a blessing on the one to whom they went, before he packed them tenderly in their box.

Christie was deriving daily joy now from Hazel Winship's friendship. Sometimes when he remembered the tender little sentences in her letters his heart fairly stood still with longing that she might know who he was and yet be ready to say them to him. Then he would crush this wish down, and grind his heel upon it, and tell his better self that only on condition of never thinking such a thought again would he allow another letter written her, another thought sent toward her.

Then would he remember the joy she had already brought into his life, and go smiling about his work, singing,

> "He holds the key of all unknown,
>   And I am glad."

Hazel Winship spent that first summer after her graduation, most of it, visiting among her college friends at various summer resorts at seaside or on mountain-top. But she did not forget to cheer Christie's lonely summer days — more lonely now because some of his friends had gone North for a while — with bits of letters written from shady nooks on porch or lawn, or sitting in a hammock.

"Christie, you are my safety-valve," she wrote once. "I think you take the place with me of a diary. Most girls use a diary for that. If I was at home with mother, I might use her sometimes; but there are a good many things that if I should write her she would worry, and there really isn't any need, but I could not make her sure. So you see I have to bother you. For instance, there is a young man here —" Christie drew his brows together fiercely. This was a new aspect. There were other young men, then. Of course — and he drew a deep sigh.

It was during the reading of that letter that Christie began to wish there were some way for him to make his real self known to Hazel Winship. He began to see some reasons why what he had done was not just all right.

But there was a satisfaction in being the safety-valve, and there was delight in their trysting-hour when they met before the throne of God. Hazel had suggested this when she first began to try to help Christie Christward; and they had kept it up, praying for this one and that one and for the Sunday school.

Once Christie had dared to think what joy it would be to kneel beside her and hear her voice praying for him. Would he ever hear her voice? The thought had almost taken his breath away. He had not dared to think of it again.

The summer deepened into autumn; and the oranges, a goodly number for the first crop, green disks unseen amid their background of green leaves, blushed golden day by day. And then, just as Christie was beginning to be hopeful about how much he would get for his fruit, there came a sadness into his life that shadowed all the sunshine, and made the price of oranges a very small affair. For Hazel Winship fell ill.

At first it did not seem to be much — a little indisposition, a headache and loss of appetite. She wrote Christie she did not feel well and could not write a long letter.

Then there came a silence of unusual length, followed by a letter from Ruth Summers, at whose home Hazel had been staying when taken ill. It was brief and hurried, and carried with it a hint of anxiety, which, as the days of silence grew into weeks, made Christie's heart heavy.

"Hazel is very ill indeed," she wrote, "but she has worried so that I promised to write and tell you why she had not answered your letter."

The poor fellow comforted himself day after day with the thought that she had thought of him in all her pain and suffering.

He wrote to Ruth Summers, asking for news of his dear friend; but, whether from the anxiety over the sick one, or from being busy about other things, or it may be from indifference, — he could not tell, — there came no answer for weeks.

During this sad time he ceased to whistle. There grew a sadness in his eyes that told of hidden pain, and his cheery ways with the Sunday school were gone.

One day when his heart had been particularly heavy, and he had found the Sabbath-school lesson almost an impossibility, the little dusky girl who had spoken to him before touched him gently on the arm.

"Mistah Christie feel bad? Is somebody you all love, sick?"

Almost the tears filled Christie's eyes as he looked at her in surprise, and nodded his head.

"Youm 'fraid they die?"

Again Christie nodded. He could not speak; something was choking him. The sympathetic voice of the little girl was breaking down his self-control.

The little black fingers touched his hand sorrowfully, and there was in her eyes a longing to comfort, as she lifted them first to her beloved superintendent's face and then to the picture above them.

"But you all's fathah's not dead," she pleaded, shyly.

Christie caught her meaning in a flash, and marvelled afterwards that a child should have gone so directly to the point, where he, so many years beyond her, had missed it. He had not learned yet how God has revealed the wise things of this world unto the babes.

"No, Sylvie," he said quickly, grasping the timid little fingers; "my Father is not dead. I will take my trouble to Him. Thank you."

The smile that broke over the little girl's face as she said good-night was the first ray of the light that began to shine over Christie Bailey's soul as he realized that God was not dead and God was his Father.

When they were all gone, he locked his doors, and knelt before his heavenly Father, pouring out his anguish, praying for his friend and for himself, yielding up his will, and feeling the return of peace, and surety that God doeth all things well. Again as he slept he saw the vision of the Christ bending over him in benediction, and when he woke he found himself singing softly,

> "He holds the key to all unknown,
>   And I am glad."

He wondered whether it was just a happening — and then knew that it was not — that Ruth Summer's second letter reached him that day, saying that Hazel was at last past all danger and had spoken about Christie Bailey, and so she, Ruth, had hastened to send the message on, hoping the far-away friend would forgive her for the delay in answering.

After that Christie believed with his whole soul in prayer.

He set himself the pleasant task of writing to Hazel all he had felt and experienced during her illness and long silence. When she grew well enough to write him again, he might send it. He was not sure.

One paragraph he allowed himself, in which to pour out the pent-up feelings of his heart. But even in this he weighed every word. He began to long to be perfectly true before her, and to wish there were a way to tell her all the truth about himself without losing her friendship. This was the paragraph.

"I did not know until you were silent how much of my life was bound up with yours. I can never tell you how much I love you, but I can tell God about it, the God you taught me to love."

The very next day there came a note from Ruth Summers saying that Hazel was longing to hear from Florida again and that she was now permitted to read her own letters. Then with joy he took his letter to the office, and not long after received a little note in Hazel's own familiar hand, closing with the words: "Who knows? perhaps you will be able to tell me all about it some day, after all." And Christie, when he read it, held his hand on his heart to still the tumult of pain and joy.

"Have you written to Christie Bailey that you are coming?" said Victoria Landis, turning her eyes from the window of the drawing-room car, where she was studying the changing landscape, so new and strange to her Northern eyes.

"No," said Hazel, leaning back among her pillows; "I thought it would be more fun to surprise her. Besides, I want to see things just exactly as they are, as she has described them to me, you know. I don't want her to go and get fussed up to meet me. She wouldn't be natural at all if she did. I'm positive she's shy, and I must take her unawares. After I have put my arms around her neck in regular girl fashion and kissed her she will realize that it is just I, the one she has written to for a year, and everything will be all right; but if she has a long time to think about it, and conjure up all sorts of nonsense about her dress and mine, and the differences in our stations, she wouldn't be at all the same Christie. I love her just as she is, and that's the way I mean to see her first."

"I am afraid, Hazel, you'll be dreadfully disappointed," said Ruth Summers. "Things on paper are never exactly like the real things. Now look out that window. Is this the land of flowers? Look at all that blackened ground where it's been burnt over, and see those ridiculous green tufts sticking up every little way, varied by a stiff green palm-leaf, as if children had stuck crazy old fans in a play garden. You know the real is never as good as the ideal, Hazel."

"It's a great deal better," said Hazel positively. "Those green tufts, as you call them, are young pines. Some day they'll be magnificent. Those little fans are miniature palms. That's the way they grow down here. Christie has told me all about it. It looks exactly to a dot as I expected, and I'm sure Christie will be even better."

The two travelling companions looked lovingly at her, and remembered how near they had come to losing their friend only a little while before, and said no more to dampen her high spirits. This trip was for Hazel, to bring back the roses to her cheeks; and father, mother, brother, and friends were determined to do all they could to make it a success.

It was the morning after they arrived at the hotel that Hazel asked to be taken at once to see Christie. She wanted to go alone; but, as that was not to be thought of in her convalescent state, she consented to take Ruth and Victoria with her.

"You'll go out in the orange-grove and visit with the chickens while I have a little heart-to-heart talk with Christie, won't you, you dears?" she said, as she gracefully gave up her idea of going alone.

The old man who drove the carriage that took them there was exceedingly talkative. Yes, he knew Christie Bailey; most everybody did. They imparted to him the fact that this visit was to be a surprise party, and arranged with him to leave them for an hour while he went on another errand and returned for them. These matters planned, they settled down to gleeful talk.

Victoria Landis on the front seat with the interested driver — who felt exceedingly curious about this party of pretty girls going to visit Christie Bailey thus secretly — began to question him.

"Is Christie Bailey a very large person?" she asked mischievously. "Is she as large as I am? You see we have never seen her."

The old man looked at her quizzically. "Never seen her? Aw! O," he said dryly. "Wall, yas, fer a *girl,* I should say she *was* ruther *big.* Yas, I should say she was fully as big as you be — if not bigger."

"Has she very red hair?" went on Victoria. There was purpose in her mischief. She did not want Hazel to be too much disappointed.

"Ruther," responded the driver. Then he chuckled unduly, it seemed to Hazel, and added, "Ruther red."

"Isn't she at all pretty?" asked Ruth Summers, leaning forward with a troubled air, as if to snatch one ray of hope.

"Purty!" chuckled the driver. "Wall, no, I shouldn't eggzactly call her purty. She's got nice eyes," he added, as an afterthought.

"There!" said Hazel, sitting up triumphantly. "I knew her eyes were magnificent. Now *please* don't say any more."

The driver turned his twinkly little eyes around, and stared at Hazel, and then clucked the horse over the deep sandy road.

He set them down at Christie's gateway, telling them to knock at the cabin door, and they would be sure to be answered by the owner, and he would return within the hour. Then he drove his horse reluctantly away, turning his head back as far as he could see, hoping Christie would come to the door. He would like to see what happened. For half a mile down the road he laughed to the black-jacks, and occasionally ejaculated: "No, she ain't just to say *purty!* But she's *good.* I might 'a' told 'em she was good."

This was the driver's tribute to Christie.

Chapter 9
The Discovery

Hazel walked up to the door of the cabin in a dream of anticipation realized. Here were the periwinkles nodding their bright eyes along the border of the path, and there the chickens stood on one kid foot of yellow, as Christie had described.

She could almost have found the way here alone, from the letters she had received. She drank in the air, and felt it give new life to her, and thought of the pleasant hours she would spend with Christie during the weeks that were to follow, and of the secret plan she had of taking Christie back home with her for the winter.

They knocked at the door, which was open, and, stepping in, stood surrounded by the familiar things; and all three felt the delight of giving these few simple gifts, which had been so little to them when they were given.

Then a merry whistle sounded from the back yard and heavy steps on the board path at the back door, and Christie walked in from the barn with the frying-pan in one hand and a dish-pan in the other. He had been out to scrape some scraps from his table to the chickens in the yard.

The blood came quickly to his cheeks at sight of his three elegant visitors. He put the cooking-utensils down on the stove with a thud, and drew off his old straw hat, revealing his garnet-tinted hair in all its glory against the sunshine of a Florida sky in the doorway behind him.

"Is Christie Bailey at home?" questioned Victoria Landis, who seemed the natural spokesman for the three.

"*I* am Christie Bailey," said the young man gravely, looking from one to another questioningly. "Won't you sit down?"

There was a moment's pause before the tension broke, and then a pained, sweet voice, the voice of Christie's dreams, spoke forth.

"But Christie Bailey is a young woman."

Christie looked at Hazel, and knew his hour had come.

"No, *I* am Christie Bailey," he said once more, his great, honest eyes pleading for forgiveness.

"Do you really mean it?" said Victoria, amusement growing in her eyes as she noted his every fine point, noted the broad shoulders and the way he had of carrying his head up, noted the flash of his eyes and the toss of rich waves from his forehead.

"And you're not a girl, after all?" questioned Ruth Summers in a frightened tone, looking with troubled eyes from Christie to Hazel, who had turned quite white.

But Christie was looking straight at Hazel, all his soul come to judgment before her, his mouth closed, unable to plead his own cause.

"Evidently not!" remarked Victoria dryly. "What extremely self-evident facts you find to remark upon, Ruth!"

But the others did not hear them. They were facing one another, these two who had held communion of soul for so many months, and who, now that they were face to face, were suddenly cut asunder by an insurmountable wall of a composition known as truth.

Hazel's dark eyes burned wide and deep from her white face. The enthusiasm that could make her love an unseen, unlovely woman, could also glow with the extreme of scorn for one whom she despised. The firm little mouth he had admired was set and stern. Her lips were pallid as her cheeks, while the light of truth and righteousness fairly scintillated from her countenance.

"Then you have been deceiving me all this time!" Her voice was high and clear, tempered by her late illness, and keen with pain. Her whole alert, graceful body expressed the utmost scorn. She would have done for a model of the figure of Retribution.

And yet in that awful minute, as Christie met her eye for eye, and saw the judgment of "Guilty" pronounced upon him, and could but acknowledge it just, and saw before him the blankness of the punishment that was to be his, he had time to think with a thrill of delight that Hazel was all and more than he had dreamed of her as being. He had time to be glad that she was as she was. He would not have her changed one whit, retribution and all.

It was all over in a minute; the sentence gone forth, the girl turned and marched with stately step out of the door down the white path to the road. But the little ripples of air she swept by in passing rolled back upon the culprit a knowledge of her disappointment, chagrin, and humiliation.

Christie bowed his head in acceptance of his sentence, and looked at his other two visitors, his eyes beseeching that they would go and leave him to endure what had come upon him. Ruth was clinging to Victoria's arm, frightened. She had seen the delicate white of Hazel's cheek as she went out the door. But Victoria's eyes were dancing with fun.

"Why didn't you *say* something?" she demanded of Christie. "Go out and stop her before she gets away! See, she is out there by the hedge. You can make it all right with her." There was pity in her voice. She liked the honest eyes and fine bearing of the young man. Besides, she loved fun, and did not like to see this most enticing situation spoiled at the climax.

A light of hope sprang into Christie's eyes as he turned to follow her suggestion. It did not take him long to overtake Hazel's slow step in the deep, sandy way.

"I must tell you how sorry I am —" he began before he had quite caught up to her.

But she turned and faced him with her hand lifted in protest.

"If you are sorry, then please do not say another word. I will forgive you, of course, because I am a Christian; but don't ever speak to me again. I HATE deceit!" Then she turned and sped down the road like a flash, in spite of her weakness.

And Christie stood in the road where she left him, his head bared to the winter's sunshine, looking as if he had been struck in the face by a loved hand, his whole strong body trembling.

Victoria meanwhile was taking in the situation. She espied Hazel's photograph framed in a delicate tracery of Florida moss. Then she frowned. Hazel would never permit that to stay here now, and her instinct told her that it would be missed by its present owner, and that he had the kind of honor that would not keep it if it were demanded.

"This must not be in sight when Hazel comes back," she whispered softly, disengaging herself from Ruth's clinging hand, and going vigorously to work. She took down the photograph, slipped off the moss, and, looking about for a place of concealment, hid it in the breast pocket of an old coat lying on a chair near by. Then, going to the door, she watched for developments; but, as she perceived that Hazel had fled and Christie was dazed, she made up her mind that she was needed elsewhere, and, calling Ruth, hurried down the road.

"If you miss anything, look in your coat pocket for it," she said as she passed Christie in the road. But Christie was too much overcome to take in what she meant.

He went back to his cabin. The light of the world seemed crushed out for him. Even the organ and the couch and the various pretty touches that had entered his home through these Northern friends of a year ago seemed suddenly to have withdrawn themselves from him, as if they had discovered the mistake in his identity, and were frowning their disapproval and letting him know that he was holding property under false pretences. Only the loving eyes of the pictured Christ looked tenderly at him, and with a leap of his heart Christie realized that Hazel had given him one thing that she could never take away.

With something almost like a sob he threw himself on his knees before the picture and cried out in anguish, "My Father!"

Christie did not get supper that night. He forgot that there was any need for anything but comfort and forgiveness in the world. He knelt there, praying, sometimes, but most of the time just letting his heart lie bleeding and open before his Father's eyes.

The night came on, and still he knelt.

By and by there came a kind of comfort in remembering the little black girl's words, "You all's Fathah's not dead." He was not cut off from his Father. Something like peace settled upon him, a resignation and a strength to bear.

To think the situation over clearly and see whether there was aught he could do was beyond him. His rebuke had come. He could not justify himself. He had done wrong, though without intention. Besides, it was too late to do anything now. He had been turned out of Eden. The angel with the flaming sword had bidden him no more think to enter. He must go forth and labor, but God was not dead.

The days after that passed slowly and dully. Christie hardly took account of time. He was like one laden with a heavy burden and made to draw it on a long road. He had started, and was plodding his best every day, knowing that there would be an end sometime; but it was to be hard and long.

Gradually he came out of the daze that Hazel's words had put upon him. Gradually he felt himself forgiven by God for his deceit. But he would not discuss even with his own heart the possibility of forgiveness from Hazel. She was right, of course. He had known from the first that her friendship did not belong to him. He would keep the memory of it safe; and by and by, when he could bear to think it over, it would be a precious treasure. At least, he could prove himself worthy of the year of her friendship he had enjoyed.

But, thinking his sad thoughts and going about the hardest work he could find, he avoided the public road as much as possible, taking to the little by-paths when he went out from his own grove. And thus one morning, emerging from a tangle of hummock land where the live-oaks arched high above him, and the wild grape and jessamine snarled themselves from magnolia to bay-tree in exquisite patterns, and rare orchids defied the world of fashion to find their hidden lofty homes, Christie heard voices near and the soft footfalls of well-shod horses on the rich, rooty earth of the bridle-path.

He stepped to one side to let the riders pass, for the way was narrow. Just where a ray of sunlight came through a clearing he stood, and the light fell all about him, on his bared head, for he held his hat in his hand, making his head look like one from a painting of an old master, all the copper tints shining above the clear depths of his eyes.

He knew who was coming. It was for this he had removed his hat. His forehead shone white in the shadowed road, where the hat had kept off the sunburn; and about his face had come a sadness and a dignity that glorified his plainness.

Hazel rode the forward horse. She looked weary, and the flush in her cheeks was not altogether one of health. She was controlling herself wonderfully, but her strength was not what they had hoped it would be when they brought her to the Southland. The long walk she had taken under pressure of excitement had almost worn her out, and she had been unable to go out since, until this afternoon, when with the sudden wilfulness of the convalescent she had insisted upon a horseback ride. She had gone much further than her two faithful friends had thought wise, and then suddenly turned toward home, too weary to ride rapidly.

And now she came, at this quick turn, upon Christie standing, sunglorified, his head inclined in deference, his eyes pleading, his whole bearing one of reverence.

She looked at him, and started, and knew him. That was plain. Then, her face a deadly white, her eyes straight ahead, she rode by magnificently, a steady, unknowing gaze that cut him like a knife just glinting by from her in passing.

He bowed his head, acknowledging her right to do thus with him; but all the blood in his body surged into his face, and then, receding, left him as white as the girl who had just passed by him.

Victoria and Ruth, behind, saw and grieved. They bowed graciously to him as if to try to make up for Hazel's act, but he scarcely seemed to see them, for he was gazing down the narrow shadowed way after the straight little figure sitting her horse so resolutely and riding now so fast.

"I did not know you could be so cruel, Hazel," said Victoria, riding forward beside her. "That fellow was just magnificent, and you have stabbed him to the heart."

But Hazel had stopped her horse, dropped her bridle, and was slipping white and limp from her saddle to the ground. She had not heard.

It was Sunday morning before they had time to think or talk more about it. Hazel had made them very anxious. But Sunday morning she felt a little better, and they were able to slip into her darkened room, one at a time, and say a few words to her.

"Something must be done," said Victoria decidedly, scowling out the window at the ripples of the blue lake below the hotel lawn. "I cannot understand how this thing has taken so great a hold upon her. But I feel sure it is that and nothing else that is making her so ill. Don't you feel so, Ruth?"

"It is the disappointment," said Ruth with troubled eyes. "She told me this morning that it almost shook her faith in prayer and God to think that she should have prayed so for the conversion of that girl's soul —"

"And then found out it was a creature, after all, without a soul?" laughed Victoria. She never could refrain from saying something funny whenever she happened to think of it.

But Ruth went on.

"It wasn't his being a man, at all, instead of a girl. She wouldn't have minded who he or she was, if it had not been for the deceit. She says he went through the whole thing with her, professed to be converted and to be a very earnest Christian, and pray for other people, and talked about Christ in a wonderful way — and now to think he did it all for a joke, it just crushes her. She thinks he deceived her of course in those things, too. She says a man who would deceive in one thing would do so in another. She does not believe now even in his Sunday school. And then you know she is so enthusiastic that she must have said a lot of loving things to him. She is just horrified to think she has been carrying on a first-class low-down flirtation with an unknown stranger. I think the sooner she gets away from this country, the better. She ought to forget all about it."

"But she wouldn't forget. You know Hazel. And, besides, the doctor says it might be death to her to go back into the cold now in the present state of her health. No, Ruth, something else has got to be done."

"What can be done, Victoria? You always talk as if *you* could do *any*thing if you only set about it."

"I'm not sure but I could," said Victoria, laughing. "Wait and see. This thing has got to be reduced to plain, commonplace terms, and have all the heroics and tragics taken out of it. I may need your help; so hold yourself in readiness."

After that Victoria went to her room, whence she emerged about an hour later, and took her way by back halls and by-paths, and finally unseen, down the road.

She was not quite sure of her way, but by retracing her steps occasionally she brought up in front of Christie's cabin just as Aunt Tildy was settling her spectacles for the opening hymn.

She reconnoitred a few minutes till the singing was well under way, and then slipped noiselessly through the sand to the side of the house, where after a few experiments she discovered a crevice through which she could get a limited view of the Sunday school.

A smile of satisfaction hovered about her lips. At least, the Sunday school was a fact. So much she learned from her trip. Then she settled herself to listen.

Christie was praying.

It was the first time Christie's voice had been heard by any one but his Master in prayer. It had happened simply enough. Uncle Moses had been sent away to the village for a doctor for a sick child, and there was no one else to pray. To Christie it was not such a trial as it would have been a year ago. He had talked with his heavenly Father many times since that first cry in the night. But he was not an orator. His words were simple.

"Jesus Christ, we make so many mistakes, and we sin so often. Forgive us. We are not worth saving, but we thank Thee that Thou dost love us, even though all the world turn against us, and though we hate our own selves."

Victoria found her eyes filling with tears. If Hazel could but hear that prayer!

Chapter 10
Victoria Has a Finger in the Pie

During the singing of the next hymn the organist came within range of the watcher's eye, and she noted with surprise the young man to whom she had been introduced in the hotel parlor a few evenings before, Mr. Mortimer. He was a cousin of those Mortimers from Boston who roomed next to Ruth. He would be at the hotel again. He would be another link in the evidence. For Victoria had set out to sift the character of Christie Bailey through and through.

She was chained to the spot by her interest during the blackboard lesson, which by shifting her position a trifle she could see as well as hear; but during the singing of the closing hymn she left in a panic, and when the dusky crowd flowed out into the road she was well on her way toward home, and no one save the yellow-footed chickens that had clucked about her feet were the wiser.

Victoria did not immediately make known to Ruth the events of the afternoon. She had other evidence to gather before she presented it before the court. She wanted to be altogether sure of Christie before she put her finger in the pie at all. Therefore she was on the lookout for young Mr. Mortimer.

She had hoped he would visit his aunt Sunday evening, but if he did he was not in evidence. All day Monday she haunted the piazzas and entrances, but he did not come until Tuesday evening.

Victoria in the meanwhile had made herself agreeable to Mrs. Mortimer, and it did not take her long to monopolize the young man when he finally came. Indeed, he had been attracted to her from the first.

They were soon seated comfortably in two large piazza chairs, watching the moon rise out of the little lake and frame itself in wreaths of long gray moss which reached out lace-like fingers and seemed to try to snare it; but always it slipped through until it sailed high above, serene. So great a moon, and so different from a Northern moon!

Victoria had done justice to the scene with a fine supply of adjectives, and then addressed herself to her self-set task.

"Mr. Mortimer, I wonder if you know a man by the name of Bailey down here, Christie Bailey. Tell me about him, please. Who is he, and how did he come by such a queer name? Is it a diminutive of Christopher?''

She settled her fluffy draperies about her in the moonlight, and fastened her fine eyes on Mortimer interestedly; and he felt he had a pleasant task before him to speak of his friend to this charming girl.

"Certainly, I know Chris well. He's one of the best fellows in the world. Yes, his name is an odd one, a family name, I believe, his mother's family name, I think he told me once. No, no Christopher about it, just plain Christie. But how in the world do you happen to know anything about him? He told me once he hadn't a friend left in the North.''

Victoria was prepared for this.

"O, I heard some one talking about a Sunday school he had started, and I am interested in Sunday schools myself. Did he come down here as a sort of missionary, do you know?''

She asked the question innocently enough, and Mortimer waxed earnest in his story.

"No, indeed! No missionary about Christie. Why, Miss Landis, a year ago Christie was one of the toughest fellows in Florida. He could play a fine hand at cards, and could drink as much whiskey as the next one; and there wasn't one of us with a readier tongue when it was loosened up with plenty of drinks —''

"I hope you're not one of that kind?'' said Victoria, earnestly, looking at the fine, restless eyes and handsome profile outlined in the moonlight.

A shade of sadness crossed his face. No one had spoken to him like that in many a long day. He turned and looked into her eyes earnestly.

"It's kind of you to care, Miss Landis. Perhaps if I had met some one like you a few years ago, I should have been a better fellow.'' Then he sighed and went on:

"A strange change came over Christie about a year ago. Some one sent him an organ and some fixings for his room, supposing he was a girl — from his name, I believe. They got hold of his name at the freight-station where his goods were shipped. They must have been an uncommon sort of people to send so much to a stranger. There was a fine picture, too, which he keeps on his wall, some religious work of a great artist, I think. He treasures it above his orange-grove, I believe.

"Well, those things made the most marvellous change in that man. You wouldn't have known him. Some of us fellows went to see him soon after it happened, and we thought it would be a joke to carry out the suggestion that had come with the organ that Christie start a Sunday school; so we went and invited neighbors from all round, and went up there Sunday, and fixed seats all over his cabin.

"He was as mad as could be, but he couldn't help himself; so, instead of knocking us all out and sending the audience home, he just pitched in and had a Sunday school. He wouldn't allow any laughing, either. We fellows had taken lunch and a case of bottles over to make the day a success; and, when Armstrong — he's the second son of an earl — came in with the case of liquor, Chris rose in his might. Perhaps you don't know Christie has red hair. Well, he has a temper just like it, — and he suddenly rose up and fairly blazed at us, eyes and hair and face. He looked like a strong avenging angel. I declare, he was magnificent. We never knew he had it in him before.

"Well, from that day forth he took hold of that Sunday school, and he changed all his ways. He didn't go to any more 'gatherings of the clan,' as we called them. We were all so proud of him we wouldn't have let him if he had tried.

"The fellows, some of them, come to the Sunday school and help every Sunday — sing, you know, and play. We all stand by him. He's good as gold. There's not many could live alone in a Florida orange-grove from one year's end to another and keep themselves from evil the way Christie Bailey has. Wouldn't you like to see the Sunday school sometime? I'll get Chris to let me bring you if you say so."

Victoria smilingly said she would enjoy it; and then, her interest in Christie Bailey satisfied, she turned her attention to the young man before her.

"You didn't answer my question a while ago, about yourself." There was pleading in Victoria's voice, and the young man before her was visibly embarrassed. The tones grew more earnest. The moon looked down upon the two sitting there quietly. The voices of the night were all about them, but they heard not. Victoria had found a mission of her own while trying to straighten out another's.

But the next morning early Victoria laid out her campaign. She took Ruth out for a walk, and on the way she told her what she intended to do.

"And you propose to go to Christie Bailey's house this morning, Victoria, without telling Hazel anything about it? Indeed, Vic, I'm not going to do any such thing. What would Mrs. Winship say?"

"Mrs. Winship will say nothing about it, for she will never know anything about it. Besides, I don't care what she says so long as we straighten things out for Hazel. Don't you see Hazel must be made to understand that she hasn't failed, after all, that the young man was in earnest, and really meant to be a Christian, and that the only thing he failed in was in not having courage to speak out and tell her she had made a mistake? He didn't intend any harm, and after it had gone on for a while of course it was all the harder to tell. Now, Ruth, there's no use in your saying you won't go; for I've *got* to have a chaperone, you know; I couldn't go alone, and I *shall* go with or without you; so you may as well come.''

Reluctantly Ruth went, half fearful of the result of this daring girl's plan, and only half understanding what it was she meant to do.

Christie came to the door when they knocked. He looked eagerly beyond them into the sunshine, hunting for another face, but none appeared. Victoria's eyes were dancing.

"She isn't here," she said mockingly, rightly interpreting his searching gaze. "So you'd better ask us in, or you won't find out what we came for. It is very warm out here in the sun."

Christie smiled a sad smile, and asked them in. He could not conjecture what they had come for. He stood gravely waiting for them to speak.

"Now, sir," said Victoria with decision, "I want you to understand that you have been the cause of a great deal of suffering and disappointment."

Christie's face took on at once a look of haggard misery as he listened anxiously, not taking his eyes from the speaker's face. Victoria was enjoying her task immensely. The young man looked handsomer with that abject expression on. It would do him no harm to suffer a little longer. Anyway, he deserved it, she thought.

"You were aware, I think, from a letter Miss Summers wrote you, that Miss Winship has been very ill indeed before she came down here — that she almost died."

Here Ruth nodded her head severely. She felt like meting out judgment to this false-hearted young man.

"You do not know perhaps that the long walk she took from your house last week, after the startling revelation she received here, was enough to have killed her in her weak state of health."

Christie's white, anxious face gave Victoria a flitting twinge of conscience as she began to realize that possibly the young man had suffered enough already without anything added by her, but she went on with her prepared programme.

"You probably do not know that, after she had controlled herself the other day when she was riding horseback until she had passed you by, she was utterly overcome by the humiliation of the sight of you, and slipped from her horse in the road, unconscious, since which time she has been hovering between life and death —"

Victoria had carefully weighed that sentence, and decided that, while it might be a trifle overdrawn, the circumstances nevertheless justified the statement, for truly they had held grave fears for Hazel's life several times during the last two or three days.

But a groan escaped the young man's white lips, and Victoria, springing to her feet, realized that his punishment had been enough. She went toward him involuntarily, a glance of pity in her face.

"Don't look like that!" she said. "I think she will get well; but I think, as you're to blame for a good deal of the trouble, it is time you offered to do something."

"What could I do?" said Christie in hoarse eagerness.

"Well, I think perhaps if you were to explain to her how it all happened it might change the situation somewhat."

"She has forbidden me to say a word," answered Christie in white misery.

"O, she has, has she?" said Victoria, surveying him with dissatisfaction. "Well, you ought to have done it anyway! You should have *insisted!* That's a man's part. She's got to know the truth somehow, and get some of the tragic taken out of this affair, or she will suffer for it, that's all; and there's no one to explain but you. You see it isn't the pleasantest thing to find one has written all sorts of confidences to a strange young man. Hazel is blaming herself as any common flirt might do if she had a conscience. But that, of course, though extremely humiliating to her pride, isn't the worst. She feels terribly about your having deceived her and pretending that you were a Christian, and she all the time praying out her life for you, while you were having a good joke out of it. It has hurt her self-respect a good deal, but it has hurt her religion more."

Christie raised his head in protest, but Victoria went on.

"Wait a minute, please. I want to tell you that I believe she is mistaken. I don't believe you were playing a part in telling her you had become a Christian, were you? Or that you were making fun of her enthusiasm and trying to see how far she would go, just for fun?"

"I have never written anything in joke to Miss Winship. I honor and respect her beyond any one else on earth. I have never deceived her in anything except that I did not tell her who I was. I thought there was no harm in it when I did it, but now I see it was a terrible mistake. And I feel that I owe my salvation to Miss Winship. She introduced me to Jesus Christ. I am trying to make Him my guide."

The young man raised his head, and turned his eyes with acknowledgment toward the pictured Christ as he made his declaration of faith.

Victoria and Ruth were awed into admiration.

"I almost expected to see a halo spring up behind his aureole of copper hair," said Victoria to Ruth on the way home.

Victoria had arranged to send him word when he could see Hazel, and the two girls went away, leaving Christie in a state of conflicting emotions. He could do nothing. He sat and thought and thought, going over all his acquaintance with Hazel, singling out what he had told her of his own feelings toward Christ. And she had thought he had done it all in joke! He began to see how hideous had been his action in her eyes. Knowing her pure, lovely soul as he did through her letters, he felt keenly for her. How could he blame her for her saintly condemning of him? And it was that day that he found in the breast pocket of his old working-coat the photograph of Hazel so much prized and so sadly missed since the day of her visit. He had supposed Victoria took it, but now he recalled her words about it as she ran after Hazel; and, smiling into the sweet, girlish face, he wondered whether she would ever forgive him.

The next day there came a note from Victoria, saying he might call at seven o'clock on Saturday evening, and Hazel would likely be able to see him a few minutes. A postscript in the writer's original style added: "And I *hope* you'll have sense enough to know what to say! If you don't, I'm sure I can't do anything more for you."

And Christie echoed the cry too deeply to be able to smile over it.

Victoria had laid her plans carefully. She arranged to spend more time with Hazel than she had been doing, pleading a headache as an excuse from going out for a ride in the hot sun, and sending Mrs. Winship in her place more than once. She found that Hazel had no intention of opening her heart to her; so she determined to make a move herself.

Hazel had been very quiet for a long time. Victoria thought she was asleep until at last she noticed a little quiver of her lip and the tiniest glisten of a tear rolling down the thin white cheek.

Without seeming to see she got up and moved around the room a moment, and then in a cheery tone began to tell her story.

"Hazel, dear, I'm going to tell you where I went last Sunday. It was so interesting! I wandered off alone out into the country, and by and by I heard some singing in a little log cabin by the road, and I slipped into the yard behind some crape myrtle bushes all in lovely bloom, where I was entirely hidden.

"I looked through a crack between the logs, and there I saw three rows of black children, and some older people, too, and at the organ — for there was a nice organ standing against the wall — sat Mr. Mortimer, that young man we met in the parlor the other evening, Mrs. Boston Mortimer's nephew, you know. There were some other white young men, too; and they were all singing.

"And after the singing there was a prayer. One of the young men prayed. It was all about being forgiven for mistakes and sins, and not being worth Christ's saving. It was a beautiful prayer! And, Hazel, it was Christie Bailey who prayed!"

Chapter 11

A Daring Manoeuvre

Hazel caught her breath, when she heard of Christie's prayer, and a bright flush glowed on her cheek; but Victoria went on:

"Then he taught the lesson, and he did it well. Those little children never stirred, they were so interested; and just as they were singing the closing hymn I came away in a hurry so they would not see me."

Victoria had timed her story from the window. She knew the carriage had returned and that Mother Winship would soon appear at the doorway. There would be no chance for Hazel to speak until she thought about the Sunday school a little while. The footsteps were coming along the hall now, and she could hear Ruth calling to Hazel's brother. She had one more thing to say. She came quite near to the couch, and whispered in Hazel's ear:

"Hazel, I don't believe he has deceived you about everything. I believe you have done him a great deal of good. Don't fret about it, dear."

Hazel was brighter that evening, and often Victoria caught her looking thoughtfully at her. The next day when they were left alone she said, "Tell me what sort of lesson they had at the Sunday school, Vic, dear."

And Victoria launched into a full account of the blackboard lesson and the queer-shaped little cards, which she could not quite see through the crack, that were passed around at the close, and treasured, she could see. Then cautiously she told of the interview with Mr. Mortimer and his account of Christie's throwing the bottles out the door. The story lost none of its color from Victoria's repetition of it; and, when she finished, Hazel's eyes were bright and she was sitting up and smiling.

"Wasn't that splendid, Vic?" she said, and then remembered and sank back thoughtfully upon the couch.

Victoria was glad the others came in just then and she could slip away. She had said all she wished to say at present, and would let things rest now until Saturday evening when Christie came.

Victoria had arranged with Mrs. Winship to stay up-stairs and have dinner with Hazel on Saturday evening while the family with Ruth Summers went down to the dining-room. She also arranged with the head waiter to send up Hazel's dinner early. And so by dint of much manoeuvring the coast was clear at seven, Hazel's dinner and her own disposed of, and the family just gone down to the dining-room, where they would be safe for at least an hour.

It was no part of Victoria's plan that Mother Winship or Tom or the Judge should come in at an inopportune moment and complicate affairs until Hazel had had everything fully explained to her. After that Victoria felt that she would wash her hands of the whole thing.

Mother Winship had just rustled down the hall, and Victoria, who had been standing by the hall door, waiting until she should be gone, came over to where Hazel sat in a great soft chair by an open fire of pine-knots.

"Hazel," she said in her matter-of-fact, everyday tone, "Christie Bailey has come to know if he may see you for a few minutes. He wants to say a few words of explanation to you. He has really suffered very much, and perhaps you will feel less humiliated by this whole thing if you let him explain. Do you feel able to see him now?"

Hazel looked up, a bright flush on her cheeks.

Victoria betrayed by not so much as the wavering of an eyelash that she was anxious as to the outcome of this simple proposal. Hazel's clear eyes searched her face, and she bore the scrutiny well.

Then Hazel sighed a troubled little breath, and said: "Yes, I will see him, Vic. I feel quite strong to-night, and — I guess it will be better, after all, for me to see him."

Then Victoria felt sure that it was a relief to have him come, and that Hazel had been longing for it for several days.

Christie came in gravely with the tread of one who entered a sacred place, and yet with the quiet dignity of a "gentleman unafraid." Indeed, so far had the object of his visit dominated him that he forgot to shrink from contact with the fashionable world from which he had been so entirely shut away for so long.

He was going to see Hazel. It was the opportunity of his life. As to what came after, it mattered not, now that the great privilege of entering her presence had been accorded him. He had not permitted himself to believe that she would see him even after he had sent up his card, as directed, to Miss Landis.

Victoria shut the door gently behind him, and left them together. She had prepared a chair not far away, where she might sit and guard the door against intrusion; and so she sat and listened to the far-away hum of voices in the dining-room, the tinkle of silver and glass, and the occasional burst from the orchestra in the balcony above the dining-room. But her heart stood still outside the closed door, and wondered whether she had done well or ill, and feared — now that she had done it — all evil things that can pass in review at such a time for judgment on one's own deeds.

Christie stood still before Hazel. The sight of her so thin and white, changed even from a week ago, startled him, — condemned him again, took away his power of speech for the moment.

She was all in soft white cashmere draperies, with delicate lace that fell over the little white wrists as petals of a flower. Her soft brown hair made a halo for her face, and was drawn simply and carelessly together at the back. Christie had never seen any one half so lovely. He caught his breath in admiration of her. He stood and did her reverence.

For one long minute they looked at each other, and then Hazel, who felt it hers to speak first, as she had silenced him before, said, as a young queen might have said, with just the shadow of a smile flickering over her face, "You may sit down."

The gracious permission, accompanied by a slight indication of the chair facing her own by the fire, broke the spell that bound Christie's tongue, and with a heart beating high over what he had come to say he began.

And the words he spoke were not the carefully planned words he had arranged to set before her. They had fled and left his soul bare before her gaze. He had nothing to tell but the story of himself.

"You think I have deceived you," he said, speaking rapidly because his heart was going in great, quick bounds; "and because I owe to you all the good that I have in life I have come to tell you the whole truth about myself. I thank you for having given me a few minutes to speak to you, and I will try not to weary you. I have been too much trouble to you already.

"I was a little lonely boy when my mother died —" Christie lowered his head as he talked now, and the firelight played fanciful lights and shades with the richness of his hair.

"Nobody loved me that I know of, unless it was my father. If he did, he never showed it. He was a silent man, and grieved about my mother's death. I was a homely little fellow, and they have always said I had the temper of my hair. My aunt used to say I was hard to manage. I think that was true. I must have had some love in my heart, but nothing but my mother ever called it forth. I went through school at war with all my teachers. I got through because I naturally liked books.

"Father wanted me to be a farmer, but I wanted to go to college; so he gave me a certain sum of money and sent me. I used the money as I pleased, sometimes wisely and sometimes unwisely. When I got out of money, I earned some more or went without it. Father was not the kind of man to be asked for more. I had a good time in college, though I can't say I ranked as well as I might have done. I studied what I pleased, and left other things alone. Father died before I graduated, and the aunt who kept house for him soon followed; and, when I was through college, I had no one to go to and no one to care where I went.

"Father had signed a note for a man a little before he died, with the usual result of such things, and there was very little remaining for him to leave to me. What there was I took and came to Florida, having a reckless longing to see a new part of the world, and make a spot for myself. I never had known what home was since I was a little fellow, and I believe I was homesick for a home and something to call my own. Land was cheap, and it was easy to work, I thought, and my head was filled with dreams of my future; but I soon saw that oranges did not grow in a day and produce fortunes.

"Life was an awfully empty thing. I used sometimes to lie awake at night and wonder what death would be, and if it wouldn't be as well to try it. But something in my mother's prayer for me when I was almost a baby always kept me from it. She used to pray, 'God make my little Chris a good man.'

"I began to get acquainted with a lot of other fellows in the same fix with myself after a while. They were all sick of life, — at least, the life down here, and hard work and interminable waiting. But they had found something pleasanter than death to make them forget.

"I went with them, and tried their way. They played cards. I played, too. I could play well. We would drink and drink, and play and drink again —"

A little moan escaped from the listener, and Christie looked up to find her eyes filled with tears and her fingers clutching the arms of the chair till the nails were pink against the finger-tips with the pressure.

"O, I am doing you more harm!" exclaimed Christie. "I will stop!"

"No, no," said Hazel. "Go on, please;" and she turned her face aside to brush away the tears that had gathered.

"I was always ashamed when it was over. It made me hate myself and life all the more. I often used to acknowledge to myself that I was doing about as much as I could to see that my mother's prayer didn't get answered. But still I went on just the same way every little while. There didn't seem to be anything else to do.

"Then the night before Christmas came. It wasn't anything to me more than any other day. It never had been since I was a mere baby. Mother used to fill my stocking with little things. I remember it just once.

"But this Christmas I felt particularly down. The orange-trees were not doing as well as I had hoped. I was depressed by the horror of the monotony of my life, behind and before. Then your things came, and a new world opened before me.

"I wasn't very glad of it at first. I am afraid I resented your kindness a little. Then I began to see the something homelike they had brought with them, and I could not help liking it. But your letter gave me a queer feeling. There seemed to be obligations I could not fulfil. I didn't like to keep the things, because you wanted a Sunday school. I was much more likely to conduct a saloon or a pool-room at that time than a Sunday school.

"Then I hung that picture up. You know what effect it had upon me. I have told you of my strange dream or vision or whatever it was. Yes, it was all true. I never deceived you about that or anything else except that I did not tell you I was not what you supposed. I thought it might embarrass you if I did so at first, and then it seemed but a joke to answer you as if I were a girl. I never dreamed it would go beyond that first letter when I wrote thanking you."

His honest eyes were on her face, and Hazel could not doubt him.

"And then, when the writing went on, and the time came when I ought to have told you, there was something else held me back. Forgive me for speaking of it, but I was trying to be perfectly true to-night. You remember in that second letter that you wrote me, where you told me that you were praying for me, and — you —" Christie caught his breath, and murmured the words low and reverently, "You said you loved me —"

"Oh!" gasped Hazel, clasping her white hands over her face, while the blood rushed up to her very high temples and surged around her little seashell ears.

Chapter 12

The Whim Completes Its Justification

"Forgive me!" he pleaded. "It need not hurt you. I knew that love was not really mine. It was given to the girl you thought I was. I knew without ever having seen you that you would sooner have cut out your tongue than write anything like that to a strange man. I ought to have seen at once that I was stealing something that did not belong to me in appropriating that love.

"Perhaps I would not have put it from me even if I had seen it. For that love was very dear to me. Remember I had never been loved in the whole of my life by any one but a mother who had been gone such years! Remember there was no one else to claim that love from you.

"And remember I thought that you would never need to know. I never dreamed that you would try to search me out. Your friendship was too dear to me for me to dare to try; and, too, I knew you would consider me far beneath you. I could never hope to have you for the most distant friend, even if you had known all about me from childhood.

"My hope for your help and comfort and friendship was in letting you suppose me a lonely old maid. Remember you said it yourself. I simply did not tell you what I was.

"But I do not take one bit of blame from myself. I see now that I ought to have been a good enough man to have told you at once. I should have missed a great deal, perhaps, as human vision sees it, have missed even heaven itself, unless the very giving up of heaven for right had gained heaven for me.

"I can see it was all wrong. The Father even then had spoken to my heart. He would have found me in some other way, perhaps; and it would have been your doing all the same, and I should have had the joy of thanking you even so for my salvation. But I did not, and now my punishment is that I have brought this suffering and disappointment and chagrin upon you. And if I could I would now be willing to wipe out of my life all the joy that has come to me through companionship with you by letters, if by so doing I might save you from this annoyance.

"For I have one more thing to tell you, and I will ask you to remember that I have never but once, in so many words, dared to tell you this in writing, and then only in a hidden way, because I thought if you knew all about me you would wish me not to say it. But now I must tell it. The punishment to me is very great, not only that you suffer, but that I have merited your scorn — for I love you! I love you with every bit of unused love from all my childhood days, in addition to all the love that a man's heart has to give. I have loved you ever since the night I read from your letter that you loved me — a poor, forlorn, homely girl as you thought — and that you thought I loved you too; and I knew at once that it was so.

"I want you to know that since that night I have had it ever before me to be a person worthy of loving you. I never dared put it 'worthy of your love,' because I knew that could never be for me. But I have tried to make myself a man such as you would not be ashamed to have love you, even though you could never think of loving in return. And I have fallen short in your eyes, I know. But in what you did not know of my life I have been true.

"Can you, knowing all this, forgive me? Then I shall go out and try to live my life as you and God would have me do, and remember the joy which was not mine. But you gave me one joy that you cannot take away. Jesus Christ is my Friend.

"Now I have said all there is to say, and I must go away and let you rest. Can you find it in your heart to say you forgive me?"

Christie rested his elbow on the arm of the chair, and dropped his head on his hand, while the firelight flickered and glowed among the waves of ruddy hair again. He had said all there was to say, and he felt he had no hope. Now he must go forth. The strength seemed suddenly to have left him.

It was very still in the room for a moment. They could hear each other breathe. At last Hazel's little white hand fluttered timidly out toward him, and rested like a rose-leaf among the dark curls.

It was his benediction, he thought, his dream come true. It was her forgiveness. He held his breath, and dared not stir.

And then, more timidly still, Hazel herself slipped softly from her chair to her knees before him. The other hand shyly stole to his shoulder, and she whispered: "Christie, forgive ME. I — love — *you.*"

Then Hazel's courage gave way, and she hid her blushing face against his sleeve.

Christie's heart leaped forth in all its manhood. He arose and drew her to her feet tenderly, and, folding his arms about her as one might enfold an angel come for shelter, he bent his tall head over till his face touched her lily face, and he felt that all his desolation was healed.

There were steps along the hall that instant, lingering noisily about the door, and a hand rattling the door-knob, while Victoria's voice, unnecessarily loud from Ruth's point of view, called: "Is that you, Ruth? Are the others through dinner yet? Would you mind stepping back to the office and getting the evening paper for me? I want to look at something."

Then the door opened, and Victoria came smiling in. "Time's up," she said playfully. "The invalid must not talk another word to-night."

Indeed, Victoria was most relieved that the time was up, and she looked anxiously from Hazel to Christie to see whether she had done more harm than good; but Hazel leaned back smiling and flushed in her chair, and Christie, standing tall and grave with an uplifted look upon his face, reassured her.

She led him away by another hall than that the family would come up by and was in so much hurry to get him away without being seen that she scarcely said a word to him. However, he did not know it.

"Well, is it all right?" she laughed nervously as they reached the side doorway.

"It is all right," he said with a joyous ring in his voice.

Through the hall, out the door, and down the steps went Christie Bailey, his hat in his hand, his face exalted, the moonlight "laying on his head a kingly crown." He felt that he had been crowned that night, crowned with a woman's love.

"He looks as if he had seen a vision," thought Victoria as she sped back to "view the ruins," as she expressed it to herself.

But Christie went on, his hat in his hand, down the long white road, looking up to the stars among the pines, wondering at the greatness of the world and the graciousness of God, on to his little cabin no longer filled with loneliness, and knelt before the pictured Christ and cried, "O my Father, I thank Thee."

Quite early in the morning Hazel requested a private interview with her father.

Now it was a well-acknowledged fact that Judge Winship was completely under his daughter's thumb; and, as the interview was a prolonged one, it was regarded as quite possible by the rest of the family party that there might be almost anything, from the endowment of a college settlement to a trip to Africa, in process of preparation; and all awaited the result with some restlessness.

But after dinner there were no developments. Hazel seemed bright and ready to sit on the piazza and be read to. Judge Winship took his umbrella and sauntered out for a walk, having declined the company of the various members of his family. Mother Winship calmed her anxieties, and concluded to take a nap.

Christie had gone about his morning tasks joyously. Now and again his heart questioned what he had to hope for in the future, poor as he was; but he put this resolutely down. He would rejoice in the knowledge of Hazel's forgiveness and her love, even though it never brought him anything else than that joy of knowledge.

In this frame of mind he looked forward exultantly to the Sunday-school hour. The young men when they came in wondered what had come over him, and the scholars greeted their superintendent with furtive nods and smiles.

During the opening of the Sunday school there came in an elderly gentleman of fine presence with iron-gray hair and keen blue eyes that looked piercingly out from under black brows. Christie had been praying when he came in. Christie's prayers were an index to his life. During the singing of the next hymn the superintendent came back to the door to give a book to the stranger, and, pausing in hesitation a moment, asked half shyly, "Will you say a few words to us, or pray?"

"Go on with your regular lesson, young man. I'm not prepared to speak. I'll pray at the close if you wish me to," said the stranger; and Christie went back to his place, somewhat puzzled and embarrassed by the unexpected guest.

He lingered after all were gone, having asked that he might have a few words with Christie alone. Christie noticed that Mortimer had bowed to him in going out, and that he looked back curiously once or twice.

"My name is Winship," said the Judge brusquely. "I understand young man, that you have told my daughter that you love her."

The color softly rose in Christie's temples till it flooded his whole face, but a light of love and of daring came into his eyes as he answered the unexpected challenge gravely, "I do, sir."

"Am I to understand, sir, by that, that you wish to marry her?"

Christie caught his breath. Hope and pain came quickly to defy one another. He stood still, not knowing what to say. He realized his helplessness, his unfitness for the love of Hazel Winship.

"Because," went on the relentless Judge, "in my day it was considered a very dishonorable thing to tell a young woman you loved her unless you wished to marry her; and, if you do not, I wish to know at once."

Christie was white now and humiliated.

"Sir," he said sternly, "I mean nothing dishonorable. I honor and reverence your daughter, yes, and love her, next to Jesus Christ," and involuntarily his eyes met those of the picture on the wall, "whom she has taught me to love. But, as your daughter has told you of my love, she must have also made you acquainted with the circumstances under which I told it to her. Had I not been trying to clear myself from a charge of deceit in her eyes, I should never have let her know the deep love I have for her; for I have nothing to offer her but my love. Judge Winship, is this the kind of home to offer to your daughter? It is all I have."

There was something pathetic, almost tragic, in the wave of Christie's hand as he looked around the cabin.

"Well, young man, it's a more comfortable place than my daughter's father was born in. There were worse homes than this. But perhaps you are not aware that my daughter will have enough of her own for two."

Christie threw his head back proudly, his eyes flashing bravely, though his voice was sad: "Sir, I will never be supported by my wife. If she comes to me, she comes to the home I can offer her; and it would have to be here, now, until I can do better."

"As you please, young man," answered the Judge shortly; but there was a grim smile upon his lips, and his eyes twinkled as if he were pleased. "I like your spirit. From all I hear of you you are quite worthy of her. She thinks so, anyway, which is more to the point. Have you enough to keep her from starving if she did come?"

"O, yes," Christie almost laughed in his eagerness. "Do you think — O, it *can*not be — that she would come?"

"She will have to settle that question," said her father, rising. "You have my permission to talk with her about it. As far as I can judge, she seems to have a fondness for logs with the bark on them. Good afternoon, Mr. Bailey. I am glad to have met you. You had a good Sunday school, and I respect you."

Christie gripped his hand until the old man almost cried out with the pain; but he bore it, grimly smiling, and went on his way.

And Christie, left alone in his little, glorified room, knelt once more, and called joyously: "My Father! My Father!"

"This is perfectly ridiculous," said Ruth Summers looking dismally out of the fast-flying car-window at the vanishing oaks and pines. "The wedding guests going off on the bridal tour, and the bride and bridegroom staying behind. I can't think whatever has possessed Hazel. Married in white cashmere under a tree, and not a single thing belonging to a wedding, not even a wedding breakfast —"

"You forget the wedding march," said Victoria, a vision of the organist's fine head coming to her, "and the strawberries for breakfast."

"A wedding march on that old organ," sneered Ruth, "with a row of black children for audience, and white sand for a background. Well, Hazel was original, to say the least. I hope she'll settle down now, and do as other people do."

"She won't," said Victoria positively. "She'll keep on having a perfectly lovely time all her life. Do you remember how she once said she was going to take Christie Bailey to Europe? Well, I reminded her of it this morning, and she laughed, and said she had not forgotten it; it was one thing she married him for, and he looked down at her wonderingly and asked what was that. How he does worship her!"

"Yes, and she's perfectly infatuated with him. I'm sure one would have to be, to live in a shanty. I don't believe I could love any man enough for that," she said reflectively, studying the back of Tom Winship's well-trimmed head in the next seat.

"Then you'd better not get married," said Victoria. She looked dreamily out of the window at the hurrying palmettos and added: "One might — if one loved enough;" and then she was silent, thinking of a promise that had been made her, a promise of better things, signed by a true look from a pair of handsome, courageous eyes.

Christie and Hazel watched the fast-flying train as it vanished from their sight, and then turned slowly toward their home.

"It is a palace to me now that you are in it, my wife!" Christie pronounced the words with wonder and awe.

"You dear old organ, it was you that did it all," said Hazel, touching the keys tenderly, and turning to Christie with tears of joy standing in her eyes she put her hands in his and said, "My husband."

Then as if by common consent they knelt together, hand in hand, beneath the picture of the Christ, and Christie prayed; and now his prayer began, "Our Father."

Because of Stephen

Chapter 1

The room was full of blue smoke from bacon sizzling on the stove when Philip Earle came in.

Philip was hungry, but there was a weirdly monotonous reminder of preceding meals in the odor of the bacon that took the edge from his appetite.

The lamp was doing its best to help both the smoke and the odor that filled the room; any other function it might have had being held in abeyance by the smoke.

The lamp was on a little shelf on the wall, and under it, half hidden by the smoke, stood another young man bending over the stove.

There was nothing attractive about the room. It was made of rough boards: walls, floor, and ceiling. The furniture was an old extension table, several chairs, a cheap cot covered with a gray army blanket, and a desk which showed hard usage, piled high with papers and a few books. A wooden bench over by the stove held a tin wash-basin and cooking-utensils in harmonious proximity.

Several coats and hats and a horse-blanket hung on nails driven into the walls. A line of boots and shoes stood against the base-board. There was nothing else but a barrel and several boxes.

The table was set for super: that is, it held a loaf of bread, two cups and knives and spoons, a bag of crackers, a paper of cheese, a pitcher of water, and a can of baked beans newly opened.

Philip added to the confusion already on the table by throwing his bundles down at one end. Then he stood his whip in one corner, and tossed his felt hat across the room to the cot, where it lay as if accustomed to staying where it landed.

"A letter for you, Steve!" he said as he sat down at the table and ran his hands wearily through his thick black hair.

Stephen Halstead emerged from the cloud of smoke by the stove, and examined the postmark on the letter.

"Well, I guess it can wait till we've had supper," he said carelessly. "It's not likely to be important. I'm hungry!" and he landed a large plate of smoking bacon and shrivelled, blackened fried eggs on the table beside the coffee-pot, and sat down.

They began to eat, silent for the most part, with keen appetites, for both had been in the open air all day. Stephen knew that his partner would presently report about the sale of cattle he had made, and tell of his weary search for several stray animals that had wandered off. But that could wait.

Philip, however, was thinking of something else. Perhaps it was the texture of the envelope he had just laid down, or the whiff of violet scent that had breathed from it as he took it from his pocket, that reminded him of old days; or perhaps it was just that he was hungry and dissatisfied.

"Say, Steve," said he, setting down his empty cup, "do you remember the banquet in '95?"

A cloud came over Stephen's face. He had reasons to remember it of which his friend knew not.

"What of it?" he growled.

"Nothing; only I was thinking I would like to have the squabs and a few other little things I didn't eat that night. They wouldn't taste bad after a day such as we've had."

He helped himself to another piece of cheese, and took another supply of baked beans.

Stephen laughed harshly. He did not like to be reminded of that banquet night. To create a diversion, he reached out for the letter.

"This is from that precious sister of mine, I suppose," he said, "who isn't my sister at all, and yet persists every once in a while in keeping up the appearance. I don't know what she ever expects to make out of it. I haven't anything to leave her in my will. Besides, I don't answer her letters once in an age."

"You're a most ungrateful dog," said Philip. "You ought to be glad to have some one in the world to write to you. I've often thought of advertising for somebody who'd be a sister to me, at least enough of one to write to me. It would give a little zest to life. I don't see why you have such a prejudice against her. She never did anything. She couldn't help it that her mother was your father's second wife. It wasn't her affair, at all, nor yours either, as I see. When did you see her last?"

"Never saw her but once in my life, and then she was a little, bawling, red thing with long clothes, and everybody waiting on her."

"How old were you?"

"About ten," said Stephen doggedly, not joining in the hilarious laughter that Philip raised at his expense. "I was old enough to resent her being there at all, in my home, where I ought to have been, and her mother managing things and having me sent off to boarding-school to get rid of me. I could remember my own mother, Phil. She hadn't been dead a year when father married again."

"Well, it wasn't her fault anyway, that I can see," said Philip amusedly; "and, after all, she's your sister. She's as much your father's child as you are."

"She's nothing but a half-sister," said Stephen decidedly, "and of no interest in the world to me. What on earth she's taken to writing me long letters for I can't make out. It's only since father died she's done it. I suppose her mother thought it would be well to appease me, lest I make trouble about the will; but I knew well enough there wouldn't be much of anything father had for me. His precious second wife did me out completely from the first minute she set eyes on me. And she's dead now, too. If it hadn't been for what my mother left, I wouldn't have had a cent."

"Who's the girl living with?" asked Philip.

"O, with an aunt,—her mother's sister,—an old maid up in New England."

Then Stephen tore open the letter, and shoved his chair back nearer to the lamp. There was silence in the room while Stephen read his letter; and Philip, emptying the coffee-pot, mused over the life of an orphan girl in the home of a New England maiden aunt.

Suddenly Stephen's chair jerked about with a sharp thud on the bare floor, and Stephen stood up and uttered some strong language.

He had a lot of light hair, originally a golden brown, but burnt by exposure to sun and rain to a tawny shade. He was a slender fellow, well knit, with a complexion tanned to nature's own pleasant brown, out of which looked deep, unhappy eyes of blue. He would have been handsome but for a restless weakness about the almost girlish mouth.

He was angry now, and perplexed. His yellow brows were knit together in a frown, his head up, and his eyes darker than usual. Philip watched him in languid amusement, and waited for an explanation.

"Well, is she too sisterly this time?" he asked.

"Altogether!" said Stephen. "She's coming to see us."

The amusement passed rapidly from Philip's face. He sprang to his feet, while the color rolled up under his dark skin.

"Coming to see us?" he ejaculated, looking round and suddenly seeing all the short-comings of the room.

"Coming to see us?" he repeated as if not quite sure of the sound of his own words. *"Here?"*

"Here!" asseverated Stephen tragically with outspread hands, and the two looked about in sudden knowledge of the desolation of the place they had called "home" for three years.

"When?" Philip managed to murmur weakly, looking about in his mind for a way of escape for himself without deserting his partner.

Stephen stooped to pick up the letter he had thrown on the floor in his excitement.

"I don't know," he said dejectedly. "Here, read the thing, and see if you can find out." He handed the letter to Philip, who received it with alacrity, and settled into the chair under the light, suddenly realizing that he was tired.

"She'll have to be stopped," said Stephen meditatively, sitting down on the cot to study it out, "or sent back if it's too late for stopping. She can't come here, of course."

"Of course!" agreed Philip decidedly. Then he read:

"My dear Brother Stephen: — "

Philip suddenly felt strong jealousy of his friend. It would be nice to get a letter like that.

"It is a long time since I have been able to write to you, but you have never been out of my thoughts for long at a time. Aunt Priscilla was taken ill the day after I wrote you the last time. She was confined to her room all winter, and some of the time a little flighty. She took queer notions. One of them was that I was going to run away and marry a Spaniard. She could not bear me out of her sight. This tied me down very much, even though we had a nurse who relieved me of the entire care of her. I could not even write when I was in her sight, because she imagined I was getting up some secret plot to send her away to an old ladies' home of which she had a great horror.

"I don't like to think of those long, dreary months; but they are all over now, and I will not weary you with talking of them. Aunt Priscilla died a month ago, and now I am all alone in the world save for you. Stephen, I wonder if you have any idea how dear you have grown to me. Sometimes it has seemed as if I just could not wait any longer to see you. It has kept me up wonderfully to know that I have a lovely, big, grown-up brother to turn to."

Philip's eyes grew moist, and he stopped to clear his throat as he turned the page and glanced surreptitiously toward the unloving brother, who sat in a brown and angry study, his elbows on his knees, his chin in his hands.

"So now, Stephen, I am going to do just what I have wanted to do ever since mother died and I left college and came home to Aunt Priscilla. I am coming to you! There is nothing to hinder. I have sold the old house. There was a good opportunity, and I cannot bear the place. It has been desolate, desolate here." Philip wondered what she would think of her brother's home. "I cannot bear the thought of staying here alone, and I know I could not coax you away from your beloved West. So I am all packed up now, except the things that have been sold, and I am starting at once. Perhaps you may not like it, may not want me; and in that case of course I can come back. But anyway I shall see you first. I could not stand it without seeing you. I keep thinking of what father said to me just before he died. I never told you. I have always thought I would rather wait till I could say it to you, but now I will send it on to you as my plea for a welcome. It was the last afternoon we had together. Mother was lying down, and I was alone with him. He had been asleep, and he suddenly opened his eyes and called me to him. 'Don't forget you have a brother, when I am gone,' he said: 'Tell him I'm afraid I wasn't wise in my treatment of him always. Tell him I loved him, and I love you, and I want you two to love each other.'

"I began to love you then, Stephen, and the longing to know you and see you has grown with the years, five years, since father died. I never told mother about it. She was not well enough to talk much, you know; and she did not live long after that. Of course, I never told Aunt Priscilla. She was not the kind of woman to whom one told things. But I have never had opportunity to claim that love, or to seek it except in just writing you letters occasionally; and sometimes I've been afraid you didn't care to get them. But now I'm coming to see for myself; and, if I'm not welcome, why, I can go back again. I shall not be a burden to you, brother; for I have enough, you know, to take care of myself. And, if you don't want me, all you have to do is to tell me so, and I can go away again. But I hope you'll be able to love me a little for father's sake."

"Have you read the whole of this, Steve?" asked Philip, suddenly looking up as he reached the end of one sheet of paper and was starting on another.

"No," said Stephen gruffly; "I read enough."

"Read the rest," commanded Philip, handing over the first sheet while he went on with the second.

"Now I have burned my bridges behind me, Stephen; and I have not let you know until just the last thing. This letter will reach you only a few days before I do; so it will not be of any use to telegraph me not to come if you don't want me, for I shall be well on my way, and it will be too late. Please forgive me; I did this purposely because I felt I must at least see you before I gave up my plan, or I should never be able to give it up. And I am hoping that you will be glad to see me, and that perhaps I can be of some use to you, and put a little comfort into your life. You have never told me whether you are boarding or housekeeping or what. It is strange not to know more about one's brother than I do about mine, but I shall soon know now. I am bringing all the little things I care about with me; so, if you let me stay, I shall have nothing to send for; and if I have to go back, they can go back, too, of course.

"I shall reach your queer-sounding station at eight o'clock Friday evening, and I hope you will be able to meet me at the train, for of course I shall be very lonely in a strange place. Forgive me for surprising you this way. I know Aunt Priscilla would think I was doing a dreadful thing; but I can't feel that way about it myself, and anyway I have myself to look out for now. So good-by until Friday evening of next week, and please make up your mind to be a little glad to see your sister,

                                                    "MARGARET HALSTEAD."

Philip handed over the last sheet to Stephen, and sat up, looking blankly at the wall for a minute. He could not deny to himself that he was wholly won over to the enemy's cause. There was something so fresh and appealing about that letter written from a lonely girlish heart, and something so altogether brave and daring in her actually starting out to hunt up a renegade brother who had shown no wish to brotherly, that he could but admire her. But what could they do with her there? Of course she must go back. A pity, too, when she seemed to have her heart so set. But, if she stayed, she would be disappointed. Philip looked at Stephen sadly. It was a good thing she must go back, and would not need to know how little worthy of her love and admiration this unknown brother of hers was. He was a good-hearted fellow, too. A pity for the girl she had not some one to care for her.

Suddenly a new thought came to him as he looked idly down at the envelope of the letter Stephen had carelessly flung aside. The date on it was a week old.

He picked it up excitedly.

"Steve, what day was that letter written?"

"The twenty-eighth," said Stephen, looking up to see what caused the unusual note in Philip's tone.

"Man alive!" exclaimed Philip, "that letter's lain in the office for more than a week now, or else it's been off up to Humstead's ranch, lying around till some one had time to bring it back to the office. Such a postmaster as they have out here anyway! Get up, Steve, and do something! This is Friday night! Don't you realize that your sister's almost here? If it wasn't that the Northern Central is always an hour or more behind time, she would be standing alone down there on the platform, in the dark, this minute, with all that howling mob of loungers that congregate near by. What are you going to do?"

"I don't know," said Stephen in a dazed way.

Philip towered over him fiercely. "Well, you better know. Get up. It's five miles away, and the express due now if it's on time."

Chapter 2

Margaret Halstead stood alone on the narrow board platform that seemed to float like tiny raft in a sea of plains and darkness.

The train on which she had come her long and interesting journey had discharged her trunks, and taken up some freight, and wound its snakelike way out into the darkness, until now even the last glimmer of its red lights had faded from the mist that lay around.

The night winds swept about her, touching hair and cheek and gown, and peering solicitously into her face as if to inquire who this strange, sweet thing might be that had dropped, alien, among them, and then, deciding in her favor, softly kissed her on the cheek and ran away to tell the river of her coming.

A few lights dotted here and there the murk and gloom about her, and loud, uncultured voices sounded from the little shanty that served, she supposed, as a station. She dreaded to move a step toward it, for a strange new terror had seized upon her in the darkness since the friendly train had disappeared from view.

She remembered that the porter had been solicitous about leaving until her brother arrived to claim her, and had paused beside her until the last car swept slowly up and began to travel by; then, eying dubiously first the silver piece she had put in her hand, and then the fast-gliding train, he had finally touched his cap and swung himself onto the last car, calling back to her that he hoped she would be all right. She had not realized till then what it was going to be to be left alone at night in this strange place, with no assurance whatever, save her own undaunted faith, that her brother had even received her letter, much less, would meet her.

Apprehension and alarm suddenly rose and began to clamor for attention, while she suddenly realized how rash she had been to follow a fancy half across a continent, only to bring up in this wild way.

What should she do? She supposed she ought to go over to that dreadful group of rough men and ask some questions. What if, after all, she had been put off at the wrong station? She half turned to walk in that direction; but just then a wild shriek followed by a pistol-shot rang out in the air, and she stopped, frightened, a whispered prayer on her lips for help. Had she come all this way on what her heart had told her was a mission, to be forsaken now?

The clamor was heard by Philip as he rode through the night.

Stephen heard it also, and hastened his horse's footsteps.

Then from out the gloom and horror there came to the young girl's ears the soft regular thud, thud, thud, of horses' hoofs, and almost at once there loomed before her out of the mist two dark shapes which flung themselves apart, and appeared to be two men and two horses.

She started back once more, her heart beating wildly, and wondered which way to flee; but almost at once she heard a strong, pleasant voice say:

"Don't be afraid. We are coming!" and what seemed a giant landed before her. With a little gasp in her voice that sounded like a half-sob she said,

"O Stephen, you have come!" and put her hands in those of Philip Earle, hiding her face against his shoulder with a shudder.

Philip felt a sudden gladness in his strength, and it was revealed to him in a flash that there were sweeter things in life than those he had counted upon.

Instinctively his arm supported her for just an instant, and a great wave of jealousy toward her brother went over him. His impulse was to stoop and give her the welcoming kiss that she was evidently expecting; but he held himself with a firm grasp, though the blood went in hot waves over his face in the darkness.

To have the unexpected and most unwelcome guest of his partner thus suddenly precipitated upon him, and to find that she was not altogether undesirable, after all, was a circumstance most embarrassing, as well as extremely delicate to handle. He blessed the darkness for its hiding. It was but an instant and Stephen was beside them, and he managed in some way—he never could describe it to himself afterward—to get the young women faced about toward the real brother and her attention turned in that direction, and then stood watching while Stephen, the impressible, welcomed the new sister with open arms.

It was like Stephen, though he had grumbled all the way to the railroad about what a nuisance it was going to be to have her come, that he should succumb at once to a sweet voice and a confiding way.

Philip's lips were dry, and his throat throbbed hot and chokingly. He felt the pressure of little, soft, gloved hands in his hard ones. He turned away angry with himself that he should be so easily affected and by some one whom he had never met except in the pitch dark. Yet even as he said this to himself he knew the face would fit the voice and the hands when he should see them.

So, after all, though Philip, because he rode the fleeter horse, had been the first to greet her, and though his was the cool head, and he had expected to have to explain why they had been so late to meet her, it was Stephen's eager voice that made the explanations.

"You see I never got your letter until an hour ago. It was miscarried or something, and then we don't get to the office often when we're busy. So, when I took it in that you were really coming and looked at the time, your train was already overdue; and, if it had not been for their habit of being always two hours behind time, you might have stood here alone all this time."

Stephen said it gayly. He was beginning to think it a nice thing to have a sister. He had forgotten utterly how Philip had to insist on his coming at once to meet her, and that he had been most reluctant and ungracious.

It occurred to him at this juncture to introduce his partner.

Philip came to himself as he heard his name mentioned, and was glad again for the darkness. Margaret Halstead blushed, and wondered whether this giant knew how extremely near she had come to greeting him with a kiss, and hoped that he had not noticed how her head had rested against his shoulder for an instant when she was frightened. What would he think of her?

Her voice trembled just a little as she acknowledged the introduction; but her words were few and frigid, and made Philip feel as if she had suddenly held him off at arm's length and bade him come no nearer. She said:

"I did not know you had a partner, Stephen. You never said anything about it in your letters. I am afraid I have been wrong in coming without waiting to hear from you before I started."

But Philip had noticed the tremble in her voice, and he hastened to make her most welcome as far as he was concerned.

Nevertheless, a stiffness hung about the trio which made it hard for them to be natural; and, had it not been for another pistol-shot from the shanty down the road and another clamor of voices, they might have stood still some time longer.

Margaret started in spite of herself, and asked nervously:

"Oh! what can be the matter? What a dreadful place this must be!" And Philip found in himself a new instinct of protection.

"We must get your sister out of this, Steve," he said. "We must take her home."

And somehow the word "home" sounded a haven as he pronounced it. The thoughts of the two young men galloping furiously on their way to the station had been but of how they should reach there as soon as the train. They had made no plans. It was impossible for them to realize the importance of the charge that was about to be put upon them.

But now the manners of the world from which they had come some years before, and from which this young woman had but just come, suddenly dropped down upon them as a forgotten garment, and they knew at once the wretchedness of their limitations.

"It isn't much of a place to call home," said the brother, apologetically, "but I guess it's better than this. If we had only known before, we'd have had something fine fixed up someway."

He made the statement airily, and perhaps he thought it was true. Philip found himself wondering what it would have been. There was not a house where she might have been lodged comfortably within fifty miles.

"How do you think we'd better arrange the journey?" said Stephen, suddenly brought face to face with a problem.

"You see," said he in explanation to his sister, "we had no time to hitch up, if we had thought of it, though I'm blamed if it occurred to me but that we could carry you in our pockets. Say, Phil, guess I'll go over and see if I can get Foxy's buckboard."

"Foxy's gone over to Butte in his buckboard with his mother. I saw him go this afternoon," answered Philip.

Stephen whistled.

"I'll ask Dunn for his wagon," said Stephen starting off.

"Hold on!" said Philip shortly. "I'll go myself. You stay here."

"Couldn't we go down to the station and see after my trunk, Mr. Earle?" said Margaret timidly. And to his ears the name never had so sweet a sound.

"Give me your checks, and stay here, please," he said in quite a different tone from that in which he had addressed Stephen; and, turning, he left them standing in the dark, while the mist closed in behind him and shut him from their sight as if he had left the world.

Alone with her brother, Margaret suddenly put out her hands appealingly to him.

"You are a little bit glad I've come, aren't you, Stephen?" she said.

"I'm no end of glad," he answered, rousing out of his sulkiness that Philip would not let him go. He knew that Philip had good reason for making him stay. "But we're a rough lot out here. I don't know how you'll stand it."

His voice had lost a shade of the gayety, and she thought it was touched with anxiety. She hastened to assure him.

"O, I shall not mind a bit. And I shall try to make things a little pleasanter for you. You think I can, don't you?" This in an anxious voice.

"I'm sure you can," said Stephen heartily. There was something in her voice that appealed to his better self, and reminded him strangely of his childhood. It could not be his father; for his father had always been silent and grave, and this voice was sweet and enthusiastic, and flowed out as if it loved to speak. And yet it must be the likeness to the father's voice he noticed.

"I am so anxious to get you in the light and see how you look," she said ardently, and then added softly, " My dear brother."

Stephen slid his arm about her awkwardly, and kissed her on the forehead. He felt embarrassed in doing this; yet it was by no means the first time he had kissed a girl. Perhaps it was the memory of those other kisses hovering near that shamed him now. He half felt this, and it made him awkward. He was glad to hear Philip's step coming toward them.

"Dunn's wagon has broken down, and both the front wheels are off for repairs. There isn't a thing we can get in town to-night," said Philip anxiously. "Miss Halstead, can you ride? Horseback, I mean."

"Why, I can try," said Margaret a little tremulously. This was a rather startling proposition to even her dauntless courage. Involuntarily she glanced down at her city-made gown in the darkness. She felt hampered by it.

"It's too bad, Miss Halstead," he said apologetically, while Stephen in the dark wondered at his new tone and manner. "But there's no other way, and I think you'll enjoy getting out of this, anyway. There's going to be a big row over there," he added in a low tone to Stephen. "Jim Peters is on his high horse. Hurry!"

Then in a cheery tone he said:

"It won't be so bad. You can rest your foot in the stirrup, and Steve and I'll take turns walking beside the horse. She'd better ride your horse, Steve. He's the gentler of the two."

Margaret Halstead felt herself suddenly lifted in the dark by strong arms and seated on a horse. She clung to the saddle, and left her foot obediently in the stirrup where it was placed by a firm hand; but she was not certain whether her brother or his friend had put her there. It was bewildering, all in the dark that way, and neither of them spoke till both were standing by her side. She was glad the horse stood quite still. She expected him to start nervously. She felt timid about Western horses. They had a reputation for wildness. But it was Stephen who after a moment of low talk came and stood by her side and placed his arm about her as they started.

"My suit-case and my bag," she murmured.

"Phil has them all safe," said her brother.

"And the trunks?"

"They are locked safe in the station, Miss Halstead, and we will get them early in the morning," said a voice out of the mist before her.

Then there was silence as she looked anxiously into the darkness, and could not see a spot of road for the horse to place his foot.

The road was rough and her seat unsteady. A man's saddle is not the surest thing to ride sideways upon. She put her hand timidly on her brother's shoulder, and the touch seemed to give her courage. It gave Stephen a strange new sense of his power of protection.

They went slowly, for the night was dark and the mist lay thick about them. The road was so rough that horse and leader could keep together only by moving slowly. The sounds of disturbance behind them grew fainter as they went on, but now and then a shriek or a fragment of an oath would reach them as if it had been flung out wildly in the night and lost its way.

Margaret shuddered when this happened, and said in a half-frightened tone:

"What awful people they must be, Stephen! Isn't it unpleasant to live in their neighborhood?"

And Stephen somewhat uneasily answered:

"O, they never bother us. They've got a little too much to-night, that's all; and, when they get like that, they can't stand a difference of opinion."

"How dreadful!" said Margaret in low, awestruck tones. Then after a minute she added:

"O Stephen, I'm so glad my brother is not like that. Of course it wouldn't be likely, but they must be somebody's brothers, and how their sisters must feel — and their mothers!"

Stephen felt his face grow hot. He said nothing for a long time. He could not think of anything to say. There was a strange feeling about his throat, and he tried to clear it. The mist kept getting in his eyes. He was glad when his sister began to tell of her aunt's illness and the long, weary months when she had been chained to the sick-room at the beck and call of a whimsical, wandering mind.

She did not say much about herself, but he felt touched by her sweet self-sacrifice and her loneliness. It reminded him of his own lonely boyhood, and his heart went out in sympathy. He decided that it was a nice thing, after all, to have a sister. It was like Stephen to forget all about the end of their journey and the poor accommodations he had to offer her, utterly unfit for a woman, much less fit for one who had been brought up in luxury. He grew gay as they went on, and talked more freely with her. When Philip suddenly appeared out of the silent darkness ahead of them, and said it was time to change guides, he was almost loath to leave his sister.

Margaret, too, would rather not have had the change; but she could scarcely ask her brother to walk the whole of the five miles. There was something about him that reminded her, even in the dark, of their father, and so he did not seem strange; but this other tall man, who had taken control of the entire expedition, frightened her a little. She wished she could get a glimpse of his face and know what kind of a man he was. It was hard to know what to say to him, and still more embarrassing to keep entirely still.

But the road was growing rougher. The new guide had to give a good deal of attention to the horse, and she to keeping her unsteady seat. The road was steadily rising before them now. She could feel that by the inclination of the saddle. It seemed to be stony also.

Once she slipped, and would have fallen from the saddle if Philip had not caught her. After that he placed his arm about her and steadied her. She could not object, for there was nothing intimate or personal in the touch. She concluded that Philip was a gentleman, whatever else he might not be.

She gripped the saddle in front of her a little tighter, and looked into the darkness, wondering whether this journey would ever end. She essayed one or two sentences of conversation, but the young man beside her was distraught, and seemed to be more interested in looking ahead and guiding the horse.

The road was even steeper now. Margaret wondered whether they were going up the Rocky Mountains. It seemed as if they had come far enough to have almost reached them, according to her vague notion of the geography of that land.

"Wouldn't it be better if I were to get off and walk?" she asked timidly, after the horse had almost stumbled to his knees.

"No," answered Philip shortly; "we'll soon be over this. Put your arm around my neck and hold on now. Don't be afraid! Steady, there, steady, Jack!"

The horse scrambled, and seemed to Margaret to be walking on his hind legs up into the air. She gave a little scream, and threw her arm convulsively about her companion's neck. But she was held firmly, and seemed to be riding upon Philip's shoulder with the horse struggling under her for a moment. Then like a miracle they reached upper ground, and she was sitting firmly on the horse's back, Philip walking composedly beside her, his arm no more about her.

It was lighter too, here; and all the mist seemed to have dropped away and to be melting at their feet.

"It's all over now," said Philip, and there was a joyous ring in his voice quite different from the silent, abstracted man who had walked beside her for so long. "I hope you weren't much frightened. I've been afraid how Jack would act there. That is an ugly place. It must be fixed before you come this way again. You see the bridge was broken down the way we usually go, and we had to come around another way. You were perfectly safe, you know; only it was bad to frighten you when you have just come, and you are tired, too. But we are almost there now. And look! Look ahead!"

Margaret looked, and saw before her a blaze of light flare up till it made a great half-circle on the edge of the horizon. Not until it rose still higher — like a human thing, she thought — did the girl recognize the moon.

"O, it is the moon!" she said awestruck. "Is it always so great out here?"

Philip watched her as she looked. He felt that for the first time in his life he had companionship in this great sight of which he never tired.

"It is always different," he said musingly, "and yet always the same," and he felt as he was saying it that she would understand. He had never talked to Stephen about the moon. Stephen did not care for such things except as they were for his personal convenience or pleasure. Moonlight might be interesting if one had a long ride to take, in Stephen's economics, but not for purposes of sentiment.

"I see," said Margaret. "Yes, I recognize my old friend now. It seems as if it wore a smile of welcome."

"Do you mean the man in the moon, or the lady? Which do you claim?"

"O, both!" laughed Margaret, turning toward him for the first time since there had been any light. And now she could see his fine profile outlined against the moon, the firm chin, the well-moulded forehead and nose, and the curve of the expressive lips.

"Now, look down there, back where we have come!" said Philip, as she looked.

The mist was glorified like an expectant one waiting to be redeemed from the state where it was put till its work was done.

"O!" breathed the girl in wonder. "You can fairly see the darkness flee away!"

"So you can," said Philip, looking off. "I never noticed that before."

And they started forward round the turn in the road where Stephen was waiting impatiently for them to come up with him, and almost at once they saw before them the outlines of the rude building the two young men called home, lying bathed in the new-risen moonlight.

Chapter 3

The moonlight was doing its best to gild the place with something like beauty to welcome the stranger, but it was effective only out-of-doors, and the two young men were painfully conscious of the state in which they had left the inside of their house, as they helped their guest from the horse and prepared to take her in. All the impossibility of the situation suddenly came upon them both, and made them silent and embarrassed.

Stephen took on his sulky look, which ill became him, while he stumbled over the moonbeams that followed him when he opened the door, and lighted the wicked little oil lamp. He had no mind to welcome his sister there. What did he want of a sister anyway? His foot caused the crisp rattle of paper as he threw the match down, and he knew it was her letter lying on the floor. The same mood that had seized him when he read it was upon him again; and he turned, scowling, determined to show her that she had made a serious mistake in rushing out here unbidden.

Margaret Halstead turned from the brilliant moonlight to the blinking lamplight bravely, and faced the scene of her self-chosen mission.

There may have been something in the half-defiant attitude of her brother that turned her from her purpose of having a good long look at him and making sure of her welcome. She may have seen that she had yet to win her way into the citadel of his heart, and wisdom or intuition taught her to break the embarrassment of this first moment in the light by a commonplace remark.

Her eyes roved anxiously about the dreary room in search of something to bring cheer. They fell upon the old desk in the corner.

"O Stephen! There is the desk from your old room!" she cried eagerly, going over to it and touching it tenderly. "I used to go up into your room and sit by it to study my lessons. And sometimes I would put your picture on the top, — the one you sent father when you were in the military school, — and sit, and admire you, and think how nice it was to have a straight, strong brother dressed in a military suit."

Stephen turned toward her with a look of mingled astonishment and admiration. His ugly mood was already exorcised. The soft rustle of hidden silk, made by her garments as she moved, created a new world in the rough place. She stood by the old desk, loosening the hat-pin and taking off her hat: he could see the grace of every movement. And this beautiful girl had cared for him enough to look at his picture once in a while when he was just a boy! He half wished he had know it then; it might have made some things in his life different. His voice was husky as he said, "You don't mean you ever thought of me then, and called me your brother!"

"Yes, surely," she said, looking at him with a bright smile as she ran her fingers through the soft hair over her forehead, and settled it as if by magic into a fitting frame for her sweet face. "O, you don't know how I idealized you! I used to put myself asleep at night with stories about you, of how brave and good and true you were, and how you did all sorts of great things for me—I'll tell you them all some day. But now, do you know you haven't welcomed me home yet? You're sure you're going to be glad I came?"

She looked up anxiously, a sweet pleading in her lovely eyes as she came over to him, and held up her face. Stephen bent over her awkwardly, and kissed her forehead, and then turned away in embarrassment, knocking down the tin basin from the bench as he moved; but Margaret felt she had her welcome, and set herself to win this brother.

Philip would fain have escaped to the barn from the confusion of the first few minutes, but had been drawn back to the door for very shame at deserting his partner in time of embarrassment, and had heard the little dialogue.

He turned silently away from the door, and slipped back to the horses thoughtfully. He had never seen that look on Stephen's face before, nor heard his voice so huskily tender. Perhaps, after all, there was something in a sister.

Margaret Halstead folded her wisp of a veil as carefully and precisely as if she had just come home from a concert in the East, instead of being dropped down in this land that knew her not; but all the while she was taking mental note of the place, its desolation, its need of her, its paucity of material with which to work, and wondering how these two men had lived and been comfortable.

"And now you are hungry," she said in a matter-of-fact tone, just as if her brother were the guest and she the hostess, "and what can we get for supper?"

Stephen had returned from a chase after the tin wash-basin, which had chosen, after the manner of inanimate articles, to take a rattling excursion under the stove. He was looking helplessly about the room. He did not know what he ought to do next.

"There isn't much but bacon and beans, the same old stuff. We have it morning, noon, and night."

Margaret came over to the table and began to gather the dishes together. It was a strange assortment, and she felt like laughing as she extracted the hammer from under the paper of cheese and looked about for a place to lay it; but she kept her face as sober as if that were the proper place for hammers and cheese, and said thoughtfully:

"Haven't you any eggs? I think you mentioned poultry in one of your letters."

"O yes, there are eggs. There are always eggs and bacon. They would be good if they weren't always the same."

"How would you like an omelet? Do you ever make them?"

"Yes, we've tried, but they lie around in little weary heaps, and won't 'om' for us," said Stephen, laughing at last. "I'll go out and get some eggs if you think you could make one."

"Yes, indeed!" said Margaret with alacrity. "Just show me how this stove works first, and fill the tea-kettle. I always use boiling water for my omelets; it makes them fluffier than milk. Where is your egg-beater kept?"

"Egg-beater!" said Stephen with a shrug of his shoulders. "Don't ask me. I wouldn't know one if I met him on the street. Can't you make an omelet without an egg-beater?" he added anxiously.

"O yes," said Margaret, laughing; "a fork is slower, but it will do. Bring me the eggs now. I will have them ready by the time the kettle boils and the frying-pan is hot."

Margaret worked rapidly while he was gone, and managed to clear the table and wash three plates and cups before he returned. Then she went to her bag that Philip had put just inside the door, and after a little search brought forth four large clean handkerchiefs, a supply of which she usually took with her on a journey. These she spread, one under each plate and one in the centre. At least, it would not seem quite so uncivilized as did that bare table.

An examination into her lunch-box showed a glass of jelly still untouched and half a dozen sugary doughnuts, the farewell contribution of an old neighbor of her aunt's. These she arranged on the table with a plate of bread cut in thin slices, and was just searching for possible coffee when she heard the voices of the two young men.

Stephen went whistling out to the barn for the eggs. "Christopher Columbus, Phil! She knows how to make omelet ! Hustle there, and help me get a lot of eggs. We'll have something worth eating again if it takes every egg on the place."

Philip had been wondering whether he might not be excused from going back to the house that night at all. But at the appetizing sound he went to work with a will.

They stopped in astonishment at the door, and gazed at the table as if it had been enchanted, and then gazed anew at the cook. They had left her there a fashionably attired young woman of a world that was theirs now no longer. They found her now a busy woman, with frock daintily tucked up and a white towel pinned about her waist apron-fashion, her sleeves rolled up, revealing white, rounded arms, and her cheeks pink with interest over her work.

"That lamp smokes horribly," she remarked, looking up at it vindictively; and there was something so true and human about her voice and words that both young men laughed.

The stiffness was broken, and did not return; but the relations were established and the guest was commander-in-chief. She told her hosts what to do, and they did it. She took the eggs, and deftly broke them, the whites into one dish, the yolks into another; and giving Stephen one dish with a fork to beat them, she took the other herself, meanwhile commanding Philip to find the coffee and make it.

They enjoyed it as much as three children at play, and their appetites were keen, when a few minutes later, having watched the puffy omelet swell and billow and take on a lovely brown coat, they drew up to the table to supper.

Margaret told little incidents of her journey, and described the people who had been her fellow travellers, showing a rare talent for mimicry, which entertained her audience exceedingly.

It was late when the meal was finally concluded and the room put into what Margaret thought was a poor apology for order. The problem of the night was now to be faced, and Margaret wondered what was to become of her. She suddenly realized how very weary she was, and that her nerves, long over-strained by new experiences, were ready to give way in tears.

Stephen knew that something must be done about sleeping now; but he had no idea what they were going to do with the new sister, any more than if she had been an orphan baby left upon his door-step. He turned helplessly to Philip. Philip always knew what to do in emergencies, though Stephen did not like to admit that he depended upon him.

Philip had done some thinking while he stood by the horses in the moonlight. There was little log lean-to opening off this large one-roomed cottage of theirs. It was divided by a board partition into two fair-sized rooms. One of these had been Philip's room and the other Stephen's. There was little furniture in them besides a bunk with heavy blankets. Blankets were the only bedclothing the house possessed, and with them beds were easily made. Philip turned toward the door of his room now, and in the dark went about the walls, hastily gathering an armful of clothing from the nails driven into the logs, which he threw out the window. Then he struck a match, and picked up a few things thrown here and there in confusion, and decided that was the best he could do toward clearing up.

He explained to Stephen in a low tone that he was to give his sister that room, and he himself would sleep in the hay. Then, saying good-night, he went out.

Margaret almost laughed aloud when she looked about her primitive bedroom a few minutes later, and by the light of the blinking lamp took an inventory of her surroundings. Then her eye caught a photograph pinned to the wall, and she went over to study it. It was Philip's one possession that he prized, and he had forgotten it in his haste. It was a sweet-faced woman with white hair and eyes like Philip's that followed one about the room sadly.

She had been shocked, even prepared as she was for the primitive, to find her brother living among surroundings so rough. Nevertheless, her determination was firm. She had come to help her brother, and now that she had seen him she would not turn back. There might be some hardships; but in the end, with the help of God, she would win. She felt shy of Philip, and inclined to wish him away. Perhaps he did not have a good influence over Stephen. He seemed to be very dictatorial, and the strange part about it was that Stephen yielded to him. It might be that she would have to help Philip in order to help her brother. That would complicate matters.

She knelt down beside the hard gray cot, and put the work she had come to do at the foot of the cross, asking help and guidance. And she wondered as she prayed whether she had been rash and taken her own way, instead of waiting for heavenly guidance, in coming to this strange land where evidently, to say the least, her presence had not been desired. Then she added, "O Jesus Christ, if this work is of Thee, bless me in it; and, if it was merely a wild impulse of my own, send me back where Thou wouldst have me."

Then with a feeling of contentment she lay down wrapped in the gray blankets, and was almost immediately asleep.

"Is she there?" asked the wind, whispering softly.

"Yes, asleep," said a moonbeam peeping through a crack between the logs, and then stealing in across the window-ledge.

"And will she stay?" sighed the night wind again.

"Yes, she has come to stay," affirmed the moonbeams; "and she will be a blessing."

Out in the sweet-scented hay lay Philip, but he was not asleep. There was planning to be done for tomorrow. Would the guest choose to stay, or would she fly from them at the morning light? Could she stand it there, so rough and devoid of all that had made her life what it was? Of course not. She had come only on a tour or curiosity. She would probably give it up and go back reasonably in a few days. But in the meantime, unless she came to her senses by morning and knew enough to go back to civilization at once, what was to be done?

In the first place, there must be a woman of some sort found, a servant, if you please. A chaperone she would be called back in the East. Here perhaps such things were not necessary, especially as she was really Stephen's sister; but it would be better to have a woman around. She must not be allowed to do the cooking, and surely they could not cook for her. It had been bad enough for them, men as they were, to eat what they cooked. How good that supper had tasted! The omelet reminded him of his mother, and he drew his hand quickly across his eyes. What would his mother think of his staying out here in the wilds so long? And all because a pretty girl had chosen to flirt with him for a while and then throw him aside. But was it all that? Did he not stay for Stephen's sake? What would become of Stephen without him?

But perhaps, now, Stephen's sister had brought him a release. He might just pretend to have business calling him away and leave them together. Then a vision of the frightened hands that came through the mist to greet him at the station recalled him sharply. No! He could not leave her alone with her brother! It would not do. And at once he knew that his mother, if she were able to know of what went on in this life, would approve of his staying here.

But where was a woman to be found who would be a fit servant for Miss Halstead?

He searched the country in his mind all round and about, and at last came to a conclusion.

The hay settled and crackled about him, and the hens near by clucked anxiously in their sleep; the horses moved against the stall now and then, and away in the distance came the sharp, vigilant bark of a dog. Philip dropped asleep for a little while, and dreamed of a small hand clinging to his neck and a wisp of soft, sweet hair blowing across his face, and awoke to find the hay hanging over and touching his cheek and a warm ray of morning lighting the sky.

The morning was all cool and fresh with sleep yet, when he rose and rode away, hurrying his horse onward through the dewy way. He found himself wondering what Stephen's sister would say to this or that view or bit of woodland that he passed, and then checked his thoughts angrily. She was nothing to him, even if she had understood his thoughts about the moon. Women were all alike, heartless—unless it might be mothers. With these thoughts he flung his horse's bridle over the saddle-horn, and sprang down at the door of a rude dwelling, where after much ado he brought to the door a dark-faced woman with straggling black hair and a skin that told at once of Mexican and Indian blood.

What arguments he used or what inducements he offered to bring the curious creature to promise she would come, he never told. But when a half-hour later, with the additional burden of a large, greasy-looking bundle fastened to his saddle, he again started homeward, he smiled faintly to himself, and wondered why he had done it. Perhaps, after all, by this time their guest had made preparations for her departure. And this wild woman with her lowering looks and her muttering speech, would she be any addition to their already curiously assorted family?

A fierce rebellion, often there before, arose in his breast at the Power, whether God or what, that made and kept going a universe so filled with lives awry and hearts of bitterness and sorrow. Not even the breath of the morning, nor the rich notes of wild birds, could quite dispel this from his heart. A sky like that above him, so peerless, and earth like this around him, so matchless, and only lives like his and Stephen's and that dark-faced old hag's to enjoy them. He ran over the whole rough crew of friends who sometimes congregated with them, and saw no good in any.

Still, there was Margaret Halstead. She seemed a fitting one to place amid beauty and joyous surroundings. She would not mar a scene like that this morning with anything her heart or life contained.

Yes, there was Margaret. But it might be only seeming. Perhaps she was like them all. Doubtless she was. It remained to be seen what Margaret really was. But what were they all made for anyway?

The old question that had troubled Philip for a long, lonely time; and he drew his brows in an unhappy frown as he came to a halt at the only home he now owned.

Chapter 4

When Margaret Halstead came to the door a little later to view the morning and look by daylight upon the new land into which she had come a stranger and a pilgrim, she still carried with her the atmosphere of her Eastern home. She had changed the long, dark, close-fitting travelling-gown of the night before to a simple gown of light percale which she had wisely brought in her hand-baggage; and, though the garment was plain and of walking length, and must have occupied little space in the satchel, it hung with a grace and finish unknown in those parts; and there was still about her as she moved that soft atmosphere of refinement.

She opened the door wide, and stood for a moment enframed. The dark, big-boned creature who was huddled on the steps sprang up and gazed at her in wonder. Her eyes had never met a sight like this before. The golden hair, touched with the sunshine into finer threads of spun glass, the blue eyes like rare stones that hold the colors of a summer night, the fair face, the pleasant mouth, the graceful form in the soft blue cotton gown, made a picture for which an angel might have sat.

Margaret looked at the woman in amazement, and then at the dirty bundle that lay upon the steps at her feet.

"Who are you?" she asked after a moment of silent scrutiny between the two.

"Man come get. Say heap work. Man say big pay."

"O, my brother has been after you. I see. He brought you here this morning before I was awake. That was kind of him. And I thought he was asleep yet."

She was thinking aloud rather than speaking to the woman. Philip, coming around the corner of the house, heard and halted, and his lips settled sternly. A curious expression crossed his face, and then he turned and went back to the other side of the house without being seen. Let her suppose this was the work of her brother if she would. It ought to have been. It was as well she should think so.

But Margaret was grappling with the problem of breakfast, with the addition of this unknown quantity who had come to assist her. Would it be possible for those grimy, greasy hands ever to be clean enough to touch food that was to be eaten by them?

She hit upon the plan, however, of setting the newcomer at some much-needed scrubbing about the doors and windows until they should have breakfast out of the way, and she drew a sigh of relief as she looked about the one living-room and noted how large it was. The woman would not have to be in too close proximity to them while they ate. That was one thing to be thankful for.

She smiled to herself as she hastily laid the table. It was nice of Stephen to go out so early in the morning and get a woman to help. It was dear of Stephen! He was going to justify her utmost ideal of him, she felt sure.

They all felt a strain of embarrassment over them during breakfast. The morning light displayed the crudities of the rude home. Margaret's beauty showed in stronger contrast as she moved about in her dainty blue and white, and seemed some rare bird of paradise dropped into their midst. The two young men in their dark flannel shirts felt ill at ease. They were all facing the problem of what was to be done next.

Margaret felt that the crucial moment for the desire of her heart was coming, and she must walk carefully. She realized, more than did they, the changes it would make in their lives if she remained here as she wished. As for her companions, it seemed to them by the light of morning wisdom an impossibility that she should stay, and they discovered to their own surprise that there was a growing disappointment in their hearts. She had given them a peep into their former lives, and they would turn from it now the more reluctantly.

At last Margaret ventured.

"I don't intend to be a bit of bother when I get settled," she said brightly, "and I will be as patient now as can be; but I would like to know when you think it will be possible for my things to be brought up."

The silence grew impressive. Stephen looked at Philip, and Philip looked into his plate. Margaret watched them anxiously from the corners of her eyes. At last Philip spoke.

"How many things are there?" he asked, merely to make time and give Stephen a chance to tell her what he knew he ought to tell, that this was no place for her to stay.

Margaret would rather her brother had taken the initiative. It was awkward to have to ask favors of a stranger. She wondered how much of a partner he was anyway, and what right he had in the house. Could it be possible that he was part owner? If so, it was more complicated than she had expected.

"O, I'm afraid there are a good many," she answered humbly. "You see I had to bring them or sell them. There wasn't any good place in town to store them where I felt sure they would be safe. It is just a little country town, you know. And some of the things I love. They belonged to my old home. I thought Stephen would like having them about him again, too." She glanced wistfully over at her brother. These old things had been part of the ammunition she had brought with which to fight her battle for the winning of her brother.

"Of course!" said Philip brusquely, scowling across at Stephen. He was disgusted with Stephen for not being more brotherly.

"And there's my piano!" said Margaret, brightening at this slight encouragement. "I couldn't leave that!"

"Certainly not!" said Philip, looking about at the rough room in a growing wonder of what was coming to it. The impossibility of it all! A piano in the wilderness!

"Great Scott!" ejaculated Stephen, looking up at last, and struggling to express his feelings. "What did you do it for? You can't put a piano and things in here! Think of a piano in this barn!" and he waved his hands eloquently toward the silent, dejected walls.

"O we'll make something besides a barn of it, Stephen," said Margaret, laughing almost hysterically, she was so glad he had spoken at last, even if it was only to attempt a veto to her plans. "I thought it all out this morning when I woke up. This room is lovely, it is so large. It needs a few more windows, perhaps, and a fireplace to make it perfect; but unless you are very much attached to this primitive simplicity you won't know this place after I get it fixed. Just wait till my materials come, and we'll have a real home here. Couldn't you boys build a fireplace, the old-fashioned kind, with a wide chimney in the room? Isn't there any rough stone around here? It would be grand to sit around winter evenings while I read aloud to you, or we all sing. It ought to go right over there!" and she indicated a space between two windows rather far apart, and directly opposite the front door.

"No doubt!" said Philip, looking blankly at the wooden box that now occupied that position and trying to imagine a great stone fireplace in its stead. His fancy failed him, however. He could not see an angel in a bit of rough marble. But the picture of the reading aloud around the open fire on winter evenings, and the music, was alluring.

"Charming," he added, seeing that the weight of the answers all fell upon him. "I never built stone chimneys for a living, but I think I could assist if you would be so good as to direct the job, Miss Halstead. I can't bring my mind to comprehend anything in this room being lovely, but if you say so I suppose it is   possible."

"Great Scott!" ejaculated Stephen again in amazement. He was not certain whether Philip was in earnest or not.

"And the piano ought to stand there," said Margaret after the laugh had subsided.

"Certainly," answered Philip again, more amazed than ever. "But might I inquire what you would do with the stove? You couldn't cook on the piano, could you? Or would you expect to use the fireplace?"

The old half-breed peered in from the window she was washing to see what all the laughter and shouts meant. This seemed to be an exceedingly jolly household into which she had come. She had not heard sounds so light-hearted and merry, so utterly free from the bitter mirth that tinged most of the jollity in this region, in all her life, not since she was a little child and played among the care-free children.

"The stove," said Margaret, "must go into the kitchen, of course."

"Ah!" said Philip meekly. "Strange I didn't think of that. Now, where, might I inquire, is the kitchen?"

Margaret arose and went to the back window, and the two followed her. "It ought to be right here," she said, "and this window should be made into a door leading to it. What is that little square building out there? Can't we have that for a kitchen?"

"That edifice, madam, was originally intended for other purposes, the housing of certain cattle or smaller animals, I forget just what. It isn't of much use for anything. It is in a tumble-down condition. But, if your fairy wand can transform it into a kitchen, so it shall be."

"Say, now that's an idea, Phil!" said Stephen interestedly.

"Then we could use a corner of this room for a dining-room, you know," said Margaret, turning back to the house again. "I have a pretty little cupboard with glass doors that will just fit into that corner, and there are screens and draperies. It will be just charming. I've always wanted to fix up a lovely big room that way. Can't you imagine the firelight playing over the table-cloth and dishes?"

"We haven't seen a table-cloth in so long I'm afraid it would be a strain on our minds to try to do that," said Stephen bitterly. All this talk was alluring, but wholly impossible. Such things could never come into his life. He had long ago given over expecting them. A look of hopeless longing went across his face, and Philip saw and wondered. He had felt that way himself, but somehow it had never seemed to him that his comrade would understand such feelings, he seemed so happy-go-lucky always.

"But what would you do with the roughness of everything?" asked Philip doubtfully. "Pianos and corner cupboards wouldn't like to associate with forests of splinters."

"O, cover them" said Margaret easily, as if she had settled that long ago. "I brought a whole bolt of burlap for such things. It is a lovely leaf-green, and will be just the thing for a background. I don't suppose I have enough; but I can send a sample to New York, and have it here before we need it. I've been thinking this morning what beautiful moulding those smooth, dry corn-stalks would make tacked on next the ceiling. You see, when the walls are covered with something that makes a good background, this will look like a different place."

"You see, Steve, that's what's the matter with you and me. We've never had a suitable background," said Philip slowly.

And thus it was that, amid laughing and questioning, Margaret won her way, and finally saw Philip go off with two horses and a large wagon. She was much troubled that Stephen had not gone with him. It seemed so strange when he was her brother, and Philip would need help, surely, in loading up the furniture. Philip certainly was a queer man. Why did he presume to dictate to Stephen, and, strangest of all, why did Stephen sulkily submit? When she knew her brother better, she would find out, and spur him on to act independently. Again she wondered uneasily whether Philip was not a hindrance to her plans. A man who could so easily command her brother was one whose influence was to be feared.

So Stephen stayed behind, followed his sister about, and did what she asked him to do. In the course of the morning much scrubbing and putting to rights was done, and a savory dinner was under way in spite of the marked absence of needed culinary utensils.

Philip Earle drove away into the sunshine at high speed. He was determined to make all the time he could. He felt uneasy about Stephen, lest he should mount his horse and come after, in spite of injunctions to stay about the house and take care of his sister until they got things into some sort of shape. There were more reasons than one why Philip should be uneasy about Stephen to-day. Nothing must be allowed to happen to startle the newcomer on this her first day. Perhaps she would be able to make things much better. Who knew? It certainly would be great to have something homelike about them. Though it would be all the worse when she would get tired of it, — as of course she would sooner or later, — and take her things and herself off, leaving them to their desolation once more. But Philip would not let himself think of that. With the gayety of a boy of fifteen he called to his horses and hastened over the miles to town.

Margaret and Stephen went out to walk around the house, and plan how the kitchen could be brought near enough for use. Margaret suggested, too, that there ought to be another bedroom built on the other side of the house. She tried to find out how much of a share in things Philip owned, but Stephen was non-committal and morose when she talked of this, and did not seem to take much interest in any changes she would like to make in the house; so she desisted.

She wondered why he acted this way. Could it be that Stephen was short of money? She knew that he had a good sum left to him by his own mother, and her father had also left certain properties which had gone to him at the death of her mother. Could it be that they were tied up so that he could not get at the interest, or was it possible that he had lost some of his money by speculation? Young men were sometimes foolhardy, and perhaps that was it, and he did not like to tell her.

Well, she would just be still on the subjects that she saw he did not wish to talk about, and work her way slowly into his confidence. She had accomplished even more than she had hoped for right at first, for Stephen's letters had not led her to think she would be very welcome, and she had come with a high heart of hope that she might first win his love for herself and then his life for God.

For several years now she had been praying for this stranger brother, until, when she was left in the world alone, she had come to feel that God had a special mission for her with him; and so she had dared to come off here alone and uninvited. She was not going to be daunted by any little thing. She would try to be as wise as a serpent and as harmless as a dove. Meantime she thought she understood Philip Earle somewhat, and she wished that he did not live in the same house with her brother. He might be interesting to try to help, taken by himself; but she was fearful that he would not help her with her brother.

Philip had succeeded beyond his wildest expectations in getting help to bring the freight that he found waiting in the little station. For Margaret had laid her plans well, and knowing the ways of delays on railroads, had shipped her household goods to this unknown land much in advance of herself, that when she arrived, there might not be so much possibility of sending her away, at least, until she had had opportunity to try her experiment. A girl with a little wider experience of the world, especially of the wild Western world, would not have dared do what she had attempted.

Two stalwart ranchmen Philip enlisted to help him, with their fine team of horses. They were the wildest of the wild men, who drank heavily, and gambled recklessly, and cared not at all that man's days are as grass and he is soon cut off, but took life as if they expected to hold it forever against all odds and have their wicked best from it.

Not a word said Philip about Stephen's sister to them. Something innate made him shrink from speaking of her to them. They were men such as he would not like to have his own sister know. Not that he objected to them himself. They were good fellows in their way. They could tell a story well, though not always of the cleanest sort, and they were fearless in their bravery. But they were men without any moral principles whatever.

Philip, as he drove back home, silent for the most part while the men talked, reflected that his own life was not faultless, and that in the three years that had passed since he came to this country to become a part of it his own moral principles had fallen quite perceptibly. He had not noticed it until to-day, but now he knew it. Somehow the coming of that girl had showed him where he stood. But he still knew what those principles were.

And these two men must, if possible, be kept from knowing that Miss Halstead had come.

But how could he manage that? Stephen ought to have been warned. What a fool he was not to have taken Steve out to the barn, and had a good talk with him before he went away, for Steve would never think to be careful. He had no idea of the part he ought to play in the protection of his sister.

The two men had joked him curiously on the amount and kind of furniture they were putting into the wagons, but Philip had only laughed and put them off with other jokes; and in the code of the wild, free life they accepted for the time, and questioned no more. They knew that when Stephen came he would tell all. Stephen could not keep a thing to himself when he got among his boon companions. They were a trifle curious to know why Stephen did not come along when he expected so important a shipment of goods, and they were exceedingly curious over the piano, feeling sure that either Stephen or Philip was about to be married and was going to try to keep the matter quiet. But they were obliged to content themselves with Philip's dry answer, "Steve couldn't get away this morning."

Just in sight of the house Stephen came out to meet them, still half-sulky that Philip had insisted on going away alone; and Philip said a few low words to him as he halted the forward wagon, the other two men being together on their own wagon just behind. Stephen demurred, but Philip's insistent tones meant business, he knew, and without waiting to do more than wave a greeting to the two in the other wagon, he walked reluctantly back into the house.

In his heart he was rebelling at Philip and at his sister's presence once more. He could see plainly that it was going to hamper his own movements greatly. His friends were good enough for him, and why should his sister be too good to meet them? If she would stay here, she must take what she found. But he did as Philip told him. He told his sister that he thought she had better go into her room and shut the door until the wagons were unloaded, as they were rough fellows that Philip had brought up with him to help, and she would not want to be about with them. He said it gruffly. He did not relish saying it at all. The men were his especial friends. Had it not been that he knew in his heart that Philip was right, he would not have done it at all.

Margaret wondered, but reluctantly did as he suggested, and went thoughtfully over to the window to look out.

She was right, then. Philip was wild. Stephen knew it. Stephen was trying to help him, perhaps, to reform him or something; and that was why he was so reluctant to speak about Philip's share in the household. And now Philip had brought some of his friends, some rough men that Stephen did not approve and did not wish her to meet, to the house; and he was trying to protect her.

It was dear of Stephen to care for her that way, and she appreciated it, but she felt that it was wholly unnecessary. She felt that her womanhood was sufficient to protect her from insult here in the house of her brother. She was not in the least afraid to be out there and direct where things should go. If Stephen was trying to help Philip to be a better man, then she ought to help, too. It would be another way of helping her brother to help what he was interested in. And these friends of his, could they not be helped, too? It was a pity for Stephen to feel so about it. She wished she had had time to argue with him, for she really ought to be out there to tell them where to place things. It would save a lot of trouble later.

Thus she stood thinking as she heard the stamping of the horses' feet about the front door, the creaking of the wagon-wheels as they ground upon the steps, and then the heavy footsteps, the voices of men, the thuds of heavy weights set down.

She wearied of her imprisonment the more that there was no window in her room from which she could watch operations; and at last, when she heard them discussing the best way of getting the piano out of the wagon, she could stand it no longer. She felt that she was needed, for they had made absurd suggestions, and her piano was very dear to her heart. She must tell them how the piano men in the East always did. It was ridiculous for her to be shut up here, anyway. Stephen might as well learn that now as any time. For an instant she knelt beside the gray cot and lifted a hurried prayer, — just why she knew not, for there was nothing to be afraid of, she was sure, — and then with firm hand she turned the knob of her door, and went out among the boxes and barrels of goods that were all over the room, until she came and stood framed in the sunny doorway, the brilliant noonday glare upon her gold hair and shining full into her eyes, her little ruffled sleeve falling away from her white wrist as she raised her hand to shield her eyes.

"Stephen, wait a minute," she called; "I can tell you just how to move that. I watched the men put it in the wagon when it started. It is very easy. You want two rollers. Broomsticks will do."

Chapter 5

There was sudden silence outside the front door. The two strangers turned and stared admiringly and undisguisedly. Stephen looked sheepishly triumphant toward Philip, and Philip drew his black brows in a frown of displeasure.

"My sister!" said Stephen airily, recovering himself first, and waving his hand comprehensively toward the two men. He felt rather proud of this new possession of a sister. His own eyes glowed with admiration as he looked at her trim form in its blue and white drapery framed in the rough doorway, one hand shading her eyes, and the animation of interest in her face.

But now Margaret was surprised. Why did Stephen introduce her if he had considered these men too rough for her even to appear in their presence? It was curious. Was he afraid of Philip? Ah! They must be friends of Philip's whom Stephen did not admire, and yet whom he had to introduce on his partner's account, and so he wished to evade it by keeping her out of sight. Well, what mattered it? A mere introduction was nothing. She would let them see by her manner that they were strangers still.

So she acknowledged Stephen's naming of them as "Bennett" and "Byron" with a cool little nod, that only served to increase their admiration. Perhaps the coolness of her manner was to them an added charm. Stephen rose in their estimation, being the possessor of so attractive a sister.

After she had given her wise, clear directions, — which proved to be exceedingly sensible ones, they could not but acknowledge, — she vanished into the house once more, but not, as they supposed, from hearing. She went quickly into Stephen's bedroom, from whose small window she could watch their movements. She intended to see that her directions were carried out and that piano safely landed in the proper place.

Just one short instant she was out of hearing as she opened the other room door, and closed it softly after her, and drew the torn paper that served as a window-shade slightly aside so that she could see out. During that instant Byron, who was famed among his associates for the terribleness of his oaths and the daring of his remarks, broke forth with a remark to Stephen, prefaced by a fearful oath. The remark was intended to convey the speaker's intense admiration of Stephen's sister, and Stephen himself would have been inclined to take it in the spirit in which it was meant; but Philip, standing close by with darkened countenance, laid a heavy hand on

Byron's shoulder, and said in low tones, which yet carried in them a menace, "That kind of talk doesn't go down here!"

It was just then that Margaret's ear became quickened to hear, and her intuition told her that she was the subject of the conversation.

"What's the matter with you, man?" said Byron, shaking off the hand. "Can't you bear to hear a woman praised? Perhaps you'd like a monopoly of her. But she don't belong to you — " with another oath; "and I say it again, Steve, she's a — "

But Philip's hands were at Byron's throat, and the word was smothered before it was uttered. Margaret dropped the paper shade, and stood back pale and trembling, she knew not why. Was Philip against her? Did he hate to hear her praised even, and did he wish her away, or was he defending her? She could not tell, though there had been something strong and true in the flash of Philip's eye as he sprang toward the other man, that made her fear lest she misjudge him.

What kind of a country was this to which she had come, anyway? And why, if there was need to defend her, had Stephen not been the one to do it, seeing it was Stephen who had warned her to keep away? It was all strange.

She sat thinking, on the hard little cot bed, looking around on the dismal room, and the pity of her brother's life appealed to her more strongly than it had yet done. She resolved to put away any foolish misgivings, and make a home here that should help him to live his life the best that it could be lived. She turned and knelt a minute beside her brother's bed, and asked help of her unseen Guide, a kind of consecration of herself to the mission that had brought her to this strange country.

Then she went once more to the window, and looking out saw the work of unloading the wagons going on as calmly as if nothing had happened. There was a firmness around Philip's mouth and chin that was not to be trifled with, and his eyes seemed to look apart from the others; but the rest were gayly at work, whistling, calling to one another merrily. Margaret watched them awhile. The one called Byron had a handsome face with heavy, dark waving hair, and big black eyes that were not true, but were interesting. She shuddered as she remembered the oath he had used to Philip and Stephen, a much milder one than the first, which she had not heard. The name of her Saviour, Jesus Christ! She had never heard it spoken in that way. It seemed to her the depth of wickedness. She had not yet dreamed of the depths to which wickedness can reach.

It rushed over her in a great wave of pity and sorrow as she watched the muscular arms lifting her furniture, saw the play of fun and daring on the handsome features, and thought that it was the name of his Saviour, as well as her own, he had used. His Saviour, and he did not know Him, did not recognize, perhaps, what he was doing. O, if he might be shown! If she might help to show him! It might be there would be a way.

And suddenly her mission widened, and took in Byron, Bennett, Philip, and an unknown company of like companions; and her heart swelled with the magnitude of the possibility that God might have chosen her to help all these as well as Stephen.

She watched a long time, and listened, too; but there were no more oaths, and no more fights. She studied the faces of the four men as they worked, especially the man who had spoken that awful word, and she prayed as she watched. It was a way that she had been acquiring during her last three or four years of loneliness. And by and by a plan began to open to her mind.

Then she went quietly out to see that the dinner she had started was doing as it should, and prepared to set the table for five instead of three.

By this time some packing-boxes and trunks were where they could be reached, and with Stephen's help she opened one containing some table-linen. It gave her much satisfaction to be able to have a table-cloth the first time she gave a dinner party in her new home.

The goods were all unloaded from the wagons and set under cover, and the two helpers were mopping their perspiring brows, while Philip drove his own wagon to the barn, when Margaret came to the door once more.

"Dinner is ready now," she remarked, quite as if they had all be invited, "and I suppose you would like to wash your hands before you come in. You will find the basin and towels out by the pump at the back door, Mr. Byron and Mr. Bennett." She had watched long enough from the window to know which was which, and she let the slightest glance of her eyes recognize each now, a glance that set them at an immeasurable distance. "And, Stephen, please hurry, because everything will get cold."

Stephen's eyes lit up with pleasure. This was the kind of thing he liked; but it was not what Philip would like, and he knew it. There was no telling but Philip would pitch the two guests out the door and down the hill when he came in and saw them preparing to sit down at the table.

They drew a long and simultaneous whistle when they entered the door together and saw the table draped in snowy white. They were none of them used to table-cloths.

Margaret had cleared a space around the table and arranged boxes for seats where there were not enough chairs; so there was room for all. Before each place she had laid a snowy napkin. To the young fellows so long unused to this necessity of civilization they looked of a dazzling whiteness, and each became immediately conscious of his own poor appearance. She had opened her trunk and found silver knives and forks and spoons, and all were set as she would have set the table in the East for a luncheon of a few friends.

She knew no other way. There was enough in this to awe the two wild Western cowboys, who under other circumstances might have proved to be unwelcome guests.

There was a touch of refinement, too, in the few green leaves and blossoms that Margaret had gathered in her morning tour around the house, wild blossoms, it is true, and nothing but weeds in the eyes of the men who daily and unheedingly trod over their like; but here, set in this snowy linen, held in a tiny crystal vase that had also been carefully packed in Margaret's trunk, they took on a new beauty, and were not recognized as belonging to the world in which they lived.

It was like the girl, impulsive and poetical, that she had kept the whole dinner waiting just a minute while she found that vase and added the touch of beauty to the already inviting table. Who knew but the flowers might speak to those men of the God who made them?

And the flowers lifted up their pink, dainty faces, and breathed a silent grace about that board at which they all sat down, creating a kind of embarrassment among the strangely selected company.

It was just as they were sitting down that Philip entered, and paused in the doorway at the sight, his brow darkening.

"Please sit over there, Mr. Earle," said Margaret, passing a plate of steaming soup to the place indicated; and Philip, hesitating, half-reluctant, sat silently down; but his eye ran vividly around the table like the threatening of lightning, in one warning glance.

Philip's look, however, was not needed. The spoons and the napkins and flowers, and above all the young woman, had awed for once the undaunted souls who were noted all about that region for their daring and wickedness. Margaret had rummaged among the tin cans on the shelf of the little cupboard in the corner, and had compounded a most delicious soup with the aid of a jar of beef-extract, a can of baked beans, and another of tomatoes. To be sure, its recipe was not to be found in any cook-book ever published; but it was none the less appreciated for that.

There was half a loaf of baker's stale bread, which she had toasted and cut into crisp little squares for the soup, and there was corn-meal wherewith she had made a johnny-cake or cornbread of flakiness and deliciousness known only to New England cooks. Not even the old mammies of the South could equal it.

It was not exactly a menu for an Eastern lunch party, but with the aid of another glass of jelly from a box hastily pried open it seemed a feast to the hungry young men who had been their own cooks for long, weary months of famine.

Bennett was tall and lanky, with freckled face, red, straight hair, and white eyelashes heavily shading light-blue eyes. He had a hard, straight mouth, and a scar over his left eye, and was known among his associates as a dead shot. His voice had a hard, cruel ring when he spoke. Margaret did not like his face.

She sat at her end of the table, pouring coffee, or slipping quietly over to the stove, waiting upon their needs, diffusing a softening, silencing influence about the table.

The old woman crept from her duties in the new kitchen which she was scrubbing and purifying, to peep inside the door, and wonder at the strange hush that hovered over the usually hilarious company. She knew the reputation of those young men, and could not understand their silence. Then she looked at the sweet presence of the girl as she presided over the meal, and shook her head, wondering again as she crept silently away.

It was after the last crumb was finished and they had risen from the table,—a mingled look, half of satisfaction in the meal, half of relief that it was over, in their faces,—that Margaret dared her part.

She had made up her mind to do it while she was preparing dinner, and her heart had thumped sometimes so hard that she had scarcely dared try to eat after she had decided upon it. Some rebuke must be given to the man who had uttered the name of Jesus Christ in that awful way. What she should say she did not know. "Lord, give me courage, give me words, give me opportunity!" had been the silent plea during the dinner-time.

And now, as she lifted her brave eyes, stern with the purpose she had in mind, they met the bold, handsome ones of Byron. He was trying to think up something appropriate to say to the hostess for giving them this delightful dinner. He was noted for his hilarious speeches; but the usual language in which he framed them would not be according to Philip's ideas, and he did not care to rouse Philip twice in a day. It would scarcely put him into this young woman's good graces to engage in a free fight with Philip Earle before her face.

Something in her troubled gaze embarrassed him as he lounged across the room to where she stood. He was conscious of Philip's forked-lightning glance upon his back, too, as he went; yet he swaggered a little more and held his head higher. He would not be put to shame before a girl. He ran his fingers through his abundant black hair, drew tighter the knotted silk handkerchief about his bronzed throat, and came gallantly forward with a few gay words of thanks on his lips, which were unusually free, for him, from profane garnishings.

He even dared to put out his great brown hand to shake hands with her. He had a fancy for holding that little white hand in his.

But Margaret looked at his hand, and then faced him steadily, putting her own hand behind her back.

They did not see Philip, his eyes like a panther's, unconsciously move toward them. Bennett and Stephen drew off by the door to watch what would come.

Her voice was very low, but clear. Philip, standing behind Byron, could hear every word she said; but the two by the door could not.

"Mr. Byron," she said, and there was pain in her voice. "I cannot shake hands with you. You have insulted my best friend."

The red flashed up under the bronze in the young man's cheek, and he drew back as if struck.

He stammered and tried to find words.

It was nothing but a passing word, a flash, he said; Philip and he were as good friends as ever. He did not know, or he would not have spoken. He would apologize to Philip.

Margaret caught her breath. She had not expected to be misunderstood.

"I do not mean Mr. Earle," she answered quietly and steadily; "he is but a new acquaintance. I mean my best friend. I mean Jesus Christ, my Saviour. I heard you speak his name in a dreadful way, Mr. Byron."

She lifted her eyes to his now, and they were full of tears.

The man was dumb before her. What had been a flash of anger and embarrassment grew into shame, deep, overpowering. He had nothing to say. He had never met a thing like this face to face before. It was not something he could point the barrel of his revolver at, nor could he grapple with it and overcome. It was shame, and he had never met real shame before.

The fire in Philip's eyes went out, and he turned half away, as if from something too holy to look upon. He had seen the tears in the girl's eyes, and the real trouble in her voice. Into his own heart Rebuke had sent a shaft as it passed to meet this other man whose guilt was greater.

At last the careless lips, so deserted of all their gay, accustomed words, spoke.

"I did not know—" was all he could say, and he turned and stumbled out of the room, not looking back.

And Margaret, trembling now, with the tears blinding her, took refuge in her room.

Chapter 6

The next few days were strenuous ones in the house of the unbidden guest. Philip and Stephen arose early and retired late, and did their regular work at odd times when they could get a chance, while they entered like two boys into the plans of their young commander.

They moved the little cattle-shed near to the house and floored it with some lumber that had been lying idle for some time. They took down the cook-stove and set it up in the new kitchen, where it soon shone out resplendent in a coat of black under the direction of Margaret and the wondering hand of the old woman.

A box of kitchen utensils which Margaret had considered indispensable to her own career as a housekeeper, and was now thankful she had not left behind, was unpacked, and soon there began to appear on the table wonderful concoctions in the shape of waffles and gems and muffins, which made each meal the rival of the last one, and kept the two young men and the old woman in a continual state of amazement.

Into the midst of all this work came the first Sabbath of Margaret's new life.

A storm had burst in the night, and was carrying all before it, seeming to have made up its mind to stay all day; so there was nothing to do but stay in the house as much as possible.

At the breakfast-table Stephen began to speak of the work they would do that day, and to say what a shame it was raining, as they could not work on a little room to accommodate the old woman, who had now to hobble home at night to her shanty a mile and a half away.

"You forget what day it is, Stephen," said Margaret, smiling. "You couldn't work if it didn't rain. It is Sunday, you know."

Stephen looked up in surprise. He had almost forgotten that Sunday was different from any other day, but he did not wish to confess this to his sister. He drew his brows, scowling, and answered, "O, bother, so it is!"

Then Philip scowled too, but for a different reason, and looked anxiously at the sky to see whether it was really to be a rainy Sunday. He grew suddenly thankful for the rain. But what would he do with Stephen all day?

They were compelled to do some work, after all, for the old woman did not hobble over at all that day, and no wonder: the rain came down in sheets; thunder rumbled; and lightning flashed across the heavens; and Philip blessed the rain again.

"Go into the kitchen, Steve, and wash those dishes," said Philip laugh-ingly, "and I'll help. We're a lazy lot if we can't do the work one day out of seven for our board. It is enough for Miss Halstead to do the cooking." And so they worked together, and Philip hunted around, and managed to make work, little things that Stephen must do at once, and which Margaret kept telling them could wait until the morrow; but Philip insistently kept Stephen helping him at them till dinner was out of the way and it was nearly five o'clock.

The sky was lighting up, and showed some signs of clearing.

Stephen wandered restlessly to the door, and looked down the road, and then at his watch.

Philip was on the alert, though he did not have that appearance. He glanced at the big piano-case still unopened.

"Miss Halstead," he ventured, "why didn't we open that piano yester-day? If we should knock off a couple of those front boards and get at that keyboard, don't you think you might play for us a little, and while away the rest of this day? Steve will be off to gayer company than ours if you don't amuse him."

He laughed lightly, but there was a troubled something in his voice that caused Margaret to follow his glance toward her brother. She saw the restlessness in his whole attitude, and took alarm. Was it for one or both of the young men she was troubled? She could not have told.

"O, yes, if you can do it easily," said Margaret eagerly. It would be a delight to her to touch the keys of her piano again; it would drive away any lingering homesickness.

Philip's voice again called Stephen's wandering attention, and soon their united efforts brought the row of ivory and black keys into view.

Margaret, seated on a kitchen chair, touched strong, sweet chords while the two young men settled down to listen.

Sweet Sabbath music she played from memory, a bit from some of the old masters, a page from an oratorio, a strain from the minor of a funeral march, a grand triumphant hymn. Then she touched the keys more softly, and began to sing low and sweetly; and by and by there came a rich tenor and a grumbling bass from the two listeners as she wandered into familiar hymns that they had sung as little boys.

The rain came on again, and it grew darker, and still they sang, until at last Philip drew a sigh of relief, and realized that it was bedtime and Stephen had not gone to the village. Then Margaret stopped playing, and they all went to get a lunch before retiring.

Margaret, before she slept that night, asked a blessing again on the work she hoped to do, and never dreamed that already she had been used to keep the brother for whose sake she had come this long journey.

After they finished the old woman's room Philip came in with his arms full of great rough stones, and announced that he was ready to begin the fireplace, and he thought it would be best to get the muss and dirt of plaster out of the way before they put things to rights in the living-room.

Margaret had almost forgotten the doubts she had about Philip when she first came, and his strange actions on the morning after her arrival, and was prepared to accept both the young men as good comrades, or brothers. Laughingly they all went to work, Margaret drawing the outline of the fireplace that she thought should be built, and Stephen mixing mortar while Philip brought in stones from a great pile that had been collected by the former owner of the place to build a fence.

"There's nothing like being jack of all trades," said Stephen as he slapped on some mortar with the blade of a broken hoe, and settled into it a great stone that Philip had just brought in.

Margaret's eyes shone as she watched the chimney being built. She saw in her mind's eye a charming room, and she was anxious to get it into shape before another Sabbath, that they might have a quiet, restful time. While she had been playing and singing the night before, there had been revealed to her ways in which she might point the way to her Saviour, and she longed to begin.

There was much to be done in teaching the strange servant new ways, and in keeping clean the things they used every day: but Margaret was one of those whose hands are never idle, and she had put her whole soul into the making over of her brother's home; so she accomplished much in her own way while the young men worked at masonry and the stone fireplace grew into comely proportions.

By the time it was finished she had rooted out from the boxes and barrels most of the things she would need in the immediate arrangement of this living-room, and had cut and sewed cushions and fixings ready to put into place when the time came, so that the work of refurnishing went rapidly forward. Indeed, the two helpers became fully as eager to see the room finished as was the young architect.

Margaret had bought a number of things before she left the East that she thought she would be likely to need in arranging her own room, which she wanted to make as pretty as possible to keep her from getting homesick. All this plan she now abandoned, and set herself to put these pretty things into the adornment of the great, bare living-room which she meant should be the scene of her labors.

Among other things there were bright materials for cushions, and there were rolls of paper enough to hang the walls of a reasonably large room. A careful calculation and much measurement soon made it evident that this paper would cover the most of the walls of this room, which was the size of an ordinary whole house without any partitions. She puzzled a while to know whether she should risk sending for more, but finally a bright idea occurred to her as she looked at the large bundle of green burlap that was lying in the box with the paper. This she had intended for draperies, or floor covering, if necessary, or maybe covering for a chest or a cushion. Now all was plain before her.

The paper had an ivory ground on which seemed to be growing great palms as if a myriad of hothouses had let forth their glories of greenery. There was enough of this paper to cover the two sides and front of the room. That was delightful. It would look as if the room opened on three sides into a palm grove. On the back end, in the centre of which was the great stone fireplace, she would put the plain moss-green burlap, fastened along its breadths with brass tacks. Two or three good coats of whitewash would give the ceiling a creamy tint, and she could cut out a few of the palms from the paper to apply in a dainty design in the centre and corners.

The two young men looked bewildered when she tried to explain, and she finally desisted, and issued her directions.

They covered the back of the room first; and, when the mossy breadths were smoothly on over the rough boards, fastened at intervals with the gleaming tacks, the old stone fireplace stood out finely against the dark background.

"Now, if you have any guns and things, that is the place to put them," said Margaret, pointing to the wall about the fireplace, and Philip proudly brought out a couple of guns, and crossed them on the wall to the right, while Stephen fastened a pair of buffalo-horns over the door to the left that led into the new kitchen. This side of the room was at once denominated the dining-room, and Margaret unwrapped a handsome four-panel screen of unusual size, wrought in black and gold, and stood it across that corner.

They turned with avidity to follow her next directions, having more faith in the result than they had before. And another day or two saw the walls papered and the ceiling smiling white with its green traceries here and there.

It did not take long after that to unpack rugs and furniture. Margaret had brought many things from the old home, rare mahogany furniture and Oriental rugs, that a wiser person might have advised her to leave behind until she was sure of making a home in this far land. But the girl rejoiced in the beauty of the things she had to give to her "life-work," as she pleased to call it, and had brought everything with her that she intended to keep at all.

The rough old floor with its wide cracks and unoiled boards did not look too bad when they were almost covered with a great, soft rug of rich, dark coloring, and set off here and there by the skin of a tiger or a black bear, or by a strip of white goat-skin.

A wide, low seat, covered with green and piled with bright cushions, ran along the wall to the right of the fireplace. In the corner beyond the window was a low bookcase, which Margaret had intended for her own room, and again beyond her bedroom door another low bookcase ran along to the other bedroom door. These doors were hidden by dark-green curtains of soft, velvety material; and no one would have suspected the rough, cheap doors behind them. By each one there stood on the top of the bookcase, half against the green of the curtain and half mingling with the lifelike palms on the wall, a living palm in a terra-cotta jardiniere, which made the pictured ones but seem more real.

The piano stood near the front of the room, across the right-hand corner; and a wide, low couch invited one to rest and listen to the music.

The rest of the room that was not dining-room was filled with easy chairs, a large, round mahogany table with a most delightful reading-lamp in the middle, and more books, while Stephen's old writing-desk stood across the left-hand front corner.

It was all most charming to look upon, this finished room, when the weary workers at last sat down to a belated supper Saturday evening, and realized what they had accomplished during the week.

There was much to be done yet. Margaret, as she ate her supper, glanced around, and planned for a row of little brass hooks against the wall, whereon should hang her tiny teacups, and wondered how she should manage a plate-rail for the saucers, in this country without mouldings. The little glass-faced buffet that was to hold the china still stood on the floor in the corner, waiting its turn to be hung, and the pictures were as yet unpacked; but there was time enough for that. There was a room in which to spend the Sabbath, and she prayed that her work might now begin.

Softly there crept up through the darkness of the sky the dawn of another Sabbath day, and Margaret arose with eager anticipations. In the first place, she meant to make Stephen, and Philip, too, if possible, go with her to church. That, of course, was the right place in which to begin the Sabbath.

Before she left her room she laid out upon her bed the things she would wear to church, choosing them with care that she might be neatly and sweetly attired in the house of the Lord, and that she might be as winsome as possible to those she wished to influence.

She did not acknowledge even to herself that she had some doubt in her mind as to whether she should accomplish making Stephen and Philip attend church, for she meant to accomplish that in spite of all obstacles.

Nevertheless, she went about her self-set task with great care and deliberation, prefacing her request with the daintiest breakfast with which they had yet been favored.

It was just as they finished that she brought forward the subject that was so near to her heart and about which she had been praying all the morning.

"Stephen, what time do we have to start for church? Is it far from here? You don't go on horseback, do you?"

Stephen dropped his knife and fork on his plate with a clatter, and sat back in astonishment; and there was a blank silence in the room for some seconds.

Chapter 7

"To church!" Stephen uttered the words half mockingly. "What time do we start! Well, now, Phil, how far should you say it was to the nearest church?"

A mirthless laugh broke from Philip. It was involuntary. A wave of bitterness rolled over him as a wave of the ocean higher than the others might break over the head of one who was bravely trying to breast the tide. As soon as he had uttered the laugh he was sorry, for he felt the shock this would be to Margaret even before he saw her start at his harsh laughter.

These two young men were alike in the bitterness that each carried in his heart, but Stephen's had been caused by the hardness of his heart toward his earthly father, while Philip had hardened his heart, for what he considered just cause, toward his Father in heaven; and of the two his bitterness was the more galling.

Philip checked the laugh, which had really been but the semblance of one, and answered steadily with his eyes on his plate, "About forty miles by the nearest way, I should judge."

Stephen's eyes were twinkling with fun as he tipped his chair back against the wall and watched his sister. He had no inkling of the desolation this would bring to her, and he could not understand, perhaps did not notice, the whiteness of her face as she looked at him, only half comprehending. It was given to Philip, the stranger, to feel with her the appalling emptiness of a country without a church. Dismay dropped about her as a garment.

"But what do you do?" she faltered. "Where do you go to service on Sunday?"

"Same as any other day," laughed Stephen carelessly. " 'The groves were God's first temples,' " he quoted piously; "suppose we go out in search of one. This will be a first-rate day for your first lesson in riding horseback. It won't do for you to stick in the house at work all the time."

But Margaret's face was flushed and troubled.

"Do you mean you don't go anywhere to church?" she asked pathetically. "Is there no service in the town? Are there no missionaries even, out here?"

"There isn't even a town worth speaking of, Miss Halstead," answered Philip, feeling that some one must answer her earnestly. "You do not know what a God-forsaken country you have come to. Churches and missionaries would not flourish here if they came. You will not find it a pleasant place to stay. Men get used to it, but women find it hard."

She lifted her troubled eyes to his, wondering in an underthought whether he was hinting that she should go back where she came from; but she saw in his kind face no eagerness to get rid of her, as his eyes met hers. She turned sadly toward the window, looking out on the stretch of level country away down the hill, thinking with despair of the place to which she had come and the hopelessness of carrying out her plans without the aid of a church and a minister.

She had thought her part would be simply to make a good home for her brother, to speak a quiet word when opportunity offered, and to use her influence to put him under the power of the gospel. But out here it seemed there was no gospel, unless she preached it. For this she was not prepared.

Perplexed and baffled, she hardly knew with what words she declined her brother's urgent request to go riding with him, to which were added the most earnest solicitations of his partner when he saw that Stephen was not going to succeed. She wondered afterwards at the anxiety and annoyance in Philip's eyes when she told him firmly that she did not ride on Sunday, and would rather stay quietly at home. It seemed strange to her that he should try to interfere between her and her brother. Then she went into her little log room and shut the door, and knelt in disheartened prayer beside her bed. Had she, then, come out on a fruitless mission? For what would it avail if she did bring palm-covered walls and pianos and books into her brother's life, if there were no means by which he could be brought to see the love of the Lord Jesus Christ?

She was scarcely roused from her disappointed petitions by the sound of a rider leaving the dooryard. She wondered idly whether it were Philip, but soon she heard another horse's quick tread, and, going to the window, was just in time to see Philip fling himself upon his horse and ride at a furious pace off down the road.

Quiet settled down upon the house, and Margaret realized with disappointment that both the young men had gone away. Why had she not tried to keep Stephen with her? Perhaps he would have listened to her while she read something, or she might have sung. Philip, it was quite evident, had intended going off all the time, and was only anxious to get her and Stephen out of the way so that he could do as he pleased. The tears came into her eyes, and fell thick and fast. How ignominiously had she failed! Even the little she might have done she had let slip by because of her disappointment that God had not arranged things according to her expectations. Perhaps it might have been better for her even to go on the ride with Stephen rather than for him to go off with some friends who never had a thought of God or His holy day.

Thus reflecting, she read herself some bitter lessons. She had forgotten to ask for the Spirit's guidance, and had been going in her own strength; or she might have been shown a better way and been blessed in her efforts.

By and by she went out where the old woman sat outside the kitchen door, mumbling and glowering at the sun-clad landscape. Perhaps she might essay a humble effort with this poor creature for a Sabbath-day sacrifice.

"Marna, do you know God?" she asked, sitting down beside the old woman and speaking tenderly.

The woman looked at her curiously, and shook her head.

"God never come at here," she answered. "Missie, you—*you* know God?"

"Yes," answered Margaret earnestly. "God is my Father."

"God your Father! No. You not come off here; you stay where you Father at. God, you Father, angry with you?"

"No, my Father loves me. He sent His Son to die for me. God is your Father, too, Marna."

The old woman shook her head decidedly. "Marna have no father. Fathers all bad. Fathers no love anybody but selves. Brothers no much good, too. All go off, leave. All drink. I say, stay 'way. No come back drunk. Knock! scold! hate! I say stay 'way! Drink self dead!"

Marna was gesticulating wildly to make up for her lack of words. Suddenly she turned earnestly to the girl, with a gleam of something like motherliness in her wrinkled, wicked old face.

"What for Missie come way here? Brothers no good. All go own way. Make cry!" and Marna's work-worn finger traced down the delicate cheek, which was still flushed with the recently shed tears.

Margaret instinctively drew back, but she did not wish to hurt the old woman's feelings; so she answered in as bright a tone as she could summon.

"Brothers are not all bad, Marna. Some are good. My brother was lonely here, and I came to take care of him."

" 'Take care! Take care!' " muttered the old woman. "And who 'take care' of Missie? Men go off, stay all day. Drink. Come home drunk! Ach! No, no, Missie go back. Missie go off while men gone. Not see brothers any more."

Margaret was half frightened over this harangue; but she tried to be brave and answer the poor creature, though her heart misgave her as a great fear began to rise.

"No, Marna," she said, smiling through her fear; "I cannot go back. God sent me, and until He tells me to go back I cannot go."

"God love you and send you here? Then He never come here. He don't know—"

"Yes, He knows, Marna, and He is here, too," she answered softly, as if reassuring herself. "Listen!"

And Margaret began at the beginning of the story of the cross, and told it all to the wondering old woman as simply as she knew how. But, when she had finished, the listener only shook her head, and murmured:

"No, God never love Marna. Marna have bad heart. No love for good in heart. No heavenly Father love."

It was time to get dinner ready, and Margaret arose with a sigh, a great depression settling on her heart. Not even to this poor old woman could she show the light of Christ.

She gave herself to the preparations for the noon-day meal for a little while, thinking soon to hear the sound of horses coming up the road; but, though the dinner got itself done and sent forth savory odors on the air, and Margaret stood with anxious, wistful eyes shaded with a hand that had grown strangely cold with a new fear, there came no sound of horses.

The girl ate a few mouthfuls, and had the dinner put away. The old woman went about muttering:

"Men no come. Men off. Have good time. Missie cry. Missie go home. Not stay."

The stars came out thickly like sky-blossoms unfolding all at once, and the sky drew close about the earth; but still there came no sound of travellers along the long, dark road.

Margaret went in at last from her vigil on the doorstep and lit the great lamp. It was a disappointing Sabbath. It was more than that; it seemed a wasted Sabbath. She might much better have been riding with Stephen if perchance she might have said some helpful thing to him. And the old woman rocking and muttering to herself in the back doorway, what good had she done to her?

At last she could bear the silence and her fears no longer.

She called to Marna to come in. "Sit down," she said gently. "I will sing to you about Jesus."

Marna sat down with folded hands on a little wooden stool, and listened while Margaret sang. She chose the songs that were in simple language, that told of Jesus and His love; songs that spoke to weary, burdened ones and bade them rest; songs that told of forgiveness and a Father's love.

A long time she sang; and then, yearning for a help, she knew not what, feeling as if she must have a companionship in her need, she came over to the old woman, took her hand, and drew her down beside the fireplace seat.

"Come," said she. "We will talk to God."

Wonderingly, half fearfully, the old woman knelt, watching the girl with wide-open eyes the while; and Margaret closed her eyes, and said:

"O God, show Marna how her Father loves her. Make Marna love God. Make Marna good, for Jesus' sake."

As under a spell the old woman stood up; her eyes, half frightened, half fascinated, were upon the girl's face.

Margaret smiled and said good-night, but Marna went out under the stars, and muttered wonderingly, "Make Marna good?" as if it were a thing that had to be and she could not see how it could be.

Then Margaret locked the door, and turned out the light, and sat down at the window to watch and pray. During that time there was revealed to her a part of what she might do in this land without a God or a temple. Out of her darkness, her fear, and her feebleness came a strength not her own.

It must have been long past midnight — her watch had run down and she could not tell — when at last faint sounds came slowly up the hill; and silently, slowly there crept past her window and wound around the house to the barn two horsemen, strangely close together. One seemed to be supporting the other. They spoke no word; but one of them turned his head as he passed her window, and looked, though she could not tell which one it was.

Neither of them came to the house that night, though she lighted the lamp and waited awhile for them. She concluded they did not wish to disturb her.

Then, not caring to take off her clothes, she lay down and wept. After all the long, hard day the tension was loosened at last, but what yet did she know? Was one of her new-found fears dissipated? Was she sure that Stephen had come home with Philip, and was now in the barn lying in the hay? Was she sure that it had been Philip? They might have been two tramps — but no. Tramps would not come to a desolate land like this. They would tramp to more profitable places for plying their beggarly trade. Somehow for herself a strange peace settled down upon her. She was not afraid that anything would happen to her. She feared only for her brother — and — yes, she must admit it — for his friend. For, after all, he was her brother too, in a larger, broader sense, but still the son of her heavenly Father.

And those words of Marna's, what had they meant? Did the two with whom she had come to make her home, drink? And, if so, how could she ever hope to help and save them, just she alone in that country without a church? For the absence of a Christian church and a Christian minister seemed to leave her most inexpressibly alone.

And yet not alone, for out of the darkness of her room came the words to her heart, "And lo, I am with you alway."

Then she prayed as she had never prayed before, prayed until her soul seemed drawn up to meet the loving Comforter, Strengthener, and Guide. In that consecration hour she laid down herself, her fears and wished, and agreed to do what God would have her do here in this lonely place, against such fearful odds as might be; herself alone with God.

Out in the hay lay Philip, body and mind weary with the fight of the day, in which he had not won, yet too troubled to sleep now that he had the chance.

With anxious eyes he peered through the darkness toward the house, and wondered how it had fared with the one who had waited all day while he had been in the forefront of battle. Was she frightened at being left so late alone? Had she seen them when they came in? Had she guessed at all what the trouble was, or had she coupled them both in deserting her? Philip's heart was very bitter to-night, and against God. He felt like cursing a God who would let a woman, and so fair a woman, suffer. Poor, straying child of God, who knew not the comfort of trusting and leaning on the everlasting arm; who knew not that even suffering may bring a beauteous reward!

Chapter 8

Stephen slept late the next morning; and when he came heavy-eyed and cross to the breakfast-table, he complained of a headache. But Philip sat silent, with grave lines drawn about forehead and mouth. He was too strong a man to show the signs of fatigue or loss of sleep in any other way.

Margaret had come out from the horror of the night with peace upon her brow, but her eyes looked heavy with lack of sleep. Philip gave her one long look while she was pouring coffee, and saw this. It angered him to think she had suffered.

Margaret was sweetness itself to her brother. She insisted upon his lying down on the long seat by the chimney, while she shaded his eyes from the glare of the morning, and brought a little chair near by, and read to him. When he turned his head away from her entirely because for very shame he could not face this kindness, and know what in his heart he really was, she laid the book aside, and, bringing a bowl of water, dipped her cool, soft hand in it, and made passes back and forth across the temples that really throbbed in earnest.

Something was working in his easily stirred heart, something that went beyond the mere surface where most emotions were born and died, with him; and, as her hand went steadily back and forth with that sustained motion that is so comforting to sick nerves, he reached up a shaking hand, and caught hers, and his voice choked as he said,

"You are a good girl, —a good sister!"

Then Margaret stooped over, and kissed his lips, and murmured softly, "Dear brother, now go to sleep; and when you wake up, you will feel better."

Stephen had much ado to keep back moisture that kept creeping to his eyelids with stinging, smarting stealth; and he was glad when she finally thought him asleep and tiptoed away. Not for long years had he felt a lump like that that was growing in his throat till it seemed it would burst. But by and by the quiet and the darkness brought sleep; and Philip, looking anxiously in, went out quickly with a relieved sigh.

The dinner was late that day, for Stephen slept long, and Margaret would not have him disturbed. But when it came it was delicious. Strong soup seasoned just right, home-made bread, delicious coffee, and a quivering mound of raspberry jelly, cool and luscious with the flavor of raspberries from the old New England preserve-closet. It was marvelous how many things this sister could make from canned goods and boxes of gelatine. There seemed to be no end to the variety.

But Stephen was restless as the dinner neared its close, and Philip looked anxiously toward him.

Stephen shoved his chair back with a creak on the floor, and said crossly that he believed he would ride down to the village for the mail. He needed to get outdoors; it would do his head good. Philip frowned deeply, and set his lips for a reply; but before he could speak Margaret's sweet voice broke in eagerly.

"O, then, give me my lesson in riding, Stephen, please. It is a lovely afternoon, and will soon be cool. I don't want to be left behind again. I was sorry I had not gone with you yesterday. Please do; I am in a great hurry to learn to ride so I can go all about and see this country."

Philip's face relaxed. He waited to see what Stephen would do, and after a bit of coaxing Stephen consented, although Philip felt uneasy yet.

The horses were saddled and brought to the door, and Philip held the bridle of the gentler horse while Stephen helped his sister to mount, giving elaborate advice about how to hold the reins and how to sit. Then they were off.

"Go the east road, Steve!" called Philip as they rode away from him; but Stephen drew his head up haughtily, and did not answer. Then Philip knew he had made a mistake, and he bit his lip as he turned quickly toward the barn. There was still another horse on the place, though it was not a good riding-horse, and had some disagreeable habits, which left it free generally to stay behind when there was any pleasure riding to be done. Philip flung his own saddle across her back now, and, hardly waiting to pull the girths tight, sprang into it and away after the two, who were turning westward, as he had been sure Stephen would do after his unfortunate remark.

He urged the reluctant old horse into a smart trot, and soon caught up with the riders, calling pleasantly:

"Made up my mind I would come along too. It was lonely staying behind by myself."

Stephen's only answer was a frown. He knew what Philip meant by following. His anger was roused at Philip's constant care for him. Did Philip think him a fool that he couldn't take care of himself with his sister along?

Margaret, too, was a little disappointed. She had hoped to get nearer to her brother during this ride, and perhaps to find out where he had been the day before, and have a real heart-to-heart talk with him. But now here was this third presence that was always between her and her brother, and hindered the talk.

Philip, however, was exceedingly unobtrusive. He rode behind them or galloped on before, dismounting to gather a flaming bunch of flowers, and riding up to fasten them in the bridle of the lady's horse, and then riding on again. Stephen ignored him utterly, and Philip gayly ignored the fact that he was ignored. Margaret came to feel his presence not troublesome, and in fact rather pleasant, hovering about like a guardian angel. Then she laughed to herself to think of her using that simile. To think of an angel in a flannnel shirt, buckskins, and a sombrero!

It was Philip's quiet hint — no, not a hint, merely a suggestion that a certain turn would bring them to a view of the river — that caused Margaret to plead for going that way just as they had come to a critical turn in the road. Stephen, all unsuspecting, turned willingly, thinking they would go back soon and find their way to the village; but wary Philip tolled them on still further until the town with its dangers was far behind them. Then Stephen awoke to the plot that had been laid for him, and rode his horse sulkily home; but the deadly fiend that slumbered within him was allayed for the time, and he went to his room and slept soundly that night.

There was plenty of work to be done yet upon the house. Philip surprised them all a few days later by driving up to the door before breakfast with a load of logs, several men and another load of logs following after him. The sound of the axe, saw, and hammer rang through the air that day, and by night a good-sized addition of logs, divided into two nice rooms, was added to the right-hand side of the living-room.

Margaret's eyes shone. It was just the addition she had spoken of to Stephen, to which he had seemed so opposed. Her heart swelled with gratitude toward him. It seemed she did not yet understand this brother, who was sometimes so cold, but who yet was trying to do all in his power to please her. She watched the work some of the time, and was surprised to find that, while Stephen worked with the rest, he yet took all his orders from Philip as did the others, and seemed to expect Philip to command the whole affair. It was still more strange that all the orders were just what she had suggested to Stephen on the first walk around the house.

It was as they were coming to the supper-table that evening that she attempted to tell her brother how good it was of him to do all these things that she suggested. She thought they were alone; but Philip had come in behind them while they were talking, and Stephen saw him. The back of Stephen's neck grew red, and the color stole up around his golden hair as he said laughingly:

"O, thank Phil for that. He's the boss carpenter. I couldn't build a house if I had to stay out in the rain the rest of my life."

Margaret looked up brightly, and gave Philip the first really warm smile he had received from her, a smile that included him in the family circle.

"I will thank him, too," she said and put out her hand to grasp his large one, rough with the handling of many logs. But she left her other hand lovingly on her brother's shoulder, and Stephen knew she had not taken back the gratitude she had given him. It somehow made him feel strangely uncomfortable.

In a few days the addition to the house was in good order and the windows draped in soft, sheer muslin.

There seemed to be good cheer everywhere. The three householders took a final survey of the premises before the sun went down.

"If we could only grow bark on the outside of the old boards on the main part of the house!" said Margaret wistfully."

"Nothing easier," answered Philip quickly. "It shall be done."

"What do you mean?" asked Margaret.

"Why, cover it with bark," answered Philip. "Steve, get up early with me in the morning, and we'll strip enough bark down in the ravine to cover one side of this front before breakfast."

"Won't that be beautiful?" said Margaret, clapping her hands childishly, and the stern lines in Philip's face broke into a pleased smile. He was glad he had suggested it. What was it about this girl that always made one feel glad when he had done her a favor? Other girls he had known had not been that way.

That night he slept in the house for the first time since Margaret came to live there. The front room of the addition was fitted up for him. Margaret had just found out that his only bed had been in the hay, and that he had permanently and quietly given up his room to her. She had supposed before that there was a room over the barn, large and comfortable, which he called his own, though she had indeed thought little about it. She took especial pains with the furnishing of Philip's room. She felt it was due to him for turning out of his own for her. It was not difficult to make it beautiful. There was enough fine old mahogany furniture left. She picked out the handsomest things, and arranged them attractively. She had not yet fixed up her own room further than to have her own bedstead set up in preference to the hard little cot, but she wanted to make Philip's as attractive as possible.

As a final touch she went to her room, and unpinned from her wall the photograph of the sweet-faced woman with the white hair, and framing it in a little leather case of her own, set it upon the white cover of Philip's bureau. And it was his mother's eyes that looked at Philip in the morning as he opened them for the first time in his new abode. He lay for a moment, looking at the picture, wondering how it got there, blessing the thoughtfulness that had so placed it, wondering what his mother would think of him now in this strange, wild life. Wondering, too, what she would think of the girl who was bringing to pass in this desolate house such miracles of change. He touched the smoothness of the sheet and the pillow-case, and realized that he had missed such things as these for a long time, and had not known it.

Those were busy, happy days. At times Stephen seemed to be wrought up to the same pitch of enthusiasm and violent effort that kept the other two at work. He did not seem to want to stop for his meals even, until all was finished. And one night, when they were standing off, looking at the almost completed outside of the house, he said,

"We ought to have a housewarming when it gets done."

"Certainly," said Margaret. "We will do it by all means. How soon can we have it, and whom will you invite?"

But, as she turned to go into the house, she caught that look of disapproval on Philip's face, the look she had not seen for several days, and wondered at it.

"Let's have it next Sunday," said Stephen enthusiastically. "It's getting cooler weather now, and by evening we can have a fire in that jolly new fireplace of Phil's. And we'll ask all the fellows, of course."

Philip stood still, aghast. If Margaret had not been there, he would have fairly thundered. But his tongue was tied. This must be managed, if possible, without letting her know what a precipice she was treading near. She would be overcome if she knew all.

"Is there no other day but Sunday, Stephen, dear?" asked Margaret, and her troubled voice was very soft and pleading. "You know I always make the Sabbath a holy day and not a holiday. I would much, *much* rather have it some other time."

She did not say no decidedly to his proposition, remembering her Sunday's experience when she had declined to ride with him. Perhaps there was some way out of the perplexity better than that. She would not antagonize her brother yet, and she would ask her Guide. There surely would be a way.

"No, there isn't any other time when they all can come," answered Stephen shortly. "But of course if you have your puritanical notions, I suppose it's no use. I can't see what harm it would do for the boys to be here that day more than any other day. You can go off into your room, and pray if you want to; and the boys won't be doing any worse than they would do down in the village carousing round."

Stephen was angry, and was forgetting himself. Philip's cheeks flamed with indignant pity for the girl who winced under her brother's words.

"Oh, Stephen, *don't*, please! Let me think about it. I want to do what you wish if there is a right way." She spoke pleadingly. There were tears in her voice, but her eyes were bright and dry.

"Well, then, do it," said Stephen sulkily. "It won't hurt your Sabbath to give us some tunes on the piano. The boys will like that better than anything else. They don't hear music about here."

Margaret looked up troubled, but thoughtful.

"I'll think about it to-night, Stephen, and tell you in the morning. Will that do? I'll really try to see if I can please you."

Stephen assented sulkily. He had very little idea she would do it. He remembered her face that Sunday when she declined to ride with him. He set her down as bound by prejudices and of very little use in such a country as that.

But Philip, troubled, hovered about the door.

"Miss Halstead," he called pretty soon, "the moon is rising; have you noticed how bright the stars are? Come out and look at them."

"Come, Stephen," said Margaret.

"What do I care for the stars?" said Stephen sulkily, and he went into his room and shut the door.

Margaret's eyes were filled with tears, but she winked them back, and came to the door, anxious to get to the kindly starlight that would not show her discomfiture.

"Miss Halstead, I beg you will not think of doing what Steve asks," said Philip low and earnestly.

"Why not, Mr. Earle? Have you any conscientious scruples against company on Sunday?" Her voice was cold and searching.

"No, of course not," said Philip impatiently.

"Then why? You spent all day one Sunday off somewhere, presumably on a pleasure excursion."

"It was anything but a pleasure excursion, Miss Halstead," said Philip, his face growing dark with anger in the starlight. "But that has nothing whatever to do with the matter. I beg you will not do this for your own sake. You do not know what those fellows are. They will not be congenial to you in the least."

"Does that make any difference if they are my brother's friends?" Margaret drew herself up haughtily. "I thank you for your advice, Mr. Earle; but this is my brother's house, and of course I cannot stop his having guests if he wishes. I do not like company on Sunday; but, if they must come, I shall do my best to make it a good Sunday for them. More than that I cannot promise. Do you think I can?"

There was a mixture of coldness and pleading in her voice which would have been amusing at another time. But she had silenced Philip most effectually. He bit his lips, and turned away from the house to walk out into the starlight with his vexation.

Chapter 9

Margaret slept but little that night. A great plan had come to her, born of anxiety and prayer. At first she thought it seemed preposterous, impossible! She drew back, caught her breath, and prayed again; but over and over the idea recurred to her.

It was this. Perhaps God had sent her out here into these wilds to witness for Himself, yes, even among rough men like the two that had taken dinner with them that first day after her arrival.

Could she do it? Could she make that proposed Sunday gathering into a sanctified, holy thing? She, who had never spoken in public in her life, except to read a low-voiced essay from a school platform? She, who had always shrunk from doing anything publicly, and let honors pass her rather than make herself prominent? She who had never been taught in ways of Christian work, other than by her own loving heart?

Could she do it?

And *how* could she do it?

The utmost she knew about Christian work was learned in the class of boys she had taught in Sunday school at home. But they had been boys, most of them still in knee-trousers, and under home discipline. They had loved her, it is true, and listened respectfully to her earnest teaching. Even their mischief had given way before her hearty, trusting smile. They had learned their lessons, and thought it no disgrace to answer her questions. They had come to her home occasionally, and seemed to enjoy it, and she had talked with several of them about holy things. Two she had labored with and knelt beside while she heard their first stumbling acknowledgment that God was their Father and Jesus Christ their Saviour.

But this was all very different from bringing the gospel to a lot of men who knew little and cared less about God or their own salvation. She shuddered in the dark as she remembered the sound of that awful oath that Byron had let fall. How could she do it? Was it right and modest for her to try?

Then out of the night she seemed to feel her Saviour's eyes upon her, and to know that such things must not count against the great need of souls when she was the only one at hand to succor. And she bowed her head, and answered aloud in a clear voice.

"I will do what you want me to do, Jesus; only let me help save my brother."

The sleeper in the next room stirred, and started awake at the unusual sounds, and thought over the words he had heard, trying to put a meaning to them, but thought he had dreamed; so he slept again, uneasily.

After Margaret had said, "I will," to her Master the rest came easily. The plan, if it was a plan, was His. The Spirit would guide her. She had asked for such guidance. If it was of God, it would be crowned with some sort of success. She would be made to understand that it was right. If it was her own faulty waywardness, it would fail. It surely could do no harm to try to have a Sunday-school class of any of Stephen's friends who would come; and, if they refused or laughed at her, why, then she could sing. The gospel could always be sung, where no one would listen to it in other form. It would be a question of winning her brother over, and that might be difficult.

Stay! Why need she tell him? Why not take them all by guile, and make the afternoon so delightful to them that they would want to come again? Could she?

Her breath came quickly as the idea began to assume practical proportions and she perceived that she was really going to carry it out. She had ever a spirit of strong convictions and impulsive fancies; else she would have stopped right here. But perhaps in saying that too little weight is given to the fact that she had given herself up to the guidance of One wiser that herself.

Just before the stars paled in the eastern sky she lay down to rest, her mind made up, and her heart at peace. As for Philip's words of warning, she had forgotten them entirely. Philip she did not understand, but neither did he understand her.

The two young men were both surprised the next morning when she told them, quietly enough, that she would be glad to help them entertain their friends on Sunday afternoon, provided they would allow her to carry out her own plans. She thought she could promise them a pleasant time, and would they trust her for the rest?

It was very sweetly said, and her dainty morning gown, a touch of sea-shell pink in it this time that made her look like an arbutus blossom in the greenery of the room, sat about her so trimly that her brother could but admire her as he watched her put the sugar into his coffee.

It must be admitted that Stephen was surprised, but he was too gay himself to realize fully the depth of earnestness in any one else; so he concluded that Margaret had decided to let her long-faced ideas go, and have a good time while she was here; and he resolved to help her on with it. She was certainly a beauty. He was glad she had come.

But Philip's face darkened, and the little he ate was quickly despatched. After that he excused himself, and went out to the barn. He was angry with Margaret, and he was troubled for her. He knew better than she what she was bringing upon herself; moreover, her brother, who should have been a better protector of so precious a sister, knew even better than he. Why did not Stephen see, and stop it?

But Philip forsaw that matters had gone too far for it to be wise in him to say a word to Stephen. Former experience had taught him that Stephen took refuge from pointed attacks in flight to his companions in the village, which always ended in something worse.

Philip was so angry that after he had done all the work about the barn-yard that was ready for him he concluded to take himself away for a while. There was enough in the house to keep Stephen busy and interested for the day. The fear that had made him keep guard ever since the arrival of Margaret Halstead was for the time dominated by his anger at both brother and sister; and he took his revenge in going off across the country many miles on a piece of business connected with a sale of cattle which he had proposed to make for some time, but had put off from week to week.

He did not stop to explain to the household except in a sentence or two, and then he was off. Margaret noticed the hauteur in his tones as he announced his departure at the door, but so full was she of her plans for Sunday that she took little heed of it. It did not matter much about Philip anyway. He was only an outsider, and, besides, he would feel differently, perhaps, when Sunday came.

Philip's anger boiled within him, and grew higher and hotter as he put the miles between himself and the cause of it. He wished himself out of this heathenish land, and back into civilization. He decided to let people take care of themselves after this. Of what use was it to try to save this girl from a knowledge of her brother's true self? She was bound to find it out sooner or later, and she would perhaps only hate him for his effort.

But Stephen, after teasing his sister to discover what plan she had for the entertainment of their guests, made up his mind to make the most of Philip's absence, and get his guests well invited before that autocrat interfered. It was marvellous that he had not done so already. Therefore he slipped away to saddle his horse while his sister was busy in her room, and, only leaving a message with Marna, rode away into the sunlight, as gay of heart as the little insects that buzzed about his horse, and with less care for the morrow than they had.

Margaret was disappointed to find her brother gone when she presently came out, for she had planned to get him to do several little things about the house that morning, and while he was doing them she had intended to sound him on the friends he would invite. She wondered whether there were many and whether among them there would be any who could help her in the work of establishing her Sunday school. There must be some good women about there. Surely she could get a helper somewhere.

But perhaps this first time it would be only two or three of Stephen's best friends. He had spoken of "the fellows," and it would be better not to have any complications of womankind till she was well acquainted and knew on whom she could count for help. She admitted to her own heart, too, that she could open up the plan to them, and teach a class in her own way, better stilling the flutter of her own frightened heart, if there were no women or girls about to watch.

She was disappointed, it is true, but after a moment she reflected that perhaps even Stephen's absence was an advantage. She would take this quiet hour to study up a lesson and plan her programme, though it would be much easier if she knew just what kind of scholars she was to have. She spent a happy morning and afternoon planning for the Sunday, and only toward night did she begin to feel uneasy and hover near the door looking down the road.

Marna came in, shaking her head and muttering again, and it required all Margaret's faith and bravery to keep her heart up.

The night closed down like that other night when she had kept a vigil, and still neither of the young men appeared. Margaret wished that Philip would come, so that she might reassure herself by asking where he supposed Stephen had gone and when he would return. She acknowledged to herself that after all there was something strong and good to lean upon in Philip.

She prayed much that evening, and by and by lay down and tried to sleep. After several hours of restless turnings she did finally fall into an uneasy sleep.

But, when the morning broke with its serene sunshine, and neither of the two men had returned, she grew more restless. In vain did she try to settle to anything. She constantly returned to look off down the road.

Marna said little that day; but Margaret remembered her former words, and her old anxieties returned to clutch her till she was driven to her knees. As she prayed, a great, deep love for her new-found brother grew and grew in her soul till she felt she must save him, for instinctively she knew that he needed saving more than many.

And the second day wore away into the night, but still they had not returned.

Margaret lived through various states of mind. Now she was alarmed, now indignant that they should treat her so; and now she blamed herself for having come out here at all. Then alarm would succeed all other feelings, and she would fly to her refuge and find strength.

When the third day dawned and seemed likely to be as the others had been, she questioned Marna as to where she thought they could have gone; but the old woman shut her lips and shook her head. She did not like to tell.

She had watched the young girl long enough to have a tender feeling of protection toward her.

This third day was Saturday. Margaret had had some wild ideas of trying to saddle the horse and go out into the strange, unknown country to seek knowledge of her brother; but her good sense told her that this would be useless. She must wait a little longer. Some news would surely come soon. Resolutely she sat down to study the Sunday-school lesson just as if nothing had happened to disturb her, and to plan out everything for the morrow, trying to think that her brother would surely return for Sunday; but her heart sank low in trouble as the night came on once more, and she left her supper, which Marna had carefully prepared, untasted on the table while she stood by the dark window looking down the road.

Philip's anger had carried him far toward his destination. When at last it cooled with his bodily fatigue, and he began to reflect on the possibilities of what might happen during his absence, he would have been minded to turn back, but that his horse was weary and the day was far spent. Besides, it would be foolish to go back now when he had almost accomplished that for which he came. A few minutes with the man he sought would be all he needed, and perhaps he could exchange horses, or give his own a few hours' rest and then return. He hurried on, annoyed that it was growing so late.

There was some difficulty in finding the place, after all, for several old landmarks had been removed by a fire, and it was quite dark before he reached the lonely ranch of the man with whom he had business.

He had not known his own strong desire to return until he discovered how he was to be hindered. He found that the man whom he sought had gone to another ranch a few miles further on, and would probably not return for three or four days. It would be ridiculous to turn back and have his long journey for nothing. He must press on now and accomplish what he had come for. He got a fresh horse, and, taking only a hasty supper, spurred his horse forward through the darkness, trusting recklessly to his own knowledge of the country to bring him to the desired point.

Of course he lost his way, and brought up at the place the next morning when the sun was two hours high, only to find that the man whom he had come in search of had started back the afternoon before, and must be at home by this time.

Another delay and another fresh horse, and he was on his way back, too weary to realize how long a strain he had been under. And, when he reached the first ranch and found his man, he was so worn out that he dared not start home without a few hours' sleep. So, the business disposed of, he lay down to sleep, his mind tormented the while by thoughts of Stephen and his own discarded trust.

But worn nature will take her revenge, and Philip did not awake until almost sunset on the second day. Then his senses came back sharply with a vision of Margaret, a dream perhaps, or only his first waking fancies. She seemed to be crying out in distress and calling: "My brother! Stephen! O, save him, Philip!" And with the sound of that dream voice there came a great desire in his heart to hear her speak his name that way.

But he put this from him. He tried to remember that he had been angry with her, and that this whole thing was her fault anyway for not following his advice, and then he remembered that she had no knowledge or reason to follow his advice — a stranger. What did she know of him and his reasons for what he had said? In some way she must be told, but how could he tell her?

All these thoughts were rushing through his mind as he went out and was hunting up his own horse, hastily preparing to go home. He would not have stopped for something to eat even, had his host not insisted. Then it was only because the reasonableness of this act appealed to him that he finally yielded and ate what he was given.

And all the long miles back, most of it in darkness, Philip was thinking, thinking, cursing himself for a fool that he had left Stephen alone with his sister, almost cursing God that such a state of things was possible.

It was toward morning when he neared the handful of buildings that constituted the village near their home. The horse quickened his pace, and familiar things seemed to urge the travellers forward. Distant discordant sounds were in the air. A pistol-shot rang out now and again. But that was not unusual. Shots were as common as oaths in that neighborhood. They were a nightly occurrence, a part of a gentlemen's outfit, like his generosity and his pipe. Nearer the sounds resolved themselves into human voices, the deep bark of dogs, singing, the clinking of glasses, a slamming shutter, the gallop of a rider whirling home after a night of revelry, to strike terror to the heart of any who waited for him.

The muscles around Philip's heart tightened as a sickening thought came to him, and he put spurs to his willing beast, making the road disappear rapidly behind him.

Near the one open house in the village, where lights were still burning and whence the sounds came, he drew rein, and the patient horse obeyed, having felt that anxious check to his rein before. Close under the window he stopped. Listening and then rising in his saddle, he looked to make sure of what his heavy heart had already told him was true.

There in the midst of the room, on a table, his golden curls all dishevelled, his jaunty attire awry, his fine blue eyes mad with a joyless mirth, and his whole face idiotic with absence of the soul that lived there, stood Stephen. He had evidently been entertaining the company, and he was speaking as Philip looked.

"Jes' one more song, boys!" he drawled. "I got a go home to my sister. Poor little girl's all alone, all aloney. Zay, boys, now that's too bad, ain't it?" His voice trailed off into unintelligibility.

A great anger, horror, and pity rose within Philip. Pity for the sister, anger and horror over her brother. He had seen Stephen like this before, and had sadly taken him away and brought him to himself, excusing him in his heart; but he had never before felt more than a passing disgust over the weakness of the man who put himself into such a condition. He had gone on the principle that, if Stephen liked that sort of thing from life, why, of course he had a right to take it; but he had always tried to save him from himself. Now, however, the thought of the sweet, trusting girl alone in the night waiting for him — how long had she waited? — while the brother she had come to help and love bandied her name and her pity around among a set of drunken loafers — Philip stopped his thoughts short, and sprang into action.

Not in the quiet, careless way in which he usually entered upon such scenes and took possession of his partner did he come this time. His soul was roused as great men's are when they have a deed of valor to perform.

He strode into that maudlin company, and dashed men right and left. They rose from the floor in resentment, or reeled against the wall, and shook trembling fists, and felt for ready weapons; but Philip's wrath was mighty. They quailed before him. One word he uttered between set teeth and white lips.

"Fiends!"

Then he grasped the shrinking Stephen firmly, and dragged him from the table and from the room before the fiery men around him had realized and drawn their revolvers. One or two wild shots whistled harmlessly into the air after him, but he and Stephen were gone.

He put Stephen — already in a senseless state — upon his horse, and took him to a shanty where he knew that no one was living now; and all the rest of that night and through the brightness of Saturday he stayed guard over him.

Stern lessons of life he read to himself as he sat there watching the tainted beauty of the face lying before him. All Stephen's gay, winning qualities were hidden behind the awfulness of what the man had become. He had never seen it so before. He had simply borne with Stephen till he came out of one of these states and became his gay, companionable self again. Now all at once Philip looked with disgust upon him. And the difference was that up on the hill five miles away there sat a sweet, pure woman, whose trust and freely lavished love the man before him had basely betrayed.

When Stephen had slept long, Philip brought water, bathed his face, and made him drink. He was determined to make Stephen perfectly sober, and he was anxious to do this as soon as possible, that they might get home and relieve the anxieties of the girl who waited there. But it was a stern face that Stephen looked into from time to time, and it was a silent journey that they took that night when darkness had come down to cover them. Only one sentence Philip spoke as they neared the house, and it was in a tone that Stephen was not likely to disregard.

"Be careful what you say to your sister!"

Then Stephen wondered what had happened since he left home, and how many days he had been away, and sat soberly trying to think as he rode up to the house.

Margaret's white face met them at the door, and Philip spoke first, his tone anxious and earnest.

"I am afraid you have been lonely, Miss Halstead. I am sorry it happened so. You see, Stephen thought he must come after me, and we were delayed by the absence of the man we went to see. The ride was too much for Stephen. He is played out, I am afraid. He ought to go right to sleep. If you have any coffee there, I will carry him in a cup. It will do him good. No, he isn't sick, just used up, you know. Nothing to worry about."

Philip's voice was quite cheerful. If Margaret could have seen his face, she would have wondered at his tone. But Margaret had been sitting in the dark, and it took some minutes to light the lamp with her trembling fingers, shaking now from the relaxation of the strain.

"Hope I didn't scare you, Margaret," Stephen spoke, his gay, easy manner settling upon him like an old coat he had plucked from its familiar nail and fitted on. "You know one must not wait where duty calls. But I'll take Phil's advice, I guess, and turn in. I feel mighty seedy. All knocked up with the long ride."

Philip was soon back from caring for the horses, and took the smoking coffee from Margaret's hand. As she handed it to him, she looked into his face.

"How about you, Mr. Earle? You look as if you needed the coffee more than Stephen," she said kindly.

The tender tone was almost too much for Philip after the grim strain he had passed through. It had in it a note of his mother's voice when he used to come home with a bruise from a fall or a fight. He smiled faintly, and said most earnestly,

"Thank you!"

And when he came out from Stephen's room he found that she had set him a tempting supper on one end of the table.

She hovered about, waiting upon him till he was done, and told him to sleep late in the morning when she said good-night. Then she went to her room, buried her face in the pillow, and cried. She did not know why she was crying. It was not from trouble. Perhaps it was relief. When she grew calm, she thanked God for saving her from some nameless trouble that she felt, but did not understand, and begged of Him again, help for the morrow and the work she was going to try to do for Him.

Chapter 10

The healing of sleep settled down upon the little household late that Saturday night, and lasted far into the morning.

When Margaret awoke, the sun shone broad across her floor, and a sense of relief shone into her heart. As she went about her preparations for the day, an awe settled down upon her in remembering what she was going to try to do for Christ. She dared not think of any words she would speak, and she had not yet made up her mind how she would set about it to introduce her plan to the expected guests. She shrank as she remembered Byron's bold, handsome eyes, and wondered whether he would be among those invited, or whether he was Philip's friend alone. She shut her own eyes, and prayed that she might put away such thoughts and think only of the message she had to bring.

The two young men literally did as she told them, and did not awake until almost noon. Margaret had kept their breakfast waiting until it was too late, and then she hastened the dinner preparations; and so the first meal they ate together was dinner.

After dinner Philip hastened to the neglected horses, and to see after some matters at the barn, and Stephen threw himself upon the couch. The day was chilly, and Marna had kindled a fire on the hearth. It crackled pleasantly, and Stephen was feeling the relief that comes after a throbbing headache has ceased. He took up a book from his sister's case, and began to read. He seemed to have forgotten all about his company, and Margaret thought perhaps he had not invited them after all, and it would be best not to speak about it. He was tired, and it would be much better for him.

There was immense relief to her in the thought that her task, which at times assumed proportions impossible, would be put off indefinitely. And yet there came a strange pang of disappointment, for her careful study of the lesson had revealed to her hidden blessed truths which the Spirit had made her long to impart to others. She wondered whether she could muster courage to suggest to Stephen that he and she, and perhaps Philip, too, if he liked, study the lesson together. She was sitting shyly by the piano, looking at her brother behind his book, and meditating whether she should ask him about it, when the door burst open most unceremoniously, and three young men stood upon the threshold.

To be sure, they knocked uproariously upon the opening door, and their greeting was loud and hilarious. Margaret arose, startled. But they stopped as suddenly as they had begun, and looked about upon the strange, changed place. This was a room with which they were unacquainted, many times as they had ascended the hill to make good cheer for Stephen. And the woman who stood silent by the piano was a lady, and was beautiful beyond any question.

It was as if they had come expecting summer weather, and were suddenly plunged into a magnificent snowbank. They stood embarrassed and for the moment silent, just as the other two strangers had stood, a little while before. All the effrontery of their brave, outlandish Western attire deserted them. The instinctive feeling of each man was self-defence, and involuntarily their hands sought the place which held the inevitable weapon. Not that they meant to draw it, only to feel the cold, keen protection of its steel assuring them.

They had been gentlemen born, these three, at least in appearance, but had long ago forgotten what that word meant. Perhaps it was the harder for them, therefore, to understand the beauty of purity and art, having once known it and wandered so far from its path, than if they had never seen it.

They were wordless for the moment, not knowing how to occupy the new position.

Stephen came airily forward. He was glad Philip was out of the way for the time. He hoped he would remain away until things were well going.

"Welcome!" he said with a wave around the place as if it were a palace and he the king. "My sister, Margaret Halstead, gentlemen. Margaret, this is Bowman, and Fletcher, and Banks."

Margaret bowed in a stately way she had, which made her seem much taller than she really was, and kept at a distance any man whom she chose to keep so. Nevertheless, there was in her manner a smile of welcome, which seemed to the three strangers something like a cold bit of sunshine that had fallen their way and charmed them, but did not belong to them.

They came in and sat down, trying to assume their natural voices and easy speeches; but a mist of convention was enveloping them round, which they could not drive away. All but Banks.

Banks was small, slightly hard of feature, with an unfeeling slit of a mouth and hateful, twinkly black eyes that were not large enough to see anything wonderful. He carried about him an ill-fitting self-complacency that belonged to a much larger man. His collegiate career had been cut short by his compulsory graduation to an inebriate asylum and later to the West.

Banks essayed a remark to Margaret which would have caused Philip to sling him out the door if he had been there. It was complimentary and coarse in the extreme. Fortunately Margaret did not understand it, and stood in dumb amazement at the shout of laughter that was raised. She was glad when the door was darkened again by other guests, for she felt there was something painful in the atmosphere. She looked for Stephen to stand beside her; but he was already slapping shoulders with a newcomer, and her gaze met Byron's bold eyes bent in admiration as he came forward and attempted to take her hand by way of greeting, having a desire to show to the others his superior acquaintance with the queen of the occasion. But Margaret drew her hand behind her, and held him back with the gentle dignity of her greeting. He felt that she had not forgotten their last meeting and the words she had spoken to him. Her glance reminded him reproachfully of it. He saw he must not expect to be her friend with that between them. The blood stole up his swarthy cheeks, and he stood back conquered, to see Bennett — whom he knew to be no better than himself, but whom she did not know — greeted with a welcoming smile.

Bennett's white eyelashes fell beneath the glory of that smile, and his freckles were submerged in red. He sat down hard in a Morris chair that was several inches lower than he had expected, while Banks carolled out a silly song appropriate to the moment. This happened to be Bank's role, the bringing in of appropriate songs and sayings at the wrong minute, and causing a laugh.

Margaret looked about the room bewildered. The place seemed to be swarming with great, bold, loud, men. She remembered Philip's warning, and gasped. One moment more, and she felt that her head would be whirling dizzily. She must get command of the situation or fail. Surely her Strength would not desert her now, even though she had made a mistake. She lifted her soul to God, and wished while she prayed that Philip would come in. Philip somehow seemed so strong.

There were but seven men invited, though they looked so many. They were for the most part the pick of the country thereabout, at least among Stephen's friends. He had intended to be careful on Philip's account, for he knew Philip would not stand any one that would be outrageous. But Stephen's discretion had forsaken him with the first taste of liquor that passed his lips, and two had crept into the band worse than all the rest. Well for Margaret that she was strong in her ignorance of this.

"Well," began Stephen, and Margaret saw that now was her opportunity if she would not let this strange gathering slip from her control.

"My brother asked you to come this afternoon because he thought you might enjoy some music and reading," she said in a clear voice that commanded instant silence, "and I shall be very glad if I can give you any pleasure."

Then she smiled upon them like an undesired benediction, and each man dropped his eyes to his feet, and then raised them, wondering why he had dropped them.

"Won't you all sit down and make yourselves comfortable?" she went on pleasantly. "We should like to have you feel at home."

"Be it ever so humble, there no place like home," sung out Banks flippantly.

"Shut up, Banks!" said Bennett, turning redder, and glaring from under his white eyelashes at his neighbor.

"I want to get acquainted with my brother's friends, of course," went on Margaret, not heeding this accompaniment to her words. She had suddenly the feeling that she was holding a pack of hounds at bay, much as one feels when starting a mission school of wild street arabs. She must say the right thing at once and work quickly, or her cause would be lost.

"I don't know what kind of music you like best; so perhaps you will excuse me to-day if I play you my own favorites. I'm going to begin at once, please, so that we shall have plenty of time for them all, because by and by I want you all to sing."

They looked at her as they might have watched some new star in a theatre, wondering, awed for the minute by the strangeness, but not permanently. It takes a great deal to awe a Western cowboy.

Margaret turned with a sweep of her white draperies, and sat down at the piano. As she did so, she caught a glimpse of Philip standing in the doorway, his rugged face written over with disapproval and anxiety. It spurred her to do her best; and, laying her fingers upon the keys, she imparted her own spirit to them.

Some music lay upon the rack before her. It was not what she had intended to play first, but it would do as well as anything. She felt she must waste no more time in beginning, for Philip's face looked capable of almost any action if there was suffient cause.

It was Handel's "Largo" that sounded forth through the room with swelling, tender strain. She felt that perhaps it was not the right thing with which to hypnotize her audience, but she put her soul into it. If it were possible for music to express sacred things and true, then her music should do so. But, had she known it, music of any kind was so rare a treat and so unique that she might have played even a common scale for a few moments and had her audience until the strangeness wore away.

She gave them no time, however, to grow restless; for she glided from one thing to another, now a great burst of triumph, and now a tender sympathetic melody, and all of them connected in her own mind with sweet days of worship in her childhood's church at home. Instrumental music might not convey anything of a Sabbath nature to these untamed men, but it certainly could be no worse than no attempt at it, and she was feeling her way.

Philip stood like a grim sentinel in the doorway. The company felt his shadow and resented it, but were engrossed with the music at first. Philip could not let himself enjoy it. He stood as it were above it, and let it break like waves about his feet. He felt that he must, or some wave might ingulf them all.

He watched their faces as a great watchdog might eye intruders, mistrusting, lowering, a growl already in his throat.

The wonder of the spell the girl had cast about them had not yet touched him. He was guarding her.

Suddenly she felt the pressure of emotion too strong for her. With a chord or two she dealt "one imperial thunderbolt that scalps your naked soul," as Emily Dickinson has put it, and stopped.

They caught their breath, and, coming out from under the charm, turned toward Philip to take their revenge for his attitude.

But Margaret was all alert now. She felt the disturbance in the air. She moved quickly.

"You must be thirsty," she said, unconsciously using a term that meant more to them than she dreamed. "I'm going to give you a cup of tea. Stephen, call Marna to bring the kettle, please; and Philip, will you pass the cups?"

There was a gentle deference in her tone as she addressed Philip, almost as if she would ask his pardon and acknowledge that he was right about what he had told her.

There was something more also, a pleading that he would stand by here and help her out of this scrape into which she had allowed herself to go.

The soul of Philip heard and responded, and his quiet acquiescence sustained her all through the afternoon. It was as if there were some unspoken understanding between them.

The men watched her curiously as she moved about the room, collecting strange, thin, little dishes, the like of which some of them had never seen, and others had almost forgotten. There was enough of the unexpected and interesting about it to keep them moderately subdued, though a muttered oath or coarsely turned expression passed about now and again, and Banks tried a joke about the tea which did not take very well.

Margaret, however, was happily ignorant of much of this, though she felt the general pulse of the gathering pretty accurately.

The tea came speedily, for Marna had obeyed orders implicitly, and had been hovering near the door with a curious, troubled expression and shaking head. With the tea were served delicious little cakes of sugary, airy substance, olives, salted almonds, and dainty sandwiches.

The whole menu was just what Margaret would have used at home with her own friends. She knew no other way. Extravagant and unusual? O, certainly, but she did not realize this, and the very strangeness of it all worked for her anew the charm she had broken when she ceased to play, and kept the wild, hilarious spirits she would tame quiet till she had the opportunity for which she had been praying.

They vanished, these delectable goodies, as dew before the sun. The capacity of the company seemed unlimited. The entire stock of sweet, dainty things from carefully packed tin boxes that Margaret had brought with her would scarcely have sufficed to satisfy such illimitable appetites.

"They eat like a Sunday-school picnic," thought Margaret to herself, laughing hysterically behind the screen as she waited a minute to catch her breath before going out to try her hand at the most daring move of all her programme.

Then she looked across to where Philip stood watching her with faithfulness written in every line of his face, and saw that he was eating nothing. She motioned him to her, and gave him with her own hands a cup of tea. It was well she gave it behind the screen; for, had the others seen it, a bitter rivalry would have begun at once for favors from the lady's hand.

He took it from her as one might take an unexpected blessing, and drank it almost reverently, if such a thing can be.

Then he looked up to thank her; but she was gone, and he saw her standing, palm-surrounded, near the piano again, her soft white draperies setting her apart from the whole room, and her golden hair making a halo about her head, the rays of the setting sun just touched her with its burnished blessing like a benediction upon her work. Philip felt, as he looked, that she was surrounded by some angelic guard and needed no help from him. His stern expression relaxed, and in its place came one of amazement.

She was talking now in low, pleasant tones, as if these men were all her personal friends. Each man felt honored separately, and dropped his gaze, that the others might not know.

She was telling them in a few words about her home, and how she had come out there alone to her brother, now that she was alone in the world. She was putting herself at their mercy, but she was also putting them upon their honor as men, if they had any such thing as honor. Philip was doubtful about that, but he listened and wondered more.

Then she told them about the first Sabbath she had spent here, and how shocked and disappointed she had been to find no church or Sabbath services going on near by. She told them how she missed this, till they could not but believe in her sincerity, though such a state of mind was beyond their ken entirely; and she spoke of her Sabbath-school class at home, and how she loved the hour spent with them, until each man wished he might be a little boy for the time being, and offer her a class.

"I haven't asked my brother if I may," she said with a girlish smile, turning toward Stephen as he sat disturbed and uncomfortable in the corner. She felt intuitively that Stephen would count it a disgrace to be implicated in this manner, and thus honorably exonerated him. "But I am going to ask whether you would not be willing to help me make up for this loss I have felt. Perhaps some of the rest of you have felt it too."

Here she gave a quick, searching look about the circle of sunburnt faces.

"I wonder if you will help."

They straightened up, one or two, and looked as if they would like to assent, but Margaret went quickly on. She did not want to be interrupted now till she was done; else she might not have courage to finish.

"I am going to ask if you will help me have a Sunday school, or Bible service, or something of that sort. I will try to be the teacher unless you know of some one better—"

There was a low growl of dissent at the idea that any one could equal her, and Margaret flushed a little, knowing it was meant for her encouragement.

"We could not do much as they do at home in the East, but it would be keeping the Sabbath a little bit, and I think it would help us all to be better. Don't you?"

She raised her eyes, at last submitting the question to them, and the slow blood mounted in each face before her, while shame crept up and grinned over each shoulder. When had any one ever supposed that they wanted to be helped to be better?

"Now, will you help me?" She asked it in a sweet, pleading voice, and then sat down to wait their decision.

Chapter 11

But shame does not sit easily upon such as Banks. He roused himself to shake it off. He seldom failed in an attempt of that sort. He saw his opportunity in the intense silence that filled the room.

> "I am a little Sunday-school scholar, lah, lah,
> I dearly love my pa and ma, ma, ma, ma;
> I dearly love my teacher, too, too, too, too,
> And do whatever she tells me to — to, to, to,
> Teacher, teacher, why am I so happy, happy — "

He had chanted the words rapidly in his most irresistible tone, and he expected to convulse the audience and turn the whole gathering into a farce; but he had sung only so far when strong hands pinioned him from behind, gagged him with a handkerchief, and would have swiftly removed him from the place but that Margaret's voice broke the stillness that succeeded the song. Her face was white, for she realized that she had been made the subject of ridicule; but her voice was sweet and earnest.

"O, not that, please, Philip. Let him go," she said. "I'm sure he will not do it again, and I don't think he quite understood. I don't want to urge anything you would not all like, of course. I want it very much myself, though, and I thought perhaps you would enjoy it too. It seems so lonely out here to me, without any church."

She sat down, unable to say more, it must be left with God now, for she had done all she could.

Then up rose bold Byron. It was his opportunity to redeem himself.

"My lady," he began gallantly, "I ain't much on Sunday schools myself, never having worked along that line; but I think I can speak for the crowd if I say that this whole shootin'-match is at your disposal to do with as you choose. If Sunday school's your game, we'll play at it. I can sit up and hold a book myself, and I'll agree to see that the rest do the same if that'll do you any good. As for any better teacher, I'm sure the fellows'll all agree there's not to be found one within six hundred miles could hold a candle to you, so far as looks goes; and as for the rest we can stand 'most anything if *you* give it to us."

It was a long speech for Byron, and he nearly came to grief three times in the course of it because of some familiar oath that he felt the need of to strengthen his words.

Philip, as he held the struggling, spluttering Banks, glared at Byron threateningly during it all, and wondered whether he would have to gag the entire crowd before he was through; but Byron stumbled into his chair at last, and Margaret, to cover her blushes and her desire to laugh and cry both, put her hands up to her hot cheeks, and wondered what would come next. Then a wild, hilarious cheer of assent broke from the throats of the five other guests, and Margaret knew she had won her chance to try.

"O, thank you!" was all she could gather voice to say; but she put much meaning into her words, and the men felt that they had done a good and virtuous thing.

"Then we will begin at once," said Margaret, almost choking over the thought that she was really going to try to teach those rough big fellows a Bible lesson. "Mr. Byron, will you pass that pile of singing-books? And let us sing 'Nearer, my God, to Thee.' You must all have heard that, and I'm sure you can sing. Philip, please give this book to your friend, and release him so he can help us sing," and she actually was brave enough to smile condescendingly into Banks's mean little eyes.

Philip took the book, and let Banks go as he might have given a kick and a bone to a vagrant dog; but he looked at this most remarkable Sunday-school superintendent with eyes of wonder.

And they could sing. O, yes, they could sing! From their great throats poured forth a volume of song that would have shamed many an Eastern church choir. They sang as they would have herded cattle or forded a stream, from the glad, adventurous joy of the action itself; and more; they sang because they were trying to help out a lonely, pretty girl, who for some mysterious reason was to be helped by this most pleasant task.

As she played and listened to the words rolled forth, Margaret found in her heart a flood of uncontrollable desire that they all might know the meaning of those words, and sing them in very earnest.

The lesson, the same one that she would have taught, had she been at home with her class of little boys, began with the grand and thrilling statement:

"There is therefore now no condemnation to them that are in Christ Jesus, who walk not after the flesh, but after the Spirit."

They listened respectfully while she read the lesson in her clear voice. But the words conveyed very little to their minds, and it is doubtful, when she began to talk about a prisoner condemned to death and a pardon coming just in time to save him, whether they connected it in the least with the words she had been reading, or whether they even recognized them as the same she had read, when she repeated them later after having made the meaning clear.

It was simple language she used, with plain, everyday stories for illustrations; for she was accustomed to teaching little boys. But a doctor of theology could not have more plainly told the great doctrines of sin and atonement than did she to those men whose lives were steeped in sin, and to whom the thought of conviction of sin, or of condemnation, seldom if ever came.

They felt as if they had suddenly dropped into a new world as they listened, and some of them fidgeted, and some of them wondered, but all were attentive.

She did not make her lesson too long. For one thing, her own trembling heart would have prevented that. She had feared that she would not have enough to say to make the lesson of respectable length; but, when she began, the need of the souls before her appealed to her so strongly that she found words to bring the truths before them.

Philip watched her in amazement. She reminded him of a priestess robed in white, the palms behind her and her gold hair crowning her. He could think of nothing but Hypatia and her wonderful school of philosophy of old, as she opened up the simple truths. Looking about on the hard faces, softened now by something new and strange that had come over their feelings, he felt her power, and knew her way had been right; yet he feared for her, was jealous for her, hated all who dared to raise their eyes to her.

What power was it that made her able thus to hold them? Was it the mere power of her pure womanhood? Or the fascination of her delicate beauty? No, for that would have affected such men as these in another way. They would have admired, and openly; but they would not have been quiet or respectful.

Another thought kept forcing itself to his mind. If the God whom she was preaching, whom she claimed as her Father, should prove indeed to be the one true God, was he, Philip Earle, condemned? But this thought Philip put haughtily aside.

"I have been thinking," said the teacher, "as I sat here talking, how beautiful it would be if Jesus Christ were yet on the earth so that we could see Him. What if He should walk into that door just now?" and she pointed to the doorway where they had all entered.

Involuntarily each man lifted his eyes to the door, and Philip with the rest.

"He would come in here, just as He used to come into households in those Bible times, and we would make room for Him, and you would all be introduced."

Some of the men moved restless feet. Their thoughts were growing oppressive.

"And you would all see just what kind of a man, and a Christ, Jesus is," went on the sweet voice, "You could not help admiring Him, you know. You would see at once how gracious He is. You would not be—I hope—I think—none of you would be like those people who wanted to crucify Him—though we do crucify Him sometimes in our lives, it is true; but if we could see Him and know Him it surely would be different. He would call you to be His disciples, just as He called those other disciples of His, Philip and Andrew and Matthew and John and Peter and the rest."

Unconsciously Philip Earle flushed and started at his name. She had never called him Philip until that afternoon, and he thought for the moment she was speaking to him now.

There were others who looked conscious, too, for Bennett's name was Peter, and Fletcher's name was Andrew, and two others bore the name of John. Because of these little coincidences they were the more impressed by what she said.

"And what would you answer Him?" She paused, and there was stillness for just a minute in the room.

"I am going to tell you what I want for you all." She said it confidingly. "It is that you shall know Jesus Christ, for to know Him is to love Him and serve Him. And suppose as we study in this class that you try to think of yourselves as men like those disciples of old, whom He has called, and that you are getting acquainted with Him and finding out whether you want to answer His call. Because until you know Him you cannot judge whether you would care enough for Him for that. Will you try to carry out my fancy?"

She had struggled much with herself to know what she should do about prayer. It did not seem right to have a service without it, and she did not feel that she could pray. It was unlikely that the others would be willing to do so. She had settled on asking them all to join in the Lord's Prayer until she saw them, and then she knew that would not do. She even doubted whether many of them knew it. Her faint heart had decided to go without prayer, but now in the exultation of the moment she followed the longing of her heart to speak to her Father.

"Please, let us all bow our heads for just a minute and keep quiet before God," she said, and the silence of that minute, wherein seconds were counted out by great heart-beats, was one whose memory did not fade from the minds of the men present through long years of after experiences.

Awful stillness, painful stillness! Banks could not bear it. All his weak flippancy seemed singled out and held in judgment by it. He wanted to escape, wanted to break forth in something ridiculous, and yet he was held silent by some Unseen Power, while the terrible seconds rolled majestically and slowly around him.

"O Jesus, let us all feel Thy presence here, Amen!" said Margaret as if she were talking to a friend.

Then she turned quickly to the piano, and before the raising of the embarrassed eyes that dared not look their comrades in the face, lest they should be discovered as having been bowed in prayer, soft chords filled the room, and Margaret's sweet voice rang out in song.

"Abide with me," she sang; "fast falls the eventide."

The room had grown quite dusky, lighted only by the glowing fire in the fireplace, which Philip had quietly replenished from time to time with pine-knots that sent fitful glares upon the touched and softened faces of the men, while they sat rapt in attention to the music.

A few more chords, and the melody changed,

> "Weary of earth, and laden with my sin,
> I look at heaven and long to enter in;
> But there no evil thing may find a home,
> And yet I hear a voice that bids me, 'Come,'
>
> "So vile I am, how dare I hope to stand
> In the pure glory of that holy land?
> Before the whiteness of that throne appear?
> Yet there are hands stretched out to draw me near."

Soft chords came in here, like angel music that seemed to float from above them somewhere. It was a way she had with the piano, making it speak from different parts of the room and say the things she was feeling. The listeners half looked up as if they felt there were white hands stretched toward them.

The sweet voice went on:

> "It is the voice of Jesus that I hear,
> His are the hands stretched out to draw me near,
> And His the blood that can for all atone,
> And set me faultless there before the throne.
>
> "O Jesus Christ, the righteous! live in me,
> That, when in glory I Thy face shall see,
> Within the Father's house my glorious dress
> May be the garment of Thy righteousness.
>
> "Then Thou wilt welcome me, O righteous Lord;
> Thine all the merit, mine the great reward;

Mine the life won, and Thine the life laid down,
Thine the thorn-plaited, mine the righteous, crown."

"And now will you all sing a few minutes?" said their leader, turning toward them in the firelight, her fair face filled with the feeling of the prayer with which her song had closed.

"Philip, will you give us some light? Now let us sing 'I need Thee every hour' before you go home."

They growled out all their superfluous, bottled-up feelings into that song, and made it ring out, till Marna crept around and peered into the window to watch the strange sight. She stood there muttering in amazement, for such a miracle she never saw before. Perhaps Missie could work charms on even her, if she could make those wild fellows sit quiet there and sing that way.

And then they found themselves dismissed.

"I shall expect you next Sunday at the same time," she said, smiling, "and thank you so much for helping. It has been so good, almost like a Sunday at home. I have a delightful story and a new song for you next Sunday."

Greater marvel than all the rest, they went out quietly beneath the stars, mounting their horses in silence, and rode away. One attempt on Banks's part came to a dismal failure. Philip, standing at the door, heard the silly, swaggering voice rollicking through the night. "I dearly love my teacher, too, too, too, too," and Bennett's unmistakable roar, "Shut up, you fool, can't you?" as the song was brought to a summary close.

Byron had dared to linger a moment by the teacher's side, and with an expression almost earnest on his face had asked,

"Aren't you ever going to forgive me?"

"You must go to the One you insulted for forgiveness," answered Margaret gravely. "When you have made it right with Him, I will be your friend."

Then Byron dropped his boastful head, and walked away silent and thoughtful.

They turned, then, Philip and Margaret, and found themselves alone. They could hear Stephen slamming around in his room, the thud of first one boot and then the other thrown noisily across the floor. Stephen evidently was not in a good humor.

Margaret's face grew sad, and she realized that through the whole afternoon her thoughts had been more taken up with the others than with the brother she had come to try to save. Had the message reached him at all?

Seeing Philip standing in the door watching her, the look of wonder still upon his face, her expression changed. She went over to where he stood, and, putting out one hand, touched him gently on the coat-sleeve. "I did not understand," she said simply. "You were right. I ought to have listened to you."

He looked down at the little hand with finger-tips just touching the cuff of his sleeve, as if it had been some heavenly flower fallen upon him by mistake; and then he said, his voice all strange and shaking, "No, it was I who did not understand. You have been *wonderful!*"

Chapter 12

The days passed busily now. The queer little dwelling on the hill grew in beauty and interest with every passing hour. Stephen did his part, and seemed pleasant enough about it, although the first few days after the Sunday school he was strangely moody and quiet. Margaret could not tell whether or not he was pleased with what she had done.

And now she lured the two young men to gather around the hearth in the evenings while she read aloud to them in carefully selected books which touched their experiences of life and made them forget themselves for a little while. Margaret's power of song was equalled only by her ability to read well; and no dialect, be it negro or Scotch, was too difficult for her to enter into its spirit and interpret it to her readers. So long had they been out of the world that some of the best books about which people had raved for a few days and then forgotten had passed them by entirely. These were among her favorites, and now she brought them out and read them, while the two sat by and listened, much moved, but saying nothing except to laugh appreciatively at some fine bit of humor.

Thus she read "Beside the Bonnie Brier Bush," "A Singular Life," "Black Rock" and "The Sky Pilot"; and then went further back to George Macdonald, and chose some of his beautiful Scotch stories, "Malcolm," "The Marquis of Lossie," and "Snow and Heather." Over this last they were as silent as with the rest, but now and then Margaret noticed that Stephen covered his face with his hand and Philip turned his eyes away from the light while she was reading about the "Bonnie Man."

This sort of thing was all new to the two lonely fellows, who were used to making companions of the woods and fields and dumb beasts, and letting life go for little. This world of the imagination peopled life more richly. But ever when a book was finished Stephen would grow restless, and sometimes go off upon his horse, and Philip too would disappear. When they returned, — it might be late the same night, or after a day had passed, — Margaret could not tell which of the two, if either, had been the one who started first, and her heart grew heavy.

She rode with Stephen or with both of them quite frequently now, and was getting to be an expert horse-woman. She knew the ways about the country, and had seen some beautiful views. But not once had either of her escorts taken her near to the railroad station where she had arrived, nor pointed out what she fancied must be the semblance of a village. When she asked them, they always put her off, and more and more she wondered why.

With some trepidation she faced the next Sabbath, half fearful that her class would come again, half fearful lest they should not. But they came, every one, and brought two or three others along. There was not much need for Philip to stand guard, as he did, at the rear of the company, ready to spring should any slightest insult be offered to the teacher.

They had odd ways, these rough scholars of hers, and were as undisciplined as a company of city ragamuffins; but they respected the beautiful girl who chose to amuse herself by amusing them, and they listened quietly enough.

After the first wonder wore away they had the air of humoring her whimsical wishes. It pleased them to take it this way. It helped them to humble themselves into respectful attention. But ever, now and again, some word of hers would strike home to their hearts; and there would come that restless, noisy moving of the feet, that dropping of the eyes and avoiding one another's gaze, as each tucked his own past away within his breast, and fancied no one knew.

They grew to love the singing, and put their whole souls into the hymns they sang together; but they liked it more when Margaret sang to them the songs which sometimes brought back to them the days when they had been innocent and pure.

There was always, too, that solemn hush, that moment of silent prayer, before the one trembling but trustful sentence Margaret spoke to God. And sometimes, as the weeks went by, this or that man would find himself saying over in his own heart that sentence she had prayed the week before. It was not often she used the same sentence. Always it was something that touched the heart-experience or impressed the lesson-thought upon the mind.

The first prayer she had uttered in that house would always remain with Philip — "O Jesus, let us all feel Thy presence here." And, as he looked about the glorified room, it did seem as if a Presence had entered there, and come to stay. He often thought, as he sat waiting for the reading to begin in the evenings, of how that room had looked the night her letter came, and of how much he had hated the thought of her coming. Now, how light would go out of his life, should she go away! She did not know that. She never would, most likely. She was as far above him as the angels of heaven, but her coming had been as a gift from heaven. Would it last? Would she care to stay and keep it up? And Stephen, sitting on the other side of the hearth! Who could tell what were his thoughts as he alternated between his fits of moody silence and gay restlessness?

There came a day when Philip and Stephen were at work upon some fences, mending weak places where the cattle had broken them down. And in the afternoon Margaret put on a thin white dress with a scarlet jacket, and wandered out to where they were at work.

The day was bright and warm for late October, really hot in the sun. The light scarlet jacket was almost superfluous, but it served to intensify the scarlet in the landscape; and so she came, a bright bit of color into the prosaic of their work.

She had meant to talk to Stephen. In her heart she had been keeping some precious words she meant to say to him as soon as an opportunity offered. She longed to see him give himself to Christ. As yet she saw no sign that he had even heard the call to become a disciple.

But Stephen was in his most silent mood. He answered her in monosyllables, and at last gathered up his tools and said he was going to the other end of the lot. She saw it would do no good to follow him, for he was not in a spirit to talk; so, saddened and baffled, she walked slowly along by the fence toward the house. Until she came close to where he stood she had not noticed that Philip was working now right in the way where she would have to walk.

He stood up, and welcomed her with a smile, and offered her a seat on a low part of the fence, where the rails had some of them been taken down.

It came to her that perhaps her message to-day was for Philip rather than Stephen; so she climbed up and sat down.

He stood leaning against the supporting stakes near her, and the breeze caught a fragment of her muslin gown, and blew it gently against his hand. It was a pleasant touch, and his heart thrilled with the joy of her presence so near him. The muslin ruffle reminded him, with its caressing touch, of the wisp of hair that had blown across his face in the dark the night she had come.

A great, overpowering desire to tell her that he loved her came to him, but he put it aside. She was as cool as a lily dropped here upon this wayside, and talked with him frankly. But there was a something in their intercourse this afternoon more like their first brief talk about the moon than there had been since the night she came. She seemed to understand what he was saying, and he to interpret her feeling of the things in nature all about them. He dropped his tools, and stood beside her, willing to enjoy this precious moment of her companionship.

She looked across the fields to the valley, the other hills beyond, and a purple mountain in the distance, while he followed her gaze.

"You see a picture in all that," he said briefly, as if reading out her thoughts.

She smiled.

"Was it for all this that you gave up your home and friends, and came out here to stay?"

His face darkened.

"No," he said, "I was a fool. I thought life's happiness was all in one bright jewel, and I had lost mine."

"O," she said, looking at him searchingly, sorrowfully. "And, when you found out that was not so, why did you not go back?"

"Perhaps I was a fool still." He spoke drearily. He would not tell her the reason why he had stayed.

There was silence for a few minutes while each looked at the dreamy mountains in their autumn haze, but neither noted much of what was to be seen.

"There is a jewel you might have, which could not be lost. It is a pearl. The pearl of great price. Do you know what I mean?"

"Yes, I understand," he answered, deeply moved, "but I am afraid that would be impossible."

"O, why?" said Margaret, with pain in her voice. "Don't you care the least in the world to have it? I thought I saw a look of longing in your face last Sunday when we talked of Jesus Christ. Was I mistaken?"

Then she had been watching him and cared. Last Sunday! The thought throbbed in his throat with a delirious joy. He lifted his hand, and laid it firmly on the bit of fluttering muslin on the rail beside him. It was all he dared do to show his joy that she cared even so much.

"No, you were not mistaken," he said, his voice choking with earnestness. "I would give all I own to feel as you do, but I cannot believe in your Jesus as more than a man of history. If it were true, and I could believe it, I would be His slave. I would go all around the world searching for Him till I found Him if He were upon earth. But I cannot believe. I would not shake your sweet belief. It is good to know you feel it. It makes your life a benediction to every one you meet. Don't let my skepticism trouble you, or make you doubt."

"O, it couldn't!" said Margaret quickly, decidedly. "You could not shake my belief in Jesus any more than you could shake my belief in my mother, or my father, you know. Because I have known them. If you should tell me I had not a mother, and she was not really good or kind to me, I should just smile, and pity you because you had never known her. But *I have*, you know. I do not blame you, for you have never known Jesus. You have not felt His help, nor almost seen Him face to face. You don't know what it is to talk with Him, and know in your heart He answers, nor to be helped by Him in trouble. You think I imagine all this. I understand. But you see I *know* that I do not imagine it, for I have *felt*. You may feel too, if you will."

"I wish I might," said Philip with a sigh.

"'And ye shall find me, when ye shall search for me with all your heart,'" quoted Margaret softly, wistfully. "And there is another promise for such as you. God knew you would feel so, and He prepared a way. 'He that doeth His will shall know of the doctrine, whether it be of God—' "

"Do you really think that is true?" asked Philip, looking into her eager face.

"I know it is. I've tried it myself," she replied with emphasis.

There was silence broken only by the whisperings of some dying leaves among themselves.

"Won't you take that promise, and claim it, just as you would take a bank-bill that promised to pay so much money to you, and present it for payment? Won't you do it—Philip?"

She had never called him that before except the first day of the Sunday school. It seemed to have been done then as a half-apology to him for not following his advice. After that day she had gone back to the formal "Mr. Earle" when she was obliged to address him by name at all.

Philip started, and crushed the bit of muslin between his fingers.

He was deeply affected.

"How could I?" he said softly.

Margaret caught her breath. She felt the answer to her prayer coming.

"Just begin to search for Him with all you heart, as if you *knew* He was somewhere. You never have tried to find Him, have you?"

"No."

"Then try. Kneel down to-night, and tell Him just how you feel about it, just as you have told me. Talk to Him as if you could see Him. You may not feel Him right away; but by and by, when your whole heart is in it, you will begin to know. He will speak to you in some way, until you are quite sure. Take as many other ways to find out, too, as you can, all the ways there are, of course; not that it matters so much, though, about your mere reason's being convinced; for, when you have felt Him near, you will know against any kind of reasoning. But take the way of talking with Him. It is the quickest way to find Him."

"But should I not feel like a hypocrite, talking to One in whom I do not believe, of whose existence I have even no assurance?"

"No, for you said you wanted to find Him. It would be reaching out for what your heart desires, just as the untaught heathen do."

Philip flushed.

"You think I am a heathen," he said reproachfully.

"No, Philip, only a child of God, lost in the dark. I want you to find the way back."

"But suppose I do this, and nothing comes of it. Then you will be disappointed."

"What has that to do with it?" she said with a motion as of putting any thought of herself aside; "and something will come of it. No soul ever went to God in that way and nothing came of it. Besides, there is more you can do. There is the other promise. 'He that doeth His will.' After you have come to Him, and told Him that you want to find Him, but you cannot believe, and have asked Him to show you how, you can set to work to do His will. For through the doing what He would like to have you do a part of Himself will be revealed. Now, will you go to Him and tell Him all about it, to-night, and begin to try to find Him? Will you?"

Philip had drawn his hat low over his eyes, and stood looking off to the crimsoning sky. The sun had sunk low as they talked, and the air was growing chill. Margaret, in her intentness, did not know how grateful she was for the warmth of the little scarlet jacket. She waited silently and prayed while Philip thought.

At last he turned to her, and held out his hand with a grave smile.

"I will try," he said.

"With all your heart?" asked Margaret, as she laid her little white hand in his.

"With all my heart," he said reverently, as he looked into her eyes and pressed the hand he held.

Margaret let him know by the quick pressure of her hand-clasp how glad she was.

"And I shall be praying, too," she said softly.

Philip's heart quickened. It seemed to him like a holy tryst.

The young man picked up the idle tools, and they started toward the house, walking slowly through the twilight. They did not say much more. They were thinking of what had been said and promised. It was enough to walk quietly together thus and know what had passed. Stephen was not in sight. He must have gone to the house some time before.

But, when they came in and were ready to sit down to supper, he had not come yet, and Philip went out to call him.

Margaret listened to his shouts, strong, deep, full, with a note of earnest purpose in them. They grew more distant, and she thought he must have gone back to the lot where they were that afternoon to see what was keeping Stephen. She waited a long time by the door, and they did not come, and then she went in to search out the book she wanted to read to them that evening. Marna was keeping supper hot in the kitchen.

Suddenly there came a sound of rapid horse-hoofs down the road. She rushed to the door, and looked out. Down against the western sky, which still kept a faint blush from the sunset, now gone on its way to conquer other days, she saw a rider, hatless, galloping, etched for a moment against the sky. Then he was gone.

A sudden fear filled her heart. She put her hand to her throat, and rushed to the kitchen.

"Marna," she cried insistently, "did my brother come to the house before we did?"

The old woman shook her head.

"Brother rode off fast 'fore dark," she said doggedly, as if she did not wish to tell, but had to.

"Marna," said the girl, catching the old woman's arm in a grasp that must have been painful, "you talked about brothers drinking. I want you to tell me true if you know anything about it. Does my brother go where they drink?"

The old woman shut her lips, and a stubborn look came into her eye. She did not reply.

"Quick! Tell me at once," said Margaret, stamping her foot in her excitement. "Do they both drink? Is that why Stephen and Philip go away so suddenly sometimes? Do they both drink?"

"No!" said the old woman quickly. "Not both drink. One all right. Pretty good man. He take care. Bring other home. Heap good man."

"Which one, Marna?"

"Big man, heap good," answered Marna.

"And my brother drinks?" demanded Margaret, the sad truth hers now. "Answer me."

The old woman hung her head and nodded. It was as if she felt responsible.

Margaret had let fall the arm she held so tight and was standing still for one brief minute with her hand upon her heart, too frightened to cry out, too bewildered even to frame a prayer; but her heart was waiting before God to know what she should do. Then swift as thought she turned, and, snatching up her little scarlet jacket as she ran, fled toward the barn.

The old woman looked up to try to say something comforting, and saw her vanish through the open door. She hobbled after her, some faint idea of protection coming to her withered senses. She found her in the barn with white, set face, struggling with the buckles of the saddle-girth. The two empty stalls beside the one remaining horse had made good her fears.

It was the poor old horse that had been left, for Philip needed the best in his chase through the night. Margaret had never ridden this horse, but she did not stop to think of that.

"Buckle this!" she commanded, as Marna came wondering into the barn, and she held the lantern that Philip had left lighted to find his own saddle.

"Missie no go out 'lone," pleaded Marna after she had done the bidding of the stern little voice. "Missie get lost. Big man find brother. Bring home. Missie stay with Marna."

"I must go," said Margaret quietly in tones of awful purpose. She swung herself into the saddle without stopping to think, as she usually did, how she was ever to get up to that great height. And she was doing it alone now.

"Now had me the lantern!" she commanded, and Marna obeyed, her hand trembling. Tears from the long-dried fountains of her soul were running down her cheeks.

The old horse seemed to catch her spirit, and started off snorting as if he felt battle in the air. Some instinct carried him after the others who had sped along that road but a few minutes before. Or perhaps he had been that way before so many times that he could think of only one direction to take as he flew along.

Margaret held her seat firmly, grasping the lantern and the bridle with one hand, and tried to think and pray as the night wind, wondering, peered into her face, then turned and gently crept with her, protectingly, as if it thought she needed guarding.

Chapter 13

Margaret had forgotten all her fears of former rides, lest the horse should stumble or take fright, lest the saddle should slip or she be thrown. Even the dark had lost its terror.

Somewhere near here the road cut away sharply at its outer edge, and went down to a great depth. She might be even now close upon it, and any moment the horse's feet slip over the precipice. But her heart trembled not. The Father was watching. She must go to find her brother.

Just why it was strongly borne in upon her that she must go herself, and not wait for Philip to find Stephen, perhaps Margaret could not have told. It may have been a wish to see for herself just what was Stephen's danger. Possibly, too, it was fear for Philip. Were Marna's words true? "The big man no drink." O, what comfort if she might be sure of that! What a tower of strength would Philip then become!

Riding, and praying, and trusting to God, she was carried safely through the dangers of a short cut that Philip, knowing and fearing, had avoided, and she galloped into the main road only a moment after Philip had passed the spot.

The moon stood out like a silver thread hung low and useless against the horizon. It made but little difference in the darkness.

Margaret felt anxious to catch up with Philip if possible, or at least get within sight of him. It would not do to catch him too soon, or he would send her back; and that she could not bear. So she pushed on and after a short time could hear the sound of his horse and catch fitful glimpses of a dark form riding hard.

By and by she came out upon a bridge across a gully deep as darkness; how deep she could not see as she peered down for one awful glimpse, and then closed her eyes, and dared not look again. It was too late to turn back, for the way was scarcely wide enough for that, and the bridge swayed horribly with the horse upon it.

She held her breath as if that would make her weight the lighter, and dared not think until she felt the horse's feet touch solid ground. Then behind her came a snap, as sharp as if some giant tree had parted, and something, a bit of timber from the rail, perhaps, fell far and long below.

If the bridge had been one foot longer, or the horse had been going a little slower, horse and rider might have been lying down below in that sea of dark trees. The lantern slipped from her trembling hand, and fell crashing in the road; but the horse flew on, frightened, perhaps, by the danger he must have felt, following habit, too, in these long, wild rides to a certain goal he knew, and had travelled toward many a time before the new third horse came to be used in his stead.

But Philip had not crossed the crazy bridge that had been for some time now discarded, and indeed was supposed to be blocked by logs across its entrance. Either the old horse had jumped the logs in the dark, or some one had dragged them away to use somewhere else.

Philip, further down the road, had crossed by the new bridge, and had not known of the rider rushing along through dangers so profound.

He heard the crashing of the falling rail, and the sound of flying hoofs a moment later. He checked his horse, wondering who could be riding behind him. For a moment the possibility that Stephen had not got ahead of him, after all, but had tried to blind him by going another way, passed through his mind; but he looked back and saw only the darkness, and heard the steady thud of the horse's feet. It was not like the gait of Stephen's horse. He pushed on; but occasionally he halted once more, pursued by the feeling that he ought to wait till that rider came up with him.

Then from out the darkness twinkled the lights of the village below him. In a few minutes he would be at his journey's end. He could see the flare of the saloon lights now, and almost hear the tinkle of the glasses and the sliding of the wooden chairs upon the wooden floor. He paused once more, for the other horse was very near now. It would do no harm to wait a second.

Then from out the night he heard his name called once, in a wild, frightened cry, like a sob, as of some one whose breath was almost gone,

"Philip!"

He stopped and waited as the horse came swiftly toward him, something white taking shape upon its back, till he saw the girl, her face white like her dress, her hair all loosened by her ride, unheld by any hat.

One word he spoke.

"Margaret!"

He had never used her name before in speaking to her. He did not know he used it now. But she did, even in her fright; and it seemed to give her courage and renewed strength.

"Don't stop; keep on!" she cried as her horse almost swept by him and he was forced to start his own horse again to keep alongside of her. "Don't lose a minute's time. I know all about it now. Let's hurry!"

"But, Margaret, you must not go!" he cried, putting out his hand to catch the bridle. "Why did you come? And how? It cannot be you crossed the broken bridge."

"It broke just after we got across, I think," she shuddered. "But do not think about it now. I am here. I cannot go back alone, and you must not turn back with me. Let us hurry on to save Stephen."

"But you cannot go down there. It is not safe for a woman."

"I am going, Philip. I am going to save my brother. And God is with us. There is no danger." In some way she managed to impart her eagerness to the old horse, and before Philip knew what she was doing she flew down the road far ahead of him.

It of course took but a moment for him to catch her again; but their gait was too rapid now to admit of talking, and the lights of the saloon were straight ahead. The horses knew their goal, and were making for it with all their might.

They stopped by the open window, from which coarse laughter was issuing into the night, foul with words and thick with oaths. Margaret raised her eyes, and saw what she had come to seek, her brother Stephen, standing gayly by the bar, a glass of something just raised to his smiling lips.

Stopping not to think of her unbound hair or the rough men staring all about, she slid from the horse, cast the bridle from her, and ran to the open door, from which a wide shaft of light was lying on the darkness of the pathway.

Like a heavenly Nemesis she appeared before their astonished gaze, and some who had already drunk deep that night thought she was the angel of the Lord sent to strike them dead.

She stood there in her limp white drapery, with long golden hair and outstretched arms, and only the vivid scarlet of the little jacket gleaming here and there like a flame among the glory of her hair.

She rushed to her brother, and dashed the glass from his hand even as he held it to his lips; then, turning to the roomful, she looked at them with one long, mournful, pitying, condemning glance. There were the Sabbath class to a man, standing before her. They were not drunk, for most of them could stand a good deal of liquor.

She said not one word to them, but just searched each face with a quick, heartrending glance, then turned, and drew her brother away.

Philip had tried to stop her as she flew from her horse to the open door; but she vanished from his hand like a thing of the air, and now he stood behind her ready to protect or help, even with his life. But she needed no help. Like darkness before the light they fell at her coming; and no one, not even Banks, raised a word or a laugh at her expense.

Even Stephen yielded unwillingly, and followed her from the room. Out into the night she led him, silently to Philip, with none to hinder or scoff. It was as if a messenger from God had walked into that saloon and plucked Stephen away, searching each soul that stood there with one glance of flame.

The little cavalcade started out into the night; and as the sound of their going died away from the silent throng inside the lighted room, each man drew apart from the rest, moving noiselessly out into the darkness, and went his way by himself. The saloon was utterly deserted except by one or two old topers too sodden with drink to understand. The barkeeper cursed the girl who had thus descended and stopped business for that evening. But he soon put up his shutters and turned out his lights.

All silently the three rode, and the tired horses moved slowly.

Stephen went ahead with bowed head, whether in anger or in shame they could not tell. Margaret and Philip rode abreast. Not a word they spoke as they went through the dark. Once Philip turned and looked at the frail girl by his side, her white face and gown lighting up the darkness. He thought she was shivering, and he silently took off his own coat, and buttoned it around her. She tried to protest by a lifted hand; but he would not be denied, and she smiled wanly, and let him fasten it around her. By common consent their communication was wordless. Stephen was close in front.

When they came out on the road near where Philip had first heard Margaret's call, he reached out, took her cold, white hand that lay limp on the saddle-cloth, and held it in his warm, strong one all the rest of the ride. Again she let him have his way, and took comfort in the reassuring pressure.

When they reached home, she did not burst into tears and hang about Stephen's neck, begging, pleading, and reproaching. She was too wise for that, and her trouble much too deep.

She made him lie down on the couch by the fire. She brought some strong coffee that Marna had ready, and an inviting supper, and tried to make him eat. But, when she bent over him to ask whether he would sit up, she saw that upon his face there were tears that he had turned away to hide. Then she stooped and kissed him; and, kneeling there beside him with her face near to his, she prayed. "O Jesus Christ, save my dear brother!"

She kissed him again, and drew a little table close with the supper upon it, leaving him to eat it when he would, while she prepared something for herself and Philip.

Unreproached by any words, Stephen went to his room a little later and laid him down, more miserable than he had ever been in the whole of his gay, reckless life. Thoughts that till now had been too grave to be admitted to his mind entered and had their way. Searching questions he had never asked himself were poured upon him. Through them all he heard, and could not keep from hearing, his sister's voice on the other side of the thin board partition as she prayed and pleaded for her brother's salvation.

All night long he wrestled with the two spirits that were at war over him; the spirit of the demon that cried for drink, aroused by the few drops that had but wet his lips ere the glass was dashed from them; and the spirit of God's Holy One who strove to have him for eternity.

He sat dejectedly beside the fire the next morning after breakfast. His young face showed the wear of the night in haggard lines. He looked up as Margaret came over to him, and smiled wearily.

"I'm not worth it," he said. "You'd better give me up."

Margaret came and sat down beside him.

"I will never give you up, Stephen, until you are safe," she said.

He reached out and took her hand.

"You are a good sister," he said. That was all, but she felt that hereafter he would not be against any effort she made in his behalf.

It seemed as if he could not let her out of his sight the next few days; if she left the room, he followed her, and when he closed his eyes he saw a vision of his sister in white with burnished golden hair like some sweet angel of mercy come to save.

When the Sabbath came, Margaret doubted whether she would have any class but Stephen and Philip. Her heart was heavy over them all. More than she knew had she hoped that they were being led near to Christ. Now all her hopes were gone. Of what use was it to pray and preach and sing to men like this? Men who can stand about and watch quietly or help on the degradation of one of themselves. She had been reading deep lessons of the morals of that country ever since she came, but not until that night in the saloon had she realized how little she had to build upon with any of them. She even looked at Philip doubtfully sometimes. How could he be different from the rest, since he was one of them?

Philip had not presumed upon the intimacy of that night's wild ride. He was the same quiet, respectful gentleman, only with this difference: there was a promise between them; and, when he looked at her, his eyes always seemed to let her know he had forgotten it.

But contrary to her expectations the entire company of men trooped in at the regular hour, and seated themselves, perhaps with a little more ostentation than usual.

Margaret welcomed them gravely. She was not sure of them, even though they had come. Marna had been telling her just before dinner about the circus, and a painted lady who was to dance in the saloon that afternoon.

"Men no come to-day," she had said. "If come, no stay late. Go see dance-woman."

Margaret's heart had sunk. Of what use was it for her to try to help these men if they were going straight to perdition as soon as she was through?

Margaret's fingers trembled as she played, and she had chosen minor melodies with dirge-like, wailing movements. The singing even was solemn and dragged, for the men only growled instead of letting out their usual voices.

They turned to the lesson, and Margaret read the text; but then she pushed the Bible from her and lifted troubled eyes to them, eyes in which tears were not a stranger. There was a helpless despair in her attitude.

"You came here because I asked you to help me start a Sunday school, but I am afraid I have done you more harm than good," she said. The tragedy of it all was in her voice.

"You have been studying for a good many weeks now about Jesus Christ. I have told you how He loves you, and wants you, and how He took the trouble to leave His home and come down here to suffer that you might be saved from sin, and come home to live with Him. It hasn't seemed to make a bit of difference. You have listened just to humor me, but you haven't done a thing to please Him, my dearest Friend, for whom I did it all. You have kept right on in your wrong ways. You have gone to places that you knew He would not like. You are planning, some of you, perhaps, to go to a wicked place this afternoon when we are through with the lesson. I have been showing you the right way, and you have chosen the wrong. It would be better for you that you did not know the right than, knowing it, that you should not take it. I have made a great mistake. I have shown you the loveliness of Christ, and you have treated it with indifference."

Her lips quivered, and she turned away to hide the tears that came. The nights of anxiety and the days of excitement were telling on her nerves. She could not for the moment control her sadness. She put up both hands, and covered her face.

The silence was profound.

Then up rose Bennett in his might, he of the white eyelashes and the red hair. His face was mantled with blushes, but there was a true ring to his voice.

"My lady," he said, — it was the way they spoke of her with a deferential inflection that made something different from the ordinary way of saying that, —"we're pretty rough, I know, and you can't say anything too bad about us, perhaps; but we ain't that bad that we're ungrateful, I know. We promised to stick by this thing, and we're a-going to do it. I don't know just what it is you want, and I don't think the other fellows sense it; but, if you just speak up, we're with you. If it's the drinking you mean, we'll shut up that saloon if you say so, though it'll be a dry spot for some of us without it. And if it's that there dancing-woman, if a single feller goes out of this room with intentions of visiting her scene of action, he goes with a bullet in him."

Bennett paused, and held his deadly weapon gleaming before him, covering the whole room with it. Banks started back in terror, and then recovered himself and laughed nervously; but the other men faced Bennett steadily; and their silence lent consent. It was evidently understood so by

Bennett, for he put the revolver back in his hip pocket, and resumed the unusual labor of his speech.

"As fer treating any One with indifference, we ain't meant to. It's just our way. We've listened respectful like to what you said about Him, and ain't questioned but what it's all so. But we ain't just up to this Sunday-school act, and don't know what to do. If you'd just say plain what 'tis you want, we might be able to please."

Margaret turned her eyes all bright with tears to the young man, and said with earnestness:

"I want you to be like Him, Mr. Bennett, to live like Him, to love Him, to grow to look like Him. That is what He wants. That is why He sent the message to you."

Bennett stood abashed at the awful disparity between the One spoken of and himself. He looked at her helplessly.

"I'll be gashed if I know what you mean," he replied with fervor; "but, if you'll make it all out easy fer us, we'll try."

It was late that night before she sent them away, for she had prolonged the lesson and the singing, and then had read them a tender story, full of the tragedy, the love, and the salvation of life.

They rolled forth their closing song with their magnificent voices as if they meant it. The words were,

> "Just as I am, without one plea,
> But that Thy blood was shed for me,
> And that Thou bidst me come to Thee,
> O Lamb of God, I come, I come."

They were all there yet. Not one of them had stolen away to the revelries in the village. If Banks had entertained thoughts of doing so, he had not dared.

She had asked them to sing the words as a prayer if they could, and each man sang with his eyes on his book, and a strange new look of startled purpose was dawning in some faces.

Then they went out into the starlight silently, but first each man paused and shook hands with Margaret as she stood by the door. They had never done this before. They would not have dared to touch her lily hand unless she gave it them now.

The hand-clasps were awkward, some of them, but each one was a kind of pledge of new fealty to her.

Last of all came Byron, his bold eyes dropped. He did not know whether she would touch his hand or not. He stood hesitating before her. It was something new for him to be embarrassed.

"Will you take my Christ for yours?" she said, looking up and comprehending.

"If I know how," he answered brokenly.

Then out came her eager hand, sealing the promise with a warm grasp of friendliness, and Byron walked out of that door, a new sense of honor dawning in his breast.

She turned back to the room, her face bright with feeling. Stephen stood behind her, and, bending as if he had come for that, kissed her on the forehead, and went quickly into his room, shutting the door behind him.

Then Margaret stood alone with Philip.

Chapter 14

"Had I the grace to win the grace
Of maiden living all above,
My soul would trample down the base
That she might have a man to love.

"A grace I have no grace to win
Knocks now at my half-opened door;
Ah! Lord of glory, come Thou in;
Thy grace divine is all, and more!"
—George Macdonald

"I have been thinking, " said Philip, a strange new light in his eyes, as he turned toward her from the firelight into which he had been looking, "of what value are unbeliefs? They do not change facts. I will throw away mine. I will take your Christ. If there is no Christ, I shall lose nothing. If there is, I shall have gained all. Margaret, I take your Jesus to-night to be my Saviour."

He said it solemnly, as one utters a vow for eternity; and the girl stood looking up at him, the radiance in her face reflected in his own.

When he had gone to his room that night, he closed the door and knelt down. A strange gladness was in his heart. He found that he did not shrink from praying, but longed to register his vow, to begin his new life.

"O Christ!" he murmured, reaching out longing arms as if to grope for and find the desire of his heart, "O Christ! Come to me! Show me! Let me know Thou art there. Let me never go back to doubting. I will give Thee all myself, though it is worth but little. Only come to me! Jesus! Jesus! I take Thee as my Saviour!"

It was a different prayer from what he might have prayed if he had not known Margaret. Even if his will and desire had been stirred to praying at all without her influence, he would not have used such language, he would not have spoken to Jesus, the Christ, if he had not heard Margaret's simple, earnest talks of Him every Sunday. He would naturally have spoken to God more distantly, his praying would have been less insistent, and perhaps he would not so soon have received the blessing.

Some one has said that prayer is the throwing of the arms of the soul about the neck of God.

Philip had laid his soul before the Christ, and all tenderly, as if the great arms of God had folded about him, there came to his soul a sense of the presence of Jesus.

"How sweet the name of Jesus sounds in a believer's ear!" they had sung once in the Sunday class, and Philip had curled his lip quietly, in his corner behind the piano, over the sentiment. How could it be possible that the name of One who has never been seen could be dear, no matter how much one believed?

But now in the new, sweet dawn of his own second birth he suddenly knew that the name "Jesus" was sweet to him. How it had come about, he could not explain. He said it over and over, gently at first, for he feared the sweetness might depart, and then more confidently, as his soul rang with the joy of it. It was true, after all, and one could feel Jesus' presence just as Margaret had said.

With a sense of great peace upon him he lay down at last to rest, but before he closed his eyes in sleep he murmured,

"I thank Thee for sending—Margaret!" and he spoke the name lingeringly and reverently.

They did not say much to each other, Philip and Margaret, about the wonderful change that had come into Philip's heart; but there was a secret understanding between them that made their eyes look glad when they met across the room, and Margaret's heart sang a little song of triumph as she went about her work. It was not for several days that Philip dared to tell her he was beginning to get the answer to his prayer that she had promised, and how he knew that now what she had said was true.

The days went by in much the same way that the preceding ones had gone, save that both Margaret and Philip exercised a more vigorous watchfulness over Stephen. The evenings were spent in delightful readings, and Margaret invented all sorts of little things she wanted made, which the young men could work at while she read.

Margaret was getting to be a good rider since her adventure by night. It seemed to have freed her from all fear, and constantly the three rode about the country together, enjoying the clear, crisp days as the winter hastened on.

It was about this time that there came to that region a young minister, who had broken down in his first charge, and who had come out to the West to fight nervous prostration on a cattle-ranch. He was an earnest young fellow with no foolish notions, and he had not been long at his new home before he had made friends of the men with whom he was constantly thrown. He had a desire to do them good in some way, though it must be confessed he saw little hope for any such thing. He did not feel well enough to preach, even if there had been any encouragement for starting religious services on

Sunday. There seemed to be no church within possible reach, and he pondered much as he rode, and laughed, and learned, of the rough men who gave him no easy lessons, how to rub off the "tenderfoot" looks and ways.

At last, one day he questioned a man from his own ranch. Was there no service of any kind held in the whole of that region? Did they not know of even a Sunday school? Surely there were some Christian people.

The man whom he happened to question was Banks.

Now Banks had been growing exceedingly unpopular among the members of the select Sunday class which met with Margaret Halstead, because he did not take kindly to the extreme principles she taught, nor yield up his rights in the matter of drinking and gambling as some of the others were discussing the possibility of doing. He had made one or two attempts to raise an opposition to the power of the fair young priestess, but they had not been successful. He felt his loss of prestige, and with a half-idea of revenge by getting the minister on his side, and running him in opposition to the young teacher, he began to tell him about the Sunday school.

Banks had a gift of imitation, and a vein of what he supposed was humor. He used them both in this case, and the result was not to the advantage of the Sunday school. However, the young theologue was not altogether without some insight into character. He did not take all that Banks told him as strictly true; and, when the fellow wound up by offering to take him around to the school the next Sunday, he decided to accept the invitation. It would at least give him a chance to study the men and see what influence was able to hold them. It also held out the only opening for a religious service that the neighborhood afforded.

"But you must wear your outfit things, or the boys'll get on to you bein' a preacher, an' make it hot fer ye," said Banks. "They won't have any snobs around. The teacher might think you'd come to break up the meeting, and Earle might take a notion to put you out the back door."

The minister wondered what kind of a strange Sunday school this might be to which he was to be taken; but he quietly accepted the advice, and the next Sunday just as the opening hymn was being sung — Banks had timed his coming well, when all would be occupied and there would be none to dispute the appearance of the newcomer — they walked into the room and sat down.

The minister looked about him in wonder on the beauty and refinement everywhere visible, but his eyes were held at once by the loveliness of the girl who, dressed in soft white, presided over this motley gathering. His eyes went from the hard faces of the men to her pure profile, in wonder, again and again.

There was an ease and mark of the world about the minister, even in his cowboy garb, that Philip noted at once. He drew his brows together in almost his old frown of displeasure as he watched him covertly, jealous of the looks the minister cast at Margaret, jealous of his easy way of smiling and accepting the book that Banks handed him open to the place. It was not till the name "Jesus," repeated several times in a chorus that was being sung, reached Philip's heart, and felt for that vibrating chord that was learning to thrill with joy over the name of his Master, that he realized what an ugly feeling toward this utter stranger had sprung up within him all unbidden. He tried to down it, and looked about for some hospitality to offer the visitor, but in spite of himself he felt dismay at the presence of this man. He was different from the other fellows, and Margaret would see it at once.

Fortunately for Margaret she had no time to look the stranger over closely until after the lesson was done; else she might have been disconcerted. She had long ago overcome her fear of the men she taught every Sabbath, through her intense desire to lead them to the Saviour; but, had she known that her audience that afternoon contained a full-fledged minister fresh from a long theological training, she would have trembled and halted, and perhaps have had no message to deliver that day.

She went through it all as usual, the solemn, silent waiting, and the simple, earnest prayer; and the young minister felt that there were things he had yet to learn about preaching which might not be learned in any theological seminary.

She found him out as soon as he spoke to her, however, which was at the close of the lesson and while they were passing the usual cups of delicious tea and the cakes. She knew him for one of her own world, and welcomed him pleasantly.

Now the minister was small and slight. In contrast with Philip and Stephen and the others he looked insignificant to Margaret's eyes, newly grown accustomed to this giant build of men. So, when he asked permission to come to the class sometimes, she did not feel the trepidation that she would have felt before she came out here. He positively declined to teach. He said his physician had forbidden anything of the sort, and he thanked her warmly for all the help she had given him that afternoon. She found afterwards that he had left her with the impression that he needed help, too. He did not seem to have the same idea about a personal friendship with Jesus Christ that had grown so dear to her.

She felt strengthened, however, at the thought of another Christian to help in the work, and began at once to plan how she would ask him to explain deep points in the lessons that she might in turn explain them to the class. He seemed a bright, interesting young man. Margaret was glad he had come. He was from near her own home, also, and knew many of her intimate friends. That made him doubly interesting.

As the winter went on, the minister began to drop in upon them at sunset, occasionally, to spend the evening. Stephen had taken a fancy to him, and encouraged his coming. Margaret rejoiced at this, and made the minister more welcome because Stephen liked him.

During the long evenings they would read and talk and have music, much as when they were alone.

The minister naturally gravitated to a seat beside Margaret. It was his hand that turned the music for her when she played, and his voice that joined in the duets they sang, for he was something of a musician as well as theologian.

He was also a good reader, and often took the book from Margaret, and read while she rested or busied her hands with a bit of embroidery.

Occasionally the entire Sunday class would be invited for an evening of reading and song. At such times the minister proved to be an admirable helper always ready with some witty saying or a good recitation. He had the power of whistling in imitation of different birds, and would whistle wild, sweet tunes to a running accompaniment on the piano.

He was not altogether unpopular among the men. He had the sense to keep any extra self-esteem he might have brought out West well locked away in his breast, carrying about with him always a hearty friendliness. The men could not help liking him, and Margaret more and more turned to him for advice and looked for his help in planning for her different gatherings. But when he was present Philip was always silent and gloomy.

Three times during that winter did Stephen grow restless and slip away. Twice his faithful guardians came galloping after him when he was scarcely out of sight of the house, and took him on a long ride that ended only late at night, when they all were worn out; but they brought him safely back, sober. The third time he met Bennett on his way, who immediately suspected and shadowed him till he made sure, whereupon he laid strong hands upon Stephen, and insisted on riding home with him.

Margaret had hoped and prayed. She had even ventured to talk with Stephen at dusk sometimes, when he would come in and throw himself down upon the couch by the fire. He always listened, but he said very little. Not much hope had she ever received from him that he was paying heed to her earnest pleading to come to Jesus Christ and be a new man.

And the winter wore away into the spring.

Chapter 15

"All I could never be,
All, men ignored in me,
This, I was worth to God."
— Robert Browning

It was one day in early summer that the minister and Stephen set out on a long ride. They were to return in time for supper, and Margaret had planned a pleasant evening for them all. "The boys," as the Sunday class were now called, were all coming.

She stood watching them ride away into the pleasant afternoon light, and wondered whether the minister would improve his opportunity to say a word to Stephen. She felt very sad about her brother. He did not seem to get any further toward eternal life.

Philip was to have gone with the riding party; but a message in the morning had called him in another direction to attend to some business, and he would not return till evening.

Margaret watched the two riders out of sight, and then went in to finish her plans for the evening. There were one or two little things she wanted to do for an unusual attraction. She was always thinking of new things to win these men into another world than the one they lived in every day.

The two riders went to a distant ranch famed for its superior cattle. They passed spots of marvellous beauty on the way, and stopped to look and wonder; and the minister did improve his opportunity to speak a few earnest words to Stephen, as Margaret had hoped he would do.

Stephen answered sadly, half wistfully, but would not commit himself. He did not repel the words, and seemed to like his companion even better that he had dared to speak.

They spent some time going about the ranch, and late in the afternoon turned their horses homeward.

They had gone about half-way back when a messenger overtook them to beg the minister to return. A whisper had gone around the place that one of the visitors was a minister. The mother of one of the men was lying very ill, not likely to live, and she begged that he would return to pray with her. The message, scrawled feebly, was so pitiful that no one, least of all the kind-hearted young minister, could refuse.

Stephen insisted upon going back with him, but this Mr. Owen would not allow. He said that Stephen must go home and tell his sister the circumstances. He would come as soon as possible. The messenger offered a fresh horse and an escort for returning, and the minister said he would be with them before the evening was over. It would not do for Stephen to go with him, as his sister would wait supper and it would spoil all their plans.

It was a disappointment to the young man, and a deep one. All day as he rode through the brilliant air his heart had been rejoicing over the thought of the evening. He had formed a little plan during the past week, that to-night he would ask Margaret to ride with him some day soon. Then he could have her all to himself, and perhaps — that was as far as he let his thoughts go in the presence of others. He liked to be by himself when he thought of Margaret.

Many miles away there rode another man, thinking of Margaret, too, and of the minister, sometimes letting his heart rejoice over the smile the girl had given him and the little wave of her white hand in farewell as he rode away that morning, sometimes feeling the heavy gloom of foreboding as a vision of the delicate, spiritual face of the minister rose before him. For Philip had long known that he loved Margaret better than his own life. Now and then he lifted his eyes up to the clear blue overhead, and called from his heart to his Father, and her Father, not praying, not asking for anything for himself, for he did not dare do that, but just to assure himself that there was a heavenly Father who belonged to them both, who loved them both, and would do well. More than this he did not venture to think.

Stephen sat in his saddle, watching his friend out of sight on the road they had just come together. He felt a strong impulse even yet to turn and follow him. Something told him it would be better. Something whispered that here was his safety. He half called to them as they disappeared around a knoll; and then, remembering that Margaret would be watching anxiously for them, and determining for once to show he was a man and could be trusted, he reluctantly started his horse on alone.

But the devil came also.

The devil had not had so good a chance at Stephen for nearly a year. He had been watching his opportunity, and had almost given up this soul that was once so firmly in his clutches. But now he came swiftly, and attended him with all his old arts and many more beside. He whispered:

"You'd better ride around by the town, and go through, and then you can tell Margaret how strong you are."

That was the first thought. Ride through town, and not go into the saloon, nor stop once to talk to any one! He would enjoy knowing that he could do that. He might even try to be the Christian Margaret and the minister wanted him to be if he could do that once. He would not be so ashamed. He half decided he would do it, and turned it over in his mind, that mind so easily influenced by his own imagination that to think of going through town was almost as much of a temptation as going. He could see how the saloon-keeper would stand at the door and look, and wonder, and perhaps call. He could smell the odor of the familiar room as it was wafted out into the road from the swinging blind door.

Something wild seized him with the thought of that odor. A spirit that would not be downed. He forgot that he had intended to ride safely through town to astonish and please his sister by his strength. He forgot his half-desire to be a Christian. He forgot the words the minister had spoken, which indeed had taken deep hold upon his wavering nature. He forgot everything save that one fiendish thirst for strong drink, and he set the spurs cruelly into his faithful horse, and rode like mad, his breath coming in great, hot waves through his lungs. His eyes grew blood-shot, and all the devils in the service of the arch-fiend flew to urge him on. There were miles yet to be covered, but that was nothing. He was alone and unsuspected. He had time to get there and get all he wanted. All he wanted! For once no one could stop him, for no one would know until the minister came back, and that might not be to-night.

He turned upon a road that would not lead past home, and galloped on. It was the road his sister had taken in her wild night ride after him and Philip.

It was quite dusk when he neared the bridge that she had crossed in safety and but just escaped with her life. He knew the bridge had long been disused. He knew that it was considered extremely unsafe. He did not know of the great supporting timber that had parted and fallen into the ravine below on the night Margaret had crossed. But he knew enough about it to make him feel even in his most daring moods, heretofore, that he would rather not try to cross it.

But something stronger than reason was urging him to-night. This bridge would lead to a crossroad where he would not be in danger of meeting any of the fellows coming up to Margaret's gathering. The fellows had of late been a sort of self-constituted watch-guard. He could not shake them off. They had kept him many a time from himself. He would escape them all to-night. The fever in his blood had taken fire through all his veins. A blind purpose took possession of his reason.

With sudden quick jerk of the bridle he turned his trembling horse, and put him at the bridge, nor would he let him lessen his gait. He half knew in his wild folly that his safety lay in getting over quickly, if safety there was. And so under full gallop the panting horse flew at the bridge in the fast-gathering darkness.

It wavered and cracked, and wavered long, and then suddenly, too late, the horse drew back upon his haunches with a frightened snort almost human in its anguish, and poised a moment in mid-air! The bridge did not reach across the chasm! One whole section had fallen! The last support was tottering in decay!

One awful second Stephen realized his position, and saw in vivid panorama the follies of his life and the sins of his heart. Saw, and cried out in one wild cry to God, in acknowledgment and late submission. The cry rang through the upper air, down into the dark ravine; then all was blackness of unconsciousness to Stephen as bridge, horse, and rider fell crashing below!

The supper had stood waiting for some time when Philip came. Margaret was growing restless, and was glad to see him. His face was anxious when he heard that the riders had not returned, though he tried to laugh it off and say the minister was not used to long rides. Perhaps it had been too much for him, and they had had to stop to rest; but in another half-hour Mr. Owen, his horse all covered with froth, rode gayly up to the door, and dismounted.

He made his apologies, explained his lateness, and then looked around for Stephen.

"Isn't he here yet?" he asked in surprise.

But there was more than surprise in the faces of the other two. There was trouble. Philip excused himself immediately, and went toward the barn. His own horse was weary with the long, hard day. He must take the other horse. He saddled it, and quickly led it out into the darkness; but at the door stood Margaret, her face white and drawn, a steady purpose in her eyes. Philip could see it shining through the starlight like another star. She had followed him to the barn, intending to ride with him after Stephen.

He dropped the horse's bridle, and came over to her. Taking both her cold little hands in his strong ones, he looked down into her face.

"Margaret," he said, and there was deep tenderness in his tone. "I know what you would do, but you must not. You must promise me you will stay here and pray. You cannot go out into the night this way. There is no need, and I will not let you. I will not go myself until you promise."

She caught her breath in a half-sob, and dropped her face miserably upon his hands that held hers so firmly.

He drew her to him in the shadow of the great, dark barn, and, bending over her, kissed reverently the silken coils of hair upon her head. "Margaret, I love you; will you do this for me? Will you promise to stay at home and pray?"

He was half frightened afterward that he had dared to speak to her so, but she did not shrink away. Instead, she stood very still, and held her breath for a moment, and then answered low and sweet,

"Yes, Philip!"

He longed to take her in his arms, but he dared not. He gave her hands one long, tender clasp, and sprang into his saddle; but Margaret's white face looked up now, and she ran a step or two beside the horse. She clasped her hands in pleading.

"You will be careful, Philip—for yourself," she said brokenly, and his heart leaped with joy as he promised. Yet, after all, he told himself it might be only a sisterly care.

She watched him ride away through the dark, her hand at her throat to still the wild, sweet, fluttering thing of joy that had come to thrill her soul. And for the minute she half forgot her fears for Stephen in love and fear for Philip. She stood still several minutes, and let the memory of his kiss flow over her and cover her with its glory and its joy. Then she went swiftly in, and tried to entertain the minister, who was wondering and rejoicing that he had her to himself for a little while. Poor soul, he did not know her thoughts were far out down the dark road, following a rider through the night.

As Philip rode along, he could not believe that he had really dared to tell Margaret that he loved her. It seemed too strange and wonderful to be true that she had not repulsed him when he kissed her. As the tumult in his heart quieted a little to let him think, he told himself that perhaps she was excited about Stephen, and had needed comfort. She had not realized what his words of love had meant. It might be she only took his meaning as a kind and brotherly feeling. If that were so, he would never take an advantage of her. That moment they had spent together should be a sacred thing between them. He would rejoice always in that kiss and that chance to hold her dear white hands.

But wild and sweet through such thoughts thrilled the joy of loving her and the song of hope in his heart. For something every now and then made him sure that she loved him, marvellous as it might seem.

So he rode down through the dark into town, and, finding no trace of Stephen nor any one who had seen him, turned his horse back to the house to see whether he had come; anxious now and grave, canvassing every possible way to turn next for the finding of Stephen. Then he remembered and began to pray for guidance and help.

Stephen's wild cry had reached the ears of two men travelling along the upper road above the ravine with a wagon. They stopped, listened, and heard the crashing timbers and fall of horse and man.

Instinct taught them what the accident must be, and they went to find out who it was that had fallen to a death so sudden. They carried a lantern; for the night was dark, and one was old, and the road they had to go was treacherous in some places. So now, when they could see only the blackness of horror below, they climbed down another way, leaving their horse tied above, and found the place where Stephen lay.

The horse was dead, and lay quite motionless with all his four faithful legs broken and a great beam of rotten timber across one temple, where it struck and mercifully ended his life.

But Stephen lay a little further off, flung, partly by the struggles of his horse, perhaps, or it may have been by some wild leap of his own in the moment of falling. He was stretched upon a grassy place, the kindest that the old ravine could offer, and lay unscratched apparently, the damp gold waves of hair lying loose upon his forehead, his hands flung out as if he were asleep. He was profoundly unconscious of the majesty in which he lay.

The men held the lantern to his face, and one muttered with a great oath:

"Steve Halstead! Drunk again!"

They tore his shirt open, and felt for his heart, but could not tell whether he was dead or living. Finally they carried him with great difficulty up a sloping, circuitous path, and put him in the wagon.

Bennett and Byron and two or three others had just arrived when they brought him in. Margaret turned away in sick horror. She had never seen her brother drunk. She could not bear to look now. They motioned her from the door, and laid him upon his own bed; but something in his face made Byron stoop down. There was no breath of liquor upon him. They listened with shocked faces as the two who had found him told their story. Then Byron flung himself upon his horse, and galloped off into the night for the doctor, while the others worked in desperation to bring him to consciousness, with the door closed against his sister.

It was Bennett who told Margaret that her brother had had a fall on the way home, and that he had not been to the village at all, but was found on his way there. Her face lighted at that. She understood his meaning. She was glad Stephen had not been drinking. They sent the minister to stay with her; and she was wide-eyed and brave, and would talk but little, looking anxiously through the open front door.

There came a sound of horses presently, and she rushed out into the night. Mr. Owen thought she was looking for the doctor, and let her go, thinking it might be well for her to have something to do, even if it were nothing but to watch for the doctor, who could not possibly have come so soon.

It was Philip who had come.

She ran out to him, and looked anxiously through the dark.

"O Philip, is it you? And are you safe?"

And Philip's heart warmed with hope.

"They have brought him home, Philip. He had fallen through the bridge. I was afraid you had fallen, too. I do not know how badly he is hurt; but, Philip, he had not been drinking!"

There was a ring of triumph in her last words, as if it could not be all bad, whatever might be coming. Then together they went into the house.

"She is a wonderful girl, isn't she?" said the minister to Philip in subdued tones a little later, as he watched her go quietly about getting a cup of tea for Philip. "It seems so strange that I should have had to come away out here to find her, when our native towns were but twenty miles apart." In his voice was a tone of possession and pride, and Philip's heart sank as he listened.

Chapter 16

The doctor came by and by, and was able to bring back the spirit into the form that had lain so still and deathlike. Stephen opened his eyes, and looked about him with a bewildered gaze as of one who had expected a different scene. He looked first at his sister, who had come into the room with the doctor, and then he smiled.

"I didn't get there, though, Margaret," he murmured. "God stopped me on the way. It was the only way He could save me."

He closed his eyes, and they thought he had fainted again; but he opened them with his old, careless, mischievous smile, and looked around upon the boys, his eyes lingering lovingly on Philip's face.

"I've been a coward, boys," he said, "and I've tried to get away from Him all the time; but still He kept drawing me, and you all helped. And now He's going to take me to Himself. There won't be any more drinks up there, and maybe I can begin over again."

The words were faint, and the doctor bent over him and administered a stimulant.

He made a thorough examination, and told them that Stephen was hurt internally and could not live long. They thought he was not conscious; but he opened his eyes, and smiled at them.

"It's all right, doctor. It's better so," he said feebly. "But can't you give me something to strengthen me up for a few hours? I've got something I want to say to the boys."

The doctor turned away to rub his hand across his eyes; and the men moved, choking, away from the bed, and went to the windows or slipped into the other room.

"I'll try!" said the doctor huskily. "If you'll lie quiet and rest a little, you may live through the night."

Stephen obediently took the medicine, and lay quiet for a few minutes; but as soon as the artificial strength came to him he began to talk. The gay, reckless tongue that had been the life of so many gatherings had but a little while longer to speak.

It was Philip who came to him first, and tried to quiet him with that strong personality that had so often saved him from himself.

But Stephen's mind was abnormally active. He seemed to think of things he had neglected all his life. He spoke of this and that he would like to have Philip do for him, and he talked tenderly of his sister.

"You'll look after her, Philip?" he asked anxiously. "You know she'll have no one now when I'm gone. She will be sorry. You like her, don't you?"

Philip's eyes filled with tears, and his strong chin quivered.

"I love her, Stephen, with all my soul," he said with choking voice. "I will care for her as far as she will let me care. I will make her my wife if she will consent."

"Consent?" said Stephen, his voice rising and his old petulant manner coming back to him, as ever when his will was crossed in the slightest. "Consent! Of course she will! Why shouldn't she? No one could help admiring you, Phil. Why can't you be married right away, before I go? I'd like to see it. I'd like to give you my blessing."

He looked up eagerly into Philip's face.

Philip almost groaned.

"Why can't you, Phil?" he urged again.

"I have not asked her yet," said Philip. "She may not love me at all. Sometimes I think she loves the minister."

"Then ask her now," said Stephen, and he called in the high, thin voice of those who are almost done with life, "Margaret!"

She heard his cry through the slight partitions, and came at once.

Stephen had almost exhausted his breath with his eagerness, and lay panting, looking up first at Philip wistfully, then at his sister.

"Phil—has something—to tell you," he gasped, and then swallowed the spoonful Philip gave him from the glass the doctor had left, and closed his eyes.

Philip scarcely dared to look at Margaret. It seemed almost a desecration in this hour of death to speak of what meant life and joy to him.

"I have been telling Stephen of my love for you," he said, trying to control the tremble in his voice. "I have been saying I would like to make you my wife. I would not dare intrude this upon you now, but Stephen longs to know how you feel about it."

Philip had come near her, and they both stood close to Stephen's side. There was an undertone of pity for her in Philip's voice as he spoke, and a slight touch of formality in his words because of the presence of a third person, that made it seem like a contract in writing. But Margaret remembered his impassioned tones a little while before in the shadow of the night, and did not doubt his deep love for her.

With the tears brimming her eyes she looked up to Philip, and tried to smile. Her lips were trembling with emotion, but she said simply,

"I love you, Philip!" and put her hands out to his.

Then Stephen's great brown hand, so weak now, came groping out to them and clasped them both, and the two with one consent knelt down beside his bed.

"Be married now, while I am here," he whispered. "I can leave you better so." He looked pleadingly at them.

Margaret caught her breath with a sob, and Philip put his arm tenderly about her.

"Can you bear to—dear?" he asked.

She was still a minute with drooping face and downcast eyes, and then she whispered softly,

"Yes."

Philip stooped and kissed her forehead reverently, and Stephen smiled his old joyous smile. For a minute the shadow of death that was beginning to hover over his face was chased away.

"Where are the boys?" he asked. "I want the boys and the minister. I'll tell them. No, it won't be too hard. I'd like to. Go and get ready."

They came trooping in, the great, rough men who loved him, and who had tried so hard to ruin him and save him both. The minister came behind them, and the doctor hurried in and felt Stephen's pulse. But he did not notice the doctor. He was all eagerness.

"Boys, we're going to have a wedding!" he said in a cheery, weak voice. They thought his mind was wandering, and looked sorrowfully at one another.

"That's all right, boys," he said as he saw they did not understand. "It's sure enough. I want you to carry me into the other room for the ceremony. No, don't say they can't, Doc. I'll stay alive long enough to say all I need to say. I must go out there where we've had so many good times. I'd rather die out there. Take me out, boys; we've no time to waste. Philip and Margaret are out there waiting, and the minister will marry them."

His old impatience was using up his strength fast. The doctor looked grave, but said in a low tone:

"Take him out. It cannot make much difference."

They gathered up the mattress tenderly, the clumsy fellows, and carried it out to a cot that was placed across in front of the fireplace. Almost they thought he was gone when they laid him down; but he rallied wonderfully, and, smiling, whispered,

"Go on."

Philip and Margaret, quiet and white, stood together, hand in hand, in front of the mass of summer blossoms that Margaret had arranged a few hours before for the expected evening gathering. It was just where she had sat to teach their first Sunday class, and she was all in white as then. There was a glorified light in her eyes that defied the sadness even of death. Stephen wondered as he looked at her whether she was looking up to and speaking with the unseen presence of her Christ.

The room was beautiful, and only Stephen as he lay with partly closed eyes and watched them, half impatient for the ceremony to be over, remembered the bare old room filled with the odor of lamp-smoke and bacon into which they had brought his sister on the night of her arrival. And in his heart he thanked God for her coming.

The minister with stricken look and trembling voice performed the ceremony. It was hard for life to take away his love just as death was stealing a good friend. He had begun his portion of sorrow, and would learn his lesson; but it was bitter at the start.

There in the "chill before the dawning, between the night and morning," while the angel of Death delayed a little, to watch, they were married. The night was black around the little house, and the stars kept watch above.

As soon as it was over and the short prayer ended, Stephen made a movement as if to rise, and then, remembering, dropped his head again.

"Boys, I can't stay long," he said eagerly. "I only stayed for the wedding," and he smiled in his old, reckless way. Then, growing sober, with an honest ring to his voice that sometimes came in his speech so winningly, he said:

"There's something I want you to do, boys. You can if you only will. I want you to promise me before I go. I want you to build a church here, and get the minister to run it. You can do it well enough if you don't go to the saloon. It's the saloon, boys, and the gambling, that has taken all our money, and made us into such beasts. It was the saloon that ruined me. You all know that. You all know how I came here and bought this place, and then drank it all up and everything else I had, and would have gone to the devil at once if it hadn't been for Philip coming out and buying back the place, and keeping me half-way straight."

His breath was growing short. His sentences became more broken.

"You all know what my sister's done for me," he went on. "God bless her. But even she couldn't save me. The devil had too tight a hold. I'm sorry I didn't do as she wanted me to, and take Jesus Christ — it might have done some good — but now it's too late — He'll just have to take me. I guess He'll do it. I've made a clean breast of it — but it's been a wasted life. Don't wait any longer, boys. I've thought if there'd been a church here when I came — and a minister — who lived right up to what he said — it might not have been so with me. Now, boys, will you build the church?"

They had turned away to hide the tears that were coursing down their bronzed faces; but they went solemnly, one at a time, and took his cold hand in a strong grasp, and made the promise in hoarse, broken murmurs.

"That's all right, then, boys. I know you'll do it," said Stephen; "and, boys," with almost a twinkle of the old mischief in his eyes, "I want them to put me on the hill here under the big tree, and mark the place so you'll remember your promise. I'll maybe be able to help a little that way by reminding, and so make up for all I've wasted."

He was still a minute. His voice kept its strength wonderfully.

"Sing, boys," he said, opening his eyes. "Sing all the old songs. It will make me feel more at home where I'm going to hear your voices on the way."

They looked helplessly at one another. They did not know what to sing.

"Sing 'Jesus, Saviour, pilot me,' boys," he said. "I didn't live for Him, but maybe I can die with Him."

Trembling the great voices started, like some grand organ that has lost its player, and creaks on feebly at the touch of sorrow with a broken heart.

When they were through, he said:

"Sing 'Safe home in port.' I always liked that. And, boys, sing it as if you were glad. Sing it as you always do."

Then they mastered themselves and sang:

> "Safe home, safe home, in port!
> Rent cordage, shattered deck,
> Torn sails, provisions short,
> And only not a wreck:
> But, O, the joy upon the shore,
> To tell the voyage perils o'er!"

They were singing as they used to sing it in those first bright Sundays, now. Something of the spirit of the triumph in the song had caught them.

> "No more the foe can harm!
> No more the leaguered camp,
> And cry of night alarm,
> And need of ready lamp;
> And yet how nearly had he failed,
> How nearly had the foe prevailed!"

"That's right, boys! That's me! It's all true," called out Stephen to them. They could see the shadow deepening about his eyes now.

Their voices grew softer with tenderness, but they sang on. They would sing him right grandly into heaven if that was what he wanted, even if it broke their hearts. Their voices should not fail him while he could listen.

> "The exile is at home!
> Oh, nights and days of tears!"

Stephen pressed Margaret's hand that lay in his, at these words, and she tenderly kissed him.

> "Oh, longings not to roam!
> Oh, sins and doubts and fears!
> What matters now grief's darkest day
> When God has wiped all tears away?"

It was the minister who started other hymns, words that he had heard them sing in their gatherings. They needed no books, nor could they have looked at them with their tear-blinded eyes, if they had them.

Stephen was sinking fast. He did not talk any more, nor look at them. Once he opened his eyes, and, looking at Margaret, murmured, "Dear sister!"

He had lain so still for a long time that they thought he had ceased breathing, when he suddenly opened his eyes, and with a strength born of his flight into another world raised himself from the pillow, calling in a loud, clear voice:

"Did you call, father? Yes, sir, I'm coming!"

Then he fell back dead.

Was it some memory of his boyhood that came to him at last, or did he hear his heavenly Father's voice?

It was the minister that started to sing,

> "Safe in the arms of Jesus,
> Safe on His gentle breast;"

and with choking sobs that did not need to be suppressed the men joined in the song that Stephen loved. Just then the sun shot up behind the hills, and laid a touch of glory on the gold of Stephen's hair.

"He is safe home in Port," said the minister. "Let us pray."

They knelt about him in their grief, and heard him pray for them, and then went out and left Philip and Margaret with their sorrow and their joy.

They went out to a new world wherein were vows to be kept and a goal to be attained, and each man was resolved to do his best to keep the sacred trust that Stephen had left to them.

They went about among Stephen's friends, and gathered up a goodly sum. They brought it to Margaret on the day of the funeral service, and told her it was for the church, and that it should be built at once. Margaret, smiling through her tears, thanked God, and knew her prayers were being answered.

They laid him in the place he had spoken of under the great tree that crowned the hill, and to mark it they put a stone whereon were engraved Stephen's name, the date, and the simple words,

"SAFE HOME."

Beside the grave up rose the little church, its spire pointing heavenward, its doors stretched wide to save both day and night, its bell calling over the lonely country at set times of worship, and over the door, cut into the stone, the words,

"STEPHEN HALSTEAD MEMORIAL."

The minister has found his church; and Stephen's life, though gathered safe home, is going on in the memory of those he is helping.

Lone Point

Chapter 1

Rachel Hammond sat by the open window with her Bible on her knee. The muslin curtains did not blow with the breeze, for there was no breeze that hot morning in June. The air seemed breathless. Rachel had put her pretty room in order, finished all her little morning duties, and now had sat down for a quiet minute with her Bible before she began the day.

Her sister Maria, two years older, sat in the adjoining room, her door open for all possible circulation of air. Indeed the door between the sisters' rooms was scarcely ever shut by day or by night. But Maria was trimming a hat instead of reading her Bible. Not that Maria did not read her Bible, for she did, but she never had a set, quiet time for doing it as Rachel had.

The hat was white sailor and had been very stylish and consequently very expensive earlier in the season, but now the mass of people were supplied with millinery for the summer, and poorer people were enabled by the great reduction in prices to indulge their taste for pretty things. It went very much against the grain with Maria Hammond to have to wait until late for the pretty summer things she wanted, and even then to be obliged to buy with careful hand and long-hoarded savings, for until recently she had been used to buying when and what she pleased since she could remember. Maria had taken more bitterly her father's change of fortune than any of the other members of the family. The others had looked on the bright side of things and cheerfully told each other how good it was that matters were no worse; that the father had not fallen ill physically under the heavy burden that had been placed upon him by the fraud of a trusted partner; that the dear beautiful home where the three children had been born was saved to them, with a little — a very little, it is true, but still a little — with which to keep things going; and best of all, that all the creditors had been fully paid. But Maria could only see the dark side. From a rich man, who was able to do what he pleased, and who intended soon to build a home lovelier even than their present one, and who could afford to place his daughters in the best society, her father had become a poor man. Thus to her the present home had lost even the charms which it had possessed before she looked forward to the finer one.

This present home was by no means an undesirable one. It was located on a quiet, pleasant street where the neighbors were staid and old-fashioned, people of fine old families. It was built of stone in a comfortable manner, with ample room and broad piazzas, vines peeping in the windows in summer, and lawn enough about it to give the feeling of plenty of room.

It was in the plainest end of a fashionable suburb, but it was not fashionable. The house had none of the modern twists and turns which art and fashion have decreed shall adorn the modern handsome dwelling, and for this reason Maria despised it and pitied herself for having to live in it. A look of discontent had settled down upon her pretty white forehead which was gradually but surely changing her expression permanently.

"Oh, dear!" sighed Maria, as she jerked a loop of white ribbon into place behind the many cheap white wings she was arranging on her hat. "What's the use of fussing and fixing up things to wear after all? There won't be a place to wear them except church, and all the people we know or care about will be out of town by another month. One might as well wear one's old duds after all."

Rachel looked up from her Bible, through the open door where she could see her sister at work.

"Oh, yes, there will be plenty of places. Don't be so disheartened, dear," she answered brightly. "How pretty that hat will be, 'Ri! It looks just like you."

"Does it, indeed?" responded the elder sister. "Then my face must be badly snarled up, for this ribbon is. I can't get the right twist to it any way I put it. I do wish I could afford to take it down to Haskins' and have it trimmed by our old milliner. It is awfully vexatious to have to do everything one's self or else go without. But I'd be willing to do it myself if we could only go out of town for a little while, Ray; it's so horribly plebeian to stay in the city all the year round. Everybody else is going."

"You forget, 'Ri, we don't live in the city, we live in the suburbs, and plenty of people stay all summer in the suburbs. Some people prefer to take their trips away from home in the winter, you know. Look at the Adamses and Monteiths, they don't go away at all, and even Mrs. Burbank told me the other day that they didn't care to take any vacation, they enjoyed their home in the summer so much."

"Oh, yes, I should think they would. They have a park surrounding them, a great, cool house with plenty of servants, all the guests they want, and are up on a high hill besides, with plenty of shade about. Besides, it's nonsense for them to talk about not going away. They are hardly at home two weeks in succession all the year around. Mrs. Burbank and Tilly spend a week at a time at Atlantic City every time they sneeze or have a headache, and Mr. and Mrs. Burbank took a trip to California last winter, while Tom and his aunt went to Florida. When they don't run up to New York or out to Pittsburgh for a few days they go up to that sanitarium in the mountains for their health for a month or take a trip to Bermuda. I don't know that I should care either about going away in the summer if I only knew I could go whenever I pleased, and what is more, knew that everybody else knew it. I tell you, Ray, the hardest thing to bear is to feel that folks are saying we can't go anywhere now, and pitying us! I just can't stand it," and Maria threw her half-finished hat on the bed beside her and lay back on one of the snowy pillows in a discouraged attitude.

Rachel by long experience with her sister knew that it was of no use to argue with her, so she tried to cheer her as best she could, sighing a little regretfully as she closed her Bible and came into her sister's room. She had been reading the verse, "For me to live is Christ," and she wondered wistfully if she would ever know what that meant, and wished that Maria felt more of the spirit of it, so that her life would not seem so hard to her.

"If you want to go away so much perhaps we might go to the same place Marvie Parker told me about yesterday," said Rachel, seating herself on the foot of Maria's bed and resting her chin thoughtfully in her hand.

"No, thanks!" said Maria promptly and decidedly. "I don't think I should care for any place where Marvie Parker goes. I don't see what you find in that girl to attract you, Ray. She is the dowdiest thing I've seen in a long time. Her father is nothing but a clerk in his brother-in-law's store. There are plenty of nice girls for you to go with without choosing her for a friend."

"But she is nice, 'Ri," said the younger sister, her eyes flashing bright in her eagerness to defend her friend. "You don't know her or you wouldn't talk that way. She is very bright and has read and studied far more than either of us. The whole family are very bright. I never enjoyed myself more in my life than I did the evening I spent with them last week. She has a brother just home from college who is as full of life as can be, and Marvie is the sweetest girl I know, next to you."

"She may be sweet enough," answered Maria, ignoring the earnest compliment, "but she is not of the same social standing with you, and it is a great deal wiser and pleasanter not to try to upset the world and drag people out of their spheres." This with an air and expression of long experience with the world.

"Well, I think you might wait until you have known them before you judge them; but listen. Let me tell you where they are going. It sounds very interesting. The place is an island right between the bay and the ocean, not very wide either, so you get the view of both. Marvie says it is beautiful there, and the sunsets are go gorgeous. It is a real, old-time beach such as you read about, with no boardwalks and no merry-go-rounds, and everybody does as he pleases, and lots of bathing and boating and fishing and sailing. I think it would be delightful. Marvie says there are cottages down there for seventy-five dollars for the season, just think of that! They are not fine, of course, but are real comfortable, with big rooms, and lots of corners and shelves and places to fix up. I think I should like it immensely."

"Now Rachel Weldon Hammond, what in the world do you mean?" said Maria, sitting upright on the bed and looking at her. "Seventy-five dollars for the season! The very idea of our living in a cottage that costs only seventy-five dollars for the season! You must be crazy. Why the cottage the Johnses lived in last year at Atlantic City was twelve hundred, and even the Pattersons paid a thousand. I think you are nothing but a child, in spite of your seventeen years."

Just then a servant came to announce that a young lady was in the parlor to see Miss Ray, and Rachel with a bright spot on each cheek went down to find her friend Marvie.

It was not until dinner that evening that the subject was renewed. Maria had spent the afternoon in town hunting among the bargain tables and had come home thoroughly tired. There is something in a disappointing day of shopping which particularly exasperates some people's nerves. Every subject that came to Maria's mind seemed to be productive of discomfort. At last something was said about Rachel's morning caller. Then Maria burst out:

"Was that Marvie Parker here again? I think she is rather running things into the ground. Mamma, do you know what kind of a girl is getting an influence over Rachel? I think the friendship ought to be stopped. She isn't in our set at all, and Rachel will feel most uncomfortable in a year or two if she makes a special friend of a girl like that, whom she can't invite nor go with, of course, when she gets old enough to care about things."

"What is the matter with Miss Parker?" questioned Mr. Hammond, turning his sad gray eyes to his elder daughter's face. "It does not seem to be a good reason for objecting to her merely because she is not in your set. If she isn't in, bring her in; that is, if the set is worth her coming. If it isn't, it might be a good thing for Rachel to have a few friends outside it, in case of an emergency. Miss Parker ought to be a good girl. Her father is a fine man, and I used to know her mother years ago when we were children. The girl ought to be well brought up. What is the matter with her, aside from that senseless notion?"

Maria's face grew red. She did not like to have her father against her, neither did she feel fully prepared to face his keen eyes or his searching questions. She was on the point of reminding him that she and Rachel were no longer in a position to say who should or should not belong in their set, and that their own footing there might at any time grow insecure, but she remembered just in time to save herself this disgrace and her father the pain of such a remark. Instead she flew at once to some defense of her own statements.

"She may be a good girl, papa, I presume she is," she replied; "but you will surely acknowledge that she is putting queer notions into Ray's head.

Why this morning she actually confided in me that she would enjoy going to some out-of-the-way place, on an almost desert island, where the Parkers are going to seek solitude for the summer, and live in a shanty at seventy-five dollars for the season. Just think of it! I don't know where she thought even the seventy-five dollars was to come from, with the railroad fares and all, but she would really like us to go. Did you ever hear of such of an idea!"

Rachel's fair face had grown rosy red during the conversation.

She was an exceedingly sensitive girl, and shrank from being the center of observation, even in her own family, and now as the glance of father, mother, and brother were turned upon her, she could scarcely keep the excited tears from rushing to her eyes. But she tried to smile in answer to her father's encouraging look as he asked for an explanation.

"Why, papa, I didn't really say I wanted to do it," said Rachel, her cheeks flushing redder, "I only said I thought it would be real nice. And of course I'm perfectly happy here where I am. But if we were to do it I suppose we'd have to in the same way that the Parkers do. They rent their house here, and they get two hundred and fifty dollars for the season for it from some people who have to stay in town on account of business all summer and have to be at their store at seven o'clock, so they couldn't get in from far away from the city in time. Marvie said her father knew a lot of men who wanted just such homes as ours for the summer, where they could bring their families out of the rows of brick houses. I thought maybe there would be come one who might want our house that way, and it ought to bring more than the Parkers', because it is larger and has more ground and is on a nicer street. But I didn't really mean ever to say anything about it, for 'Ri seemed to think it was all so dreadful that I didn't mention the renting of our house."

Rachel dropped her burning face from the exclamations which she knew would follow.

"Rent our house!" said Maria aghast. "Whatever can you be thinking about? Are you crazy? I guess we have not quite come to that state of disgrace!"

"My dear child!" exclaimed the mother, not so much in horror as astonishment at the new thought. "How could we have people using our carpets and our dishes?" There came a little distressed pucker between her eyes, showing that the idea was not an impossibility to her after all and she was really considering it.

"And what did you propose to do with father and me, Ray?" asked her brother Winthrop, who was a little older than Maria and in business with this father, struggling to bring back the name and the fame which the former firm had lost through the treachery of one of its members. "You know we are obliged to be in town at a set hour everyday, as well as some other folks!"

Rachel's cheeks flushed anew at the implication that she, the quietest member of the household, had taken the family affairs into consideration and assumed to make the plans, but she answered shyly:

"I hadn't thought it all out, but Mr. Parker and his son go in to town every day. Marvie said there was a train leaving the island early enough to get here before nine, I think, and there are special season tickets for business men, so it doesn't cost much, and the store closes early during the summer anyway, doesn't it? But I didn't mean to plan. I am happy where I am. I wouldn't have said a word, only 'Ri was worrying because we had to stay in town all summer, and I thought maybe mother would enjoy the coolness by the shore."

"She is nothing but an absurd child! " exclaimed her sister. "Papa, surely you are not going to encourage her in such plebeian notions. I'm sure I'd rather die respectably than go away for the summer in such a disgraceful manner." And she sat back in her chair with a sneer.

"My daughter," said Mr. Hammond, looking straight at Maria, "I am ashamed if a child of mine has come to the place where she can say such a thing as that. You do not mean it. And as for this 'notion,' as you are pleased to term it, it is nothing new to me. I have long thought that I could save a good deal and make matters mend in our pecuniary affairs much more quickly if I could rent this house. Indeed, I had an offer last week of four hundred dollars for this place, stable and all, from now till the first of October. The reason I declined the offer was not on account of any such frivolous and unworthy motives as you have expressed, but simply because I knew of no cheaper place where my family could be comfortable while the house was earning the four hundred dollars."

"I should think not!" put in Maria with red, excited face. It meant a great deal to her, this question of fashion, and what her little world of "they" would think and say. It meant all that she now cared for in life, though she would not have believed it if she had been told that this was true of her. But her father went on in his calm tone:

"Now if the Parkers have found a place for seventy-five dollars where they can be comfortable, I should think we might do so as well. The Parkers are respectable people and used to having the necessaries of life, at least, if not all of the luxuries. I should think it might be worth the looking into at least. Don't you think so, mother?"

And the wife, with a troubled look at her eldest daughter's face, and a sigh of longing for the cool air of the ocean, assented that she thought they ought to make inquiries, at least.

Maria, with tears of chagrin in her eyes, suddenly left the table, and Rachel, whose tender heart was sorely distressed at having been the cause of the trouble to her sister, went soon to her own room, where for once she found the connecting door between her room and her sister's closed, and upon softly turning the knob a few minutes later she discovered it was also locked. This was something that had not happened since the two girls were very little and first had rooms to themselves, and Rachel could not keep the tears back. She betook herself to her Bible for comfort and through blinding tears she found it, and resolved to try to make Maria happy that summer no matter what happened, seashore or home, heat or cool breezes, pleasure or disagreeableness. And so she slept.

Chapter 2

Maria Hammond was a girl of very determined nature. When she liked or wanted a thing she liked or wanted it intensely, and bent all her energies to get it. What she disliked she was equally persistent in opposing; and when it happened, as it often did in her life, that her plans and desires were frustrated, it took a great struggle of will before she could give up and yield to the inevitable. Even then, should the least chance occur, she would try for her own way again. She insisted that it was not her own way, however, which she desired, but merely to have things right about her, and as they ought to be; and that if the way were another's and it seemed right to her, she would be just as eager to have it as though it had been her own. With such sophistry did she excuse herself to herself and to others for her persistency and headstrong, stubborn willfulness, and because of a discontented nature, which was always desiring the unattainable, she was constantly in trouble.

When she went to her room after her stormy speeches at the dinner table the tears of anger, defeat, chagrin, and disappointment swelled into her throat and eyes. Locking her door, she threw herself on her bed in a torrent of weeping. It is true she had attained the years when young ladies are supposed not to weep violently, unless for some great grief of life, and she would not for the world have had any one, even a member of her own family, see her thus; but her nature was so uncontrolled that when it burst out upon her in this way she could but give way to it. Moreover, in her eyes very little things often seemed important, and thus it came about that what to another might simply be an annoyance to her became a great and overwhelming grief. It was, as it were, her very life that was in the balance. For what else was life to her but the good opinion of the world? And so Maria lay upon her bed crying for a long time. It was not merely what had occurred at the dinner table which caused her trouble, nor even the prospect of spending the summer in a most unfashionable retreat, though that seemed to her mind very unlikely, even after what had been said by father and mother, "For surely," thought she, "their reason will see that it would be dreadful, simply dreadful"; but it seemed to her a sort of climax of all the disappointments which had come since her father had lost his money. In consequence, she mourned and cried and pitied herself, and perhaps pitied the rest of the family a little with what heart she had left after her own need was lavishly supplied. By and by she grew more calm, and then there came to her a shadow of her religion to question why it could not help her in this trying time, for she had a religion, this stormy-natured girl, in spite of all her will and her fear of what "they" would say. And with the thought of her religion came the reflection of all she had meant to do to help in the church work during the summer, of the class of delightfully bad little boys she had promised to take in the Sunday-school; of the young people's meeting she had promised to lead; and of the tennis picnic in the park she was planning for those same young people, which was to close in the dusk of evening with a short prayer meeting under the trees, and which she hoped would do much good. Then she told herself it could not be that she was to be removed to an out-of-the-way place where there would be no possible opportunity for anything of the kind when she had planned to do so much. Thus she magnified her own projected goodness until she seemed a very martyr.

Now such a nature as Maria's is not one which long remains under a cloud. She began to persuade herself by and by that things could not possibly be as bad as they seemed about to be, and to silence her own uncomfortable conscience, which was beginning to reproach her keenly for the way in which she had spoken to her father and sister. She resolved with a large sigh of conscious martyrdom to go to her father the next morning and tell him she was resigned to being a hermit if it would conduce to his financial comfort. Having thus resolved, and being comforted by the thought that if she pursued such a course her father would by no means be likely to accept her sacrifice, she went to sleep.

Meantime the father and mother had been holding a consultation. Money matters had been coming to a crisis during the last few weeks. Business was very dull at the store. Mr. Hammond hoped if he could tide affairs over until fall that he might be able to weather the gale. He now felt that a serious talk with his wife was necessary, though she was such a frail little woman that he always spared her all he could because she took every burden at twice its weight, and went about with her face sad and anxious. The result of this talk, however, was that Mr. Hammond took his breakfast a half-hour earlier than usual in order that he might stop in and speak to his friend Mr. Parker on his way to the office. And so it was that Maria did not get an opportunity to speak to her father until evening.

It was just as the dinner bell rang through the house, and Maria, hastening down the stairs that she might speak to her father as he entered the dining room, heard her mother's voice speaking to him as she passed the door of the library. She spoke with an anxious sigh: "Yes, it would be very nice and just the thing. I would do it in a minute if it only were not for the girls' sake. I hate to do it when they are so opposed."

And her father's weary tones answered: "It is Maria that is opposed, not both of them, remember, and things are as they are. Maria may come to worse trouble if we do not do this."

"Yes," said the mother sadly; "but Maria is the oldest, you know, and just at the age when everything of this sort makes so much difference to her. It might hurt her future life, my dear."

"Nonsense!" said her father rather sharply, although he felt the truth of what his wife was saying, keenly enough. "If Maria's future is to be hurt by the fact that her father rented his home to good, respectable people for a few months, and went to a quiet, unfashionable place to stay during that time, I think it had better be hurt. It seems to 'me that friends who are affected by such things are not worth the having." But he sighed again as he came down the stairs, his face wearing a careworn expression.

Maria's heart beat fast and the tears came into her eyes. She had not realized that she was making her loved father so much trouble. Her impulsive nature at once forgot all about any personal sacrifices, and rushing up to her father, she drew him into the door of the sitting room they were passing, and throwing her arms about his neck, begged him to forgive her for all she had said, and not to mind her in the least in anything he wished to do, that she would try to be as helpful as she could.

And so it came about after all that it was through Maria that the Hammond home was rented to a family who would pay well for four months' use of it, and the Hammonds themselves migrated to the seashore. It must not be supposed that Maria was changed all in a moment. She had many evenings of weeping over the inevitable, but the memory of her father's weary face and her mother's anxious tones was sufficient to keep her from demurring any further to the family plans, and it was only to her sister Rachel and her brother Winthrop that she permitted herself to grumble. Winthrop had long ago said that his sisters were well named: Rachel was like a ray of bright sunlight everywhere, always, cheery, never cross, while Maria, or 'Ri, as they all called her, "always took things awry and kept a wry face much of the time."

"I say 'Ri, do let up a little, can't you?" said her brother one day when Maria had finished one of her sarcastic speeches about their summer outing. "It's too late now to give up, so you'd better make the best of it. Where's the Christian fortitude I hear most church-members talk so much about? Can't you summon up a little bit to help you through this vale of tears? I'm sure you've taken every grain of pleasure out of this summer that it might possibly have contained for Rachel and me, so do be satisfied, for you surely can't wish father and mother to suffer."

This somewhat caustic speech from her usually good-natured brother sent Maria to her room weeping. The days had been very hard for her even before this. She had endured, in imagination, the heavy trial of coming home to find her room treasures spoiled by ruthless alien hands. She had pleaded that certain necessary articles — necessary to the thorough furnishing of the house — be put away under lock and key, but had been made to understand that this could not be. She suffered a great deal while clearing out her bureau drawers and closet and all her little private "cubby-holes," realizing how in a few days these places would be filled with some other girl's belongings, and she felt that when she returned she never could feel the same toward the home-corners again after strangers had called them their own. She had also been obliged to help in packing cushions and cretonne draperies that could be well spared from the home, with curtains, pictures, screens, and a few such things as were considered essential to make the summer cottage, to which they were going, habitable.

This had also gone much against the grain. To think of having to spend one's summer amid things that were merely fit to put in a bedroom! It was humiliating. If they were to have a cottage, why couldn't they at least have it look comfortable, cheery, and furnished with taste? Maria was the artist of the family, and so had been called upon to select the draperies they should take, but when her mother found that Maria's choice would be to carry silk-chenille portières and satin embroidered sofa pillows and a plush hand-painted screen, she was obliged to do the selecting herself, or quietly put it into Rachel's hands, for Rachel had been down to the little beach cottage. Her friend, Marvie Parker, had invited her for over a Sunday, and her father thought this would be a good opportunity for some member of the family to judge of the fitness of the cottage for their abode. It is true Rachel had hitherto been considered the child of the family, but her judgment was usually good, and her father and mother felt her to be a much more unprejudiced judge than her sister would have been, for Rachel would tell not only the best but also the worst, which Maria would not have seen at all, had she desired to go as much as her sister did. So Rachel had accepted the invitation, much to the chagrin of Maria, who told her that if she did this she would open the way to the Parkers to be entirely too intimate with them for the summer, a thing she, for one, did not intend to countenance. But Rachel, having the consent of father and mother, went and enjoyed her two days immensely, coming home with glowing accounts of all the pleasures in store for them, as well as an accurate description of the cottages for rent. They were rough, she admitted; not finished inside except for a high facing of heavy manilla paper. The ceilings were high, reaching indeed to the peak of the roof, and thus giving the rooms a lofty appearance. She felt sure that Maria could make of the parlor or sitting room, or whatever they chose to call it, a perfect summer bower, and the rooms, though few, were all large, indeed quite spacious for a place so cheap. It was all on one floor, with a wide piazza for hammocks and a view of sea and bay. But when Maria — a slight interest awakened for the moment — began to select silk and velour portières, Rachel laughed and then looked troubled. She saw endless difficulties in making her sister understand.

"They will look incongruous, 'Ri," she said. "You ought to have gone in my place and then you would know just what to take, for you always know how to make things fit; but really I should think some of that pretty printed burlap we bought to make cozy-corner cushions for our bedrooms would be just the thing."

"If I had gone," said Maria severely, "I should probably have brought back such an account as would have made the family understand it was no fit place for us to live in. However, you seem to be having everything your own way this time and I suppose we will take what curtains you say. I wish with all my heart we were not compelled to spend the summer entirely in a burlap atmosphere. I didn't suppose things would be quite so rough."

And so had Maria gone on, fighting every step of the way, contesting every inch of the plans that were made, until all who asked her to help were glad to see her go away and leave them to finish alone.

Poor Maria! Don't be too hard upon her. Her heart was very heavy during these days. She discovered a day or two before they flitted to the shore that the place selected was but a mile from a fashionable summer resort of which she had often heard as being at the very height of refined and aristocratic summer haunts. She also discovered to her dismay that the De Veres, of the West End of the city, who were very wealthy and literary and cultured, had taken a cottage there. Now Maria had met the Misses De Vere and their brother some three or four times at various social functions, and she felt that their acquaintance would be worth cultivating. But she knew she should shrink into herself with shame if they discovered her whereabouts and came to see the kind of place in which she was summering. She had really taken quite a liking to those young people, and it was hard for her to think of them as looking down upon her. Why she did not feel that people who would look down upon her because of the house in which she lived were not worth her caring for, is hardly explainable, unless it was because she knew that she should look down upon any one similarly placed, and so judged them by herself. She had listened to a bit of talk between George Parker, Marvie's brother, and her sister Rachel, wherein he described some of the cottages at Lone Point and told how the Spray View people laughed at them and called them "Lone Point Barracks," and all sorts of funny names. Maria's spirit writhed within her as she pictured to herself Roland De Vere driving by their cottage some day and laughing with other strangers about their home. The blood crimsoned her whole face, and she resolved that by no word of hers should the De Veres find out where she was to spend her summer, even though she missed many a pleasant invitation thereby.

One more experience Maria had to complete her wretchedness before they left for Lone Point. She had been with her sister on some last errands prior to their departure from civilization for a time, and just before they took the car for home, stopped at the public library to secure a store of books for summer reading. It was while they were waiting at the desk for their cards to be marked, that Roland De Vere, with his arms full of books, stepped up to them and touched his hat. Maria introduced her sister, of course, and the three walked out together.

"By the way, where do you spend your summer this year?" asked the young man as they paused at the corner to wait for a car.

Maria's cheeks grew rosy. She never could keep her face from telling tales which she would rather were untold, but she caught at her presence of mind and answered:

"Papa is talking of the seashore somewhere," rather vaguely, and then looked eagerly to see if the car were not coming.

But Rachel, not noticing her sister's vague response and not understanding in the least its intention, turned in her eager, girlish way and said:

"Why, yes, we're going quite near to where you will be, if I have heard aright. Are you not going to Spray View? Your sister told a friend of ours. I hoped I might meet your sisters this summer. I have heard so much about them, and Maria is quite in love with both of them. Our place is only a mile from there, Lone Point; do you know it?"

Maria's face was crimson now. She motioned violently to the car which was still half a block away, and telling her sister the car was ready, never even turned her eyes to see what Mr. De Vere was thinking. She had so often rehearsed in her mind how under such circumstances his face would grow astonished, and he would utter a very expressive "Oh!" and turn away, that her imaginings became a reality to her, of which the true scene which followed was not able to efface the impression. So with a vexation and embarrassment that amounted almost to an agony she stepped out into the street with the other waiting passengers, thinking to prevent all further conversation.

This, however, Mr. De Vere did not notice. He was entirely taken up with talking to Rachel. His face lighted with pleasure and he said: "Know it? I should think I did. It is a delightful little place. I had a good friend there last year. I hope we shall see each other often. You go to-morrow, you say? How pleasant! We go the first of next week, and sooner if mother can get ready. Good-afternoon, Miss Rachel; Miss Hammond, good-afternoon. I am glad there is a prospect of our seeing one another often this summer."

He touched his hat; they stepped on the car and were soon speeding away. The car was crowded and the two girls had difficulty at first in finding seats, but as they neared the suburbs the passengers grew fewer, and Maria found opportunity to seat herself beside Rachel, who in blissful unconsciousness of her sister's state of mind had been letting her eyes dance and her heart rejoice in the innocent pleasures in store in the possibilities of the summer. Maria had been bottled up for nearly twenty minutes and the vials of her wrath had not cooled during the process. She always showed her feelings to their full extent in her face, so Rachel had a sudden and unpleasant awakening from her girlish dreams.

"Rachel Hammond!" said Maria, trying to lower her excited voice so none of their fellow-passengers could hear, "I should think you might learn to keep your mouth shut occasionally. I never introduce you to one of my friends but I regret it bitterly at once. It seems as if you might be old enough now to know how to behave."

Poor Rachel! Her sensitive face flushed and she roused herself at once to remember what terrible breach of etiquette she had been guilty of, but could think of nothing. She dreaded one of Maria's tirades beyond almost any experience that came into her life, and was constantly studying to avoid them, and perhaps as a consequence she was the one who had to receive the larger number of them.

"What did I do, 'Ri?" she faltered, and if Maria had not been too angry she would have been touched by the pitiful quiver of the pretty, sensitive lips, and the grieved, troubled look of Rachel's large eyes.

"What did you do, indeed! You little tattle-tale! You need not tell me you don't know, for you did it just to annoy me, you know you did, or else from some high and mighty notion that you would rebuke me for not telling everything I knew. You will have to learn that it isn't necessary to tell all you know in this world in order to avoid telling a falsehood. Why was it necessary for you to explain fully to that elegant Mr. De Vere in what a humiliating state we were to spend our summer? I should think things were being made uncomfortable enough for me already without that being added. I shall simply die of shame if they come over to that horrid little place and find us rusticating in a cowshed. I think you have fully overstepped the mark this time. You have chosen your friends and I have a right to mine. I shall ask papa to let you know hereafter that you are not to interfere with me and my friends."

Maria had grown angrier as she talked. She had kindled her imagination during the silent ride with fancied scenes of meeting between herself and Fannie De Vere at Spray View, until she scarcely could contain herself. Rachel's fair face grew almost white at her sister's words. She tried to explain, but Maria was in no state to be reasonable.

"But, Maria dear," she pleaded, "I didn't dream I was saying anything unpleasant to you."

"Then you must be very blind," snapped Maria. "You certainly must have seen from the way I answered him that I would have bitten out my tongue sooner than have him know."

"But I didn't, 'Ri, indeed; indeed I didn't dream of such a thing! I was only delighted for your sake, for I thought you would have some company, and he seemed so pleased about it."

"Oh, yes, he was pleased!" sneered Maria. "He's too polite to let anything else appear, but he's probably laughing in his sleeve this minute. You needn't worry. We shall not see either him or his lovely sisters at all this summer. As soon as he said he was acquainted with Lone Point I knew what to expect. I heard a man from Spray View talk about Lone Point the other day, and they don't consider the place fit for Spray Viewers to wipe their feet on."

Poor Rachel quivered under her sister's upbraidings, until when they reached home she could bear it no more and went to her room to do an unusual thing for her, have it out with her tears. And then she went to her Heavenly Father with her little bruised heart and found comfort.

Chapter 3

Meantime Roland De Vere was walking down Walnut Street reflectively.

"Strange," he said to himself. "What could have been her reason? Was she ashamed of going to a quiet, unfashionable resort? She was angry with her sister for telling me. I could see that. Her face struck me as being a very intellectual one when I first saw her, and a pretty one too, but I didn't notice that discontented curl to her lips. However, I have never seen her in the daytime before. Gaslight makes a wonderful difference. It is not so good as I thought at first. But the other face is like a flower. The youngest sister must be worth cultivating. I did enjoy her frank eagerness. Fannie would like her. I mean to take her over to call as soon as possible after we get to the shore."

How Maria's eyes would have opened in surprise could she have known his true feeling. It is a pity that some inventor could not give us a little instrument for divining occasionally what others really think of us. It would sometimes save a world of worry. But how careful we should then have to be of our own thoughts of others. Perhaps some one greater than Edison will arise one day who will search out the hidden law that governs thoughts and let us look into one another's hearts, and then how much better—or how much worse, alas—we shall be! For surely the kingdom of heaven will be near at hand when men's judgments of one another are kind and loving.

The Hammonds' journey to Lone Point was taken on a Saturday, for then they might have the escort of father and brother and their assistance during the day in unpacking and arranging their belongings for the summer. Maria looked sadly about on familiar objects as she walked toward the nearest station in the early morning. She felt as if she were going out of the world, and that when she returned, if she ever survived the humiliations of the summer, all would be different to her, and she could never be the same girl again.

Rachel, however, had gone ahead with Winthrop. He had seen how her bright spirits were clouded by her sister's gloomy countenance and had made a pretext of some errand to get her with himself. He had in some way found out from Rachel all that her sister had said to her on the street-car the night before, and he was indignant with Maria for being so hard upon the sensitive younger sister. He resolved upon the first opportunity to give her a plain talking-to, and save Rachel from further annoyance of that sort. He managed the seats in the cars so that Rachel should be with him, his father and mother together, and Maria installed with a fresh magazine and a pile of hand-baggage in a third seat. This suited Maria exactly, and as Rachel was in front of all she did not have to think about Maria and her troubles during the journey. Rachel looked a little pale that morning from her unusual vigil of the night before, and Winthrop set himself to make her forget it. He succeeded wonderfully, for soon her face lighted up and her silvery laugh could be heard occasionally, which made Maria look up and frown, to think that any member of the family could make merry on such a journey as this. She felt as if she were attending her own funeral, and the procession would never cease. However the magazine was interesting and she soon forgot herself for a little.

Through pleasant villages of gardens, and then through wastes of sand and scrub they sped, and the time seemed to Rachel short until they wound their way out at last upon the lovely bay and ran for several miles with water on either side and the sea breeze blowing fresh in their faces through the open windows of the car. Rachel and her mother drew in long, life-giving breaths, and even Maria aroused to a sense of relief from the heat and her heart seemed not to be quite so heavy as before, though she did not stop to explain to herself why it was so. Finally they came in sight of Spray View in the distance, its cottages and hotels seeming quite imposing beyond the blue waters of the bay and with the deep green sea as a background; and Maria, when she heard the name of the place, was looking enviously ahead and wishing that that tallest dark green cottage with the trumpet vine in full bloom over its lordly piazza were to be theirs, instead of—when suddenly the train came to a halt and the brakeman called out "Lone Point," and they were all hustled suddenly out upon a bare platform in the sand, and the train sped on toward the towers of fair Spray View a mile ahead.

"What did we get out for?" questioned Maria querulously. "We haven't got there yet. They said that was Spray View ahead there. Isn't the place (scornfully) the other side of it? This isn't any place at all apparently," and she looked about with curling lip on the waste of sand with the cluster of small buildings nearer the beach.

But no one was paying any attention to her, and she was obliged to pick up her umbrella and hand-satchel and follow the rest.

"Here we are, and there it is!" shouted Rachel gleefully, in her excitement clapping her hands and going back to her childhood ways of several years before. "There! that's ours, that green one over there with the white trimmings. And there comes Marvie to meet us, and her brother George. Oh, I'm so glad we're here!" and she flew to meet her friend.

It was all fully as humiliating as Maria expected. To have the "Parker boy," as she designated him—though he was fully as old as young Mr. De Vere—come and meet them, and offer assistance and insist on taking her hand-bag from her; then to be under obligations to the Parkers, whose

cottage was next door and who had kindly prepared dinner for the Hammonds and had it served on the table by the time they had their hats off! It
was simply unheard-of and dreadful, and Maria had no appetite to choke
down the delicate fish and fresh vegetables prepared so nicely. She wished
her mother had declined any assistance whatever and would rather have
starved until their own servant could prepare some kind of a meal. However, the others of the family did not share her feeling and did ample justice
to the dinner.

The afternoon found plenty for even troubled Maria to do and left her
no time for thought. The one poor servant whom they had brought down
with them and upon whom they depended to make everything move
smoothly and bear all the burdens had, it would seem, ideas also about
watering places. She went out and took a brief survey of the place, and above
all of the terrible ocean, heretofore unseen by her. One swift gaze over the
turbulent blue waves, and with a wild look in her eyes she turned and fled.
Returning to the cottage where the family had improved her absence to fit
up an impromptu partition in the kitchen and so make her a bedroom, she
took a hurried invoice of that, exclaimed in dismay over the roughness of
things, said "My land!" several times, went out on the porch and took in the
narrow stretch of land between ocean and bay, and going in told Mrs.
Hammond she must go right back to town by the next train, she "couldn't
stand it nohow," that she was "sure that there water would meet and flood
the place." Nor could any amount of persuasion on the part of the united
and dismayed family change her firm decision. No, indeed, she would not
stay over-night! She would never expect to see the morning light. She did
not wish to let the sun go down and darkness settle upon her with that awful
ocean roaring and surging back and forth so near her. What mattered it to
her that the Hammonds had paid her fare down from the city, had indeed
bought her a return ticket? What cared she for losing her place? Fear had
taken hold upon her, and her frenzied soul cared but to flee; and flee she
did on the two-o'clock train.

Then the family sat down in dismay to consider what they should do
next. Rachel was cheery. She had been to the beach and it had filled her
with exhilaration. She was ready for anything, and to call it fun, even if it
meant washing dishes and peeling potatoes. They all looked fearfully at
Maria. She had made her gloom felt so severely all day that each one
dreaded the effect of this last blow upon her.

Then up rose Maria with a martyr-like resignation. She had not been
to the beach, she did not wish to go. One spot on this deserted island was
just the same to her as another. As she was condemned to stay here, what
mattered it where she stayed or how she was employed during that time?
If one must have a disagreeable time, why not have it just as disagreeable

as possible, and so get greater credit for one's endurance? (This, however, not audibly.) She would do the work. She was perfectly capable of doing as much as that good-for-nothing girl had been. If she wasn't, she would learn. She could at least save a few more cents from the girl's wages to add to the family treasury and so increase the vast sum which they were to make during this summer of humiliation. Their downfall was complete; why not accept it and go to the bottom gracefully? They had to live in a hovel; of course they must do their own work; it was no more than she had expected.

Now Maria did not say all this; instead her sentences were very short, her words were few, but by tone and manner more than by words, she contrived to convey her meaning to the family and made them feel it to the heart's core. The father's face took on a gray look, and the mother's grew old and careworn. Rachel's brightness faded. It seemed as though Maria would manage to dampen the spirits of them all.

But Winthrop was determined that this first day should not be spoiled. Without an instant's hesitation he took Maria's proposal up, not in its spirit, but in its words.

"Why certainly, why shouldn't we? Mother, we can all help. I can't do much all day, but I fancy I can make it up evenings. I'll see that the wood is cut and the coal handy, and make the fire in the morning, and get the ice in the refrigerator, and go errands. There'll be plenty of time for errands before breakfast and train time if I get up a little earlier. And Sundays I'll agree to wash all the dishes three times a day to make up for what I can't do on week days. I can wash dishes beautifully. It will seem like old times when I was a little chap and 'Ri was a baby and mother had no girl, and I helped wipe dishes. Mother, don't you remember? I used to be as proud of the shining white dishes as if I had been a girl, prouder I fancy. Then I can go errands over to Spray View evenings after supper. We don't need to live high, anyway, and there can't be much housework to do in such a small house."

"Of course we can do the work," echoed Rachel eagerly. "I'm sure both Maria and I have had cooking lessons; and besides, here is mother, who knows how to do everything in the world, and can direct us in anything we have forgotten or never learned. I think it will be delightful fun. I'm all ready for it. Come on and let us wash those dinner dishes right away, Winthrop, and then there'll be more room in which to get to rights." And so saying, she ran humming out of the room followed by her brother, and the two had a gay time clattering the dishes.

Maria, with scornful dignity befitting the occasion, followed them, and was soon engaged in stirring up some mysterious concoction for supper and starting some bread for the morrow, as it was found there was no bakery nearer than the neighboring town, and all were too busy to go there for anything.

It was perhaps a half-hour later when all were deep in work; the girls with their sleeves rolled up and hastily improvised kitchen costumes snatched from the open boxes and trunks, Mr. and Mrs. Hammond unpacking and sorting out the most immediate necessities, and Winthrop in his shirt sleeves with a large checked apron tied about his waist and a wiping towel over his arm engaged in mopping dry a thick white-ware soup plate — he was whistling a merry tune and calling out comical sentences to his sisters between times — when a light rig drew up in front of the door and some one got out and came up the steps, but no one in the house heard.

"I say, 'Ri!" called out the diligent brother in a cheery tone, "don't look quite so cross or that bread'll be too sour to eat. It'll be 'rye' bread. See?"

Just then came a distinct knock on the open door, and the irrepressible brother disappeared through the calico portière which belonged to the house and separated the dining room from the parlor, to answer the knock, supposing the intruder to be a butcher or a baker or a candlestick maker, and caring little as to his appearance. Was he not on a lark and on a desert island where he knew not a soul? Besides, his was a spirit that did not feel degraded by a gingham apron and a dish towel.

He had hardly, however, bargained for the immaculate apparition that stood before the door trying to keep a smile from playing politely round his well-shaped, merry lips.

"I beg your pardon; I hope I'm not intruding," said the young man on the porch, with a graceful touch of his hat, "but is not this Mr. Hammond's..."

"Shanty? Certainly," finished Winthrop with a low bow and mock solemnity. "Walk right in. Things aren't quite ship-shape, yet; but I think we can find you a chair."

Winthrop Hammond was not to be embarrassed by any strange gentleman in fashionable driving costume. He dusted off a chair with a flourish, using the dish towel as a duster. Rachel, with a merry face, appeared in the doorway, one cheek well dabbed with flour and her arms dripping with soapsuds. Her dark hair, a trifle rough and loose about her face, had curled itself into little rings, and her cheeks were flushed with excitement and work. She heard Winthrop's gay talk, and never doubted he was making fun for their benefit with some grocer boy or fish man. The young man at the door with a laugh entered into the occasion and stepped willingly into the room, then catching sight of Rachel in the doorway, he came forward with easy grace.

"Good-afternoon, Miss Rachel," he said. "Welcome to the shore. Have you just arrived? You didn't expect to find me here ahead of you, did you?

But you see mother sent me on ahead to attend to some arrangements and make everything ready for them on Monday. Up to your eyes in work, aren't you? Is this your brother? I thought so. Glad to meet you, Mr. Hammond. Having a jolly time, aren't you? I envy you. I'd like nothing better than to pitch in and help. Haven't you something for me to do? Come, now, I've got a horse here and can run all the errands you want. Do put me to work. I've got my own garden all weeded and not a thing to do till the folks come Monday. I'm lonesome, and should enjoy it. Is your sister here?"

"She's in the kitchen making bread," laughed Rachel, entering into the spirit of their guest's speech. "Maria!" she called, and started laughing to find her sister; but Maria had listened to the voice at the door in dismay and had fled.

Chapter 4

Into the midst of the turmoil of work and settling came the calm of the Sabbath. There was a little church near by, and at the appointed hour they could see the neighbors in simple dress wending their way thereto. Rachel, having completed her morning work and helped all she could in the preparation of dinner, announced her intention of going to church, but the others were too weary, and even Mrs. Hammond thought it as well to wait until the next week to begin their acquaintance with the place. However, Winthrop took up his hat and followed his sister down the steps, when she came out a few minutes later arrayed in dark serge skirt, clean shirt waist, and sailor hat.

"For pity's sake! Rachel Hammond! You're surely not going to church in a strange place in that rig?" called the horrified Maria as she caught sight of her sister going out the door. "You haven't any gloves, either. I do think you have taken leave of your senses. You might have a little sense of decency left, at least."

But Rachel, happily, was out of hearing and went serenely on her way, drinking in the salt air and the Sabbath quiet as she walked.

Maria, looking after her, wondered how her sister could be so happy, half envied her her sweet, happy nature, and then went by herself to shed some tears of discontent. They had not been able to make her listen to any account of the visitor of the day before. She had kept in hiding during his short stay and disappeared as suddenly again when he returned with some packages which Rachel had laughingly sent him after. Maria did not approve of taking Mr. De Vere into their family at this stage of events and letting him see all the ins and outs of the rude cottage and the makeshifts of the family life. She wanted to receive her guests in the right way or not at all, and so she had left herself severely out of yesterday's affair. Her soul writhed within her at the thought of the laughing account Mr. De Vere would give his stately mother and elegant sisters of his visit to Lone Point. She resolved to keep away from their sight as much as possible, and wondered why it had been considered necessary to add this humiliation to her list of troubles for the summer. After her little cry she went to the kitchen, where her martyr spirit bore her up grimly, while she made the rest of the family uncomfortable with the elaborate dishes she prepared, and of which she tasted but little herself. She did not intend to make them all unhappy, but she was not averse to their knowing how extremely uncomfortable they had succeeded in making her and how well she was bearing herself under the circumstances. She continued this conduct during the week, even carrying it so far as refusing to go to the beach, when she could have gone as well as not. She declared she had no wish to meet the people of the place; they were a common lot, anyway, she could tell that from their appearance on Sabbath, and as for the sea, she never cared much for it. There were none of the usual enjoyments of seaside life here to make this place endurable, and she would rather stay at home and let others who could enjoy things go to the beach. And so she stayed in the cottage and cooked, and arranged the cheap draperies into graceful fashionings, not taking pleasure and pride in her pretty work as she might have done at another time, but urged to it from fierce necessity. If there were danger that the De Veres might call at any time she would at least make things as presentable as possible that they might not see an utterly barren place, though she firmly resolved to always absent herself and be unfindable when they did call. Thus she wrought, and the room grew truly beautiful in spite of the rebellious spirit of its artist. She asked little help from any one, but her brother and sister were both watching to be of assistance and supplied the needful help without being asked. In one corner of the parlor there grew up a cosy-corner or divan of vast dimensions, composed on one side of the woven-wire cot on which Winthrop slept, and on the other of the packing-box in which the curtains and tin dishes had traveled. This was upholstered deftly in dark blue burlap bearing a wreath and crest design, and the whole was united by a deep valance around the sides. In the corner were many cushions, some only filled with straw or excelsior from the packing, others being the pillows used for Winthrop's bed at night and stuffed during the day into calico and chintz covers of gay design. Two or three were genuine eiderdown with embroidered denim covers, and the effect was not only lovely but luxurious. Maria manipulated pretty screens out of cheap torn paper ones, and one corner was curtained off in a most novel way with a heavy bamboo pole Winthrop found on the beach, and curtains of green and brown figured burlap hanging in fold from it. Behind this no one would have suspected Winthrop's washstand and a few hooks on which he hung some of his clothes. It seemed terribly low to Maria that some one had to sleep in the parlor, but as there was no help for it, there being but two other sleeping rooms in the house, she disguised the fact as prettily as possible. Crêpe paper lampshades and a quaint little bookcase of odd shape and original workmanship, which knew its origin in a shoe box and an old peach crate, also gave touches to the room, which when done was pronounced to be a perfect gem of beauty, comfort, and coziness by the entire family.

"Isn't this beautiful! What a transformation!" exclaimed Roland De Vere, as he entered the room the next week to announce that his family were coming over to call as soon as the Hammond girls were willing to receive them.

"I declare I never saw such a change. Who is the fairy that has waved her wand so effectually?" he asked, and looked at the sweet-faced Rachel, who immediately disclaimed any part in the work and gave it all to Maria. Meanwhile Maria continued invisible to all callers. Mr. De Vere did not notice this fact so much, however, as he would have done had he been less well pleased with the company of her brother and sister. They began planning numerous excursions and moonlight sails, in which she was always included, but in the preparation of which she did not figure. She felt very much cut at heart at the way things were going and blamed it all on the others, not seeing that it was her own doing. She persisted more than ever in her purpose of isolating herself. She would not even go to the beach, though the others entreated her and invented various ways of trying to get her there. He headstrong, stubborn will had set itself up against all their pleadings and she would not be coaxed by anything or any one, so at last they gave it up. Maria arranged her hair in the most unbecoming way possible, took on hard, drawn-down lines about her mouth, significant of her martyrdom, and went about in an old work apron most of the time. Rachel grieved over it as much as she had time for amid the merry round of delight that was open to her. She found a great deal of joy in wandering over the beautiful beach in search of shells with her friend Marvie Parker and Marvie's brother George, who proved to be fully as bright and interesting a companion as she had prophesied, though he was a busy student and had little time, even that summer vacation, for a frolic. She enjoyed her brother Winthrop's merry talk in the evenings, and rejoiced in going to the seven-o'clock city train to meet him and their father every evening. She looked upon the delight of a visit from Maria's friend, as she called Roland De Vere, as some great treat which did not belong to her, but by special privilege she was permitted to share with the others. The summer seemed to be unfolding before her with a beautiful promise.

She sat one evening just at sunset in her room. She could look out on the beautiful bay in the distance and see the softly rippling waters calming down for the glassy effect of sunset. The white sails here and there were speeding homeward. In a few minutes the evening train would slip silently along by the water and she would run down to meet her father and brother. Supper was nearly ready. The bisque of clams was perfect. That had been her work and she was proud of it. Maria was busy with some one of her special concoctions and seemed to desire the kitchen to herself, and Rachel had been glad to slip away for this little silent minute to rest and think and pray. Since they had been doing their own work she seemed to find so little uninterrupted time for her Bible and thought that she was glad to find it anywhere. The mornings were now so full of work, and as soon as the work was done Marvie Parker was sure to run in and claim Rachel for some scheme. To be sure it was not yet a week they had been by the sea, and yet it seemed to Rachel that things had settled down into a routine. She thought sadly of it, for Maria, her dear sister, seemed left out of everything. She would not have anything to do with the Parkers, and she seemed fully as loth to have to do with her own friends, the De Veres.

Rachel wondered what it meant and if there was anything she could do, if perhaps she was to blame in some way for having suggested this summer scheme. But no, when she thought of her mother's face taking on a glow of health from the life-giving breezes, and of her father, whose face had dropped its load of anxious care, and who seemed to be really enjoying life once more, she could not feel that she had done wrong; for surely it had turned out to be the best for all of them. No, it was clearly not her fault and she must not mourn over it as such. The next question came: What could she do for Maria? for she was ever one who was looking out to be her brother's keeper. She took up her Bible, from habit perhaps, for her own heart could not answer the questions that multiplied upon her. She felt it fully laid upon her to do something for her sister; but what could it be? Coaxing would not do, sacrifice would avail nothing, and neither would pity; she had tried them all. They merely seemed to irritate the loved one. The Bible opened of itself as it often did, to the sweet old call, "Come unto me, all ye that labor and are heavy laden, and I will give you rest. Take my yoke upon you, and learn of me; for I am meek and lowly in heart; and ye shall find rest unto your souls." Rachel had marked those verses when she was but a little girl with her new pen and some bright red ink. She had turned to them many, many times since, at first because they were familiar words and seemed like old friends on account of the red lines about them, and afterward because they had comforted her and had grown dear for their own sakes.

It was not strange that she opened to them now, and as she read them mechanically, though reverently, she did not linger there, for at first thought their message seemed more for her sister than herself, and she sighed as she half turned the leaf and wished that Maria could find rest, so that her life would be all peace and a joy that she could reflect everywhere. Then suddenly a thought stopped her hand as it slowly turned the leaf. Wait! Was not that message for her after all? She was burdened with the gloom of her sister. Might she not find rest from that as well as from some burden of her own? The dear Lord surely would not have her carry that burden. He would show her if she "came to him" what it was, if aught, she could do, to help lift the cloud that was over Maria, and she could come to Jesus and find rest and strength, so that even the burden of her sister's attitude would not disturb her calm, for it would be his calm. She turned the leaves slowly to another verse also marked and which had been her help many a time before. "Ye have not chosen me, but I have chosen you, and ordained you, that ye should go and bring forth fruit, and that your fruit should remain, that whatsoever ye shall ask of the Father in my name he may give it you." Then it was not her business to look after the fruit. She was to do his work because he had chosen her. She would do whatever he put into her hands to do, and meanwhile she had forgotten that whatsoever she would ask of the Father he would do it for her, and she might trust him to do it in his own good way and time. She would trust him with this dear sister. And so she knelt and poured out all her heart, full of worry, that had been so anxiously filling from day to day with the many little petty irritations that had arisen in kitchen and parlor and all over the house, and which she had tried to bear patiently but which had worn on her sweet spirit till now and then sharp words had escaped her. She told her Heavenly Father all and then asked for her dear sister's happiness as the greatest joy that could come. After that she smoothed her hair and rushed out into the kitchen with her heart full of love for Maria and trust for the answer to her prayer, and putting her arms impetuously around her warm and weary sister's neck gave her a great big hug and whispered softly: "'Ri, dear, forgive me. I've been awfully cross and teased you a great deal to do what you don't want to, and I have not helped you half enough. Will you forgive me? I'm sorry."

Now Maria was frying fish and was just in the act of turning over a large beautiful piece so that its perfections should remain unmarred. Besides, she was very warm and the stove had been acting abominably all the afternoon, and the brownness of the fish was only due to repeated shakings and coaxings on Maria's part with kindlings and bits of paper. Maria's hair was coming down, or was so nearly so that any movement on her part was precarious. Also she had burned her wrist and the pain was quite severe, aggravated as it was by the heat of the stove. Therefore Rachel's eager hug was scarcely pleasant just then, and Rachel's willingness to confess her fault, when she herself, the greater offender, was very unwilling to do so, irritated Maria more than words can tell. Perhaps she was not so much to blame, poor child, for she certainly was having a very uncomfortable time, largely her own fault though it was. She had just received a letter from one of her dear friends describing in detail the delights she was enjoying in a popular hotel in a lovely mountain resort. It was no wonder perhaps that her tone was ungracious.

"For pity's sake, do get out of my way, Rachel!" she said crossly. Don't you see what you're doing? You'll make me break that lovely piece of fish. I do wish you would ever be considerate. I'd much rather you'd show your sorrow by your actions than your words. Words are cheap."

With that Maria jerked the fish over and pushed the tea kettle and two or three pans around on the stove with such a nervous clatter that there was no chance for any more words even if Rachel had chosen to speak them, and Rachel, with the tears brimming over in her eyes, went her way to the train, full of sorrow that she had made another mistake. "I never seem to know what to do or say to please her," she said to herself. "I'm sure if she had spoken crossly to me and had asked me for forgive her I should have been so happy and forgotten it all, but it only seemed to make her feel crosser with me." Then Rachel remembered that it was not her work to look after results, and that she had taken her burden to her Heavenly Father and given it to him to carry. She must not pick it up again and bear it away with her; it was hers no longer. So she cast it all aside and hurried toward the station with a lighter heart.

Chapter 5

Maria stood on the piazza later that evening. The sunset glow was fading over the bay. The supper dishes were all washed and put away. There was nothing more to be done in the kitchen that night. She was at liberty to watch the pearl-colored sail that floated lazily on the pink and gray waters. Winthrop and Rachel had gone over to the pavilion directly after supper with Marvie Parker and her brother. They had not thought it worth while to ask Maria to join them to-night. Indeed, Rachel had hinted to her brother that perhaps it would be better to say nothing of their purpose to Maria, as everything of the kind seemed only to make her feel badly, and so for the first time since they had been at the seaside, they had gone off without coaxing her to go with them. Although Maria had declined these invitations quite curtly every time, she nevertheless felt cut by the omission to-night. Tears filled her eyes and blurred the pearl-colored sail as she thought how easily they could get along without her. Heretofore she had been the life of the family, the center of every excursion, the witty talker, the graceful leader in all. Now Rachel, her younger sister, hardly grown up as yet, seemed to have taken her place. She was not then so indispensable as she had thought. Even her father and mother had strolled away, arm in arm, like a pair of lovers, pointing out a bright star overhead or calling one another's attention to a sail in the distance. Maria felt very lonely.

Things had proved a great deal worse even than she had feared. She had supposed that after the family saw how uncomfortable things were going to be they would set about to right them in some way. They would perhaps go over to Spray View and take some sort of a respectable cottage where they could live in some decent style, as she phrased it to herself; there would be some enjoyment in that, and perhaps they would try to get another servant, though she herself would be willing to help in the kitchen and get along with a very poor one, if they might so save enough to be able to live in what seemed a respectable manner and, what was more important to her, would seem so to her friends. Then she would gladly welcome the De Veres and enjoy whatever they could offer her in the way of pleasure. Now, however, all was different. The family seemed entirely indifferent to their surroundings. They were actually happy. As she thought over it she realized that she could not remember to have ever seen her father and mother so thoroughly enjoying themselves before. She wondered that they did not see how unhappy she was. Oh, if she could but go away to that mountain resort where her friend Nellie Mayhew was having such a delightful time! To be sure she couldn't hope to share in everything because she could not buy the clothes in which to go to many of the entertainments and social affairs participated in by her friend, but she told herself that if she could but get there, be in that great hotel, one of its guests, she would trust herself but that with a very few dollars she could construct a wardrobe that would make her look well enough to vie with the others. But what was there here? She cast her eye about. Nothing but views and air! She curled her lip. And a father and mother and sister and brother who were too absorbed in their own pleasures to think of her or know that she was at home moping alone after a long day of hard work in the kitchen.

Now at that very minute father and mother, as they pointed out the stars and the sails, were discussing whether or not they could possibly manage to scrape together money enough to send Maria to the mountains in the style she wished to go. The mother, strange to say, was the one who objected this time.

"No, Richard," said she, "I cannot help feeling, even if we felt it right to afford it, that it would not be best. Maria is young yet, and while I think she is perfectly to be trusted to behave herself and take care of herself in every way, I am not sure but it is much the best thing for her to have the discipline of this summer. Already she had shown traits of character which I did not dream that she possessed. It has grieved me to the heart to see it. She has behaved in an utterly selfish and inconsiderate manner. You do not see it all day long as I do. She works, oh, works like a slave, harder than she ever worked before. I shall put a stop to that overwork pretty soon, for it is utterly unnecessary, a great part of it; but she is unlovely to me and to her sister, and as disagreeable as she knows how to be. I have been meditating how to go about it to have a talk with her, but it seemed best to wait a little while and study her present mood. Sometimes I am afraid she never has understood what it means to be a true Christian, she is so utterly rebellious at her lot."

And then in tender tones the father tried to excuse her and pity her, and so they talked and walked much farther and longer than they had expected to do, and the evening wore on while Maria sat alone, until from very weariness of herself and her own thoughts she was forced to go to bed.

It was the very next day that Maria was at last driven to the beach. It was Saturday. Winthrop had remained at the shore as his father felt he would not be needed that day at the store. The dinner being out of the way, and Maria's dress being soiled beyond hope of further use until it was washed, she retired to her room to make a severe but crisp toilet. If she could have found anything ugly to put on she would have done so, but fortunately for her nearly everything she possessed was tasteful and pretty, and the ugly things brought along for rainy weather or hard usage she had entirely used up for that week, therefore she was obliged to betake herself to a dainty sheer dimity, clear blue and white. The belt and collar of this dress were light blue ribbons with fluttering bows. Maria tried to fit on a linen collar and go without a belt, but the effect was so incongruous that she finally gave in to her own innate sense of beauty and put on the blue ribbons. Then her hair did not seem to harmonize with the costume, and by this time her sense of fitness had been sufficiently aroused to make her loosen her hair and coil it in the old way which was so becoming. Altogether she was quite like the familiar Maria when she was ready to leave the room. As she passed the window to pick up a novel that she had been reading, her eye caught sight of a double surrey, drawn by handsome horses, just turning the corner by their cottage. There were three ladies and a young man in the carriage and the elder lady was leveling a lorgnette at the unpretentious little dwelling. That lorgnette made up Maria's mind. That carriage contained the De Veres — mother, daughters, and son. They had come then, at the son's instance, to patronize the Hammonds. Maria, for one, did not intend to be investigated through a lorgnette. Her soul boiled at thought of it. Quick as a flash she caught up her book and a white parasol belonging to Rachel lying on the bed and flew out of the back door, straight across the sand lot to the next street and in line with the house so that she could not be seen from the carriage, which was now standing in front, and then turned and went swiftly to the most unfrequented portion of the broad beach she could find; there she established herself behind her parasol and a fortification of sand, and gave her mind to the reading of her book, assured that no unwelcome visitor could find her here.

Meanwhile Rachel, as she opened the door all smiles and played the gracious lady to the elegant Mrs. De Vere, remembered with satisfaction, not for her own sake but for Maria's, that she had caught a glimpse of Maria's blue dimity on the bed as she had passed the door, and that by this time she must be arrayed in it, for of course Maria would be obliged to come out of her shell now. But lo, when the anxious mother, who felt that Maria would need an extra word from her in order to make her put aside her new and foolish notions, came in search of her elder daughter, she could find her nowhere, and Rachel, being sent in search, though she looked in all Maria's former places of retreat, could find no trace of her. Much puzzled, Rachel returned to enjoy the call and forget all about her sister's disappearance.

Perhaps the De Veres thought it strange that Maria was absent from the house, especially as they knew from their brother and son that she had always been absent when he had called; but if they did so think they were far too well-bred to let any one know it. They were not nearly so overpowering in grandeur of manner as Maria had anticipated. Mrs. Hammond was quite charmed with the gracious and cordial friendliness of Mrs. De Vere, and a mutual liking seemed at once to draw the two elder ladies together. Meantime the young people planned innumerable pleasures in company, and the time flew by and the call was prolonged far beyond the usual length prescribed by fashion. In a most unceremonious manner, and one that would have shocked poor Maria beyond believing had she been present, the three De Veres followed Rachel through the sand and gayly fell upon George and Marvie Parker with a demand that they join their moonlight sail planned for the coming week. How it had come about Rachel could hardly understand, but they had found out she had friends in the Parkers and had delicately suggested the invitation and then proposed that they go at once and give it. Rachel wondered as they went whether Maria would blame her for it, and if she would make trouble about the Parkers going with them, and finally resolved to say nothing about it to her sister, letting things come about as they would.

Meanwhile Maria, clothed daintily, as was her habit to be, and having attained her purpose of getting away from her visitors unseen and unsuspected, felt much more at peace with the world than she had done for many a day. She settled herself without the usual hard cloud upon her brow to really enjoy her book. So much are the clothes of value that the subtle consciousness of being well-dressed has often power to lift one for the time at least above a seeming fret of circumstance or sordidness of surroundings.

Now had Rachel Hammond been consulted as to the answering of her earnest prayers for her sister, she would have said that the most unpromising thing that could happen for Maria was to have her run away from the De Veres and spend the entire afternoon by herself in a lonely part of the beach, reading a highly-wrought novel wherein the heroine suffered impossible things and was crowned with untold rewards for her pains. Rachel would have said a pleasant afternoon in the company of pleasant people, planning a delightful excursion, forgetting things that might have been, and learning to be interested in things that are and are to be, would have been the best thing for her sister. But God knew better. He was leading this child of his through a narrow thorny path, it is true, but through the only straight road that would take her home. She sat there and read, and as she had not visited the beach before and knew little the peculiarities of wind and tide, she did as most newcomers do, settled herself by the edge of the surf, as near as seemed safe and pleasant, that she might watch the water. Then after a good look she forthwith forgot to watch the water in the tide of the fortunes of her heroine. The ocean's tide at that time was going out, but almost at its turn. It receded a little and a little, and Maria read on, and by and by it did not recede, and then it gained a little and a little, until it crept nearer and nearer to the seat upon the sand and the straying blue ribbon that fluttered out from the white silk parasol. Now a larger wave came and almost stretched its lip of foam to kiss the foam of white lace on the blue dimity ruffles; then it went back again for a while to gather force, and now another came and did just touch the dainty ruffle and dampen it, but still the wearer read on oblivious to recession or approach. She had turned herself sidewise to keep the ocean glare from her page and did not notice. Moreover, the heroine was just on the point of being rescued from a desert island on which she had been cast with a noble hero who loved her, by an ignoble lover who had come in search of her. The situation was a thrilling one and Maria had no eyes for aught but the story. Neither did she see a young man who was sauntering leisurely down the beach toward her from the direction of the lighthouse, a mile or two away.

The Rev. Howard Fairfield, in the most unclerical dress he could find in his very unclerical wardrobe, had been visiting the Point Rock lighthouse, and joking with its keeper, entering with zest into all the stories the old man told of his wild life as a young sailor, himself posing as a young man who understood and enjoyed all such escapades. Now he was walking slowly along the beach and, wholly unconscious of any inconsistency or incongruity, was engaged in weaving the wonders which he had just seen and heard of God's providence and man's skill into a fine illustration that should well set off the conclusion of the address, both eloquent and learned, which he was preparing for the first sermon he should preach after his vacation was ended. He was a very young man for the important charge he occupied, and he had chosen this simple, quiet summer resort as a suitable place for him to spend his vacation, with the idea that the absolute quiet if not loneliness of it would conduce to the rest and study which he meant to alternate so judiciously, and thus send him back to his city church thoroughly fortified in health and with a store of material for sermons for the winter's campaign.

He was not an unspiritual minister, neither was he ashamed of his calling; but in college and seminary he had acquired some "advanced" notions concerning the doffing of clerical clothes and the "clerical manner" which, while they might be good in a degree, had been carried by him to their utmost extremity. He delighted, on going to a place, to keep the people from finding out that he was a minister. Indeed, he carried this so far that he would sometimes allow himself to be taken for almost anything else rather than let others know his true character or profession. He had a fancy that he could do a great deal more good in this way, by entering into other people's lives and sympathies and not letting them feel that the good he did was because it was his business to do so. Perhaps there was truth in this, the great drawback being that he spent so much time in entering into people's sympathies and lives that he frequently forgot or found it awkward to do the good that might have resulted from the influence he had gained thereby. Sometimes too, others felt that he allowed the line between right and wrong to be glossed over a trifle in this "entering-in" business. He called it "being all things to all men." However that may be, he was a student, an eloquent preacher, somewhat conceited because of the extraordinary praise he had received during his short pastorate, and very much opinionated, but nevertheless very much in earnest. He considered himself very spiritual indeed, and in his heart longed to be all that his Lord would have him be. In person he was handsome, with a scholarly air, graceful in manner, a little distant but exceedingly attractive to most people, especially when he chose to be so. Rachel Hammond, had she known him, would have considered him the most unlikely person to help her sister Maria that could be found, and yet he was coming toward her on the beach and the waves were creeping toward her on the sand, and the Lord was ordering it all. For the winds and the waves obey his will, even in so seemingly slight an affair as this.

The young man had advanced quite near to Maria and without particularly noticing her, except to realize that his favorite combination of light blue and white was lying over there on the sand making a pretty picture against the background of sky and sea. As he drew nearer he saw it was a young woman with a shapely hand that held a book, and he wondered, because he was a student of human nature, what sort of a young woman she was, reading thus alone so close beside the sea, and what was the book which so absorbed her that she did not mark the approach of the hungry waves. He thought he must warn her if she did not look up before the next wave, and lingered a little to see if she stirred. Then, before he could think further, there came one of those unexpectedly large waves which take people, and almost themselves it seems, by surprise, and rush and tumble in mad glee far beyond any predecessor. It not only touched and soaked the crisp ruffles of the dimity, but it merrily dashed into the young lady's lap, wetting her feet and book and sending her flying back from the spot in alarm. And then it calmly seized the white silk parasol which was a treasured present from a rich uncle to Rachel, and boasted a solid gold handle, and hurled it out in its retreating arms, a toy upon the billows. Maria, finding herself on solid ground and seeing her sister's precious parasol tossed on the water, made another dash to catch it on the crest of the next wave, but the water was again too quick for her and it floated out, this time a little farther, where the breakers tossed the delicate thing so rudely that Maria despaired for its frail structure. At this juncture the young man standing by took two strides in the saucy waters and brought the wet and dripping thing to Maria with as much dignity as he could command considering the wet and flapping condition of his white duck trousers.

It was certainly an embarrassing situation for both young people, but the Reverend Howard Fairfield rather enjoyed carrying off trying situations in a graceful manner, and he certainly did himself justice in this instance, to the admiration of the young woman concerned.

"Oh, not at all, let me carry it home for you," he said, as she reached her hand for the sunshade. "Your cottage is near by, is it not? Nothing is very far away from anything else in this place, is it?" Here he stopped to pick up her book, actuated more perhaps by a curiosity to know its name than anything else. "No, no, let me carry it. You will have enough to do to walk in this sand with your wet gown. I am going this way, you know, and it's no trouble whatever."

And so Maria, much against her will, walked the length of the beach to her home with a stranger, a young man, her dress wet and bedraggled, her borrowed parasol and book carried by him, and his own costume rather the worse for water. It was altogether too dramatic for Maria's liking to appear at home in this condition after the lofty way in which she had been acting. She knew her brother would never cease teasing her. She was trying to plan some way of retreat, or getting rid of the stranger who was chatting pleasant nothings to which she need not reply except by monosyllables, when lifting her eyes she saw her sister, accompanied by the Misses De Vere, their brother, and Miss Parker, coming toward them. There was no escape. They were on the point of meeting. It was horrible! Maria caught her breath, and then she heard her sister's exclamation and knew there was no hope but to turn and face the situation.

Chapter 6

It turned out that Howard Fairfield was an old college friend of Roland De Vere, and the two young men met with great delight and gayety. Introductions followed all around, and Maria's chagrin was covered by this ceremony, until she had time to recover herself and smile an apologetic retreat, leaving the minister to make explanations. The merry little party, however, followed her, Rachel, who had hurried on with her sister, was kind and eager to help, solicitous lest she might catch cold, and plied her with questions as to how it happened. The others came more slowly to the cottage and chatted a little till Rachel and Maria, who had hastily replaced the dimity skirt by one of black serge, again appeared. Then the De Veres said they really must be going home, and drove away with promises for the next day and many merry words about the moonlight excursion. The minister lingered a little after the departure of the carriage, politely saying he hoped no harm had been done Miss Hammond by her unexpected sea bath; thanked her for his part in the affair which had resulted in so pleasant a meeting with his old friends; and bowed himself away to the hotel, leaving a good impression behind him.

As he walked he reflected:

"Two very pretty girls. I had not bargained for friends this summer. Perhaps it may interfere with my plans for hard study; but, after all, why shouldn't I take a little recreation? I can't enjoy ladies' society at home, because if I look at one young woman more than another, I feel as though all the gossips of both sexes were proclaiming marriage banns from the housetops for us; but I don't believe it is good for a man to be forever with men alone. One forgets how to treat one's sister after a while. It was a pleasant interruption to the monotony of the place to meet De Vere. I always liked him in college. Well, things are turning out better than I had expected. I don't know but that I shall stay the month out, after all. At any rate, I won't give up my room yet until I have time to decide."

Then he went in to prepare for supper.

The afternoon's experience had done this for Maria: she was drawn out of her shell at last and by necessity pledged to go on the moonlight excursion. She reluctantly gave up her role of martyr little by little, and by Sabbath evening was sufficiently herself to go to church. It really would be more bearable than this continual staying in the house, which was beginning to wear on her patience. Besides, her brief glimpse of young, merry company the day before had made her restless for more.

There was no settled minister at Lone Point. The church itself had been built by the donations of visitors, who had spent their energies one summer in raising the money and making as pretty a little house of worship as could be desired for the chance sojourner by the sea. Some of those who lived for a large part of the year in the place took it upon themselves to keep the services going all the summer. Occasionally there were ministers visiting over Sunday who preached, to the great delight of the little audiences; but during the rest of the time, earnest workers from city churches, who were not taking a vacation from their religion as well as from their other work, took turns in either reading a sermon or making a short talk to the little company gathered there, and the songs of praise swelled forth from worshiping hearts as truly thankful as if they had been feeding on the bread of life dealt out by regularly ordained hands. These services were divided among several men, who were always willing to do with their might what their hands found to do. Rev. Howard Fairfield, in spite of his experiences of the day before in finding old friends, had succeeded in keeping his incognito so thoroughly that no one dreamed of asking him to preach, for which he was in his heart truly thankful, since he really needed the rest. He had perhaps, though, a little of the natural feeling of a man who was fresh from the ecclesiastical atmosphere of the seminary, a slight doubt as to the genuineness of Sabbath services conducted by a man who not only had not been through a seminary course, but who was not even college bred. It amounted almost to a feeling of sacrilege, as though they were "playing church" as children do, to have the laymen handle sacred phrases and forms. Young theologues are apt to feel at first more anxious for the orthodoxy of the worship than for its spirituality, though if you asked them, they might tell you it could not be truly spiritual unless it was thoroughly orthodox. Mr. Fairfield sat through the morning address, given by a white-haired brother who had served his church for full fifty years, and was amply competent, by reason of his wide Christian experience, to have ministered even to the needs of a theological student. His face wore a look of gentle toleration, which scarcely masked the critical impatience he was feeling all the while. He told himself that an hour spent at home with his Bible would have been more profitable. But by reason of the command of his Lord, which he reverenced, not to "forget the assembling of yourselves together," he went again in the evening.

Now in the evening the service was led by a younger man who had spent some time in a training school for Christian workers, and who, though thoroughly versed in the Bible, was yet not so thoroughly trained in the English language. He did not attempt a sermon. The service was largely composed of song. His own part in it was two or three gentle, earnest talks interspersed with illustrations, carrying home to the heart the true meaning of as many Bible verses, whose practical teachings were linked together into a single, fully developed theme. There was singing between each of these talks. They seemed to scarcely belong together, and yet when the hour was passed, the thoughtful soul went forth with something to carry into daily life to help in making ready for heaven.

The service was short. No one need complain that he grew weary. They issued forth into the bright moonlight from the cheery little chapel, some with kindly greetings, some with earnest words or merry ones upon their lips. The minister, quite as a matter of course, walked along beside the two young ladies he had met the day before, and they chatted pleasantly as they walked. He stopped a moment on their piazza to watch the moonlight on the bay, and they began talking, for want of any other topic of common interest, about the place, the people, the church, and the day itself with its services.

"I supposed, of course, we should hear you preach this evening, Mr. Fairfield," said Maria pleasantly. She was regaining her good-humor and quite liked the young man. She had never had a ministerial friend. It was something new and interesting.

"Oh, no indeed," said the minister laughingly. "I took good care no one should know that I was anything other than the most ordinary of idle young men on a pleasure trip. I don't want to preach. It isn't fair when one is off on a vacation. It isn't fair to my people, either, you know. They expect me to rest and not use up my strength on some other church when they are sending me away to recruit it. You don't know how a minister feels when he gets away from his work. I have a clerical friend who said last year, when he started off on his vacation, 'No more preaching, no more praying, no more reading of the Bible, for six whole weeks,' with a sigh of relief. I wouldn't go quite so far as that myself," laughingly; "but at the same time it is a relief to get away from all reminders of work when one goes off to rest."

Maria laughed gayly at the story. She thought the young minister very clever. There was a prospect of something enlivening, after all, in this desolate place. But Rachel glanced up quickly. "Did he really say that?" she said with a troubled look in her eyes; "a minister of Jesus Christ?"

There was something embarrassing in the anxious expression of those clear eyes that made Mr. Fairfield, for the first time since he had told that story, reflect that it was not altogether the feeling for a minister of Jesus Christ to have, even if the expressing of the thought had been merely in fun. He was a trifle vexed with himself for having told the story and began excusing his friend, and finally mildly condemning him. But there was an uncomfortable consciousness of something, the minister did not exactly know what, which he was certain he would have to face out with his own conscience after he got by himself.

"Well," said Maria, hastening to cover what she considered to be an impoliteness on her sister's part, "I suppose it's all very well for the poor ministers who have to work all the time, but I must say I don't enjoy hearing a man who doesn't know how to conduct a service. Did you ever see such a hash as that meeting to-night? Upon my word, I began to wonder if they wouldn't ask us all to get up and recite some little verses or stories next." She ended in a bubble of laughter over her own fun. She was in the habit of saying bright, daring things and of having them laughed at. The young minister was no exception. He laughed. He was tired of loneliness and her laugh rested him.

"Well," he said, "that man did very well for a layman. I fancy he got some of his thoughts out of some one of Moody's books, or something like that, but really that first bit of a talk he gave us on what we live for was not so bad. I never heard that story about the old sea captain before. It did sound odd when he kept repeating 'When I'm at the North Pole I live sperm whale, when I'm at the South Pole I live sperm whale.' It was well expressed too, and a good illustration. I suppose some of those old fishermen would say for them to live was fishing. I know a man in the city whose entire life is for money, just like the man he was speaking of to-night. It really was a good thought to bring before those young people."

"But," said Maria laughing again, "did you hear him say 'opportoonity'?" She brought out the broad "oo" in exact imitation of the tone in which it had been uttered so earnestly a few minutes before. But her laugh was interrupted by Rachel.

"Mr. Fairfield," said she, lifting those clear, thoughtful eyes of hers with the moonlight shining into her pure face, "do you suppose that it is possible for any one — that is, for young people — well, say for — me, to be able to say with perfect truth, 'For me to live is Christ'?"

The minister felt once more that strange embarrassment, mingled this time with a desire to answer the question aright and a feeling of inability to do so. His pastorate had been a short one, his experience was small, and there had not come to him many times in this earnest way an inquirer who seemed to be searching for the light. It is true, in a theological sense, the question was easy enough to answer; but he knew by the look on Rachel's face that she meant more than an ordinary question asked out of curiosity. She really wanted to know in order that she might if possible use the knowledge.

He searched his mind and his catechism for a suitable reply, but none would come. At last with his usual tone of positiveness, which carried weight with so many who questioned him, he replied: "Why, yes, surely; why not? If you are a Christian, you certainly can say that."

"No," said Rachel, shaking her head in a thoughtful, troubled way, "I can't. I have been thinking about it ever since Mr. Brown told that story about the sperm whale. My life isn't 'sperm whale,' but I am afraid I would have to say if I answered truthfully, for me to live is having my own way, having a good time, and having everything go just as I planned it. I'm afraid I put that above Christ. I certainly must, or I would be happy with whatever Christ gives me, if for me to live were Christ."

Maria listening was surprised. She had thought uncomfortably that evening during the meeting that for herself to live was to have her own way, but she would never have laid that charge at her gentle sister Rachel's door. Rachel, who was always willing to give up when others insisted on having their own way! But Maria did not like to have the conversation drift into so solemn a theme, and she hailed the coming of her brother upon the porch with relief.

"Mr. Fairfield," she interrupted just here, "you have not met my brother yet."

During the introduction that followed, Rachel slipped away. She felt that she wanted to be quiet and think. Perhaps sometimes she could find that minister alone for a few minutes and he would have some help for her; ministers all knew how to help, and he was young and she would not be afraid to ask him, unless—unless he should be like that other dreadful minister, who had said that awful thing about not wanting to read the Bible or pray for six whole weeks. She shuddered as she thought of it again, and her literal soul was greatly disturbed that a minister should be so like the rest of the world. But just now she wanted her Bible to answer her, and she went softly in and lighting her little shaded lamp went to her Rock for help.

Mr. Fairfield did not remain long that evening. It was Sunday, and he did not as a rule make calls on the Sabbath, unless it were an errand of necessity or mercy. He looked about for Rachel as he left, and was both troubled and relieved to find her gone—troubled, because he felt in some indistinct way that he had not done his duty; relieved, because "what business had duty to follow him around on his vacation?"

After all, the little girl's question had been true enough. How many people were there in the world who really could say that? Could he himself? Was it Christ for him to live, or was it fine sermons, a good name, a large church roll? Did he think most when he preached of whether he was speaking to the hearts of men and leading them to see Jesus, or was he looking after the praise of men? Was he not sometimes looking about to see if there were a committee from that big Chicago church sitting in some dim corner of the room and wondering what they thought of that rounded sentence? Could it be possible that for him to live was getting to be whether he would in a few years receive a call to a better church with a larger salary and a greater name?

He wandered down by the sea in the deep moonlight where he could be alone with his conscience and his God. As he walked to his retired musing place he said to himself: "How strange it is that that man, who is evidently not a highly educated man, can with his few words so touch a heart that it will ask itself such questions as that girl asked me to-night! Did any one ever go home from one of my sermons and ask himself such searching questions as that, I wonder? There it is again. I am looking out to see what other people think of me and my words. No, not all that either. Perhaps I'm looking out now to see what God thinks of me. I must find that out to-night."

Chapter 7

Does Satan also walk sometimes beside the sea? Perhaps he saw the trend of this young man's thoughts, and hoped to turn them aside. Perhaps he feared too much the searching questions that would surely come to this thoughtful heart, which if once awakened to itself and its possibilities would be a dangerous enemy to the powers of darkness and of this world. Or it may be that what happened next was just another link in God's wonderful chain of influence that was to draw this disciple nearer to himself.

"Ho! I say! Stop a minute!" shouted a voice, that at last made itself heard above the roar of the waves, sufficiently at least to attract the attention of the preoccupied man.

The voice proved to belong to a fellow-boarder at the hotel. "Is that you, Mr. Fairfield?" called the man, hurrying along the sand almost out of breath with his efforts; "I wasn't sure in this uncertain moonlight. There's a telegram down at the hotel for you and they've been hunting all over creation for you. They went to church but found it closed. The boy came over from Spray View with it and he is almost frantic to get back and seems to consider it a part of his duty not to surrender the message till the right man turns up, though a number of us offered to pay the requisite fifty cents, the ridiculous price they charge to bring a message over to this forsaken spot."

The minister thanked his informant, turned hurriedly and retraced his steps along the beach to the hotel, wondering meanwhile if aught had befallen his mother or sister far away on a foreign trip, or if some member of his church was lying very ill, or perhaps dead.

Telegrams may mean so much or so little, they always set one's heart beating faster till he has them safely read.

It proved to be only a notice of a special business meeting of importance to himself and his church, to which he was called home early the next day to accommodate a member of the church committee who was himself called suddenly away and wished some matters attended to before he left. The minister stood on the moonlit piazza a moment after he read it, and crushed the yellow paper irritably between his fingers. It did not suit him to rush back to the city in the heat just now. He had expected that meeting to be deferred until the first week in September. It annoyed him too, to have such a message as this sent on Sabbath evening. He did not stop to analyze why, except to think that it might have waited, or have been sent the night before. A feeling came over him of how utterly it lacked harmony with the day's quiet resting and his evening's high thoughts. So much was he disturbed in mind that he did not again go back to his musings by the sea. His line of thought as well as his walk was broken off. The hour was late. He must take a very early train in the morning. He must prepare his mind for the business in town which awaited him, and there were a few preparations he must make for his hurried journey. So he went reluctantly up to his room, wondering vaguely whether he would ever get back to the time and place to have that talk out with himself alone by the ocean and resolving that he would take the first opportunity for it. He remembered the moonlight sail planned for that week, and new friends he had found and the old ones he had discovered to be near by, and resolved to leave his baggage here in this secluded place beside the sea and return on the evening train or by the next day if possible, rather than pack up and move on to some new place as he had half resolved to do three days before. Somehow there seemed to be a new charm to the place now that he had found friends, even though what he had wished to get away from was all social obligations. He was interested in the family who had such a pleasant little cottage around by the bay. He believed he would like to talk further with that bright, intellectual older sister, and perhaps even hear more of the flower-faced younger sister's searching, innocent questions. He felt that they were not bad training for him in many ways.

Mr. Fairfield was scarcely seated in the uptown car the next morning on his arrival in the city when he became aware that two bright eyes were watching an opportunity for their owner to claim his attention, and looking up, he beheld across the car a young lady who was one of his parishioners. She greeted him with gushing frankness. There was always a good-natured openness about Miss Lou Marlow. Everybody called her Miss Lou, except those who went a little further and called her "Lou." She was hail-fellow-well-met with every one, as intimate on the first day of acquaintance as she bade fair to be in ten years from that time, a large, pretty girl, with good spirits to overflowing, and a laugh and joke for every one. The minister always felt as if he had come in contact with a splash of brilliant sunlight unrelieved by any softening shadows when he met her, and yet she affected no one unpleasantly; there was too much true good-nature and native humor about her. Still, one always looked with her to have their faults or virtues hauled out and laughed over with jolly, ruthless hand, and for this reason the minister rather dreaded a tête-à-tête with Miss Lou. He particularly shrank from one in a street car, as Miss Lou's voice, like her taste in dress, was not altogether subdued, but she had moved to one side and made room for him beside her on the seat, and her movement was unmistakable. Besides, she plainly showed that she had something good to tell and would scarcely be deterred from it by so small a circumstance as having to talk across a car aisle. The minister changed his seat, but as he did so put on his most dignified air in order to check as much as possible a too exuberant manner, should such appear.

"Oh, Mr. Fairfield, when did you come back? Why I'm so astonished," began Miss Lou volubly. "Really this is quite a coincidence. I had the strangest dream about you last night, and it was so real and vivid, and now to think I should meet you when I thought you were far away! It really looks as though there must have been something meant by it," and she giggled uncontrollably.

Mr. Fairfield looked nervously about the car to see if there were others of his acquaintance present, and his informant went on between her gurgles of laughter.

"Oh, it was too funny!"

"Yes?" said the minister helplessly. He hoped it was nothing connected with selecting a wife for him or anything of that sort, but he greatly feared from the young lady's tone it might be some silly dream linking him with some one of his congregation. That it would be something embarrassing he felt sure. He waited helplessly, hoping he would be given the grace to keep from looking too red and angry if it were, and prepared a hearty unfelt laugh to bring forth at need to cover her telling.

"Why, I dreamed I was riding in a car down this very street, and it was summer just as it is now, and you were away, at least we all supposed you were away, on your vacation, and suddenly you came into the car and spoke to me, and you told me that you had been called home to attend a funeral." Here Miss Lou uttered another spasmodic giggle. "And I asked you who it was and you said it was that little Lillie Hartley,-don't you know,-the carpenter's little girl who sings in the children's Sunday-school exercises so sweetly. You told me when the funeral was to take place and asked me to come and sing, and I said I would. Well, I went to the house at the hour, and we sat there, and sat there, and you didn't come, and it got awful late and still you hadn't come, and they had to go way out to Mt. Laurel to bury, so they got awfully worried, and finally they sent after you, and the girl where you board said you were in your study,-that is, she hadn't seen you come out,-and they went up to the study and found the door locked on the inside. The girl said that was the way you always had it when you were studying hard, and they called and knocked and got no answer, so at last they burst in the door and found you sitting there dead by your desk with your book of funeral prayers, or whatever you call it, beside you, with the page open to the children's burial service, and everything looking as if you were just ready to go out, and you dead! There was an awful time just beginning, but I woke up and didn't see the end. But wasn't it too funny that you should come in the car just now? Oh! here's my street; I must get off. I hope you haven't come home to any funeral. Good-bye; wasn't it funny?" and the loud-voiced young woman swung herself off the car, having completed her last two or three sentences as she moved hastily toward the door, and ended with a loud giggle in which the minister felt somewhat called upon to join, at least with a sickly smile. Then he sat back with a scowl of annoyance on his face. Of all disagreeable things to happen, this seemed among the most disagreeable just now. Not that he cared about the dream, of course not. He was neither superstitious nor nervous, but it grated on his fine sensibilities to have the solemn and ridiculous mixed in this way. He could scarcely brush it aside and forget his unpleasant entrance into the city. He bought a morning paper and tried to bury his mind in that, but he felt irritated even when he reached the house he called home, and went to his rooms for any letters or papers that might have gathered during his two weeks' absence, which had not been forwarded.

It was almost time for him to go out again to meet the board of trustees, when the house servant tapped at his door.

"Please, Mr. Fairfield," she said, "there's a man downstairs as has been here yesterday to see you, and when he found you wasn't here he come back again this morning to get your address, and I told him you had come back unexpected, and he's most awful anxious to see you."

"You don't know who it is, Jane? He didn't send up his card?" said the minister, anxiously consulting his watch. "I have an engagement in five minutes. I can't spare much time."

"No, sir," said Jane deprecatingly, "I don't; but he's a plain-lookin' body, and if you're busy I'll just tell him to come back again when you can see him."

"Oh, no, I'll go down," he said, gathering up his hat and some papers he wished to carry with him to the meeting.

It struck a chill to the minister's heart when he reached the hall to see plain, honest Mr. Hartley standing there, heavy-eyed, his whole figure dropping with unmistakable sorrow.

"Mr. Fairfield," he said, the tears beginning to start to his eyes, "I'm so glad you're here. I made certain you'd come when you heard; but I didn't have the face to trouble you so far; but the wife she did want you and say she couldn't have Lillie buried without her minister she loved so much, and it's to be to-morrow afternoon. And could you get somebody to sing? The wife, she wanted 'Safe in the Arms of Jesus,' same as Lillie sung herself last Children's Day in the church."

There was something very strange about it all. The minister thought of it after the man had gone, tarrying until he had to hasten not to be late to his meeting. The broken-hearted father had had so much to say about his little girl and how she loved her minister and how ready she had been to go to heaven! He laughed a mirthless laugh as he walked down the street in the hot sunshine and told himself that if he were a superstitious man this would be a good chance for him to run away. He held his head high and rather gloried in the fact that he was not superstitious, but in spite of it all he could not get away from Miss Lou's dream and the strange coincidence of the death of the child. He wiped the perspiration from his brow and longed for the cooling sea breeze he had left behind, half wishing he had told the father he could not stay and suggested a brother minister for the funeral. Then his heart accused him sorely as he remembered how the father's face had lighted up when he saw him coming down the stairs. He knew in his heart he never could have done such a thing, and was glad with his better nature that he was here and able to be at least of so much comfort to the stricken parents.

It was strange too, after the day's business was over and he had time to think about the funeral and remember the father's request for a singer, that the only singer to be found in the city who could possibly be at leisure at the hour of the funeral was Miss Lou Marlow. He knew she would come, and that her voice was rich and sweet, though not so highly cultivated as some others. He knew that her generous nature would be willing to do anything in her power for the sorrowful family, and that she often went to funerals to sing, and people liked her singing then because she sang with so much sympathy in her voice. There were good things about Miss Lou, and her pastor knew it. Nevertheless he searched far and thoroughly before he made up his mind that there was no one else to ask. He told himself it was not in the least for his own sake he did this, but merely because he shrank from what she might say in her blunt way, and the giggles with which she would intersperse it, whatever it was. He sent a message by Jane at last with the request of the father and mother, leaving himself out entirely. He did not care to have Miss Lou see any more likeness to her dream than was necessary.

Then he shut himself into his study, and as he turned the key, he remembered Miss Lou's words vividly, how they had come and knocked and called with no answer, and how they had burst in the door and found him dead. Nevertheless, he locked the door as usual and sat down in the study chair, as was his custom, beside his desk and tried to think. A strong feeling of destiny laid hold upon his mind. He felt as if he were living out something that had been laid down for him to do. He felt as if he could not help it, but must go on living it out to the end, even to dying. He could not shake it off. He had heard of people dying with less cause than this, just dying because they thought the time had come. He didn't feel afraid that he should, but in spite of him, he began to wonder what he would do, what he would like to do before he died, and to realize if it all should prove to be true, what a short time he had in which to prepare! There were papers to be put in shape, if he knew he was going. There were messages to leave; there was his mother and sister and his church. How could he leave his church? His work was not completed. He had not carried out his plans; he had not won the souls he hoped, intended. There were those young men who sat in the back seat by the door and whispered sometimes and never listened. Something ought to have been done for them. He had in times past thought seriously of applying for a policeman. Now it seemed as if he might have won them some other way. Was it forever too late?

There was—why, there were all his people, as they started up one by one! He might have brought comfort to one and a word of warning to another; and what had his preaching been, now that he faced the thought of its being over forever? True he had spent hours of labor and study upon his sermons; but while the sentences were finished and perfect as to grammar and rhetoric, and sometimes even eloquent, would that stand before God? And then he looked upon himself. Was his soul ready to meet his Master? Had he not been living selfishly, serving the Master as second and himself as first, living a self-life, gratifying his desire for the intellectual, filling his soul with ambitions for a high calling on earth rather than one in heaven? Then the souls he had been set to keep! What of them? While he had supplied them with the flowers of his oratory, or sought to, had they starved for lack of a little of the plain bread of life? He was searching his own heart and accusing himself now as he never had done before. He seemed to realize all that was about him, to know that the time was near for the funeral, that he must prepare, and yet he could not turn his thoughts to anything else. Once he reached out his hand for the book of forms and funeral services, and opened it, finding, as if by necessity, the little child's funeral service, but he could not read the words. He could only think that he must set his own heart right. If some one had stepped to the door just then and asked him the questions, "Are you afraid you are going to die in a few minutes? Are you nervous about this dream and the strange coincidence?" he would have answered almost wonderingly; "No, certainly not. I am not afraid to die. I know that these strange coincidences cannot hasten or delay the day of my death one second. I know that all is just as it was with me before I heard of these things. But in some way I have suddenly realized what it would be to leave this world and my work—my unfinished work—with these few moments' notice. I know that it is not impossible that I may die at any moment. If not now, it may come, *will* come, at some equally unexpected moment, and I feel that I am not ready—not so ready as I *would* be."

That was the undercurrent of his reasoning as he sat in the study chair, his face buried in his hands, and thought. And now he heard footsteps below, and it reminded him again that the time of the funeral was near, perhaps was almost come. In a few minutes, if he did not hasten, some one would actually come to his door to see why he had not come, or to say the carriage had been waiting and the people were wondering where he was.

Down upon his knees he dropped and spent those last few minutes in prayer, such prayer as he had never known before. Out of the far depths of his soul rose a mighty cry for forgiveness for his past, a great longing for the Saviour to come into his heart and cast out the self in him. Yet, as he knelt, the room was still as death. Not one audible syllable did he utter. It was perhaps such preparation as he had never made before for any of his public duties of the ministry. And when a few minutes later Jane did tap at the door to say the carriage had come, he rose from his knees, his face shining with a holy light of something deeper than he understood, and found that he had forgotten the curious dream and had not watched to see if he should die at all, but had been getting ready to live. He took the little book of services and went to the funeral, feeling utterly unprepared, and yet, strangely enough, not worried about it. He knew that preparation was worth all he had felt it to be, but that there were times also when God took that out of his messengers' hands and made them look at him for a while, and then supplied the words. And the words were supplied now. Verse after verse of comfort from God's holy word, with now and then a comment of tender explanation, were all he essayed; but surely the Lord himself guided his selections, made as he rode along in the carriage, for the broken hearts were comforted and the sorely wounded spirits bound up, and many other hearts not so sore wounded, but there from sympathy, were touched, and made to feel how near and sure and grave a thing is death, and the life to come.

As the clear, rich voice of Miss Lou broke the stillness of the room that followed the minister's prayer, in the tender old refrain of "Safe in the arms of Jesus," the minister, listening, remembered the dream, and bowed his head in thankfulness that he was yet alive with a hope before him of better living and better work, Christ living in him, the hope of glory, and no longer the hope of the glory of his own intellectual powers.

Chapter 8

It was night, and along the coast the wind raged wildly. The ocean fairly thundered its waves against the stolid black sands. The sky was of black velvet, slashed here and there with vivid flashes of lightning. Above the roar of the waves and the voice of the wind came the distant roll of the thunder as it muttered its approach.

In the cottages the dwellers nestled closer in their beds at thought of the comfort about them which seemed all the more delicious as they slept, indistinctly aware of a storm without. Mrs. Hammond gave a sigh as she turned over on her pillow, a sigh of relief that now there would be rain water in the cistern again and they would not be obliged to scrimp and save water on account of having to carry it so far, from the hotel well. It was a little thing to give comfort, perhaps, but she felt that lack of water had been one thing which had made Maria's life so hard the last few days, and the mother was troubled on Maria's account. Now it seemed as if things might be a little easier, and Maria was getting in with pleasant young friends, and perhaps their summer would be a happy one after all. It was such a comfort that this pleasant little house had been procurable, so cheap that they need not feel they were extravagant in taking this vacation. Then she slept soundly again, aware that the storm was almost ready to break, and glad of the refreshing sound thereof.

The great raindrops came at last and pattered rapidly down on the high roof, sounding almost like tumblers full, they were so large, and soon the rain fairly poured down. Rachel was awakened by the cold wet touch of a great drop falling plump upon her cheek. It startled her at first and she could not make out what it was, but before she was fully awake it was followed by another, and they fell at regular intervals. Rachel remembered having read somewhere about criminals who were sentenced to be executed by a peculiar method, the falling of a drop of water at regular intervals upon the person from a great height, for a certain set length of time. She had wondered at the time how this method could possibly cause death, as she knew it did, the long-continued strain upon the nervous system of even so little an annoyance as this, being awful to endure. She lay still, trying to see how it would seem, so interested for a few minutes that she hardly realized that her pillow was growing quite wet. Then she heard movements in her mother's room—her father and mother conversing in low tones, a match struck—the pushing of furniture about. She realized the roof was leaking in there as well. She could hear drops falling out in the room on the floor, and now a new one that sounded on the dressing bureau. Suddenly her sister Maria started up in bed with an angry exclamation that "there was water falling on her head." It all struck Rachel as exceedingly funny. Somehow such things always showed on the humorous side to Rachel, quiet and sober as she usually was. This was one thing which often irritated Maria very greatly, this having Rachel laugh at a trying time. Rachel always said it was better to laugh than to cry or be cross, and she must do something, and Maria replied that she had a "hystericky nature." She should control her feelings. Then Maria would proceed to control hers by being cross. But Rachel always forgot about hysterics and laughed, a pure, mirthful laugh.

It gurgled forth now, sweet and amused, as she hurriedly got out of bed and brought her sun umbrella, raising it over their heads as she got in again. It was very funny to camp out in real picnic style and have to go to bed under an umbrella. She enjoyed it.

Maria lay down again angrily.

"Rachel Hammond, I do wish you would grow up and learn not to giggle when anything happens. I'm sure I don't see anything funny in being leaked on when you are fast asleep."

That was the beginning. Before many minutes had elapsed the movements of furniture in the next room together with the conversation back and forth and the various excursions for waterproofs and awning cloths with which to protect the beds from the constantly increasing drops, had thoroughly awakened Maria and roused her temper to a pitch quite beyond endurance. She found fault with the house, and the landlord, and said it was what might have been expected of the cottage at the ridiculous price they paid for it. Then when the family had hushed into silence she began at her sister, in a low whisper:

"Rachel, I think you really ought to try to realize that you are grown up in years if you are not in mind yet. I meant to speak to you about a thing you did Sunday night that made me so ashamed I didn't know what to do; but I haven't had a chance to talk to you about it; you manage to keep yourself so busy away from us except just when you are helping with the work, that I never have any chance to see my sister any more," this in an injured tone. "I'm sure I hope the Parkers appreciate your society. Perhaps you manage to make yourself more agreeable there than here. But at any rate, please confine yourself to being polite when you are with me and my friends, whatever you do when you are with yours."

"What in the world have I done now, Maria?" asked Rachel in a troubled voice. She really wanted to please her sister, though she found it much harder work than usual these days.

"Done!" said Maria growing irritated at the remembrance of her discomfiture two days before. "Why, you've acted like a perfect little prig, and almost insulted a minister. What in the world did you think Mr. Fairfield would think of you, Sunday night, turning around and as much as contradicting what he said? It didn't make it the least bit more polite that you put it in the form of a question. He is bright enough to see through that. Who are you to set up to rebuke a minister, anyway? You might as well try to find fault with the Bible."

"Why, 'Ri, I didn't rebuke him. I only asked him a question that honestly puzzled me. What do you mean? I never intended—"

"Nonsense!" said Maria sharply. "You were rude and you know it. If a man doesn't seem to come up to your standard you immediately set about telling him so. You will simply get yourself set down as an insufferable little prig for your trouble if you keep on in that way. I was surprised that Mr. Fairfield didn't tell you that you were a child who didn't know what you were talking about. For my part, I hope I shall not be called upon to endure another such insult to a caller of mine; if I am, you may be sure I shall call mother to come and take you in. It is the only fit rebuke for such actions. You talk religion too much, anyway. It isn't ladylike to stick it in every one's face. A minister hears enough of it in his profession without being called upon to talk about it in his social life. Religion is much better acted than talked, I think. I should hope you would take that to heart. If you attempt any of that sort of talk with the De Veres you will find you won't be tolerated in their society very long. I'm sure I'm ashamed of you. Now do go to sleep if you can. I don't want to talk any more," and Maria turned over with a twitch and pretended to go to sleep herself.

But for Rachel sleep was effectually routed. She lay there thinking. The tears chased each other down her cheeks. It hurt her so to have her sister talk to her in this way. She felt as if she ought to make some protest, but what could she say that would help matters? Her protests always seemed to anger her sister more. Was Maria right after all, and did the minister feel in the way she had said he would about the questions she had asked? If so, was she all wrong in her way of feeling about things? Of course a minister must be right, for he had spent his life in getting ready to preach Christ's gospel, and had given up all to that work. He ought to be consecrated if any one was. But surely he ought also to be one to whom any one could go with a question about Christian living.

Then she remembered Roland De Vere and how differently he had talked about religion, just the few words he had happened to speak on the subject. Somehow she felt that Maria was mistaken about Mr. De Vere at least, and she wished that he would talk to Maria and perhaps he would be able to influence her. Perhaps this minister would know how to help Maria by and by. Ministers' lives ought to be an influence on those around them, without any words, as Maria had said. She would pray for that. Meantime, was there not some little thing she could do for her Master? She felt that her life was so full of pleasure this summer, that without some definite, special work to do, she would be apt to grow selfish. She had tried to help Maria, but all help seemed only to irritate her. Perhaps it was wrong in her to set up to help an older sister. She would just pray and try to keep her tongue from doing aught to make her sister trouble. Her tongue did seem to be a very unruly member. So she closed her eyes and prayed to be shown what to do, and then, like a tired child, threw off her burden and went to sleep.

In justice to Maria be it said that she had been feeling deeply chagrined that Mr. Fairfield had neither called nor come upon the beach when they were there, nor in any way appeared since to claim his acquaintance with them, which he had seemed eager to do on Sabbath evening. It puzzled Maria greatly, for while she cared nothing about the man in particular, still she was deeply sensitive to the opinion of any one, either stranger or friend, whose manner and appearance seemed to make his judgment of value in her eyes. She feared that he had set them down as a family of fanatics, and that the whole fault lay with Rachel's babyish way of talking religion, as if it were an every-day matter.

Having nothing else to do, she brooded over the matter until it appeared very large to her. She felt that the minister was intentionally slighting them, and that now as he had found his friends at Spray View, he wished to show them that he had only been polite to Maria on account of the very awkward accident which had thrown them together on Saturday. Maria's imagination was so vivid, that as the days went by—which, by the way, continued to be rainy, the clouds pouring down water in a very deluge at times—she began to think that the end of all pleasant times had come even as they had just begun. Of course there was no moonlight excursion.

Maria stood on the piazza one afternoon, toward the end of the dreary week, gazing discontentedly at the desolate landscape. The mist of fine rain was still falling, when it was not varied by terrific showers. A stiff breeze was blowing, first from one direction and then from another, as if in fitful mood, uncertain what to do. Off at her right Maria could see the banks of sand piled high, looking almost like cliffs in places, with their low undergrowth of huckleberry and wild sage and laurel, the only growth which the island seemed to afford, for there was not a tree in sight. Now and again the waves of the ocean would dash so high that the spray would be carried up in clouds above these sand banks. There was one break in the banks, just at the end of what was supposed to be their street or "avenue," in the parlance of the place, where one could gaze far out over the wild, turbulent ocean in its dull gray and brown tones, with a seething touch of vivid green here and there and froth of maddened yellow-white. It all looked so cold and wild and awful.

Maria turned from it, shuddering; on her left there stretched the steel-colored bay, once so bright and gay, reflecting tints like an opal, now an almost interminable stretch of mist and desolation. The long reaches of waste sand, and heavy, wet-headed, salt marsh grass, bending with the wind, only added to the dismal character of the scene. The girl walked back and forth on the green piazza, which was wet with the mist, and looked with horror, almost with hatred, at the whole view. Yes, for one can hate even sky and grass and water when one is in the right mood for it. The scene embodied to her the desolation that seemed to have come into her life. It was like that waste of water and sand and dark-leaden sky. There seemed in it no hope of brightness for the future, just as it seemed impossible now, after these days and days of rain, that the sky could ever be bright again or the waves would ever grow soft and lovely and the bay take on its gemlike look. God seemed nowhere to her. She felt a kind of desperation, as if she could not endure another hour of this hateful existence.

It almost frightened her to realize that she felt so. She knew it was wrong. She had been too well brought up not to have been conscious during the days that had passed just how wrong and hateful she had been in her feelings and actions. She began to wonder if she ever had really loved God, or been a Christian, and whether there was anything in it. Wild ideas ran through her brain. Where was God, anyway? Why did he want her to be so unhappy? Had he forgotten her? Over and over in her mind kept going a verse of an old hymn learned in childhood, or rather one line of the verse, she could remember no more. It ran like this, "Has God forgotten to be kind?" She tried to shake it off, but it came again and again. She brushed back the hair that clung wet with the mist to her hot temples and went into the cottage.

Anything was better in this vast desolation alone. She went to the kitchen and in desperation took out her recipe book, to find the most difficult thing she could make for supper. It would at least occupy her hands and her mind. There were books, to be sure, but she felt dissatisfied with them all. She could not interest herself in one of them. A book was all very nice and cozy on a rainy day, when all was cheery indoors and there were visions of bright days in the hopeful future after the rain should be passed, but Maria felt that for her there were no such visions.

The trouble was deeper than these few days at the seashore. It went back to the time when her father lost his money. She was rebellious. She was not willing to give up that money and the position which it carried. Now that it was gone, she felt there was nothing else in the world worth living for. She had been a pretty good Christian, according to her own way of thinking, in those days when things had been prosperous. Why had not God seen that? She could have done much more in the world for him if he had left her life as it was. Now she was no Christian at all, and he must see how he had made a failure of her Christian work by taking away her father's money and her social position. She did not say these things even to herself, in so many words. She would not have dared, because she had been taught to be reverent in her speech, and in a degree this teaching had reached to her thoughts, but she felt them strongly, deeply, fiercely.

And Rachel sat in the other room and apparently read her book, while all the time she had been uneasily watching her sister and quietly praying for her. Oh, why was it that this her great, longing prayer for the beloved sister could not be answered? Had she not prayed earnestly enough? Or must she be willing to pray longer? What was the matter? God had promised to give what the believing heart should ask for. She laid down her book and went into the bedroom, carefully fastening the curtain behind her against interruptions. She would kneel down now and pray again for Maria. But though she knelt and prayed fervently, she felt no sudden sense of answer such as she had heard other people talk about, and when she listened, she could hear Maria rattle the pans and kettles as fiercely as ever in the kitchen. There was no sign as yet in her of any spiritual change. Rachel's was a sweet nature, struggling for light, and she was not being guided by human help perhaps as much as would have been good for her. She believed everything intensely and at once, and wanted to see a vindication of her belief, like many another eager, impatient one, but she was willing to be led. She took her little Bible. It had aided her many times in perplexity. She turned to it now from habit and read one of her favorite psalms. "Delight thyself also in the Lord, and he shall give thee the desires of thine heart."

She had read that verse over without thinking about it, when a thought seemed to arrest her attention. Was it possible that God had sent her that very promise now? Did he want her to delight herself in him first before he gave her what she had been asking? Perhaps that was true and she had not made him her chief delight. She slowly closed the book and went out again to the sitting room and her story, but though she held the book before her eyes, she was not reading. She was going over her life and thinking how she might make the Lord her chief delight, and how she had not done it. It was a revelation to her of herself, for had she been asked a little time before reading that verse, she would have said that Christ and his life-work were her chief delights; but now she saw that she had made other things chief and Christ's work only a part — a very small part — of the pleasures of her life. She saw that there was something which needed a radical change in her whole soul, so that Christ would be in her pleasures, the source and center of everything, instead of a mere outside pleased observer, as she felt she had been wont to regard him heretofore.

Meantime, she remembered that there were peaches to be peeled for supper. She disliked this work intensely, and was not always prompt to remember that it belonged to her; but to-night she arose with alacrity, saying to herself, "He wants me to peel those peaches; I will try to remember I am doing it for Him and then perhaps I can take delight in it." And she succeeded so well in what so few succeed at all that presently she was singing a happy little song:

> "There is sunshine in my soul to-day,
> More glorious and more bright,
> For Jesus — "

"For pity's sake," snapped Maria, "do select something more appropriate, if you *must* sing. It doesn't look as if there would ever be any sunshine any more anywhere."

And for once Rachel was enabled to laugh and make a pleasant reply and then go on with her singing, instead of closing her mouth and letting the tears steal up to her eyes at the sharp words, as she usually did. And so supper was prepared in much more peace than usual.

Chapter 9

The sun shone out at last bright and clear as though he had never thought of anything else. The bay, blue in the distance, sparkled in the sunrays like a wondrous sapphire set in emeralds. White-winged sailboats, like great birds, floated lazily across the glassy surface, carried hither and thither by the light winds, in the very joy of life and motion. As one gazed westward toward the bay, not a sign could be seen of the gloom that had shrouded the landscape for days. Turning toward the sea, radiant with brilliant coloring, bordered by a shining garment of newly washed sand, the late rage of the elements was more apparent, for the sea, slower in rousing to terrible wrath, is more reluctant to cease from its anger, and long after nature smiles, pours thunderous billows upon the unresisting shore.

Had Howard Fairfield been there, his whole day would have been passed at the very edge of the surge, gazing far out to sea over the majestic spectacle, still more striking by reason of the contrast it presented to the calm sky overhead, until his soul had been filled with the wonder of the scene. But much to his own disappointment, a series of unimportant details still held him in the city. It was Saturday. Rachel sat on the piazza peeling peaches. Her father had brought from the city the night before a quantity of fine fruit, for in their island home all such luxuries had to be imported. In the salt-laden atmosphere they decayed rapidly, and to Rachel therefore had been assigned the task of preparing them for preserving and canning. Although this was a task always especially distasteful to her, yet the morning was so bright and beautiful that she caught the spirit of its gladness and sang blithely as she worked.

Moreover, was not her life henceforth to have a new motive, to be filled with a joy not of this world? Jesus was now to be to her a delight, and to her surprise, perhaps, she discovered that that delight shone up at her through the most commonplace tasks. It seemed wonderful. She rejoiced in the brightness of the morning because he had made it bright. Thus she sat thinking her happy thoughts, working with deft fingers at her task, and as she worked, caroled forth a little song.

Maria felt very differently about the change in weather. Of what good was the sunshine when one did not care to go out into it? She had no place to which to go if she did go out; no one for whose companionship she cared, who was likely, as she said to herself, to care enough about hers to seek it. To be sure, there was the beach to visit, mother and sister for company, books and embroidery for occupation, to say nothing of the kaleidoscopic scenery of sea and sky; but these went for nothing with her, having no place in the catalogue of her desires.

A fierce resentment filled her at the mockery of the day's brightness contrasted with the gloom of her own mood. It was plain, now, even to her mind, that she had been taking a sort of grim, self-pitying satisfaction in the melancholy of the weather. It had stood for a distinct grievance, and now she was almost angry that it was taken from her. As her mother passed through the room, she sighed at sight of the discontent that sat now so often on her elder daughter's face. Rachel's song floated in through the open doorway and made her wonder why one daughter should seem to find all the sweetness while the other persisted in drinking only the bitter. It was the more difficult to understand because it had not always been so, for in her younger days Maria had been as sunny as her sister. It was unlike her to cling to her self-conceived wrongs for so long a time, to show to others only the thorny side of her nature.

Could it be that Maria was on the verge of illness, and that here was the hidden reason for her discontent? With this idea stirring in her heart, the mother passed again into the kitchen and urgently begged Maria to resign her place at the stove to her and Rachel for the day and to lie down in her own room. Her advances were met with scorn, and Maria prepared to cook a more elaborate meal than usual, as a proof that there was nothing the matter with her health. The mother, repulsed, went sadly away again to her sewing, on which more than one tear dropped, as she anxiously asked herself what *could* be the matter with Maria. She found herself wishing that that handsome young Mr. De Vere would pay a little less attention to Rachel, who seemed to care nothing about him, and a little more to Maria, who, with the keen intuition of a mother, she feared did; or else that that intellectual-looking minister, who had brought her home that day she got the drenching, would come again — anything to take her child out of herself and infuse a new interest into her life, that she should not brood over her misfortunes so much, and perhaps thus give a permanent bent to her character in the unfortunate direction of melancholy. She had hoped that even the sunshine would cheer her, but it seemed to have rather the opposite effect.

Across a strip of neatly mowed marsh grass, not many rods distant, stood a small unpainted cottage surrounded by a well-kept vegetable garden. The wide piazza, peculiar to the place, ran across its front, and around this, in attempting to cope with the mosquitoes, some one had at one time tacked a blue mosquito bar which now hung tattered, waving in the breeze. This was the home of the Higginses, little and large.

The family was one of many and varied occupations. The father fished a little, and gardened a little, and drove parties of three in his rickety old green spring wagon over to Spray View on errands, at the rate of ten cents per head, or three for a quarter. Rachel, when she heard this, had rejoiced that they might often take the beach drive, it was so cheap; but Maria had curled her lip in such scorn at the idea of driving past the elegant De Vere villa in the old green wagon that Rachel had not mentioned it again. Mrs. Higgins washed for a living, besides sewing and cooking for her large family, carried tomatoes, which she called "tomats," delicious beets, fresh eggs, and chickens, to the few people who lived near enough to purchase them; went into the bay when requested to dig clams, which she sold at a ridiculously low price, and was the delight of all 'curio-loving' people who came in contact with her, by reason of her quaint dialect, a mixture of Irish, German, and Jersey.

There were four grown sons with their wives and children, who lived, some in the same house, some near by, and others came often to visit, on which occasions the eggs, "tomats," and fresh fish were scarce for the time being. There were two young women, daughters, who plodded through the sand every morning at five to reach the Spray View Hotel in time to perform their daily duties there of chamber-maid and nurse-girl, respectively. There was a son who worked on the railroad when the trains ran (which was only during the summer) and fished between times, and last but not least were Katy and John, the two youngest children. They solemnly and silently appeared at the door from time to time, bringing milk or eggs or other things which had been ordered, but fled in dismay if any questions were asked them.

Rachel had found out all this about their neighbors during the first few days of their stay at the shore. She was always interested in every human being that was within her sight. The rest of the family knew of them only as a convenience for the performance of odd jobs and for the supplying of cheap vegetables, fish, and clams. Maria knew them but to despise, because they never by any means happened to have the thing she wanted at the time she ordered it. But Rachel was really and truly interested in watching their movements and realizing that they were human beings, with emotions like herself, in spite of the fact that they were such queer people and seemed to exist and be happy under such very different circumstances from her own, which in contrast with her father's former condition in life she had unconsciously come to regard as none of the best.

In one of Rachel's intervals of song, when she had been on a trip to the kitchen in search of more peaches and another dish, which latter was of course not to be had in this cottage of few conveniences, Rachel heard a burst of song from over the way. I will not say it was music, though it was evidently meant for that. The singer was one of the young women members of the Higgins family. Rachel could see that she was sitting in the wide porch behind a tattered remnant of the blue mosquito netting swinging a much-used hammock, which evidently contained a baby, probably one of the many Higgins grandchildren. Her voice was loud and sharp and clear, with a decided nasal twang. The song was a lullaby improvised for the occasion, but sung in such a tremendously high key as to seem to be intended for the benefit of some baby up in the clouds, or away beyond Spray View.

Rachel broke into a low soft gurgle of laughter and called her mother and Maria to listen, as the loud twang of "Sleep, sleep, sleep, baby, sleep, Hush-a-bye, sleep, hush-a-bye, sleep," rang out above the voice of the majestic waves. The song continued for some time, and Rachel hushed her own singing, partly to listen and partly because the metallic tones grated on her delicate musical susceptibilities. By and by the singer changed her song, while the hammock still rocked violently. The baby was evidently being brought up to be a sailor, for certainly no other vocation would be more suitable after spending one's infant days in such a turbulent cradle.

> "There's a land that is fair-rer than da-ay,"

rang out the words distinctly,

> "An' by faith we c'n see it a-fa-ar."

All through the verses sang the girl, her lungs apparently as unwearied as when she began, and the energy with which she brought out each word distinctly, making a listener sure that she enjoyed her own music, whatever might be said of others.

She finished one song and went on to another, a gospel song, of date so many years back that Rachel could remember it only as having been familiar with it in her very early girlhood. Her eyes grew dreamy as she thought of various occasions when she had sung these very words which now seemed a little out of date because of the many new jingles which had superseded them in a way. She wondered where this girl had become acquainted with all these songs, that she could sing them from beginning to end. The family, she had heard, had been on the island both summer and winter for several years. She had heard that they never went to church or Sunday-school. Indeed, Sunday seemed to be a sort of merry-making time with them, for there were sure to be several sons with their wives there to spend the day, and Rachel had noticed a case of beer bottles outside the porch once when she went to get some clams to make clam bisque for supper.

Where, then, had this girl gotten her knowledge of religious song? She had words enough of the way of salvation at her tongue's end, to save a whole family, if words could save. It must have been acquired before the family moved to this deserted place. It would be interesting to know where and how. Perhaps she had sometime been an attendent at Sunday-school, or perhaps she had gone to a series of Moody meetings and the songs had grown familiar there. Rachel was a bit given to letting her imagination have free rein, and when she had thought out the possibilities thus far she began to grow intensely interested in the family over the way and to wish to know more. She would talk with that girl the next time she came over with the milk and perhaps find out something.

Meantime, how grand a thing it would be if through those very songs some day the whole family should become Christians. What a nice story that would make. Rachel dropped her peach and looked dreamily off over the bay. She liked to scribble little stories herself, just for her amusement sometimes. She never showed them to anyone. This would be a splendid start for a plot. But how would this marvelous change be brought about? The Spirit of God could do it, of course, but he would be likely to use some earthly instrument. Some one must come who would speak words, or do some helpful thing, or get an influence over them, perhaps some young minister on his vacation, like Mr. Fairfield, or even some young lady, or—

Here Rachel's thoughts came suddenly back to the practical from the imaginary and a soft pink color stole up into her cheek. Why sit and plan a story when, perhaps, there was really an opening for work? She had been asking God for some work for him, maybe he was showing it to her through that loud-voiced singing over there. It was not, at first thought, as attractive work as some she might think of, not nearly so interesting in reality as it would be in a story; but perhaps it was work she could do, at least she could try a little of it. She picked up her peach and began to peel it rapidly again, revolving in her mind whether there really was anything she could do after all. She felt herself shrinking from the undertaking when it was presented to her and she wished she had not thought of it at all, nor listened to the horrible grating singing. How could she do anything, anyway? It would only be another trial for Maria if she should associate herself with any of those despised Higginses. They would be less to her sister's liking than even the Parkers. Then she had never been introduced, and perhaps the girl would resent anything she might do or say as patronizing. Rachel had a horror of seeming to patronize any human being. There was not the least danger that her gentle, loving smile and winning way would ever be mistaken for that, but in her true modesty she did not know this.

Finally she cast aside the thought with this feeling: "If God wishes me to do anything in that way he will show me. Perhaps I am as mistaken about this as I was about trying to help Maria." With an upward turning of her heart she cast the thought at her Saviour's feet. He knew best. If he wished her to do anything he would show her.

By this time the peaches were finished and so was the song from over the way. The baby probably had succumbed at last to the boisterousness of hammock and song. Rachel carried her peaches into the house, washed her hands and came out again with her little work-basket of dainty lace which she was making for the border to a center piece, and two little books, still in the paper wrappings as they had arrived that morning, by messenger, for her from Spray View. The handwriting of her own name in bold, manly characters had told her who was the sender, and Rachel postponed the opening of the package until her work was done that she might the better enjoy what was to be found therein. Perhaps too, there was a shy, sweet pleasure in opening the package by herself, and was it to keep up a show of work that she also carried her basket and lace work out with her, or did she really intend to make lace and not read? Anyway, the morning was charming and it was so nice to have a package to open and her pretty work lying beside her, and nothing to do but enjoy it all. Slowly she untied the knots of the string, tracing meanwhile the graceful, strong letters of her fair name, "Rachel Weldon Hammond."

And then she undid the wrapping and brought the two books to view. She had known they were books, for Roland De Vere had told her he had two books which he wanted her to read, as he felt sure she would enjoy them, and they would perhaps lead her into lines of reading which were new to her. Now she looked curiously to see what they were. One was of a dark red paper cover, but attractive in print, short of paragraph and brief of chapters. It was called "A Castaway." A glance through it told her it was the one he had told her would be of special use to help spend the long Sabbath afternoon, and aid her in her Christian life. She smiled with pleasure in her eyes as she turned the leaves a few minutes, snatching a sentence here and there that seemed to have been written just for her, so perfectly did it fit her circumstances and thoughts, and then she laid it aside. Sabbath reading like this, aside from the Bible, did not often come in her way. She must treasure it for the Sabbath. She would just take a few peeps into it and leave the rest of it for a Sunday treat.

Then she turned to the other book, a daintily bound volume all in pale green and gold. The paper was thick and creamy, the print clear, and the whole appearance of the book exquisite. Rachel loved the feeling and the look of such a book. It was poetry. She opened at random. One poem was styled "Day's Parlor." She read, and it seemed to her that that day had been fashioned in just the way described.

The day came slow till five o'clock,
Then sprang before the hills
Like hindered rubies, or the light
A sudden musket spills.

The purple could not keep the east,
The sunrise shook the fold,
Like breadths of topaz, packed a night,
The lady just unrolled.

The happy winds their timbrels took;
The birds, in docile rows
Arranged themselves around their prince
(The wind is prince of those).

The orchard sparkled like a Jewel,
How mighty 'twas, to stay
A guest in this stupendous place,
The parlor of the day!

Rachel caught her breath and looked up at the bay and the blue, blue sky, drinking in all their loveliness. How those jeweled words had brought out the beauties! She turned a few pages and read again:

She sweeps with many colored brooms,
And leaves the shreds behind;
Oh, housewife in the evening west,
Come back and dust the pond!

You've dropped a purple raveling in,
You dropped an amber thread;
And now you've littered all the east
With dust of emerald!

And still she plies her spotted brooms,
And still the aprons fly,
Till brooms fade softly into stars —
And then I come away.

Ah! Rachel drew her breath again as if she had caught some delicate perfume that was new to her, and she feared to lose a single atom of the delightful sensation. This poetry suited her dreamy imagination, which was always personifying nature. She felt that she would enjoy this book to the full. This last poem was just a description of that exquisite sunset last week. She was grateful for the gift of the book, and dimly felt the high, fine perceptions of the young man who had selected it for her. The music of these words and their coloring gave her pleasure clear to her finger tips.

And then in the mist of these thoughts appeared her answer from Heaven and her work ready laid out for her. It was a contrast, perhaps, but a well-tuned nature should always be ready to turn from the high to the low and feel none the worse for it, and sometimes even recognize that what is rated the low is in reality the highest of the high, while the high is merely a picture of what pleasure may be after all.

"Did your ma want any clams to-night?" It was the clear metallic voice of the singer from over the way who asked the question, and the voice was so sharp, and her coming had been so silent that Rachel, lost in her beautiful dreams, started. But the girl seemed not to notice this. Her eyes were intent upon Rachel's work-basket and the beautiful lace work on its pretty blue cambric background pattern.

"Oh, what a pretty thing that is!" exclaimed the girl. "Did you do that?" and as Rachel took up her basket to bring the work nearer for her inspection, "Ain't it awful hard work? You must be just dreadful clever. Does it take a long time? Now I'll just guess that stuff costs an awful lot. I see a woman over to the hotel the other day workin' at a thing like that. You don't say! That's the way you do it. Just sew that braid onto them lines! Why that looks easy! My, but I suppose it's all in knowin' how!" and the girl sighed wistfully. "My! but I would like to know how to do some of them pretty things! I never have no time in summer; but land! in winter, time just drags and drags. Seems like I was fifty years old every winter I go through in this place. I wish I could do something to shorten it."

And thus it was that Rachel's work came to her, and of all things! That it should come through a bit of renaissance lace work! She looked at the gray old cottage with its flapping, faded mosquito bar, after the girl had gone, and then down at her delicate blue and white work, and thought how incongruous the two were, and how little she would have dreamed of beginning to get an influence over a girl from that house through anything as fine as that. God knew best. It was really wonderful, when you left it all to him, how he made that to appear. Why had she never tried that before? It might not be that she would accomplish so very much, for after all she had only promised to teach an ignorant girl how to make lace and that might not lead to anything else, but she felt that she had been given a chance to try, and she thanked her Father for it.

Chapter 10

Howard Fairfield had not lingered in the heat of the city because it was his wish to do so. He had found an aged member of his church very ill and wishing to see him; and the man who was to have supplied his prayer meeting sent word that he could not come, so he stayed for that; then afterward he lingered by the old saint's bedside till he had gone where spiritual help was needed no more. Thus had come another funeral in that one short week, which yet had seemed to stretch itself out to such a length.

Saturday afternoon saw him free at last, for the pulpit was supplied for the morrow and the man on the ground. There was no need for him to linger longer. There was just time to catch the last train back to the quiet shore. He laid his head wearily against the cushion of the seat while the train whirled him on, and thought over all the experiences of the week. How he had been led! That girl with her dream, and the little girl's funeral, and his own experience in waiting for the hour to arrive! And then those hours by the bedside of the dying saint, where he had gained, more than given, spiritual help. He had a new feeling toward the old man who had just entered heaven, which he had never felt for any person who had died before. It was as if he had been given to know one of the apostles for a few short hours, and to talk with him, and have his eyes opened by him, and to grow to love him, and then the heavens had opened and he had seen the man carried up to Jesus.

Heaven had a new interest for him now. He felt nearer to it. He loved it more than he had ever before realized he could. He could not help wondering what sights and scenes that dear servant of God was passing through at that moment, while his friends were mourning his absence from the earth. To him the coffin which he had seen lowered into the earth but two hours before contained no thought of the grand sweet soul, who was not buried there, but was high in heaven with the angels. How he wished that he had known the old man better during the time he had been on earth. Oh, those wasted months, when such companionship and help might have been his. It reminded him of the days when the disciples had Jesus with them and had not half known how to value his daily companionship. To know intimately one who was like Jesus was, in a limited sense, like having known and walked with Jesus when he was in the body on the earth.

Perhaps there were others in his congregation who were like this man. Now that he could think over the list, there were several families whose simple, trustful Christian life had evidently strong faith behind it, and rich experience from which he might learn much. There were the Clarks! He had looked upon them as good souls, but had thought them ignorant. Ignorant, perhaps they were in some things, but they read their Bibles and they lived their Bibles, and now that he thought of it there were many ways in which he felt sure they could help him. How foolish he had been! How wise in his own conceit! He had felt that because he was fresh from the seminary he knew more than they all. Now he saw that he had not half learned the true heart-knowledge, which should have gone hand in hand with his head-knowledge.

Had he then wasted his preparations so far this summer? There was that series of sermons he had planned out and half developed on the mystery of the Trinity, and there was the other series which he had worked carefully over and had almost ready for use on "The Life and Works of the Prophets." They seemed empty and useless to him now. There were doubtless many good things in them. It might be that at some time they might even be useful to him for the especial purpose of helping certain minds over perplexing places, but in the light of his new experiences they seemed so wide of the mark, so almost unnecessary when one thought of the tremendous truths which needed to be presented, yes urged, yea, thundered from the pulpit day and night.

He had thought that a quiet summer by God's sea, with his own intellect and God's good teacher, nature, would be of vast assistance to him as a preacher: but perhaps he might have gone somewhere else, to one of those wonderful spiritual gatherings of which there were so many far and near, beginning with Northfield and Mr. Moody. He had always thought he might like to go to Northfield, but it had been in a lofty, condescending way, more out of curiosity than anything else. Now he longed for something of which he had heard, and which he knew by instinct might be found there. Perhaps he ought to give up his present plans and go there at once. It might be the best thing he could do. He closed his eyes restfully, and wondered what his Heavenly Father would have him do about it, and he prayed to be guided; for while he wanted to go, and felt it would be good, he yet had a longing for the quiet and rest of the still seashore place and the chance to talk with God alone. He would wait there at least till he was sure what God would have him do, or whither he would have him go in his great school, for he felt like a new pupil just entering a higher grade to be taught things he had not dreamed there were for him yet to learn.

As the train rushed on and drew nearer to his destination he began to open his eyes and look for landmarks. He had not realized how tired he was, nor how eager for a sight of the mighty ocean. He thought of the few friends he had met and wondered if they would be there; and if they would be helpful; and then, with a strange new feeling, if he could be helpful to them. There was that girl, there were those two girls in fact, whom he had met under such peculiar circumstances. He hardly knew where to place them, he had seen so little of them. The younger girl had asked some strange questions. And now there came back to him vividly his last walk and reverie by the sea. He would go back there and walk and think, but he felt with a grateful thrill in his heart that there would be answers to his questions now which he had not been able to give then. Now his eyes were open and he was beginning to see things differently. He thanked God for this. Meanwhile, if there was aught of good that he could get or do, he wanted to be ready for it. He watched eagerly in the deepening twilight, as the train drew near the station, for the few little cottages, bathed in the sunset glow of the bay, and sprang out on the platform, breathing in the salt air, glad that he was back again. After supper he took his way out beside the sea in the darkness of the starry night alone to think and be with God, and he came back from that walk to deep, dreamless sleep and awoke to the restfulness of the Sabbath.

Now the Saturday which had brought such brightness to the shore, and had blown such a life-giving breeze from across the bay had also brought the little mosquito. On the wings of that delicious breeze he came – not alone. He brought his entire family and all his relatives with him. They were small and sharp mosquitoes. They were harmless and unmusical mosquitoes, but they were wise. They knew those cottages of old with their wide cracks and roomy ceilings for daily hidings. They had been blown across the bay on just such breezes for years, at least if not they, then their ancestors, and they went as straight to their several stopping-places as if they had telegraphed ahead and had rooms reserved for them and meals ready. They arrived all at once and took possession. They swarmed through the piazzas and drove the helpless sitters there inside the screen doors; but they did not stop outside, they rushed in also, and those who failed of the door were not long in finding the other vulnerable points in the cottages. By night, when the lights had begun to appear, they had managed to make their presence almost unbearable.

Maria, like many other people of fair skin and highly strung nervous organization, was particularly susceptible to stings of any kind, whether of insects or tongue. She became irritable at once. Perhaps no one would have wondered who saw the enormous red and white swellings which immediately responded to the attack of the little insect. Mosquito bites poisoned Maria, and she really suffered intensely. Therefore it need not be wondered at that her temper was strung to its highest pitch. She actually sat down in the sitting room before the whole family and cried in vexation and despair over the torment of the little pests. She declared she could endure it no longer, that she would rather die, and a dozen other extravagant things which she did not mean, and then went to bed, sick and sore, to fight them there, and find little sleep to restore her calmness.

Sabbath morning found her aching in body and mind. The mosquitoes still continued. Maria refused to go to church, though the entire family condescended to urge her to do so, hoping that it would in some way soothe her troubled spirit. They had reason to be glad, however, that she had refused, when they arrived at the church door and entered, attended by thousands of the little insects, and found that they were thick on the white plastered walls, and that the assembled congregation looked more like a lot of dancing dervishes than a company of quiet and respectable church-goers, bent on the worship of God. Indeed, the mosquitoes kept up their part of the performance until people were nearly distracted, some going home in desperation. The speaker of the morning drew his remarks to a speedy close and the people hastened home remarking on the unusualness of the visitation of mosquitoes, and the wind, weather, and state of tempera-ture as causes of the plague. Those who had plastered houses hastened indoors and those who had not took refuge in penny royal oil and the smoke of various herbs, and then in despair betook themselves to the beach. There at least was a place of refuge. Even Maria was driven thither very soon after the noonday meal. She would not have gone if it had been tolerably comfortable at home, for she felt in that perverse mood in which she dreaded seeing any one or speaking pleasantly. She even felt a strong distaste to making herself look neat and pretty for the day.

Nevertheless, she finally consented to change her dress and smooth her hair and go to the sand with Rachel. Rachel, in her sisterly solicitude that the afternoon should be a time of comfort to Maria, loaded herself down with cushions, parasols, fans, and a beach chair. Then with her own little Bible and the new book, which had come to her the day before and which she had kept for this precious Sabbath afternoon's reading, she walked cheerfully through the sand and swarms of mosquitoes to find just the right spot on the beach where the breeze and the view were most pleasant, while Maria scolded with every step and declared she would go back, but nevertheless went on.

Rachel pitched her tent, as it were, arranged the beach chair comfor-tably, fixing cushions and sand for herself, declaring she preferred them, and pressed the chair upon her sister. Rachel opened her Bible first. Maria sat gloomily looking out on the smooth water which had calmed itself into one of those transparent blue-green sheens which look innocent of any possible boisterous to-morrow. Certainly the coloring of the ocean was worth watching to-day, and the sky and air seemed perfect. But Maria was in no mood to enjoy it. Presently she closed her eyes drearily on it all. She felt so weary, poor child. Her life seemed so empty. She was impatient of the day and of the summer, and even of the outlook of her whole life as she seemed to see it stretching before her.

Rachel felt her sister's gloom. It could not but be apparent, and Rachel was so impressionable that it made her quite unhappy. She knew there was nothing she could do to lighten her sister's heart, and yet she could not enjoy her own reading nor her own pleasure in the day. She read one of the short chapters in her new book, wondering over the helpfulness of every word, charmed with the plain, everyday language and tender sympathy expressed by the writer, but in spite of her interest in the book, her mind kept wandering to Maria and she was conscious of every movement her sister made. At least she thought she was asleep and instantly she gave thanks. Sleep would be the best thing for her in her present state of mind. Unconsciously Rachel relaxed her tension of muscles and resting back among her pillows enjoyed the day and her own happy thoughts for a little. She let her mind wander to the Higginses and the promised lesson in lace-making, and wondered how she could get a lesson on something else besides lace. By and by two little figures, which she had been watching for some time when they were but mere specks away down toward the lighthouse, came nearer, hand in hand, and now were near enough to be distinguished as the two younger members of the Higginses household, Katy and John, wandering along, bareheaded and barefooted, picking up a shell now and then and trotting on again.

Rachel watched them interestedly. How different the sea must seem to them, who lived there all the year and knew it at its wildest! It was evidently their friend and they loved it. Rachel could tell that from the way they looked out upon it, pointing now and then to a distant sail, or cloud of smoke from some steamer far-off against the horizon.

The girl, watching, wondered if the sea ever spoke to them of God, and what idea they had of its majesty and its Maker. Did they associate the two? Had they been taught enough for that, she would like to know; or did they perhaps have some natural instinct which would lead them to feel this without the teaching? She began to frame questions which she would like to ask them, and grew eager to know how they would answer.

And then her second opportunity came, as the children sat down on a great broken spar which had been washed ashore some time ago and been half buried in the sand. Katy dug her bare feet in the sand, making a soft sailor instinct of his family stirring within him. They evidently meant to sit there some time. Rachel might go over and talk with them. They looked lonely too, perhaps they would like her to tell them a story. She missed her class of little girls at home in Sunday-school which met at about this hour. It would be a real pleasure to her to teach the lesson of the day, which for the sake of keeping in touch with her class during her absence she had been studying all the week. What if she should go over and talk to those two children and God should open a way for her to tell that beautiful Bible story to them? Might she? Would Maria miss her? She glanced at her sister, who seemed to be fast asleep, and then moving gently she laid her books by Maria's side and rose and slipped away. She would go for a few minutes, anyway, and see how she was received. And so with beating heart, for she was young and this seemed a grave and responsible mission to her, Rachel went to see what her first opportunity had for her of possibility in the way of soul winning.

Katy and John were startled when they found the pretty young lady sitting down beside them on their spar, and actually speaking to them, and they picked up their shells and prepared to flee, but Rachel's winning smile and her eagerness over the pretty shells they had gathered soon made them forget this intention, and before they knew what they were about they were sitting on the sand at her feet, listening with large, wondering eyes and wide-open mouths to a story she was telling them. She had found that the questions she wanted to ask would have to be deferred until she had won a place in their hearts and had been able to loosen their tongues, for they were shy of speaking any words at all but yes and no, and blushed deeply even at these. They evidently were not used to being talked with much by any one except their own family, and perhaps not much by them. And so Rachel's art of story-telling stood her in good stead. She made a shell lead up to the story, and she soon had them interested in it.

Then from that story she went on to tell of Jesus making a fire by the seaside and cooking the fishes for his disciples' supper. As they grew interested she forgot everything in her joy of teaching. She drew a bit of a diagram in the sand, using a razor fish's shell for a crayon, and the children, who had never seen anything of the kind before, bent eager heads over the picture and drank in her words as if they had been listening to music. Perhaps it was not the best lesson she might have selected for a first in religious instruction, but she presently succeeded in making those two young hearts beat with longing to have been of that weary boat load coming in to the supper and the dear and gracious Master.

And then, wonder of wonders! they heard from this beautiful young lady's lips that they also might be his children! his, cared for by him. That great, good Jesus, who was no more associated with their idea of God than they would have associated him with some of their own family, and whose name they never heard but in profanity, he might be theirs. If the young teacher could have looked into those darkened little hearts and known what they really did think and feel about God, and how very little they knew about him, her heart would have sunk at the impossibility of her task, and her words might have grown less eloquent in her hopelessness; but mercifully she did not know, as mercifully none of us know just what is before or about us, and the Father in heaven knew that they were filled with a great longing for the first time in their little lives to know Jesus Christ.

So Rachel talked on and on, and the children did not grow weary, and the sun was setting in the west before she realized how long she had kept her Sabbath-school, and how long she had been away from her sister, who would doubtless blame her for the neglect.

That night when Rachel opened her Bible in her own room she read these words, "Therefore, my beloved brethren, be ye steadfast, unmovable, always abounding in the work of the Lord, forasmuch as ye know that your labour is not in vain in the Lord." And she wondered wistfully just what those words meant, and if it were wrong for her to claim them and think her Father in heaven sent them as a message to cheer her heart in this new work.

Chapter 11

But Maria was not really asleep. She had closed her eyes because she did not wish to talk. She did not wish to see her sister bending over her Bible. It made her uncomfortable to think Rachel could enjoy the Bible. *She* could not. She told herself plainly that she never had; that she only read it from a sense of duty, as of course all church-members would do. It irritated her to think that Rachel pretended to enjoy it. In her heart she knew that there was no pretense about Rachel, and that she really did enjoy it, but it pleased her to say this to herself. It made her own unhappy, rebellious life seem less black in contrast. When Rachel laid down her books and slipped softly away Maria felt relieved. She wanted to be alone. She felt too utterly ugly in her heart to be near any one. Presently she wondered where her sister could have gone, and why she did not return, and raising herself and peeping under the parasol, she looked up and down the beach and saw Rachel with her young class gathered about her. Maria understood what it meant. She curled her lip a little. Rachel was always doing such queer things. What would the De Veres or some of the hotel people think if they came along now and saw her sitting in the sand with those two barefooted little heathen beside her. She half made up her mind to call her back and reprove her, and then sat back again, asking herself what was the use, and feeling a little relieved that she was likely to be by herself for some time, albeit there was growing in her heart a determination to charge her sister with neglecting her for two little vagrants when she did return.

She settled herself a little more comfortably with the help of some of Rachel's pillows, and seeing the red paper-covered book that had been left lying closed on the Bible beside her, she took it up. It surprised her a little that Rachel should bring a paper-covered novel out on Sunday along with her Bible, for Rachel was apt to be a little puritanical about such things; but she knew that Roland De Vere had sent some books over to Rachel yesterday; doubtless this was one of them. She reached for it, reflecting that Rachel's scruples would be easily overcome by that handsome young man, who seemed to have made up his mind to devote himself to her, even if she were nothing but a little girl.

She read the title, "A Castaway." It looked exciting—that is, the title seemed so. It was probably a story of the sea. She turned the pages and opened at the beginning, a look of satisfaction on her face that here was something to make her forget herself for a little while. But the look rapidly changed to disappointment as she read. A Bible verse at the beginning! It was nothing but a sermon after all, or worse still, one of those devotional books. She flung it carelessly down in her lap and leaned back again. How exasperating! Just when she thought she was going to have a little relief from the monotony and enjoy herself. She picked up the book once more and read half-way down the first page, but it was as if she were reading Hebrew. She knew not what manner of speech this was, and she did not take in the sense of the words. They meant nothing to her, and she closed it again and went on with her own thoughts, her fingers carelessly between the pages, but the look of settled discontent upon her face. It was well for her that the parasol was placed at such an angle as to thoroughly hide that expression on her face else she might have missed what had been sent her that afternoon.

Howard Fairfield had come out on the beach to walk and be alone. He had gone out at once after dinner, feeling that he wanted to get away from the gay chatter of the hotel guests, for the few guests that there were made much of themselves and of each other and chattered indiscriminately. He had walked up by the lonely lighthouse, and now had turned and was retracing his steps, thinking to go to his room to rest or read a little, perhaps. He had gained an uplifting in his walk by the sea. His thoughts had been with God, and there was a softened, sweet expression upon his face, an expression which in a man's face, seldom as it is seen, makes it the more noble and manly, as if he were growing more like the man God meant him to be.

He walked on slowly as he neared the part of the beach in front of the hotel and began to meet one and another of the guests there strolling and chatting in lazy fashion. He guided his own steps farther away, that he might not be drawn into conversation with any of them and break the solemn quiet which had stolen over him. Thus he passed just back of Rachel and her little group of listeners, and catching a word or two of her earnest lesson, walked more slowly and listened too. He recognized the tact and skill with which this mere girl was talking to these two ignorant little children, and wondered thereat. There were things he might learn from even a young girl's teaching, he said to himself, as he passed wistfully on, wishing he dared linger and hear more without danger of spoiling the lesson for the other two.

Then he turned his steps straight down to the sea and stood as close to the waves as might be, looking out and thinking. It seemed to him that his past life was rolling out there before him, wave after wave of it, too far away from him to ever come at and change it, rolling carelessly but certainly on to eternity to meet him again on the other shore. He numbered each wave with a year or period of his life, and saw its glaring mistakes, and wished he might ride over the waters and bring those farther ones back and live them again that they might be better lived. At last he turned with a sigh. It was no use looking back. He must go forward and see that the waves which followed these should be stronger and more resistless with endeavor for Christ. And so walking deep in thought up the sandy bank he came face to face with Maria Hammond, who had of course seen him, in fact, had been watching him for some minutes, and who while she was too proud to arrange her dress or alter her position as if she expected him to greet and talk with her, had nevertheless risen more to a sitting posture, and changed her expression from one of scornful discontent to one of quiet, dignified Sabbath thoughtfulness.

The young man, realizing suddenly that he was in danger of walking over a lady and sun umbrella, raised his head and recognized Maria. Of course there was nothing to do but pause a moment and speak to her, though in his present mood he would have avoided any one — especially a gay young girl, as he had imagined her to be — if he had had the choice beforehand.

But while pausing and exchanging the word of greeting, his eyes fell on the Bible and the little paper book. He looked up quickly, almost surprised, and yet glad, at the young girl's face. He had not somehow thought of her as one who would be likely to bring her Bible to the shore where others were. He must have been mistaken. She as after all a Christian, an earnest one, perhaps, like her sister over there who was doing her best to work for Jesus. He felt glad in his heart instantly that he had stopped, said to himself that perhaps he had been led to her for help, for he recognized in himself just then a great need for help. His face lighted up.

"May I sit down?" he asked, "or are you expecting some one else to occupy this luxurious chair in the sand? I'm a little tired from my long walk."

And Maria, all smiles and graciousness, though with not a shade too much earnestness for maidenly decorum, told him that he was welcome, and that the seat was Rachel's, but that Rachel had gone on a missionary trip to some little heathen, and there was no telling how late it would be before her return. If Maria had not seen a certain something which seemed new to her in this new acquaintance of hers, she might have put a shade of scorn for Rachel and her menial service into this sentence, but there had been that in the young man's face which had reminded her that he was a minister and that ministers were wont to respect and praise such acts as Rachel's present one, therefore her tone told nothing of the scorn she felt, and she spoke of Rachel's work as a natural, perfectly praiseworthy occurrence. She wondered afterward why she had done this and how she had been kept from saying several things which had been on the tip of her tongue and yet had not seemed quite to be what Mr. Fairfield would expect of her, as they would have seemed two weeks before, during their first few days of acquaintance.

"She is doing her work over there well," said the minister, his face growing grave again. "I could not help hearing a little of her lesson as I passed, and wishing I were a barefoot heathen too, for what I heard helped me. She must have remarkable talent as a teacher of little ones."

Maria was somewhat astonished, it is true, but accepted her sister's compliment with sisterly pride. Mr. Fairfield stretched out his hand while they were talking and took up the little paper volume. Maria's face flushed slightly, and she was about to disclaim any connection with the book, and to tell how miserably disappointed she had been a few minutes before over the contents, when again something held her back and she sat still while Mr. Fairfield turned the leaves.

"Ah! Mr. Meyer!" he said, as he opened the title-page. "You have been reading this?" He flashed his bright dark eyes up into hers again with that sudden pleasure and surprise that had confused her a moment before. "I never read it myself, and I was foolish enough to lose my opportunity of hearing the man when he was in this country, through listening to some adverse criticisms upon him, which I have since come to believe were utterly false and unfounded. I wish I could undo that loss and hear this address as it was delivered in my own city. A saint who has just gone to heaven told me of it."

Maria listened in respectful, surprised silence, glad that some intuition had kept her mouth closed a moment before. This certainly was not the same young man whom she had known, or thought she had known, two weeks before, and she prided herself on being a quick judge of character, and on being able to read faces readily. What had made the difference? She watched him while he turned the pages slowly.

"Have you been reading this?" he asked again suddenly. "Have you read it all? Perhaps you would not mind reading it aloud to me, if you have not. I never have any one to read aloud to me now that my sister is abroad. Are you fond of exercising yourself in that direction for other people's pleasure?"

"No, I have not read it all," Maria admitted, her face flushing slightly, and she wondered whether, if he knew the fact he would call that the strict truth to answer so, "but I am very fond of reading aloud and shall be delighted to read it if it will be any pleasure to you."

Now it happened that Maria was gifted in the art of reading aloud. It is true her family very seldom had the benefit of this gift, for there were few occasions when she thought it worth while to exercise it, and they seldom asked favors at her hand. But on occasions, when her audience was appreciative and worth while, she could charm a friend, or a whole room full of friends, as she read from story or poem, and bring their tears and their laughter at her will. Her voice was low and sweet and clear, and her expressive face helped to interpret whatever she read, by flashes of fun or earnestness. Everybody liked to hear Maria Hammond read, and in her younger days when she was a little child, guided by the wishes of her family, the father and mother and brother and sister had been exceedingly proud of her powers.

There was something exceedingly interesting, not to say romantic, to a girl who had been moping at a dull seaside with nothing to do but cook and be cross, in the situation of sitting by the lovely sea with a very handsome, evidently cultured, young man and being asked to read aloud something in which he was deeply interested, and which had to do with his own especial, personal lines of thought, all for his benefit. Even though the book was one which she had just now scorned, and the theme chosen was to her uninteresting, what mattered it? Religious writing was always easy to read and capable of much good expression in an elocutionary way. She took the book with alacrity, much pleased over the turn the afternoon had taken, and wondering why the sea looked so much more beautiful that it had done a half-hour before.

She read impressively the wonderful Bible text with which the address began, and then went on as naturally as if the writer of the simple, earnest sentences had himself been present delivering them. She was aware constantly of the pair of earnest eyes which watched her, listened intently to what she read, taking in every slightest turn brought out by her good rendering, appreciating to the full the homely, apt illustrations with which the short sermon was sprinkled, and unconsciously to herself, she was thinking most about what he thought of her reading, though as the reading went on, she could not fail to be interested too, for a good reader, like a good singer or a perfect actor, for the time being throws his whole soul into what he is voicing, and lives it and believes it with all his heart.

On to the end she read without interruption save an occasional half-articulate emphasis from the listener as some peculiarly good point was noted by him, and as she finished the impressive prayer with which the address closed, she raised her eyes to his and they were full of tears.

There seemed to be something almost dreadful about those tears to Maria, as she thought upon them afterward, as if she had given an impression she had no right to give, and she dropped her eyes quickly. There had been a strange, a kind of exalted, look upon his face too, as if he were pleading for forgiveness with his eyes from one unseen, and realizing something in his life which hurt him. He had hardly seemed conscious of the young girl by his side. But then he spoke slowly, quietly; he was very grave, with a strange light in his eyes, she saw, as she glanced shyly up again.

"Miss Hammond, I cannot thank you enough for the help you have been to me in reading that. It seems somehow to fit my life better than anything

I ever heard. Do you know, it touches me in a vital spot. I have been fearing within the last few days that I myself have been a castaway, even before I have ever been of any real use. I did not think an hour ago I could have spoken of this matter to any one, but perhaps it will do me good to tell it to some one, and you have been so kind and helpful. In fact I can see that you know just how to help some one in trouble." Here he looked up with a pleasant smile, not in the least the smile of the ordinary young man of society who is giving a young woman a compliment, but more a sweet, grave acknowledgment of her womanhood and its natural province of helper, comforter, sympathizer.

"I have had a strange experience since I left the beach so suddenly. I never thought to tell it to any one, but I believe I will tell you if you do not mind."

And then he went on and gave the astonished Maria an account of his hasty summons to the city, of his meeting with the dreamer, and of the strange fulfillment of the dream. He even told her of his own feelings as he waited for that summons to the funeral, and of his full surrender to God, and the following experiences by the bedside of the dying saint.

And when he had finished and they rose by tacit consent to walk slowly toward home, he gathering up the cushions and parasol and silently assisting her in getting her things together, she walked subdued and wondering beside him. Not that she was utterly silent. Oh, no; she was naturally too tactful for that. She knew how to sympathize with people in other things than religion, she knew how to put in the quiet, helpful word and to listen with rapt attention.

Moreover, she was wonderfully interested in this young man and his story. She had never listened to a real heart history like this before. No one had ever before given her his confidence to such an extent. She could not help but be sympathetic and to feel that there was something in all he said that was true for her as well as for him. She murmured, "It is all very wonderful," as they neared her home, and Mrs. Hammond, awakened by approaching voices from an uncomfortable nap in the mosquito-netted hammock on the piazza, looked up to see a strange new light on her elder daughter's face and to wonder over Maria once more.

They paused at the steps and the minister said earnestly, "You have helped me this afternoon. I should like to talk with you more about this matter. May I hope to have some more of that wonderful reading soon?" And then something was said about attending the evening service in the church. The mother, behind the porch screen did not hear nor heed. She was wondering how it was that Maria, the Maria whom they had known since their stay at the seashore, could possibly be of any help to anybody in her present state of mind.

Chapter 12

"That is a remarkable girl," said Mr. Fairfield to himself as he walked slowly back toward his hotel. "Her acquaintance will indeed be a help to me, I can see that at once. And what a fine reader she is! She seems utterly unconscious of the fact. She is as sweet and natural as a flower. She must be an unusual Christian!"

It is a good thing that people are blind sometimes, else much of the good of this world might be left undone because the workers would think it was hardly worth while. God in his mysterious kindness makes us see each other, now worse, now better than we really are, in order that we may help and be helped. It is doubtful whether the Hammond family, had they been permitted to know the young minister's conclusions about Maria, would not have thought it their duty to warn him how mistaken he was. And yet nothing that could have come to Maria would have been likely to do her so much good as this afternoon of being happily misunderstood and the consequent impression she made upon the minister. How, if this had not been, could she have ever spent those days which followed in reading and talk such as she had never dreamed of taking part in before, and of pleasant companionship of a higher character than any which had been permitted to fall to her lot before? God had just as surely sent Mr. Fairfield to be a missionary to Maria Hammond as he intended Maria Hammond to awaken and help the young man. And yet a weak human judgment would have kept these two utterly apart for the spiritual growth of each.

For the first time since her coming to the shore Maria entered the low door of the despised green cottage without a thought of the cottage or its shabbiness, or her own hatred of the surroundings. She went thoughtfully to her own room and laid down the two books she had been carrying on Rachel's little table, making a few slight changes in her toilet preparatory to getting supper, but her face did not wear its now usual expression of distaste and weariness. Instead, she really looked bright and happy.

It is true she was not thinking of the deep spiritual things she had read from the little book, nor yet entirely of the young minister's experiences which he had given her, though they had impressed her strongly. She was instead pleasing her own starved love for admiration with thinking that the young man had cared to confide in her, had thought her worthy of such confidences. She recognized that they were unusual confidences, and her own conscience, which was a well-educated one, soon began to trouble her that she had let him suppose her to be better than she was. She went back over the afternoon talk, and while she realized that she had not told any falsehoods, not indeed done anything or said anything out of keeping with actual truth, still she acknowledged to her own soul with crimsoning cheeks that she had remained silent several times, when, in order to have been perfectly honest, she ought to have spoken out and told him that she was not at all what he thought, that he must go to her sister, or others, whom she had half despised for their very eagerness about such things, if he wanted any help.

And yet, if she had done this, she would have lost the privilege of that talk, and she began to realize that it had been a privilege to her. Nor was it wholly on account of her desire for companionship and pleasure. There was something deeper in her heart, which had been so restless, which said to her, "Here, here is something you have been longing for. This man may show you a way to get it. He is different from what you thought him at first. and perhaps you are a little disappointed that he is, for you fear you cannot have quite so much of what you call 'fun' with him if that is the case; but underneath it all you know you like him better that he is of a higher type than you at first thought him."

What queer conversations people carry on with themselves, and how they analyze their own feelings and think they know themselves, and yet can only read a little piece of their own hearts and know not its follies, nor its goodness either, and then straightway forget what manner of men and women they are and go on committing the very same follies again.

But Maria's cheerfulness lasted while she prepared the evening meal. Rachel coming in and expecting a storm on account of her desertion, was astonished, almost uneasy, and finally felt called upon to explain to her sister how it was she had not come back sooner. But Maria answered pleasantly that she had been listening to an account of the delightful little lesson she had been teaching, and she hoped it was not all thrown away on those poor ignorant children. It was a pity Rachel had not some better material to work upon down here, but it was good of her to be willing to help those poor children, she supposed. Then Maria went out to the refrigerator actually humming a little tune under her breath while she took out the butter for supper.

And Rachel went to the piazza where sat her mother, and said: "Mamma, is Maria sick, do you think? She doesn't seem to act like herself. I wish I had not left her alone this afternoon, but I thought she was asleep."

The mother glanced up anxiously, always full of foreboding for her children, and then remembering, smiled and answered: "No, dear, I fancy she has been having a little glimpse of pleasure, and perhaps it is doing her good. She has had a hard time, poor child, though of course we could not help it."

"Well, mamma," said Rachel, a little careworn wrinkle coming in her smooth brow, "I think she is working too hard, and I wish you and papa would make her stop and go out on the beach and let me take my turn awhile. I know I can't do so well as she, but I will try my best. I don't feel happy having Maria work so hard."

"You dear child!" said the mother, drawing Rachel toward her and smoothing her hand. "I know just how much that means for you to say. You do not like kitchen work one bit, and you have been brave and good at it too, thus far. But it is not necessary for you to do any more than you have been doing. Your father and I have talked over the same thing, and have been worried about your sister's health. We decided last night to have that Higgins girl come over every day. She is not skilled, and will need help and watching, but she will learn; and she is willing to come for very little if I will teach her our ways, she says; so you need not think the expense will be too great. That will set both you and Maria free for most of the time, and I am much relieved."

Maria called her mother just then to ask some question about the supper, and Rachel was left standing in the dying twilight pondering. How wonderful was everything! God was actually going to send the girl whom she had planned to help a little, right into their daily life, and she would have endless opportunity. She closed her eyes and lifted her heart in prayer that she might be shown how to live so that her life would show forth God's glory, and that she might be given power to lead that ignorant girl to Jesus. It was sweet to her to remember the eager little faces that had listened to her lesson that afternoon, and now that she could not think of them without reproaching herself for having left her sister alone, she could not drive them from her mind, but went over and over again their questions and her answers and the way they had been received, her heart leaping within her at the thought of really telling the story of Jesus for the first time to two little human waifs for whom he had died.

Maria saw the minister only a few minutes more that night. The mosquitoes were too merciless for them to linger outside the house or to dare light up the cottage and invite people in, and the minister was not one who would propose a walk. He felt that both their hearts had received a benediction, and that the young woman would sympathize with him in wanting to be alone with God a little while after the Sabbath blessing.

But Maria's conscience had grown decidedly prickly. He had thanked her again as he bade her good-night for the help she had given him, and she felt guilty as she let him go away thinking of her in this way. She felt that her natural honesty would not long allow her to accept quietly this homage to her supposed goodness. She must explain soon, and then good-bye to all friendship with him, for he was evidently much in earnest. He would hardly waste time on such as she had been. Well, what did she care? She could go on as she had done and endure the summer to the end. The man was but a stranger, anyway, and not of her kind. Her restless spirit was returning. She knew nothing of the proposed domestic help. She remembered the morrow and all the petty miserable cares which she had of her own free will taken upon herself. The mosquitoes again began to be a terrible thorn in the flesh, and she saw in imagination the piles of greasy dishes which would have to be washed in the morning, and the struggle with the grocery boy to get him to send the yeast in time for the morrow's baking, with probably the necessity for buying some of the miserable baker's stuff offered under the name of bread which all the family cordially detested.

And then the brother came in with his never-ending flow of fun and capacity for teasing, and choosing the wrong time, proceeded to poke questions at her about Mr. Fairfield. Maria's replies were short and sharp; she said with freezing dignity that she cared nothing whatever for Mr. Fairfield and wished he would keep away; that she supposed he was some nobody, anyway, as no one else would come to such a place for the summer unless he had to. Then she went to her room with tears of vexation in her eyes and thought of the same man's earnest "thank you" spoken a few moments before, remembered her own gentle, subdued good-night, her assent to his works of Christian friendliness, how she had so evidently deceived him as to her character, and felt herself a very hypocrite indeed.

It is no wonder then that the morning found her unrested and unhappy as in the days that had passed. She was even disposed to resent the new arrival in the kitchen instead of being glad and relieved, and after repeated attempts to monopolize the entire work and so show that girl was a room with a sweep of her head, declaring that if they would not let her work she supposed she could sit down and endure life in some way with folded hands. No, she would not go to the beach, and she would not go bathing, and she would not fix up her muslin dress to wear to Spray View that afternoon for she was not going to Spray View to call on those two stuck-up girls. She did not care to be patronized if Rachel did, and as for Roland De Vere, she thought she had been greatly mistaken in him. He did not seem nearly so intellectual as she had at first supposed. Then when Rachel in despair had left her, she had barred the door and burying her face in the pillow had cried as hard as her overwrought nerves demanded.

Fortunately for her, she had not cried long when Rachel's voice called to her again that there was some one in the parlor to see her. This stopped the tears suddenly, but not the stubbornness. She would not go to the parlor to see anyone. Rachel might make any excuse she pleased, that she was too busy or sick, but she would not come out, and she would not unfasten the improvised door which the father and brother had contrived for more privacy than the cottage afforded. Nevertheless, she rose from beside the bed and went to the small disfiguring looking-glass. She knew by former experience that the few moment crying in which she had indulged must have left its marks already on her face. Yes, her eyes and nose were red and swollen. She could not go out if she wished to do so, without disgracing herself. She began to wonder who it could be who wished to see her; perhaps some of those De Veres, now become hateful, because she fancied they were looking down upon her and hers; perhaps, the minister. Well, if it was the minister, what did she care? she asked herself fiercely and she went nervously to the wash bowl and began to dash the cold water on her swollen eyes.

Then at the other door came the mother's voice, always low and sweet, but very low now lest the caller in the parlor of this very "open" house should hear. There was also a note of command in the voice which Mrs. Hammond seldom used toward her children, but which Maria did not dare disregard.

"My daughter, let me in at once. I have something to tell you."

Maria with the wet towel in her hand answered her mother's summons then, and quickly let her in, mopping her face violently the while:

"Are you ill, daughter?" asked the anxious mother as she saw the traces of excited tears on her elder daughter's face.

"No," answered Maria, choking suddenly at the tenderness in her mother's voice; she almost wished she were really ill and lying in bed to be petted and taken care of. It made the tears start again to her eyes.

The mother wound her arm about the daughter's waist.

"Well, then, dear, is there any reason why you do not care to see Mr. Fairfield? Tell me all about it. I must know the reason, you know, before I can excuse you."

"Is it Mr. Fairfield?" asked Maria, a little gleam of satisfaction showing in her voice in spite of herself. "But you see, mother, I can't go out. Look at my eyes. I am a perfect sight. It will be hours before I get over being a fright. You will have to tell him something." There was disappointment in Maria's voice, very evident to the mother, and she determined that she would make a strenuous effort to get Maria out of herself, and into the fresh air, where her overwrought nerves might have a little chance for rest.

"Nonsense! Your eyes will be all right in a few minutes, dear!" she answered quickly. "Bathe them and brush your hair. Here, slip on your pretty beach dress. You have not worn it since you came and the air is quite fresh this morning. I want you to get out and have the air and sunshine. You will be ill if you do not, and that we are not going to allow. Now hurry, dear, Mr. Fairfield is quite anxious to see you. I will excuse you for a few minutes, and Rachel shall take him down to the new clam beds while you are getting ready. Now hurry," and the mother hastened out to do what she had promised with more confidence in her manner than she felt in her heart that Maria would do her bidding.

But something seemed to have come over Maria. She desired suddenly above all things to go out with her pretty beach dress, walk beside Mr. Fairfield, have him think her good for a little while, and say she helped him. It would not do any harm just for once and she was tired of the hateful way things had been going. She washed her face feverishly and furiously and hastened her toilet as much as possible and between times took hurried trips to the disfiguring little glass to see if there was any hope of her eyes and nose soon assuming their proper color and shape, and the mother, coming back, was relieved to find that Maria was ready.

And so it came about the Maria and the young minister started out on a tramp to the life-saving station, two miles away, on that lovely summer morning, with a fresh breeze blowing in their faces, and Maria looking her very prettiest in her dark blue and white yachting suit, her cheeks becomingly pink from the recent tears, and her whole face as expressive of sudden happiness as could well be, for when Maria gave way after a fit of stubbornness she was often really lovely and subdued and humble, and somehow her mother's tones and wistfulness had conquered her that morning.

Moreover, she felt humiliated in her heart and the humility sat well upon her face, where there had been so much haughty pride of late. The minister, looking at her in the Monday morning light decided that she was very fair as well as good, and he was glad to walk with her and talk beside the sea, and before the morning was over they found many points of interest in common. Maria coming back did not feel half so much a hypocrite that she had not confessed to him how unworthy she was of his praise, because the talk had not been on things in which she felt she was lacking. The Lord in his wisdom saw that this child of his needed a little of the brightness and joy of life and he had given it to her, weaving, as he gave it, about her the cords of his own love which were to draw her to himself. Let no skeptical one fancy all this beneath him. We barter away the whole comfort of life if we so think. For these things, and things like them, are among the "all those" the Master promised should be added to those seeking first the Father's kingdom.

Chapter 13

The afternoon was warm and lovely. It was several days since Maria and Mr. Fairfield had walked to the life-saving station together, and since then there had been several like expeditions. Maria lay in the screened and netted hammock on the porch with a book before her, but she was not reading. Instead, she was thinking. Her troubled conscience had pursued her day after day through all the pleasant walks and sails and rides and talks. She felt herself to be more and more a hypocrite. She had tried feebly, two or three times, to explain to the minister that she was not "good" as he seemed to think, in fact that she was very wicked and worldly and unlovely in her character; but her efforts had failed, for it had been so pleasant to have some one think well of her, and make her a part of his pleasure as this man had done.

This afternoon her conscience had arraigned her most strongly.

Something ought to be done. She must not go on reading religious books and pretending to be devoted to them, though the fact was growing plain to her that the books themselves were not so wholly without interest as they had seemed to her last Sabbath. She had learned that there was much that was intensely interesting in them, and she liked to hear the minister talk of these things. Her own part in these conversations had been a meek assent to what he said, but still she had managed to assent in such a manner as to keep unchanged his first impression that she was heart and soul with him in what he said. She had even added a word or two now and then when he had seemed to expect her to say something, and when something quite original had occurred to her which seemed to fit into the discussion. He thought her an exceedingly bright young woman, and so she was; those little additions of hers to the religious conversations had been apt and striking ones. She knew that her bringing-up had been largely the cause of her ability to say such things well, and to know when to say them.

But she also knew that her life for some time had run counter to her words and she hated hypocrisy above all things. She had planned conversation after conversation in which she should tell her new friend exactly the truth about herself. In some of these imaginings she was humble and begged him to teach her to think as he did. But for that she was too proud. In others she withdrew from his acquaintance entirely, told him she was not of his kind and that he had been mistaken in her. And then it occurred to her, "Why not turn about and try to be what he thought she was?" She had reached that point this afternoon for the seventeenth time, and she had asked herself over and over again whether she could do it and how she should begin, and whether if she did, it would be exactly honest in her to do so? And then, why, after all, should she do it? Mr. Fairfield was a pleasant acquaintance, but in all probability he would go away in a few days and she might never see him again. Why did she care to try to appear well before him, and not only to appear well, but to really be what she appeared? She could not understand why he seemed to bring out the best and highest longings her soul contained.

Well, supposing she should set herself the task of being good, what should she do first? She might refrain from being cross, it is true, and saying sarcastic things; but that seemed rather a hopeless task, for her tongue was so used to bitter words that she scarcely knew when she spoke them. Then too, there was nothing interesting in that. Still of course that would come in as a necessary part of any such change in her life. She might take up some philanthropic work. But what could it be? Rachel seemed to always be able to find some work to do for others, but now that there was help in the kitchen. Maria felt that her life had been made too easy for her to show forth her good works by any great sacrifices such as she was seeking.

It was just at this point in her conversation with herself that her sister came upon the porch with low rocking-chair, work-basket, scissors, and thimble, and in the distance across the sandy dunes could be seen the lank, awkward from—arraying in a neat blue calico and white apron—of their new serving-maid, bearing in her arms a bundle of old hats, apparently. Her work was done for the afternoon and Rachel's first lesson, instead of being in lace work, was to be in millinery, for it appeared that Annie Higgins' greatest desire in the line of worldly possessions was a nice hat to wear to an entertainment that evening over on the mainland, to which her cousin's wife's brother had asked her to accompany him in his sailing vessel, along with some other members of the family. Rachel, through tact and kindness, had discovered this need and desire of Annie's and had readily offered her assistance, sighing as she thought how much better hat Annie might have if only Maria were to make it instead of herself; but she quietly kept the matter to herself, as she supposed, dreading Maria's scornful looks and words which would be sure to come if she knew.

She had reckoned, however, without remembering the cracks in the kitchen wall. Maria had heard the entire arrangement that morning as she sat in her room mending a rent in her blue dress, and had thought for other people. Had Rachel been there and known that she heard it, Maria would have felt called upon to show her scorn of such a proceeding, but away from sight Maria was able to appreciate something of her sister's kindness, although she wholly disapproved, and wished she would not do such queer things. Now as she saw Rachel come out and Annie also issue forth from the little unpainted house across the marsh she remembered, and half wished she were gifted with doing things for other people so that she might not feel so utterly unworthy of the friendship of a good and earnest Christian minister. She languidly watched Rachel as she put on her little white work apron and selected the needle with which she expected to work. She knew that to Rachel the task of making a hat was a great one. Rachel would much rather write a description of the hat, or draw a picture of it, than go through the necessary manipulations in order to produce one. It was not likely to be an artistic affair when done, either, as both the sisters well knew from former experience. However, Rachel would do her best, hoping for the best results.

Just at that moment around the corner by the little church came two beautiful horses drawing an elegant carriage in which sat Roland De Vere and his two sisters. The two sisters were on the back seat and the front seat beside the young man who was driving was evidently left vacant for some one they expected to pick up. The carriage drew up at the little green cottage doorsteps and its occupants greeted Rachel effusively. Maria was glad that she was well screened from their view, for somehow she felt as utterly out of sympathy with them as she did with herself or anybody else, though several months before her heart would have jumped with joy at their appearance and she would have done anything to be the fourth member of that riding party. Now she knew that they had come for Rachel, and she saw by the sudden rush of glad color to her little sister's cheek that Rachel knew and was glad, gladder perhaps than they had any idea of, for Rachel was always so quiet about her likes and dislikes that sometimes she was in danger of being allowed to lose much that she cared for in life through other people supposing that she did not care. Maria's eyes were opened a little by the look on her sister's face as she quietly laid aside her basket and went down the steps to greet her callers and ask them to come in. Maria was glad that they immediately declined, for she could not get away unobserved and she did not wish to be seen; but she could not well help listening to the conversation.

Roland De Vere, in his gallant and courtly way, invited Rachel to put on her hat and get into the carriage at once, as they were off for a long drive up the beach and must have her company else their pleasure would be spoiled. Maria saw, through the cracks in the porch screen, how the soft color stole again into Rachel's cheeks and then how her bright face clouded over with disappointment.

"Oh, I'm so sorry I can't go," she answered instantly; "I would love it so, and it is such a perfect day for a drive on the beach. I have often thought how delightful it would be to fly along on the edge of the waves with horses like those. But I can't, I really can't."

"Now we won't have any 'can't' at all. What is it in the way?" asked the young man earnestly; "because whatever stumbling-block there is, I shall remove it. Have you been a naughty girl and won't they let you get up out of your chair till you're good, or are you mending and can't leave your task till it's finished? If that's it, give me a needle, and I'll help and we'll have the work done in less than no time."

Amid the laugh which followed Rachel's perplexed face grew firm.

"No, it isn't anything like that," she answered, laughing, and yet sorry and troubled. "It's the Higgins girl."

"The Higgins girl! What has she to do with it, and who is she? Bring her along, that'll be all right; we can stow her in somewhere and make her comfortable, I guess. Fannie, can't you and Evelyn make room back there?"

But Rachel hastened to explain, with an irrepressible smile at the idea.

"No, no it's her hat. I promised to help her make a hat to wear to an entertainment to-night. She is the fisherman's daughter who lives over in that little house, and she wants to go to an entertainment with a friend to-night. I have promised her and she seems very happy over it, so I must not disappoint her."

Mr. De Vere emitted a prolonged whistle and the Misses Fannie and Evelyn looked curiously at Rachel, making Maria's blood boil within her.

"Dear me!" said Evelyn shrugging her shoulders, "can't you put her off?"

"Yes," put in Fannie seeing her brother's evident disappointment and Rachel's firmly-set red lips, "tell her it is a great deal more smart to go bareheaded to entertainments this time of year and wear a flower in her hair."

These girls were well-bred and liked Rachel very much, and moreover desired to please their brother, but they were not quite equal to giving up an afternoon's pleasure for the sake of making a hat for a fisherman's daughter, it was evident. Rachel felt this more than saw it. Meanwhile she also felt that she had the brother's sympathy in her perplexity.

Maria, listening, saw it all and suddenly resolved. This was her opportunity. Without her usual calm deliberation, she acted impulsively, almost as Rachel might have done. She called her sister's name.

"Rachel!"

Poor Rachel! No small part of her perplexity, embarrassment, and trouble had arisen from the fact that Maria was listening on the porch, unable to get away, and that she would let fall all sorts of sneering comments upon her, ruthlessly, as soon as the visitors should be out of sight. But she had not supposed that Maria would dare speak at the moment, bringing out the fact of her presence, for she knew Maria's hair was tumbled with lying in the hammock, and Maria's gown was not the one in which she would array herself to appear before the De Veres. With cheeks crimsoning and eyes burning with tears she was too proud to let be seen, she excused herself a moment and went to her sister, trembling as if she had been a little child lest Maria was about to reprimand her severely in the hearing of these friends, as she had once or twice threatened she would do if Rachel persisted in her puritanical notions.

But to her utter amazement, instead of the proud, scornful look she expected to see upon Maria's face there was one of interest, and Maria's tone was low and sisterly as she said: "Rachel, go! I will trim Annie's hat. Yes, go on at once; it's all right. You know I can do it as well as you. Get ready right away."

Rachel could hardly believe her ears. Maria offering to trim a servant girl's hat! Maria giving up her ease, without being urged, to do a work of kindliness for one she despised!

But the friends in the carriage were waiting and Maria was hastening her. She must go and explain. She hesitated but a moment. She saw her sister meant it, and would be displeased if she did not accept it, so she went back to the carriage with a happy face and explained that Maria would see to the hat and then ran in to make her hasty, simple preparations and soon drove away with a bright face. Roland De Vere as he touched his whip to his gay horses said to himself: "I must have been mistaken in Maria after all. I would not have expected her to do so kind a deed."

It seemed that Maria was fated to give false impressions of her goodness nowadays, in spite of herself and of her honest endeavor to right matters with her conscience. As soon as the carriage was out of sight she went in to the kitchen to the solemn-faced girl, who had slipped around to the back door with her pile of old hats and soiled ribbons and funny bright artificial flowers, watching the expected helper drive away in the beautiful carriage with growing dismay gripping her heart, the thought of her own expected pleasure dimmed by the shade of the old worn-out hat.

She was only a poor girl after all, and of course Miss Rachel wouldn't stop for her when she had pleasure of her own on hand! Then she sighed and told herself Miss Rachel was no better than other folks after all, if she did teach the children a whole lot of religion last Sunday. Christian folks were all alike. She had been almost tempted to believe Miss Rachel was different, but now she would never believe in anybody again who had pretty clothes and lots of friends and pleasures. Then she had sat down disconsolately in the back door and looked off at the sea, and felt gloomy, and thought of the long dull winter which would come so soon.

Maria explained how it was that Rachel had gone, and said pleasantly that she would do the work, inviting Annie at once to bring her materials that they might look them over; but Annie had not formed so charming an idea of Maria's character as yet that she did not feel a trifle afraid of her, so she only sat still and said she needn't bother, it didn't matter, anyhow. Maria found that her services, which she knew were so much better than her sister's in this particular line, and which she had expected would be accepted with overwhelming joy, had actually to be urged upon this poor fisherman's daughter. It made her indignant and she told herself that she wouldn't touch the hat if she had not promised Rachel, that the girl deserved no hat at all.

However a promise was a promise, and so she set herself to win Annie out of her glumness and soon had her interested in the hat. And while Annie heated irons, according to her direction, for steaming velvet, she hunted among her own ribbons and flowers for something suitable to help out the meagre array of trimming, and she pondered within herself why she had done this. Was it for Rachel, or for the minister, or for her own conscience' sake?

Chapter 14

The porch was the only comfortable place in which to work that warm afternoon, so after a brief struggle with her pride, Maria transported Annie and her trimmings to a place behind the screen. It was true there was a possibility of some neighbors passing, or of the return of the driving party, or that the minister might come by before she had completed her task. But for the neighbors she cared little, and her feeling toward those De Vere sisters was such that she would rather enjoy shocking them, and, as for the minister, well, she was not sure but she had done this for him, and if he did not understand, her work would have been in vain.

She settled down determined to make a pretty hat and be friendly with this uninteresting girl if she could. She was determined for once to try her hand at philanthropy. On the whole, after the first half-hour she found it not so uninteresting. Trimming hats was always pleasant work to her. She enjoyed thoroughly making "a whistle out of a pig's tail," figuratively speaking, and to make this old hat into something respectable, nay even into a work of art, was as good as playing a new game. She really liked it when once she got into it.

Annie was kept so busy steaming velvet for the first few minutes that she had not time to talk, for which she was thankful, for she felt half resentful at Maria for touching her hat. She had had no reason as yet to like Maria, and would almost rather have done without a hat than take a favor from her. She felt as though she were being patronized. But when she at last emerged from the kitchen with the carefully brushed and steamed velvet and saw the hat which had looked such a hopeless, shapeless mass to her but a few moments before, assuming under the skillful hands of the manipulator the shape of hats she had seen in the stores and on the heads of the ladies of fashion in the hotels, her heart gave a great bound of joy and her allegiance forthwith went out to Maria even more warmly than it had done to Rachel. Such is the vanity of all flesh. Shall we say feminine flesh? To watch those white fingers tastefully twist the renewed velvet folds about the now gracefully shaped straw, was a wonder. Annie sat and gazed in speechless delight, proving herself a sharp and foreseeing helper, because of the quick, alert way in which she always seemed to anticipate the needs of the milliner, handing her a pin or the spool of thread at just the right moment, and restoring the scissors when they slipped to the floor, as scissors have a habit of doing. Maria could but notice and appreciate this, and felt an impulse to speak a kind word, but could think of nothing except about the hat.

"I think it will look very well when it is done," she said at last, holding the hat off to survey it, and feeling that this admiring silence was becoming oppressive.

"It's jes' perfec'ly lovely!" exclaimed Annie effusively, her eyes shining with the delight of possessing anything so altogether satisfying. "I jes' don't see how you can do it so good! Don't you feel awful proud to be able to? How did you learn how? Did you ever work at a milliner's store?"

Maria's cheek flushed. She did not like this question. She felt inclined to be indignant and take the girl's words for an insult. The idea of her working in a milliner's shop! This came of their hiring such a ridiculously cheap cottage and making even the poor fisher folk think they were from the common walks of life. Then she glanced up and seeing the evident admiration in Annie's face, reflected that the girl had lived on the island much of her life and knew little of the different strata in society. Of course she had no intention of insulting her. Indeed, she perceived from the girl's face when she answered no, that she would have stood a trifle higher in her estimation as a skilled artisan if she could have boasted that advantage. So she let the little discomfiture pass, a fact which almost surprised herself and would have astounded her family beyond measure; she even smiled at the queer questions which followed, getting a little quiet amusement out of them.

"Your sister Rachel says you know how to do most everything," went on Annie, clasping her hands about one knee and rocking back and forth on the broad low step on which she was seated. "She said you could paint pictures. Say, did you ever do any of them crayon pictures of live folks? What they hang in best parlors, I mean, that look just like the folks, only all dressed up better than they gen'ally are when they're alive? They have two of them over to my friend's on the mainland. They've got red plush and gold frames, awful pretty, and they hang over the organ and the sofa. It's of her ma and pa when they was first married. I'd like awful well to get one of my oldest brother, that died when he was ten, for ma. She hasn't never forgot to mourn about him. Jes' seems if none o' us could take his place. Do you s'pose you could do one if I was to tell you how he looked? You see he never had no photograph taken, cause they didn't even have a tin-type place here when we come here to live, nor in Spray View either. Could you do one o' them kind o' pictures, do you think? If you could I'd work all summer jes' fer nothin' to get that picture, fer it would please ma and pa so; and I know where I could get a real pretty frame made cheap; a friend of mine is in a store where they make 'em."

Annie's eagerness quite overcame the milliner. She tried to repress the smile that would keep coming and to explain that no one would be able to make a likeness of a person who was dead, without some kind of a photograph to go by, especially one who had not known the person in life. Annie looked disappointed. She had gone from one extreme to the other and felt that a person capable of transforming her old hat could do anything. She was silent a few minutes watching the deft fingers at work, and then she began again.

"Your sister says you made them couches and pretty stuffings and curtains in your parlor. I think you must be awfully smart. You're sort of a 'Jack at all trades' as the sayin' is, aren't you?" She laughed heartily over this intended joke, and Maria could not refrain from joining in. Maria coupled with her powers of elocution a rare ability as a mimic of the tones and manners. She began to think she would have rich material in this girl for quite an amusing entertainment of her friends if she should choose to give it to them.

Annie, in a wistful sort of way, finally asked: "Say! if I was to get some caliker, would you kind o' pin it up fer me like that there green stuff hangin' in your dinin'-room door? I'd like awful well to fix up our front room a little. I hate it the way 'tis. I never knew how to do them kind of things, but I always knew it looked horrid. I tried once or twice. I sent all the way to New York for a motto I saw advertised in a paper I had. It was "Little Church around the Corner." That was just the year they built the chapel there and I thought it would look kind of nice to have that motto in the parlor. It said it had the directions how to make it, and the stuff an' all fer twenty-five cents, so I got it an' it took me a good part of the winter workin' evenin's to finish it. I done it in blue with green trimmin's and a brown steeple, them was the colors they sent, and it looked real pretty and I stuck some shells on pasteboard and made a frame for it, but I ain't never had anything else to go with it. I would jes' give anything if we had a organ. It would look so nice under where it hangs, an' Jim and the girls would all like the music so much. I guess they could play it too after tryin' a little, for Jim can play the accordion real good. He plays 'Swanee River,' and 'Home Sweet Home,' an' 'Sweet By an' By' every Sunday night when he don't have to go down the bay. Say! How did you get them cushions in that corner to stand out so pretty with them ruffles all around? Do you s'pose I could fix up our house a little like this if I tried real hard?"

Maria could not help being interested in the poor, forlorn little house and this girl's helpless, hopeless attempt to "fix it up." She began to suggest some simple things which seemed to Annie quite too simple to make any effect, but as Maria went on and grew interested herself in describing the changes she should make in a bare room if she had but limited means,

Annie's eyes began to sparkle and her cheeks to grow red with eagerness. She really saw ahead of her some chance that their home might have a few bright, cheerful things some day as well as others.

"Why, I could do that," she said, as Maria paused with a pin in her mouth to try the effect of the ribbon she was arranging on the hat.

"Jim, he could saw the boards. I know he wouldn't mind helping. He has lots o' time Sundays."

Maria's strict training as to the Sabbath as a day of rest made her feel a little doubtful of the good she might be doing if she were but starting a family to work on the Lord's Day, but Annie's eager tongue went on, leaving her little time for reflection.

"Say! would you mind coming over some day soon and jes' lookin' at that room an' tellin' me where you thought that shelf you said how to make, would look pretty, and how far down the side of the wall the seat had ought to reach? It ain't very far over there, you know, an' I could show you some cunnin' little chickens and ducks if you'd come."

Maria began to see that her philanthropy was expected to last beyond this afternoon, and she was doubtful whether she relished the idea. She had been willing enough to make a hat, but as for enduring much of this cross-questioning, and being taken on such a friendly social level, she did not have any such intentions. She already felt herself swelling in her own estimation until she almost came up to the minister's ideal. Surely she must be pretty good, after all, to smilingly undergo such a storm of talk as she had been sitting under for the last hour.

But worse was to follow. She did not like to refuse the girl's eager request, so she said perhaps she would come some time, in what she meant to be an indefinite time, but the eager Annie accepted it all in good faith and began to thank her in most intense terms. Suddenly she turned full upon her. "Say!" said she earnestly. "You're one of them church folks too, ain't you? I didn't think you was at first, because you didn't go so much to the chapel, nor seem to run around talking Bible like your sister, but I knew quick as I saw you at that hat so nice an good that you was. I never thought much of them church folks till lately. Pa he thinks they're all frauds, 'cause some of 'em have treated him mean; but then folks ain't all alike, an' I always used to say that folks that is mean will be mean even if they are church folks, an' the church can't make 'em any worse, only it looks worse, them pretendin' so much; but when that there minister come along and was so awful nice about our boat an' all, — I s'pose he told you how it was, — why I jus' made up my mind it wasn't the church that made 'em all so mean, 'cause he bein' a minister an' a kind o' head of it all, he would be meaner than the hull lot of 'em if 'twas the church made 'em so, an' I began to tell pa that he must uv made some mistake. Well, he did allow that if that young feller should run the chapel awhile he would go an' hear him preach himself. He's awful nice, ain't he? Say! ain't you an' he goin' to marry? Folks says you are. I heard it over to Spray View. It's awful nice you like the church an' are so good if you're a-goin' to marry a minister!"

Before Maria could lift her flaming face, or steady her voice to reply to this remarkable series of questions and remarks, she heard a step on the single board which formed a walk over the sand in front of their cottage, and looking up, annoyed beyond measure, to see who was coming and perhaps overheard the last remarks, she saw Mr. Fairfield standing before her. His face was a study, to say the least, perhaps a trifle too grave; but it was evident that the gravity was put on to hide a twinkle which Maria felt must be in his eye. It was impossible to tell how much he had overheard. He betrayed no sign whatever of anything having been over-heard at all, but the irrepressible Annie arose from her step in confusion, adding to Maria's consternation.

"Goodness gracious me! If here he ain't now! 'Talk of angels an' you hears their wings,' as the sayin' is." And she disappeared most unceremoniously into the cottage and began rattling the cook stove to hide her embarrassment.

Chapter 15

The minister sat down on the step vacated by Annie. His acquaintance in the Hammond cottage had progressed so far that he felt sufficiently at home to be seated without an invitation from the young hostess, who was evidently too perturbed to think of offering him any seat less lowly. He looked her over with a new and curious expression upon his face. She was appearing to him in a light in which he had not as yet considered her. Her blushes were certainly becoming. He rather enjoyed her embarrassment. He was quiet for a moment, not caring to interrupt his study of her face. She meanwhile was earnestly engaged in struggling with her thread, which had snarled in the most unaccountable way just as she was taking the final stitch in the completed hat. Her cheeks instead of cooling down grew fairly purple, and her horror and indignation over what that impertinent girl had dared to say to her grew with every minute, as she realized how much the man before her might, yes, must, have heard.

"What are you supposed to be doing?" at last questioned Mr. Fairfield, with an amused expression upon his face.

At the first sound of his voice the spell which had been cast upon Maria's tongue seemed to be broken. She ignored his question. Indeed, she did not know a word he had said:

"Mr. Fairfield," she burst out impetuously, "I do hope you will not believe from the last words that impertinent girl said that *I* have been discussing *you* and your affairs with *her!*" She emphasized each pronoun a little more till the final one was intense and well expressed the scorn she felt.

"And if you had, am I to understand that my humble self would have been a subject so far beneath your notice that you should speak of me in that tone?"

Howard Fairfield's tone was light and cheerful. It was more the tone in which he used to speak to his young associates ten years before when he was just entering college, and before the grave things of life had as yet reached him. Something in this afternoon's occurrence had seemed to put him back again for a little and make him feel young and full of mischief. Besides, he was one of those rare beings who possess wonderful tact, and he saw that Maria was extremely embarrassed and could only hope to regain her composure through being able to laugh it off. He proved himself correct in this conclusion, for his tone, so different from the grave, earnest one he had been accustomed to use in their intercourse, roused Maria from her painfully overwrought feelings to look up and wonder, and even laugh. She essayed to make him understand once more that she had not been discussing him, but had been treated to a catalogue of his virtues,—something connected with a boat,—and she suddenly remembered to her relief that Annie had suggested that he might have told her the story, therefore she at once asked an explanation. Although the young man was evidently annoyed that a mere act of kindness on his part should have been so brought out that he was obliged to tell of it himself, he saw that it would help Maria to regain her composure if he did, and so in a few words he told her how he had helped the father with a bit of advice and a trifle of a loan of money when their fishing boat, their largest source of revenue, had been in danger of being confiscated for a small debt. Had Maria been less upset in her mind she might have read much between the lines which was to the young man's credit, for she must have seen how little he made of the affair and how lightly he told of it. And then he launched into an account of a walk he had taken that afternoon and a most beautiful spot he had discovered, and made Maria forget her discomfiture entirely in the charming powers of description which he exerted for her benefit.

Suddenly he asked, "And what have you been doing all the afternoon? What is that creation you are holding? It looks as if it might be pretty, and certainly is marvelous in its construction. Are you preparing to leave this desert island, and fly back to civilization, and is that a part of your plumage?"

Maria had to laugh again, although the color mounted in her cheeks as she looked at the hat, now grown contemptible in her eyes, and wished she had never seen it nor ever might again—realizing that it had been the cause of her discomfort. It came to her at the same time that she had made an utter failure of trying to do good, and she made a resolve, to be honest with herself and him and everybody else and not let people think her better than she was. She would show everybody just how mean and contemptible she was. Then at least she would be no longer tormented by her conscience, whatever other unpleasantnesses she might have to endure.

"No," she answered half laughing, half troubled, "it represents a vain attempt on my part to right myself in the eyes of the world and be honest. I have been trying to be 'good' and do unto others—well—as they would have me do to them, at least, if I did not do as I would have them do to me. But I think I will give it up. I am not constructed on those lines, I see, and seem to have made a failure in every way. And, indeed, Mr. Fairfield, I have been rarely punished for my attempt to deceive others and myself."

"I don't understand," said the minister comically, puzzled and reaching out his hand for the hat. "It seems to be all right as far as I can judge, though I own I'm not a judge of millinery; but I was told that a hat to be all right must have so much straw, so much ribbon, so much velvet, and so many flowers or feathers, put together in the right proportions. You seem to have all those things. Isn't it becoming? Is that the matter?"

Now Mr. Fairfield had seen at once that there was behind Maria's half-laughing, troubled face something deeper, something which he felt he would like to know. Their intercourse together had been of the sort which draws human hearts to sympathize with one another. He saw she needed help, or thought she did, and as he felt she had helped him, he wished to help her. But he would find out what she meant from her own lips, he would not ask her questions, for he judged from his own nature that that method might only serve to shut the truth from him forever, so he continued his bantering tone.

But although Maria laughed, her face sobered suddenly.

"The hat isn't mine," she answered him quickly. "I am supposed to be doing it for the love of doing good to others. It is for Annie Higgins. It is some of my sister's philanthropy. I never originated any, not to carry it out, in my whole life. Ray had promised to trim this hat so that girl could go to some sort of a picnic to-night, and then her friends came for her to take a drive, and I acted on a sudden impulse and offered to do it for her. I think the real reason I offered to do it was to see if I could just for once be as good as you have persisted in telling me I am. But I'm not. I want to tell you the truth. I can't be miserable any longer at being thought to be good, and helpful, and all that, when I don't know nor care the first thing about it. I let you misunderstand me in the first place and then it went on, and I began to see it was all just as bad as if I had started out to act a lie. I have not had the usual experience of the rich reward of doing good that you find in the Sunday-school books. I may have succeeded in making a respectable looking hat, but I have had a most uncomfortable afternoon, in addition to having been almost insulted by questions and an intimacy which is exceedingly disagreeable thrust upon me, and which I can foresee will cause me endless embarrassments. Now you can see just how much of a fraud I have been. Of course it does not matter to you, for there are other people in the world who are really what you thought I was and can talk with you on these subjects you enjoy and be honest, but I cannot rest comfortably to have any one think me what I am not."

Maria had tumbled these words out one on top of another, scarcely realizing what she was saying, only being anxious to get the horrid explanation over and have the visitor go, so that she might escape to her room and cry as she had never cried before. The tears were already coming to her eyes, and as she raised her face to make her meaning more impressive Mr. Fairfield saw them. He became aware also at that moment of what neither of them had noticed before, that the carriage containing the De Veres and her sister Rachel was just driving up to the door. His heart went out to the overwrought girl before him with sympathy and something deeper — a longing to help which he could not understand. His ready tact stood him in good stead now. He arose with a graceful bow and came forward to the carriage and shaking hands with the young ladies and saying a bright word to his friend Mr. De Vere, thus gave Maria time for recovery before she came forward. He spoke of the charming day and how delightful the drive must have been, and said in a loud cheery tone that he had just dropped in to see if Miss Hammond would not like to walk to the pavilion and watch the double sunset on bay and ocean for a few minutes, that there was to be something rare that evening. Then he half turned toward Maria, and said in an aside:

"Are you nearly ready to go, Miss Hammond? I am afraid that we shall miss the best of it unless we hurry. Just get your hat and let us go without waiting longer, can't you?" and he turned again to the carriage to help Rachel out.

It was a venture almost doubtful in his mind, for he felt one could scarcely tell what Maria in such a mood might or might not do, but he was relieved to see that she took his words as a cover for a hasty retreat into the cottage, ostensibly to get her hat, and he hoped she would there get her equilibrium as well, at least enough to come out and meet and pass the De Veres and go with him to some secluded spot where they two could understand each other and where he might if possible help this young woman who had seemed before so strong in faith and without need of help.

When Maria reached her room and the tears came tumbling down with more prepared to follow, she was tempted, nay she was almost determined, not to go out of that room that night, but to give herself utterly over to misery. And yet, so queer a thing is human nature, she wanted to go out and walk with the minister to the beach and see what he would say to her — for she knew that he had some intention in his kind and strangely given invitation — more than she wanted anything in life. And so without the least delay she dashed the refreshing cold water over her flushed face, smoothed her hair, and seizing her hat made haste out to the piazza, relieved to find that the ordeal of speaking to the visitors was made a short one by the evident haste of her companion to get away and see the sunset.

And the walk to the beach was a brisk one in which the minister talked incessantly, letting Maria have no chance for even a word, pointing out a cloud over the bay, or the etching of a lonely deserted fisher's hut in the distance, against a sea of pink and gold off at the right. He even joked about the shape of some of the cottages, and indulged in a humorous remark or two on some of the inhabitants of the small town, not in any malicious way, only a little laugh, just to keep Maria from thinking of herself or what she had said, or what she meant to say. He was scarcely aware of what he was saying as he strode along. His one aim was to talk. And so he guided her to a quiet knoll a little way up the beach, too far to be disturbed by loiterers at this late hour. He even talked on while he arranged a seat for her in the sand, with two pillows, and shawl which he had not forgotten to take from the hammock on the porch, and he made her sit down in the purple and golden light which hung between the glittering bay and the opal-tinted sea. Then he stopped a moment and turning to her with a quiet smile, as a reminder that their friendship was deeper than the talk of the afternoon had been, said:

"And now, will you explain just what you wanted me to understand by what you said a few minutes ago? I think you are troubled in some way, and I couldn't get quite at it. You surely did not mind my hearing those foolish things that poor girl said. It was something deeper. May I understand?" His tone was gentleness itself, a tone Maria had never heard him use before except once; and that to a little frightened child they had passed one day running in terror from the incoming waves. She felt as if she were a little child adrift and now that he had found her, somehow she would be brought ashore. She dropped her eyes to the sand and tried to tell just what was in her heart.

"I mean that I am not 'good.' I am not like Rachel, or like you, or anybody that *loves* good things. When I first knew you, I did not feel that I was so different. You seemed to enjoy fun and I did not think you cared very much for grave, solemn things. But when you came back and were in some way changed, I was quite surprised. I understood the difference after you honored me by telling me of your strange experience. You were good before, I think, only I had not seen that side of your nature brought out yet. You took me for better than I was because, when we first met, I had my sister's Bible and a religious book which Mr. De Vere had sent her, lying beside me on the sand. I saw you thought more highly of me because they were there, and it pleases me always to please those with whom I am thrown. You asked me to read, and I like to read. I am afraid I am proud of my reading too, and it was mere selfish pride that made me read that book well, for I had scoffed at it a few minutes before, having taken it for a novel at first and thinking I would enjoy reading it. I let you think that I had been reading and enjoying it before you came. Then you told me all those wonderful things about yourself, and I felt ashamed to think I had let you do so, for I knew I was not worthy of so grave a confidence. Well, there isn't any more to say only that I have let you go on from day to day supposing that I was interested in religious things more than in anything else, just because I was lonely and it was pleasant to have an intellectual person to talk with who could make anything, even religion, interesting. I have been ashamed of it every day, but I did not know how to get out of it, and there seemed to be a sort of a spell upon me when I was with you which prevented my showing you my real character. I have tried once or twice to see how it would seem to really act out what you thought I was, but I don't succeed. I'm nothing but a frivolous creature who loves a good time and her own way. I feel very much relieved that at last I have mustered up courage to tell you the truth; but I would like to thank you for the very pleasant hours we have had together before we part, for I feel sure that they *have* helped me, and you have been very good to spend so much time in making it pleasant for me." All this in a torrent of words as though it had been one long sentence.

She started to rise, as if she were ready now to bid him farewell and go, but he detained her.

"Please sit still," he said quietly. "I want to ask you just a few things. In the first place, you surely do not suppose that because of what you have said that you and I are going to be any the less friends than before? Friendship cannot be cut in two by a few words and a farewell. You have come into my life, and have helped me, in spite of all you say, and if you have felt as you say you have there is all the more reason that I should try to help you if I can. Will you tell me one thing, Miss Hammond? Do you mean by all this that you do not love the Master?"

It is very strange how hard a simple little question is to answer sometimes. Maria had heard and read that question so many times, and in her childhood had answered it glibly and carelessly, taking it as a matter of course that she did. Now her eyelids and voice trembled and she hesitated long before the earnest question. At last she said:

"I'm afraid I don't," in a very low voice, almost inaudible above the sound of the waves.

"And do you mean you do not *want* to love him?" went on the quiet voice.

This time the hesitation was longer than before. Maria was questioning her own heart carefully, and shuddering at the thought of answering it in the affirmative. Very slowly came the words, by and by:

"No, I do not mean that."

"Thank God for that!" said the listener under his breath, and Maria looked up to see a light in the minister's face which awed her into silence and made her drop her eyes again and wait for him to speak.

One step further the minister dared to go as he breathed a prayer for guidance, so much concerned was he about this young friend, who suddenly seemed in his sight one very precious to his Master.

"Wouldn't you *like* to belong to him, to rest in him, just as we have talked about so many times? I cannot think that all we have said together has been utterly without interest to you. Do you not care in the very slightest to be his dear child?"

And Maria answered in an unsteady voice and humbly, "Yes, I *care*. I believe I care about that more than anything else on earth. I didn't know quite what it was before, but that is what I want. But, oh, I cannot get it. It doesn't belong to me," and the cry of her soul reached out to her Father in heaven, as she seemed to be groping in the darkness for his hand.

Chapter 16

The sunset flashed and faded unnoticed. The twilight crept softly over the ocean and stole up the sands; the young moon looked out and began to climb the sky; and still they sat and talked.

What they said is recorded above, and it meant much for both lives. The minister was going through his first real experience of leading an immortal soul to Christ, and the girl was face to face with the Master. Out of the gathering shadows on the waters it seemed to her that he came, as of old, and spoke peace to her troubled heart. Many days after, she found a poem among others in a book sent to her sister, which seemed so to fit into her memory of that evening and her experiences that she copied it on the margin of her Bible. These were the words:

> Out in the night on the wide, wild sea,
> When the wind was beating drearily
> And the waters were moaning wearily,
> I met with him who had died for me.

And there was a sense in which for a little space the existence of each to the other was blotted out as these two held converse concerning the things of the kingdom. The man felt that he was conveying a message of vital import from his Master, the first of the sort ever entrusted to him, perhaps, or at least the first whose importance had ever so impressed him. He must not think of himself, he must choose only the words, the Spirit spoke, he must not let his faith waver, he must pray as he breathed every instant, for he felt that Satan might set in at any moment and thwart the work. It was wonderful beyond any experience of his, this overpowering anxiety, this trembling joy, as she seemed to yield hers to her Saviour's will.

To the young woman who sat thus reviewing her life and her motives, the man beside her but carried a heavenly message. She forgot that he and she stood in mutual relations in the world which made it natural that she should desire to appear well in his eyes, and that she should admire his earnest, well-spoken words and be pleased that he cared to spend his effort upon her. Her heart-hunger for something better in her life than had ever been there before had at last spoken and she was recognizing its eternal right to be heard. She heard Jesus pleading through those words spoken without any excitement, and yet with such tremendous earnestness.

And yet each knew that there was a sense in which Maria was already a Christian, that is, before the world. She had taken Christ's vows upon her. She had been brought up to keep the commandments outwardly at least. She had even not been inactive in Christian work, to the extent of being zealous at certain times, when the work was particularly pleasant to her. And yet she sat and waited and hesitated, and knew that if she once gave over her will the decision would mean that her whole life hereafter must be changed.

They sat so long upon the sand that their figures, etched against the fading sky, became blurred by the mist of the evening, and when the great decision was finally made and the minister sealed it with a prayer whose few low-spoken words were from the deep new joy of his heart that God had blessed his message, the quiet night shut out their bowed heads from view.

Supper in the hotel was long over when they walked back along the sand and passed the gay piazza, filled with the merry talk of guests who watched the new moon travel its silver pathway over the waves, and laughed and made commonplace remarks, as though it were a common night and a common sight.

Supper in the green cottage was long over also, although it had been delayed for Maria's coming for some time. Rachel had gone over to the Parkers' with her brother, the father and mother had taken a stroll to the bay, and could be seen in the distance slowly walking up and down the little platform by the water, the sky, lit by the last memory of the dead sunset, making a clear background for their dark figures. The Higgins girl was seated on the front steps impatiently waiting to tell Maria, when she should come, that the hot biscuits were in the oven covered with a tin plate and the butter was in the top of the refrigerator, and the rest of the things were on the table for her supper, before going home to join in the merry evening attendant upon the arrival of several brothers-in-law and other relatives. Boisterous laughter issued across the marsh from the little house. Her errand accomplished, the Higgins girl hastened away. She felt embarrassed before the minister and Maria after what had happened in the afternoon.

Maria was relieved to find the house empty. She wanted to understand herself before she met any of the others. She paused at the top step to say good-night, and then bethought herself that the minister had missed his supper. She asked him to come in and have something to eat, and to her surprise instead of declining he hesitated and said: "May I?"

Maria scarcely knew whether she was glad or sorry he had accepted her invitation. It was rather an embarrassing position, this eating supper together, after foraging in the refrigerator and the oven, exposing the crudeness of their dwelling to this young man evidently used to luxury, and yet it was pleasant too. He entered into it like a boy and held the lamp for her while she got the butter, and stirred the fire to make the kettle boil for a cup of tea which he declared he should enjoy if she did not mind making it. It covered her shyness too, for after their long, serious talk, and the solemn words she had spoken, it had seemed to her she would scarcely dare to attempt common every-day living again at once lest she should do something to mar the wonder of the great peace which filled her soul. She did not take her change of heart as Rachel would have done, with a bubble of joy that entered into everything that touched her life. It was too new, and her nature did not so quickly accept and appropriate new situations. She felt that her experience was too sacred even to think about yet awhile. Indeed, it could hardly be called an experience. She felt no joy though she did feel at peace; she did not think that life was now to be all rose-colored. She was not perfectly sure but to-morrow she might fall from her high resolves. The only difference in her feelings from two hours ago was this deep peace, a peace which comes of decision, and a fixed purpose to surrender her will and to trust. Henceforth her life was to be different. Not because she could make it so, but because she had chosen another motive for its center. Now she only knew that her life was to be ordered for different ends, and whatever of joy or sorrow came, they were alike to be brought to Christ, the end to be his glory.

It was a novel experience to Maria, this free and easy getting supper together with the minister. Heretofore her intimate friends had not been of the sort who were admitted to the kitchen, and indeed the kitchen in their home had always until lately been under the rule of a regiment of good servants. There was a homelikeness, a comradeship, in their sitting down together. Maria felt embarrassed at first at the idea of it, fearing lest Rachel should come in, or her brother, and find what was going on and be surprised at her, for she had always looked down upon such proceedings as plebeian in the extreme and not to be encouraged — more like what the Parkers might be expected to do. And yet here she was actually enjoying it. She wondered why it was, and then forgot to wonder. Mr. Fairfield seemed boyishly happy, and Maria could but catch the infection of his spirits and be happy too. Each realized that there was deep feeling in the heart of the other, and the minister fully intended to go away at once as soon as they should have put away the remains of their impromptu repast, thinking that Maria needed the rest and quiet and a time alone with God after the long strain of the struggle of decision. They were just going to the piazza, the minister to say good-night and leave Maria with her own thoughts, when they heard steps and merry voices. Maria hastily set the lamp, now turned low, on the little shelf back in the kitchen, where its light would but dimly reach the front door, and so tell no tales of the tête-à-tête supper, and quietly, with all possible speed, followed her guest to the piazza. She did not wish her brother and sister to find room for teasing in anything that went on to-night, for it seemed to her she could not bear it. It was Rachel and Winthrop, with the Parkers and some others, come to sit on the veranda and sing.

In the little change that took place while the quartet grouped themselves on the steps and Rachel brought the lamp for them to see the penciled words of a recently written song, Mr. Fairfield drew nearer to Maria and said in a low tone; "You are tired."

He did not put it with the rising inflection of a question that demanded an answer, nor was there time for an answer before the singing began, but Maria felt that he was reading her thoughts and feelings with a fine sympathy, anxious to aid her. She smiled gratefully. Then the singing began. All at once Maria realized that these were the people to whom she had most clearly showed her dislike and disdain. With a sudden resolve, which seemed to her to be in response to a hidden, bidding voice, she determined to take the first step in a new direction at once. Throwing aside the distant manner which she had worn ever since coming to the shore, except then in the company of the minister or the De Veres, she forthwith joined in the talk and laughter, when the song was ended.

The Parkers were delighted with her bright words and ready assent to any plans they might propose. She was indeed a charming girl, and why had they been so deceived in her at first? Rachel and Winthrop sat silent through sheer amazement, and the minister wondered and divined the reason. It was strange how well he was beginning to understand this young girl who had been to him a stranger a few short weeks before. He sat looking at her in the dim lights and shadow thrown by the flickering lamp, as she talked, and he saw a gentle, softened look which was not wholly stirred by the pleasant things she was saying. He remembered now her face at different times as she had been pondering his questions down by the shore that evening, and the grave sweetness in her eyes, when she at last decided. To him she seemed all sweetness. He had not yet realized that she had indeed been hateful, as she told him. Isn't it blessed, sometimes, that there are people who cannot and who will not see our faults, even though we tell them they are there?

Maria was glad when they all rose to leave; not that she was not enjoying the talk. It was pleasant, and she was surprised to find herself interested in those Parkers; but she longed for the quiet of her own room.

Mr. Fairfield had been watching her during the last few minutes and now, as they rose to go, he took her hand for good-night and said in an undertone: "Are you any happier, Miss Hammond, than you were this afternoon?"

"I think so," she answered softly. "And oh, I want to thank you. I never should have found the right way if it had not been for you."

The young man bowed his head humbly. Said he:

"I think that is the most welcome thanks I ever received, for I never before to my knowledge was the means of leading any one to Christ. That seems a terrible admission for me, a minister of the gospel, to make, and perhaps, oh, I hope, it may not be true! But I never knew it at least and I have not been the sort of minister I should have been, you remember. You have helped me, you know, in spite of all you have said to the contrary, and so I am grateful beyond expression to be allowed to bring a little of the same blessed comfort to you."

Then Maria went in to the quiet moonlit window of her room and sat there in wonder, thinking of all that had passed since she left that room so hastily a few hours before; of the kindness of the minister, his earnest face and tender words, of the quiet lovely night about them, then of the walk home, and the pleasant little supper together. Somehow the fact of their eating alone together had made them better friends. There was something about the thought of that supper which she did not like to put into words yet, a strange, pleasant something, into which she dared not look for explanation. Perhaps sometime she would think it all out and see if there was any foundation for real pleasure in it, but now it was to be allowed to hover on the horizon of her mind, a pleasant memory connected with this wonderful night. Then she thought of the coming of the young people, and their songs. And there had been a new duty for her in their very fun. She must learn to join in it. She realized that perhaps this might be one of the hardest things for her to do, this letting down of her prejudices and being agreeable when her heart was not in what was going on. Would she be able to do it? She trembled at the mountain of difficulties which rose before her untried feet.

Of the great central event of that day, the decision that she had made to make Christ the center of her life, she almost feared to try to think as yet, it seemed so new and sacred. She could not begin to get used to it. She must wait till all the others were asleep before she could let her thoughts dwell much upon that.

Rachel came in soon and softly stealing up behind her, put her arms around her neck and kissed her, and she returned the caress lovingly and rose to prepare for rest. She felt she could not sleep soon, there was so much to think about, and when she knelt to pray, as was her habit, the act and the words meant so much more than they had ever meant before. Then, contrary to her expectations, she fell into a deep dreamless sleep, for her Father knew she was wearied and needed rest, more than to think of high resolves and to plan difficult paths. Now that she was willing to walk as he would have her, he would choose her paths and carry her over the hard places without the resolves which are sometimes merely signposts for Satan to read which way we are intending to go, that he may lie in wait for us there and intercept our progress. If she would but put her hand in Christ's all would be well.

> Trusting the one great Pilot of the deep
> To be for aye my tender, low voiced Guide,
> I look aloft and say—
> Though tossed upon life's ocean wide—
> "All's well! All's well! By day or night, all's well!"

Chapter 17

"She is a great friend of Maria Hammond's," said Fanny De Vere, as she skillfully opened an egg at the breakfast table. "I suppose that is the reason she chooses that place for the remainder of the summer."

"Well, I should imagine she would be just about Maria Hammond's stamp," said Evelyn; "they must have a good many interests in common. Nannette Davenport cares for nothing whatever but her own pretty self. She is the most self-centered person I know of. I suppose it's very unkind in me to say so, but positively, I don't believe her grief over her mother's death is more than skin deep. She never seemed to care for her in the least when she was alive."

"I am sorry she is coming," said Fanny. "Of course we shall not necessarily have much to do with her, but at the same time there will be a certain amount of civility which must be exchanged for decency's sake. It is a great pity she could not have gone somewhere else, but truly I suppose the real reason of her selecting Lone Point this summer is because she is in deep mourning and the society in which she moves would be scandalized if she were to appear anywhere else. Here she can do as she pleases. She is supposed to have retired from the vain world. If she chooses to indulge herself in a little amusement no one is a whit the wiser. I suppose Maria Hammond could not stand it any longer without some of her friends about her. Roland, I wonder why it is that girl is so different from her sister. You never would dream they were of the same family, would you?"

Thus appealed to the young man hesitated a minute before answering.

"I'm not sure," he said. "I've seen several things lately that led me to think she might be other than we at first thought. There must be something about her that's interesting or Fairfield would never waste his time on her. He isn't a lady's man, by any means. In college he would never have anything to do with shallow, insipid girls. There had to be some intellect before he would look at them, much less talk with them, unless he was absolutely compelled to do so."

"Oh, I suppose she is bright enough, as far as that goes," said Evelyn; "but for my part I think she is decidedly disagreeable, and I can imagine that she will be twice as much so when backed up by Nannette Davenport. I can't think how Nannette will endure the simplicity at the Lone Point Hotel. She never washed out her own bathing suit in her life, nor waded through deep sand to get to the beach. As for the rude cottages there, she will probably take the next train back home when she has seen them. Are you sure, Roland, that Miss Hastings said she was going to Lone Point?"

"Perfectly sure," answered the young man. "Miss Hastings had been up there yesterday afternoon to engage her room for her at her aunt's request. The young lady in question is coming unchaperoned, as her aunt considers that in so quiet a spot, so near Miss Davenport's intimate friends, a chaperon is hardly necessary."

Evelyn laughed.

"If she is the same Nannette who went to Boston a year ago, she will need a chaperon more in Lone Point than she does in a crowded city. She is kept somewhat in check there by custom and her position, but Lone Point she will consider good game. If you have the least friendliness in the world for your friend, the intellectual minister, you would better warn him to flee, for in spite of his intellect and his devotion at present to Miss Hammond, he will shortly be in the wiles of Miss Nannette. Why, consider, my dear brother. He is about the only eligible young man in the whole of that lonely Lone Point, unless perhaps Mr. Hammond and Mr. Parker might be counted in. But she counts it nothing to have three or four on hand at once."

"Well, if Fairfield can't take care of himself, I'm sure he deserves to suffer, that's all I have to say," said the young man with a laugh as he arose from the table and took up the morning paper.

It was by the morning mail Maria received a letter from her quondam friend, Miss Nannette Davenport. It was gushingly characteristic of her. She was always gushing when she had a point to gain. Just at present it suited her purpose to spend a few weeks in a quiet place, and Maria would be very useful to her in helping to pass the time. The letter expressed great delight over the thought of a quiet summer in which to hide the deep grief she professed. She said she wanted to get away from the world and had decided to come near to her friend. She had delayed to send Maria word until the day before her arrival that her coming might be a pleasant surprise, but her room was already engaged at the hotel and Maria might meet her at the Lone Point Station at three the next afternoon.

That this was a surprise to Maria need not be doubted; but it was anything but a pleasant surprise. Nannette Davenport had never been a deeply loved friend. She had a certain prestige because of her mother's wealth and standing in society which Maria had thought she could not well afford to ignore. Through Nannette she had gained entrance to several homes in a high social circle where she feared she would not have been able otherwise to go since her father's failure. Indeed it was through Nannette she had met the De Veres. The two girls had been thrown together not a little at the beginning of their friendship, if it could rightly be called a friendship where there was no real love nor even very strong liking, when they were both away at school. Maria knew just how much real friendship Nannette held for her. She knew what a shallow, heartless girl she was. And she did not rejoice at the thought of her coming to Lone Point.

Had the letter come three or four days before it did, she would have worried greatly that Nannette should come and see her in such humble surroundings, but somehow the events of the past few days had made surroundings seem of less importance; so that now, as she read the letter and pondered over it with a distressed little pucker between her eyes, it was not because of the little green cottage nor yet of their straitened circumstances that her first objection was raised. Her first thought was for her new life. How hard it would be to mix thought and feelings so utterly at variance! Her utter distaste for Nannette's pleasures was a sort of a revelation even to herself as she read. She had not known how much her own likings and longings were wrapt up in her desire to carry out her new aim in life.

She sat down and began to ponder what she should do. It would not do to be rude to Nannette. Christ would not wish that. Was her trouble that she was afraid to stand out against her and say decidedly that her motives in life were changed? Or was it that she feared her own self and dreaded lest she might lose this wonderful calm that had come into her life three nights ago? Did she think that it might be she would be tempted back to old ways, old thoughts, old bondages? There came to her suddenly with this thought a remembrance of a verse she had read that morning from Rachel's Bible. Rachel's Bible was always lying open somewhere about, and Rachel's Bible always had marked verses to catch her eye when she was in a hurry. She used to say she kept her Bible near at hand that she might snatch a thought now and then as she was going by, as it helped to keep her from temptation. Maria had not yet gained the courage to bring forth her Bible openly as Rachel did. She wanted to read it by herself first and get used to the thought of her new way of living, and so she had chosen a verse from her sister's Bible as she dressed. It was:

"God is faithful, who will not suffer you to be tempted above that ye are able; but will with the temptation also make a way to escape that ye may be able to bear it."

How strange that that verse should have come in her way that morning! How wonderful to think God was actually answering her thoughts in his own words! Surely, this girl's arrival was nothing she was responsible for, and therefore she was not to blame. He had allowed the temptation; could not she trust him to make a way of escape for her? She arose and fastened the door, and then knelt down to ask for faith. She knew it would seem very strange to Rachel to come in in the daytime and find her praying. She was still in bondage. Her fetters had been forged tight, and it was hard for her to drop them even now that they were broken.

She did not feel that she knew how to pray very well, but she knew that God would understand; and as she rose she began to wonder if perchance he would in some way turn the decision of Miss Davenport and send her somewhere else even at the last minute. Or had he other ways of working? Of course he might mean that this was a discipline through which she was to pass before she was fit to be his child. If so she would try to do what was right, but it seemed much harder even than to take in the Parkers. They had grown quite tolerable, even to pleasantness, and it was only three days since she had decided to become acquainted with them. With the remembrance of the Parkers came the question, "What would Nannette think of the Parkers? Would she make it very unpleasant?" Maria knew that Nannette possessed, among other uncomfortable qualities, that of sneering at people and things, and making one feel that one would rather do anything than confess to a friendship for the person or a liking for the thing which she had scorned. What was she to do with Nannette?

It must not be supposed that Maria had grown good all in a night. By no means. To all outward appearance she was the same Maria grown a little sweeter tempered, a little more willing to give up her wishes for those of others, and in one respect rather surprising, in that she freely mingled with the young people and notably with the Parkers, making them feel perfectly at their ease and happy in her company. She had lost her temper once or twice. She had forgotten to refrain from a scornful remark about the pump on one occasion, which, while she felt no peculiar animus at the time, had still grown to be such a habit with her that she scolded without realizing it. She had noticed the weary look about her mother's eyes at the time the words were spoken and she instantly knew the mother was sighing over her. There had come an impulse then to throw her arms around her mother and tell her how different she meant things should be, but something within restrained her and the next instant her mother had passed out to talk with the grocer's boy and her opportunity was gone. She reasoned also that it would be better for her first to show some "works meet for repentance" before announcing to the others what she was going to do. Moreover, she felt that her recent experience, if it could rightly be called an experience, was too sacred yet to be talked about, and that it was no question of witnessing for Christ in this case, as they already knew she was his professed follower. It would be much wiser for her to let them see that she was different. She forgot that to the mother and sister there would have been great relief in the fact that she was willing to try to be different: that they would have overlooked many things in her and helped her in numberless ways, if she had once taken them into her confidence. If people only understood each other in this world there would be much less of friction, less sighing, and less worry about one another. And so the mother was

praying daily for her daughter, and wondering why it was her prayers were
of no avail — whether because she was unworthy to be answered, or because
of her lack of faith; while all the time the dear Lord had prepared a loving
answer and put it down beside her and she was too taken up with worry to
notice it. It would be well, in our praying, to sometimes lift the head and see
whether the answer to our prayers is not shining in the heavens or standing
joy-clothed beside us, or even lying at our feet waiting to be recognized.

Maria pondered deeply over what to tell her new friend the minister
about her old friend Nannette, and finally decided to let him judge for
himself. However, she had no opportunity to tell him anything, as it turned
out, for Mr. Fairfield was all that day and the next away attending to some
business on the mainland, and only arrived at Lone Point on the very train
which carried Nannette in her black robes.

The three days which lay between Maria and her decision had been
bright ones to her. Her friendship with the minister was growing to be an
exceedingly pleasant thing to think about, not that the intimacy had as yet
grown into its larger possibilities as personal; but there was growing in each
of their hearts something warmer than a mere interest for the other, and
occasionally little glimpses of alluring perhapses would flit across the
mental horizon of each. It is just possible that underneath Maria's distaste
for the arrival of Miss Davenport there was an undertone of uneasiness lest
the pleasant friendship between herself and the minister might be broken
in upon, but if this was so she did not even confess it to herself. She was
never a girl who was quick to think a man wished to pay her special
attention, nor to seem to appropriate one to herself. She rather erred in the
other direction; and he on his part, while he admired her for this, was, in a
certain sense, kept at a distance by her, even though they talked more
intimately than most young people are apt to do about that most sacred
emotion of life, one's personal love for his Saviour.

Chapter 18

Maria waited on the little platform the next afternoon for the incoming train. Her emotions were not pleasant. She seemed to see Nannette's curling lips as she first took in the situation and observed the rude cottage life. She seemed to hear her sarcastic comments, and strange to say they were, in her mind, much what her own had been on arriving here. Suddenly there flashed over her the thought that she had changed, in this respect at least, for she seemed to have in her heart some real love for the place, some desire to protect it from what scornful strangers might say. Why was it? Was it because she had found Christ here? Or was it, perhaps, on account of her new friendship with the strong true man who was becoming her friend? She looked up at the blue sky and smiled in answer to its heavenly look. She gazed over the yellow-green waves of the marsh grass, so bare to her once, and lo! they had taken on beauty, and she felt a sense of gladness in their smooth stretches of level green, and discovered that in a night they seemed to have burst into a million stars of meadow pinks dotted all over among the grass as far as eye could reach. She stooped and gathered a handful of them and placed them in her belt, adding a very pretty touch to her toilet. Nannette's influence had already begun to be felt in her careful arrangement of that afternoon's toilet. She had worried more about her dress and taken more time for it that day than she had done altogether since she had come to the island. Even now she looked down at herself doubtfully. She hardly cared to come in for sarcasm herself just at the outset. She had chosen, after much indecision of mind and careful scrutiny of her wardrobe, to wear for that day a white duck costume. It was plain, of course, and in a sense inexpensive. Its great beauty in her eyes was its exquisite cut and fit. She had committed her greatest extravagance of the summer by taking that duck dress to a notable tailor to be cut, and in her eyes and in the eyes of Nannette as well, she knew that fact would cover a multitude of sins in other directions. She half intended Nannette should soon discover that Melton had cut her dress. Nannette would then be sure to admire it. And yet, do her the credit to observe that she was annoyed over finding herself so deeply concerned about her dress, and descending so low as to actually think how she could tell where it had been cut. She sighed and wondered if this were a sign that Nannette was going to win her forever back to worldly things. Then before she went out she knelt and prayed. She had seen Rachel kneel often before going out, when she thought she was by herself, and she felt that now perhaps such a habit might be a good thing for her. Certainly she needed much help.

She did look fresh and pretty and thoroughly in keeping with her surroundings, all in white with black velvet belt and collar and band about her sailor hat. Even the most exacting taste could have found no fault with her. The fresh ocean breeze had blown loose a few soft strands of a waving lock about her forehead and flushed her cheeks, and the touch of pink blossoms in her belt made her look exquisitely pure and sweet. At least so thought Mr. Fairfield as he alighted, hot and dusty from his ride in the train, and his face lighted with a sudden joy that was pleasant to see. In spite of herself, the color would come into Maria's cheeks as she bowed to him. She was a trifle embarrassed too, for just a moment, since it must look to him, until Nannette appeared, as though she had come to the train to meet him.

But now the porter handed Nannette, with her bag, and her dress-suit case, and her bundle of golf sticks, and her tennis racquet, and several other accessories of the fashionable girl at a summer resort, down upon the platform, and the train moved on toward Spray View, and Maria found her hands full.

Nannette's greeting was effusive, a mingling, of kisses and adjectives, and a few stylish tears which necessitated the pushing up of the very becoming black veil in which her head was swathed in spite of the heat. This over, Miss Davenport turned her dark eyes upon the minister who stood by Maria as if he belonged there, and an introduction of necessity followed.

Maria felt annoyed beyond measure that she had not ere this told the minister of Nannette's expected arrival. Just why she should feel so much annoyance she did not then look into her heart to see. As a matter of course the minister rode with them in the surrey which had been sent down from the hotel to convey the new guest from the station, and though Maria also went with them and sat in the back seat with her friend, Nannette monopolized the conversation entirely and addressed it all to Mr. Fairfield. She spoke gushingly of her friendship with Maria, dating its origin much farther back than Maria had supposed it could be, showing reasons why Maria was her warmest friend, and therefore had been the one to whom she turned in her deep trouble. Here she punctuated her remarks with a few tears wiped carefully away with a correct handkerchief, deeply bordered with black.

She was a dashingly handsome girl; tall, slender, with black eyes and reddish brown hair. She wore her hair loose over her ears and coiled low at the nape of the neck which gave her an innocent, childlike appearance. She was an excellent actress when she chose to be. Mr. Fairfield was non-plussed and disappointed. He felt instinctively that this girl would have little sympathy for the quiet walks and talks in which he and Maria had been indulging of late. He feared that her presence at the shore would be anything but a good influence for the girl in whom he was becoming so deeply interested.

Maria, on her part, was greatly distressed. What would Mr. Fairfield think of her friends? What would he think of her past life? She must hasten to explain, at the first opportunity, how little of real friendship there ever had existed between them; and yet how could she, without deliberately making the other girl out a liar? It was all very unpleasant. She was glad when the surrey drew up to the hotel and they could get out. She was more glad than she dared say, even to herself, that no conversation concerning the place, and the various cottages they had passed during the short ride, had come up, for at least she was spared having the truth dawn upon Nannette while the minister was with them. She went upstairs with Nannette at her request, though she would have preferred going straight home to have a good cry, or wandering off on the sand and telling Mr. Fairfield all about it. She felt a childish desire to tell him her troubles and ask him what she should do, but she shut her lips tightly and walked up the stairs like a soldier, so that he thought she was only too happy to have one of her own sort with her again and he would have no more opportunities to see her.

Nannette's several trunks were at last deposited and unstrapped and she was at leisure to take off her hat and talk with her friend. She laid her hat on the bed and settled herself in a rocker by the window: "Now, 'Ri, tell me all about this hole," she said familiarly. "Is there anything going on to keep one alive? Isn't it dreadfully dull? But you see Aunt Mortimer is old-fashioned and terribly rigid, and she wouldn't at all consent to my appearing at any interesting place. She wanted me to stay at home with her all summer! Just fancy! She said I ought not to want to go anywhere when my mother was dead, but dear me!" — with a shrug of her shoulders — "what good would it do mother for me to mope? I told aunt I should die of grief among those associations of mother, and that seemed to touch the right spot, and she consented to my going away. She would have come with me if she could, but Cousin George is worse this summer and not able to be moved and she couldn't leave him. I think she would have liked me to stay and devote myself to him, read to him and make messes for him; but Cousin George is altogether too devoted to the memory of his dead wife to make it interesting to waste one's time on him. Besides I hate sick people and he isn't likely to get well, anyway. So I'm here. First of all, who is that very handsome Mr. Fairfield? A minister? Dear me! Is he very good? Because that would be dreadfully tiresome."

"I'm sure I don't know," said Maria; "you'll have to find that out for yourself." Her voice showed her disgust plainly, but Nannette was too much interested to notice. She went rattling on.

"Say, 'Ri, is he very devoted? I thought he looked at you as if he was. Are you engaged?"

"No, *indeed,*" answered Maria freezingly. It flashed over her then that there was something about Nannette's face that reminded her of Annie Higgins and she thought if the two were compared there would be a balance in favor of the Higgins girl.

"Not engaged? Then I give you fair warning, 'Ri dear, I shall do my best to have a good time. You don't mind, do you, dear?"

"Certainly not," said Maria again, in a voice which the minister never would have recognized.

Nannette seemed to feel that it would be just as well to change the subject. She leaned out of the open window nearest her, looking toward the cottages.

"And now do tell me where the town is, what there is of it. Of course I know it's small, but I've seen nothing but cow-sheds so far. What in the world do they need so many of them for? Or are they bath-houses? No, they are too far from the ocean."

The Maria of a few weeks ago would have blushed crimson and hesitated, tried to apologize and explain, or even have invented some way out of the truth, perhaps; but the Maria of today was too deeply stung and disgusted. She was shown herself and just how low she had fallen in being ready to bow down to a girl whose thoughts and feeling were as low as this one's. It was so great a contrast with the high and holy thoughts in which she had been dwelling with the minister lately that she was in great danger of going to the other extreme and despising this girl for motives really lower than belonged to her. For Nannette Davenport was only selfish, that was all. But that is perhaps enough.

Maria arose and with grave dignity walked to the window and pointed out.

"Those are cottages," she said, trying to control her voice steadily. "That white one nearest to you is where our friends the Parkers live. The green one trimmed with white next to it is ours. The others belong to very nice people. You will meet them all soon. There is no reason why one should not have a pleasant time here if one chooses."

Maria remembered her own actions of two weeks ago, and was amazed at herself. Nannette looked curiously at her, and then without further remark turned toward her trunks, saying with a sigh:

"You don't say so! Well, I suppose I've no choice but to make the best of it this year, with these horrid black things on, but I shall make up for it next year, you may be sure. And I warn you I'm going to be just as wicked as I please, so look out for your own interests. By the way, 'Ri, haven't you a brother? Is he nice looking? How old is he? One must have friends, you know, in such a desert as this. They say Roland De Vere is over at Spray View. He and I had a terrible quarrel a year ago, but I may be able to patch that up. He is so old-granny particular! Now what shall I put on for dinner, and what hour do they have that meal in this out-of-the-way place?"

"They have dinner at one o'clock. It is over four hours ago. Supper is at six," answered Maria severely. She somehow took a fierce pleasure in shocking this girl. She felt glad that this feeling possessed her instead of the fear which she had been afraid would tempt her to do things out of accord with her new views. She felt so little trust in her own self, poor child, and her trust was so recently given to her Saviour, that she did not realize that he would hold her and she would not need to worry lest she should not hold to him. She was anxious to get away now, and the many elaborate dresses which Nannette began to take out and spread upon bed and chairs for her admiration, wearied her. She felt as if she had always given an undue amount of time and thought to clothes. No doubt these things were pretty, yes, they certainly were. She could not help letting her eye dwell in pleased delight upon an elaborate waist of black taffeta. Nannette certainly had good taste, there was no denying that, and plenty of money with which to exercise it. It was hard, of course, this gay season when everybody was flaunting bright colors, to get up a beautiful and varied outfit with only black and white, with strict severity and much crêpe a necessity, but Nannette had succeeded, and Maria, in spite of dislikes and resolves, began to grow interested in the pretty clothes. Nannette insisted upon her remaining until she had arrayed herself in a severely plain white gown with black ribbons, and Maria was obliged to say, at the demand of the new-comer, that she was bewitchingly pretty even in the trying dead black and white.

"Now, you may go, dear, for I suppose you are awfully tired of me. But please tell me first," — holding Maria off at arm's length, — "do you think I shall captivate him? I mean that young minister, of course. I must have something to amuse me, and I should hate to fail at the very beginning."

"I'm sure I don't know," answered Maria in her most sober tone. She drew back, stung deeper than she realized.

"Ha, ha!" laughed Nannette, "he must be good and have infected you. Never mind. I shan't hurt him much, you know, and I'll let him go in the end. Don't blame me much, dear. It's all I have to live for now, you know." And she put her mourning handkerchief to her laughing eyes in the smart little pat which she affected.

Maria coldly promised to come back that evening and walked away. She could stand no more. All she had to live for! Flirting! How boldly she had confessed it.

Was it possible she had ever admired a girl like that? She bowed her head and was ashamed.

The minister, standing at the window of his room in the hotel, saw her, watched her down the street, wondered and sighed and turned away thoughtfully.

Chapter 19

When Maria reached the cottage her mother looked at her searchingly, expecting to find her face wreathed in smiles on account of the arrival of Nannette. Instead she saw a gray, weary look about her eyes, and felt the anxious tugging at her mother-heart again which had been there so often the last few weeks. Was Maria plunged again in gloom because of the talk and dress of her gay friend? Was she contrasting her own life with that of Miss Davenport?

When at supper her brother Winthrop asked some laughing question about Nannette, Maria looked up at him anxiously and answered him more shortly than she had spoken to him for at least three days. The family could not understand it. They had expected her to be pleased at the accession of a friend in this lonely place. She ate very little supper, and when Winthrop proposed going with her to the hotel to call upon the young lady, she promptly declined his escort, saying Nannette must be tired and would not want to see any one that evening. Her conscience gave her a sharp twinge as she said that, but she looked after her brother with a sigh as he whistled and left the table. Then she went quickly out to the piazza and stood alone in the purple and pink twilight with tears blurring her vision. There had suddenly stirred in her heart a new feeling of love for her brother. She saw a possible danger to him lurking in the future and she felt herself inadequate to ward it off. Oh, if she had but always been such a sister to him that a word from her would have been as a shield to him. But now she felt that if she should point out to him her fear he would walk straight up to it laughing, more perhaps to tease her than anything else. Things were becoming complicated. There was her brother, and there was the minister, and there was Nannette, and there was she, and where was the Lord? She thought it reverently. She stood looking up into the clear opal tints above and wished she might see him, if only for one little second of time, that her poor weak faith might have something to bind itself to forever. She felt a great longing for Christ to come and touch her. She wanted him more than anything else just then.

Her mother came softly out behind her and putting her arms about her daughter drew her head down to her shoulder.

"What is it, little 'Ri, tell mother," she said tenderly, just as she used to speak when Maria was but a baby and came in with bumped head or bruised knee from a fall.

Then Maria hid her face in her mother's neck and cried, and tried to tell her all her troubles, and of how she wanted to live a changed life.

The mother's heart grew glad and light suddenly. It seemed too good to be true. She drew her down to a chair beside her on the porch, stroking her hair, talking low and tenderly with her as they had not talked together for many a long day. Yet even as the mother talked and comforted and was glad, there came and stood beside her the shadow of a possibility of happenings for the future which held in them both sorrow and joy, and she put away what she heard to think of by and by. She was not a mother who often talked with her children about personal religion, therefore it would have been hard for Maria to tell her mother of her changed feelings on the subject if it had not been for this sudden letting down the bars of her nature and her mother's opportune coming. It was hard too for the mother to talk on religious subjects and therefore her words of comfort were not many, but to Maria who well knew her mother's nature, they meant much, and carried true solace with them. When she said, "Maria, I am glad," Maria knew that she meant more than if she had used a whole dictionary full of adjectives, and when she advised her daughter to "give over worrying and take her trouble to her Heavenly Father," then Maria felt that her mother spoke whereof she knew.

One load the mother carried on her heart when her daughter finally kissed her and went to the hotel, which she had not had before. Maria had dropped a hint as to possible danger for Winthrop in the coming of Miss Davenport, and the mother-heart grew anxious at once as soon as she had time to think, and she had need to take to herself the advice she had given her daughter.

Winthrop, her only boy, was very dear to her, and she knew him to be fond of bright company and very susceptible to its influence.

When Maria reached the hotel, she began to frame an excuse for being so late, but on ascending the steps of the long wide piazza which ran all around the building she saw in the distant corner, standing out against the background of moonlit ocean, the figures of Miss Davenport and Mr. Fairfield. The sudden chill which crept over her made her pause and draw about her shoulders the light shawl she had carried on her arm. She half turned to go away again, thinking Nannette was in no need of her presence and she would come again in the morning, but Nannette had seen her, and waved her handkerchief and called, so there was nothing for it but to go over and sit down in another large rocking-chair beside them.

"You dear naughty thing, you deserted me!" said Nannette in her most gushing voice. "Why in the world were you so long coming? If it had not been for Mr. Fairfield I should have been so lonely that I should have wished to take the morning train back to the city. But he had been so exceedingly kind that I actually forgot this place was called Lone Point."

It had been no part of Mr. Fairfield's intention to have any more to do with Miss Davenport than was absolutely necessary. The feeling of dislike he had experienced for her at first sight only deepened as they rode along to the hotel. But a gentleman cannot be actually rude to a lady, especially if that lady is a professed friend of one who has his deep friendship and respect. Therefore, when, by some skillful maneuver, the old lady who usually occupied the place at the right of Mr. Fairfield in the dining room, was placed across the room, and Miss Davenport was found seated beside him, he was obliged, in ordinary courtesy, to talk with her. It could not be said that he exerted himself to any great degree to make the conversation pleasant for her. Indeed, this was not necessary. Nannette was vivacity itself. She was an adept in small talk and almost made the studious young man feel ill at ease. His replies grew short. But the young woman perceiving her mistake at once subsided, grew meek and inquiring, and presently discovering that books were a delight amounting almost to a passion with the gentleman, molded her conversation accordingly. Before the meal was over she had professed an overpowering desire to read and have explained to her a certain book about which there was a great deal of talk in the literary world. To Mr. Fairfield's exceeding disgust he found that he had not only promised to lend her the book, but to give her at no late date an exhaustive explanation of the discussion in current magazines over certain passages in the book. How they had come to get quite so far as this he was not able to explain, but he awoke to the fact as Nannette was thanking him most sweetly for being so kind as to be willing to help her.

As they rose from the table she said innocently enough, "What in the world do you do here in the evenings? Won't you show me where to go? I don't know a soul but you, you know." She flashed her fine eyes up at him confidingly and he felt in duty bound to take her to the piazza. He went there rather than to the parlor, in a vain hope that Maria might soon come and redeem the situation. But time passed, the sunlight faded from the sky, the moonlight came over the water, and still the young woman by his side gave him no opportunity to leave, without absolute rudeness on his part. He was growing more and more uneasy, when Maria at last arrived, and if she had not been so engrossed with her own feelings at the sight of him and Nannette sitting together in such evident good fellowship, she must surely have noted the joy that broke over his face at sight of her, and the warm welcome he gave her. Be assured Miss Davenport saw it, and ground her pretty white teeth, that in spite of all the charms she had exerted she had not once been able to bring to his face that true pleasure which was there now. She resolved that before many days should have passed this should be different, and thenceforth Lone Point was no longer a desert island to her, for there was a man there who must be conquered, and added to the long line of conquered admirers in the past.

Maria, however, in spite of her mother's comforting words, was ill at ease again the moment she came into Nannette's atmosphere. If she roused herself to reply to Nannette it at once threw her back into a past which she did not like to feel had ever been hers, and with which she did not wish Mr. Fairfield to know she was familiar. If she should speak to Mr. Fairfield, what should it be about? Not Mr. Meyer's book! Not the Bible verse about which they had been talking so freely but yesterday, for what would Nannette think, and how could she drag sacred things into a conversation so filled with the froth of that young woman's remarks?

Mr. Fairfield finally settled back to wait till Maria should go home, thinking he would walk with her and they could have a little quiet word together after all, and he found his mind wandering out of the talk so that he was often silent. He was thinking what he should say to Maria.

Did Nannette read what was passing in his thoughts? Certainly she acted as though she did. When Maria rose to say good-night, she followed her to the steps and then, as if the thought had just occurred to her, she put her hand lovingly on Maria's arm and said: "Why, I guess I'll walk over with you, 'Ri, if Mr. Fairfield doesn't mind bringing me home. I should get lost, you know, if you didn't." she said, turning laughingly to him, and she looked him straight in the eyes in the full moonlight and saw that he was disappointed.

When Maria reached her room that night it was late, for Mr. Fairfield had determined that he would take his revenge upon the new arrival and therefore he proposed a walk. He knew that Maria was used to the sand, and could stand it well, and that to the young woman from the city streets it would be harder work. He hoped perhaps to tire her out and take her back to the hotel before Maria had been taken home, and still have his quiet half-hour with her.

He had reckoned without his host, however, Nannette possibly perceived his intention, or it may be that she was stronger than he had judged possible. She bravely waded through the sand wherever he led the way, exclaiming in delight over scenes which only half pierced to her mental retina at all, and still saying she was not tired. On he took them, this way and that, now nearer the ocean. Not to the walks which he and Maria had taken together; they were full of pleasant thoughts and should not be marred by the memory of this walk. He grew quite gay in his effort to gain his point, and Maria wondered at him and grew more silent herself. And now he perceived that she was growing very weary, for there was a white droop about her mouth he had not seen there before, and for her sake he proposed that they go straight home.

There was triumph in Miss Davenport's eyes as she faced herself in the mirror of her room at a late hour, and her lips had a firm set. It had been a hard race, for she was very tired, but she had not given up, and she had gained her point. She would win him yet even if she had to be "good," as she phrased it, to get him.

Maria in her room, with only the moon to light her to her couch, threw herself on her knees beside her sleeping sister who was tired out, soul and body. She was too weary to pray and too weary to cry. She felt as if it would be so good if the dear Christ could just come to her gently, as her mother had done, and tell her what all this meant and why she was so very unhappy. She did not want to try to think and reason it all out. She supposed there was an ugly feeling of jealousy in her heart. It must be that her trouble was because she wanted that young minister to admire her and be with her all the time. It was all very humiliating. She had not known before that she was so selfish. He had helped her to a better life, why did she not want Nannette to have the same opportunity? Was it possible that she had made that great decision just because she admired the man who asked her to do it? Had she fallen so low that her motive was only self-pleasure, after all, and that she did not give up to Christ but to a man whom she admired? Did she not love Christ? With this question came a surge of feeling. Yes, she did love Christ. She felt now as if her all depended upon him. She would give up everything for him. She only wanted his rest, his peace. He had promised it. She had accepted it. It was hers. No one could any more take it from her. Nannette could not touch it. The minister might turn his entire attention to Miss Davenport and forget her. It would be as well if he did, for evidently she was beginning to think too much of him. He might help to bring Nannette to Christ, and then perhaps have a deeper feeling for her, marry her, perhaps. It ought to be nothing to her. She was Christ's. Henceforth she would do as he bade, go where he sent her, live as he would live in her. What a glorious, what a precious thought that was! Would it last till morning? Could she trust it still to be there when she awoke, and could she go to sleep saying, "I am Christ's, I am Christ's. He is mine?"

Strangely, wonderfully, it seemed to her, came an answer from her innermost soul, "I can," and she feel asleep.

If the minister could have known her thoughts as he stood disappointedly beside his window, looking out on the now dark night with only a glimmer of light here and there of a belated cottager, for the moon had set, he might have prayed for her a prayer whose words he knew and loved, instead of wondering gloomily why everything seemed to have gone wrong:

Rest her, dear Master!. . . draw very near
In all thy tenderness and all thy power.
O speak to her. Thou knowest how to speak
A word in season to thy weary ones,
And she is weary now. Thou lovest her—
Let thy disciple lean upon thy breast,
And, leaning, gain new strength to "rise and shine."

Chapter 20

Mr. Fairfield, as he looked out over the sparkling waves the next morning, felt new life and joy come into his soul. What was the use in being downcast when the world was so lovely? He was a child of the living God. He would be given all that was needful for his good and happiness in life. Why should he begin to doubt and grow gloomy because he feared the Lord would take some pleasure from him? Surely it was not worth while to begin to fear anything until he saw it plainly before his eyes? What was it he feared, any way? Was his anxiety wholly unselfish? He recognized clearly that there was a danger menacing Maria's new-found joy in Christ, but could not he and she both trust the One to whose keeping she had committed herself? He remembered the words, "He is able to keep you from falling and to present you faultless," and knew that he was wrong to fear for her.

No, that was not all, though there had been a quick recognition of Maria's danger. What was this other feeling which came and went, a warm, rich, new current in his heart? Miss Hammond had grown to be more than a mere acquaintance; more than one to whom he was trying to bring a message from God, though that relation is a very precious one. There had grown up a personal tie. He told himself that she was the first really intimate friend he had had since his chum in college died, and tried to be satisfied with that way of putting it, but somehow he knew there was something not altogether sincere about that statement either. He decided to go for a quiet stroll along the beach in the early sparkling morning and think it out. There he would be quite alone with God. There was something serious here which ought to be settled at once, he felt sure. Strange he had not thought of it before! Was it possible that this girl, an acquaintance of but a few weeks' standing, was growing indispensable to him? Before he had walked very far, or turned that thought over many times in his mind, he knew that it was so, and that he loved Maria. He sat down on the sand and looked off at the ocean without seeing a single wave of it, to take in the wonder and the beauty of this thought. It fairly overwhelmed him. It was another day and another experience something like the one when first he had realized that he loved his Saviour. He remembered now to have heard Henry Drummond once say that an earthly love was the highest and best example of, and the only thing really approaching at all, the soul's relation with Christ. "Get acquainted with Jesus just as you would with an earthly friend," the great simple man had said, and the young theologue had been rather inclined to call him irreverent then. But now he saw it in all its beauty, the earthly love, so real and warm and dear, a type of the heavenly, just as close and warm and dear and real, only infinitely more in every way than the human heart could comprehend. Was this what God had made earthly love for, that he might the better show us what his love for us must be?

The thoughts rolled past him, rather than were thought by him. He felt, as he sat there in the midst of the lovely morning, as if God spoke to him out of his grandeur and beauty, and was very gracious to him. Most gracious of all because of this wonderful gift of love which he found in his heart for another of his children. He felt that he loved his Heavenly Father more intensely, more intelligently than he had ever done before, because of the sudden blessed realization of another love.

He arose from his hour's meditation feeling that whatever came after, he should always be a better man for that sacred experience, and that he would be able better to preach of the love of God now that he could understand a human love, like the love of a man for a woman; aye, he would be a better man for having harbored this love in his heart, even though he might fail to win her — though, please God, he would *not* fail if he could help it.

As he walked back toward the hotel he suddenly remembered Miss Davenport and her proximity to him at the table. He wished that he had remembered sooner. It must be late. He would like to get his breakfast and get away before she came. He did not care for a tête-à-tête with her just now. He felt that her rattling conversation would be a desecration to his joy-filled mood. How hard it was to have to come down from the heights to every-day living, and every-day disappointments and perplexities! And yet, that was the discipline of life and must be cheerfully borne. He hastened his steps, hoping that she would be late to breakfast, as indeed she was, and he hastened his breakfast, to get out before she came. He did succeed, but little good it did him.

Miss Davenport awoke with a feeling that she had slept later than she intended, for she had business of moment on hand that day and must not let the enemy get any small advantage at the beginning. She found to her dismay that her watch had run down, and she had no means of telling the hour. Glancing from the window, she saw Mr. Fairfield, watch in hand, hurrying toward the hotel, and rightly concluded that breakfast must be ready. With unusual alacrity for a girl of her ordinary lassitude she hurried through a charming toilet prepared with much forethought and intended to deepen the interesting pallor of her supposedly grief-stricken face. Then she hastened to the dining room.

She found to her chagrin that the prize had already escaped her, and the maid was clearing the dishes away from Mr. Fairfield's place at the table. He must have breakfasted hurriedly, or else she had been longer than she thought. As she sat biting her red lips in vexation, she saw him through the opposite window at the other end of the long room, going with determined steps down the sandy path. One comprehensive glance at the landscape told her that he was going in the direction of the green cottage. She watched him a moment and saw that her guess had been correct, for he ascended the steps, knocked at the door, and then sat down in one of the big rockers standing on the piazza. Her purpose was taken in a moment. Taking a few swallows of coffee from the cup just set down beside her, she slipped up to her room for her parasol and hat and followed the path he had just taken.

Mr. Fairfield had felt during his brief breakfast that the thing he wanted most in life just then was to look upon the face of the one whom he had just discovered he loved. Not that he intended to tell of his love just now; no indeed! He saw instantly that it was too soon for that. She had not known him long enough. She might not love him — how could she? — and he would not startle her by telling her of it abruptly. No, he would teach her daily to love him. He would wait and see if there was any chance for him, before he told her. But whatever came of the telling, the fact, the precious fact, remained that he loved her, and he wished to see her in the light of the knowledge of that fact. He had hastened his morning meal that he might go to her home and ask for a walk, before Miss Davenport could be around to claim her time, and thus he had gone happily down the path, whistling a few notes of a popular song, then humming a line of a hymn, and so, joyously, scarcely knowing what his thoughts might be. Rachel answered the door and told him her sister had run in next door on an errand for her mother but would be back almost immediately. He sat down to wait while Rachel went on with the work she was doing, which she could not leave just then. The acquaintance between the Hammonds and Mr. Fairfield had grown sufficiently intimate for Rachel to feel privileged to go on working and occasionally come to the door to make some pleasant remark or answer something Mr. Fairfield called in to her.

Maria coming in the back door with the basket in which she had just carried some fish to Mrs. Parker, a present from her mother, who had purchased more than she needed, heard the minister's voice and answering Rachel's motion slipped into her room to change her dark working calico for her beach dress. Rachel, buzzing about in the kitchen finishing Maria's morning work that she might not be kept from her friend any longer, did not see the tall black-robed young woman who presently came up the steps, on the veranda, and greeted its occupant with such effusiveness, seating herself in the next rocker and entering into an immediate discussion of the morning and its charms.

It seemed to Mr. Fairfield as if some black cloud had suddenly been cast across his sky, but he tried to remember that this was Maria's friend, and while she was not in the least like Maria, she might have a great many delightful qualities if one could only get at them. At least she had a soul, and if he could not be interested in her in any other way, he would try to remember that, and let his courteous treatment of her reflect his Master's example. If he had but known her heart he might have felt more tempted to assume a scourge of small cords with which to drive her out from the temple of that day, into which she had set tables for her barter in hearts. If good was to reach her soul, at least he was not intended to bring it, not in the way in which he brought it to Maria. This one was not capable of receiving the good word, not yet at least, for the ground was stony and shallow and barren.

Maria, coming with a bright face to meet her friend, found the two seated side by side. Nannette was bending over the other's chair to inspect a tiny gold ring which he carried on his watch chain, and which she had herself asked about. That this action on Nannette's part was greatly to the annoyance of Mr. Fairfield Maria could not possibly be expected to know. She would never have been willing to ask about a gentleman's personal adornments, nor to reach out and handle them of her own accord, and she naturally judged that no other girl would so far forget herself, especially with an acquaintance of barely one evening. The natural inference was that he was telling her the story of the charm, and had invited her to examine it. Of course it was evident that they had come together from the hotel to see her, anybody would know that. She half wished in her heart that they had gone off together, and not brought her in at all, then her life and her troublesome feelings would not perplex her so. Nevertheless they had come, and her part was to be pleasant and polite. She hastily drew to her the memory of the night before, as a child will reach out its hand to its father when in fear and remind him of his promise to protect. She understood the swift upward look of her soul to the Saviour, asking him to help her to forget all but that she was his, and her heart thrilled with the answering strength that came to her need.

Nannette instantly saw her advantage. Indeed she had hastened her steps and given up her breakfast, scarcely hoping she might succeed in gaining the porch before Maria came out, but wishing, if possible, to give her the impression that she had come with Mr. Fairfield. If Maria would draw off and leave the minister to her, her task would be more than half done. It was Maria's presence which hindered her own charm from working. It piqued her to think that Maria could be supposed to be more charming than she, but then Maria had been there first, and there was no telling what a man might not take a fancy to if he had nothing else at hand. Nannette's idea of a man was that he must always have a woman to amuse him, as her idea of a woman was that she could never be happy without an adoring man or two about.

"You were so long coming last evening, dear, that we thought we would run right over after breakfast and stir you up," said Nannette gayly.

It occurred to the minister that Nannette must have eaten her breakfast long before he had, or else had gone without. He gave her a searching look and decided for the latter theory. Then he wondered what was her object. He was not a conceited man, and therefore her real object had not yet dawned upon him. He took her merely for a disagreeably bold, worldly girl, and decided to keep away from her as much as possible. He did not know yet how much control this skillful coquette had over the possible when she chose.

Maria sat down clothed in her new strength. She tried to look at Mr. Fairfield merely in the light of a chance acquaintance in whom she had no interest at all, and to heartily enter into Nannette's talk, at least in so far as she conscientiously could. She did not talk to Mr. Fairfield this morning. It was easier for her not to do so.

Mr. Fairfield was disappointed at the way things had turned out, and solaced himself by retiring from the conversation, as he had done the evening before, except when absolutely pressed into it by Miss Davenport. He was studying the fair lines of Maria's face, and thinking how lovely she was, and wondering why he had never noticed her beauty as being so unusual before. He thought there was a new touch of gravity and earnestness about her too, which sat well on her countenance. As he watched her and noted her replies, he made up his mind that she was in no present danger from Miss Davenport's influence.

But Nannette perceived that the conversation, of which she had the monopoly, was becoming strained, and casting about for something to change the situation she discovered in the distance along the Spray View road a carriage containing the De Veres. She immediately began to dilate on the excellencies of that family, and remembering that quality in man, jealousy, which had often served her a good turn, she professed especial delight in the coming of Roland De Vere.

"We always were such good friends," she said, turning her eyes sweetly upon the minister; "we used to play together by the hour as children, and as we grew older our friendship was really something lovely till he went away to college. Don't you think he has a very remarkable mind, Mr. Fairfield?"

Maria, remembering Nannette's account of her quarrel with Roland De Vere, listened in wonderment. Nannette had omitted to state that her intercourse with Roland De Vere from their earliest childhood had been strictly upon a war footing. He had never been afraid to tell her of the shams and falsehoods he saw in her, and this had made her almost hate him.

Nevertheless, it was sometimes expedient to seem to love your enemies, at least for a time. This was one of the unwritten commandments in Miss Davenport's code.

Maria felt greatly relieved at the appearance of the De Veres. So did Mr. Fairfield, and so did Nannette, but each for a different reason.

A sailing party was the order of the day, and the De Veres had driven over to secure their Lone Point friends to join them. The yacht was to be at the Lone Point wharf in an hour to wait for them, and they were to send the carriage back by the driver, and go out across the bar and fish in the open sea, returning by moonlight. It was a thoroughly delightful plan. Maria could not help but be happy, and forget all her troubles. Somehow they seemed to melt away in the light of the genial company. She hastened in to call Rachel, and consult with her mother about some additions to the ample lunch which the De Veres had brought with them.

"We'll go in and tell the Parkers," said Fannie De Vere, catching Rachel's hand in quite a girlish fashion, and starting off through the sand.

"The Pahkahs! And who are the Pahkahs?" asked Nannete, amid the pleasant hurry that prevailed. Nannette always used the Southern drawl when she wished to be interesting.

"They're nobodies, Nannette; just nice, pleasant people, not at all like you and me. You won't care for them in the least," answered Roland De Vere with a touch of the old rudeness which had characterized his conversation with her always.

Chapter 21

Mr. Fairfield, during the preparation for the excursion, had been diligently studying how he might secure Maria's company on the way to the boat, and for as much of the day as possible. But although he made himself variously useful, offering assistance to Maria and Rachel in numberless little ways, and gladly taking upon himself all the burdens of wraps and lunch baskets that he could find belonging to the green cottage, he did not seem to succeed. Maria was busy and dignified. If he essayed to walk beside her she suddenly discovered an errand with another member of the party, or rushed back for her forgotten parasol. Laden as he was he could scarcely follow her, and when he waited behind the rest he was at once pounced upon by Nannette, who called him a "poor, lone man," and sweetly insisted upon holding her parasol over him and carrying Maria's blue jacket, in the possession of which he had taken especial delight. He could do nothing but submit, for he was helpless. There was nothing for it but to walk grimly on to the wharf as fast as possible and hope for better fortune. Maria did not seem to see all this. In fact she was remembering just then that Mr. Fairfield had never told her the story of the dainty little gold ring he wore, nor even spoken of it. He took her for a girl who did not care for such things. Well, it was as well. He had helped her, he was a minister, a — no, it would not do to call him her friend. There must be a more dignified name for their relation than that. The Catholics had a good name for it: "Spiritual adviser," that was what he was. As such she could enjoy his conversation, and feel that she did right to take pleasure in his company; but not when Nannette was about. Maria, therefore, walked forward and began to talk eagerly with the first unoccupied one of the group. This happened to be Marvie Parker, and Maria silently blessed her for her bright, girlish conversation, which in spite of her, cheered her thoughts and turned them in another direction from the one which they were constantly tempted to take.

George Parker at the last moment joined the group on the wharf. Nannette had given his sister a comprehensive sweep of her big, brown eyes, and ignored her beyond the slightest possible inclination of the head. When the brother arrived, tall, grave, somewhat diffident in his manner toward strangers, and with a rather homely face and figure, by some mischance she was not introduced. It was as well, perhaps, for she stood in the shadow of a sail, and curled her lip as she looked at him. Of the happy little party standing about and warmly greeting the new-comers only Marvie saw that glance. Instantly her warm, loving heart resented if for her dear brother, and her anger flamed up till she was ready to blaze out in a well-deserved reproval, for Marvie Parker was a girl of tremendous impulses. But fortunately her impulses were under the control of One wiser than herself. A moment more, a hasty prayer, and she was ready to look again at the silly, conceited miss, and forgive her, and say, "Poor thing." Then she set herself to see if she could not in some way do a kindness to the one who had smitten her so hard upon the one cheek. She knew her brother far too well to carry revenge in her heart for his sake.

Maria took care to place herself between Fannie De Vere and Marvie Parker when they seated themselves in the boat, and when Mr. Fairfield cast about to get near her he found no opportunity. Miss Davenport had not been so discreet. She took good care that there should be a vacant place beside her, but the disappointed young man for once got the better of her. If he could not sit beside Maria, at least he would not subject himself for an entire morning to the chatter of her disagreeable friend. He went to the bow of the boat and seated himself among the coils of rope. Here he could be quiet and think and watch Maria without being observed.

Roland De Vere swung himself aboard at the last minute and took his seat, without noticing, beside Nannette, and when he discovered her proximity he was fully as dissatisfied as she with the arrangement. He began to wonder what he had done to deserve such punishment, but as Rachel was at his other side, with George Parker next, he devoted himself as much as possible to them.

Like some beautiful, intelligent creature, the boat spread her white wings, and turning glided from the bank. There seemed something almost unearthly in the beauty of the day and the flying of the boat along the shimmering bay, swiftly, swiftly to the place where the soft, benignant blue of the sky came down to meet the water. Perhaps Mr. Fairfield was the only one who thoroughly enjoyed it all. He was by himself and with pleasant thoughts for company. The others were arranging themselves comfortably and answering one another, as bright shafts of sarcasm and bubbling mirth went answering one another. Nannette was cross. She had missed her aim. True, she had managed to separate Maria and Mr. Fairfield, though she felt pretty sure that Maria had done this herself, and she could not even claim the credit of it. But she had not gained his company. She had felt certain that a whole day by her side amid such lovely surroundings would surely fix her in Mr. Fairfield's good graces by night. Now she had no one but that hateful Roland De Vere, and she saw instantly that he was not disposed to be forgetful or friendly. She decided to show her pique by making fun of those ungainly Parkers. If the young man had been just the least bit better looking, or seemed at all to glance at her with admiration, she might have been driven to flirt with him, but with such a man as Mr. Fairfield by, unwon, she felt she could not stoop so low. She decided, however, that Mr. Fairfield must not see her making fun of that solemn looking Parker boy, for as he was a minister she supposed he would be obliged to disapprove. She had a theory that young ministers always disapproved of wrong things because their churches obliged them to do so, and not at all because they felt any strong convictions on the subject.

Her opportunity to practice on young Parker came soon, and for want of better material she fell to work at once. Roland De Vere as early as possible during the morning made an excuse to change seats with George Parker. He felt sorry for George when he did it, but George Parker was one of those people who always have the disagreeable people and places thrust upon them in this world, and who seem to be given the grace to accept them pleasantly. His sister watched him as he sat down and turned his keen, gray eyes upon Miss Davenport, with a remark about the beauty of the day. Nannette had fancied him shy, and was astonished to find that he had a fine voice and spoke with perfect ease and unusual grace of manner. She plunged into a conversation with him, her most disagreeable expression upon her face, determining to put him to embarrassment as soon as possible. She had found from the talk of the others that he was something of a musician, and fancying him wise in his own conceit as a superficial amateur, she thought this would be as good an opportunity as any to "take a rise out of him." Summoning all her slight knowledge of the truly musical world, which amounted in all to the names of a few leading performers, with perhaps the titles of a number of brilliant productions, though it is doubtful if she knew which piece was being played without her programme, she began.

"Did you say you lived in the city?" she asked him, turning toward him with one of the cold stares which was usually so disconcerting to the poor victim whom she chose to transfix with it. "Then I suppose if you are so fond of music you heard Josef Hoffman last month."

Her expectation was that he would hardly know to whom she was referring, but to her amazement his plain face lit up with joy, thinking he had discovered a kindred spirit. "Yes, I did," he answered at once. "I heard him both times. It was a treat I would not have missed for the world. I was unable to get a seat, to be sure, as I had to rush there just at the hour, and there was scarcely standing room left. However, I might have been standing on my head for all I knew about myself while he was playing. Wasn't it fine? What did you think of his rendering of Beethoven's E-flat major sonata? Wasn't that first movement absolutely perfect? Didn't he bring out the orchestral effects most marvelously in Liszt's transcription of the overture to 'Tannhäuser.' "

It was Nannette's turn to be embarrassed. She had not heard Josef Hoffman, and would not have understood him if she had, for she was not a musician. Worse than that she had not one atom of delicate appreciation of good music; it was a bore to her and nothing more, unless it was the accompaniment for dancing. Then, and then only did it find an answering chord in her soul.

She flushed slightly, paused, but rallied and tried again. Her malice was stirred. She never quite forgave any one who made her feel uncomfortable. She flew to a subject in which she felt more at home.

"Were you at the opera house last month? Did you see 'The Wife's Revenge'?" she asked, a wicked look flashing across her face.

The young man looked at her with instant comprehension of the mistake he had made at first.

"Yes," said he, "I was at the opera house last month: but I did not go to see a play. I was with Mr. Moody."

Now Miss Davenport was so utterly out of the religious world that she did not at first know who Moody was.

"Moody," said she puzzled; "who is Moody?"

"Moody, the evangelist. Surely you heard of the two weeks' series of meetings held in the opera house."

"What! Moody and Sankey Sunday-school songs?" she exclaimed with a disagreeable laugh. "Oh, you're good, are you?" The sneer on her face was decided this time; but to her disappointment it did not seem to have any effect whatever upon her listener.

He turned his grave, gray eyes full upon her. "Just what is your definition of goodness, Miss Davenport?" he asked quietly.

Nannette was nonplussed. She had not expected to be answered like that. She had looked for a wave of color over his face, and immediate disclaiming of any right to the adjective she had applied, in the midst of which she would laugh scornfully and make him to feel that to be "good" was above all things else a thing for one to laugh at and disclaim.

"Oh, I never deal in definitions," she answered uneasily. "I leave that to the dictionary."

"The dictionary gives some ten or twelve different meanings to that word, if I am not mistaken," said he; "but the one I like the best was given years ago by Paul: 'For scarcely for a righteous man will one die; yet peradventure for a good man some would even dare to die.' If I might claim that sort of goodness, Miss Davenport, I would count it the highest honor."

After that, conversation between these two languished. Nannette had really nothing to say. She felt that she had been worsted from the first, and with weapons which were new to her. She took refuge in teasing the fish which they presently began to catch. Strange to say, she was among the successful catchers that day. The line she held was often taken by some poor unwary fish, and she would jerk him out of the water and let him down again, only to give the line a stronger jerk and keep the poor creature in agony. The girls protested once or twice, and at last Roland De Vere turned with sudden vehemence upon her;

"Nannette, stop torturing that poor creature. It will rise in judgment against you at the last day." He perhaps did not mean his words literally, but he was angry at the cruelty of her action.

Nannette laughed scornfully and gave the fish another jerk. "Your theology is all wrong. They don't have fishes in heaven," she responded saucily. "Mr. Fairfield," she called laughingly, "do set Mr. De Vere straight. He thinks we shall have fishes in heaven. Do tell him they haven't any souls."

"I leave it to you, Fairfield," said the young man, turning toward the minister, "if some animals haven't more soul than some human beings."

Thus appealed to, the minister recalled his thoughts from their pleasant wanderings and answered: "Certainly, De Vere, I fancy animals will have some part in the future life. Whether they have anything answering to souls or not, I cannot say; but I surely do think they will have their part, with all of God's creation, in the heaven that is being prepared."

This statement aroused much discussion and many exclamations from the rest of the party, and Nannette and her fishes were left to themselves while the others contemplated the new thought. Maria, who was charmed with the idea, which was a new one to her, found herself looking at Mr. Fairfield with her old admiration and thinking what a delightful talker and deep thinker he was. She wished he would go on and tell more about this; but he was not inclined to say much. He seemed to be changed somehow from the genial friend she had known so well for a few weeks. She wondered what had made the difference, and if Nannette had been the cause. How pleasant it would be if she could have him by herself just for a little while, so that she might ask him some questions about her new life which were perplexing her; but she supposed that must not be, for it was better for her not to see too much of him. What if he had seen how much she had enjoyed his company and had drawn off from her on that account, to save her from the shame of showing him her heart. Her face burned at the very thought. How dreadful that would be! Surely she could not have seemed to care for him! How could she when she did not know it? Of course she did not really care for him, she only feared she might. But she would not, now that she saw her danger. That would be terribly unwomanly. It was bad enough to have to realize her own danger. If she had been more careful she would not have had to endure the humiliation of that thought. But then, she might have missed this blessed joy of finding Christ. And her heart was really happy with the feeling of the perfect peace she had with God. She could be willing to endure even to have him think humiliatingly of her for the sake of that sweet peace. But she would take care to show him in the future that she had no interest in him apart from the spiritual help he had given her.

What a happy day this would have been if these two could have looked into one another's hearts! But God knew best, and he had some wise end in view through this discipline.

I cannot say, beneath the pressure of life's cares to-day, I joy in these
But I can say that I had rather walk this rugged way, if Him it please;
I cannot feel that all is well when darkening clouds conceal the sun;
But then I know God lives and loves; and say, since it is so, "Thy will be done."
I cannot speak in happy tones; the teardrops on my cheek show I am sad;
But I can speak of grace to suffer with submission meek, until made glad.
I do not see why God should e'en permit some things to be, when he is love;
But I can see, though often dimly, through the mystery, his hand above!

Chapter 22

Altogether Nannette felt very much discontented and dissatisfied with her first week at Lone Point. The weather had been perfect, but what is weather when there is a storm within? The party had been a merry one, but somehow she felt utterly out of harmony with it. Perhaps they felt this inharmoniousness more that she did.

The fishing had been abundant and successful. What fishing party could ask more? The sea had been calm. The sunset was one of the most magnificent ever seen at Lone Point and the moonrise was equally resplendent. They had floated slowly home, drawn by zephyrs that seemed willingly to obey the hand that held the helm. But one thing had been lacking in it all for Nannette, the only thing that made fishing parties and moonlight trips home again filled with pleasure, and that was an adoring man at her side who would chatter nothings and feed her vanity by likening her eyes to the sparkles on the wave and her complexion to the dazzling whiteness of the moonbeams. Mr. Fairfield had persisted in keeping a dignified distance, at least as far as was permitted by the length of the boat. Once, during a change of places she had gotten beside him as they came back from supper at the hotel on the mainland and were re-embarking for their homeward ride, but he had after a few words abruptly excused himself and gone to the aid of one of the sailors, who she felt sure needed him not at all. It was all very humiliating to her pride.

Any one, even George Parker, would have been better than no one at all. She was absolutely tied down to the companionship of the girls, and to her that was as low as she could fall. She had never taken pains to make any true friends among the girls, and felt, what was true, that she was only tolerated out of politeness. This she cared not one straw for when she had plenty of men at hand. She looked over at George Parker and wished she had been less disagreeable to him in the morning. It would at least have amused her to subjugate him, she felt it would have been an easy task, and to have enjoyed the dismay of that pious little sister of his. Altogether, Nannette was as thoroughly unhappy and disagreeable as she ever had been in her life. All the way home there had been singing. She had asked for one or two songs, but no one seemed to know the airs she called for, most of them society sentimentalities, or if they did, they did not care to break the harmony of the evening by bringing them in. The songs they sang were old ballads mostly; soft, low, sweet strains which seemed to be in tune with the murmur of the waters. By and by some one started a hymn, and they sang on from one to another favorite. It was wonderful how much more the words seemed to mean when sung on the water.

> "Far, far away like bells at evening pealing,
>   The voice of Jesus sounds o'er land and sea."

Nannette had an uncomfortable feeling that there might be a supernatural voice going to speak to them pretty soon. The songs chosen seemed all to follow one thought:

> "Jesus, Saviour, pilot me,
>   Over life's tempestuous sea,"

and as the last words died away Rachel's voice took up the words of another:

> "Jesus, Jesus, visit me,
> How my soul longs after thee.
> When, my best, my dearest friend,
> Shall our separation end?"

Then Roland De Vere started with

> "My Jesus, as thou wilt."

and his sister took it up at the close with the lovely tune of "Dorrnance" in the words,

> "Jesus calls us, o'er the tumult
> Of our life's wild, restless sea;
> Day by day his sweet voice soundeth,
> Saying, Christian, follow me."

Maria sang the words, feeling every one in her heart. She was enjoying this service of song more almost than she was able to endure, for tears of deep, unspeakable gladness would come to her eyes now and then, as she said over to herself: "He is my Jesus. I can feel it. I know it. I love him." And she realized at that moment that all her Christian life she had been dissatisfied with herself and longing for just this thing to come to her, only she had not been willing nor known how to take the necessary steps to bring it about.

As they neared the shore and the lights of Lone Point began to shine out over the water, Rachel and Marvie, sitting together, started the sweet strain:

"One sweetly solemn thought, comes to me o'er and o'er,
I'm nearer my home in heaven to-day, than ever I've been before."

Nannette felt the hush that hung over the little company as the boat silently slipped up to the dock when the last words were ended, and she was reminded so strongly of her mother's funeral that she felt tempted to jump overboard in order to create some kind of an excitement. Just as the boat touched the wharf, Mr. Fairfield repeated in the clear rich voice which had hushed a congregation to instant attention so often:

"And I pray that every venture
The port of peace may enter,
That safe from snag and fall,
And siren haunted islet,
And rock, the unseen Pilot
May guide us one and all."

It seemed like a benediction at the close of a beautiful meeting.

They landed in silence and went toward their homes with a hushed reverence upon them.

Nannette, seated before her mirror—she always made a practice of sitting before her mirror after she had been anywhere, that she might see just how she had looked and what sort of an impression she had made—curled her lip in intense scorn.

"I feel exactly as if I had attended a revival meeting and been sitting on the mourner's bench all the evening. I declare this is worse than reading to Cousin George. I have half a mind to go home. If it were not for making that stuck-up minister come down a peg I believe I would, but he must be conquered! If I could only catch Maria at a disadvantage when he was along! I must see if I can't work something up along that line. I see plainly, however, I shall have to try the pious dodge before I can do very effective work. Ah me! What a bore! I shall make up for this next summer!"

Then she went to her bed, but not to sleep. She lay there planning a campaign which meant victory and the downfall of the ministry in Lone Point at least.

The days passed by with much the same relation between the three, Maria, Mr. Fairfield, and Nannette, that there had been the first day of Miss Davenport's arrival. Nannette annoyed Mr. Fairfield not a little, asked services of him, and accepted them in a gracious manner, as if it were a favor to him to be allowed to run her errands. She circumvented his plans to meet Maria in the most ingenious ways, often making it appear perfectly natural that it should be so, so that he had not even yet begun to suspect how deeply laid was her plan.

Nannette had not forgotten her wish to show Maria off to disadvantage before him, and constantly her mind was trying to discover some means of doing this. She went about her work with an ingenuity which was worthy of a better cause. One day at the table she began a conversation with a view to ascertaining his views on certain questions.

"Mr. Fairfield, what do you think of cards? Aren't they awfully wicked? Don't you find they do a great amount of harm?"

She asked the question one morning at breakfast. Mr. Fairfield turned in amazement from the contemplation of his plate. This was not a subject in which he would have supposed Miss Davenport interested. As for discussing the right and wrong of card-playing, he did not deem that it would be at all profitable. He supposed, of course, she must be a card-player, as indeed she was, though she chose this morning to pose as one greatly disapproving the folly of it.

"I find that card-playing among Christians, as a rule, leads to worldliness," he answered stiffly. He judged Miss Davenport's object in asking the question to be to force him into an argument, and he did not care to discuss worldly amusements with a person who professed to belong wholly to the world. He was a little surprised that she did not further pursue the subject, but thought no more about it. He had more important things to think of. There was to be a concert by a fine orchestra on the veranda of one of the Spray View hotels. The Lone Point young people were invited over to spend the evening and attend it with the De Veres. Mr. Fairfield was hoping that the evening would give him an opportunity for at least a few minutes with Maria, so that he might ask her to walk with him the next day. He had a new address by Mr. Meyer which he was sure she would like to see, and he wanted the pleasure of reading it with her for the first time. It must — it surely could be planned. It was absurd that he actually could not get a chance to speak to her alone any more. He would have to resort to writing pretty soon if things went on as they were going, though he feared that for him to write would appear strange in her eyes, and precipitate matters before the time was ripe. He wondered, with a sigh, how long Maria's friend would stay in Lone Point. Perhaps he could ask her and find out the limit to this, to him, most distasteful state of things.

The fact was, if it had not been that Maria was resolved that Mr. Fairfield should not imagine her anxious for his company, Nannette would not have been able to contrive so many separations as she did; but with them both at work to keep him from his object it was a difficult thing for him to gain his point.

It was about this time that Winthrop Hammond had remained in town continuously for some days, taking care of a friend who was alone in the city and was ill with typhoid fever. The young man's parents had at last arrived and Winthrop felt at liberty to leave him, and so had come to the shore for a few days to stay, without going up to the city, as he felt he needed rest after his many nights of nursing and wakefulness.

It so happened that this concert at Spray View was the first one of the gatherings of the young people at which Winthrop had been present, and therefore was the first time Nannette had met him.

Strange to say they had never happened to meet in town.

Maria prayed earnestly before going out that evening. She asked Winthrop anxiously several times if he would not rather remain at home and rest, saying she would gladly stay with him; but as he seemed to be really anxious to go, she ceased talking about it.

Perhaps Nannette was so interested in Mr. Fairfield that she would not set any snares for Winthrop. At any rate she had put the dear brother into God's keeping, and nothing more could be done. She hovered about Winthrop and tried to be as cheerful and interesting as possible. Indeed, Winthrop noticed how she had changed and wondered what it meant. It was pleasant to have her seem to care to be with him, though it was unlike her too, for she was one who always had plenty of admirers of her own.

Nannette's plans were not thoroughly made, though she knew she meant to make some decisive move that evening. She had a shadowed outline of a plan which should depend upon circumstances, and upon this occasion circumstances favored her. Early in the evening, she met a company of young people with whom she was well acquainted. Among them was a particularly fast young fellow, whose face showed plainly what his life must be. Nannette took pains to introduce them to Maria. This young man in particular seemed to be greatly taken with her, and whispered in an aside to Nannette:

"I say, Nan, she's a 'beaut'! Where'd you pick her up? I like her style. She's not so slow as a 'looker,' is she? Say, give a fellow a chance to talk with her for a while."

"All right, I will," she agreed readily enough, "if you'll do something for me in return. Promise me to get up a set for whist or euchre with her in it in the small card-room to the left of the office, the one with the wide windows on the piazza, you know. I have a special reason. I'm setting up a little joke on some one, that's all. I think she knows how, all right, but anyway, if she doesn't, you offer to teach her."

"You're a jewel, Nan," he responded eagerly, glad of the chance to teach so pretty girl as Maria anything; "just command me and I'll obey."

"Well, you be in there with the girls in five minutes and I'll manage to send her in," and Nannette went airily on her way. She was by no means so sure of Maria, as she pretended, but she would do her best. Fortune favored her a second time as she walked back to the end of the piazza, where the De Vere party was seated. Winthrop Hammond met her near the parlor door. He stopped her and begged that she would send the others to him as he had secured better seats for the music, but could not leave them lest some one else would pre-empt them. Here was one more aid for her scheme. A few minutes' delay one way or another would make no difference about the seats, and Winthrop Hammond would never find out. Yes, she would try it.

"Maria dear," she said in a low tone as she came up to the party, who had not noticed her absence, for she had only walked away with her old friends for a few moments, "Maria, I just met your brother and he wished me to ask you to come to him. You will find him over there in that small room to the right of the office."

Maria rose at once and went in the direction she had pointed, wondering what in the world her brother wanted, and feeling a glad little thrill of joy that he did want her instead of some one else. As she walked away, Mr. Fairfield broke off in the midst of a sentence to Marvie Parker and rose to go with her, but Nannette quickly stepped to his side and, in a tone which all could hear, said sweetly: "Oh, Mr. Fairfield, would you be so good as to help me find my friends again? I have lost them and I am very anxious to see them once more before the music begins."

Of course there was nothing else to do as a gentleman but to offer her his arm and march away down the wide piazza, inwardly fuming at his trying position and, let us admit it, at its pretty cause.

Now Nannette could not, for her own purposes, have better timed their coming to the part of the piazza where the little card-room window opened out upon it, if she had been gifted with supernatural powers.

"I think I heard them say they would be near here. Would you just look in that window, please, and see if you catch a glimpse of them?" With her quick eye she had already seen the forming tableaus within and knew that time and scene were ready for the intended auditors. A table stood in the center of the room, around which sat the company of young people whom Nannette had recently introduced to the Lone Pointers. One seat was vacant and the fast young man was just bowing and holding it ready for Maria to be seated as Mr. Fairfield looked in. From where they stood in the darkness, gazing into the brilliantly lighted room, he could plainly see the cards on the table and in the hands of those about it, and then a soft little hand stole quickly over his eyes and Nannette, in the gayest of shocked laughs, said; "Oh, please come away. I'm so sorry. I wouldn't have done it for the world if I had known. She wouldn't have you see her in there, I know; but you won't think hardly of her for it, will you? She has been having such a hard time keeping up, you know, and one can't be good always. One must have a little fun occasionally. Besides, Maria has done bravely. She isn't used to such a straight-laced life, you must remember. She has been telling me how hard it was for her. But she would be terribly broken up if you saw her. She had been telling me about your — well, perhaps, I would better not say any more, for she might not like it, you know," Nannette broke off hesitatingly. They had been walking on toward a secluded end of the piazza, entirely deserted now, for the guests were gathering for the music. Nannette determined to strike while the iron was hot, for she thought she saw that Mr. Fairfield was greatly taken aback at what he had seen. Here were seats and the loud dashing of the waves. No place could be better for confidences and a pleasant little flirtation. What if the music did go on and pass, no matter if she fought for and won this trophy.

"Let us sit down just a minute, please," she said as if out of breath, putting her hand to her heart; "I feel so upset by this; I am afraid she would blame me for it, and I should feel so sorry. She has been telling me all about it, you know, and well — excuse me, but I have these little turns with my heart ever since mother's death. It will soon pass away. There — oh, please sit down just a minute." She leaned her head back against the wall and let it incline till it almost rested against her escort. Only just an instant did she let it remain, and then she seemed to come to herself and gain strength to sit up, and to beg his pardon. She had hoped, that he might feel impelled to do as other young men had done before when she had been attacked in a like manner, but as she saw no sign of any such movement on his part, she concluded to discreetly withdraw.

Mr. Fairfield, on his part, was startled almost out of his accustomed composure. He would not have thought it so great a thing to see Maria playing cards, for she had told him herself that she had lived a worldly life, and she would not be expected to have thought over all these questions and to have decided them, in so short a space of time. But to be told that she had thought about it, and had deliberately gone in there to play, planning that he should not know about it — that she was actually trying to deceive him and appear better in his eyes than she was, was another matter. Worst of all, was it to know that the sacred words which had passed between Miss Hammond and himself about a better, nobler life, had been recited in detail to this worldly, unsympathetic listener. This was what cut him to the quick. He sat dumb for a few minutes with the pain of it.

Chapter 23

One might have supposed that Howard Fairfield, a minister of the gospel for three years, had lived long enough in the world, and had experienced enough of it, not to believe all that such a girl as Miss Davenport told him. Indeed he had never put much faith in anything she did or said from the first, but somehow the little that he had seen with his own eyes to-night had suddenly broken down his good common sense, and he began to doubt Maria. This was what Nannette had hoped for. She had thought that with his first doubts of Maria he might turn to her, and then she would have gained an influence over him which she well knew how to use. But Nannette showed in this that she was not a good judge of human nature. She did not understand the pure, high nobility of such a man's heart or she would never have thought to thus turn him to herself.

Miss Davenport, when she saw that the minister was sitting by her side and waiting, got out her little black-edged handkerchief and began to sob softly.

"It frightens me terribly when I get one of those heart attacks," she said in a soft, childish voice. She was a very good actor when the occasion demanded private theatricals. "I feel as if I were not good enough to die."

She paused. She thought if there was a spark of the true minister in him he would turn now and try to preach to her, but instead he sat quite silent beside her.

After a moment in which nothing could be heard but the beating of the waves, he spoke in a stern, controlled voice:

"Are you quite able to return to your friends now, Miss Davenport?" It was all that he could bring himself to say. He had detected the false note in her voice instantly. He could not try to talk to her of spiritual things. He felt instinctively that it would be casting pearls before swine. "If you do not feel able to go back, I will go in search of assistance for you," he added.

Nannette rose hastily from her chair, stung by anger and defeat, and during the long walk down that piazza neither of them spoke a word.

It was a pity that Mr. Fairfield could not have lingered just an instant longer before that brightly lighted window and have seen Maria coldly decline the seat at the card table, and after a glance about the room as if she were searching for some one, and a dignified word or two of inquiry about her brother, leave the room again. He might have been spared the pain which continually surged back and filled his heart, for then he would have seen that the whole thing was manufactured in the fertile brain of Miss

Davenport. Perhaps too, it might have dawned upon him sooner that the young woman in question had an end of her own to gain, namely himself. But the man's nobleness of character cannot better be described than by saying that such an idea did not even occur to him. It was not until he was in the quiet of his own room, and remembered that head almost laid upon his shoulder, that he began to see what sort of girl Miss Davenport really was, and a blush of shame mantled his brow for her sake, and for the sake of the womanhood which in his thought she, even in that slight act, had dishonored.

Meantime Nannette, humiliated and resentful, directed the party to where Winthrop Hammond was waiting for them, and disappeared for a while from the room as she saw Maria approaching.

Mr. Fairfield slipped away as the music began. His excuse was that he had promised to preach the next day, and needed the time for preparation. No one thought it strange, though all were sorry to lose his companionship. As he walked down the long piazza, intending to walk home by the beach instead of the road, he espied two people ahead of him. They were some distance away, and he could not see them distinctly. In the mingled, uncertain light of moon and dashing spray, he scarcely noticed them at first, except to know that the dark figure was a man, and the white draperies belonged to a woman. But as they turned out into the brighter moonlight to walk on the silver sand close beside the waves, his rapid steps gaining upon their lagging, lover-like ones, the man's dark arm stole out and encircled the waist of the white dress beside him; then in the settling, confiding, unresisting attitude of the woman he suddenly realized a familiar memory, and as suddenly became aware of two long, black sash ends, with fluffy little black chiffon ruffles about them, which he recalled noticing on Miss Davenport's dress as she walked before him on the way from the De Vere home over to the hotel. It had occurred to him as he first set eyes upon them that he had felt morally certain if her bereavement had not positively forbidden it, that sash would have been a bright red.

He was drawing nearer, and could see their faces now. Nannette was looking sweetly up into the man's eyes so close above hers, and he saw that the man was the same one who had but a few moments before placed Maria's chair at the card table. At least it was a relief to know that Maria was not playing with that man. He half wished he had remained to see what became of Maria, but he would not go back now. Moreover he had witnessed all the flirtations he cared for in one evening, and he turned abruptly off over the sand and struck straight across the country to the carriage drive, regardless of hillocks or wire fences, or even quicksands.

It was not a pleasant walk, and he felt as if perhaps he had lost rather than gained strength for his work on the morrow. He went straight to his knees, and in communion with his Heavenly Father he by and by lost the heavy strain that the events of the evening had put upon him, and was able to think of what he intended to say on the morrow.

He had chosen for his text, "For me to live is Christ"; that verse had been deeply impressed upon his mind since the first evening when he had visited the Hammond cottage, and Rachel had asked her innocent, earnest question.

By the hour of church service, the rest of the night, the beauty of the morning, and above all the peace which Jesus Christ had given him, had lifted him above his troubled thoughts of the evening before, and he felt "in the Spirit on the Lord's Day" as he went forth to speak in Christ's name.

For just a moment after he was seated in the pulpit, while the congregation were gathering, he felt a disagreeable sensation as Miss Davenport came in and seated herself before him in her elegant black robes. Perhaps he was hard upon her, but he was a noble man with high ideals of womanhood, and his very soul shrank from the thought of what he had seen of that young woman the night before. He caught however a glimpse of Maria's face, on which unconscious loveliness sat so sweetly, and of Rachel's calm brow, and he remembered that there were women in the world who would not stoop to what was beneath them. He wondered, as he looked at the sisters, why he had never noticed before how much alike they were. Happily for him he forgot for the moment the trouble about Maria that had come to him the night previous, for the sight of her face in its Sabbath peace seemed so foreign to anything deceitful that it was not until his work for the morning was over that the occurrence suddenly came back to his memory. There is no time when God's servants need so earnestly to watch and pray as when they have just finished some special work for him which required attention, and nerves on the alert. The tension is over, and they feel no more need for the watching and prayer immediately, and Satan steals up unaware when they are all unprepared for attack and takes them in their weakest place, sometimes undoing or rendering useless all the work of the time of action.

So after the hour of exaltation, when Mr. Fairfield almost stood upon the mount with his Saviour, and face to face with him gave forth the message of life, when as he spoke he felt in his heart that though to live for Christ was glorious, yet to die for him would be better than all, and that he would welcome death at once if Christ should send it; after all this Satan stole upon him on his way home and told him his preaching was of no effect, that his dearest hopes were vain; that the woman whom he felt was the one of all the earth for him was vain and deceitful, and possessed a number of other qualities he could not bear to think of.

However, as Satan was busy with the preacher, he had not time just then to go about picking up the seeds of good that had fallen upon the open mellow ground, and when he did get back to that work he found that much of the seed had already taken root and was growing. It was only that which had fallen upon the rocks that he could pick up and destroy.

Maria felt the uplifting of the morning sermon. It had helped her beyond anything she had ever heard before. It may have been because the preacher had written his sermon just for her. He had in mind her heart experience and he seemed to have anticipated all her doubts and perplexities and answered them. He had been much with God during the days when he had not been able to talk with her as he had done before and perhaps this separation had been good for them both for this very reason. They were learning each to first find help in God and only after that in one another. She thanked God over and over again that day for that sermon. She was not unaware that the preacher's face, in its high intellectual refinement, had worn a look of spiritual illumination which in her eyes made it more beautiful in a manly way than any face she had ever looked upon. It troubled her that the realization of the speaker's personality came so often to her mind, but after several vain attempts to put it away she decided to enjoy the day and the sermon and not trouble herself about this part of it, which apparently could not be helped.

There was just one speck of trouble on the bright surface of the day to her. Her brother Winthrop had walked beside Miss Davenport back to the hotel from church, and after dinner had declined Rachel's earnest request that he should attend her to the Sabbath-school and gone directly back to the hotel. From the piazza of the green cottage she had soon thereafter seen him emerge from the hotel carrying Miss Davenport's shawl and parasol, and with her by his side they had sauntered down the beach. She had evidently made up her mind that so spiritual a preacher would hardly be good material for a jolly Sunday afternoon and looked about for other prey.

As Maria had watched her during the past week or two, she had become more and more convinced of the shallowness and perhaps wickedness of her heart. She felt assured that she was an utterly unprincipled girl, and she could not bear to see her brother Winthrop walk into the net spread for him. In this fear she was evidently joined by Rachel, although neither said nothing to the other; but Rachel stood by her side on the piazza, her calm brow for once clouded with trouble and the ready tears gathering as she watched their brother. Maria had turned and looked at her and as their eyes met she obeyed the warm impulse of her heart and kissing Rachel gently, said "Come with me." Almost in amazement, Rachel had understood, though up to this time there had no word of any change in Maria passed between the two. Rachel followed her sister to their room and together, hand in hand, they knelt down beside their bed. They spoke no word aloud then, nor after they rose, but Rachel kissed Maria this time and then slipped softly away to the Sabbath-school. Because of this little incident, Maria felt that the day had been a wonderful one, and so did Rachel. It had touched Rachel's heart beyond anything that had even happened between them, to have Maria tell her in this way of her new deep feelings. She was a remarkable little sister or she might not have understood.

It may be that some little seed of the morning's word dropped on Miss Davenport's heart. She felt troubled. She was reminded unpleasantly again of her mother's death. She always avoided solemn things if she could, but that had been the one solemn incident of her life thus far that she had been unable to avoid. She did not wish to think about it, because while in her life that mother had not been so strong and faithful as she ought to have been, yet in her death she had aroused to the sense of her responsibility and had spoken a few dreadful words to her daughter, which by night and by day pursued her, unless she could keep her mind occupied with worldly things. However, her mind was shallow and she easily turned the tide of her thoughts to light things.

She had not been without some recognition of the illumination of the minister's face as he preached that morning, though in her words he was judged "decidedly handsome and distingué." She remembered his severity of the evening before, and a blush of actual shame crept over her face, unused to such blushes as it was. Then to drive out this unusual feeling she began to wonder if after all there was not yet hope that she might conquer this man. He had held out so long that it would really be quite interesting if she could bring him to her feet now. She might even fall in love with him. She really felt nearer to falling in love than she had for four or five years. And if he had a good church and large salary it might not be so bad a "catch" after all. She began to speculate upon just what the position of a minister's wife was, and how much would absolutely be required of her, for propriety's sake. The only drawback she could think of would be that she might be occasionally called upon to attend funerals, and *that* she *would not* do. She would never do it to please any one! Horrid places! She shuddered involuntarily and took up her fan, deciding that she would put her foot down upon that at once and declare she would not go. After all, as she had plenty of money, and probably would have more than he, there would be no danger but that she might have her own way about everything. Thereupon she looked up to the minister's face to see how it would seem to look at him in the light of a possible husband, and perceived that he had hushed the audience into tears by a simple story of pain and loss and love and loyalty to Christ which he was telling. She took up her handkerchief and tried to listen with the others as he recited impressively the words:

"When his steps
Were on the mighty waters—
When we went with trembling hearts through nights of pain and loss,
His smile was sweeter and his love more dear;
And only heaven is better than to walk
With Christ at midnight over moonless seas."

During the prayer that followed the sermon's close she formulated the plan which she carried out that evening, her final plan for his capture. Then with the benediction, she rose, satisfied with her morning's worship, and turned to Winthrop Hammond with her sweetest smile. If the plan should fail, there was this one left, and he was handsome and of a good family, and not very hard to subdue as she could easily see.

As Mr. Fairfield passed down the aisle, his exaltation yet upon his face, his thoughts hardly called back to earth from the message he had delivered, she stretched out her daintily gloved hand and just touched his coat sleeve with the tips of her fingers:

"Oh, Mr. Fairfield," said she with a sweet and reminding quiver in her voice, "thank you for that sweet sermon. It was just perfectly lovely. I did enjoy it so much."

And the minister suddenly remembered that he dwelt yet upon the earth.

Chapter 24

Mr. Fairfield received two letters of note in the Monday morning's mail. One had no postmark. The other was from his city home, telling of the severe illness of a woman who belonged to his church. He read this first, naturally anxious to know the home news, and sat with it in his hand pondering whether his duty did not call him home, at least for a day or two. Then he suddenly remembered the other letter. It was written in high, angular hand on a thick cream, violet-scented paper, and as the handwriting was very "high" indeed, and the letter long, it was consequently bulky. It read as follows:

My Dear Mr. Fairfield: My heart is filled with conflicting emotions as I sit down to write you this note. I feel as if I had come to a crisis in my life. The moment that I met you I realized that you were one who was to wield a great influence over me, and have something unusual to do with my life. This morning when I sat entranced listening to your words of eloquence I realized this still more. More than any one I have ever met, I believe you have influenced me. I was deeply affected. I have been thinking the matter over, and have decided to ask your help and spiritual advice. My dear mother used to tell me that some day I would meet with some one who would have the power to reach my stony heart religiously, and I now see that she was right. Oh, I am very wretched and miserable! If you can bring me any consolation from the religion which you so beautifully preach, I shall be forever grateful to you. I know you will not leave a poor girl who has no one else to whom to turn, comfortless. You will come to me and let me tell you the story of my life, and you shall teach me how to be good like yourself. I cannot endure yet to have any of my friends know that I have taken this step. It is too new and too sacred a thing to me. Therefore I ask you to meet me by the inlet, up toward the lighthouse, where the old mast is buried in the sand. There we can sit and talk to our heart's content without being observed. I shall be there at half-past ten in the morning, and I know you will not fail me. Until then farewell. Yours penitently,

Nannette M. Davenport.

The minister felt a cold chill creeping over him as he read this letter. He was more and more convinced of the insincerity of the writer as he thought over the matter, and read and re-read the letter. There was not in his heart one particle of response to that summons for help. He tried to examine himself and see whether it was his prejudice which made him feel so; but no, he could not think of any one else, no matter how humble, whom he would not gladly have gone to meet and help. He could not feel that the Spirit of God was sending him to this one. Saturday night's experience stood out too plainly in his mind, and the horror that he felt, grew as he thought about it. If there had been no one to talk with her, the case would have been different. He would have risked all on the mere chance that she was in earnest. Or if she had not worded her letter so strangely, and chosen so secluded a spot for their talk, he would not have been half so suspicious. What should he do? He felt strongly that this letter was written in much the same spirit as one a tramp had brought to him some months before, poorly spelled and ungrammatical in wording, purporting to be from a scholarly member of his church. It was to the effect that if he, the minister, would give the man some help from the church funds, this church-member felt sure that they might win the man to Christ. He was disposed to beware of this letter in the same way that he had been of that, for in the former case his suspicion that the man was an arrant fraud and the letter a forgery had proven entirely correct.

He felt now that for the sake of the love he bore Maria he ought not to meet this strange young woman. What if Maria should be walking upon the sand, and come upon them? Perhaps Miss Davenport meant to plan just such a *rencontre*. Now that his eyes were open there were no depths to which he felt she might not descend to gain her end, whatever it was. Then the letter had no genuine ring. There was too much talk about himself and his influence on her. There was no confession of having sinned. Why had she seen it necessary to write at all? Why had she not boldly asked him to talk with her upon the porch or anywhere? There were plenty of opportunities. Why, if she wanted religious help, had she not gone to Maria who, according to her own statement, had talked with her on these topics? He went to his room and asked his Heavenly Father's advice. This was a matter too important for his own inclination to decide. He could not easily refuse a call for help, even though he did doubt it. He prayed, trusting that an answer would come, and it did.

As he rose from his knees the other letter, the one about the sick woman, fluttered from his hand upon the floor, and on the back of the sheet where he had not noticed it before he saw a short postscript, asking him, if possible, to come home, as the woman had wished for him and seemed to have something on her mind to tell him.

Quick as a flash he felt that this was his heaven-sent answer, and he must obey. A glance at his watch told him that the next train was due at the station in one hour, just ten minutes before the time set by Miss Davenport in her letter for him to meet her at the inlet. He would go home. He certainly ought to go home, for his church was his first duty, and this woman was dying. Hastily he gathered together his belongings, and settled up the few matters which had to be attended to before he left, trying all the while to think what to do about Miss Davenport's request. He might ask someone else to meet her. He thought of a dear old Christian woman at home and wished she were here, but she was not. He thought of Maria, but disliked to ask her to go on such an errand to her own friend, lest she might suppose he had formed an intimate friendship with Miss Davenport, the circumstances of the past week well bearing out such a supposition. Nevertheless, he at last made up his mind that Maria was the only one to whom he could turn now. He went at once to the green cottage, leaving his orders about baggage at the hotel, so that he would not have to return.

Nannette was far up the beach practicing pretty little maneuvers with her deepest bordered handkerchief, and thus failed to see him go. But when Mr. Fairfield reached the green cottage he found to his dismay that Maria, with her mother, had been driven over to Spray View in Mr. Higgins' green wagon to do some Monday morning marketing, and would not be likely to return before the city train left. His heart was filled with a great regret when he thought of leaving her so abruptly, so that for a few minutes the thought of Nannette in her self-appointed trusting-place did not come to him.

Rachel was at home and had given him writing materials, and he was trying to construct a note of farewell to Maria. Perhaps he ought to write a note to Miss Davenport. It was only courteous to do so, but when he started he found in his innermost soul he shrank from addressing a word to her. He glanced up at the earnest face of Rachel as she sat shelling peas on the upper step of the piazza. Her far-away, dreamy expression told that her thoughts were upon high and lovely things.

Suddenly a new idea came to him. It would be late when Maria returned, too late for her to reach Miss Davenport at the inlet before she had left there. Here was Rachel. She would know how to help that girl. There passed through his mind the verse about how the Lord had kept some things from the wise and prudent and revealed them unto babes, and while Rachel was no babe, still she was a child at heart. He remembered how well she had taught the little boys upon the sand. She had the root of the matter in her, and could surely bring the message of salvation to another soul. He would send her.

In a few words he explained the situation to Rachel, telling her only what was absolutely necessary, that Miss Davenport had been affected by the services of yesterday, and had written him a note, in his capacity as a minister, asking his help spiritually. He was called suddenly to the city by sickness in his congregation, and might be detained he knew not how long. Would she go and meet Miss Davenport, and help her to find Christ?

Rachel's face beamed with a holy light to think she was to be sent on an errand of mercy. She was genuinely glad that Nannette wanted to be a Christian. She had been secretly praying for her ever since her arrival, she seemed to Rachel to be so much in need of a Saviour. She promised eagerly to go at the appointed time, and immediately went away to get ready, such a joy upon her face at thought of the work before her that the minister was put to shame and felt he ought not to have shrunk from it. However, he reflected that as Rachel had no such doubts of the would-be inquirer as he held, she might be able to do much more good, for she was going trusting that her mission would be blest, and perhaps it would. He pledged himself to pray for this.

Then he found to his dismay that he had very little time left and could only write a line to tell Maria he was sorry to leave without seeing her. He left the Meyer book for her, asking that she would read it with him on his return, if he was able to return that summer. Then he heard the train whistling at Spray View, and hastily bidding Rachel good-bye went to the station, feeling that he was leaving behind him all that was precious in this world. It certainly was very hard for him to go. If only he could have had a little word with Maria and one of her lovely smiles to light him on his way!

Rachel, with exalted expression and her little Bible in her pocket, walked swiftly up the beach. She was praying as she went that she might be led to say the right words.

Nannette was seated on the sunken mast, her back turned toward the entrance of the secluded amphitheatre-shaped place she had selected for her morning's confessional. Her idea was to be deep in meditation of an affecting character when the young man should arrive, and thus make a good impression at first. She reasoned that if any one else came by and saw her sitting thus they would think she wished to be alone and pass on.

Rachel came with eager steps almost up to Nannette before she realized that any one was near, and then hearing the rustle of a dress, Nannette turned quickly to see who was there.

"Oh, Nannette! I am so glad!" exclaimed Rachel, stooping down and kissing the astonished girl on her forehead. "I am so glad for you, but I wish there was some one better than I to help you."

"What do you mean?" said Nannette coldly, pushing her back and looking at her strangely. It had been so long since any girl had cared to kiss her that it made her feel queer.

"There! I have done just as I always do, and plunged into the middle of things without any beginning," said Rachel distressed. "Why, Mr. Fairfield had to go away to the city this morning. He was called suddenly to a woman who is sick, and he stopped at the cottage and told me you were troubled, and you wanted to know how to be a Christian; and he asked me if I would come and tell you the best I could about it. I am sorry it is only I. If Maria or mamma had been at home one of them would have come; but he was anxious some one should come to explain at the hour, why he was not here, so I have come and I'll do my best, dear. I do love Jesus, and I think I can tell you a little about him," she said sweetly; "and oh, I am so glad you are going to belong to him too."

Nannette looked at Rachel blankly.

"And so he is gone!" she exclaimed, and broke into a harsh laugh. "Well, I have taken a lot of pains for nothing. It was awfully good of you, Ray, to travel way out here in the sand and sun, and you are doubtless just as good a talker as any one else, so don't worry your righteous little soul about that; but indeed you needn't trouble yourself to talk religion to me. I'm not in the mood for it, and it really wouldn't pay you. You'd better keep it for the fisherman's children. I hear you are quite converting them." Nannette arose to go back, a disagreeable look on her face. She felt that she was foiled again, and this time pretty badly. There was no longer any hope of reducing the minister to admiration of her charms; he was gone. He had evidently run away. She laughed aloud again. "Rachel, I have driven him from the ground. He didn't dare to stay and fight. It is a sort of victory, after all."

Rachel, who had been watching her in puzzled silence, was now completely mystified, and began to wonder if Nannette was losing her mind. "What do you mean, Nannette?" she asked.

"Oh, you dear little goose," laughed Nannette. She had not the energy to keep up her "pious dodge," as she called it for the benefit of a girl; what would be the use? She told herself it would make her no end of trouble, so she frankly admitted the part she had been playing.

"Did you really suppose I was anxious about my soul? Well, you must have known very little, indeed, about me. Don't look so worried, I was doing no harm. Your nice little words that you had all fixed up, will come in quite handy for some one else. If you were not such a blessed little goose, I would be very angry that he had dared to send some one else in his place."

"But, Nannette, he couldn't come, and I was the only one at hand he could send," said Rachel, with her troubled eyes looking earnestly at the other girl. "Perhaps he had not time to explain it all out to me. What was it you did want of him? I don't understand."

Nannette was very much amused, indeed. She laughed and laughed, using the black-bordered handkerchief to wipe away tears, genuine for once, even if they were born of mirth instead of grief.

"Well, I would have been a fool indeed if I had lured the minister out here just for the sake of talking religion at me, my little innocent," she said when she could control her laughter sufficiently to speak. "My dear, I wanted to bring him out here for a nice, little, harmless flirtation, that's all. Don't be so shocked. I wouldn't have hurt the poor man for anything."

"Oh, Nannette!" exclaimed Rachel in a horrified voice, "don't say that; you surely don't mean it, that you would plan such a flirtation with a minister?"

Nannette fairly shrieked with laughter now. "And did you suppose, my dear, that because he was a minister he had no heart?" she said between her peals of laughter.

Rachel was silent for a moment, taking in the meaning of what had been told her. "But, Nannette—" she hesitated as a new thought came to her. "Aren't you engaged to that other man? The one we met last night? Excuse me, but I couldn't help seeing. I stood on the piazza with Fannie De Vere as you went down the beach and I saw—him—put—his—arm—" She stopped. She could not bring herself to say more, and the tears were coming to the surface now with the effort she was making to do her duty.

A blush of as much shame as this girl could feel stole suddenly upon her cheek as she saw her own act, which had seemed to her an every-day affair, standing out in the light of this sweet, pure soul's ideals. It was perhaps the first time that Nannette had ever felt any real shame in allowing such familiarity with comparative strangers.

"Oh, little Ray! You are good fun!" she tried to say carelessly. "Why that was nothing. Any nice man would do that and think nothing of it. Just wait till Roland De Vere tries it with you and you'll understand."

And then Miss Davenport was treated to a touch of such righteous wrath as made her see that the gentle-hearted Rachel Hammond had more spirit in her than she had thought.

"Mr. De Vere would never do such a thing!" said Rachel, her bosom heaving and her face flaming, and then, her eyes flashing, she added, "But if he _did_, he would never try it again." She turned and walked a few steps with dignity. But Nannette rebuked, and not wishing to show it, sprang up.

"Oh come, now, Ray, don't be too hard on people who haven't risen to your heights. We can't all think alike, you know. I guess you're right about Roland. He's too much of an old granny to do anything of that sort. Come, let's be friends and go home, this sun is broiling. Don't tell your good mamma about this escapade of mine, I beg of you, or else she might write to my prim old auntie and have me sent home in disgrace."

Rachel walked along in silence. Of her in her every-day life it might be said:

"Other hope had she none, nor wish in life, but to follow meekly, with reverent steps, the sacred feet of her Saviour." It was not often that anything stirred her soul to the depths as this experience of the morning had done. And yet, as she grew calmer she realized that the girl beside her did not know Jesus, and that she had started out on a mission to help her to find him. She remembered how she had committed her cause to her Master before starting, and that she had confidently trusted in him to bless what she should do. And now she was going home without even having said one word that could make this other girl think more of Jesus Christ. Was the fault in her? Would it be casting pearls away to speak now, after what had passed between them? And yet could she in conscience leave her without having at least tried to fulfill her trust? All the way along the beach she was silent, letting Nannette talk as rapidly and vapidly as she would. Suddenly, as they came in sight of the hotel, Rachel paused beside a little side path that turned off from the beach and went down toward the green cottage, a shorter cut than going around by the hotel.

"Nannette," she said, putting out her hand gently to detain her companion, "I came out this morning to bring you a message from Jesus. I thought you were waiting for it, and would be glad to get it. I found you were not. I am very sorry. But I believe that Jesus sent that message to you all the same, even if you did not want it, and I must give it to you. Nannette, Jesus loves you, and he wants you to love him." The tears were in Rachel's eyes, and she felt that she could not trust herself to say another word, so she turned and sped swiftly down the sandy path toward home, and Nannette stood still looking after her, a strange smile upon her face, half of wistfulness and half of ridicule. As Rachel disappeared from sight behind the sand dunes she turned toward the hotel again, murmuring to herself, "She's a good little thing."

And who shall say but that Rachel's words were as the seed that often lies long in the cold, black earth before it gives sign of life? But at last it bursts and grows and brings forth fruit.

Chapter 25

After that Nannette plunged into a mad flirtation with Winthrop Hammond. She kept him by her side morning, noon, and evening. He was certainly devoted enough to make up for all the chagrin she had felt in the lack of admiration she had found in Mr. Fairfield. He bought her candy, and flowers whenever such were procurable in Spray View, regardless of the fact which he had heretofore kept before him that money was an article not to be carelessly spent by any member of the Hammond household just now. Nannette discovered a company of friends at Spray View who were altogether gay enough to suit her. There were little private gatherings for card playing and dancing, and Nannette, unrestrained by onlookers, took her part now and again, and began to feel that the summer was not such a bitter failure after all.

Having reduced Winthrop Hammond to subjection she set herself to make him drink wine. The young people with whom she went always drank it at their gatherings. She took him among them on all possible occasions where it was forthcoming. She ridiculed him when he declined it, and when he allowed his glass to be filled she dared him to drink with her. He had been brought up with a strong feeling against the use of wine, and he did not readily overcome it. Once or twice he drank to please her, because she made such a point of it. He was out very late at night these times, and his mother was troubled about him. His father even went so far as to suggest that it might be as well for him to return to his business, if he was going to use his rest hours to so poor an advantage. But he answered them all laughingly, and went on.

It was evident to the family that he had fallen in love with Nannette Davenport, and each wondered at it. They did not know how very charming she could be when she chose, and they could not know that she was choosing just now to very good purpose. Having been foiled in her first attempt she was angry, and determined to take her revenge out of the next victim. She appeared to think a great deal of her admirer, but in truth Mr. Fairfield's intellectual face and severe eyes turned full upon her, often rankled in her soul, and she felt deeply ashamed of herself and her whole life.

Things had been going on in this way for about two weeks. No word had come from Mr. Fairfield save an occasional paper or book addressed to Maria, and once a large box of beautiful flowers, which came by express and contained no card. Maria treasured all these things, but of course said no word to Nannette concerning them.

Maria's life just now was a little hard. She worried daily about her brother, and prayed often. She tried to make a friend of Nannette, that she might, if possible, prevent the intimacy between her and her brother. Nannette apparently had grown quite discreet. She asked one day as they were walking together: "Say, 'Ri, you wouldn't write to that minister, would you, if you were I? I should hate to hurt his feelings, but really I don't like letter writing, and when a man's gone, why he's out of it, you know. If he should come back, of course I'd be nice to him, I suppose, but I hardly like to go so far as to correspond, it seems to mean so much, you know. A man always means a good deal by asking for the privilege, especially a man like that. I haven't written him but once, and I don't believe I shall again, would you?"

And Maria answered, "I should do as I thought best," and turned the conversation to other topics, but she could not help thinking that Mr. Fairfield had never asked her to correspond with him. And she never knew that Nannette had been prompted to these remarks by a chance sight of the box of flowers at the express office addressed to Maria in a handwriting she recognized.

Winthrop Hammond was to return to the city to his business the next morning. He was out, and it was very late. Both his sisters had silently kept the watch, which was also being kept by the anxious mother in the next room, for his footsteps Rachel, as she lay quiet, lest she should rouse her sister from what she supposed was a happy sleep, wondered if her brother could ever fall so low as to treat Nannette in the way that other young men had done. She shuddered at the possibility, and yet she had seen enough in the face of that daring girl on the day when she met her at the inlet, to feel that her influence over any man would be a tremendous power should she choose to exercise it.

She and Maria had both spent much time in praying, during the past few days, for their brother. Rachel felt that an answer would surely come soon.

Winthrop came at last, but his steps were slow and lagging, and did not sound like him. He came into the sitting room and instead of going directly to bed sat down heavily in a chair. Once Rachel thought she heard a groan, and then, as all was still, she waited. Presently her brother threw himself upon the couch and groaned again, this time quite audibly. Rachel sprang to her feet, and, throwing a shawl about her, hurried out to the sitting room, but she found that her mother was there before, and Maria not far behind her. There was no mistaking the fact that their brother was ill. He was suffering too much pain to talk or give them any idea of what was the matter, but he had a high fever, they could tell that for themselves. The father started almost immediately for the doctor, while the mother and sisters got him to bed, heated water, and gave various simple home remedies. They then waited anxiously the coming of the physician.

It was as they feared — typhoid fever. The evenings of pleasure following the nights of nursing had told upon him. The doctor warned them that it was likely to be a severe case. Then the household settled down into that forced quiet where there is the dread anxiety of critical illness. Maria insisted upon staying with her brother night and day, and, strange to say, though Rachel had always been his favorite, he seemed best satisfied with Maria in the room. During the nights and days of waiting and watching and breathless anxiety, Maria had no time to think of herself. Whenever she had a moment to herself she spent it in prayer. Her life now was one long prayer.

She sometimes looked back on the days when all was bright and happy and she had been unhappy and unreasonable, and wondered at herself.

Then she thought gratefully of Mr. Fairfield and the change he had been the instrument, in God's hands, of making in her. She wondered how she could have gone through this long, tedious trial without Jesus as her friend. She seemed literally to be living in his presence now; to be bearing all she bore with his strength, not her own; to be watching his face to see if her brother was to be spared to live more years with them, or to be taken away. She felt an assurance that if God took him he would at least first give him time in which to take Jesus as his Saviour. He was delirious now for days, did not know one of them, and then lay in a sort of stupor. The time of the crisis had come. Maria was sitting by his side, while her mother rested near at hand, to be called should there come a change. She scarcely dared to breathe lest she should disturb the one so dear, who lay hovering between life and death. Her every breath was a prayer for him. Suddenly he opened his eyes, and in a feeble voice that was scarcely audible, whispered, " 'Ri, can you pray?"

Maria thought he must be dying, but without daring to wait, so momentous seemed that instant, she dropped upon her knees, and in low, controlled tones, prayed that Jesus might stand by her brother, and loving him, might take his hand and hold him in that moment, for life or death, for time or for eternity. She scarcely knew what she said, as with upturned face and eyes that seemed as though they saw the Lord, she prayed on. The burning, unnaturally bright eyes upon the pillow watched her, drinking in every word eagerly, as though thirsty, while Maria, praying, pleaded promise after promise from God's word. By and by the restless look faded from his eyes and there came a calm like a shadow of peace, and at last the eyelids fell, and Maria knew by the soft, natural breathing that he was asleep. By and by she dared to rise and call the others, and the doctor coming in told them that the crisis was past and the young man would live. Then the sister went away and thanked God.

But her work was not yet done. As the invalid grew able to talk he wanted Maria, and long converse he held with her about the things of life. Maria felt that she was having her reward for the days and nights of watching, and her soul rejoiced in God her Saviour.

All this experience had been so hard that it seemed to put the summer, with its pleasure and brightness, and its disappointments too, far behind her. She looked back to those days when she and Mr. Fairfield had walked and talked together beside the sea, with a wistfulness sometimes, but still with all the sting gone from heart.

Nannette, as soon as she learned the nature of the malady that had now befallen her devoted admirer, in dire dread and haste, picked up her belongings, tumbled them into her trunks, and fled. She had a horror of sickness at all times, and a superstitious fear that she would take typhoid fever if she were exposed to it. Besides her conscience troubled her. She knew that it had been her fault that the young man had spent so many evenings out late and had been drinking wine, a thing to which he was unaccustomed; and she began to fear that this had been partly the cause of his illness. Rachel was grateful that she was gone, yet indignant to think that the girl to whom her brother had devoted his entire attention for three weeks should depart at once without so much as a good-bye or an inquiry for him when she heard of his serious illness. The rest of the family felt nothing but relief.

The De Veres came daily to inquire and to offer aid, and in many ways showed their true friendship. Rachel often wondered that no word came from Mr. Fairfield, and felt sorry on Maria's account, for she recognized that he had been the means of making a change in Maria, and she was disappointed that he had left so suddenly, for she had liked him. She laid it all at Nannette's door, however, and tried to forget it.

One day in September, when Lone Point was almost deserted and only one guest left at the hotel, Maria was sitting on the piazza reading aloud to Winthrop, who was convalescent. The city train stole softly up the length of the island, its line of smoke, black against the sky, the only warning of its coming till the whistle blew near-by, for the sand seemed to dull all sound of rushing engine and whirling wheels. The two on the piazza were so deep in their reading that they did not stop to glance at the train, though they could easily have seen from the piazza who arrived or departed. It was the morning train too, and few ever came at that hour so late in the season.

Presently a step was heard upon the walk, and looking up they saw Mr. Fairfield standing before them. The pink rose to Maria's cheek, and the instant flutter of her heart told her that she had not forgotten, as she had hoped. Her embarrassment was heightened by his steady, earnest gaze, which seemed to be searching her face for some answer to an unspoken question. He took his eyes from her long enough to shake hands with her brother, who welcomed him most heartily, and then he looked back at Maria once more, with a glad, hungry look. Something, perhaps it was her downcast eyelids and the color in her cheeks, brought a half-satisfied expression to his face.

Explanations followed. Mr. Fairfield had suddenly gone to Europe, as much, perhaps, to his own surprise as to theirs. When he reached the city he had received word by cable that his sister was to be married at once in Berlin, and earnestly beseeching him to come over, if only for a few days. It was a sudden change of plans, for she was not to have been married for another year, but her intended husband was about starting on a trip through Palestine, Egypt, and the Mediterranean, and she and her mother were to accompany him. He had decided hastily, having very little time for choice as the only steamer which could possibly bring him to the other side in time for the ceremony sailed the next day, therefore he had had no time to send them a message telling them where and why he was going and for how long.

It occurred to Winthrop Hammond that it would have been rather an unnecessary proceeding to send them word, and he did not understand why Mr. Fairfield thought he should have done so. Then, as he looked at the young man, and beyond him at his sister's pink cheeks, a new idea began to dawn upon him. He whistled softly under his breath and drew his brows down. He did not want to lose this sister now that he had just found out what a sister she could be, but then — here he looked up at the minister — if she must marry, Fairfield was a fine fellow. He could remember some things in that sermon he preached just before he left. They had come to his mind during those awful days of fever and he had wished then that he had taken heed to them before. His face brightened with the thought that Mr. Fairfield would be one who would help him in that way now, and he was glad in his heart that he had come, whether he meant to take away Maria or not.

Then it was Maria's turn to explain how things had gone in Lone Point. She told in a few words the story of her brother's illness, and he, with a voice full of tenderness, added words in praise of her which brought a still richer color to her cheeks and made Mr. Fairfield look steadily at her once more, till she invented an excuse to slip into the house and bath her burning face.

By and by Mr. Fairfield went to the hotel, and when he returned he asked Maria to walk with him. All the long afternoon Winthrop was left to the tender mercies of his mother and Rachel, who did their best to fill her place.

Maria had taken out with her the much-read and treasured copy of Meyer which Mr. Fairfield had left with her when he went away, thinking to grant his request and read it to him, but though they walked or sat upon the sand the whole afternoon, they did not read Meyer. They had something even better and brighter and more delightful than that to read—and they read it in each other's eyes.

As once before, they lingered long upon the sands, till the sun went down and the moon came up, and when they rose and started toward the green cottage they understood one another.

> There comes a day when Love, that lies asleep,
> The fairest island in the mighty deep,
> Wakes on our sight;
> There do we stay awhile; but so on again
> We trim our sails to seek the open main;
> And now, whatever winds and waves betide,
> Two friendly ships are sailing side by side.
> In port of Love 'twas happy to abide,
> But, oh! Love's sea is very deep and wide.

Maria thought something like this as she stood that night, somewhat later, out on the piazza alone, and looked up into the quiet starlit night. She did not put it into these words, but her heart felt it all and more. She was very happy. Her whole soul went out to God in thanksgiving for the wonderful beauty he had suddenly put into her life. It occurred to her, as it had done before, only more forcefully, to thank God that he had not permitted her to have her way and go somewhere else for the summer, but had set her just here. How otherwise could she have been brought to know Jesus Christ as a dear personal friend? And, oh, suppose she had never met the minister—her minister!

Chapter 26

Rachel Hammond sat in her room by the open window with her Bible on her knee once more. It was summer again, and they were in their own home yet. Maria's door was open and a light breeze stirred the muslin curtain just a little and blew the breath of honeysuckles in, but Maria was not seated in the other room, for Maria was gone. It was just yesterday that she stood in that open doorway in her white robes and bridal veil and kissed Rachel. Upon her bed lay the identical white sailor, whose wings and ribbons had been such a trouble a year ago. By some mischance in the packing it had been left lying there, for Maria did not want to take it with her. Rachel looked up, saw it, and remembered their talk of a year ago.

Perhaps it was because she was used to opening her Bible at that place that the leaves that morning had fallen open of themselves to the very verse she had been reading when Maria began to grumble about the summer arrangements and she had left her reading to try and brighten her up. "For me to live is Christ." How strange it seemed to Rachel as she mused. She remembered just how she had longed, as she laid by her Bible with a sigh that morning, that Maria might feel that verse in all the depth and beauty of its meaning. Now, it seemed to Rachel, that in all the list of her acquaintances there was not one who could so nearly truthfully say that verse as her sister Maria, unless it might be her brother-in-law, Howard. How strange it seemed to call him Howard! A real minister in the family! She remembered how she had wished she might know one well enough some time to ask him some questions and now she had not only a minister but a minister's wife, to whom she could go with all her little perplexities and doubts.

A tear stole out and down her cheek as she remembered that Maria's room was empty and Maria would not occupy it any more, nor be nearby as of old as her companion, but she laughed and brushed it away.

God had been very good. She must not weep. She had tried to claim that promise, "Delight thyself also in the Lord and he shall give thee the desires of thine heart," and surely he had kept it and given her more even than she had asked or desired. She was glad and thankful, even though Maria was gone.

Then too, there was something in the fact that Maria lived down-town, only a half-hour's ride away. And was she not going down in a few minutes with Roland De Vere behind his beautiful span of horses to the new parsonage that the church had built for their pastor, to put in place several articles and hang a wonderful picture, the gift of Roland De Vere to the bride? And was there not something about this even more personal and more wonderful still for her? Oh, life was not shadowed much after all!

Rachel rose and went about her room singing, and knew not how appropriate to her life the words were, and were yet to be:

> Judge not the Lord by feeble sense,
> But trust him for his grace;
> Behind a frowning providence
> He hides a smiling face.
>
> Blind unbelief is sure to err,
> And scan his work in vain;
> God is his own interpreter,
> And he will make it plain.